A Thousand
Ghosts

Ben Lusby

To Denese,

Best wishes.

Ben Lusby

8/12/2010.

Published by

MELROSE BOOKS

An Imprint of Melrose Press Limited
St Thomas Place, Ely
Cambridgeshire
CB7 4GG, UK
www.melrosebooks.com

FIRST EDITION

Cover designed by Eilean Moulang

ISBN 978 1 907040 39 9

FSC
www.fsc.org
MIX
Paper from
responsible sources
FSC® C013604

Printed and bound in Great Britain by:
CPI Antony Rowe. Chippenham, Wiltshire

This book is dedicated to Elisabeth Hudson, who first set me on the road to higher education and shared my great love of Dickens.

Acknowledgements

Front cover artwork:
Eilean Moulang

With love and great thanks.

Copyright Notices

Contents

PART TWO

Preface

Toby Freeman is a troubled man. Haunted by his own perceived failings and the growing evidence of mankind's relentless abuse and misuse of the natural environment, Toby unwittingly embarks upon a journey that will take him first back and then forward in time. Finding his life bound up with the Agents of Change, he travels through rural backwaters, cities, climate disaster and war to witness the emergence of a radically altered, more enlightened and sustainable society.

A Thousand Ghosts

W̲E INHERIT THE EARTH FROM OUR ANCESTORS and from nature. It is all we have to live upon – a precious green speck in the vast infinity of space. Yet in recent centuries, human beings have assumed the right to poison and plunder its gifts with little regard for the consequences of what they do. However, over the sky men will never be able to claim such rude dominion; for it is not, and never will be in the power of mortals to control the elemental forces of nature, shape clouds, or still the passage of a hurricane.

Prologue – The Storm

THE MIGHTY WINDS AND CYCLONIC RAIN THAT had devastated Britain for more than forty-eight hours, at last subsided. In their wake many hundreds were left dead, power supplies severed, transport infrastructure wrecked, and untold damage done to every town, city, sprawling suburb and rural retreat. Once famous buildings and landmarks had been torn away, uprooted or left in ruins. In London a large section of the dome of St Paul's collapsed, the lighting arc at Wembley Stadium disappeared amid stampeding clouds, and the storm ravaged "Eye", having initially resisted the ferocious onslaught of gale and torrent, first tilted, then tragically toppled into the swollen waters of the River Thames with thirty doomed sightseers trapped in its upper passenger capsules. Elsewhere: at Portsmouth Harbour, the masts and rigging of Nelson's flagship, HMS *Victory*, were again brutally levelled, as at Trafalgar, to the upper gun deck; in North-West England, much of Blackpool's famous "Golden Mile" amusement park was swept into the sea; while just south of Newcastle, the rusting "Angel of the North" survived wingless, twisted and crippled.

Ten thousand other locations were likewise cruelly affected, and in one such, the previously peaceful dormitory village of Molliton near Bedford, a weak sun, breaking through an unsettled sky of broken cloud, at last began to warm and dry metalled roads following many terrifying hours of unprecedented destruction. A noise of builders' hammers and drills could be heard upon the air – the whirr and rattle of chainsaws sounding at many points as workmen fought to clear fallen trees and open debris strewn roads.

Waking from a troubled sleep, Toby Freeman blinked a tired eye and observed his dishevelled reflection in the mirror, the enormity of what had happened seeping back, moment by moment, into his weary brain. Then, in his head he heard again the thrash of torrential rain against the windows, the spine-chilling sound of structural damage echoing upon the night air and the wind relentlessly howling among fractured trees.

* * *

The calamitous storm of 2013 began after an unusually hot, still and humid few days in late spring. Having risen steadily for a week, afternoon temperatures peaked at over thirty-seven degrees Celsius just before two o'clock on Wednesday, 24th May, the pungent air growing abnormally sticky and uncomfortable as road surfaces oozed and liquefied beneath a blistering sun.

* * *

After returning home early from teaching at the local junior school, Toby sat down with his wife Jenny to watch the news, their children, Brendan, three, and eighteen month old Sophie, propped up beside them on the sofa. Familiar items about exceptionally hot and unseasonable weather were covered: accidents and diversions on the roads, railway failures due to buckled track, passengers stuck in a broken-down London underground train, airports experiencing difficulties due to molten tar on runways – problems for the elderly, trouble on farms, fires burning on heaths and beauty spots... And then, as the cooling evening light streamed through lounge windows thrown wide against the heat, a young BBC weatherman, looking more anxious and apologetic than usual, delivered the following weather warning:

'The Met. Office would like to announce a likelihood of extreme weather conditions affecting all areas by morning. A deep depression gathering over the Atlantic Ocean will bring strong gale-force winds and heavy rain, with the threat of severe structural damage across all regions. Gusts of over 100 miles per hour are anticipated, with considerable impact to exposed trees and property inevitable in many places. Weather updates can be accessed on local television, radio stations, or on our website. Emergency contact information for those seeking help and advice with electricity and other service difficulties will be broadcast on your screen at the end of this programme.'

And so it was – for more than three minutes!

There were numbers for Telecom providers, Gas, Electricity and Water Services, Medical and Hospital Emergencies, Fire and Rescue, Road, Rail and Air Travel – even one entitled, "Food Distribution Providers".

Unsettled, Toby looked towards his partner. 'What do you make of that, Jen?... I mean, one hundred mile an hour winds – that could be serious...'

Jenny Freeman was not so easily perturbed however. There had been storm warnings before, but things were rarely anywhere near as bad as the media led you to expect. With two tired youngsters at her elbow, and the sun still shining reassuringly outside, she packed her husband off to the garden, to "batten down the hatches", while busying herself putting the children to bed.

Romance often brings opposites together and this had clearly been the case with the Freemans. Having taken marriage and motherhood in her stride, Jenny Freeman was neat, caring and well organised; patiently planning a life for her family that would prevent the darker happenings of the world from impinging upon her home and the happiness of those she loved. Toby meanwhile, presented a markedly different image; for where Jenny was invariably tidy in everything she did, taking pride in the appearance of the children and herself, he, although both thoughtful and creative, could appear casual to the point of neglect. Old jeans, a T-shirt and sandals or boots were Toby's preferred attire – for a desire to blend in, rather than stand out, was part of his nature. Moreover, he was a confirmed worrier: every day avidly reading the news and absorbing new information about the state of the environment, then pondering over what could be done to "Save the planet".

'Things change too fast,' he would say to himself. 'Men think they can act as they please on this earth, that they can use every resource to bring comfort and pleasure to themselves with little consideration for any damage that might ensue.'

* * *

By the time Toby had changed into his gardening clothes, a heavy bank of dark cloud moving up from the south-west already covered the sun. It had become appreciably cooler too, and an eddying breeze began to disturb the rich vegetation of the vegetable patch where he spent an hour or two most evenings during the growing season. Then, just before 9pm, a short break in the inky cloak on the western skyline allowed the last rays of a setting sun to illuminate his sheltered corner. Attracted by the brilliant glow, Toby looked up and was puzzled by what he saw; for in a few moments that radiant patch was again extinguished; not as it slipped below the horizon, but by a sinister fold of scudding cloud curling down from above like a moving blanket of darkness. In an instant twilight turned to gloom and a sharp gust of wind whipped down Hawthorn Drive, slamming doors as it passed and causing the garden fence to rattle. At the same time the wheelbarrow he had been using to carry grass cuttings to the compost heap keeled over onto a newly planted row of courgette plants, breaking three. These were the first victims of the storm, but would soon be forgotten amid the mayhem that followed.

Increasingly hampered, Toby quickly tidied away as lightning began to flash overhead, each slanting fork accompanied by a rumble of thunder echoing ominously into the distance. He heard the crash of falling pots, the snapping of a tree branch, and everywhere, windows – thrown wide open during the sweltering daylight hours – being tight shut against rising blasts. Then a towering column of cumulus swiftly enveloped the sky, which in the first coming of night had offered a promise of stars.

The rain came suddenly. As Toby reached up to lock the garage door one heavy drop slashed against finger and thumb, followed by another that struck his brow, and in seconds these initial spots became a deluge! A sheet of water, slanting across the rooftops and driven by a vicious wind, poured out of the darkening sky, and while dashing for the refuge of the kitchen door, he was soaked to the skin. Once inside Toby stood for a moment, shaken by the sudden onslaught, though as yet little comprehending that a climate event of unprecedented intensity had begun...

* * *

We are naturally awed and fascinated by violent weather. When we look out from behind our curtains imagining what mighty demons could cause such tumult, the power of nature reminds us that we are small and vulnerable.

The Freemans were like every other family that night. From the moment a mighty crack of thunder awoke Sophie and sent her into a screaming fit, they sat huddled close together by the bedroom window watching the developing majesty of the storm. There was much chatter at first – 'Wasn't it amazing how much rain was falling?' 'Had Mummy and Daddy ever known such strong winds?' – but a blinding flash of forked lightning and a fearful crack of thunder overhead brought another hysterical shriek from Sophie as wonder turned to fear. A dread compounded moments later when a dull thud sounded from the living room downstairs and all the lights went out!

Sophie threw her arms round Toby's neck, clinging tightly and sobbing into his ear as he looked nervously towards Jenny. 'Take the children into our bedroom,' he advised after a moment's consideration. 'Put them to bed and stay with them while I investigate that noise... They can't possibly understand all this.'

Having gathered up teddies and nightgowns with her frightened charges, Jenny carefully led the two infants onto the darkened landing and into the master bedroom, as Toby descended to discover what had happened below. A sour reek of singed plastic informed his nose before he opened the living room door and saw the damage. The television, left on standby that evening, had been struck by lightning, and a thin coil of sickly smoke could be discerned wisping up into the room. Toby immediately dived for the socket to remove the plug – but he needn't have worried about fire or shock, as a simultaneous massive strike close by had already cut power to the whole of Molliton. It would not be fully restored for more than three weeks, and Toby would never again enjoy the convenient wonders of electricity in his own home.

On hands and knees he nonetheless crawled back hopefully to try the light switch – just in case... Nothing!

Instead, a blast of wind, so powerful it seemed to shake the house, set up howling voices in every nook and cranny, as if mocking his futile hope. Outside a garden fence crashed over, and more ominously, two roof tiles clattered down onto a nearby driveway, shattering glass and setting off a car alarm.

'This is getting beyond a joke,' he said to himself. 'These conditions have lasted half an hour already... how much more must we endure?'

A siege mentality began to grip him; the rancid smell coming from the television would worry Jenny and the children, therefore it must be put outside. If the TV had to be left in the wind and rain, why worry? It was ruined anyway. The house was their home, their refuge, and must be made to feel safe.

With this resolve, Toby carried the television into the entrance hall, and having placed it by the telephone table, stood up to unlock the front door. Upon turning the handle it swung open violently, sending a rush of stinging air into his face. Outside the street was in darkness; no familiar lamps shone, but the road and pavement glistened with a steely glow that appeared to ripple and convulse like the surface of a wind torn lake. The illusion was all but real, for there was water everywhere! Huge puddles had formed in low spaces, driveways were awash, lawns submerged and drains overflowing – their heavy covers pushed aside by the gathering surge from below. The road had become a river, which separated a little further along, the major part flowing over the Green before passing between, or through several houses beyond. Fresh shafts of lightning continually lit up the scene, occasionally revealing vague spectral shapes moving in and out of the shadows as ill-advised householders ventured abroad to secure ravaged items of property. As Toby watched, a mighty crash of thunder caused him to flinch, and in the same moment, grey haired Mr Hayden, his immediate neighbour, staggered across the driveway entrance. The frail pensioner stumbled and fell full-length onto the wet pavement, to be caught by the wind, like a discarded bundle of rags, and rolled over into the base of a privet hedge. Painfully, the elderly man pulled himself to his knees and their eyes met.

'Go inside Bill, or you'll be killed!' cried Toby.

'We've lost some slates and the water's getting into the house,' the old fellow groaned despairingly. 'It's dripping through the ceiling in the bedroom. I need to call a handyman, but the telephone doesn't work. And now I find that one of the wretched tiles has broken the car windscreen, so I can't so much as drive to get help. Ivy's terribly worried... What can I do?'

Toby moved out into the deluge to help him to his feet, and together they fought their way back to the front door of Number 86, Toby endeavouring to give what reassurance he could through the strands of wet hair constantly whipping across his face.

'There's no point in taking risks, Bill! Just go inside and look after Ivy until morning. Keep warm and dry as best you can – it's sure to blow over by then. I'll pop in to see you when daylight comes. Worse things happen at sea, don't they?'

'But I'm 82 and I've never seen anything like this,' the old man mouthed plaintively. 'What are we to do if the roof comes off? Where will we go?'

'It won't! Now go inside – I'll see you tomorrow!'

With that, Toby pushed him through the porch, and Mr Hayden, with a final frightened nod, managed to close the heavy door with a click.

Battling the raging wind, and twice stumbling himself, Toby returned to the door of his own house, which had been pushed wide open by succeeding blasts. Without further delay he quickly heaved the ruined television outside, but upon preparing to shut out the night once more, a loud crack and the sound of thrashing foliage drew his attention towards the Green. A large horse chestnut tree, heavy with spring leaves and lashed by the relentless torrent of wind and rain, had lost its footing in the waterlogged soil, and he watched as it fell across the road with a splintering crash. Further down Hawthorn Drive similar falls occurred at two other points soon afterward – each tree blocking a major junction to leave local residents effectively cut off from the outside world!

* * *

Throughout the night the storm refused to abate and as dawn came, spreading a sickly glow across the fevered eastern sky, a vast catalogue of damage was revealed. But those who thought conditions would improve with the coming of day were sadly mistaken, for the onslaught continued and the gale, while occasionally moderating for a few minutes, unfailingly returned with renewed force and vigour. Toby kept his word and revisited the Haydens, but there was little he could do to comfort the old couple, except encourage them to stay indoors and keep warm.

Power lines were down, and without electricity gaining knowledge of the situation across the country proved difficult. A previously little used portable radio enabled the Freemans to stay in touch with outside events, but the news reaching them was insubstantial and sketchy. Many normal channels were off air, while those still broadcasting apparently struggled to give a useful account of what was happening.

The position everywhere was chaotic. Ninety per cent of the country was without power due to fallen pylons, with transport – road, rail and air – at a standstill. Shops and businesses were closed, "For at least the next twenty-four hours", schools and community services shut. Most hospitals had so far endeavoured to stay open, but with many able to accept only emergency admissions because of severe structural damage. Countless water mains were broken due to uprooted trees, and several million households left unable to flush their toilets in areas where pumping stations had ceased to function. Flooding was widespread, with half of all rivers bursting their banks; while evacuation of those most seriously affected would be severely disrupted due to the unprecedented conditions. Skeleton police and rescue services remained in place, though response times were "unpredictable". The weather forecast did promise an eventual lessening of the storm, but prolonged gusts of Force 12 winds might be expected to continue for up to another twenty-four hours. Residents were advised against leaving their homes, but to stay in touch by mobile phone where possible.

* * *

Darkness came early that Thursday evening, with conditions critical in many parts. Those living on the opposite side of the Green had, like many Molliton residents, suffered ground floor flooding, as the doleful light from candles and torches glowing dimly in upstairs windows gave testament. For their part, Toby and Jenny managed well enough, although the children had grown increasingly fractious and upset as the hours passed. Together the family ate a simple meal of baked beans and scrambled eggs (the last of the latter that they would enjoy for some time) before Jenny settled Sophie and Brendan in the main bedroom for the night. Toby again visited Bill and Ivy at around 8pm, and was assured by them that they could cope for the time being. Then, as he left to return home, the rain paused for a moment. There was even a gap in the clouds above his head where one bright star twinkled – a reminder of normality.

'Can it be over?' he thought. 'Perhaps tomorrow we'll be able to make a start on putting things right.' But Toby had scarcely made it to the garden gate before a redoubled rush of air, roaring up from the west like an express train, screamed out of the night sky.

A wind stronger and more destructive than any previously experienced in those parts began to lash around him as he reached the front porch. A blast, not cold with rain, but warm like the breath of some rabid beast in search of prey, tore between ravaged houses rattling every door and window. Crashing tiles shattered upon pavements as Toby crouched to look back at the street… A garage collapsed nearby, sending a shower of debris – wooden boards, corrugated panels, plastic sheets and garden furniture – cascading down the cluttered road. A caravan standing in a nearby driveway came away from the improvised anchorage that its owner had struggled to construct during the day, before toppling onto the pavement – its side and roof torn away by the howling torrent. Then Toby gazed in awe as a tall poplar tree floundered into the side of a house with a fearful grinding of masonary and glass. Part of the roof was torn off another property before falling with a thundering crash into an adjoining garden – an event dramatically surpassed seconds later when an ancient oak tree (reckoned by some to be more than three hundred years old) arced slowly over onto a parked car, crushing the vehicle completely and leaving its own mighty root system exposed to the sky.

Ominous sounds nearer at hand also began to demand Toby's attention. A tree in the rambling copse behind his garden was heard to fall, the fearful noise of splintering wood being followed moments later by a shrill cacophony of breaking glass.

'My greenhouse…' mouthed Toby, and might have attempted to force his way into the hurricane to investigate, if just then a large slate, accompanied by a substantial lump of concrete, had not landed in the driveway four feet away! Un-nerved by the close proximity of the impact, he peered warily up through the swirling pall of rain to see tiles on the western side of the Haydens' house being lifted up and flung away by the wind. Many came crashing to the ground almost at once, while others were carried aloft some distance, whirling off into the night sky to bring destruction elsewhere – the smashing of conservatory windows and fence panels recording their trail of devastation. But the clawing wind did not stop at the tiles of No. 86. Protective roof felt was also ripped away, thus exposing the contents of the loft, much of which Toby saw raised and sent spinning into the night. As a consequence, two suitcases were later found in the nearby play area; the severed head of a wooden rocking horse landed in a garden pond; and a baby's cot was discovered three weeks later among the ruins of a conservatory at No. 68. Within three minutes, all that remained defiantly resisting Nature's fury was the end brickwork, the metal water tank and a primitive framework of storm lashed wooden beams.

The savagery of the unfolding spectacle galvanised Toby, and he would have risked the clear danger to himself by returning to assist his neighbours had his attention not been drawn to another development – for he now became aware that something similar, although less advanced, was beginning to happen to the fabric of his own property. The west facing tiles were already coming away in ones and twos, and it looked as if the whole roof might likewise succumb to the snarling elements. Yet, although the rain had started to fall heavily once more, Toby sensed that the initial frenzy of the onslaught was weakening. If he could only keep the winds at bay a little longer the family might yet avoid the dismal fate of others. Another long and anxious night was in prospect as he retreated inside and closed the door, temporarily forgetting the plight of the Haydens as he focussed upon the peril near at hand.

* * *

An immediate examination of the loft space was required. Was there a gap in the roof? Could he do anything to make necessary repairs? Jenny was waiting on the landing and together they found the ladder from the spare room before placing it under the trapdoor. Equipped with a torch, Toby lifted the loft lid and squinted up at the roof above. He spied a narrow space where the tiles had gone from the west facing edge, below which water was already beginning to puddle between ceiling joists. This would soon seep through onto the landing and into the third bedroom, making immediate remedial action essential if sections of plaster were not to fall.

'Get the toolbox and some two inch nails from the spare room,' he called down. 'I think I can do something, but I'll need to act fast!'

Having found some lengths of wood left behind by the previous owner, Toby worked hard for almost three hours, cutting a number of battens and hammering them vertically into the furthest roof beam on the exposed side. This was a precarious job, perched as he was on narrow loft timbers while being continuously showered with rain and spray from outside. Next he set about securing the remaining planks to close up the gap. Some rainwater would still get in between the roof wall and his shield, but at least the majority of the loft space was protected and the ceiling saved from immediate collapse.

The dead of night had already passed before the task was finished: by now the storm had moderated further, and the rain, although still exceptionally heavy, had lost its wild intensity. Jenny found him a change of clothes and brought a mug of soup she'd prepared over the camping stove. Then he curled up with her beside the sleeping children. Yet Toby could not rest, but lay awake with eyes open listening for telltale signs and noises that would warn of new dangers. In this way he witnessed the dawning of Friday, 26th May, and again remembered Bill and Ivy Hayden.

* * *

The second full day of the storm had begun, but this would be one of excess rain rather than devastating wind. The gale was again blowing fiercely, but it was the enduring torrent continually drenching the land that did so much damage. The Freemans were not spared. Water from their flooded patio found its way into the dining room, and rivulets streaming down the walls of the spare room and stairway formed puddles in the hall. A section of dislodged guttering from No. 82 shattered the kitchen window, a considerable amount of rain getting in through the jagged opening before Toby was able to board it over.

However, these problems were not to be Toby's main worry that morning; for when it was still only 7.30am, the plight of the Haydens gripped him again. How had they managed? Why had he left them alone during the night?

'I'm going next door to check on Bill and Ivy,' he said at last, upon meeting Jenny's gaze.

She looked at him anxiously, thinking about the children and their own difficult situation. 'But what can you do, Toby? Don't go, love, we need you here.'

'I can't just leave them, Jenny,' he insisted, donning a waterproof coat. 'Trust me, I won't be long.'

As the front door swung open, the two looked out upon a chilling but now familiar sight. Slanting rain was still beating down sending a dancing haze into the air, which curled away in a dense mist over the open spaces. Foodwater was everywhere; great pools filling the driveway and a lake covering half the Green. The road itself resembled a sliding river circling and bubbling between the houses, while all around were toppled trees, damaged cars and accumulations of floating debris. A vision of the Haydens' roof being carried away the previous evening flashed before Toby's mind.

'Oh my Lord – what can have happened to them?' The words escaped his throat like a sigh of grief.

He strode out, splashing through the flood, and upon rounding the beech hedge separating the two properties, found his worst fears confirmed. The house had suffered miserably during the night and the front door stood open!

He hurried forward to call inside, but no answer came.

Many would say they are able to sense the presence of others without the evidence of sight or hearing – by this instinct Toby knew the house was empty.

Swiftly ascending to the landing he found the first floor wrecked. When the roof had been torn away the ceilings must have collapsed soon after, and every room had been ravaged by wind and deluge. Rain beat down upon his face as he stared up through dripping roof beams toward swirling clouds above.

Downstairs was little better. Most ceilings were still intact, though severely warped and streaming, and Toby discovered to his dismay that Mr and Mrs Hayden had evidently taken their final refuge in a corner of the lounge: a rumpled patch on the sofa, flanked by sodden blankets and pillows, clearly showing where the frightened couple had cowered together in a vain attempt to keep warm and dry. Close by, a small canvas groundsheet, doubtless held to provide shelter from the damp, lay cast aside in a corner.

'Where are they?' Toby whispered, rubbing his temple. 'Where can they have gone?'

It was then that he noticed a curling leaf of notepaper on the coffee table, and picking it up, saw that a message had been written upon it in the familiar spidery hand of the elderly. But the paper was wet and at first he could not read the smeared and faded words... Moving to the porch, Toby held it to the light, his heart sinking as he squinted at the faint script:

> Dear Toby and Jenny,
>
> Thank you for your kindness and support yesterday. It's still the middle of the night but I think we really need to find somewhere drier. Can't seem to keep warm and Ivy has developed a bit of a cough, so have decided to take her to the hospital – the radio said it was still open. Perhaps the exercise will do her good. Didn't want to bother you and the children during the dark hours. Take care of yourselves.
>
> Best wishes, Bill and Ivy.

Toby bowed his head. The hospital was three miles away, the roads flooded and impassable. How could two elderly people in their eighties possibly make such a journey?

'I should have invited them in,' he whispered. 'We could have managed together, somehow.'

Following his return to No. 84, Jenny gradually gleaned what had been found. 'I'm going to look for them,' Toby said at last. 'They might not have got far.'

She found his Wellington boots and saw him off once more, but his quest would be in vain. The wind had returned with renewed vigour, and rain falling in intermittent bursts from the dark underbelly of low and brooding clouds rattled against his hunched shoulders. All around both roads and pavements were virtually impassable, due to the tangle of fallen trees and piles of debris that had built up against every wall and obstacle. Trudging on, Toby searched as far as he could, calling out to the few people who hailed him from doors and upstairs windows, but learning nothing of the Haydens' fate. Nobody had seen them, and few appeared interested.

'What did the foolish old folk think they were doing, venturing out on such a night?' one woman responded, curtly. 'Hadn't they been warned to stay indoors?'

* * *

Thus his foray seemed to achieve nothing – a pointless journey through deserted streets and alleyways – until he came upon a strange and inquisitive Jack Russell dog crouching in a dry space under a broken door. The alert little fellow eyed Toby intently as he approached; head cocked on one side as if recognising him; before dashing off triumphantly through wide puddles barking sharply to the sky.

'Where did he come from?' thought Toby, feeling a little curious despite his low spirits. 'It was as if the little chap knew me... but how?'

* * *

He returned home much later, having long since put the odd apparition from his mind, and was saddened that Jenny's practical reaction mirrored others he'd heard.

'It's not your fault, Toby. The Haydens could have come here. It was very unwise of them to do what they did.'

But Toby took no comfort from her words, for he felt in his heart that the tragic circumstances they were all suffering should have brought the two families together, not led to this...

Jenny would learn later what had actually happened to Bill and Ivy.

* * *

Driven by their desperate situation they had made their way down through the village without meeting another soul, before coming at last to the old, many arched river bridge. There, finding the road flooded at both ends, they were unable to pass, and had chosen

11

instead to attempt a more circular and longer route via the bypass. Ivy's strength was now at an end however, and she collapsed a short while later, falling unconscious on the wet earth. Bill, also exhausted and confused, had stayed with her for an hour, sheltering his wife's soaking body from the pouring rain with his own. He'd continually called out for help, and as dawn approached was eventually heard by the owner of a nearby cottage. Together the two men managed to carry Ivy inside, but soon after, worn out and perished by the cold, she died.

For his part, now left alone after fifty-two years of marriage, poor Bill Hayden never fully recovered from the trauma of his loss, and having been discharged from hospital into the care of a nursing home, passed away three years later.

* * *

The storm continued through the second day, the sky dark with cloud and rain, until the winds finally moderated before evening. By then there was more activity on the radio and Toby tuned into the BBC to get a national update of the weather situation. Heavy downfalls were forecast to continue for most of the night, but by morning an improvement was promised as drier conditions moved in from the Atlantic. In the meantime, families were advised to stay at home until the restoration of services could begin in earnest the following day.

After putting the children to bed Toby and Jenny had discussed the situation, but they were both very tired and found it hard to agree on a course of action. Toby's apparent lack of focus irritated Jenny, who was anxious to make firm plans for their immediate future. She had been able to use her mobile phone to contact her parents in North London who, while themselves quite seriously affected by damage to their own home, were clearly in a much better and drier position than the Freemans.

'I want to get away from here with the children for a while,' Jenny argued. 'At least until the worst of the mess is sorted out. We are very lucky to have somewhere to go!'

But Toby could not generate any enthusiasm for the scheme. Someone would have to stay on while the insurance and building work was sorted out and he didn't much relish being left behind. Equally stressed by their difficult situation, an impasse was reached and a row followed. When Jenny told him to 'Pull himself together!' Toby left the bedroom and retreated downstairs to think things over, eventually falling asleep at past midnight disconsolately slumped before the mirror in the entrance hall.

* * *

Not until the early hours of Saturday, 27th May, did many begin to realise that so much which had seemed permanent and dependable before the storm had gone. True, almost all the damage could be repaired, and in time services would get back to normal, but in another way, no matter how hard they endeavoured to put this shock behind them, the old certainties had disappeared. If such an event could happen once – why shouldn't it happen again? Indeed, those that understood "Climate Change" considered this more than likely.

* * *

Upon waking, Toby picked himself up and opened the front door. The rain had stopped and a pale sun miraculously shone down through fleeting clouds. People were already busily beginning the long and difficult task of recovery. There was activity everywhere: cars being opened and examined for damage, ruined furniture heaved into the open and a start made on clearing the roads. But this great effort would take many weeks and months to accomplish; for the scale of destruction to homes and power supplies was far beyond anything ever experienced before. Many houses had been severely damaged, a number losing their roofs, while there were more fallen trees than those left standing defiantly upright denuded of leaves. Water filled every low area, the earth being temporarily reduced to a bog. There were worrying health hazards too. Drains and sewers had been washed out and already a faintly unpleasant odour of foul water and decay began to pervade the air. Seven local people, feared swept away by flash floods, were missing.

Toby looked wearily up at the house and then gazed sadly at the wreckage of No. 86. 'This is a nightmare,' he thought. 'Everything's turned upside down.'

Upon wandering forlornly round to the patio to survey the rear garden, his former haven, he found that it too was destroyed: every fence blown down, the greenhouse flattened, and part of the roof torn from the garage. Where would he begin the task of rebuilding?

* * *

For her part, Jenny had no such doubts. Straightway she busied herself around the house, but the lack of water was a problem. They could flush the toilet using rainwater and a bucket, but the drains were damaged and overflowing, so in a short time there would be consequences. The camping gas had also begun to run low, and although they might manage well enough on tinned food and bottled drinking water for about three days – what then? A further call to her mother confirmed that things were likely to improve more rapidly in London. There was already bread in some of the shops and power had been restored in Barnet. Engineers hoped to reopen two lanes of the M1 by Sunday morning, and a bus service would then be provided to ferry people to and from the capital if they could reach temporary staging points along the motorway.

'I'll set off with the children tomorrow,' she announced resolutely, as they sat together eating dinner.

'But the nearest pick-up point is Milton Keynes,' Toby protested. 'That's eight miles away. How will you get there?'

'The three of us will make it, even if I have to walk the whole distance. I'll wheel Brendan and Sophie in the buggy. Mum will provide us with clothes and everything else when we get to London. I've made up my mind, Toby – we really must leave here for a spell. It's not safe to stay and the children need comfort and reassurance.'

With that the matter was concluded: Jenny could be both resourceful and determined in a crisis – she would not be dissuaded.

* * *

They spent the rest of the day tidying up as much as possible, during which time the children had to be kept indoors because of the multitude of hazards outside, confirming the logic of taking them away for a while. A group of workmen made a start on logging fallen trees and by evening had established several corridors negotiable by pedestrians. News came in before dusk that much of the Molliton to Milton Keynes road had also been partially cleared, and by seven o'clock Jenny had the children safely tucked up in bed with a view to setting out early when morning came.

Toby slept fitfully during the short hours of darkness, before waking to find Jenny already up. She had fed the children and was enthusing about the adventure ahead. 'We'll be like explorers,' he heard her say as he approached the kitchen, 'and when we get there you'll see Nanna and Grandad. Won't it be lovely?'

Brendan and Sophie were less happy, however, upon learning that Daddy was not going with them. But Jenny's assurance that Toby would follow as soon as possible restored their spirits and both were full of beans when, seated in the double buggy, the time came to depart.

'You're mad, you know that, Jenny,' Toby said, as they stood quietly to one side. 'What if there are hold-ups? What if you can't get through? You could be in real trouble then.'

'That's not going to happen… I promise,' she said, smiling softly, a tear welling at the corner of an eye. 'I'm going to miss you a million too, you know that.'

He gazed at her, realizing there was little more that could be usefully said, then sadly bent down to kiss his children before rising again.

For a few moments Jenny moved into his arms, holding him tightly and looking deeply into his eyes; reading his emotions. Their lips touched briefly. 'I love you so much, Toby,' she whispered. 'But just now this is for the best. You do understand, don't

you? Come as soon as you can – the children will be longing for us to be together again…
God bless.'

With these parting words she gripped the handles of the buggy, and delaying no longer, moved swiftly away, weaving between the many obstacles still heaped on the road and pavement. Then, upon reaching the alleyway leading to the Milton Keynes road, she turned and smiled a last farewell as Brendan and Sophie waved, before the three disappeared from sight.

* * *

It was to be the last time Toby would see his family in this world.

PART ONE (1913–2013)

FIRE AND TEMPEST

Hold the blindfold down so your eyes can't see,
Now run as fast as you can through this field of trees.

from
"Smokers Outside the Hospital Doors"
Editors

Chapter One

Pilgrim and Fellow Travellers

TOBY FOUND HIMSELF ALONE AND ISOLATED. ALTHOUGH all around the sounds of urgent human activity went on, he felt no desire simply to pick up his life as before.

'They imagine this is a one off, but what if it isn't...? Am I the only one who can foresee that possibility?'

Consequently little progress was made toward restoring the family home. The day wore on, and when a light rain began to fall during the afternoon, he phoned Jenny to check that she and the children were safe – learning that they had successfully made their way to the motorway and were now on a coach to London. However, the journey would take some time, as the partially open M1 had become jammed with a multitude of traffic travelling south to the capital. There was little evidence of formal organisation and some tempers were wearing thin; nevertheless, it was certain they would be alright; Toby was not to worry; she and the children sent their love and would make contact again soon.

He spoke to no one else until the evening, when, at around 5pm, an official from the local council appeared in the Haydens' driveway. The rain had ceased once more, giving way to a muggy dampness, and Toby was in the process of opening the lounge windows to air the house when a man approached. The newcomer had obviously walked some way as his leather shoes were much caked with mud. His once smart black raincoat was spattered too, and he appeared to have been enlisted at short notice for his errand, the crudely cut yellow armband below his shoulder bearing the words, "Disaster Warden". As Toby watched the council representative rummaged in the large canvas bag slung over his shoulder, and having produced a heavy-duty office stapler, strode out of sight towards the Haydens' door.

Toby was outside in seconds to ask what, if anything, might be known concerning the old couple. But by the time he drew close, the other had already finished his task, and upon looking up, seemed both startled and annoyed to be approached without warning. Regaining his composure, he fixed Toby with a sour and accusatory stare.

'You really shouldn't go creeping up on people like that. You gave me a start!' he said in a clipped and unpleasant nasal voice.

'Oh I didn't mean to,' Toby apologised awkwardly. 'I just wondered if you had any news of my neighbours…'

Nodding slowly, the warden stepped aside to reveal a notice freshly stapled to the front door. It read:

All enquiries about the owners of this property should be
made to Greyfriars Police Station. Bedford.
Tel. (01234) 4838999
Entry into, or removal of property from these premises is
strictly prohibited.

The council man looked up at the shell of No. 86, a half-smile upon his lips. 'Not that anyone is likely to find much of use in there,' he chuckled. 'I thought my house was in a bad enough state, but this one… Good Lord, what a mess!'

He sounded both detached and offensively smug about his own relative good fortune, and Toby hesitated for a moment, clenching a palm, before asking in a faltering voice… 'Do you know how they are – the owners, I mean?'

The official dug into his bag and pulled out a list, which he proceeded to peruse absently. 'The woman, Mrs Ivy Hayden… she's dead, died of exposure. Her husband… Mr William Hayden… now let's see… he's in Bedford Hospital – taken there three nights ago. It says here they were found down by the river. Why, what's it to you?'

Toby turned away in an effort to conceal his emotions. 'Because they were my neighbours, man… because I'm concerned about them… And now you tell me Ivy's dead…'

How could such a tragedy have happened? …And how could this petty office scribe be so glib about the outcome?

If the man had noted Toby's distress he barely showed it, but the tone of his response was crisp and calculating. 'Look, my friend,' he continued, pointedly. 'I reckon that if the neighbours of these good old people had been looking out for them, they wouldn't have been walking around at four in the morning in the midst of a howling gale… Now would they?'

The obvious and deliberate intended barb pierced Toby to the heart.

'Don't blame me for being the bringer of bad news,' the other added, clearly relishing the opportunity to drive home a point. 'I'm just the poor so-and-so who struggled into work this morning to be rewarded with this job. You might like to know that there are over three hundred badly damaged houses in Molliton alone, most of them rendered uninhabitable, like this one, while more than a quarter of the whole village has been flooded out. In addition, eleven people have been killed or found drowned in and around Bedford already – while the list of those missing grows by the hour. This is a major disaster and I'm simply here to start picking up the pieces. Now, if you will excuse me I must be getting on, or I'll not finish before dark.'

With that he turned and walked off down the street, leaving Toby with his head bowed.

*   *   *

The rest of the evening passed slowly. Gradually the accompanying sounds of urgent work grew less, and just before ten o'clock, as if by common consent, most noises ceased altogether. The majority of people, weary from their endeavours and the stress of recent days, were happy to go to their beds, but they would begin again in the early light ensuring the long process of returning to normal went on.

For Toby it was different however. Left alone with his thoughts he wandered around aimlessly as twilight fell and darkness enveloped the empty house, more than once giving consideration to phoning Jenny as night descended. But with the battery of his mobile low, and thinking that she might already be in bed after a tiring journey, he let each opportunity pass. A feeling of guilt over the death of Mrs. Hayden weighed heavily, and having locked up he lowered himself into an armchair to sleep: dozing fitfully through the small hours, a sense of desolation preventing proper rest.

Thus, not long after a first pale hint of morning began to colour the eastern sky, Toby became fully awake once more as day dawned, reassuringly calm on Monday 29th May 2013, and hearing the song of birds, he recalled the season. 'Nests and eggs,' he thought. 'Nature soldiers on while vain and selfish Man seeks to have and dominate all!' Nevertheless, the lusty song of a robin heartened him and he got up to search for food and clean clothes.

Fresh produce was becoming scarce. Every drop of milk had been used up and the contents of an unpowered fridge had largely gone off. He ate cereals with orange juice out of a packet and finished with a slice of fruitcake from the larder, but finding sufficient provisions in future would be an increasing challenge.

The morning had become much brighter than the day before, with a prospect of sustained sunshine, and the familiar sounds of power saws, drills and hammers soon began to fill the air once more. Toby watched as a mobile water tank was manually hauled onto a patch of newly laid concrete on the Green, and later, as workmen heaved a generator into position beside it. Power cables were then run out in several directions, enabling the general buzz and whirr of activity to increase further. But the task was daunting, the sheer scale of the damage, and shortage of materials, ensuring that it would take many days to make a significant impression on the work to be done. Any useful movement of vehicles was still impossible; therefore everything required had to be wheeled or carried up from the main road half a mile away. Meanwhile, the local food

21

store, seriously flooded during the storm, remained shut and not expected to re-open until the end of the week – a situation replicated ten thousand times across England.

* * *

Nobody came to see Toby. He opened the windows to air the house, and having made some attempt to remove rubbish and debris from the patio, put up a makeshift clothes-horse to dry wet clothes and carpets. But his heart wasn't in it. He had reached a point where he needed to think, to escape from normal surroundings in an endeavour to clear his head. If Jenny had been there it would have been different, but left by himself his motivation waned. Something had changed. The offhand way the official had spoken, and a growing sense that he too must have become selfish and complacent, nagged at a frayed and private corner.

'What are we doing?' he said inwardly. 'We mess up our world and its climate, and then, when something like this happens, half of us just ignore the other half and set about rebuilding it all over again as if nothing is seriously wrong or needs to change.'

Once more he flicked the lid of the mobile phone, but the transmission signal had gone completely. It was a moment of deep isolation. He needed to talk, but not about the storm or clearing up – at the very least he must get away for a while.

'A walk… I'll go for a walk! Why not?' The idea came naturally. What difference would it make if he went off for an hour or two? 'Maybe I'll feel a lot more positive if I do.'

Toby was in the habit of taking long walks alone. During his hour or two away Jenny would sometimes wonder where he got to, but as he generally came home seeming refreshed and positive, she rarely questioned him about his wanderings.

Having made his decision, Toby felt the impetus to set off without delay and in little time had secured the house once more. He located some bottled water, and anticipating that the footpaths were sure to be wet and rutted after the rain, put on a pair of stout leather walking boots, finally donning an old blue fleece jacket over faded timber-check shirt and cord jeans. Then, after a last look round, he left the house and closed the front door with a final click of the latch, before walking to the front gate, and having glanced pensively towards No. 86, made his way purposefully down Hawthorn Drive. …It was just after ten o'clock in the morning.

* * *

Toby was heading for a narrow alley some two hundred metres away where a country path began. He walked quickly, not wanting to make contact with either workmen or neighbours, who would doubtless ask him how he was getting on and how he managed to find an hour for leisure at such a time. He did pass a number of people, some of whom looked up and might have spoken; but with a cursory, 'Good morning', strode swiftly on, leaving them to return to what they were doing. The only person he made eye contact with was a small middle-aged woman in a worn and mud-spattered dress. She was sitting on a leather chair in her front garden, next to a heap of wet and ruined furniture: a television, a cooker, a warped coffee table and a soiled roll of carpet; all piled together with a tumble of broken ornaments, toys and household belongings. The lady held a framed family portrait and had clearly been weeping. Toby was vividly reminded of haunting photographs he had seen many times of refugees from war zones – and those chilling black and white newsreels of people fleeing the fighting in World War Two. Yet this woman's world had been torn apart, not by war, but by the devastating fury of a "freak" storm that had ravaged her own street. …The effect was no less bewildering.

He stopped momentarily, and might have ventured to speak but for realizing that she had resumed staring blankly ahead, her hands trembling, too traumatised and overcome by her recent ordeal to be properly aware of his presence. Sounds coming from inside the house suggested the family was preparing to leave, and looking up he witnessed a roof damaged beyond repair. Moving away, Toby wondered where they would go, then, having reached the alleyway, he turned into it, passing a battered footpath sign knocked sideways by a falling tree. After a few additional strides he realised that the narrow passage was virtually impassable, for the fence on one side had been blown over, and a mass of accumulated debris, some washed there, some blown by the wind, had been deposited in a tangled pile beside an adjacent garage, blocking his path. At first, Toby considered turning back, but having no wish to abandon his intended journey so soon, decided instead to risk climbing over. So it was that, having slipped and stumbled a number of times on the precarious jumble of objects, he at last dropped down on the other side – the mass of rubbish now forming a rambling barrier between him and the devastated street behind.

Somewhat winded from his exertions he stepped forward, breathing deeply, as the sun came out from behind a cloud, bathing the spot in a patch of reassuring warmth. The atmosphere seemed to change in an instant; for some of the dampness immediately went out of the air, which became both drier and fresher. Toby spread his arms like a grateful flower and looked up as a sense of calm came upon him, allowing a moment of forgetfulness. But this pleasant reverie was all too brief, for from behind, a large crow, cawing loudly, suddenly stooped past his head – its black wing lightly brushing the side of Toby's face before it dipped out of sight beyond the trees a short way distant.

Taken by surprise, and having been rudely shaken back into the present, Toby moved cautiously forward, wary of a repeat performance, towards the pedestrian "kissing-gate" that marked the beginning of his country walk. As he did so, the noise and clatter rising from the nearby streets lessened appreciably, and in the settling tranquillity he began to hear the song of small birds round about. A promise of quiet and solitude drew him as he negotiated the barrier, but upon emerging into the sheltered corner on the other side he was surprised to see a curious little man sitting comfortably in an old-fashioned deckchair.

* * *

Before walkers strike out into the large field that Toby intended to cross, there is at this point a small patch of green next to a guide camp and a five-acre bluebell wood. The recent winds had caused considerable damage at the location, but although two or three of the hawthorn trees had been blown down and most of the growing wheat in the field was flattened, the spot still retained a tangible atmosphere of summer peace and calm. Certainly the person now looking up at Toby from beneath the brim of a curious old-fashioned wide brimmed hat seemed to find it most benign and pleasant. Their eyes met, and Toby had an odd sensation that he was being appraised with satisfaction, as if he were expected. A perceptible nod of the stranger's head did nothing to dispel this impression.

The man was of short but stocky build, and had an air of independence that contrasted strongly with Toby's uncertain manner. He wore a countryman's clothes: a slate grey check shirt, heavy brown cotton trousers supported by a wide polished leather belt, Wellington boots turned over at the top to reveal the lining, and a three-quarter length indigo travelling coat. His taste for dark colours was evident; which he wore with a style and confidence that gave an impression of relaxed self-assurance. Meanwhile, the piercing eyes that twinkled above his sharp nose suggested mischief rather than malice, although they were not such that all would trust. Black hair curled over his collar and a shimmering silver earring shone in the lobe of his left ear as he returned Toby's gaze unblinkingly, all the while slowly rolling a large stone dice between his fingers.

Feeling uncomfortable at being so obviously scrutinised, Toby decided to move on without delay, but was checked when the stranger spoke in a casual rustic drawl.

'Going for a walk then… can't say I blame you… it's just the day for one.'

His voice was deep, rounded and strangely at variance with the small frame from which it emanated.

Toby turned back hesitantly. 'Yes… I needed some fresh air… I thought it would do me good,' he replied, in an effort to pass the time of day.

The stranger smiled. 'I'm sure it will, friend. You've earned it; so take your time… for who knows what you'll come across? And in any event, there'll be no point in turning back until your journey's done.'

These comments were so ambiguous that they made Toby delay his departure once more; while for his part the little man had now risen from the chair and stood casually

24

facing him with hands in pockets, the smile previously upon his features having been replaced by a more knowing expression.

Toby looked down at his feet, then around at his footprints on the smooth, muddy earth. Clearly no one else had passed that way for some time, yet still he felt compelled to ask... 'Have any others come by today?'

'No, not recently... it would seem you're to be the only one, Toby.'

Toby nodded absently and had begun to move away before fully registering the mention of his name. The realisation of having been addressed in person – and with such casual familiarity – by someone he had no recollection of meeting previously, sent a sudden chill down his spine. 'You know my name,' he said, turning warily. 'But do I know you?'

From his outward manner the stranger seemed quite dismissive of this question, but when it came his reply was equally enigmatic and puzzling.

'I heard someone speak to you in the shop one time... and no, we haven't met before... although I expect our paths may cross again soon,' he added mysteriously. 'But whatever... for now I'll toss the dice, just to see which number comes up.' He did so, without awaiting a further response from Toby, catching it upon his open palm to reveal a three.

'The numbers?' asked Toby, stepping closer.

'The numbers from one to six,' replied the other. 'All common enough, you might say... but if this dice should roll a seven,' he added with a wink. 'Well then you'll know that the world has changed...'

'A seven?' said Toby. 'Surely no ordinary six sided dice can show a seven? May I see it?'

'Be my guest,' said the stranger with something between a smile and an artful leer.

Toby took the smooth stone dice from the man's gnarled hand and turned it, the white spots on each face showing only six numbers as expected. He handed it back, reassured that the suggestion of a seventh must simply have been intended in jest.

'You almost had me convinced there,' he said, feeling relieved. 'I thought you really meant it.'

'...So you thought I was having you on, eh?' said the little man. 'Well, perhaps I was... we'll have to try again another time, won't we?'

With these words, the stranger fell silent, and having returned to the comfort of his chair, pulled the leather hat low over his brow as if clearly indicating their conversation was at an end. Yet Toby suspected that his penetrating eyes, now veiled in shadow, were still wide open beneath the brim.

Left standing awkwardly, and with an uneasy feeling that the other already knew much more about him than he would like, Toby walked on again and began to cross the sweeping expanse that locals called the "Ninety Acre Field" – a huge prairie of monoculture farmland created between twenty and thirty years after the Second World War from a number of smaller fields formerly bordered by ancient hedgerows. The latter had all been progressively grubbed out to allow the working of the earth by ever-bigger machinery, and the previous character of the countryside lost forever. But although devoid of trees and other man-made breaks, the landscape, as it swept up to the western horizon, still retained a majesty of scale that could influence and calm Toby's spirit. It was, too, the home of a small scattered colony of skylarks that won a meagre living on the open soil. That day, in late spring, at a time when it should have been looking its best, the whole area was now a sea of broken corn, some standing defiantly in narrow ridges, but most levelled and beginning to rot due to the ravages of wind and weather. Little would be saved.

Yet Toby began to move with a lighter step, for as he advanced across the field the last eddying flecks of low cloud lifted away, and the sun, now riding high in the sky, bathed everything in its strengthening glow. But, as he drew level with the edge of the wood away to his left, he was again stopped in his tracks, this time by the sight of a young woman with a dog making her way round the distant field boundary. She too became motionless, looking in his direction – a tall slender figure, her blonde hair tied back in a ponytail with a red ribbon. He could not see her face clearly, but sensed the intent expression upon it. Although dressed for outdoors, her neat attire and precise manner seemed unusual for one walking in the mud and damp. As he watched, she looked away toward the spot from which he had come, as if hearing a call. Toby's eyes followed, expecting to see the stranger still reclining in his deckchair. But the man had gone, and the place he'd occupied not five minutes before was empty, but for a single crow languidly circling into the trees.

The woman now moved purposefully in that direction, and upon arriving at the gate, glanced briefly over her shoulder before passing through. Then her dog, having pursued his own eccentric and weaving path, scampered up also, barked once and similarly disappeared from view. Thus Toby was left alone once more, pensively looking back, having noted that the excited little fellow bore an uncanny resemblance to the small brown and white Jack Russell he had recently encountered in his search for the Haydens. Yet, having already been twice delayed, Toby was anxious to get on, and with so much already on his mind, elected to put these encounters to the back of his thoughts. …If he had decided to escape the noise and confusion of Molliton, why shouldn't others do the same?

So thinking, he turned to resume his walk, the warm sun reviving his spirits once more.

The track was becoming drier, and Toby's progress, although initially slippery, became steadily swifter and more assured. Where at first he had walked with his head down, placing each foot with care, now, buoyed by a sense of renewed purpose, he began to look confidently ahead, judging the distance to be travelled. Evidence of the storm, in addition to the damaged crop, was to be seen at various points: a distant cottage had lost its chimneystack, a line of wind blown rubbish lay scattered across part of the field to his right, and most dramatic of all, two of the mighty electricity pylons that formerly stood upon the upland to the north, had been wrenched over by hurricane force winds and sent crashing to the ground in ruins, their snaking cables scorching the earth in a wide sinuous line as they fell.

Yet despite witnessing the grim and twisted remains of these once impressive structures, Toby was able to find reassurance and solace in other things. A lone dragonfly flew past him with a soft clatter of scaly wings, and then, most wonderfully, a skylark, startled by his approach, spiralled up ahead on a current of rising air, singing lustily to the morning. Shading his eyes from the brightness of the sun, he followed the direction of its call, and saw the ascending bird, a brown speck now high up on the breeze, its unbroken chorus filling the sky. Toby could not help but smile, the first time he had done so in days, for his heart swelled with joy and wonder.

The straight path was now coming to an end and he drew near an ungated farm entrance leading out onto the country road that traverses the two miles between Molliton and Stavenham. A quiet lane in bygone years, this had become a much busier road since hundreds of motorists began using it to avoid travelling through nearby Bedford. A constant stream of cars and commercial vehicles normally made it dangerous for those on foot, as commuters and tradespeople rushed by. But today was different, for there was little on the road; all being strangely quiet and peaceful. Toby stepped out onto the hard surface and listened – nothing, no sound of rasping acceleration, just silence. Looking left down the hill he saw the turn to Oakwell further on; but no vehicles appeared at the normally busy T-junction. The radio newsreader had said many roads were impassable and it was pleasant to have the place to himself.

Toby moved back through the entrance and began walking down the inside of the hedge. He could have gone on the road, but habit and a desire to get back where he might enjoy the view guided his steps. The going underfoot became easier still, and where he had splashed through puddles earlier, he now trod a firm pathway. That the soil could have dried out so much seemed a little odd, but Toby rejoiced at the change. The land too was more sheltered in this falling corner of the field, the barley much less damaged, as if it had lifted to greet the warming sun. Moreover, the grain had developed its summer beard and as he looked, a light breeze caused ripples to float away across the surface. A soft rustle of movement could be heard as each undulation passed, and as he dropped down the gentle slope, the wide expanse of flattened corn further off gradually disappeared from view. Thus the world within his sight was transformed by degrees – the damaged landscape seemingly restored and healed.

At last Toby drew opposite the turning to Oakwell, and passing through a gap in the farm fence, stepped down onto the road once more. At other times he would have needed to exercise great caution at this point, but today only the empty junction lay before him. Then, having turned and continued westward for a few yards, he forked left onto the track bed of the old Bedford to Northampton railway line, along which a country path had been established some years before. Often a relatively busy place, this secluded corner of England now seemed a lonely spot, unaffected by the outside world or recent events. Toby stopped in the centre of a rough piece of land normally used as a car park by dog walkers. Sometimes fly tippers dumped rubbish here too and there was often a scattering of discarded litter to be found. Today however, the area was both clean and unspoiled, and as Toby noted, there was no apparent damage to the natural environment. Late blossom still covered the blackthorn trees, and a variety of colourful wild flowers decorated the banks. There were no puddles either, and as he peered over into a nearby ditch he could see that this too was dry. …Yet how could that be when so much rain had recently fallen? The strangeness of these sights gradually began to sink in, and he rubbed his forehead… wondering. There were in fact no signs at all to suggest the recent storm had happened, although he was less than a mile from Molliton…

Toby had begun to feel distinctly uneasy, when he heard the sound of a vehicle approaching along the road from Molliton. The noise it made grew quickly and he tried to imagine what might appear… a police car perhaps, or an ambulance? Or might it be a group of workmen on their way to clear the road? But the car that actually trundled into view could not have been more unexpected. It was a small two-tone green family saloon, the light pastel colour of its bonnet, roof and boot contrasting quaintly with the darker racing green of wings and door panels – a tiny four-seater Austin A35 from another age. In an effort to see the driver, Toby ducked down as it passed by and caught a glimpse of a woman's face, together with a flash of red. Then the little car was gone, leaving behind a thin trail of white exhaust smoke as it descended into a dip in the road before rising up the further slope and disappearing over the rim of a hill.

Toby scratched his head in amazement. 'Who would be out driving a vintage car at a time like this?' he thought, and might have retraced his steps to search for further clues had another sound not drawn his attention. For as the noise of the little car finally died into the distance, he became aware of a muffled scraping sound coming from close by; and turning slowly, his eyes came to rest on an old fence post standing against the skyline at the top of the bank some ten metres away. On it had landed a large crow, which stood silhouetted against the late morning sky. The bird ducked its head as if to fly away, but then straightened again and seemed to watch him. Jet black, the creature's summer plumage glistening with a purple sheen as it caught the sun. Toby felt as if it might speak at any moment, but having apparently looked its fill, the crow deliberately turned through one hundred and eighty degrees, and with a last disdainful backward glance, took flight and drifted from view. Toby did not move for almost a minute as he went over the two things – the girl in her old car and this curious bird. He had a deep sense that things weren't adding up properly, a ridiculous fancy perhaps, but…?

* * *

The ground ahead rose out of a hollow, and having emerged from this he began to make his way along the alignment of the old railway. This had been planted with trees and bushes several years before and these in turn were now colonised by dog rose and ivy. The path weaved in and out; narrow in places, then opening into wider avenues where two or three might walk abreast. The embankment soon began to shelve away steeply on either side where the track bed had been raised up to provide an even gradient for the trains that once ran there. Toby could occasionally see well beyond the screen of trees and searched for signs of the storm. Yet all seemed quiet and ordered: the barley crop to his left, on the nearer edge of the "Ninety Acre Field", appearing stoutly upright and flourishing, while the newly sown potato crop on his right just showed through freshly cultivated soil.

The further Toby went the more things closer at hand began to surprise him too. He had lived in Bedfordshire all his life and knew the flora and fauna of his native county like any other countryman. In season there were primroses, violets, mallow and white campion to brighten the day, together with half a dozen other dependable common species. Yet the sights he now saw were altogether different, for a profusion of flowers carpeted the clearings and fringes of the path: tiny sparks of red and orange, bright flashes of pink, purple and soft pale blue – perhaps twenty or thirty different flowering species met his sight. The air too had begun to fill with sounds. Not the harsh clamour of modern life – road noise, farm machinery, the drone of aircraft or lawn mowers – but the varied song of many birds: sparrows chattering in a hawthorn thicket, the staccato 'tic tic – tic tic' of a blue tit family, the melodious harmonies of courting blackbirds and a cooing of lovelorn doves; while all around the soft humming of bees and insects promised honey. The only noises of man to be heard were the distant tolling of a church bell and a farmer calling his dog.

'This is too peaceful… unnatural', Toby thought. 'Where is everyone? Why is it so quiet?'

He pondered for a few moments, then, when about to move on once more, again saw the crow curving in a wide arc above the treetops. Rising overhead it gave out a loud 'Caark!' before melting into the leafy canopy.

'That bird again… what does it want?'

He had now walked about half a mile along the track and was approaching a mound of earth left years before when the county path had been created. It straddled the line of the old railway, and was meant as a decorative feature, but over time had fallen away in places, becoming covered by an untidy growth of nettles and straggling bindweed. Toby would usually have walked swiftly round and carried on, but today something caught his eye. At the base of the mound two hunks of rusty metal stuck out – the ends of railway lines… He blinked: this was *surely* not possible, for the line had closed many years before, in 1962, the track being torn up soon afterwards. Even the ballast had long since disappeared. Toby himself had passed by dozens of times and seen nothing! He thought for a moment. Could it be that the recent rains had exposed this previously hidden feature? But the area looked unchanged… it was as if the storm had never happened.

Moving curiously beyond the familiar obstruction his jaw dropped a second time, for there were rails on the other side too! A line of rusty track running away before him… Toby retraced his steps to check his first impression, before returning again. Part of him wanted to blink and find his eyes were deceiving him… but the rails and sleepers were stubbornly real! He knelt down to touch the nearest and came away with a rusty film upon fingertip and thumb.

'This can't be true,' he said aloud, then began to move cautiously forward, wondering if he had somehow fallen into a dream and might wake at any moment. But this waking dream went on – the rails curving along the embankment up a steadily rising grade.

At first many of the rotten sleepers were without ballast and a good number would barely support his weight, but gradually their condition improved and the initial profusion of weeds between the rails lessened. In a short time he came to a fully ballasted section, and then to a complete panel of sleepers that, although dried and cracked, seemed both sound and strong. …A little further still and the transformation was complete.

Here the railway became much straighter. The vegetation had been trimmed back and the line wandered on into the distance under the arch of a bridge. Beyond this stood a single semaphore signal, beside which the rails glinted faintly in the sunlight, a sickly sweet smell of newly applied creosote, coating the sleepers, scenting the air.

'My imagination has got the better of me…' thought Toby. 'This is impossible – it can't be happening.' Absently he stepped forward, genuinely concerned about his sanity, then turned and sat down upon the nearest rail.

Many possibilities went through his head. Was he really going out of his mind? Could all the worry about his family and the Haydens have brought him to this? But as much as he tried to find a believable explanation for what lay before him, the evidence before his eyes presented another truth. The rail he sat on was real enough, and the bridge before him could not be dismissed as a vision. It was both firm and solid, having been built to serve local farms; all of which had disappeared more than fifty years before. When the railway closed the bridge had been demolished, and the deep cutting below infilled. Yet now it was restored again, along with the line it had crossed.

Toby pondered, frequently shaking his head and digging his heels into the hard ballast, while the crow, having circled down once more, landed in a nearby tree as if intent upon studying him more closely.

Perhaps ten minutes passed before a sound disturbed him – a swishing noise close by, accompanied further off, beyond the bridge, by a pronounced 'clunk'; and glancing back, Toby noticed for the first time a signal cable conduit running beside the track. The cable inside had moved, and looking towards the bridge he could see the signal was now raised!

'A train? ...Surely not...'

Yet in the calm of the midday heat there were other signs to heed. He sensed a faint vibration through the seat of his trousers, and bending down could hear a humming sound coming from the rail. There were audible noises of a different kind too – for he could clearly discern the distant beat of a steam locomotive exhaust! Then a whistle blew, shattering the peace of his surroundings. ...A train *was* evidently approaching, rolling down the gradient on its way to Bedford.

Toby suddenly felt the need for caution. Did he want to be seen? He slid back into nearby bushes, crouched down, and waited as the train slid into view. It comprised a small six-coupled tender engine with eight trucks and a brake van in tow. The locomotive whistled again as it approached the bridge, then burst into life as it rolled past, a rush of steam and smoke rising from the chimney. There was a brief rattle and roar of passing trucks, a screech of metal on the track, then the noisy apparition receded away round the bend. Toby gained a good view of the driver and fireman in their open cab, but they, both busily engaged in their duties, had not noticed him. Then, as he stood up to watch the train disappear, the guard emerged onto the brake van veranda looking in his direction. He half-expected to be admonished for trespassing, but the man merely waved a parting farewell as the last wisps of smoke melted into the trees.

Stepping back between the rails, Toby flipped a fallen nugget of coal with his toe. 'I must find out what's going on,' he said to himself. 'That, or get back home as quickly as possible. They'll never believe me, whatever I tell them now.'

He had all but resolved to do the latter when the watching crow cawed loudly again and a horse drawn hay wagon hove into sight on the bridge.

This new equipage was a complete contrast to what he had just witnessed. A huge chestnut shire horse, moving slowly and sedately in the time-honoured fashion of its breed, hauled the ancient wagon. It was loaded with several heavy tarpaulins of the kind used to cover hayricks, but although the sturdy cart and its contents must have been of considerable weight, the horse seemed little troubled by his task. The driver sat upon a raised seat, leaning forward and holding the reins loosely between his fingers. He clenched an old pipe between his teeth, and his head, on which he wore a knotted handkerchief, became periodically wreathed in smoke. The horse stopped to nibble grass for a moment, but on its master's gentle call of 'Come on Caesar!', the beast lifted its head and patiently trundled forward once more. Had the man worn a smock coat and chewed upon a piece of straw, he could not more have resembled a character from one of Hardy's Wessex tales. Toby waited as the wagon rumbled out of sight beyond the row of bushes on the skyline, then moved forward and climbed the railway bank until he reached the level of the bridge.

The cart had already rumbled on a little way, but he became aware that a woman of between twenty and twenty-five was following on foot a short distance behind. She paused upon reaching the middle of the bridge and turned to face him. The newcomer was slender – almost fragile – her complexion pale, but it was her expression that held his attention – for she met him with a look that was both grave and purposeful. The young woman lifted her head and smiled, her blue eyes seeming to cast a light upon fine features. Moreover, in that first moment of their meeting, Toby had a profound feeling that she not only knew him, but could read his thoughts.

'It was you I saw earlier...' he stammered, 'with the dog... and in the car... I'm right, aren't I?'

'You are indeed, Toby. I congratulate you for having been so observant.'

He was taken aback by her frankness. Was she patronising him... inwardly laughing at his confusion? Yet there was no mockery in her eyes... But could he trust this other stranger any more than the first?

'Who are you?' he asked '...You've followed me... I know. Why have you done so?'

'My name is Jeannie... Jeannie Denton,' she replied. 'But you must not think of me as having followed you, for that would be untrue. It is better to accept that having searched for many years... I have found you at last.'

'But why seek me of all people? What have I done?'

She fixed him with a steady gaze, her head slightly inclined to one side. 'You have begun to ask important questions about yourself and your world, Toby. You want to *understand* the way we have all become – to know the future and to see how this earth can be saved from the excess and folly of men. But to comprehend these things you must understand the past too. ...So you may think of yourself as having been chosen to venture here.'

They were now alone. The wagon, upon concluding its leisurely progress, had reached the top of the rise and was standing outside a large farm building some distance away, into which a small knot of figures were unloading the cargo it carried.

Toby indicated the group with his arm. 'Tell me... what age is this? Everything appears so different.'

Jeannie seemed to deliberate before quietly but firmly replying. 'It is haymaking time, Toby – in the year Nineteen Hundred and Thirteen.'

Toby's eyes widened and his mouth opened to form a perfect 'O'. When he spoke again, he did so in a weak voice as if exhaling the last breath from his lungs. '…1913.'

Desperation and disbelief filled his mind as he struggled to accept her words. How could it be true?

Gesturing toward the farm, a nearby wood and neat pastures round about, he fought for a rational explanation… 'All this… it's not really here… I've walked this way many times… there are only fields in this place.'

'In future years there *will* only be fields, Toby. But this is not your time – and all *is* as you see it.'

'But how can it be? How did I arrive at this moment?' he stammered.

'It was your destiny,' she replied softly after a pause. 'And now you must continue your journey as I leave you again for a while.'

Jeannie turned away, but spurred by a cry of anguish inside his head, Toby called her back.

'What… what am I supposed to do here?'

'*Learn,* Toby… that is the first thing that is required of you. It is what you must do if you are to play your part and find the answers you seek.'

They would have parted then had not one final question come to his lips.

'And… and the other one? The one in the deckchair?'

Jeannie smiled. 'Ah yes, Jasper. You will see him again too… sometimes no doubt when he is least expected – for he is a most unusual travelling companion! But for now you must go on alone to discover what awaits you.'

With that Toby's mouth seemed suddenly sealed against further utterances, and she, having retraced her steps, moved out of sight down the dusty track.

Chapter Two

The Lost Folk of Stavenham

L EFT STANDING IN THE MIDDLE OF THE bridge, Toby was at first undecided what to do next. It was just before noon and with a full sun riding high in the sky the day had become hot and cloudless. He cast his mind back forty-eight hours to when the storm had raged and the heavens were filled with rain. The contrast could not have been greater. 'Surely it hasn't poured like that here,' he thought. The earth was too dry and there were large cracks in the clay soil; a clear sign of there having been little more than an occasional shower for some time.

'Everything's different… or perhaps it's me that's changed…'

At last, conquering his indecision, and overcoming a nagging urge to return home without delay, he set off along the cart track leading to the farm.

* * *

During the present day the landscape at this point opens out as you leave the course of the old railway. The latter is still lined by thick bushes and trees, but the rising ground Toby now crossed has few features to break up the expanse of arable fields stretching into the distance. There are no buildings of any kind, though evidence of human habitation can be found, especially in autumn, when heavy ploughing turns up buried bricks and masonry. It is pleasant enough countryside, but there is little variety in what grows there. The land is managed by machine and given over to the cultivation of tough, reliable cash crops needing limited care. Outside the planting and harvesting seasons a wanderer might traverse the whole area without meeting another soul. Toby had enjoyed walking the rough tracks many times, especially on late evenings in summer as the sun dipped towards the west.

Now all was miraculously changed, the ancient bird filled hedgerows on both sides of the farm track restored. Butterflies, bees, bluebottles and numerous other insects crossed and re-crossed in front of him as he passed beneath the spreading canopies of elm, ash and oak trees, many of great age. The setting again had that mellow traditional beauty much beloved of English landscape painters.

He made his way between a clover meadow on one side, containing a dozen Jersey cows, and a small turnip field on the other, before reaching what he now realised was a substantial farm. There were several outbuildings, many of moss covered brick with tiled roofs, but dominant was a huge and ancient thatched barn with its weather baked oaken doors pushed back. On the arched end, a loft opening with hoist above indicated the entrance to a grain store. The wagon was drawn up outside and two men stood beside it deep in conversation. Other voices came from within. On a large black sign above the door the name "Warren Hill Farm" had been painted in tall white letters.

One of the men was a sturdy middle-aged farmer with a round sun-bronzed face and cheerful countenance. He had large, deep-set eyes topped with bushy eyebrows, an ample nose bristling with nasal hair, and a wide mouth from which a hearty laugh broke forth at regular intervals. A powerful man in his younger days, he was now a little stooped from years of heavy lifting and hard work, but still presented an air of contentment and self-assurance. An open shirt revealed the upper part of his broad chest, while strong boots and a pair of heavy working trousers completed his attire.

The other man was much younger, between eighteen and twenty-five, and from the likeness in their features was evidently the son of the elder. He had a boyish, eager face, but one that was also serious and kind. Of medium height and slim and agile build, his hair was dark, and he wore a grey cloth cap that shaded strong features, the eyes shrewd and intent. Like his father, he was dressed in working clothes; a red and green choker tied at his neck.

Toby's approach had been noted, and the older man turned to greet him.

'Good day to you… out walkin'?' he enquired, in a voice both genial and friendly.

'Yes…' replied Toby, hesitating slightly, '…it seemed such a good day for a stroll.'

'Going far?'

'Just a few miles… I've come over from Molliton.'

A look of genuine curiosity passed across the older farmer's countenance, as if he was trying to recall the newcomer's face, which put Toby on his guard. The younger man also eyed him up and down, clearly a little puzzled by his fleece jacket and boots. Toby decided to move the conversation on.

'I used to live in Molliton… but actually I've come up from London. My name's Toby Freeman… I'm a journalist. I work for a newspaper. They sent me to prepare an article on country life for our city readers.'

'Henry Trindle,' said the farmer, offering his hand, 'and this is my son, Mark… A newspaper man you say – and a city gent. Well that explains things.'

Any desire he might have had to enquire further apparently disappeared in a moment. If this was what London folk wore he could well believe it; for the capital, although only fifty miles away, was far off and the ways of its people strange and unusual.

'I've been there a few times,' he went on wistfully, tugging gently at the ear of the shire horse, which stood beside him chewing from a bag of oats. 'All big houses, noise and motorcars; I wonder how they stand it?'

But while the big man seemed satisfied, his son was evidently still puzzled by Toby's attire. He stepped forward and took a fold of the fleece between thumb and forefinger. 'Soft... wool, is it?' There was a perceptible note of doubt in his voice.

'Yes,' Toby replied, meeting Mark's eyes. 'It's been reclaimed and reused using a revolutionary new process.'

'Let's not have any talk of revolution around here,' piped Henry. 'Least not when there's work to be done. We'd best be getting on. My daughter Scarlet has been turning hay all morning down in "Farden's Meadow" and we needs must get ourselves down there to collect it.'

Just then two other men emerged from the barn. One, Henry introduced as his eldest son, Wesley, a man of twenty-five and already a little portly, but nonetheless tall, broad shouldered and as strong as an ox. Like his father he was good-natured and easygoing, but could develop a strong temper if crossed after enjoying a few drinks. His round face was dotted with freckles and deep smile lines had become ingrained around the corners of his dark eyes. A thick moustache, fashionable at the time, sat proudly upon his upper lip.

Wesley's companion was altogether different. He was a short, hunched up little man with stocky legs: still only forty-five years of age, but someone whom hard work and a life in the sun made appear much older. He carried a large oilcan with a very long spout, and looked up with sharp but genial eyes. The whole of his face was peppered with little wrinkles, his clothes worn and work stained, and he gave the impression of having emerged, like an undergrown troll, from the very fabric of the barn itself. Toby noticed that only stubs remained of the last three fingers on his left hand.

'This is Sam Milton, my farm hand,' said Henry. Now, how's things going, Wesley?'

The elder son turned and led the group towards "The Great Barn" with Toby and Mark Trindle following at the rear. The young farmer's curiosity still showed, and he again looked Toby up and down as they went in together.

The interior of the barn was no less impressive than its outer appearance. A vaulted roof made of heavy oak beams arched overhead, and chinks of light from the sky above slanted down in vertical shafts onto the pebbled floor; small motes of dust and insects circled in the brightness. They were in an open space used for the storage of carts and farm machinery with a low workshop area to the right. On the west wall a timeworn staircase led up through a gap in the floor to the storage area above. Through this Toby could see a number of full hessian sacks, many as big as a man, stacked neatly together, while others, now empty, were piled up against the walls. Hanging everywhere from walls and ceilings were a multitude of objects: the sweat-blackened harness of horses, heavy chains and coils of rope, hoeing and digging tools, levers and crowbars, a row of mallets, pickaxes and saws – some that shone brightly, several more rusty and beyond further use. There were wooden barrels too, a number with straps decayed and sprung, beside tubs of tar and tin containers of oil and grease. Looking higher, Toby saw hanging against the wall gin traps of various sizes, their evil metal teeth, tight closed, like the clenched fangs of sleeping demons. Everywhere the smell of dust, leather, grain and dry rot filled the mellow air, and while the barn had long since entered its years of decline; it still retained a powerful grandeur. For more than three centuries, the timeworn structure had served its function: home to owls, swallows and generations of grateful mice and rats. Toby saw how permanent it all must seem, but knew that its days were numbered.

The men now busied themselves around two lattice end boards designed to fit onto the hay wagon. They were strongly built and heavy and Toby quickly found himself enlisted to help carry them outside. For him the task was arduous, but he marvelled at the strength and agility of his fellow workers. Once the boards were heaved into position, Mark and Sam Milton shinned deftly up onto the wagon, and with the two big men and Toby lifting, guided the two foot long retaining stubs into metal slots. The same process was repeated a second time, and in ten minutes the wagon was ready for use, as Toby, his shirt having quickly become stained with sweat, found himself accepted as part of the team. The Trindles were evidently short-handed and his efforts had been much appreciated. So much so, that when dinner was announced by a short woman in a pink headscarf and floral apron, he was invited to share the meal on the understanding that he would stay to help during the afternoon. This was a welcome if unexpected offer, as he had not eaten for some time and had been wondering about food. Henry introduced Coodie, his wife, and they set off for the farmhouse together.

"Warren Hill Farmhouse" stood beyond "The Great Barn" in a courtyard surrounded by stables, a cowshed and a large covered storage area. An arched opening leading to further buildings stood at the opposite end, beside which a pile of fresh manure lay heaped. Chickens pecked about here and there accompanied by a large black magisterial cockerel and an old goose. Swallows ducked and swooped overhead, and a colony of sparrows hopped around the recently removed contents of the cowshed. The yard was partly paved with worn cobbles that sloped towards a temporarily blocked drain where a puddle of water and slurry had formed.

Coodie Trindle disappeared through the farmhouse porch and they followed her into a low ceilinged kitchen with heavy beams that the taller men ducked to avoid. A packed lunch had already been prepared for them to eat later in the fields, and Coodie set about making fresh tea for the men to drink. She was, like her husband, now in her fifties, and marked by the usual signs of a life spent out of doors. Her hair, already grey, stuck out in flowing wisps from under a scarf, and she wore a thin shawl over a rough working dress. Coodie was the family cook, washerwoman and seamstress, carrying out her daily tasks in an unending routine, measured only by the needs of the farm and the passing of the seasons. Yet, although the Trindles were clearly far from well-off and could rarely afford luxuries, Coodie never complained, but displayed a warm and practical temperament, welcoming Toby with a smile when Henry had introduced him, and cheerfully producing additional fare for his needs.

They talked a little, the conversation turning to haymaking. It had been a late spring and the haymaking season was a week or two behind schedule. Now, at last, the hay had been mown and turned and would be ready for collection that day. The hot sun would improve the crop, but it would require hard work to collect the contents of the meadow before nightfall. Scarlet Trindle, their twenty year old daughter, had been down in "Farden's Meadow" turning the drying grass since early morning, and was now raking it for final gathering.

Coodie smiled across the table at Toby. 'You give us a hand this afternoon, my lad, and I'll see you're well fed this evening. I can even put you up for the night if you don't have to go rushing back to London. What do you say?'

Toby looked round at the others, suddenly attracted by the idea of staying. 'Why not?' he replied. 'I think I can spare the time.'

'That's settled then,' said Henry, slapping him on the shoulder. 'Now let's be at it. It's gone midday already.'

They returned to the barn, and having tossed a variety of pitchforks and rakes on the wagon, prepared to leave. Henry again mounted the driving platform, his youngest son beside him, while the others clambered up onto the wagon. Then, with a single 'Get up Caesar!' they set off past the farm entrance and turned left towards the pastureland beyond.

Toby leaned against the forward end board of the wagon looking out at the countryside around him. In his time the track they were on would have led back to Molliton about a mile distant. But where he expected to see an open stretch of land leading down to Molliton Wood, he found instead an altered landscape of small fields, meadows and scattered woodland copses. They ambled past a dewpond on the right, beside which a large bull was tethered in a small paddock, and then rose up to a knoll of higher ground where the view opened out. He noted the familiar topography dipping away on three sides, but was amazed at other features. Where Toby was accustomed to seeing wide open acres, there were now dotted a considerable number of tall mature trees joined by connecting hedgerows, while to the north stood another farm, smaller and neater than Warren Hill, with recently built outbuildings and a cowshed next to it. The farmhouse there was brick built, with a tall chimney that even on this hot summer's day emitted a trail of hazy smoke into the milky sky. There were animals in the fields nearby: a dairy herd, some pigs and a flock of sheep. Two figures, a man and a young girl, were haymaking in the field beyond, and further off, a stony knoll rose up towards the skyline. A woman hanging out the family washing waved to them as Toby bent down to touch Mark's shoulder through the railings.

'What farm is that?' he asked.

' "High Dyke Farm",' Mark replied, his head swaying from side to side with the motion of the wagon. 'It belongs to Arthur Brayling and his wife. That's him in the field yonder with Kitty, his daughter. She's a great lass; only fifteen but knows more about farming than many twice her age. The young lady's strong too, and works every bit as hard as a man. The one who waved, that's his wife, Sarah. Lovely woman, do anything to help you out. Got four children between them! Took the farm on six years ago when it was about to go under. Now they seem to have turned it round. Good luck to them, I say.'

Toby thought for a moment. 'Tell me,' he said at last. 'Why do they call it "High Dyke Farm"? Surely there have never been fortifications or anything like that around here.'

His remark caused Mark to turn round with a questioning look once more. He pointed towards the distant knoll. 'Do you see that high ground?' he said. 'It's called "Wart Hill". Used to be some kind of a lookout point in the past. Apparently it was connected to the land where the farm now stands by an embankment – a dyke if you prefer – hence the name.'

*   *   *

They rumbled on a little further, and as Toby looked southward, the land dropped away before rising steeply again towards the Northampton road half a mile distant. This was screened by a narrow wood above which a gathering of rooks and crows circled. To the right, in the shallow valley, stood another farm that seemed to brood among the dark trees around it. In the bright of the afternoon it appeared to crouch amid the shadows as if shunning the light – a place closed and secretive. The buildings of a third farm could also be seen half way up the rising ground nearby.

Mark turned again and noted the direction of Toby's glance. 'That farm, the one in the valley, is "Deep Spinney Farm" – The Towsers' place. Funny lot them... The parents, Matthew and Abigail, they're alright... at least they used to be. But their children – Cregan, Barnaby and the daughter, Queenie – they're all a bit odd I reckon.'

Henry perked up at this comment. 'Bunch of cuckoos if you ask me,' he said in a low growl. 'You barely ever see them, but you know they're about. Yes, and half the time for the wrong reason. Beats me why old Matthew doesn't put his foot down. But I suppose it's too late, now they've all grown up.'

Toby was intrigued, but decided not to probe further for the moment… What he did know well enough was that nothing at all would remain at the spot a hundred years later.

'And the farm further up?'

'"Pocket Farm"… Rose and Albert Smallwood's place,' said Henry, brightening. 'They're our nearest neighbours and oldest friends… Had some bad luck five years back – lost their only daughter, Katy, in a shooting accident – really knocked them back it did. They're getting advanced in years too, both in their sixties. I can't see them staying there for much longer. We've taken on some of their land and help them out when we can.'

* * *

Pulling on the right hand rein Henry now steered Caesar into a wide, freshly cut field of hay, the scent of which filled the air. It was getting on toward one o'clock and the weather was at its best. A warm breeze coming up from the south blew across the land, lifting the rows of drying grass. Away to Toby's left a light brown shire horse, with a broad white blaze on its forehead, moved steadily to and fro pulling an ancient hay rake with arching tines. Sitting on this, upon a metal seat perched high up between the iron wheels, was a young woman in a straw hat. She expertly guided her charge, deftly raising and lowering the tines of the rake, and upon noting their arrival completed one final pass before steering towards them.

Henry turned round proudly. 'That's Scarlet, my daughter – you'll like her,' he said with a broad grin, before jumping down as she pulled up.

'Lor, my bum ain't half sore!' the girl said, laughing and rubbing her thigh. 'I wish you'd put a bit of padding on that seat, Dad.'

Scarlet was slim and wiry, her face deeply tanned by the sun. When she smiled the tiny crow's-feet around her brown eyes brought animation and character to her features. Although not beautiful, she had an attractive openness and confidence, and while caring little about her dress: wearing but a simple brown frock, a plain white blouse and working boots, her easy manner and honest good humour created a favourable impression.

Together they now sat awhile to eat the food and drink prepared for them by Coodie. The talk was all of farming and the work ahead – of sunshine, animals and the land. Then, refreshed and in good spirits, the company set about gathering the first load as Scarlet again mounted the hay raking machine to complete her task. The prepared hay had been left in lines wide enough apart for the wagon to pass between, and old Sam Milton climbed aboard to arrange and stack the loose material while the others bent and pitched the hay to him. Toby had often seen pictures and photographs depicting rural scenes such as this in museums and history books, frequently wondering at the labour intensive nature of the work. But until that day he had not realised the degree of teamwork required. Now, involved himself, he appreciated the age-old methods. His own first attempts were far from promising and caused much merriment among the others. Working with Henry Trindle on one side he endeavoured to copy the big man's technique, but initially found that his efforts to lift each loaded fork above his head almost inevitably resulted in the majority tumbling back in a quivering cascade. A gently mocking banter from the others accompanied each failed attempt, but it was always good-humoured and Toby persevered, gradually mastering both the fork and the necessary skill. By the time the initial load was put up he had fallen into a steady rhythm, first rolling the loose hay forward into a tight heap before lifting it to be received above. Mid afternoon was now upon them, the baking sun beating down from above, and although Toby had shed his fleece, sweat rolled down his back and stood upon his temples.

'Hot work, eh?' said Sam from above. 'Why not climb aboard and take a rest on the way back?'

Toby looked up, half dazzled, at the little man silhouetted against the bright sky. He saw him smile and indicate the back of the wagon with his outstretched hand. The slatted end board did indeed provide a means of clambering aloft, and following a precarious ascent of the swaying structure, Toby was hauled up the last two feet by Sam's one good hand.

'Made it!' the other said in his thick country accent. 'Just you sit along of me and enjoy the view while we hold the whole lot steady.' Then, whistling, he turned and moved forward to the centre of the load.

The cart moved off at the start of its short lumbering return journey to the farm, while Scarlet, having finished the task of raking, steered the machine to the edge of the field, and with Mark's assistance unhitched the shire horse. Then, having completed their task, the two followed on behind at a little distance. Glancing back Toby could see them in conversation, and, from Mark's occasional upward glances, sensed that part of this concerned him.

But Toby had other things to occupy him. His new vantage point provided a bird's-eye view of the surrounding countryside and final confirmation of his new circumstances. Nowhere could he see any evidence of the recent storm. The land was clothed in the fresh colours of May, the canopy of every tree decked with foliage. Lush corn crops were growing in many fields, waving tall and undamaged in the light breeze, while the farm buildings, barns and out structures he could see showed no obvious signs of weather damage. He looked back in the direction of Molliton, nestling a mile off in a shallow depression of the land, witnessing a well maintained and ordered landscape. Yet, sitting perched high up he suddenly felt uncomfortably cut off – a stranger in this once familiar place.

A line of white smoke, billowing and breaking above the trees, indicated the passage of a train now steaming through the cutting where he had recently walked, the steady beat of its exhaust echoing into the distance.

Toby gazed south at the farms identified before and noticed other structures coming into sight as they moved over the curve of the hill. One that caught his eye was an old square tower standing at the centre of a wild patch of uncultivated land dotted with grazing sheep. It was both solid and impressive, but he could not imagine the reason for it being there.

'What is that place?' he called forward to Sam, indicating with an outstretched hand.

'"Maxton Tower" – used to be an old hunting lodge, they say, but hasn't been used for years.'

Toby gazed pensively towards the structure. How often had he walked by the distant spot without realising what had once existed there? Yet virtually all the buildings he now looked upon would soon disappear – wiped from the landscape of the modern world along with the histories of those who lived in them. But one important point of reference would remain – the windmill at Stavenham that stood beyond the line of the railway on a knoll of land just outside the village. He settled upon its familiar outline, the great sails standing tall against the surrounding countryside a quarter of a mile away. In our modern day it is still an impressive structure, standing in silent testament to the life and workings of a bygone era. Now, however, as Toby watched he noticed something more – the canvas clad sails were moving – turning slowly in the shimmering haze.

* * *

After ten minutes they reached the farm and the wagon pulled up next to the empty hay barn opposite the house. The men were immediately active and Toby joined Sam Milton in heaving the load down to those below. They formed a practised chain, passing the valuable cargo back to the further side of the storage area and gradually completing the first layer before returning to the fields. Later, with the first cooling breath of evening, Coodie brought tea and fruitcake for them to eat in the meadow and the others sat a while to chat about the success of the day and work still to be done on the morrow. Toby listened mostly, only occasionally sharing in their easy talk, though feeling totally accepted among folk he now began to consider friends. Three further round trips would be made that day before the sun sank low in the sky and their task was done. All laboured with a steady purpose, a bond developing between them, and although Toby's body increasingly ached as evening drew on, his spirit was lifted by the honest toil and the satisfaction of playing a full and active part throughout. The last load was not safely brought in and stored until the twilight hour before nine o'clock, leaving the hay barn, now more than half full, to be topped up following a second cutting later in the season.

Only then did Scarlet bed the horses down for the night before joining them in the farm kitchen for dinner. They sat together over their meal, becoming animated for a while, until gradually the exertions of the day, together with the need to digest the good food they had eaten, led to a gradual falling off of conversation. Toby was very tired and his head began to tip forward each time a short silence ensued. Not slow to notice this, Coodie nodded to the others.

'This here lad looks ready for his bed,' she said kindly. 'I'll show him his room if he'll come along of me.'

Toby nodded gratefully, and was about to rise when Wesley, normally the least vocal, spoke up. 'Hold on, Ma. The lad isn't going to bed until we've bought him a drink at "The Three Eels". He's worked hard today and deserves it. So you just bring him straight back down when he's had a chance to freshen up.'

The others straightway voiced their full approval of the proposal, and as it was a statement the others would clearly not hear contested, Toby steeled himself for a further foray as Coodie led him upstairs. She had prepared a box room at the end of a narrow landing; while small, this contained a comfortable bed, a low dressing-table and an easy chair. The two lattice windows had been opened to allow a thorough airing, and a small vase of fresh flowers was placed on the window ledge.

Coodie stood in the doorway, smiling warmly as he turned. 'Hope you like it… Used to be the baby's room years ago; then Scarlet had it when she was small. It's good and quiet and you'll be able to find it easy enough when you come in later. I've put out one of Mark's clean shirts for you. He won't mind, and I'm sure it will fit, seein' as how you're about the same build as him. Oh, and there's a washroom down the corridor. You'll find heated water in the jug, which I'm sure will still be more than hot enough for your liking. We're not on the electric yet, but you can bring a lamp up with you later. Now, must be going, my love.'

And with that she disappeared downstairs.

Toby stood for a moment in the tranquil room as the shadows gathered around him. These people obviously lived very simple lives, without the comforts so familiar to him, but they showed a trust and generosity all but lost by many in his own time. The warmth of this gentle woman and her obvious care for his comfort and wellbeing both gladdened and humbled him.

* * *

When Toby reappeared ten minutes later, darkness had begun to fall in earnest and an old brass oil lamp was burning in the middle of the kitchen table. Coodie announced that she would be staying behind with Scarlet to do some mending; before seeing them off at the door with a reminder to lock up if they came in after the two had settled for the night.

The men were in good spirits. It was still well before ten and, said Henry, their walk to the pub would take little more than a quarter of an hour. The local beer was excellent and their journey thus well worth the effort. So, without further delay, the five set off and forked left down the track that would take them to the village of Stavenham half a mile away. They had not gone far, and were drawing near a large well-cultivated garden bordered by a thick hedge, when a whistle was heard away to the west. Wesley, striding along in front, stopped abruptly.

'Not a train...' he grumbled. 'I thought the last one had already gone. Now we'll be held at the crossing.'

'It's Monday,' said Mark. 'That'll be the late service from Northampton – only runs once a week.'

They moved on again, dropped into a dip and came to the railway line. Their way was barred by a closed crossing gate with a red warning light in the middle of the top spar. To the right was a short raised brick platform illuminated by three evenly spaced Victorian oil-filled standard lamps. Standing upon this was a surprisingly comfortable looking waiting room next to a small tin roofed booking office. Behind, at the top of a paved track, stood the crossing keeper's house. All was in immaculate order, with neatly trimmed hedges, well-tended rose beds and colourful hanging baskets. A single station sign announced the name "Windmill Halt" to passengers.

A very crisp and upright man, thin, slightly shorter than average height, and wearing full Midland Railway station master's uniform, stood fingering the brim of his hat and anxiously looking at the pocket watch in his hand as a fussy two carriage train came into view. It busily hissed through the crossing, a bright red glow from the open firebox lighting up the cab, and came to rest next to the platform. At the same time the stationmaster's voice rang out clearly above the locomotive noise. ' "Windmill Halt!" – Passengers alight here for Stavenham – "Windmill Halt"!'

Wesley called across to Toby with a dismissive gesture, 'Lord... you'd think this was St Pancras Station the way old George Hughes goes on. Not a piddly little station in the middle of nowhere!'

The stationmaster apparently heard this comment, for his head swung round and a prickly expression crossed his face. But his attention was quickly drawn back to the train as two passengers stepped down from separate doors of the second carriage. The first was a tall angular man with a cadaverous face. He wore a brown overcoat and a small black bowler hat, both of which seemed out of place on such a warm evening, and carried two large parcels under his left arm. He handed his ticket to the stationmaster with a curt 'Good evening, Hughes,' and quickly strode down the sloping end of the platform to the crossing. Seeing the group of figures gathered behind the gate he briefly turned towards them, slightly wrinkling his nose and fixing each in turn with a penetrating stare, like an estate agent summing up the value of real estate. Then, having acknowledged the older men with a nod, he walked away over the wooden boards of the crossing and disappeared into the gathering gloom beyond.

Mark Trindle tapped Toby on the shoulder. 'That's Christian Mandell – owns "Mandell's Corner Shop" in Stavenham. He's forty-five but has always looked ten years older than his age. Bit of a miserable bugger if you ask me! He'll have been to Northampton buying stock, as it's his half day.'

'Aye,' said Sam Milton turning round. 'And we'd best take care we don't end up paying double the price for the contents of those packages when they appear on his shelves.'

Wesley turned, slowly shaking his head. 'I don't think he'd do that. It's just what people say about him. Don't do to be too quiet or into your own company – folk just end up spreading rumours about you.'

'Well you won't catch me in there too often; what with him and his long face,' added Sam. 'Tis a pity he can't lively hisself up a bit!'

'Each to his own, Sam, each to his own,' said Wesley. 'Anyway, there's a few round here think you're a bit odd too,' he concluded with a wry smile, slapping the smaller man on the back.

By now the train had begun to move off once more and the second traveller approached the crossing. His bearing was altogether different from the first. He was ruddy faced and thick set with a surprisingly soft downy brown beard and bushy sideburns. A powerful man, his upper body, clothed in a short-sleeved shirt and leather waistcoat, had been hardened by years of heavy work. Yet there was an air of sadness about him, as of someone unfulfilled by the labours of his life. His eyes would sometimes have an absent reflective look, while his dry manner of speech could be off-putting to those who did not know him well. He was Elijah Barnes, the local blacksmith, and lived alone above his workshop near the centre of the village. Now approaching his thirty-fifth year, he had a good reputation throughout the area, since he ran a steady business and was a skilled craftsman at his trade. Yet it had been remarked more than once that he was the kind of man who might simply go off one morning never to return.

'How do, Elijah?' said Henry. 'Had a good day?'

The blacksmith looked up, a slow smile spreading across his face as he recognised an old friend. 'Good evening, Henry, Sam… boys,' he replied. 'I been down to Bedford. Someone wants a pair of gates made – wondered if I could do it for him.'

'You off home now?' asked Henry.

'That's about it,' Elijah sighed.

'Why not stop off with us at "The Eels" on your way?' suggested Henry, noting the big tradesman's slumped shoulders. 'Come on lad, I'll stand you a drink.'

The blacksmith nodded his acceptance of the offer as the stationmaster came down to open the gate. Behind him Toby noted that his wife, Morwen, in headscarf and woollen shawl, had stepped forward from the shadowed front porch of Station House and now stood motionless, watching them.

George Hughes bustled busily until both gates were swung open allowing the men to pass. He was fifty-six years old and the brightly shining company badge on his hat, immaculately polished wire-rimmed spectacles, buttons and watch chain gave him an air of sharp efficiency. No sergeant of the Guards could have been more precisely turned out. But Toby wondered at the man. As Wesley had said, this really was far off the beaten track – so little happened. All afternoon he had only been aware of five passing trains. Yet here was the stationmaster manning his wayside halt and managing the country crossing as if it were a major terminus in the city – everything kept in the best working order, with lamps lit, as if the next arrival might be royalty rather than one or two returning locals. Was this proud and fussy man aware of how little the world knew or cared about him? Again Toby pictured the site in his own time: the empty cutting and derelict, roofless house standing gaunt among tangled and broken trees.

'Now, gentlemen,' George cautioned as they passed. 'Take care to leave the gates just as they are when you come back. It wouldn't be right to let animals wander on the line, now, would it?'

Wesley turned. 'No, George, we wouldn't want the night train to London de-railed, would we?' he said, causing the others to chuckle as they moved out of sight. 'You just get straight back to Morwen this minute… before she dies of boredom living out here. Or better still, bring her down to the pub!'

The stationmaster, standing rigidly with both hands behind his back, rocked upon his heels, jangling a substantial bunch of keys. 'There's no need to make light of a serious matter,' he said, looking down the bridge of his nose. 'And don't you mind about my Morwen – she's alright.'

* * *

But Morwen was something of a mystery. She was ten years younger than her husband, and although married for more than twenty years had not raised a family, while seldom being seen far from "Station House". When she did venture out people would note her moving along the hedgerows collecting herbs and wild plants, and her talent for making natural remedies had been noted over the years; but there were those that doubted and mistrusted her. Some hinted that things in her family history "were not right", while a few among the more superstitious old worthies of the district considered her skills "dark and mysterious", warning any willing listeners to keep a prudent distance from the quiet little woman's door.

* * *

The walkers soon passed by the darkened windmill, now silhouetted motionless on the western horizon, before coming to the outskirts of Stavenham and continuing at a steady pace along a narrow road lined with stone built cottages. Then, having ascended a short rise, they arrived at last outside a modestly sized public house by the village crossroads. A welcoming glow shone out from a number of open windows and a hum of voices was heard. Somewhere nearby a church clock struck ten.

The others quickly filed inside, but as Toby was about to enter he happened to glance up at the pub sign hanging from an ornate ironwork post above. Atop it was perched a large bird, a crow, the black feathers on its head and back glowing silver in the moonlight. It turned, peering down, eyeing him beadily. Toby held back for a moment, feeling strangely exposed – like a criminal before a magistrate. But then the silent creature seemed to lose interest, and having spread its broad wings, rose up to land out of sight on the rooftop with a scratching of claws.

'The crow again,' Toby said to himself, still looking in the direction in which it had disappeared, and another minute elapsed before he remembered the others and ducked through a low doorway into the saloon bar of "The Three Eels".

This was surprisingly spacious, with a low curving roof supported by huge square oaken beams. There was a large stonework fireplace and comfortable quiet areas in the window recesses. Tables had been fashioned around the four upright timbers, while coach horns, copper and brass Victoriana of all kinds and framed prints of rural hunting scenes decked the walls. A massive pike was mounted in a wooden case above the bar, and the stuffed head of a badger looked out with a glazed expression from over the doorway to the Gents. Noisy games of bar skittles and shove halfpenny were in full swing, the air heavy with tobacco smoke and the strong aroma of ale.

'There he is!' cried Wesley heartily, as Toby appeared. 'Come here, my friend. You'll have to be sharper than that if you're to slake a good thirst before "last orders" are called.'

A pint of beer was thrust into Toby's hand and his companions watched with satisfaction as he drank.

The landlord and landlady behind the bar smiled genially too, and Toby realised that many others had taken an interest in his arrival. Several raised their glasses in greeting as he looked around.

'The lad's visitin' from London,' said Henry to the upturned faces. 'Works for a newspaper... Reckons he's going to tell all they city folk about us.'

A smattering of amused banter and wry comments went round the room.

'Lor, he's a good worker though... none better with the old fork,' continued Henry, turning to Toby with a wink. 'We'd never have finished today without him.'

There were many nods of approval at these comments before people gradually turned back to what they were doing. The pub was clearly the centre of village life for its regulars – a place where local gossip and matters of the land were the nightly stuff of conversation. The blacksmith, Henry and Wesley were almost immediately called away to talk with friends, and soon just Sam and Mark Trindle remained standing with Toby.

Taking the opportunity of a pause from serving, Davy Oldfield, the landlord, then leant towards Toby, polishing a beer glass. Now thirty, he had run the pub for eight years since taking it over on marrying his wife Goldie, who stood beside him. Davy had the gift possessed by all good landlords of being able to make easy conversation with anyone that stepped into his pub. Although casually dressed in an open collared shirt, he was smartly groomed with a neatly cropped moustache and swept back hair, the first signs of grey showing at his temples. He ran a cheerful pub, but would take no nonsense from those likely to cause a nuisance and had more than once surprised folk by forcibly expelling difficult drinkers from his premises. Because of this, and his honest efficiency, Davy was well respected by all. Yet he was not a contented man. Starting out he had hoped to go far in the trade, to progress to one of the much bigger and more prosperous town pubs. But this had not happened. The years had passed and the chance of moving on slipped by.

'There's still much more we can do here!' his wife would conclude snappishly if he should chance to raise the matter at the end of a long day. 'You shouldn't just go congratulating yourself on what you have done already. We can't be going yet!'

After three or four such arguments, doubt had inevitably been sown in Davy's mind. Was there really scope for him to be doing better at "The Eels"?

So the outward veneer of confidence and wellbeing that he portrayed to the world had become a mask for a nagging sense of professional failure, and a corrosive underlying feeling of bitterness towards his partner.

For her part, Goldie, as Toby had already noticed, was a still very attractive woman of twenty-six. Her hair, rich and golden-brown, was tightly pulled back from her forehead, and she had broad open features, a full mouth and alluring hazel eyes. Like Davy, Goldie had a welcoming manner, and it was often remarked that she was in her element behind the bar. She had an ample figure, and, as many landladies have, a taste for wearing striking low-cut dresses that revealed her shapely cleavage.

'The men like it,' she would say. 'And there's no harm if it's good for business.'

She was clearly right in this respect. When Goldie served there would always be a line of drinkers lounging against the bar, whom she constantly engaged in conversation with near to the bone anecdotes, winks and smiles, while priming them all the time to, 'Drink up and have another!' which, with such a comely view to entrance them, they rarely refused.

Born in the village, Goldie was blessed with the added advantage of having long known most of the regulars. Her parents, now both dead, were farm workers, and her marriage to Davy at the age of eighteen had lifted Goldie above the usual poverty of rural life. She had met him on market day in Bedford when he was visiting from Oxford and they'd tied the knot soon afterwards. He, a confident young man looking for his first position in the brewery trade, was captivated by her seeming innocence and good looks. At the outset everything had gone well, but in time, as Goldie's own confidence developed, their relationship gradually changed. Her initial happy acceptance of Davy's ambitions fell away and she began to express irritation at his desire to move on. Only then, when it was too late, did he become increasingly aware of her shrewish side, while the rapid fluctuations of his wife's moods left Davy fatigued and dispirited.

'I hear you work in London,' the landlord said above the rumble of voices. 'A journalist,' he nodded deferentially. 'Sounds like interesting work.'

'Oh... yes it is,' replied Toby. 'It keeps me busy.'

'And you've come here to see how the rustic folk live?' Davy continued with an ironic grin.

'You could put it that way, I suppose.'

'Well... I'd imagine some of your readers might find tales about what actually happens here a little dull – just talk about farming and the weather... and the occasional murder of course,' he added, glancing pointedly towards his wife. 'No, my friend, I'd say the lives of your average country type might be of no interest at all to city folk. You see, most are simply too set in their ways. Take old Sam here, for example. He was born and bred in "Rabbit Hutch Row", the same road as my wife as it happens, and spends his whole life between a pitchfork and the pub.'

'Aye,' said Sam, piping up. 'But that's only when I can find work to do.'

'And when he can't, we may not see him in here for a week.'

'Can't afford it!' the old labourer affirmed.

'But will he leave?' said Davy, with a tilt of the head. 'Not at all! He'd more likely prefer to starve to death before packing his bags... you see, what I mean is this,' he added, drawing closer to Toby and Sam so others mightn't hear. 'Stay too long in the countryside and it sort of wraps itself around you... put down roots here and you might never get away.'

Sam just grinned winningly, and Davy pulled him a second pint on the house in compensation for having pulled his leg.

As the labourer gratefully lifted the drink to his mouth, Davy went on. 'Just look at that mitt of his now,' he said, pointing at the stubs of the three missing fingers. 'Tell our Toby what happened, Sam.'

Sam put the half empty glass down and wiped his bristly chin with the back of his maimed hand.

'Cut them off on a swede chopper, didn't I?' he said with a toothy grin.

'Go on, tell him the rest,' said Davy, with the feigned disapproval of a village schoolmaster.

'I did it meself, see. I bin chopping swedes for the cows when a stone or somethin' got jammed in the machine so's I couldn't turn the handle no more. Well I must of bin dreamin' I reckon, for I just reached down inside while accidentally leanin' against the handle at the same time. That freed it!' he said out loud, remembering the moment and causing those nearby to turn round. 'Lord, that sharp blade went and took my fingers clean off and they dropped out the front neat as could be. I couldn't believe what I'd done.'

Toby tried to envisage the scene. 'And what happened then?' he asked.

'Well my boss, old Percy Manion – him as died a couple of years back – he went and bound it up with a bit of clean cloth. Said what a fool I'd been and as how I'd need to take a couple of days off work to recover.'

'I should think you would need to recuperate for longer than that,' said Toby, thinking about the fuss that would probably be made in his own time.

'I took a day alright and lor didn't that hand give me gip the first night. But my old wife, Susan – well she's good with things like that; she washed and re-dressed it and put some ointment on as was given to her by Morwen Hughes. And do you know what? A day later it was a good deal better! So the next morning I went back to work and I ain't really missed 'em ever since.'

Toby could hardly believe his ears. 'You went back to work after only one day away?'

'That's right,' said Sam. 'It's been all of sixteen years since it happened. If a man didn't work then he didn't get paid, and I had family to feed.'

'And no compensation either,' Toby thought, inwardly. 'How times have changed…'

* * *

A short while later Wesley returned and led Sam off to play a game of skittles, leaving Toby standing beside Mark Trindle who had remained silent throughout the recent conversation. The young farmer then ordered a final drink for them both, and as some of the regulars were beginning to drift away, suggested they might retire to the comfort of one of the vacated window snugs. The two had just sat down facing each other when the door opened and a swarthy fellow, somewhat below medium height, entered. Attired in a dark walking jacket and a waxed hat with a wide brim, he was preceded by a small brown and white dog that skipped lithely off among the table legs. The newcomer carried a double-barrelled twelve-bore shotgun, which he placed behind the bar, and wore a half-empty cartridge belt around his waist. He casually tipped his hat at one or two customers who acknowledged his arrival, then paused briefly upon glancing in Toby's direction.

Toby immediately recognised the stranger he had met earlier in the day by the gate at Molliton.

'You've just made it, George!' said the landlord heartily. 'I was about to call time. What will it be?'

'Half of cider for me, Davy, and a biscuit for the dog if you've got one,' he replied.

Noting Toby's interest in the stranger, Mark leant across to him. 'That's George Shotwell, the Tyler's new gamekeeper.

'The Tylers?'

'Local landowners – most of the land around here belongs to them. They live up at "Tyler Hall" over Cromer Hyde way.'

'And this fellow... George Shotwell, did you say? Has he been here long?' prompted Toby looking back toward the gamekeeper who was settling himself at one of the empty tables.

'Came about three months ago... just turned up in the village out of the blue. Seems to know his job, though.'

'And what is that? What does he do?'

'What you'd expect a gamekeeper to do. He takes care of his lordship's young pheasants by controlling vermin and keeping the rabbits and pigeons down. I expect he'll also organise the shoot this autumn.'

'An important man, then.'

'A good gamekeeper benefits us all,' Mark reflected. 'Do you see that little Jack Russell of his?' he added, pointing with his finger.

Toby looked across at the dog that now lay beside its master's feet gnawing contentedly upon a large arrowroot biscuit.

'Marvellous little fellow he is. Flushed out a whole family of rats in our barn. Each time they ran he just snapped them up quick as lightning! One shake of the head and that was that – dead as a doornail. A good gamekeeper doesn't need his gun much when he can rely on a sidekick like that.'

Toby could well imagine this, for even when relaxed at the end of the day and eating his snack, the little dog's muscular flanks gave an impression of barely suppressed energy, like a coiled spring.

The gamekeeper, still wearing his hat, slouched casually in his chair; his eyes meeting Toby's with a look of inward satisfaction as he rolled a heavy stone dice in his right hand.

Unnerved by the other's stare, Toby glanced back at Mark to find that he too was studying his drinking partner intently, a question upon his lips.

'Toby...' he began, 'I've been thinking... there's something that don't seem to add up about you.'

Toby looked guardedly into the other's face. Of all those he had recently met, Mark was the one who seemed most curious about him. A number of times he had chanced to find the young countryman looking in his direction, a thoughtful expression on his intelligent face.

'What would that be?' asked Toby, fingering his glass.

'Well... your clothes for a start... That blue jacket you turned up in.'

Toby thought of the fleece he had left hanging on the chair in his room. 'What of it?' he asked dismissively.

'You say it's made from wool... that you bought it in London.'

'That's right. Why?'

Mark leaned back, his brow furrowing slightly. 'Well I'll tell you,' he said, slowly shaking his head. 'I've worked around sheep all my life, sheared a good many too in my time, but I never recall seeing wool as close-knit and smooth as that.'

Toby searched for a suitable reply. The farmer's interest was perhaps motivated more by curiosity than anything else, but he realised he must steer him away from further close enquiry. The fleece, produced from man-made materials, might promote awkward questions if examined by an experienced eye. He decided to bluff the younger Trindle and trade upon his probable lack of knowledge of the city.

'You're right, Mark, my jacket is indeed made from an interesting combination of materials. I bought it in Camden Market. It contains a mixture of fibres: wool, cotton and flax, together with a little silk. Very hardwearing, the stallholder said. It wasn't cheap, but I'd just got my first wages and decided to treat myself.'

Mark smiled at this, and seemed a little more satisfied. 'But what about that label on your boots – "Rustler" it says. Who puts labels like that on their wares?'

Toby hesitated, searching for a suitable reply, and was grateful to be rescued by Davy Oldfield ringing the curfew bell. 'Time, gentlemen, please!' he called. 'Come on now – let's be off home or I shall lose my licence and the pleasures of this hostelry will cease to be available to you all another evening.'

There were some good-natured complaints about his request, but soon a steady stream of drinkers filed out through the door wishing the landlord goodnight. The Trindle party formed up too, carefully guiding Elijah Barnes, who was now more than a little light-headed due to the many drinks they and others had stood him.

Emerging into the open air Toby looked up to see the now risen three-quarter moon riding high above a bank of dark cloud in the northern sky, its pale silver light illuminating the narrow cobbled roads below. This glow was reflected from the roof tiles of the pub and the folded wings of the crow now perched, apparently sleeping, upon the topmost ridge.

Having pointed Elijah towards his home in a nearby lane, the rest set off on their return journey to the farm with Toby walking a few paces behind. The tired men spoke little and the tramp of feet became the only accompaniment to Toby's thoughts. After descending the short slope that led from the pub he was obliged to bend down to re-tie the laces of his right boot, and looking back saw the gamekeeper, the last to leave, emerge from "The Three Eels". At the same time the Jack Russell, bobbing by his ankles, barked twice, causing Wesley to turn.

'Come on, Toby!' he called. 'Don't go getting lost; there's work to be done tomorrow.'

Toby straightway stood up and came on at a good pace, aware that the gamekeeper and his dog had begun to follow in the lamplit gloom. More than once he heard the little animal scudding up close to his heels as it scampered ahead of its master. On another occasion it actually circled around his feet, looking eagerly up at him, before disappearing again. Thus, constantly reminded of another's presence, Toby made towards the open country beyond the outskirts of the sleeping village and forked once more onto the track leading past the windmill to the railway crossing. He more than half expected the gamekeeper to turn as well, but soon all sound and movement behind was lost in the darkness, the little man having apparently continued heading east along the byroad to Molliton. All was now silent as Toby followed the small group ahead of him. The windmill, standing jet-black against the sky, came into view; its huge sails like gaunt sentinels surrounded by stars; then the track dipped down into a shadowy corner before curving right again towards the railway. Lost in thought, and feeling no desire to make up ground, Toby fell behind the others once more. However, he was not to be alone at the sheltered place for long, as moments later the sound of footsteps to his left caused him to pause. A bridleway coming up from the road joins the track at this point, and drawing level with the junction of the two he saw the gamekeeper with his dog approaching less than twenty feet away. The Jack Russell looked up, sniffed, and moved forward to lick the toe of Toby's boot as the two men came face to face – the leaves of an overhanging tree dappling the moonlight illuminating the remote spot.

'We meet again,' said the darkly clad figure, his eyes glinting.

Toby did not answer, feeling perturbed by the eerie suddenness of the other's approach.

'You're staying at "Warren Hill Farm", I hear,' continued the mysterious go-between. 'It'll do,' he added, nodding slowly.

The casual satisfaction evident in the stranger's words and gestures irked Toby. It was as if his very thoughts were not his own – that the other could see into him.

'You play games!' he stammered. 'It was you I saw this morning by the gate... The one the girl, Jeannie, spoke of... what did she call you?'

'Jasper,' the little man replied laconically, looking up from beneath dark eyelids.

'That was it...' said Toby, in a shrinking voice. 'She suggested I'd meet you again.'

'And here I am,' he chuckled craftily, leaning forward to reveal the dice upon his palm. 'Jasper Farrow, your guide and servant.'

'Don't mock me,' said Toby, recovering his composure. 'Why would I need a guide?'

'Because you have much to see... and may go astray.'

'Why should I trust in you? …What kind of helper sneaks up on another in the dark and proceeds to talk in riddles?'

Looking ahead towards the crossing where the others had passed from view, Jasper seemed to consider this challenge for a moment, then said in a less distant, more conciliatory tone, 'Forgive me, my friend. We are both here for a purpose… I to assist and you to learn. Few enjoy every step of a journey, but you will doubtless be wiser at the end of your travels.'

'Jeannie spoke like this,' said Toby, softly. 'But how am I to understand what you mean?'

'You will eventually,' offered Jasper. 'As for now… I must be off, for I have tarried long enough, while you must catch up with your companions.'

'Will we meet a third time?'

'Most surely, and on other occasions too… but remember, in these parts I present myself as the gamekeeper, George Shotwell. That is how they know me here, so beware what you say. The younger Trindle in particular is astute; therefore you should not be too open with him.'

Jasper turned to go, the dog bounding off ahead down the track from which they had come. 'Wait!' cried Toby. 'The dice… what number showed this time?'

'No more than a "two",' Jasper replied, looking back.

'…And that crow? …Is it also something to do with Jeannie and youself?'

'Yes… something,' he grinned enigmatically. 'But just what, you must wait to discover as events unfold.'

Then, before Toby could enquire further, having pulled up the broad collar of his travelling jacket, Jasper slid into the shadow of the trees and was gone.

* * *

Toby stood alone for a few moments longer before slowly resuming his journey. A short time later, he came upon the others, who had decided to wait for him just beyond the crossing, and together they returned to the hilltop farm. Little was said, and only Mark seemed interested in what had kept him. Once inside, and by now completely exhausted, Toby gratefully took the glowing oil lamp offered by Coodie, and having ascended the creaking staircase to his bedroom, quickly fell into a welcome and dreamless sleep beneath the feather quilt.

Chapter Three

Meg Maddox

TOBY BLINKED AWAKE AT SEVEN O'CLOCK THE following morning and knew that he had woken again in another age. Sunlight was streaming in through the open window; and looking there he came to focus upon the wristwatch left on the ledge overnight. It was an old-fashioned one with roman numerals and a leather strap. Yet, as Toby mused upon the design, he became aware that other eyes, if given the opportunity to study it closely, might easily note clues to its modern origin. Mark Trindle, for one, would not be fooled. Thus he decided to rely upon caution that day, keeping the watch from sight – a ploy that when combined with a subsequent act of vigilance was to have unforeseen repercussions.

* * *

After shaving and taking advantage of the change of socks and underclothes provided by Coodie, Toby was preparing to leave his room when his attention was drawn to a movement below the window. A large and very handsome Golden Retriever had appeared and was sniffing enthusiastically round the nettles and docks that bordered a nearby hedge. Judging by its greying muzzle and the folds of skin around its eyes, the animal, a male, was obviously getting on in years, but it still retained all the charm and curiosity of a puppy. Having disturbed a bee or hoverfly, it would jump up and stare intently at the creature with its head on one side, as if challenging it to a game. The dog's good humour was both unquenchable and endearing, causing Toby to smile.

A young woman carrying a large enamel pail then moved into his sight. She was around twenty years of age, slim and fair-haired, wearing a bib apron, farm boots and a light brown working dress. This had a white collar, and he was struck by the way the brightness of the material set off her fine and delicate features. Although rather short in stature, as he had noticed many of the local countrywomen were, she held herself with an upright bearing that suggested independence and self-reliance. Toby was also impressed by the serious and intent look in her blue eyes as she raised her head to follow the flight of a bird.

The woman then passed from view, and having checked his own reflection in the mirror, he made his way downstairs to find Mrs Trindle clearing the breakfast table.

'You slept well,' Coodie said with a look of satisfaction. 'I'm pleased, as you seemed very tired yesterday.'

'It was welcome,' Toby replied. 'But tell me, where are the others?'

'Up and about this last hour or so,' she announced, placing a plate of bread and cheese in front of him. 'The men have gone off to the market in Bedford. They thought about taking you with them but decided to let you rest. I expect them back by half-eleven. The girls are outside working. Now you must eat up before joining them!'

They continued talking together for a few minutes longer until the girl he had seen previously walked past the window and stopped to fill her pail from a tap in the yard. As the water ran she absently stood up to wipe her brow and push a stray wisp of hair from her face, allowing Toby to observe her clearly through the open window.

He turned to Coodie, who had already noted his interest. 'That girl,' he said, 'who is she? I didn't see her yesterday.'

'That's our Meg,' replied Coodie, looking out to the yard and smiling. 'Meg Maddox, she's nineteen; comes over regular to help with the animals. She lives by herself about a mile from here – at "Silver Link Cottage", down by the railway.'

Toby watched as the girl moved out of sight. 'She lives alone you say?'

'Afraid so,' said Coodie reflectively. 'Her parents are both dead you see. Mr Maddox, he was killed in an accident several years ago; left his wife to bring up the child by herself. Then poor Sarah, she fell ill with the cancer, and that took her off six months back. So now Meg looks after herself. Her family were always the shepherds around here; Scots originally – came down around a hundred and fifty years ago they say. But there's little call for shepherding these days, so Meg makes a living where she can. We're pleased to have her for two or three hours of a morning. Takes a lot of pressure off Scarlet and me. Why don't you go out and meet her?'

Taking up the suggestion, Toby moved into the patch of sunlight illuminating the porch. The weather was clear again, with just a haze of light cloud high in the sky and an eddying breeze. It would be hot later, but the fresh scents of early morning still pervaded the air. Here and there a few domestic chickens, together with two geese and an ancient Muscovy duck, pecked about; while the self-important cockerel he had seen yesterday perched on the shafts of a cart. A little further off, a huge ginger cat lay curled up fast asleep on a sunlit wall while the voice of someone singing a popular tune could be heard coming from the direction of the nearby cowshed.

Toby moved into the yard until he reached the stables. The two shires, Caesar and Cleo, were feeding, and both ambled forward to look out as he approached. He reached up to pat Caesar's flank and had just begun to scratch the bridge of Cleo's nose when the girl appeared once more at an adjacent door, wheeling a barrow loaded with manure. She stopped for a moment without speaking; then, with a slight nod of her head, strode off through the west-facing archway to her right. She had communicated nothing, neither interest nor surprise, and Toby was slightly taken aback by this first encounter. In a few moments, however, she reappeared and came purposefully towards him; before lowering the barrow and straightening up, wiping her hands together.

'You'll be the fellow who's staying,' she said. 'Scarlet told me. Come on, I've got just the job for you.'

She led him inside the stable before turning and placing a farm fork in his hand, a half smile dimpling her cheek. 'You can load up the last of the muck and shift it round the back while I put out the straw.' With no more ado she then set to work again herself, and not seeing this as a promising opportunity for conversation, Toby joined her.

His allotted task was already almost done, but working around the horses with fork and broom he once more all but filled the heavy barrow before walking it into the yard. As he emerged Scarlet Trindle briefly appeared at the door of the milk parlour next to the cowshed opposite and wished him a cheerful, 'Good morning!' He returned her pleasantry, then following the route through the archway that Meg had taken, came upon an outer yard. There were buildings on two sides of this, one containing an old and rather melancholy grey donkey with white ears; the other housing a beautiful blue and white cow that looked placidly towards him through long eyelashes. In the open field beyond, tethered to a heavy stake, Toby also noted a magnificent bull eyeing him lazily. Yet it was the manure heap that drew his attention: a huge pile with narrow duckboards leading up to the centre. Clearly, the required technique for discharging each load was to take a run at this so as to achieve sufficient momentum to reach the top. Failure to accomplish the ascent would result in an unfortunate deviation to right or left causing the mucky load to slop out prematurely, inevitably tipping a hapless bearer into the contents of the heap! Whilst an oily slurry pooling around the base warned of the fate to be expected by any that tumbled and fell.

Swallowing nervously, Toby lunged forward with the laden barrow, miraculously completing the climb without mishap. But, having tipped the load, he lost his footing when reversing off, one boot settling deep into the fresh ooze which began to run down inside. It was an unpleasant moment, and when he reappeared in the farmyard he did so wrinkling his nose, while lifting and placing his foot sheepishly at each step.

The girls, who were now standing talking together, instantly knew what had happened and Scarlet broke into a peal of laughter that quickly brought her mother to see. Meg, more restrained, stood with hands held together, a faint smile creasing the corners of her mouth. Her expression was not only one of amusement, but also of sympathy for his embarrassment, and the impression it made would long stay with him.

It took a little time to clean Toby up. Coodie found a replacement pair of socks while he washed his foot and rinsed out the soiled boot under the tap. She told him to leave it on the wall to dry in the sun and gave him a pair of old farm clogs to wear in the meantime. Then he returned to the others.

Their work was now finished, a long list of daily tasks having been completed – milking, cleaning and feeding – each woman following a well-established routine. Scarlet was principally involved with milking the cows and chilling the milk for transport and proudly showed Toby round the cowsheds and cooling parlour. She had given names to each cow and spoke of them individually, with an affection and pride that he thought would seem out of place in his own modern age of mechanisation and mass production. But it was the cattle feed preparation barn that impressed him most of all – a dry, spacious room piled with huge hessian sacks of ground oats, barley, wheat meal and many other foodstuffs – each giving off a rich aroma.

'It's a heaven for rats and mice,' Scarlet affirmed with a smile. Yet this earthly paradise was patiently patrolled, both night and day, by three sleek, half-wild farm cats that looked down unblinking from watch posts high above in the eaves.

For her part, Meg cared for the equines, fed the domestic fowl, and looked after the pigs and calves that the Trindles kept for meat, or as future breeding stock. Yet what Toby came to realise was that although the young women formed a successful partnership and frequently worked together on shared tasks, the two were nevertheless separated by differences in character and consequently less than natural companions. Thus, although only a year apart in age, they neither joked nor made small talk, speaking little about anything other than matters to do with the farm.

* * *

By eight thirty the work was done and Scarlet went inside the cottage to help with the weekly wash. By now the comic Golden Retriever had reappeared after a long snooze on a pile of sacks in the stable, and Toby found himself alone with Meg who was preparing to leave.

She called, 'Come on, Mr Toots,' and the dog, having trotted forward to sit down beside her, looked up lovingly, his wet tongue lolling between loose jaws. 'You daft old thing,' the girl said affectionately, fondling an ear. 'What am I to do with you?'

For a moment her reserved and serious demeanour fell away, leaving Toby aware of a warmth and sadness beneath.

'You like animals?' he ventured, clearly stating an affirmative.

'Of course… doesn't everyone?' she replied wistfully, inclining her head to brush back a lock of loose hair. 'Animals are no trouble. Most always they just take you as you are – they keep it simple.' Meg pondered inwardly for a moment, before looking up with a smile, adding, 'You know, I've never met an animal I didn't like.'

It was a dry kind of humour for one so young. Yet, thought he; though she still possessed the fresh face of youth, the experiences of life seemed to have given her another kind of wisdom beyond her years.

She moved off and he fell in beside her. 'Do you mind if I walk with you for a while?'

Meg turned. 'Why not?' she said, lightening again after a quiet pause. 'It'll be company. I'll tell you more about the farm.'

She seemed to relax then, and moving towards the cat that still lay sunning itself on the wall, she stroked its head. The creature immediately came awake, arching his neck and purring luxuriantly, eyes closed. 'This is Matty,' she said, as if talking to a much-loved friend. 'And the cockerel over there – that's George. He's a bit of a boaster – the king of all he surveys, you might say.'

At this point the geese waddled by, their heads swivelling round as they appraised Toby and Meg with wary eyes. Meg curtseyed towards them, 'And these are Freda and Angus,' she added primly, '…two of my oldest and dearest friends.'

They now passed through the archway to the outer yard. 'Him out there,' Meg pointed to the tethered bull, 'that's Gladstone, perhaps the most genial of his kind in England. It's a wonder to me he manages to rouse himself to anything,' she winked. 'But this one's my favourite!' Meg had stopped beside the donkey, which looked up at her with a mournful expression as she produced half a carrot from her apron pocket. 'His name is Naffy,' she smiled, while gently stroking his drooping ear with her free hand, 'and a more doleful and melancholy old chap you couldn't wish to meet. Somebody really ought to write a book about him one day.'

So their conversation went on, and for the next few minutes he saw her animated and unguarded, but it did not last. They soon began to pass beyond the farm buildings, and Meg gradually became less voluble as they moved out into an area of rough ground overgrown with tall grass, nettles, dog daisies and thistles. Over the years this place had become the dumping ground for equipment no longer used on the farm: old carts with worn out axles, cultivating tools, rusty ploughs and broken haymaking machines. The further they went the more decrepit and indistinct these forms became, until the last few, long tucked in beside the straggling hedge, were all but swallowed by the undergrowth.

Eventually an open field was reached, beside which ran a dusty footpath that Meg began to follow. The sun had ascended higher into the morning sky and another hot day was promised. Two skylarks rose up ahead of them, beginning their long warbling ascent. Then a group of startled pigeons clattered out of an ash tree and flew noisily overhead.

Meg raised her slender arm and pointed to their right. 'I live over there… in the dip,' she said. 'You can't see the cottage from here, but it's not far.'

They were now heading downhill to where "Pocket Farm", owned by Albert and Rose Smallwood, lay tucked into the slope of rising land. Above it, on the skyline about a mile away, stood a wooded copse, the roof and chimneys of a large house discernible among the trees, while down to their left "Deep Spinney Farm" crouched in the hollow. But Toby's eyes were again drawn toward the substantial square stone structure standing in open ground nearby.

He stopped to look and Meg retraced her steps. 'That's "Maxton Tower"... It's grand, isn't it? They say it was built in the time of James I.'

'Looks like a ruin to me,' said Toby.

'Oh it is,' she replied, turning to walk on. 'But there's history locked within those weathered slabs... Perhaps I can tell you more when time allows.'

Toby spent a few extra moments scrutinising the brooding structure which even now, in the bright May sunshine, had an air of mystery.

* * *

Looking back at last, he noted that Meg had already reached the outskirts of "Pocket Farm" and trotted down to catch her up. They passed into the farmyard through a narrow entrance flanked by two aged ash trees. A sturdy five-barred gate, now broken and bleached grey by the sun, had been lifted from its hinges and discarded against the adjoining hedge. The farm itself was tiny, consisting only of a small cowshed, a pigsty, three outbuildings and a medium sized wooden barn. A pond bordered by hawthorn trees and frequented by a small gathering of ducks, geese and sparrows, stood near its centre, while a pair of ancient elm trees rose up at two corners, giving the setting shade and character.

They turned at the cowshed and came to a quaint farmhouse set slightly back from the yard and fronted by a neat garden filled with scented plants. Ivy and flowering creepers grew along deep-pitted walls and around gable ends. In our time, it might have been called an idyllic chocolate box cottage, but the moss taking hold upon large areas of the roof suggested a march of unseen decay.

Albert and Rose Smallwood, both in their late sixties, were in the garden together. They had worked the farm for over forty years but were now becoming increasingly infirm with arthritis and rheumatism. Having sold their cattle and pigs they could, as Albert said, 'But place their trust in God' while concentrating upon rearing a few ducks and chickens to pay the rent. The old farmer, white haired and bent over with age, moved forward with a cheerful greeting. He had clearly been expecting Meg to pass through and as they discussed the prospects for the day Toby sensed his affection for the young woman. He seemed very interested in Toby too, and called his wife to meet him.

'So... you've come up from London to cast your eyes over us country dwellers, have you?' Albert asked, shifting his pipe to the side of his mouth.

'That's right,' replied Toby. 'My readers will be fascinated, I'm sure.'

'Happen they will,' said the old man. 'I expect most people think we've got it about perfect out here.'

'Then they are little mistaken, I dare say,' said his wife, who had come to stand beside him. 'Folk always imagine as others have got it better than them; but few ever takes the time to find out, do they?'

Toby was struck by Rose Smallwood's appearance. Her round face was gnarled and lined by the effects of weather and time, but retained immense charm. Although she looked much older than her sixty-five years, her eyes still twinkled shrewdly and her life-long warm humour was undiminished.

'Tell me, young un,' she went on in a strong Norfolk accent retained from girlhood. 'What do they people down south in "The Smoke" think life in the shires is about when they sit readin' their daily papers and drinkin' their morning milk?'

Toby thought for a moment, conscious of the fiction he had built around himself, and suddenly aware of the inevitable gulf that existed between them. Rose Smallwood had lived her life less than two miles from his own home in Molliton; while he had passed this spot many times when out walking... but the old lady would die never knowing the truth about his own existence.

He looked down at her upturned face as she shielded an eye against the sun awaiting his reply. 'I'm sure they respect your efforts,' he answered rather lamely. 'People value the work of those who provide the things they eat.'

'Tush... come on,' she chided him dismissively. 'Albert and me have worked all these years and ain't so much as seen a London businessman. Sure they may have drunk our milk and eaten the bacon as come from our pigs, but did they give a thought for us? ...I think not.'

For all the likely truth in what she said, Toby could see that there was really no bitterness behind her words since a small smile still creased her lips. She was just stating "the way of the world".

'Perhaps I can do something to change that,' he ventured at last.

'I dare say you could try,' she nodded sagely, 'but don't spend too long or you might grow old like us.'

'You're not old,' said Meg, looking kindly at the elderly countrywoman and touching her hand. 'You mustn't talk like that.'

Rose gazed pensively up at the younger woman, and Toby noticed an expression, almost of regret, upon her face.

'Ah... we wish a lot of things could have been different, don't we, Albert? But what the Good Lord sends we must accept.'

* * *

They talked a while longer and Toby learned more about the Smallwoods' story. They were tenant farmers and lived in a tied cottage. Having been able to save nothing from a life of hard work, staying at "Pocket Farm" would depend, as always, on their ability to pay the monthly rent – now a much harder prospect since giving up their animals. Some landowners would allow ageing tenants to remain in tied accommodation at a nominal rent; but Albert intimated that this was not to be their good fortune. He gestured towards the distant copse of trees that Toby had noted earlier.

'That's where our landlord lives – up there at Cromer Hyde, in "Tyler Hall" with his young wife, Charlotte. The one as our Meg here works for during the day.'

Toby glanced at Meg, who looked down as if irritated by the reference.

'Mr Basil Tyler… that's him…' Albert went on, 'the man we've paid good money to all these years – and his father before him. But still he demands his pound of flesh.'

'You mean you could lose your home if you don't pay?' asked Toby.

Albert turned to him, a dry smile lifting his eyebrows. 'It's not just us as could lose out in future. Tenant farmers work all the properties hereabout: "High Dyke", "Deep Spinney" and "Warren Hill", where you yourself have come from. Aye, and a number more further over – even our Meg's little "Silver Link Cottage" is owned by him.'

'And what sort of man is Basil Tyler?' asked Toby.

Rose interrupted at this point. 'A cold fish!' she said, an edge to her voice. 'A man of business… A tallow faced corpse with watery eyes… No more than forty but so dead inside he might have passed away years ago. Not been here more than five times in twenty years. All soft hands and airs and graces – but those manicured nails of his are little more than signs of a sterile and selfish mind, if you ask me. He can be cruel too…' she added meaningfully. 'Loves to hunt and shoot: foxes, pheasants… anything really. When he's out with his rich friends ridin'… or with guns, it's best to keep well away.'

The suppressed note of anger and sorrow in her voice was unmistakable.

'Hush now, Rose,' said Albert tenderly. 'Don't go winding yourself up – you can't change the past.'

As if her husband's words had penetrated to a closed and private corner, Rose turned with a nod of farewell and walked slowly out of sight into the house.

'What happened?' asked Toby, as he watched her disappear. 'You seem to hint at some misfortune.'

Removing his cap, Mr Smallwood looked down and ran his fingers through the thin grey hair on his crown. He seemed to consider long and hard before answering, then looked up at Toby with sad eyes.

'It wasn't always just the two of us, son,' he said at last. 'We raised a daughter here, Katy; and if she was still alive we wouldn't be in this state. She was twenty-five when she died and I'd taught her everything I knew. You know how it is, how you have hopes for your own – to see them happy and married with children.' The old man shook his head, his face set. 'Twas the same for us... Lor, she were pretty too, I swear it! Went out courting every weekend and would have found someone...'

He fell silent, looking ahead.

'And you lost her?'

'She was killed,' he replied bluntly, swallowing his emptiness. 'Shot... six years ago. Went out along by "Deep Spinney Farm" to pick blackberries for a pie... and never came back.'

'"Deep Spinney Farm"?' Toby asked.

Mr Smallwood turned in the direction of the farm that Toby had seen on their way down – a rambling assortment of buildings among trees lower down the hill.

'The Towsers' place...' he said with a note of disgust. 'We used to get along alright with old Matthew and his wife Abigail, but not since their children grew up. Never have been able to get on with Cregan, the eldest. Clever, hard nosed bugger if ever there was one. He's thirty now, but has been a bully since before he went to school. Got married ten years ago, only for the poor woman to leave him soon afterwards – couldn't bear his evil ways I shouldn't wonder. And his brother... Barnaby!' said the old man, throwing his head up in disgust. 'He's a sadistic so and so – insane I reckon. Just a great, ignorant, dumb ox! Got expelled from school for striking the teacher when he was eleven. Never known to say sorry. ...Ah, but his interests always lay elsewhere than learnin' – shooting, trapping, ferreting and more – even dog fighting, some have suggested. It seems something has to die before Barnaby feels any pleasure. Meanwhile he happily joins in any nefarious little activity that his brother chooses to become involved with; and the older one is both careful and crafty enough to make sure neither gets found out. They seem to have friends in high places too: regularly beating and trapping for the Tylers... Cregan apparently being on good terms with his lordship.'

The stooped old farmer seemed to reflect for a few moments before going on.

'That might explain how they manage to survive at all, since the boys seem to involve themselves in precious little proper farming. Old Matthew did his best to get them interested, but seems to have been left to get on with managing the place by himself. He still keeps pigs and a small flock of sheep – grows a few acres of wheat and barley too; but not near enough for them to afford to live the way they do.'

'How do you mean?' asked Toby, becoming intrigued by the farmer's tale.

'Well...' said Albert, sucking on his pipe, 'they got piped water to the house before we did; even though they were closer to the most reliable underground supply in the district. And now I'll be blowed if old Tyler hasn't laid on the electric for them too –

whilst we're still making do with oil and candles. Yet I bet they don't pay a penny more rent.'

'Can you explain it?' asked Toby.

'I imagine it's a question of "You scratch my back and I'll scratch yours",' said the elderly countryman with a knowing look.

'You seem bitter,' said Toby.

'I am…' Albert replied slowly. 'You see, I didn't finish telling you about the day our Katy went missing, did I?' He shifted his weight from one foot to the other, as if summoning a deeper grievance.

'As I remember, she'd been gone about half an hour when the shooting started t'other side of "Deep Spinney Farm". Pheasants they were after – there's many reared from chicks in and around "Gibbet Wood" over yonder. Well, the shootin' went on for all of ten minutes, with the sound of it seemingly coming from all directions at once. I were standing in the farmyard listening and a few pellets even pattered down in the dust near me. Then it stopped – just like that, leaving a deathly silence. I did hear a few excited voices calling a little while after, but that was all for the day. Straight off I was a bit concerned about Katy; but nonetheless expected her back before long because she was always a careful girl.'

He stopped for a moment, as if recollecting.

'She didn't come back?' asked Toby.

'Evening came and night dropped in, but there were no sign of her. I went out searchin' along the footpaths, while Rose stayed waiting here. Nothing… I found no trace! Spent half the night looking… not a sign. The following day I reported her missing to the police. They asked some silly questions at first. "Had she shown signs of being unhappy in recent days?" "Might she have gone off with someone?" Things like that. But we knew she would never leave us without saying why…'

Here the old man swallowed hard, choking back a painful memory.

'They found her two days later by a hedge up near the Northampton road… She'd been shot in the head and chest. The officer who came said she must have lain there all the while. We identified her later, and that was that.

'Shootin' accident they put it down to; which may well be right… But nobody owned up to bein' responsible – though somebody must have known. They questioned them all, even Queenie, that odd fifteen-year-old daughter of the Towsers, but seemed to meet with a perfect wall of silence… So now she's buried down in "All Saints'" churchyard.'

The old man paused as if deflated and beaten.

'You must have been devastated.'

Mr Smallwood looked up. 'You can't imagine it, lad. Losing an only child like that… it's like losing part of yourself… Damn near killed Rose. And I'll tell you the worst bit,' he went on, taking the now dead pipe from between his pale lips. 'It's the feeling that the Towsers and their shooting friends did find her lying there in the sun that evening... that they all knew; Basil Tyler included. But that rather than doing the Christian thing and reportin' it to the authorities; they chose instead to stand around her considering how best to cover their tracks, before simply deciding to disperse and walk off home, leaving her to the night.

'Just imagine though; her body might have been worried by crows or a fox... it don't bear thinkin' about, do it?'

* * *

There was another silence before the old fellow; his hands still shaking, excused himself and ambled forlornly back to the farmhouse. They watched him go before Meg, who had listened quietly to their conversation, turned to Toby with a fierce glint in her eye.

'Will you be telling all that to your readers, Toby?' she asked him challengingly.

'No... I think not – some things are probably best left to the past.'

'Perhaps...' she added, looking into his face. 'Clearly not everything out here is as perfect as some might suppose... But now I too must be off, for I'm expected at "Tyler Hall" by eleven o'clock.'

'You're employed there?'

'...As a servant and ladies' maid; with a little cleaning and secretarial work for his lordship thrown in.'

'But you don't like the work?'

Meg turned, her face bearing a calmer yet still anguished expression. 'You heard what Albert said... Katy Smallwood was my best friend. We were like sisters. Now she's gone and who knows what part Basil Tyler might have played in it? And then there's Charlotte Tyler – the one to whom I must bow and minister.'

A look of sullen frustration filled Meg's eyes and she bit her lip.

'You hate her too,' Toby suggested.

'Not hate exactly... but yes, I have come to despise her shallowness and vanity.'

'Tell me about her.'

Meg looked down as if carefully choosing her words before replying. 'Have you ever been loathed by anyone?' she asked after some moments.

'Perhaps,' he said, 'but I try not to think about that sort of thing.'

'I believe Charlotte Tyler detests me.'

'Can you think why?' Toby ventured, hearing the cold note of certainty in her voice.

'Remarkably enough; in her narrow way I believe she's jealous, even now, of my few accomplishments. We knew each other at school you see, and were in the same class. Oh, she was always more popular than I could ever be! You know, pretty – in that way boys love and girls admire. But that didn't stop her being envious of me whenever I was chosen to read in class or sing at Sunday School. I think Charlotte must have seen me as a threat or something. I can't imagine why, since I was the quiet type and always had my head in a book.'

Meg breathed a slow sigh of resignation before going on.

'That's how shallow people can be, isn't it? To me Charlotte seemed to have everything, but for her, the small gifts I possessed were a source of irritation… Stupid!'

'And now?' Toby prompted. 'You must work for her?'

'Oh yes,' she nodded, 'each day the fly must go back to the spider's web.'

'But how did that come about? You say you were at the village school together. Was she rich in those days?'

Meg pursed her lips and summoned a hollow smile. 'No!' she mouthed. 'Charlotte Tyler was Charlotte Mandell then, and quite ordinary too; just like you and me.'

'Charlotte Mandell?' said Toby, recollecting the name. 'Would she be related to the shopkeeper at Stavenham?'

Meg looked at Toby askance. 'You've met the old skinflint?' she asked with a note of surprise.

'I saw him get off the train last night… Tall, thin character; doesn't say much.'

'That'll be him,' said Meg. 'Christian Mandell: a dry fellow if ever there was one: likes to give himself airs in public, although he's no better or wealthier than the rest. He's owned that corner shop for years and never made any real money – not that he won't take the opportunity to charge double if he's a mind to. His wife, Amy Mandell, she passed on at the turn of the century; some say because it must have worn her out looking at his sour face all day. So he was left to raise Charlotte all by himself… which to be fair couldn't have been easy for a man.

'So Charlotte grew up; and while others looked for work, she looked to better herself. From early on she'd always liked to cultivate the easy life. Her skills were in the arts of make-up and hairdressing rather than anything more solid. She also mastered the subtleties of dress, the tying of ribbons and those subtle arts women learn to turn a man's head. Charlotte certainly made the best of what she had and was not afraid to show it off; growing utterly vain at heart, caring only for herself. But sadly it seems to be a part of nature that men are easily attracted, and become mesmerised by such cultivated "beauty". Thus, like a patient fisherman she baited the hook with her own brightness to lure the largest and fattest catch. Oh… and along the way many a small fish did heave into sight! But Charlotte cared little about the many suitors she rebuffed or the hearts she may have broken.

'Then one day, when she'd just turned eighteen, the perfect prize seemed to turn up. She was serving in her father's shop when who should walk in but Basil Tyler. He was already a man of forty; and it was said had never taken a fancy to anyone before. But Charlotte tipped her bonnet at him, and perhaps because he was bored or who knows what, he took up with her. It came as a shock to everyone; and there were many that said there was nothing to it – that Basil was only amusing himself and would soon lose interest. Yet they were wrong, for six months later the two were married. A big society wedding in Bedford it was, and dozens of important folk came up from London, though few local people were invited. So Christian Mandell got a daughter off his hands; Basil got a wife; and Charlotte rose to greater wealth and status than she could ever have dreamed of.

'But right from the start there were those that doubted Basil's motives: folk who suggested that he had taken a wife for business reasons alone and that there was little substance in the relationship.'

Meg stopped and thought for a moment, tiny wrinkles appearing on her brow.

'I believe they were right... that it's a loveless affair – and if so I can feel sympathy for her. I think Charlotte is deeply disillusioned – that her marriage has turned into a trap. But for all such misfortune she continues to be the jewel on Basil's arm and will probably never be able to give up either the money or power she has gained over the likes of me.

'...So now I must go,' Meg concluded, turning resignedly, 'or be made to suffer for my lateness.'

The retriever, having watched all along from the shade of a nearby tree, trotted to her side, and summoning again a little of her earlier warmth, Meg looked kindly at Toby. 'Please feel welcome to visit me at the cottage. ...This evening sometime after six o'clock would be fine if you can make it. Then we can talk again.'

With these parting words she walked away across the sloping ground towards "Maxton Tower" before disappearing from sight beyond the brow of the hill as Mr Toots, meandering to and fro in her wake, sniffed inquisitively at every anthill and rabbit hole. Toby watched her go, unknowing that a descendant of this complex young woman would one day help to shape the future of the world to come.

Chapter Four

The Last Millers of England

TOBY PENSIVELY RETRACED HIS STEPS TO "WARREN Hill Farm", again impressed by the imposing size of the huge barn that dwarfed the surrounding buildings as he approached the Trindles' property. Then he made his way through the arch from the outer yard and found Scarlet standing beside the cooling parlour. A small cart, with Naffy the donkey between the shafts, was drawn up beside the loading platform and Scarlet had already rolled three milk churns onto it.

'You're back!' she called cheerfully, looking up. 'I'm just taking these down to the station and must be there in time for the eleven o'clock train. The men haven't returned yet. Would you like to come?'

'Very much,' Toby replied, thankful for an opportunity to be active once more, and together they set off – she on the driver's seat, with Toby riding on the tailboard behind.

The weather was clear and fresh as they left the farmyard and he surveyed the surrounding scene, conscious again of the familiar nature of the landscape. Although there were buildings, trees and hedgerows that he had not seen before yesterday, the rises and dips in the land were all well known; the very earth beneath his dangling feet the same.

He dwelled upon this for some moments before realising that the cart had stopped once more and turning, saw Scarlet anxiously looking towards Bedford as she jumped down and moved towards the donkey's head. Then he heard the noise – a dull roar, rapidly increasing in volume with each passing second. Toby slid from the tailboard, and shielding his eyes against the bright sun, scanned the cloudless sky above.

A primitive bi-plane was approaching from the south-east, sputtering and whirring as it battled against the breeze. He saw the rudimentary assemblage of wire and canvas duck and weave as it drew nearer, the pilot fighting to retain control of his frail charge against the unseen forces conspiring against it. Onward the waspish contraption came, bright yellow, filling the air with sound and demanding attention – a gaudy piece of airborne theatre.

The cart jolted behind him, and looking round Toby found Scarlet struggling to prevent Naffy from rearing up in terror.

'Damn aeroplane!' she shouted above the din. 'Why do they have to come here frightening the animals?'

Toby could see other evidence of this as he looked round. The Trindles' startled cows were lumbering across a nearby meadow, udders swaying heavily, and behind him, Gladstone the bull bellowing angrily.

The machine flew directly overhead, clawing its way at an angle into the wind, and Toby saw the pilot leaning out of the open cockpit. He wore an aviator's leather helmet and seemed to be grinning as he looked down through outsized flying goggles. Turning, he gave Toby a cheery thumbs up, before again gripping the controls with both hands and flying on, a thin black scarf fluttering behind his collar.

Toby smiled to himself as he watched the Sopwith pull away leaving a trail of white exhaust fumes. It was the kind of thing people would attend air shows to see in his own time – "Good old Biggles in his breezy bi-plane." He continued to follow its progress as the yellow apparition faded into the distance, becoming no more than a dot on the horizon, then walked round to Scarlet who had managed at last to calm the donkey by offering him a placatory carrot, although Naffy's flanks still twitched nervously. She began to lead the animal forward once more as Toby drew level, but was clearly shaken and angry.

'I hate those things,' she said irritably. 'They may have been fun at first, but now there seem to be one or two every week and we get no peace. Look what happens to the animals; it half scares them to death. You take them cows for instance – it'll be a wonder if they don't produce cheese tonight!'

It was a conjecture that, although he appreciated Scarlet's annoyance, caused Toby to smile. Moreover, he wondered what she would make of life in the twenty-first century, when the trails of a dozen or more airliners might be seen at any time from the same spot.

* * *

They were now approaching "Windmill Crossing" and could see the tiny station through the trees. Then, upon passing the stationmaster's garden, Toby became aware that Morwen Hughes, whom he had glimpsed standing in the doorway of "Station House" the night before, was watching them. She was a short, neat, round little woman, who stood straight backed, smiling and holding a garden fork in her hand. Her face bore a warm and genial expression; and through the bushes behind her Toby could see an immaculately tended garden full of all manner of fruit and vegetables.

'Did you see that aeroplane?' she called out.

'Indeed we did!' replied Scarlet hotly. 'If you ask me, them things is a blessed nuisance.'

The other woman replied with measured calm. 'They say it's progress, dear, – like the railway. Just imagine life without that. What would we do?'

They left her behind, pulling up at the crossing gate soon after. George Hughes was waiting there, shoes brightly polished, a silver pocket watch in hand.

'You'd better hurry!' he called peremptorily. 'The eleven o'clock is just due.'

As if on cue, the whistle of an approaching locomotive was heard, and without further prompting Scarlet hastily steered Naffy into the small wooden loading dock at the far end of "Windmill Halt". The train, the same one Toby had seen the night before, with the same crew, rolled in moments later, and the stationmaster now buzzed around importantly as, with the guard's assistance, the heavy churns were propelled into a luggage compartment of the leading coach. Several parcels and containers were also put off, including one containing three piglets, and there were many requests for Mr Hughes' signature. He personally might well have been thought officious and over fussy in a later age; but on this day his fellow railwaymen were patient throughout, exchanging small talk and banter with confident good humour. They clearly accepted their colleague's quirks ungrudgingly and without malice. Indeed, the whole operation was well oiled and efficient; and in less than five minutes all was ready, allowing the locomotive to pull away on time in a cloud of steam.

Left on the empty platform with Scarlet, Toby glanced towards the substantial station house into which George Hughes was retreating to complete his paper work. Then he took in his surroundings, first gazing down to where the recently departed train had disappeared, before turning back towards the crossing. As his eyes passed across the second location, something caught his attention. Through a gap in the trees, where the path they had followed the previous evening wound down to the village of Stavenham, he saw the old windmill, its dilapidated sails slowly turning.

Scarlet followed his glance. 'Ah,' she said casually, 'Old Silas and Tobias Flegg are attempting a bit of milling it would seem.'

'You mean it really is a working mill?' asked Toby curiously.

'One of the last – you'll not see another in these parts! Most corn is now sent to the big factory mills in Bedford and Northampton; but you could put money on the likelihood that they two barkin' old fellows won't give up until they're carried out of there. The Flegg family have been milling in Stavenham for more than two hundred years and I dare say the tradition will die with them.'

'What do they produce there now?'

'Oh, they grind a bit of cattle feed and mill some barley to scrape a living; but they can't mill decent flour no more on account of the fact that their stones is too worn.'

'Stones?'

'Millstones,' replied Scarlet, raising her eyebrows at his apparent incomprehension. 'They're too worn for quality work, and too expensive for them to replace. No... keeping a mill in good order requires money, and they haven't got more than a little. I shouldn't wonder if the whole dang place don't go and fall down around their ears before much longer.'

She paused thoughtfully for a moment. 'I could take you there now if you want. We don't have to be back at the farm straight away and Old Naffy can stay here awhile. He ain't in nobody's way.'

Toby readily accepted, and they walked together to the crossing before passing through a gap into the field beyond.

* * *

The land, as mentioned before, dips away at this point, with the track to Stavenham snaking away to the right. Growing crops of wheat, barley and potatoes could now be seen; both north and east, while directly ahead, westward across a newly mown hay meadow, the bulk of Stavenham Mill stood up grandly upon a rising fold in the landscape. In the gathering darkness of the previous evening it had been only a misty silhouette frozen on the skyline but now, as he stepped over scented lines of cut grass, it had regained life and animation.

Toby had never visited a working windmill before. There were restored mills, of course, on the Norfolk Broads and dotted around low-lying parts of the country, but these were always brightly painted, their uncanvassed sails left bare to the sun and elements – mere postcard images of a bygone age. What now lay before Toby was a structure impressive and extraordinary in both noise and movement. It rumbled and creaked like some arthritic dinosaur raising its weary limbs to the sky as each ragged sail lurched up into the air, briefly to point towards heaven, before swinging down defeated as if exhausted by a momentous effort. A heavy rumble and swish accompanied every passing movement of the blades. Fine clouds of dust, escaping from between the warped cladding of the mill tower, puffed out with every jolt and lurch of the sail arms as if the wheezy, consumptive monster was about to choke and breath its last; and coming near, he could well understand how a visually challenged knight might mistake such an apparition for a giant.

They stopped before the stone base, each ragged blade, following its perilous descent, passing two feet above their heads. Toby looked up in both amazement and wonder. You couldn't buy such an experience in the twenty-first century; the whole splendid but decrepit building would be closed down in minutes, condemned outright – cordons erected around it, *to protect the public.* Yet here he stood, in the isolation of an empty field, watching entranced.

Walking round to the far side, they found a mangy tortoiseshell cat with an infected eye sitting on the lowest step of the rickety wooden ladder that led up to a half-open door above, and together began to ascend this, gripping a rounded handrail polished smooth by ancient hands. They might have stepped onto a ship making ready for sea, so pronounced was the motion, for the whole structure gently swayed to the repetitive rhythm of its moving parts, feeling alive to the touch. The rich conflicting smells of milled grain, creosote and grease filled Toby's senses, and as they reached the entrance a plume of pipe smoke wafted out.

Scarlet, who was leading, turned to face him. 'Don't you mind these two old reprobates when you see them,' she said, with a smile. 'There's some as thinks them weird, but they're mostly alright if you're prepared to overlook their lack of manners… especially the older one.'

She then pulled the door wide and they looked inside. A swirling mist of dust and chaff was all Toby could make out at first. Then, as he grew accustomed to the dim light, other things became more distinct. There was an orgy of sound and movement: whirring cogs, grinding mill wheels, squeaking axles, and the swish of grain flowing down metalled chutes. Above this he witnessed the passage of a sail through an open window, and heard the rattle of chains overhead. All round were broad oak beams; some vertical, others braced at angles to give strength – each pegged or bolted by skilled hands to provide support for the revolving sails. A myriad of ruined spiders' webs filled every corner and crevice, each clogged with a choking covering of amber dust, and within moments the floating debris began to penetrate Toby's eyes, nose and ears. He sneezed, holding his sleeve across his face, and would have retreated outside but for noting another thick plume of tobacco smoke rising from a shadowy recess opposite.

'There you are, Silas!' said Scarlet brightly, having noted it also. 'We didn't see you at first.'

A shape took human form in the gloom, and the lined face of a gnarled old man looked up.

'Come into the middle where I can have a proper look at you,' he croaked in a wheezy voice. 'You gave me a start, enterin' so quiet.'

Amid the noise of the mill, Toby thought, a whole detachment of light cavalry might have come up and remained unheeded.

They stepped into a shaft of light facing their accuser, who leant forward to see them better. He was one of the most striking people Toby would ever see – a man of more than ninety years who might easily have been lifted out of a storybook or fairy tale; a tiny wizened gnome, with skin like parchment and beady eyes, who now surveyed them with an eager relish as if considering whether they might be good to eat. He was completely bald, except for thin wisps of dust filled white hair around nape and temples, and had an enormous brown mole upon a cracked and wrinkled forehead. But Toby was most impressed by the hoary miller's remarkable nose, a bulbous pockmarked protuberance that stood out from his features above a toothless mouth; the narrow lips crusted with dark saliva.

His clothes, moreover, might have inspired Leonardo by their eccentric peculiarity: a faded shirt embroidered with yellow roses, a red waistcoat with an elaborate coat of arms on one breast, deeply creased white trousers of ancient cut, and a pair of enormous hobnailed boots.

His name was Silas Flegg – miller of Stavenham for over seventy years.

Nothing was said for a few seconds until the old man broke silence once more.

'Well, so you've come to visit us, Scarlet... and brought a friend I see.'

'Yes, Silas,' she replied cheerfully, suppressing a sneeze. 'His name is Toby Freeman – he's from London. He wants to write an article about us.'

'Newspaper man?' said Silas suspiciously, cocking his head on one side. 'Damn fool people if you ask me... Make up most of what they write.'

'You read the papers?' asked Toby.

'Every day, young fella – it's my only pleasure now. A man should keep himself properly informed. How else can he get to know what's goin' on in the world?'

Toby agreed. 'You've worked here all your life, Scarlet tells me.'

'Man and boy, young gent – man and boy; and see where it's got me. Ah, millin' was a good business once, but it ain't no more!' he concluded emphatically.

'I'm sure you still do a good job,' added Toby, anxious not to put the old man in a bad humour.

Silas Flegg looked up from under shaggy eyebrows, a forced grin upon his ugly face.

'You don't have to humour me, son; and there's no use denying what we've come to,' he added, with a note of self-pity creeping into his voice. 'Me... I'm a wreck... a ruin... Life's left me crippled and twisted up; just living out my time with a half mad son to keep in work until I go. This old mill's shot – the stones is worn out, with no money to replace them when they finally give up. And as for what we do: it's not proper work, just bits and pieces, low-grade stuff. The town mills have taken the cream, and we've been left with the scraps.'

Just then another rattling of chains was heard and to Toby's surprise and relief the motion of the sails outside came to a gradual halt; leaving near silence. Footsteps were heard overhead, and soon a face appeared above them at the top of a ladder leading to the upper level.

'This is my son,' said the miller, inclining his head toward Toby, 'your namesake,' he added wryly. 'Come down, Tobias!'

The son, who was over seventy, seemed barely younger than his father, but was clearly still relatively agile. An old cap covered his bald head, and dust clung to his brows and eyelashes. His pale eyes and lean face, the cheeks sunken in, might have been carved from the knot of a tree, and his complexion was shot with a sickly yellow. Toby noted that he hesitated before turning and descending – like Quasimodo from the tower of Notre Dame – the spidery movement of his thin body jerking awkwardly inside shabby, ill-fitting clothes. When down; he turned nervously, tugging his lip and squinting.

'Stand still!' said Silas irritably.

Toby disliked the decrepit miller's sour tone: for he spoke as if to a despised inferior… to this old man – his own flesh and blood.

'Are you finished up there?' the father went on peremptorily, wagging a finger toward the sail loft.

The other nodded.

'So you should have… Well, you'd better go and make me a cup of tea since you're here. Off you get!'

Without looking up, Tobias shuffled past them and disappeared outside.

'The boy don't say much, do he?' said Silas with a disagreeable smirk when he'd gone. 'Not much company… and not much up top if you see what I mean,' he added, tapping his forehead.

'Has he always had disabilities then?' asked Toby, suppressing a rising sense of disfavour at the drift of the conversation.

'Disabilities?' the old man leered in a mocking tone. 'Him? Not unless you include being lazy… and a bit thick!'

'Perhaps he might benefit from some encouragement and help?'

'Listen,' said the old man. 'If I could easily get up from this chair – I might encourage him with the toe of my boot! So he's lucky I can't.'

* * *

A different picture had now emerged in Toby's mind. The mill remained open because this selfish, broken old man still needed it. It was his personal domain, the last place where he could claim the status of ownership. But for old Tobias it was no more than a prison. His father, both an invalid and a tyrant, had cowed the younger man's spirit so much that he had been afraid to leave, and was apparently condemned to spend his whole life working for a parent who gave nothing but scorn in return.

Tobias came back a few minutes later with a mug of hot tea, which he placed meekly into his father's outstretched hands.

'You put in two sugars, I hope?' said Silas, curtly.

Tobias nodded and stepped back.

The old man took a sip, paused for a moment as if remembering something, and then looked up with a satisfied smile.

'I could get him to make you two a cup, if you'd like. It would be no trouble for the young fool now he's done up above.'

'No thank you,' replied Toby. 'We really ought to be getting back.'

'Perhaps another day,' said Silas, slurping noisily. 'Any time you're passing, eh?'

'Perhaps.'

* * *

They departed then, made their way down the ladder and quickly left the silent windmill behind. Neither said another word until arriving at the railway crossing once more. The whistle of a departing train shrieked, sending a gathering of roosting pigeons clattering into the air.

Scarlet looked up as she unhitched the donkey from the post.

'It makes you angry, doesn't it? …Silas being mean and crotchety like that.'

'Yes, selfishness always does.'

'Don't judge him too hard. Part of it is down to the closed life some people live in these parts. What seems cruel doesn't always start out that way.'

'Maybe; but it's a shame others have to suffer because of it, nonetheless.'

They did not speak further until reaching the farm, but Toby's mind was filled with troubled thoughts, both of the old man manipulating his son; and of his own lack of support for the Haydens.

* * *

The first half of the day passed quickly, and it was afternoon before the Trindles set off to work on their land after an early dinner at the farmhouse. Their intention was to hoe the young turnip crop in a small enclosure towards Molliton, and each carried the necessary tools over their shoulders. Toby still ached from the exertions of haymaking the day before and found himself hopefully looking forward to easier toil. The men talked and joked constantly, and it was obvious that the morning visit to Bedford market had gone well.

Their destination lay next to "High Dyke Farm", belonging to their neighbour Arthur Brayling and his wife Sarah, whom Toby had seen while riding on the hay cart, and as they approached he saw them waiting with their children. As Toby now learned, each family clearly enjoyed the other's company, regularly mucking in together when extra hands were needed.

Arthur Brayling, a tall, handsome man of thirty-eight, was one of those good-natured countrymen who radiate cheerfulness and common sense. His wife, Sarah, was three years younger; plump, good-humoured and quick witted. They had moved into their then semi-derelict property ten years earlier, with the shared intention of making it efficient and prosperous, and although mere tenants of Basil Tyler, had invested a considerable sum of their own money to improve both the buildings and soil. The brick built farmhouse had been fully refurbished, and new outbuildings constructed, including a Dutch barn. A modern milking shed had also been installed. Their four children stood behind them: Kitty, the eldest, and Bert, twelve, both armed with hoes, while Jim and Mickey, their younger brother and sister, stood by hoping to lend a hand.

'Hello,' called Arthur, in his clipped country accent. 'Thought we would help you out; seein' as our plants ain't so well on.'

'That's kind of you,' replied Henry. 'And when do you expect yours to be ready?'

'Oh, in about a week, I shouldn't wonder.'

'Then ours'll be happy to come over,' put in Coodie. 'I see you brought the children.'

'You try to keep them away,' smiled Sarah Brayling proudly. 'You'd think a spot of hoeing was the best possible entertainment, the way they are so eager to get stuck in. Our Kitty here being keen don't surprise me none; but seeing Bert rush to grab a hoe fair took my breath away with the shock!' she laughed.

'Don't embarrass the boy,' put in Arthur, seeing his son turn away shyly. 'He'll make a damned good cowman when he's grown; and I'll tell you what, he's out of bed afore me in the morning when the milkin' is to be done – aye, rain or frost, and long before it gets light! He's alright is our Bert; and these others here look like being the same,' he added, looking down affectionately at the two smaller children.

They talked on a little longer before setting to work under the high afternoon sun, their backs bent in steady rhythm. The others often exchanged banter and comments about matters of the land, but Toby found concentration was important if the right number of plants were to be left to grow to maturity and provide a supply of winter feed for the cattle. His shoulders and back soon began to ache, and he had to arch and straighten himself periodically to gain relief; yet none of the others once complained; all simply kept methodically at their task, both young and old, in a contented and harmonious group. Only Kitty and Bert, deftly working on adjacent rows, seemed to compete with each other to see who could best keep up with, or move slightly ahead of their parents. Toby reflected later that the four hours' toil he put in that afternoon were among the hardest of his life – yet spent in such good company, they were probably the most rewarding and satisfying he would ever experience.

They laboured on until the first evening shadows began to form around nearby hedgerows. Then, having thanked the Braylings for their help, the Trindles set off home once more, with Toby wearily trudging beside Wesley at the rear.

The big farmer turned to him as they approached "Warren Hill Farm". 'You comin' down for a drink at "The Eels" tonight, Toby?' he asked, encouragingly.

'I'd like to,' Toby replied, feeling the dryness at the back of his throat, 'but I have to see someone first.'

Wesley stopped to face him. 'Oh really... and who might that be?' he enquired, inclining his head.

'Meg, the girl who works for you in the morning – she invited me to visit "Silver Link Cottage" this evening.'

Wesley seemed to consider this for a moment. 'Did she now? She's a nice girl our Meg – so don't be surprised if you find yourself with a little competition there, my friend.'

Toby looked sharply up, reminded of Jenny. 'Oh, I'm only going for a chat!' he stammered. 'She seemed to want to talk.'

Wesley smiled broadly. 'You must be doing something right then because she never wants to talk to me,' he chortled. 'Well, you do that; and if you're back in time you can still come along with us. We're not normally off before about nine thirty.'

Soon afterwards they entered the farmyard and went in for tea; and later, when Toby retired upstairs to wash and change, he sat in the twilight for many minutes pondering what the young farmer had said.

Chapter Five

"Silver Link Cottage"

Before leaving for Meg's cottage, Toby happened to look across at the blue fleece hanging on the back of his chair and picked it up to see what he had brought with him. There was little in the outer pockets: only his watch, a box of matches and two five pence pieces. The latter pair looked small and insignificant in his hand – coins that at home might seem of little value. But their design, and the dates stamped upon them, led him to pause reflectively. Both had the head of Queen Elizabeth II stamped on one side, and the respective dates, 1987 and 2001, on the other. How would these be received, should they be discovered by his hosts? He surmised that even the most unsuspecting among them would be curious.

Toby searched again, examining the folds of the pockets, discovering among the fluff a crumpled return train ticket from Bedford to London, purchased on a recent visit to the Natural History Museum. Then finally, he reached down into the inner pocket and wrapped his fingers around the familiar, smooth shape of his mobile phone. It was like nothing he had seen or held that day – an alien object, impossible to explain or pass off. Toby flipped the cover casually, half expecting the phone to spring into life; but the device was dead, registering no battery power or signal.

'I left it here all day,' he thought to himself, 'where anyone might have discovered it…'

The possibility of somehow disposing of the item came to mind; but he dismissed this option. The phone, although useless now that the battery was flat, was still a link with his own world – with another time. Destroying it would break that connection, cast him adrift; an irreversible step he was disinclined to take. Thus, before pulling on the fleece, he transferred the phone to the pocket containing his watch, inwardly vowing that in future these incriminating articles would remain concealed about his person.

* * *

Having brushed his hair, Toby slipped quietly out of the house just before seven o'clock, meeting Coodie in the porch, who wished him a cheerful good evening. The family were planning to help the Braylings with their haymaking the following day, she said, adding that Toby was most welcome to join them and stay on as long as he wished, since they would all value his continuing help and company.

'It'll give you lots to write about,' she smiled.

He thanked her for her kindness, and was about to leave the inner yard when Scarlet too called to him from the gloom of the stable entrance.

'Don't be late back, Toby,' she said. 'Remember, night draws in quickly… and we'd hate to miss you at the pub.'

It was a friendly reminder, her smile showing that it was pleasantly given, but as Scarlet lingered, watching him pass from sight, he sensed another significance behind her words.

*   *   *

Toby struck up a good pace; soon passing beyond the confines of the farm, before reaching the falling ground that led to the Smallwoods' property. But instead of going straight on towards "Pocket Farm", he forked right as the landscape opened up, heading on a new course for "Maxton Tower" which cast a deep and lengthening shadow on its eastern side. Meg had said that she lived in the dip just beyond, and the path he trod formed a short cut in that direction. Soon he neared a hedge, and passing through a narrow gap, came out on the other side with the tower directly in front of him some thirty metres away. Viewed at close quarters, the edifice, although unused and derelict, was nonetheless a dominant structure, and Toby again tried to imagine its former purpose as he moved forward towards the shoulder of rising ground before him. In this way he came to the crest of a ridge where the prospect northward opened out. The spire of Stavenham Church stood away in the distance, while closer to, beyond the trees lining the railway, the motionless sails of the old windmill rose up through a gathering haze. He also saw that his quest was over – for just below, tucked into a dip against the line of trees, lay a small thatched cottage flanked by an enclosed plot bordered with shrubs and bushes. Excited by the actions of a young woman carrying a pail, a number of chickens, geese and pigs waddled and scuttled about as she passed among them. The hollow was west facing, and sunlight still bathed it in an orange glow. The evening had become delightfully calm and still, and the thin column of smoke escaping from the cottage chimney spiralled almost vertically upwards into the twilight air. It was the time of day when a tranquil peace seeps over the land: not deathly, but filled with gentle birdsong and the soft humming of late flying insects.

*   *   *

A sudden chorus of honking and grunting broke this pleasant spell, and Meg, having looked up to ascertain the cause of the disturbance, waved towards him, before moving in the direction of the garden gate.

'You've come,' she said with a broad smile, while brushing back the hair that had fallen loose over her forehead. 'It's so lovely to see you.'

'Did you have a good day at work?' he replied, smiling back.

She frowned theatrically. 'We won't talk of that just yet, Toby, if you please. Now, do come inside and I'll show you round my little castle.'

Meg led him through a doorway, the porch of which was flanked by trellises decked with scented honeysuckle, and they descended three steps into the room below. Mr Toots, having just then bounded up, pushed past, and having plonked himself on a large much-chewed cushion, proceeded to gnaw on an ancient bone while gazing up with benevolent eyes.

Toby had entered a comfortable kitchen, small and low ceilinged, with whitewashed plaster between unpainted beams of oak. On one side was a squat bay window, fronted with padded seats, through which the strong late rays of a declining sun still illuminated the walls and floor. The latter was made of polished stone, and in the middle lay an oval carpet with a delicately woven mosaic design at its centre. A small wood-burning stove, with a cooking range above, stood at the far side, the flames flickering through yellowed glass. Yet, although the room was heated, it was neither stuffy nor over warm, but pleasantly snug – the occasional hiss and crackle from the fire mere friendly voices in the stillness.

Upon the walls hung a number of watercolours depicting local scenes; one a particularly evocative view of the tower he had recently passed. But most remarkable was the array of bookcases that lined every available space on three sides. These were filled with tomes both large and small; some of considerable age – all neatly ordered and cared for – so that the place resembled a small library: one clearly much loved and cherished by its owner.

Meg placed a copper kettle on the range before turning to face him. 'We'll have tea, if you'd like,' she said brightly.

'That would be splendid,' he replied, continuing to look around.

'Well, Toby,' asked Meg, following a short interlude during which she quietly observed his reactions, '...do you like my cottage?'

'Very much! And these wonderful books... you have so many.'

'My mother was a great reader; they belonged to her. Mother would say that those who read widely always have something to discuss... do you read, Toby?'

He was about to say, yes; and mention Ben Elton and Bill Bryson, but corrected himself in a moment.

'I'm not what you'd call a regular bookworm,' he replied. 'Just popular titles mostly… when I have the time.'

Meg smiled, 'For Mother, reading was one of the most important things in her life; and she did all she could to pass that love on to me.'

'With great success, I think… You said this morning that she died a little while ago… I'm sorry.'

'She passed away last autumn. The cancer in her spine came quickly and took her…

'My family came originally from Scotland you know, from Dumfriesshire – border country. They were sheep farmers, but moved south when times were hard in the early part of the last century. When my great grandfather first came to Stavenham there were many flocks around here, and he took over this cottage to become chief shepherd on the Tyler estate.

'Before the railway arrived much of the country on this side of Stavenham was still open. My family have made a living here ever since, but never forgot their Scottish roots. I think that's natural; don't you?' she added reflectively, 'that we should want to hang on to our heritage, and what we are.'

'I'm sure it is,' replied Toby, with thoughts of his own.

Meg now filled a delicately painted teapot with boiling water from the kettle.

'They didn't once go back, of course. People often promise themselves that they will make such a journey: this year… or next. But time went by and newer roots began gradually to settle more deeply here – you know how it is. Yet neither forgot the land they'd left behind…'

Perhaps feeling that she had allowed herself to become a little mawkish, Meg reverted to her original theme. 'My grandmother was the first big reader in the family. She, and then my mother, would buy books and poetry; mostly secondhand, and so the collection began to develop. Theirs was a nostalgic journey at first, with the works of Robert Burns and Scott initially filling these shelves. I was introduced to many of these when I was small, and you can't imagine how much they enthralled me when read with such love and longing for a lost homeland – how characters with names like Jingling Geordie, Edie Ochiltree and Hal o' the Wynd can spur your imagination. Neither did it end there: as granny loved all good stories, both light and challenging; and this love she passed down to my mother. Thus, in time, the collection grew,' said Meg, moving to the large bookshelf that lay opposite the window. 'So here we find books by the Brontes, George Eliot, Jane Austen and Mrs Gaskell; together with those by Hardy and Charles Dickens.'

She pointed to a full set of the last mentioned writer's works, filling most of one shelf. 'Such a genius, Toby – a man who could make you laugh and cry in a moment with the artistry of his words: someone who both drew and coloured the tapestry of human life with a humble quill pen. Yet there are here ,too, other perhaps even greater works,' she added, running her finger over tomes lower down: those of Milton, Shakespeare, and Bunyan's *Pilgrim's Progress*.

She knelt to retrieve the last from its position on the shelf and placed the much-thumbed book in Toby's hand. 'He was a local man, you know – a tinker. Nobody special you might say; but in his own mind he exposed human folly and weakness like no other, creating a world of giants and demons that will last for as long as men and women care to read. ...While Christian's journey is one that we all must make some day if we are to discover our destiny.'

Having allowed herself a moment to reflect, Meg turned again to the stove to pour tea, leaving Toby to marvel at the insight of this young girl, and wondering if she had a notion of the feelings that had set him upon his own travels. Soon she stood up, smiling once more and holding two cups, one of which she gave to him.

'Mother used to say that there are worlds in books; that each creative author sets out to paint pictures using a precious store of words, inviting the reader to escape into their imaginations. "But beware," she would add, "these words might cast a spell on you".'

Come inside, they say. *Let us be gone for a day.*

'I believe it's true,' said Meg with a wink, 'that great writers – like Dickens, Emily Bronte, Hardy or Shakespeare – can lift us up and transport us to another place in our heads. But it doesn't all have to be serious stuff,' she added merrily, pointing at a row of children's books in a neat case by the window recess. 'At another time a girl like me might choose to follow the White Rabbit with Alice; or else go rowing with Ratty and Mole – before renewing acquaintance with *A Little Princess*, if I accept Mrs Burnett's invitation. Then again, I could step into the world of a railway child for an hour... rather appropriate here, don't you think?'

Sunlight no longer shone through the window, and a shadowy gloom began to fill the cottage as Meg came close to Toby, holding a book that she had taken from the shelf by the door. She turned it in her hands while looking up at him.

'Do you know this one?' she said, raising an eyebrow.

He looked down. It was a copy of *The War of the Worlds* by H.G. Wells.

'Yes, I've read it,' he replied. 'It's very good.'

'A well-written and chilling vision of the future,' she concurred, '...about Martians from another world. A rather unlikely scenario no doubt; but still a clever story because it doesn't simply dwell upon the fantastic. No, it also looks at how people behave and what they do. The unnamed hero sees it all: the futile efforts of men to win by force, the destruction of London and the breakdown of social order. And while observing these unhappy events he comes to recognise how little his fellow men, now shocked and terrorised, seem to care for each other... That surely is its true warning.'

Meg stopped, as if half expecting a response.

'They... they were faced with a mortal enemy,' Toby stammered, struggling to recall the plot and suddenly feeling awkward under her gaze... 'and each was left to do whatever he could to survive.'

'Yes, that's right,' Meg averred, looking into his eyes. 'But they were lucky and were saved in the nick of time by a natural ally, a simple virus that wiped out their enemies. Now what might we learn from this?'

Toby considered her question; trying to find a satisfactory answer. '...That men are not as almighty as they imagine... that there are elemental forces in Nature more powerful than ourselves.'

Nodding, she turned away to look out of the window. 'Perhaps, Toby... Wells was a practical scientist; but his dreams too had a great deal of fact in them. Yet I feel he also had a rather good understanding of human nature; that fragile bonds, easily broken in adversity, are all that hold human society together. If so, we should take care not to assume that we can do as we please as we advance towards the future. Neither should men rely too much upon weapons and the control over nature that they believe themselves to have. Instead, we would perhaps be well advised as a species to step back and look again at our connection with the earth... and each other.'

Another short silence ensued as Meg returned the book to its place, allowing Toby a moment to scan the laden shelves. 'I wonder, could you ever bear to be parted from your books? They seem to mean so much.'

She looked back at him with an exaggerated shake of the head.

'I believe that when you sell the books you love you sell a piece of yourself,' she replied. 'No, I could never do that.'

*　*　*

Meg then took an oil lamp from the mantleshelf above the stove and, having lighted the wick, placed it upon a low table by the door.

'To guide us back,' she said, smiling. 'Now, shall we go outside? I have much more to show you.'

Pricking up his ears at these words, Mr Toots, his tail wagging enthusiastically, jumped up and preceded them out of the door; as Meg led Toby round to the northern side of the house. There they stood by a stile as the late evening train to Northampton steamed through; both waving to the passing enginemen who cheerily returned their greeting. Then, as the smoke of the locomotive dispersed and the sound died away, she led him back past the cottage door to the enclosure where they had met earlier. On the way Meg threw a stick high up in the air for Mr Toots to chase, laughing as he leaped and tumbled hopelessly in a vain attempt to catch it before pulling himself upright again with a playful bark. When he trotted back, Meg bent down to rub his ears and put her face against his cheek.

'You silly old fellow,' she said affectionately. 'What a thing it is to live with a clown like you.'

They were quiet for but a few moments however, for just then a rabbit hopped lazily out of a hedge nearby and began to graze the grass bordering the pathway. Seeing it, Meg put her lips next to Mr Toots' ear. 'Go fetch,' she said, in a low conspiratorial voice, pointing towards the rabbit, and the dog immediately sat bolt upright before bounding off in what Toby thought appeared a determined attack, intent on blood. But as Mr Toots approached, causing the rabbit to turn its head in alarm, the retriever skidded to a halt and jumped backwards, tumbling over his hind legs, before retreating once more to Meg's side, where he crouched, trembling, staring back towards the rabbit that had already resumed feeding peacefully. They both burst into laugher once more at his antics, and only stopped giggling when Mr Toots, having regained his composure, ambled away to observe a butterfly that had settled on a nearby water butt.

'You love him very much, don't you?' said Toby as they stood watching the dog intently following the movements of the bright insect.

'So would you,' she replied. 'There never was such a character…'

Here she looked up as if searching for words to describe her thoughts. 'We've always had dogs, Toby. They've been part of the family for generations… I'd like to show you something – a quiet place that lies close by… if you have the time, that is?'

'Of course – all the time in the world.'

* * *

She proceeded ahead of him to the enclosure gate, and they passed through before proceeding into a shallow dip just on from the west-facing wall of the cottage. There they came to a shady corner surrounded by gnarled blackthorn, alder and crab apple trees. Small birds hopped about in the undergrowth, while the call of a cuckoo could be heard nearby. A pungent scent of elderflower filled the air.

'Look there,' she said, pointing down to where a small plantation of rhubarb, horseradish and flowering borage had grown tall. 'Do you see the stones?'

Toby followed the line of her finger and, as his eyes became accustomed to the shadowy light, began to make out a number of shaped slabs unmistakably placed to mark the final resting place of family pets. There were perhaps twenty in all. Some had almost disappeared into the soil or were completely covered in an ancient growth of moss and lichen; their inscriptions virtually erased. But others appeared to be more recent additions: the two below his feet clearly marked.

Toby bent down to look. "Sam – Died 15th January 1900."

'A Border collie,' said Meg. 'Sam passed away when I was only five. We kept him for herding the sheep.'

'And this one... Agnes?' asked Toby, reading the next.

'Oh, she was my dog. Agnes didn't last but more than four years before we lost her... and then along came Mr Toots!'

The retriever had come to sit beside her again and she bent down to scratch his head.

'You're going to have a nice sleep here one day, aren't you?' she said, looking down at him. 'Where it's nice and peaceful, and you can't get up to any mischief. That'll be alright, won't it, my old dear?'

The dog gazed up at her, licking her hand adoringly.

Meg smiled at Toby. 'They don't ask for much, do they? ...Animals, I mean. Just a bit of love and affection. Not like us humans... There's no conniving with a four-legged creature; no pride... no jealousy. So why shouldn't they have their own proper place in the ground?'

* * *

After browsing a little further they quietly withdrew from the spot; but instead of making back towards the cottage door, Meg turned in the direction of the old tower that now stood starkly silhouetted on the south-facing ridge.

'I'll take you up,' she said, brightening again. 'It's getting near sunset and the place can seem a bit forbidding; but the view from the top is really worth seeing at this time.'

Thus, in the fading light, both walked across to "Maxton Tower" until they stood before the entrance, which was now little more than a shadowy hole in the lee of the sun. Toby looked up at the craggy stonework, pitted and weathered by the winter storms of three hundred passing years, then higher, to the castellated embrasures. The whole structure seemed to glower down upon them, dark and threatening.

'Why *is* it here?' he said at last, his curiosity once more aroused upon the subject. 'What purpose did it serve? It seems so out of place.'

They moved forward until Meg turned to face him in the doorless entrance: a dark area where horses might have been stabled lay behind her, and a worm eaten stairway was set into the brickwork beyond.

'It was built in the time of James I,' she replied, 'by Sir Francis Maxton who lived about three miles away, just outside the village of Deerden. He was a respected local landowner who had benefited from supporting the King on his succession after the death of Elizabeth I. Doubtless wishing to impress other local gentlemen by a display of newly acquired wealth and status, he applied for permission to build *an observation poynt and retreat for those engaged in sport* on this land, the licence for its construction being duly awarded. However, the structure, when erected, was on a much grander scale than many

85

had envisaged. It came to sit like a small castle dominating the surrounding landscape, and some naturally questioned the intended use of such a stronghold. But, as he was such an influential man, nothing was actually done to alter its design or remove it. So the years quietly passed until a new king, Charles I, ascended the throne. As you may know, these were years of political and religious turmoil that led, in1642, to a bloody civil war in which the armies of King and Parliament fought for supremacy over a divided land. The conflict frequently washed nearby, until, in 1644, fighting broke out locally, forcing the rich and powerful to show their hands. Much of the county of Bedfordshire had already sided with Cromwell by this time; but the King could still count upon a few who remained loyal. So it was that when a Parliamentary garrison swept through the area demanding men and supplies for the Roundheads, the new owner of "Maxton Tower", Sir Francis's headstrong son, Clarence, youthfully intent on defying the Parliamentary force, locked himself in with ten supporters.

'News quickly got around, and a detachment of Cromwell's men was sent to demand the tower's surrender. Unsurprisingly perhaps, the young landowner, having had a little time to reconsider his position, and now fully realising the inevitable penalty for his actions, decided to flee on hearing of the soldiers' approach. However, five of the more zealous among his household stayed on, and when given an ultimatum, one of these fired on the troopers below, mortally wounding their captain and causing the rest to retreat. It was an affront that could not be ignored, and later the same day a detachment of horse artillery appeared before deploying a single cannon in front of the gate. Having established this threat, the commander then demanded that the men surrender a second time – again receiving only oaths and shouts of professed loyalty to the King in reply. Seconds later the cannon opened fire at close range, destroying the door and killing one of the fugitives. Maxton Tower was then quickly taken and the four living survivors made prisoner. The culprit who had shot the captain soon being identified, a military court convened on the spot. A charge of treason then being brought; the fellow was summarily sentenced to death and taken on horseback up to the main Northampton road. There, on a tree, the sentence was carried out, and his body left hanging for three weeks as a warning to others. In time a permanent gallows was set up on the same spot to execute highwaymen and poachers, so that the wood ever after became known as "Gibbet Wood".'

Visualising the macabre scene, Toby shuddered as Meg concluded her account. Then he stepped forward to feel the broken stonework where the hinges had once been.

'And the doors were never put back?'

'Never: the magistrates made it illegal to do so on a decree of Parliament; and long after the conflict had ended nobody saw fit to rescind the directive. But that doesn't mean the place wasn't used,' she went on. 'The tower was still valued as a lookout point; and sportsmen would come here to rest and refresh themselves when out hunting. The space here below was used to shelter their horses, and up above lies a room, with a fireplace, where they could eat and warm themselves.'

She now led him into the musty interior and began mounting the uneven stairway. Toby felt some of the warped steps bend and sway under his weight, and might have thought better of making the climb if Meg had not been leading.

'It may seem as if the whole thing might collapse at any moment,' she said, as they reached a narrow landing above. 'But I've ascended a thousand times and can assure you it won't.'

Having risen to the second storey, they now came next to a wood panelled wall in which a door stood open. Beyond them another stairway led up to the platform above from where the orange glow of the late sun came slanting down. Moving forward, Meg stepped through the doorway, disappearing from Toby's sight as if absorbed by the stones. He followed cautiously, until they both stood in a panelled room large enough to accommodate about ten people. It had two small windows, one each in the south and east walls, and contained a fireplace with a blackened hearth. The usual debris found in derelict buildings – fallen bricks, plaster and splintered wood – lay scattered around the floor.

'Hunting and shooting parties frequented this room until about twenty years ago,' Meg continued. 'It was a useful place to come when the weather turned foul. But they don't any more. I imagine it's not comfortable enough for our modern lordships now.'

With little of interest to detain them long, she led him out again and moved on in front as Toby paused by the door. There was a strange claustrophobic atmosphere to the place; the stones warm in parts, heated by the strong sun of the day now ending; but there was something else – a clamminess to the air – that made him feel oddly cold and uncomfortable as he moved. He quite understood why hunting parties had stopped using it.

By the time Toby emerged onto the open stone platform at the top of the stairs Meg was already standing in one corner looking over an embrasure. Cool air caressed his cheeks, refreshing him, and he breathed deeply.

'It's lovely, isn't it?' she said, turning. 'I spend hours up here by myself on summer evenings. Nobody bothers me. Stavenham is over there,' she added, pointing beyond the thin wisp of smoke coming from the chimney of "Silver Link Cottage", 'and that's Oakwell in the distance. You can see much of north Bedfordshire from up here.'

They began slowly moving round the platform, Meg pointing out many local places and landmarks. His companion knew the views by heart and was able to provide details that Toby had only been able to guess at before.

'Over there is "Wart Hill",' she indicated, as they looked eastwards, 'the place where the ancient folk built their dyke; and beyond is Bedford, where John Bunyan wrote *Pilgrim's Progress* while imprisoned.'

Toby was happy for her to be his guide yet repeatedly wondered at what they could not see. No longer evident was the trading estate on the hilltop at Thurton; nor could he make out the twenty-first-century by-pass at Oakwell; or the mighty twin airship hangars that formerly dominated the skyline towards Cardington.

Soon they had moved through a full circle, and as Meg's glance settled upon the distant rooftop of a large house situated among a copse of trees due west of them, she became quiet, as if troubled by the sight. He knew from their discussion that morning that this was "Tyler Hall", the residence of Basil and Charlotte Tyler. Meg remained silent, but Toby became aware that she was alternately spreading the fingers of her right hand, then tightening them into a fist, her face set.

' "Tyler Hall"... the landowners' house.'

'Yes... Charlotte's palace,' Meg replied, her voice dry and full of bitterness.

'It was awkward today?'

She turned back to him, a blank, almost desperate expression on her face. 'It's always *awkward*... That's the way Charlotte makes it...'

'Do you have to be near her? ...When you are working, I mean.'

Meg looked up, tears of frustration welling in the corners of her eyes. 'Toby, if I had my way I wouldn't choose to see Charlotte ever again... no, it's her that seeks me out. You see, whatever I'm given to do she's there – always watching. I wouldn't mind if that was all, but she makes comments: tells me to move items like mops and dusters, *because they are in the way*... trivial things of no importance. It's all nonsense of course – and she only does it to belittle me so as to enjoy seeing my discomfort, knowing that I can't complain.'

'Why don't you speak to Basil Tyler? ...Wouldn't he do something?'

She shook her head, suppressing a hollow laugh. 'He's hardly ever there, Toby. Charlotte's alone in the house most of the day... except when she's away shopping for finery. And if you knew Basil you wouldn't expect him to care about such things. No, Basil doesn't have time for the affairs of women.'

'You could leave,' suggested Toby.

'I've thought about that, but I have to live, don't I? It's not easy to find paid work... so for now I must stay on.'

They said nothing for a minute, both occupied by their own thoughts, until Meg suddenly spoke again, her face becoming flushed with anger.

'It's the personal things she says that hurt most of all! When she's standing there, with a superior expression on her face, looking down at me! The way she makes comments about my hair and my clothes; so I feel small. And then she'll start on about my family, about how they were all failed shepherds – and that being the reason why I have ended up cleaning floors. The whole thing's a lie of course (just the ranting of a spoilt child with nothing better to do), but it grieves me just the same!'

Meg was now looking intently into Toby's face, as if searching for an answer. But there was something else written in the lines of her brow and the dark wells of her eyes – a sharp edge of desperation rising up from a deep wound within.

'Charlotte truly injures me,' she continued, slowly shaking her head; her voice sounding empty and defeated. 'I lie awake sometimes, thinking about her words and seeing her face. ...With her barbed comments she knowingly probes an open sore within; and although I really don't want to hate her... I do.'

The paleness of Meg's complexion spoke volumes for her inner pain and frustration, and Toby understood in that moment that for all her apparent independence, strength and fortitude, she remained vulnerable also. This intelligent and resourceful young woman had coped alone with bereavement and loss; but a sensitive thread ran through her, as it does within us all, that if too much tested might be strained too far.

*   *   *

The sun had now dipped to the horizon and they watched as it slid into a bank of cloud. Deeper shadows began to fall, and as they prepared to descend into the darkness of the stairway once more, Toby saw a figure approaching from the direction of "Pocket Farm". It moved purposefully, and was soon evidently that of a young man.

Meg had seen the newcomer too, and cheering up in an instant, waved towards him.

'It's Mark,' she said, looking over her shoulder, smiling. '...A little late as usual!'

Mark Trindle waved back, his familiar form now obvious to Toby, and they descended the tower to meet him. Toby felt that slight sense of unease which men often do when meeting one another in the company of a female companion, and stood a little uncertainly beside Meg. The farmer, also, was more formal than on their previous meetings.

'Good evening, Toby,' he said looking him up and down. 'I didn't expect to see you here.'

Meg moved to Mark's side, linking her arm with his. 'I asked Toby to come,' she said. 'I thought he might like to see my cottage, and the tower, since he's writing about us.'

'Really,' said Mark, his eyes narrowing slightly. 'Well, you'd best make better use of your notepad, Toby – or you might forget something. ...It's funny how we never see you with one.'

Toby began to feel genuinely uncomfortable under the other's steady gaze, but Meg came to his rescue.

'What's got into you?' she chided playfully, pulling Mark towards her. 'Anyone would think you were jealous. Toby was just going... weren't you, Toby?'

'Yes... I told Wesley I'd go to the pub with him.'

'There you are then,' said Meg. 'That's settled – and we might join you later, if that's alright.'

Becoming less reserved under Meg's touch, Mark nodded his approval of the proposal.

'We can't have Wesley and old Sam getting drunk all by themselves,' he said, more like his normal self. 'Oh, before you go off, Toby, have you got the time on you?'

Toby reached into his pocket – absently wrapping his fingers around the mobile phone that lay in the deep fold next to his watch. In a moment he had lifted it out, fully exposed on the palm of his hand. At no time afterwards would he be able to explain his action, other than as a simple act of carelessness, but the damage was done in an instant. Ever alert, Mark immediately stepped forward and placed his hand on Toby's fingers; staring down at the strange plastic device with fascination and awe.

'What is that?' he asked, looking suspiciously into Toby's face.

Toby did not answer, but having tugged his hand away, returned the mobile phone to his pocket. There was an uneasy silence in which Mark, still eyeing Toby with a frown, stepped back next to Meg. He seemed to carefully consider his words before going on.

'Who... are... you?' he articulated deliberately. 'You say you come from London... but there's more to you than that. Moreover, you've put around that you want to know everything about us and about places around here – yet there is a great deal you seem to know already. And now this... in addition to that coat! Two and two definitely don't make four, where you're concerned, Toby... ain't I right?'

Toby knew that a hasty explanation would not suffice, and shuffled his feet, hoping for an opportunity to get away. Meanwhile Mr Toots, who had appeared out of the shadows, trotted up beside him and Toby bent down to stroke his head.

It was Meg who broke the tension, for although she had been just as surprised as Mark by what she'd seen, her concern about the apparent rift developing between the two prompted her to make an effort to defuse the tension.

'Oh, Mark!' she said, curling her arm through his once more. 'It doesn't mean anything. There are so many new devices around these days. I expect Toby uses it in his work... don't you, Toby? We really shouldn't let this spoil such a nice evening. You let Toby be getting off and we'll be left to enjoy our evening walk. I've got so much to tell you about today. Come along, you can ask him more later – when you meet in the pub.'

She then tugged at Mark's elbow and they strolled away together, retracing his steps from "Pocket Farm", with the pale-coated retriever trotting ahead. The two quickly passed out of sight, swallowed by the darkness, but not before Mark had turned to look back more than once.

* * *

Toby remained standing a little longer at the spot where they had parted, a cold bead of sweat rolling down his back and dampening his shirt. For the first time he had felt exposed in his new guise and feared detection. What would happen if he was taken into custody or questioned by suspicious locals? How could he talk his way out if discovered to have such strange and incriminating evidence upon his person? Just then, returning to the farm seemed out of the question. He needed to find somewhere quiet, to lie low for a while and work things out.

With these thoughts, he turned and moved down again in the direction of "Silver Link Cottage", where the glow from the oil lamp shone brightly through the open door. He did not tarry there long, however, but having reached the hedge that lined the railway, climbed over the stile and dropped down into the shallow depression of the railway cutting beyond. The glistening tracks, illuminated by a clear moon above, curved away in both directions like two delicate lines of tracery, while the hoot of an owl could be heard nearby, together with the clicking of crickets in the undergrowth. But all else was deathly silent and unmoving: no human voice or sound of any kind broke the stillness.

Feeling uncomfortably out of place and isolated, Toby shuffled onto the track and began stepping along the evenly spaced sleepers. He fell to counting them, but would suddenly recall his situation and forget the number reached, thus having to start again at the beginning. In this way he walked perhaps half a mile before noticing a disused platelayers' hut just ahead. The cutting had opened out and the low building stood at the top of a steep bank overlooking fields to the north. Much of the felt on its arched roof had come loose, to hang in ragged strips, but it was otherwise sound and gave an offer of shelter. Toby stumbled closer, now suddenly fatigued, and pushed at the door which fell back, squealing on rusty hinges, to reveal a small room with a single window facing the valley. A rickety table was placed in the centre, and three rough benches were fixed along the sides. Toby sat down on the nearest of these, then lay back heavily, gazing up at the cobwebbed ceiling. Although dusty and untidy the hut was dry, and closing his eyes he decided to wait there until morning, before returning the next day, by a circuitous route, to Molliton and reality.

Chapter Six

Love and Destruction

As Toby slept he was troubled by unsettling dreams. Amid swirling clouds he once more witnessed the landscape being ravaged by storm and tempest. Emerging through the deluge he saw an elderly couple struggling onwards through rain washed streets. Then the frail old woman staggered, never to rise again, and he despaired.

Next, the faces of his lost family flashed before him – Jenny's resolute smile at their departure and the last poignant farewell wave from his infant son.

In their wake came new characters, and a small dog – each as if viewed through a smoke fringed window... and a crow, black as night, looking down from the moonlit sign of an inn. Following closely, the ruined visage of the ancient miller leered out (his derided son framed in a doorway) and as this image faded to mist, Coodie Trindle, her honest countenance wreathed in a welcoming smile, stepped forward to offer him tea. Finally, as his inner vision dimmed, Toby stood once more on the platform at "Windmill Halt" watching a train depart down a long forgotten railway.

His mind grew full of a desire for hope and truth, and the courage to face his own world again. He saw future disasters, want and disease, and wondered how it might be in the wit of men to overcome them.

During those extended and unnatural hours Toby heard and visualised other things too: the thunder of guns ringing out above the roar of battle, together with the screams of dying men... until, as this fiendish symphony played out, the cry of a newborn baby soared up into a night sky filled with snow.

Lastly, as the distorted pageant drew to a close, a jeering face appeared, together with another contorted with rage – each spinning away to leave but a trickle of blood glistening upon cold stone...

* * *

So time moved on as Toby travelled a wide sea, and the long passage of night gave way to dawn. The sun came up, and still he turned but did not wake. Blackbirds singing in the trees and bushes nearby welcomed the day, but the cheerful chorus of morning had long been in full swing before his unquiet rest was rudely terminated by the shrieking whistle of an approaching train, running fast down the falling gradient. He jerked upright to see the black engine, bigger than any he had noted before, rush towards him round the bend before passing by in a cloud of smoke and steam. Toby listened as the crescendo of noise slowly died away, another echoing whistle telling him of the train's arrival at "Windmill Halt" half a mile distant.

He was stiff… stiffer than he could ever remember – his mouth parched and bitter – and reaching up, found his chin covered by a growth of thick stubble; the corners of his eyes crusted with sleep. He would need to find water before going on; but when about to rise, the noise of an animal snuffling around the door caused him to freeze and draw back.

The head of a small Jack Russell dog appeared round the doorpost and, having raised its nose to sniff the dusty air (as if in confirmation of having come to the right place) the animal yawned widely before trotting out of sight once more. Toby blinked and scratched his head, but the little fellow had only been gone a few moments when a tall shadow fell across the doorway, and Jeannie Denton, the woman he had met on the bridge, stepped into view. She hardly seemed to notice him at first, but moved to the window and stood looking out at the fields below. Her attire was different, for she now wore a green dress beneath a delicate shawl of white lace. A cotton bag embroidered with coiling flowers hung from her shoulder, and the silky tails of a grey ribbon floated around her neck.

'So… you are awake at last,' she said in a kind voice, still looking into the distance. 'I'm pleased – you have been gone some time.'

'And how did you find me?' Toby managed to croak through dry lips.

'It was Macken… the dog,' she replied, seeing his quizzical look. 'He kept watch… I think he likes you.'

Jeannie sat down beside Toby, studying his face while offering water from a metal flask that she took from her bag.

'You look tired,' she said, touching his shoulder. 'You won't have eaten either. I must see what I have with me.'

Toby struggled to his feet, before moving painfully around trying to force the circulation back into his aching limbs, as Jeannie produced a neatly wrapped package of bread and cheese from her bag, together with a small polished apple.

'I feel as if I have slept for a week,' he said; stretching and hearing his bones creak.

'Longer…' she replied, with a look of sympathy. 'Much longer.'

He turned to face her, the food catching in his throat as he swallowed.

'What do you mean…? How can that be? I only came here last night.'

'But much time has passed while *you* slept, Toby… And the lives of many mortals have been played out forever.'

Toby walked to the window and squinted through the dusty glass, searching for points of reference.

'I don't understand... where have I come to?' he asked, struggling to voice his thoughts.

'Ten years have passed – in the time of men it is now 1923,' she replied enigmatically.

There was another pause as her words penetrated Toby's brain – his face becoming contorted with disbelief. 'But how can that be?' he blurted out. 'I... I can't have been here all that time... can I?'

Jeannie stood up and placed her hand on his temple, before replying in a voice that was older than before, 'You must now accept what has come to pass, Toby. You alone have been chosen for the journey that you make, for it is your destiny to live on the edge of reality – a patient onlooker turning the pages. Yours is like a dream within a dream... but there will be an ending.'

Having spoken, she walked past him out of the hut and he followed her into a patch of sunlight between the trees.

'Your talk is a mystery to me... like before,' he complained reproachfully. 'What you say is not possible... There is no logic to it!'

She faced him again. 'Was there any *logic* to your coming here, Toby? ...But you did. ...Therefore, if a man can travel back through a hundred years of history while walking a country mile – might he not reasonably go forward another ten, during the moonlit hours of night?'

Her listener could summon no words in reply, but stood frozen for a moment before sinking down on the grassy bank with his head in his hands. Jeannie knelt beside him, a wild rose, picked from among the varied flowers that flourished round about, held delicately between raised fingers.

'Is this yesterday's flower... or one blooming fresh this morning, Toby? Did it spring up from the soil ten years ago... or was it nurtured by the warm sunshine of 1923? ...Just now you must accept that the second is true.'

She stood again, looking up at the sky.

'For your part, Toby: you were sent to see how the story both begins and ends. Sometimes you will walk among those who inhabit the times you visit, while at others you must observe as a traveller in parallel time the ill-considered blindness of men. By doing so you will gain an understanding of their motives, come to know what is best and worst in your fellow beings, and with good fortune see how they save themselves at last.

'A saga will evolve in which you alone are called to play a special part: the story of how humans, who now dominate this planet, abuse it to the point of destruction, until one day they learn the folly of their arrogance. As such you must stand witness as the nations of the earth more than once resort to war. During this time the people will search for ministers, elected or otherwise, to guide them; but ultimately they will find salvation through mutual co-operation and their own efforts in a world that no longer has a place for leaders.'

The breeze had now loosed some strands of hair around Jeannie's face, which she held back with the slender fingers of her left hand.

'Yet you will not witness the emergence of a benign Utopia, Toby: although it will assuredly be a place in which power, egoism and greed have been cast aside in the pursuit of a common good – the preservation of our planet and humanity.'

'Then the storm *was* a sign,' said Toby, his brow furrowed.

'Undoubtedly,' she replied. 'The first warning on a long and difficult road.'

'But… can anything really change? Is there really hope?'

'There is always hope, Toby. Men control and destroy so much; yet there is creativity and strength… and *logic* within them too,' she smiled. 'Now, I must show you what has already altered.'

Jeannie offered her hand and he staggered to his feet, still stiff from long inactivity. She patiently supported him for a short time and when he was ready they moved away.

* * *

Toby gradually regained his composure as they walked back along the railway line towards the crossing. As it was now full summer, the trees and bushes were heavy with swelling elderberries, haws and sloes. Many waving grass stems had already gone to seed and the scent of ripening corn filled the air. In a few minutes they came to the stile near Meg's home and through thick foliage Toby caught a glimpse of the cottage once more. But instead of going that way, Jeannie led him over the stile on the other side and down a footpath through a field of tall oats that swayed shoulder high around them. Soon they approached "Stavenham Mill" and came at last to an old wooden seat, bleached and cracked with age, overlooking the structure.

The mill was much decayed from when he had last seen it, and had clearly not worked for some time. The four gaunt sails still remained, though stripped of any useful canvas, and that remaining hung in ragged shreds occasionally stirring in the breeze. Slates had fallen from the roof, as had a number of cladding sheets from the sides. Meanwhile, one of the nearby outhouses had evidently been destroyed by fire, while the roof of another had tumbled in.

Shocked by the scene of dereliction, Toby searched for signs of life.

'Where are the Fleggs?' he asked, 'Are… Are they dead? Silas was very old.'

Jeannie shook her head. 'They are both still living,' she replied, 'but have not been here together for a long time.'

'Did they move away?'

'The younger one, Tobias, suddenly disappeared,' she replied, pensively. 'He just went off early one morning, in the winter of 1915. There was a search, and many believed him dead, until he reappeared three months later. He was seen wandering the lanes beyond Poddington – a tramp. A policeman found him there and efforts were made to persuade him back. But he spoke little and refused them all; so they left him to his wanderings – to a kind of freedom.'

'It must be a hard life, for one so old,' said Toby. '…And what became of his father?'

Jeannie grimaced and shook her head. 'Silas was like a spoilt child at first, only wanting his son recovered so that he could scold him. But in time he was bereft. You see, he could do little for himself; not even cook a proper meal. It was clearly impossible for him to stay at the windmill, so he sold up, vowing to leave his absent son not a penny. A buyer was found at last – a businessman from Bedford who seems to have had ambitious plans to build a country residence here. Quite a lot of money changed hands, much more than it was actually worth, so Silas was able to move to a comfortable establishment somewhere near Huntingdon. He is still there: living in luxury and nursing his self-pity. …Meanness is neither a modern affliction, nor one found entirely among younger folk.'

Toby thought again about the downtrodden son who had escaped from his decrepit and spiteful father to end his life upon the road.

'And what of the other people I met?' asked Toby, 'What has happened to them?'

She looked at him kindly. 'What happens to us all, Toby? They have grown older, and some a little greyer. George Hughes continues to tend his station; and the Oldfields still serve at "The Three Eels", while, as always, Christian Mandell sits among the dusty shelves of his tiny corner shop dreaming of future wealth and riches.'

'And the blacksmith, Elijah… Elijah Barnes?' he prompted.

A sad expression now clouded Jeannie's face. 'Killed, Toby,' she replied quietly, 'in "The Great War"… like so many others.'

He remembered learning about the conflict of 1914 to 1918. 'I've read so much about it… do you know what happened to him?'

'He didn't go at first,' she said, gazing ahead. 'His skills were sorely needed here as Britain was short of food, due to the Germans sinking so many ships bringing supplies to our shores. But Elijah was never a contented man. He would say that it seemed wrong for so many young men with families to be sent to war, when he, a bachelor with no one to care for, stayed at home. It must have played greatly upon his mind, because one day in 1917 he announced that he was volunteering for duty – with a cavalry division. And so he left for the front, like a number of others round here that lost their lives; meeting his death just before the conflict ended.

'There is talk of putting up a memorial at the crossroads in Stavenham with his name and the names of others who fell, upon it,' she added.

They moved on, making for the quiet railway crossing, and shortly afterwards approached "Warren Hill Farm". "The Great Barn", though still impressive, looked more run down than before, and Toby noted that a large tarpaulin had been secured over a section of the western end in an effort to keep out the weather. He expected Jeannie to enter the farmyard, and was considering the difficulty of a renewed meeting with the Trindles, when she struck off to the right and led him down an overgrown footpath that had gone unnoticed during his previous visit. In this way they skirted the premises, before emerging beyond the outer courtyard at the corner of a wheat field. Looking back, Toby saw a huge black and white bull in the paddock formerly occupied by Gladstone; while tethered beneath the shade of a nearby tree he recognised the familiar bowed shape of Naffy the donkey.

They stopped again a few steps further on and sat down, out of sight of passers-by, in the shade of an ash tree. Toby could see the outbuildings of "Pocket Farm" away to his right; and the rambling assortment of barns and sheds that made up the Towsers' property further down the valley slope, while eastwards he recognised familiar figures at work in a large field about a quarter of a mile away. The Trindles were harvesting an early crop of barley, and he watched as a horse drawn binder, ridden by Wesley and drawn by the two ageing shire horses, Caesar and Cleo, clattered round the outer side of the newly opened field. The circling yellow blades of the binder flashed rhythmically as they caught the sun, a succession of newly tied sheaves being cast onto the stubble at regular intervals. A little further off he saw Coodie, Scarlet and old Sam methodically collecting these and standing them in stooks of nine or ten; while by the gate at the top of the field he spied the white head of Henry Trindle, stooped low over a raised frame, the steady movements of his shoulders suggesting that he was engaged in sharpening a replacement blade for the binder. There was no sign of Mark Trindle.

'How are they all?' Toby asked.

'Oh, they're managing,' replied Jeannie, 'but things could be better. The farm makes little money now, and what with constant repairs there's nothing left to invest. But the Braylings at "High Dyke Farm" are faring much better: Arthur and Sarah just seem to have the will to make it work. They bring in new ideas and keep things moving, which is just as well with their having five children.'

'I enjoyed their company,' said Toby thoughtfully. 'They were generous people, but with a light heart, if you know what I mean?'

She turned to him. '…But even they have had bad luck.'

'In what way?' asked Toby, catching the sad note in her voice.

'They lost their oldest daughter, Kitty, five years ago. She died during the influenza epidemic. It was a great shock to them all, but the recent births of Betty and Duke have helped.'

'I'm sorry,' said Toby, reflecting back to the hoeing day. 'Kitty was a fine girl, and she clearly loved life here. But tell me about the other farms,' he added, nodding towards "Deep Spinney Farm". 'What of the Towsers?'

Jeannie wrinkled her nose. 'Matthew and Abigail are old now, so Cregan and Barnaby run the farm, with assistance from their sister, Queenie. They continue to be a bad lot; too secretive – too mad about hunting anything that moves! And recently another has joined them... an outsider by the name of Declan Finch.'

She pointed across the valley towards a large copse of trees bordering the Northampton Road just above the Towsers' farm.

'Can you see there?' she said. 'That's "Gibbet Wood", where the old gallows used to stand. For years a derelict cottage lay rotting in a hollow among the trees, which now has been repaired with electricity laid on. That's where the newcomer lives. You can often see a light burning in the window deep into the night. There are visitors too – shady characters. They park their cars in the lay-by of an evening and walk down. Nobody is sure exactly where they come from, or why, but there is a suspicion that they're up to no good.'

'And this Declan Finch?' asked Toby, with growing interest. 'What do you know of him?'

'He's a squint-eyed fellow,' said Jeannie, frowning. 'About twenty-five years old, and none too honest if looks are anything to go by. I've never seen him do any work, and he's certainly not the country type... I'd say it was odd to be so secretive,' she added.

'Wasn't there also some bad blood between the Towsers and the Smallwoods at "Pocket Farm"?' asked Toby, probing further. 'How are the old couple now?'

Jeannie sighed. '"Pocket Farm" is empty. It's up for sale, but I don't expect a buyer will be found now that the land has been rented to others.'

'But what of Albert and Rose?'

'Albert died eight years ago. He just seemed to give up as the farm went downhill around him. The old fellow still greatly missed his daughter too, and never stopped hoping they'd discover the truth about her. Then one day he went out and was gone for hours, before coming home exhausted... and next morning he didn't wake up. Rose arranged for him to be buried next to Katy in Stavenham churchyard; then she herself moved away and went to live with relatives in Norfolk. She's still alive, I think, but has never come back – too many sad memories, I imagine.'

'They too were good people,' said Toby. 'I only met them once... but you can tell.'

After talking quietly together in the shade for a while longer, Jeannie rose to her feet.

'You haven't asked me about Meg,' she said. 'Would you like to hear about her?'

'Of course,' replied Toby eagerly. 'I feel I knew her best of all.'

'Come with me then, and I'll tell you what I know.'

Thus saying, she led him back onto the track and headed down towards "Pocket Farm".

They soon came to the deserted premises and passed through the silent, empty farmyard. A "For Sale" sign, now faded and at an angle, had been put up beside the front gate of the cottage, but it was clear from the flaking paint on the windows, and the rampant growth of nettles and weeds in the front garden, that nobody had been there for months. Next, "Maxton Tower" reared up in front of them; but instead of making straight for it, Jeannie skirted the massive structure on the western side before heading towards a grassy knoll commanding a view of "Silver Link Cottage". Upon arriving there they sat down to look out over the rolling countryside. The sun was now nearing its zenith and every detail of the little corner where Meg lived clearly visible. A small figure moved among the trees of the animal enclosure.

'I'm glad she's alright,' Toby said with relief in his voice, upon perceiving Meg.

'But she has changed since last you saw her, Toby.'

'In what way – what has happened to her?' he asked, sensing regret in Jeannie's voice.

'Very much,' she replied, turning to him, 'for Meg is now the mother of a young daughter.'

Toby swallowed, trying to comprehend this. Had he not been speaking to her just hours ago... but no, he had to accept the passage of time...

'The child's father...' he asked tentatively. 'Who is it?'

'Someone you came to know quite well, Toby.'

'...Mark Trindle?' said Toby, recollecting their last meeting by the tower. 'Do they live there together?'

'I am afraid not,' Jeannie replied. 'You see Mark was another sadly killed in the war.'

Toby felt cold, as if an icy blade had run down his back.

'Can you tell me what happened?' he said at last. 'This news is a shock to me.'

'Of course: it will help when you see her again, although the story is an all too familiar one.'

Jeannie then settled herself, taking a stalk of grass between her fingers as Toby listened.

'As I think you had begun to realise, Toby, Mark and Meg were more than just friends. Having grown up together an affinity had slowly developed between them – one that laid the foundation for a deeper understanding. Both enjoyed the land and natural things, but there was something else, a meeting of minds: she self-reliant and independent, he perceptive and insightful. They would talk on any subject as equals in thought and spirit.

'It was therefore natural that another attraction should grow between them; but although he courted her, the time was not yet right for marriage. A war had begun and many would make their way to the bloody battlefields of Europe. Yet for those tucked away here in the lanes of Bedfordshire, all seemed remote at first – although as the course of the conflict dragged on the call to arms became stronger. The reversals of 1916 filled the newspapers, and Mark dwelt heavily on each report. At last he told Meg of his intention to enlist. She listened sadly, but let him go, knowing his mind was made up.

'Thus Mark went for basic training in the early spring of 1917, returning only twice on leave – on the last occasion at Whitsun time, when he told her that his regiment was being trained for a new offensive that would achieve the final breakthrough to victory. Then he left her to await his return… and they were parted, forever.'

Jeannie turned and looked intently at Toby.

'His regiment was sent to a place called Ypres,' she said coldly, 'a salient on the battlefront where a complex network of trenches had been prepared. Upon arrival the soldiers were informed that there would soon be a great bombardment of the German position, before they moved forward to attack. It was to be another "Final push" to overwhelm the enemy… but by this time, Meg had important news of her own. She was pregnant – her baby expected the following January. Yet Meg did not reveal this to Mark at first, choosing to wait and hope that he might be allowed home so that she could tell him when they were together. But all leave was cancelled soon after and, as the closing days of July approached, she wrote instead to tell him that they were soon to be parents. After this the difficult process of waiting began – but no reply came, and she would never discover if he had received her letter.'

'The Third Battle of Ypres,' said Toby, reflectively. 'Passchendaele… a cauldron… a killing ground.' He thought of the mud and horror of that terrible conflict and turned to Jeannie.

'Do *you* know what happened to Mark?' he asked.

'I do,' Jeannie replied, 'although the event is sad to recount. The regiment arrived at Ypres in mid July as final preparations for the attack were being made. It was a time of waiting and apprehension. The land had been fought over twice before and the scars of war were plain to see. The noise and commotion of troop movements and the roar of distant guns filled the soldiers' ears. The town of Ypres was a ruin – the surrounding countryside a wasteland of uprooted trees and hedgerows.

'Mark's company was moved up to a reserve trench on the 29th July, and there experienced the dismal squalor of life at the front: dampness and discomfort at night, the stench of latrines, lice and rats.

'He then came to value the comradeship of those around him, of friends he had made and the leadership of those who had been with him while on exercises. One of these was a Yorkshireman named Sergeant Trent: a tall man getting on for thirty-five. He had bullied them relentlessly during training – barking his commands for hours on end in order to force the discipline of military life into their ears and aching limbs. Mark hated the man at first – the strident voice, the relentless barbed comments – but a grudging respect grew within him as he came to understand the other.

' "We are soldiers," Sergeant Trent said to them one day, as they lay exhausted on the moorland turf following a fifteen-mile route march. "We do the world's most thankless job, but we can do it as brothers, watching out for each other. So remember, if you make me proud, I won't fail you, I'll bring you all home safe."

'His words had been delivered without the usual army rhetoric; like a father to his sons – a comrade in arms – and Mark was grateful.'

* * *

'The penultimate day was one of increasing tension. They moved to the forward trenches in the afternoon, and as night fell a mood of expectancy and unease clouded every man's thoughts and dreams. Yet for Mark it was a little different, for he was permitted a precious interlude in which to read and re-read a correspondence received from Meg that day – a letter of joy:

> *Dear Mark,*
>
> *I do hope you are well and that things are not too uncomfortable. We read the papers every morning and know that something big is building up. Look after yourself and please don't volunteer to take any unnecessary risks. There are so many dangers and we long for your safe return. Your mother and father are constantly anxious about you and we often sit together sharing our thoughts.*
>
> *I hardly know how to say this next bit, but must tell before more time passes. You see it is this, my love: I am pregnant with our child. Please don't be shocked – I feel sure all will be well when you return and we can be together again.*
>
> *Coodie and Scarlet know, but we have decided to keep it our secret for now. They comfort me in the morning when I am bad; then I am able to get through the day without too much difficulty. In the meantime others need not learn of this for a little longer.*
>
> *Now, I must not keep you, but promise to write again in a day or so. You have always been my one true confidant.*
>
> *Your ever loving, Meg.*

'By moonlight, with a smile upon his lips, and pondering over each word, Mark penned a reply in his tall angular hand. When finished, he then folded the letter neatly and placed it in the breast pocket of his tunic, where it would always remain. After this he slept fitfully until dawn came and night slid away into shadow. So the veil of sheltering darkness was drawn back on his last day as a weak sun crept over the horizon.

'Gradually, its warm rays penetrated the trenches, falling upon a throng of men. Provisions were quickly eaten, bayonets sharpened – the cold barrels of sturdy rifles caressed by those clutched by apprehension and fear. Some prayed; while others chaffed their mates and exchanged ribald jokes, as men often do at times of adversity or impending bloodshed. Few considered their own last day to have come; but the cold fingers of fear clutched at many hearts. In all they were not loud, but disciplined and deliberate – like players on a mighty stage awaiting the final act. At such times in our existence all that is best in our lives, our world and natures, is distilled and recalled in the space of a few short minutes: the comforts of home, the gentle scents of a summer garden and the company of those we love most dearly on this earth. So it was that many thoughts were turned that morning to an inner world, beyond the reach of tragedy.

'All too soon the guns roared into life, splitting the air with thunder and raining death upon the German lines. An hour of destruction was laid upon the opposing side to sweep away their foes, and crouching next to his neighbour, each waiting son wondered how any could survive the fury. Then the gunfire rolled away and they moved forward to the ladders. Mark fell in beside Sergeant Trent who, with rifle in hand, stood ready to lead them. He was calm in his authority, and addressed them steadily – meeting the anxious eyes of every man in turn.

' "There's a job to be done boys," he voiced in an even tone. "A war to be won! Stay with me and have no fear… we shall do our duty."

'Very soon the whistle sounded and he climbed up before them, disappearing over the parapet of earth. Mark followed, rising from the crowd into the barbed void of "No Man's Land". Through the shattered wire he stumbled, a throng of men half shrouded by swirling smoke on either side. Shells whistled overhead, while nearer, the thud of mortars rent the air. A rattle of machine gun fire broke out ahead; and a fetid breath, as if from hell itself, seeped over the blighted landscape.

'A soldier next to him slumped forward with a sigh as Mark struggled to stay in touch with his unit; then another fell to his left, cut through by a savage shard of shrapnel. Yet he did not look back, but moved on through the deadly hail; still hearing the sergeant's words in his head.

'Sights of carnage met his eyes: men shot through, dismembered, disembowelled… dying from gaping wounds – tokens of hatred from a foe he would never see. They were cut down: melting into the ground like mown corn – the light chaff of humanity swept away in the confusion of war and conflict.

'Mark glimpsed the sergeant twenty yards away; then a shell burst at the spot, tearing at any living thing and sending a great gout of earth skywards. Concussed and felled for a moment by the blast, Mark regained his feet and staggered on half blinded to come upon what remained of Sergeant Trent, spread-eagled on the earth... all dignity gone in the moment of death – a torn remnant of humanity cast broken upon the churned and blackened soil of Flanders.

'Mark circled past... alone, his ardour cooled: stumbling on as if guided by a cold hand through a wasteland of futility. Then a final mortar burst beside him, shattering his ankle and sending a burst of shrapnel upwards. He fell sideways, collapsing onto his thigh, before rolling slowly over, pierced by a dozen splinters. Mortally wounded and beyond pain, he looked up, to glimpse the morning sun shining serenely above high clouds: then the light in his eyes died, and his spirit, like a thousand others that day, rose up from the maelstrom of battle to ascend into the waiting air.'

* * *

Jeannie turned towards Toby with an empty look.

'They brought him in the following morning, and in the process of identifying his body found the letter he'd written to Meg. However, this was considered too cut and bloodstained to be posted home and was buried along with him in the Flanders soil where he remains to this day.

'The Trindles were devastated when they received the news; but Meg had to suffer her grief in silence, though Coodie did her best to comfort her. Yet the truth about her condition had to come out, and there were many voices of moral indignation when that secret became public. Some passed her by without speaking, and Charlotte Tyler was especially cruel, calling Meg a worthless woman and goading her for her indiscretion.

'The baby was born at "Silver Link Cottage" on 23rd January 1918 – a cold snowy night – with Coodie in attendance. They named her Alice; but she seemed a poor mite at first, the doctor warning more than once that she might not survive. But the little girl had a will to live – she came through and is now strong.

'In time Meg went back to work at "Tyler Hall", taking Alice with her during the day, but her treatment did not improve. Charlotte continued to vent her spite, envious of the other's supposed happiness.'

Jeannie paused for a moment, looking down at her shoes, an enigmatic expression on her face. 'Then the strangest thing happened,' she went on.

'What? Do tell me,' said Toby, his curiosity rising.

'Charlotte vanished."

'How? What happened to her?'

Jeannie turned to him, a veiled look in her eyes. 'I told you… she simply disappeared – there is no more… she hasn't been seen since.'

'But what do we know about her last movements?'

Looking away, Jeannie breathed out slowly.

'That she left the house one evening in May, having told the maid she was going for a walk. It was the last time she spoke to anyone. The police searched for her of course, but there were rumours that Charlotte had been having an affair with one of Basil Tyler's associates and had run off to London to join him.

'The authorities seemed to think there might have been something in it, and with the whiff of scandal in the air, Basil appears to have encouraged them to quietly shelve the case. Her whereabouts remain a mystery to this day.

'For her part, Meg gave up her position at "Tyler Hall" a few weeks later and has not worked there since.'

'I wonder what she must think?' mused Toby, mulling over what he had heard.

'That is something you might ask her yourself,' said Jeannie, facing him. 'Why not? But be warned… as I said before, Meg is different now – she is both older and wiser.'

Toby looked back in the direction of the cottage, and as he watched a tiny shape appeared through the bushes bordering the railway line. Then, as if scenting – or having seen them – Macken suddenly began scampering helter-skelter up the slope. He arrived in a flurry of short barks before flopping down at Jeannie's feet, licking her fingers.

'I thought you'd lost him,' said Toby.

Jeannie smiled, shaking her head. 'This little fellow has never been a pet, Toby… Macken goes where he pleases. He is my ears and eyes… and my nose – but I am not his master.

'Now, I must be leaving, for I have talked too long; but we will doubtless meet again when you need me.'

With these words she stood up and began walking away across the wide field, heading westward, the Jack Russell trotting close by. Toby watched as they departed, before looking back toward the cottage. When he glanced round again moments later they had vanished – leaving the landscape empty except for a single black crow circling slowly above the distant trees.

Chapter Seven

An Enduring Flame

TOBY APPROACHED MEG'S HOME AND SKIRTED ROUND the animal enclosure. Several chickens and two large turkeys were pecking about among the trees but he saw no other signs of life as he made his way to the front door. This stood open, the trailing honeysuckle hanging in heavy folds around the porch; and a young Border collie, basking in a patch of sunlight, lay comfortably stretched out on the doorstep. It watched Toby approach, following him with mild, attentive eyes.

Above the door a board was now fixed, upon which the name "Silver Link Cottage" had been carefully painted in a curving script, the delicacy of the work suggesting a woman's hand.

Toby was about to call out to announce his presence, when he heard the sound of splashing water and the clang of a metal pail. The noise came from a little yard tucked round beside the railway and he moved to investigate. Passing through an opening in a privet hedge, he found Meg in the process of replacing the wooden lid of the well. She was wearing a green working dress, and he noted that her face was thinner since he had seen her last. But she looked well and broke into a smile upon seeing him.

'Toby… it's you,' she said warmly. 'You went away and nobody knew where to; I'm so pleased you've come.'

'I'm sorry to have worried you,' he replied. 'I was called away suddenly… I should have written.'

'Coodie was so concerned,' Meg went on reproachfully. 'She cares about you very much. It's been ten years, Toby… so long.'

Meg's voice trailed away, her brow becoming furrowed for a moment as she seemed to dwell upon something.

'I can only apologise,' he said. 'It was not my intention. Much that is strange has happened.'

The note of mystery in his voice did not go unnoticed; but Meg refrained from questioning him further. The smile returned to her lips, and picking up a heavy enamel pail, she invited him to follow her into the cottage. The dog still guarded the door, and seeing Meg he sat up, nose twitching with anticipation.

'You have a new companion,' Toby observed. 'What became of Mr Toots?'

She put the pail down and stopped before the threshold, gazing fondly at the animal. 'Mr Toots was old when you were here last,' she said. 'He lived another five years after you went… just as clumsy and loving as ever. But all dogs must leave us at the end; so now we have Pip. He's not so much of a character, I'll warrant you, but a lovely fellow nevertheless. I wouldn't be without him.'

Toby thought back to his meetings with the old retriever and smiled to himself. 'That name… why Mr Toots?' he said. 'It seems an odd one for a dog.'

Meg looked up at him, raising an eyebrow with the same air of feigned disapproval that he had once seen before.

'You really must read a little more, Toby. Then you would know that Mr Toots was a very good acquaintance of Paul, in *Dombey and Son* by Charles Dickens. He was perhaps the most foolish creature in the whole world, but became the best and most loving friend young Paul could have hoped for. What better name to give a pet?'

Toby agreed, yet he felt the watchful and patient collie somehow complemented Meg's character better than her previous companion.

'Pip, made famous in *Great Expectations*, simply continues the tradition of borrowing names from the author's books,' she added, as they returned to the front door.

* * *

They were about to enter the cottage when the face of a small child appeared in the doorway: a dark haired girl with searching brown eyes and a serious expression. She was barefooted, and wore a plain black dress that both set off her pale complexion and emphasised strong features. A hand-knitted rag doll was clutched tightly to her breast. No flicker of a smile turned the corners of the youngster's mouth, and she seemed to stare reproachfully at Toby for having come uninvited.

'My daughter, Alice,' said Meg, smiling down at her. 'Alice, this is Toby – an old friend of mine. Say hello.'

'Hello,' said the girl, an expression of uncertainty suddenly crossing her face as she drew back to let them pass.

They made their way inside, leaving the girl on the step, looking in. It was not until a little later, as Meg was putting a kettle on to make tea, that the child disappeared from view.

'Don't worry about Alice,' said Meg. 'She's not used to strangers, that's all. We don't get many visitors here and it takes her a little time to get used to you, but then she's fine.'

They now passed a pleasant hour discussing everyday things, and Meg told him how she had struggled to bring up the baby alone. However, through a combination of working for the Trindles and helping out at other farms, she had been able to stay on at "Silver Link Cottage". Meg also informed him that she had become increasingly respected for her skill in the care of animals, using country remedies of her own making.

Toby said little about himself meanwhile but at last, as they sat together by the stove, Meg leaned across and looked at him closely.

'You never tell me very much about your own life, do you, Toby?' she said. 'Mark always thought you were a strange fellow... I wonder what he would say now?'

'He talked a lot of me, then?'

'There you go again,' she said, wrinkling her nose in mock frustration, 'always answering a question with a question. He found that odd too... But yes, Mark did talk of you many times; always wondering where you were really from.'

'And you?' said Toby. 'What do you think of me?'

Meg shook her head slowly. 'I don't know, Toby... I'm not sure what to think. All I know is that you have come back after ten years... like a person who simply pops out of the ground.'

'You must trust me,' he went on. 'I should really be back with my own family... but my work brings me here.'

Meg started forward at this, an intent expression on her face. 'You have a wife and children?' she asked, her eyes becoming wide and animated.

'Yes,' he replied sadly. 'My wife's name is Jenny, and I have a little boy and girl.'

'But you are separated... or have lost them, perhaps?'

'For a time, it seems... I believe I must stay here for now.'

'There is no need to say more,' Meg assured Toby, with understanding. 'I will ask no further questions if they trouble you. We all have our inner secrets... you are not alone in that...'

* * *

The little girl came in at this point and her mother cut bread and made soup, which they shared together. As she diligently helped her parent prepare the meal, little Alice seldom talked at first; but in time began to join their conversation, contributing her opinions. The child's powers of concentration and depth of thought struck Toby more and more; for it was like being with someone of much older years who had shrugged off the naivety of childhood. Yet Alice was neither pert nor precocious; but rather, insightful and imaginative in her responses. Looking at her, Toby recalled her father, seeing his likeness in her features and dark hair. She had the same intent expression – always curious and desiring to know more.

As the minutes passed the little girl increasingly relaxed and a germ of friendship began to grow up between them, until at last she brought him some of her favourite books from the shelves. 'That's me,' she said seriously, pointing at a picture of Alice in a volume of *Alice in Wonderland*.

'I want to be like Alice… and have adventures,' she stammered in her excitement, looking back towards her mother.

Toby was captivated by the girl's sudden enthusiasm, and wondered what would become of her with the passage of time.

They finished their lunch, and after washing up Alice announced that she wished to make the short journey to "Warren Hill Farm" to see the Trindles. Meg and Toby saw her off at the door, and waved as she walked purposefully away in the direction of "The Great Barn"; before strolling together towards the higher ground near "Maxton Tower" in order to watch as she neared her destination.

'Perhaps I shouldn't let her go alone,' said Meg, 'but it's what she likes best, and there's no danger here.'

They sat down on the grass and she turned towards him, a strained expression wrinkling her brow. 'You see, she's such a restless young thing that I sometimes think she wants to cram into a day what others might be content to do in a lifetime.'

'But isn't that good in a child?' he ventured. 'A dull life is never best.'

'Of course,' said Meg, 'but I fear she will never be happy here… and I don't want to lose her. She's all I have… and I can never leave.'

'You could go together, perhaps,' he suggested.

'No… no that wouldn't do… It is for her benefit that I must always stay.'

Meg's manner had become strangely agitated and she now looked at him with searching eyes.

'You know the circumstances of my life,' she said at last. 'The mistake I made… and the hardship that was bound to follow when Mark was taken from me. Now all I have is Alice, who is so like her father. I would do anything for her happiness, even if it means sacrificing myself.'

She looked at him with a sudden fierce energy, her lips pressed tightly together.

'What should we be prepared to do… or give up, to protect the ones we love, Toby? And how are our deeds to be viewed? After all, we all come to judge others using our own measure of their worth. But what drives any of us? A woman may be motivated by love to protect her children, a man by ambition or a painter by art. What each will do to achieve their ends is their own decision in the end. The same woman may later abandon her family, while a man may walk away from his profession… As for the artist, why, he may finish by burning his brushes – or cutting off his ear. And what are you or I destined to do? What sacrifices will we be prepared to make to either find or conceal the truth?'

Here she broke into a strained and hollow laugh.

'One person may seek diligently all their lives for an answer to these great mysteries – the salvation of the spirit – while another does nothing and is prepared to bask all along in the easy warmth of their own complacency. But those like you and me, Toby… will always seek the truth. Although we may act another part, we must be honest with ourselves. Anything less is a lie. People may escape to follow their dreams; but the real problem with such fantasy is that there comes a time when you must wake… And reality can be a powerful antidote for any that indulge themselves too much in that other world. No, those such as us are tested always and must crack our heads against "reason" every day.'

She rose then and together they made their way back towards the cottage. Toby was troubled by her words… thinking about his own life, about his lost family and about the times when he had been obsessed with his own affairs to the exclusion of others. Did Meg know this? Was she leading him on to look deeper within himself?

'Surely you do your best,' he said, as they approached the cottage again.

'Of course… I must. But I have made many mistakes… with Mark… with Charlotte Tyler.'

Toby touched her shoulder and she turned with a look of sorrow.

'You can't blame yourself for what happened to Mark. He chose to serve – it wasn't your fault… and Charlotte?'

Meg checked him. 'Of Charlotte it is best to say little… her departure was a good thing. For me she had only jealousy and spite, which she dressed up as moral indignation. As for what happened to her, some questions are best left unanswered, for to disturb the dust would do no good… She never really loved, and was not loved.'

There was a note of finality in her words that struck Toby to the core – like an ending of hope.

They went inside and sat in silence for a while, both gazing through the glass of the stove at the flames within. Then Meg spoke again.

'I will never go from this place,' she said. 'I am destined to stay here always. To leave "Silver Link Cottage" would be impossible now.'

'And you made the sign above the door?' he queried with a smile, wishing to lighten her mood.

'Yes… it took a good deal of patience.'

'It is a pretty name. Where does it come from?'

She stood up and lifted a book from the nearest shelf. 'The name comes from Sir Walter Scott's poem, "The Lay of the Last Minstrel" – a testament to lasting love,' she replied, opening the volume to read:

True love's the gift which God has given,
To man alone beneath the heaven.
It is the secret sympathy,
The silver link, the silken tie,
Which heart to heart and mind to mind,
In body and in soul can bind.

'I was bound to Mark in that way – and will be always,' she sighed. 'He is in my thoughts every day... This would have been our home.'

Toby sat, unable to say more. This quiet, resourceful woman, so often quick and intuitive, had revealed something of a private world clouded by enduring grief and memory.

*   *   *

Their conversation was more broken then. Meg first pottered around the kitchen doing little chores, before taking him out to see where Mr Toots was buried, a wooden name board marking the spot.

Alice came home just before six o'clock, dusty but happy, having spent a day in the fields.

'I stooked a hundred sheaves and Coodie gave me a shilling,' she said proudly, opening her palm to show them.

'Coodie shouldn't have,' said Meg. 'It's not something the Trindles can really afford. But I am proud of you and you shall keep it all.'

They ate a light supper and later Alice was put to bed. Meanwhile, Toby had begun to consider what he need do for the night, and was choosing his moment to leave on the pretext of having taken a room at the inn in Stavenham, when movements were heard outside and a woman wearing a large bonnet appeared, silhouetted in the doorway. He failed to recognise her at first, but upon hearing the newcomer's soft voice and accent, quickly realised that it must be Morwen Hughes, the stationmaster's wife.

For her part, she seemed instantly to know him.

'There you are, Meg,' she said, entering and placing a large basket upon the table. 'I just stopped by for a chat and to see little Alice – and here I find you with that intriguing young man I had the pleasure of meeting once before.'

A warm smile spread across her face, and Meg responded with similar good humour.

'Now don't tease me, Morwen – Toby is only a friend. We've just been talking about the time he was here last, that's all.'

'I know, dear,' said the older woman, looking around her as she made herself comfortable in a chair by the stove, 'but it seems I'm a bit too late to see little Alice.'

'I'm afraid so,' Meg answered, rising to offer her tea. 'She came in fair worn out, but happy as a sandboy from having helped the Trindles with their harvesting this afternoon. I doubt we will see her again before morning.'

The talk continued in this easy and familiar way, and it was evident that, although their ages were very different, a great friendship and understanding existed between the two women. Meanwhile, the room became powerfully scented with the fragrance of the fresh herbs and leaves in Morwen's basket, and Toby learned that she frequently visited the cottage while making her rounds of the hedgerows during the summer months.

Yet, although the conversation was relaxed and genial, Toby gradually began to feel awkward in the other woman's presence. He noted that she would often study him closely when he spoke, while seeming to consider his every word of special interest: so much so that he had the impression she would remember everything he said in the minutest detail another time.

'How do you find my little lass?' Morwen asked at last, straightening her apron and nodding toward Meg.

'Very well,' he replied, 'and Alice is charming too.'

'Oh she is,' said the old lady sagely. 'A lovely girl... It's not easy for a mother living by herself to bring up a child.'

'But I have you,' said Meg. 'That helps a lot.'

'So you have, my dear. I won't leave you to struggle. We country girls must look out for each other.'

Here Mrs Hughes turned in her chair and leaned towards Toby, as if to emphasise her words.

'That Tyler fellow would have moved her off by now if she hadn't been able to pay the rent. But me and one or two others weren't going to let that happen. After all, where would she go? Our Meg's like me, born and bred in the country, and that's where she belongs. If either of us went to live in a village or town we wouldn't really fit in... you might say we like our own company too much!

'Take me,' she said, closing her eyes and reminiscing. 'I was born near Llantrisant in mid-Wales; sheep country, so farming was in my blood. Then old George came along – though he weren't so old in those days. "Come with me," he says, "and together we'll make our fortune on the railway." Meanin' of course that he'd further his career. So off we went to Nottingham, a great sprawling place, all factories and smoke!' She said this with special emphasis, wrinkling her nose. 'He'd have stayed there, no doubt about it, but I never could have put up with it for long. You know the saying, "You can take the girl out of the country, but you can't take the countryside out of the girl." ...Well, I suppose I must have gone on at him a bit, so eventually he took the stationmaster's position here.'

For a moment she looked down absently at the floor.

'You shouldn't do that of course… I mean, get in the way of your husband's future. But I needed the grass beneath my feet again, and I can't say I'm sorry.'

'Has it worked out?' Toby asked.

'As well as it might,' she replied. 'George has his railway and I have my vegetable garden.'

'Did you ever want a family?'

She reflected for a moment, a wan smile upon her lips.

'We can't always have *everything* we want, Toby. No, I didn't press him on that score. George was always a little too starched and proper to want to be involved with children. But I can still be of help to Meg and her little Alice, and so I am,' she added, becoming cheerful again. 'Our Coodie and me keep an eye on Meg and the child to make sure Basil Tyler and his bailiffs leave them alone. They'll come to no harm while we're around, I promise you.'

Although Toby did not say it, this assurance came as a comfort as he prepared to go. Meg seemed sad to see him depart, but at last he took his leave, having promised to return again soon. Yet this, he realised, was far from certain.

She walked with him to the door and spoke quietly as they stood together under the porch. 'I will look out for you, Toby. Please don't wait so long before you come again.' Then she squeezed his hand and kissed him tenderly on the cheek before stepping back into the kitchen.

He turned reluctantly and moved off, absently taking the footpath that led past "Maxton Tower". It seemed a wrench to leave the cottage, and more than once he had to resist an urge to return as he walked beyond the brow of the hill. Only then did he realise his error – for Stavenham lay in the other direction and he was now heading again towards "Pocket Farm".

* * *

Toby might have retraced his steps at this point, but what if Meg or Morwen were to ask him questions about his going the wrong way? Worse still, they might offer to escort him to the inn where he purported to be staying. It was a risk he would not take; yet what was he to do instead? The light was already fading, and thickening masses of watery cloud sweeping in from the west suggested rain. He would need shelter and somewhere to rest until morning.

By now he had reached the deserted farmyard, his footsteps echoing on the dry cobbles as he approached the house. The flaking "For Sale" sign creaked as he paused at the open garden gate, and a few late sparrows twittered among the rafters of the empty cowshed nearby. But apart from these no other living thing was moving.

'I could stay here,' he said to himself. 'But is the house open?'

A little unnerved by the stillness of the setting, Toby walked slowly up the pathway with an odd sensation that, even now, the old couple might still be watching from behind a closed curtain. But there was no sign of life from any window or the casement above.

Reaching the door he pushed upon the flaking paint, but it was locked from within and moved only a fraction. Toby might then have given up and moved on, had he not, upon stepping back, noticed a second door to the Smallwoods' kitchen. He went to this – a rickety affair with two glass panels – and turning the doorknob, felt it give beneath the pressure of his hand. A sharp push with a shoulder forced the door back, complaining upon dry hinges, to reveal a small pile of newspapers and unread mail that had collected beneath the letter box during the intervening months and years. A musty smell rose to his nose as he toed the debris aside and closed the door behind him.

The kitchen, which was empty apart from a few scattered newspapers and an old cooker, had that cold feeling all uninhabited places have, the absence of people leaving it a mere shell of bricks and plaster. He gingerly walked through to the living room which, similarly empty, was filled with deepening shadows. There were no furnishings except the closed curtains that he would find had been left hanging in all the rooms. Passing through he came into a small hallway with a staircase leading up to his right, which he began to ascend, the exposed boards of unpolished wood creaking loudly under his weight as if warning sleepers of an intruder. But no voice broke the silence, and only the smell of floating dust and the scurrying of a disturbed mouse beneath the floorboards met his senses.

Treading carefully, Toby made his way onto the landing where a ladder was still placed at the open loft space above, and having inched past this went to stand by the landing window. A gloom had descended here too, but he could still see well enough in the encroaching darkness. A small linen cupboard, the door wide open, was on his left hand side, while ahead, a larger room lay before him, completely bare but for a broken stool propped against the wall on its two remaining legs. Then, to the right, he saw the closed door to a second bedroom, its white paint still offering a dull sheen in the fading light. Turning the curved handle, he pushed gently and the door swung silently open to reveal a strange and haunting sight.

This last living space, but for the cobwebs that hung here and there, might have been left that very day. It contained a made up bed with a coverlet embroidered with scenes of Norfolk lakes and waterways, and a dressing-table covered with a lace cloth. Upon this were a woman's personal items: two brushes with mother-of-pearl handles, a vanity box, a pretty necklace of glass beads, and some floral ornaments – all covered with a film of fine dust as if waiting for their owner to return. There was an oval mat upon the floor with a design of swirling colours, and a doll wearing a lace bonnet sitting upon the window ledge. A wardrobe with inlaid panels stood against the wall, in which, when opened,

Toby found dresses and cardigans hanging. Finally, placed in the casement recess, he came upon a small but comfortable armchair, on the seat of which lay a delicately worked schoolgirl's sampler complete with needle and thread.

Toby had seen such sights in museums, frozen in time, everything precisely placed… hinting at a past life, and he imagined a mother's hand at work, carefully placing all these precious things to preserve the memory of a lost daughter – only to leave them there at last to whatever fate might befall when she went away towards the closing of her own life.

* * *

Feeling like an unwelcome intruder in a private place, Toby stood a while by the closed window curtain wondering whether to leave and find somewhere else to sleep. But then, just as a distant church bell struck ten, he noticed a movement outside, and pulling back the curtain a fraction, saw the form of a woman standing by the gate. Toby drew back instinctively, but knew straightaway, from the sight of her bonnet and shawl, that it must be Morwen Hughes. She had been looking up in his direction, and might, it seemed, have had some notion of his presence. Had the intuitive old lady seen him go this way earlier as she looked through the window of "Silver Link Cottage"?

He felt uneasy, and crouching down furtively, drew back the corner of the curtain a second time. Morwen was still there, and as he watched she put one finger to her closed lips before moving off through the farmyard in the direction of "Warren Hill Farm".

Much relieved to see her depart, he decided to stay, despite some inner foreboding, with the intention of leaving first thing in the morning, rather than risk an unfortunate meeting in the dark. In the meantime he would sleep by the window, and to this end moved the sampler with its needle and thread, placing them carefully on the dusty pillow of the bed. Then, as a light rain began to patter against the windowpane, having settled himself wearily in the armchair, Toby fell asleep to face another night of shifting dreams.

Chapter Eight

The Declan Finch Affair

TOBY SLEPT ON, AND NOTHING MOVED AROUND him during his uneasy slumber except eddying dust occasionally disturbed by a draught that issued through a crack in the window frame. An inquisitive mouse did once look in at the door, but on lifting his twitching nose to sniff the languid air, found nothing to excite his senses and came no more. Only spiders invaded the long silence, noiselessly weaving their webs in corner or crevice – working patiently though the quiet hours.

At last, blinking though crusted eyelashes, Toby shivered awake as a cooling waft caressed his face. The room was cold and damp, and he shifted painfully in the armchair, feeling his bones creak. Then, gradually focusing upon his surroundings, he leant forward to draw back the faded curtain. It tore as he pulled, sending a shower of dust and fine particles drifting upwards. Looking outside he saw a changed scene: a landscape of puddles and late autumn colours, of falling leaves and an angry sky. The warmth of summer had gone, and a chilly wind tugged at the remaining foliage on tree and hedgerow. Toby reached for the window latch, lifted and pushed – but warped with age and the ingress of moisture, it resisted the pressure of his hand.

Defeated, he turned away, just as the sun, breaking from behind a billowing cloud, cast a shaft of brilliant light into the room from the living world outside. Attracted back by the bright glare, Toby glanced over his shoulder, and squinting across the yard towards the disused cowshed, noted a puff of smoke rising from its open doorway. He drew near to the window again, misting the glass, and peering down made out the hunched figure of a man seated on an upturned enamel pail. The stranger, his face partly obscured by the wide brim of a weather stained felt hat, was reading a newspaper, and as Toby watched, took a pipe from between his lips and looked up as if absently surveying the scene. But, before resuming, his eyes quite deliberately slid across in the direction of the farmhouse. He was no longer alone, moreover, for a small brown and white dog had trotted into view, which upon sitting down in front of the other, was rewarded with a titbit of food taken from a roll of greaseproof paper.

'Macken,' Toby mouthed to himself, 'and I'll warrant I know the other fellow too.'

Toby retreated from the window to gather his thoughts, then made his way downstairs. Below, the sitting room smelt even more of mould and damp; while he noted that a window in the kitchen had been pushed open and recently broken glass lay upon the floor. Toby's footsteps rasped upon the scattered shards – the sound echoing through the empty house. Reaching the door, he slid round it into the open, before moving down through the abandoned garden, brushing past the remnants of summer flowers bowed in decay and leaving the empty seed heads of poppy, thistle and foxglove bobbing listlessly in his wake.

Macken became alert when Toby appeared, but instead of barking, simply ambled over as if greeting an old friend. They met as Toby emerged into the farmyard and after sniffing round his ankles, the dog trotted back towards the gamekeeper. Toby came on behind and drawing near, recognised beyond doubt the mysterious character who had followed him from "The Three Eels". For his part, Jasper did not deign to look up at first but continued reading, giving the impression that he had been expecting Toby all along.

'Hello, squire,' the little man quipped at last. 'Do you want a sandwich? I brought enough for both of us.'

He bent down to pick up the package beside him, and opened it to reveal several large cheese sandwiches and a chunk of meat pie. He also produced an enamel can containing warm tea and having filled the lid, offered it to Toby.

'You'll be dry, no doubt... Too much time in bed always leaves me parched,' he added, his lips curling into a smile.

Toby accepted the food and drink, but was again unsettled and irritated by the other's too familiar manner. A silence ensued while he gathered his thoughts, during which his companion, who resumed reading the newspaper, showed not the slightest concern. Meanwhile Macken, seated attentively on the cobbles, licked his lips as Toby ate the pie.

'George Shotwell,' Toby said at last. 'Is that the name you still wish to be known by?'

Jasper looked up, brushing back a heavy fold of black hair that had fallen across his forehead. 'That's right, Toby, none other...' he replied, his dark eyes suddenly becoming sharp and piercing. 'Oh, and Jeannie sends her regards. Things have moved on a bit... and I'm here to take you further,' he added pointedly. 'If you're ready, that is.'

The breeze suddenly chilled Toby's face. 'You say things have moved on,' he repeated in a halting voice. 'But how much? ...How far?'

Jasper closed the newspaper on his lap to reveal the front cover – dated Saturday, 14th November 1931.

Toby gazed down upon it before sinking to his haunches. '...Another eight years! ... Eight years alone in there?' he said in disbelief, looking back at the farmhouse.

'So it would seem.'

'But why wake now? ...What is there to see at this time?'

'Much,' replied Jasper. 'Things are changing across Europe. New and evil ideas have grown up which will inevitably lead to the suffering of many.' Here he again fixed Toby with an uncompromising expression. 'Yet it would be wrong to imagine that wickedness only thrives in other lands, my friend. Therefore I must endeavour to show you how callousness also manifests itself nearer at hand.'

'I have read about the rise of Nazism,' said Toby, still considering the year.

'Of course, but similar heartlessness and cruelty, if unchallenged, might easily have led to the same corruption here... Now come, we must be moving as there is much to do.'

* * *

Rising to his feet, Jasper lifted down a heavy camouflaged waterproof jacket, similar to his own, that hung from a nail inside the cowshed entrance.

'Here, wear this,' he said in a businesslike fashion. 'It may be a little bit big, but by the looks of the weather you'll be needing it. And besides – it may help to keep off prying eyes,' he added meaningfully.

Having taken up his shotgun, Jasper then threw a large leather bag over his shoulder before striding out into the farmyard as a flurry of raindrops began to fall.

'Wait!' called Toby. 'Before we set off there is something more I wish to know. You see... I have previously met people in these parts who were good to me. Can you tell me anything of them?'

Jasper turned toward Toby, his eyes narrowing reflectively. 'The young woman and her daughter... is it them you mean?'

'Yes, and the Trindles.'

Before replying, Jasper threw a fold of hessian sacking over the shotgun on his arm to protect it from the rain. 'I must warn you of something, Toby,' he went on. 'You see, something of a spreading affliction has begun to stalk the countryside since you were last here. For sure the landlords are still rich enough – but now every tenant farmer has come to know much harder times. Other farms may soon be like this one,' he said with a sweep of his free hand. 'The Trindles have tried to change but make little money and may soon move on; which is probably what Basil Tyler desires, for he has no time for "lame ducks".

'The situation of the lone woman, Meg Maddox, is somewhat different, however, for she is destined to stay here and still survives comfortably enough by hard work and goodwill. Tyler would like to see the last of her, too, but she will not go. Her good friends will see to that.'

'And the girl... Alice?' asked Toby.

'Ah, now that is another matter...' Jasper replied with emphasis. 'Alice looks beyond these few fields, and is clever too. Therefore, I doubt Stavenham will hold her long. She is both like and unlike her mother, and the two are not long destined to stay together under the same roof.'

'I would like to see them again.'

'And so you will; but for now our time is short and not to be given over to other things.'

* * *

Without further discussion they set off towards Warren Hill. Then, having taken a narrow footpath to the right that ran down into a sunken hollow, they descended in the direction of "Deep Spinney Farm". For a time their movement was concealed from general view, but as they came into the lee of an ancient elm tree Toby could see the first outbuildings of that establishment a short distance ahead. The rain was now falling heavily, sending a flurry of displaced leaves fluttering round, and splashing into the puddles now forming on the muddy track. They stopped to take what little shelter the much denuded tree had to offer, while Macken, who seemed unperturbed by the drenching conditions, skipped off round the corner and out of sight. Toby's hair was now becoming slicked down around his temples, and small rivulets of water ran down his neck.

'Here,' said Jasper, pulling an old, battered leather Sou'wester out of his pocket, 'wear this. It's a lot better than nothing, and it could be a while before we get into the dry again.'

'Why have we come this way?' Toby inquired, shaking the water from his hair.

'Believe it or not,' replied Jasper shortly, 'there's a pheasant shoot on today; and I can assure you that a little rain will not keep his lordship and his friends from their time-honoured pleasure. No, when there's a chance to kill some of God's creatures there are a number who will gladly bear the discomfort of a little bad weather to do so. Not that the guns have to do the majority of the hard work.'

'Guns?' asked Toby quizzically.

'The ones that come out to shoot: landowners and wealthy businessmen – rich folk like old Basil Tyler, my boss for the time being. Oh yes, it's a proper ritual, a diligently preserved tradition of old England. First the woods are stocked with birds in the summer months; then every effort is made to near wipe out the all but tame fowl during the subsequent autumn and winter. A gracious time is had by all, and woe betide any other creature that makes an appearance: hares, rabbits, pigeons, partridge, jays, woodcocks and so on – for all shall likewise be considered "fair game" to provide enjoyment for these worthy few.'

Jasper paused, looking steadily at Toby, before continuing with the same cool irony.

'It's a strange business – that the custodians of the countryside, and all that is beautiful in it, should take such delight in destroying the creatures that live here, don't you think? If you or any other outsider were to do it, these country gents would call it vandalism or poaching. But among their kind it goes by the name of "Sport". The masters make things as comfortable as possible for themselves of course – by driving between the shooting positions, and getting lads that need a few shillings to beat across muddy fields to flush out the quarry. Then, when the fun's been had, they lay out the kill to size up their good work: several dozen pheasants full of lead shot, a number of stiffened rabbits with milky eyes and bloodstained fur, and three or four mutilated hares with their limbs torn off. ...Such a noble and uplifting sight!'

'I gather you don't approve.'

'Nor would most decent people... But being here has led me to uncover another little secret that I hope to reveal to you later,' he added meaningfully.

* * *

Just then Macken trotted back round the corner followed by a huge black dog that appeared to be an unhappy cross between a Wolfhound and a Doberman. It stopped momentarily upon seeing them, then bounded up, barking savagely and baring its fangs. Toby drew back and would have retreated along the bridleway if Jasper had not stepped forward commanding him to stop.

'Don't move! If you run the dog will take you – he knows me!'

Toby froze as the ugly creature, its jaws slavering, rushed up and continued barking into their faces not more than four feet away. He was appalled by the onslaught, fearing that at any moment the frenzied animal would leap forward and take him by the throat; and only when he had recovered from the first impulse of terror did Toby hear voices approaching.

Three men now came into view – Basil Tyler, looking irritated by the noise and disruption, and two others, both brawny men in their thirties.

Witnessing Toby's discomfort, the foremost of the three, a surly character with a sour and aggressive expression, threw back his head with a leer and called the dog off.

'Leave him, Satan!' he commanded with a coarse laugh, showing a row of stained and uneven teeth, 'He ain't got enough meat on him to be worth your while.'

The dog now ceased yammering and fell back, but continued to bare its razor sharp canines, a look of malice in its bloodshot eyes.

Its owner was Barnaby Towser, a pugnacious lout of a man with a heavy brow, small close-set eyes and a bulbous lower lip. His face, covered by a three-day growth of stubble, was both sallow and pockmarked – the countenance, Toby felt, of one who might take pleasure in the pain or unhappiness of others. He wore a grease-stained overcoat and carried a heavy stick in his right hand, while on his head was a woodman's hat from which rivulets of water flowed onto his shoulders.

The second newcomer was his brother, Cregan Towser, a man of similar character, but of a more calculating and, Toby sensed, a more scheming temperament. He too wore a weatherproof walking coat with a high collar over which his loosely cropped hair fell. A peaked leather cap covered his head, and a silk scarf was tied neatly at his throat – both items obviously intended to give him a rakish look. Yet while his pale brown eyes and chiselled features might have been attractive in another, the corrosiveness of his inner being showed though the superficial veneer. When amused his face habitually twisted into a smirk, a malicious smile playing about his lips.

Cregan now casually shouldered the shotgun he was carrying and stepped forward, with Basil Tyler a few paces behind. He eyed Toby up and down suspiciously before speaking.

'Who's this feller, Shotwell? You know strangers aren't welcome around here, especially when the shoot's on.'

'He's a new beater,' replied Jasper casually. 'Toby Freeman – just come up from Molliton.'

'Is that right?' said Cregan, continuing to appraise Toby critically. 'I've never seen him around.'

'He's a good man; I've used him before,' Jasper lied. 'He'll do a decent job.'

'Well… Freeman,' said Cregan, with exaggerated emphasis, 'you'll certainly earn your money today, since there'll be no place to hide from the weather.'

Basil Tyler had come up beside Cregan Towser and stood lighting a large cigar, the smoke shrouding his head. In contrast to the sarcastic and sometimes threatening manner of the other two, he showed nothing but cold detachment towards Toby.

'Serve me well and I'll have you again,' he said, looking disinterestedly at a point somewhere beyond Toby's shoulder. 'Mess up and we'll not need you next week.'

Followed by Barnaby, the landowner then turned on his heels and strode back towards "Deep Spinney Farm", the now pacified Satan padding before them. Meanwhile, Cregan fell into conversation with Jasper about arrangements for the day's shooting, leaving Toby to come along at the rear by himself. Once again, Macken was nowhere to be seen.

When they entered the farmyard shortly afterwards it was crowded with upwards of thirty men and boys. A number of vehicles were parked around: some expensive limousines, others more modest vehicles of basic and robust design. There were also farm carts and a covered horse-drawn trap which would be used by the three ladies accompanying the shoot. The farm itself was set among a dozen or more mature elm and poplar trees that towered over the adjacent buildings. At the west end stood a stone built farmhouse of solid construction, which although retaining a few pleasantly ornate features from a much earlier period, nevertheless presented a generally bland exterior that made the frontage appear less than welcoming. Situated on the other three sides were tall barns and outbuildings (their walls covered in cladding) – all sombre and black painted, that seemed to overhang the yard, their interiors gloomy and forbidding. There were also stables and pigsties tucked away down slippery alleyways; and dark sheds where animals, incarcerated away from light and fresh air, were kept penned in all weathers.

Those present were clearly of two classes – the wealthy and those that had come to work. Jasper had taken a group of shabby men and boys to one side, the beaters of the group, and was telling them their duties. A tall, thin farmhand, evidently his assistant, stood beside him with a 12-bore shotgun on his arm. Many of the boys especially were ill-equipped for the inclement weather and stood, already wet through, in a resigned huddle, their dishevelled appearance contrasting greatly with the group of "sportsmen" who had gathered a little further off. Dressed in tough waterproof hunting jackets, boots and headgear, these formed a noisy garrulous group, laughing and exchanging gossip. There were bankers, landowners, businessmen and accountants, a local innkeeper and a city lawyer; and many took liberal sips from hip flasks while loudly boasting of their prowess in previous shoots, a number offering wagers on the forthcoming day's events. Several gun dogs (a rather mixed collection of breeds and heritages), stood around their masters' legs; their hot, steamy breath rising in panting clouds. Meanwhile, two other heavily built men, together with a sly poker faced character with a thin moustache, had walked into the yard from a track leading down from the main road, and stood together shoulders hunched, surreptitiously looking round.

Very soon the beaters moved off and Jasper sidled back to rejoin Toby.

'Come with me,' he said. 'There are some things I wish you to see.'

'But shouldn't we be with the beaters?'

Jasper gave him a long and meaningful stare. 'You must surely have worked out that I didn't bring you here to hunt pheasants, Toby. No, the arrangements for the shoot are all in hand; Archie, my assistant, will see to that. They're off to begin the first draw, and we'll be able to see the "fun" if we get into position. Now come on, we'll slip away while they're busy.'

So the two of them moved off, apparently following the other beaters, before passing out of the farmyard close to where the most recently arrived trio stood. One, a hard faced villain, spat in Jasper's direction as he passed by, to which Toby's companion merely responded by touching the brim of his cap and proffering a genial smile before walking on.

'What was that for?' asked Toby, a note of disgust in his voice.

'Don't worry, lad, it was just a bully flexing his muscles. But my show of good humour will have been harder for him to take than any insult traded in return.'

Having rounded a sharp bend, they soon detached themselves from the others and made their way up a steep track through dripping undergrowth. At the top a point level with the surrounding treetops was reached, and a view obtained across the roofs of the nearby farm buildings below. Further off Toby could see "Pocket Farm" lying quiet and empty on the rising ground, while on the skyline stood the gaunt outline of "The Great Barn" at Warren Hill. Nearer, and to the left, was a small open pasture field with a spinney on the far side in which several figures were forming up in a widely spaced line next to the nearer hedge.

'The guns,' said Jasper, nodding towards them. 'Archie and the lads have gone off to beat the hedgerows before coming up through the spinney. There are perhaps a hundred pheasants in there some days, so even the lousiest of shots should be able to down at least one bird. They'll flush out a hare or two as well if the draw goes to plan.'

He indicated a straggling line of beaters who, having skirted wide of the distant trees, were now moving into position.

'It won't take them long,' said Jasper. 'But come on, there is a better location for what we have to do.'

Toby followed, and after entering a wood that grew down from the Northampton Road, they suddenly came to a thick hedge bordering a half hidden thatch roofed cottage that nestled into the hillside. Jasper immediately crouched down, and having indicated with a finger to his lips that they should proceed in silence, moved stealthily forward until they had climbed into the undergrowth above.

'What is that place?' asked Toby as they entered a small clearing.

'Be patient, I will tell you soon enough,' replied Jasper. 'But first we must watch – for the sport of these worthy folk is about to begin.'

They had now reached a spot where it was possible to look out over much of the farmland to the west, and once more saw the line of guns waiting for the beaters to do their work in the pasture field below. Immediately before them in a dip ran the lane leading up from the farm; the exit from this onto the Northampton Road being above and to their left. The roof and chimney of the cottage was no more than a stone's throw away, the front garden and gate offering onto the lane, clearly visible.

Their position, Toby now realised, had the double advantage of enabling them to see without revealing their position, for by stepping back among the foliage they could remain unnoticed by passers-by, while observing everything below.

The rain began to ease and the sky lightened. Then, within the space of a few minutes, a fresh wind sprang up as a watery sun appeared through the thinning clouds, bringing a hint of warmth. By now Toby had become aware of various sounds around him: a number of rooks were cawing and circling on the fluctuating air currents over the wood behind, a dog barked in the farmyard, and an occasional car could be heard passing on the main road. But there were other, more repetitive and persistent noises coming and going upon the air – the voices of men and boys calling, and the cracking of sticks.

As he waited, Toby looked below him to where the guns were positioned and picked out five or six motionless figures virtually blending into their surroundings. Then a wave of full sunshine peeled across the field bathing everything in a yellow sheen, bringing the dead grasses and yellowing hedgerows to life. For a few moments Toby gazed upon a perfect idyll – an image of the English landscape that Constable might have sought out and captured on canvas. The transformation from a dreary autumn day could not have been more complete or charming. Even the silent guns, their weapons primed and ready, cast graceful slanting shadows where caught by the low sun. But this sylvan calm was not to last; for just then the first of the beaters' quarry flew up – a blue pheasant, dark against the sky – and the clouds, as if to blot out the softening light, closed once more overhead.

Within moments ten more of the heavy birds took to the air, then another ten, each clattering heavily upwards with raucous calls as the line of beaters emerged from the spinney and began advancing across the open field. The first gunshots punctuated the clamour – successive reports echoing and re-echoing around the tree fringed bowl. Some buckshot was aimed wildly and harmlessly into the air; but other blasts found their mark. The leading pheasant tumbled from the sky, turning as it fell, its long graceful tail feathers curling upwards. Then another was caught in the wing, a cloud of downy fragments ripped away, sending it wheeling off its intended course and spiralling to destruction in a nearby hedge. Six more were similarly brought down; while three others, maimed and torn, slanted off to die later from their wounds.

But the carnage was not yet over, for a startled and terrified hare had also broken cover. Having turned in terror to find its retreat barred by the line of arm waving beaters, it now began to dart backwards and forwards before the guns, searching for an avenue of escape. Every sinew of its body seemed curved forward in flight as it crouched low over the ground, desperate to reach safety. Toby was captured by this brief display of grace and beauty – the last seconds of a doomed masterpiece of nature – before a loud shout went up telling the beaters to remain still. Then a single gun stepped forward – discharging both barrels at close range as the hare sped by. It reared up, ripped by lead shot tearing through fur, fine tissue and bone, before sprawling forward twitching but lifeless upon the wet grass, one hind leg severed. Whoops of celebration went up from round about, congratulating the gun upon the accuracy of his shot, before the sport of the day continued. An additional three rabbits, together with a brace of partridge, were then likewise flushed from the relative safety of the field margins and hedgerows, all being gleefully dispatched during an ensuing minute of bloodlust and mayhem. Only when the last target had escaped, winged and bleeding, beyond a line of beech trees, did the gunfire cease and a semblance of calm return.

'That's one draw completed,' said Jasper who, like Toby, had watched the proceedings in silence. 'Now we'll have to wait half an hour or so before the beaters are in position again.'

'Where will they go next?' asked Toby.

'They're due to beat "Gibbet Wood" – the one we're in. They'll go round the far side and come back through, leaving the guns to stay where they are.'

'But won't we have to move?'

'Not if we stay put,' said Jasper casually. 'Don't worry, we won't come to any harm – the guns always fire high into the tree line when a wood is being drawn. Even they wouldn't want to go shootin' their own beaters. But in the meantime there's something I want to show you, so follow me.'

With this he turned upon his heels and moved off through the wood towards higher ground behind and they both pushed through undergrowth and fallen branches for a minute or so before coming to an opening in the trees close to the main road. Piles of sawn wood were heaped up around the clearing and three wooden barrels with rusty iron straps stood close by. Yet it was not these things that caught Toby's eye, for a more riveting and macabre sight now confronted him. A hurdle, similar in size and structure to a five-barred gate, had been erected on the right hand side, from which, each dangling by the neck, hung an array of dead and rotting creatures, many desiccated by the sun. There were dozens of crows, rooks and magpies, three sparrowhawks and a clutch of jays – some of these, the more recently killed, still with bright blue wing feathers and delicate heads. Other creatures were little more than skeletons, their sightless skulls turned upwards toward the empty sky. Four legged residents hung there too: ragged squirrels, stoats, weasels and a line of rats, their stiffened tails dangling limply toward the woodland floor. As Toby watched, a waft of air would occasionally turn them, sometimes individually or in strangely animated groups, so that each performed its own bobbing dance of death.

He moved forward – drawn by the silent obscenity before him.

'Why is this here?' he asked.

Jasper came and stood beside him. 'It is supposedly a gamekeeper's trick,' he said, his head tilted to one side, 'to frighten off predators that might steal his lordship's pheasants.'

'So, you did it?' said Toby, turning towards him.

'Oh no, not me – that's not my lark. If a creature's dead it should be buried and put out of sight, that's my opinion. No, I'd say the people that produce this kind of handiwork have an altogether different temperament to mine.'

'Then you didn't kill these animals?'

Jasper shook his head. '...You don't fully appreciate why I'm here, do you, Toby?' he said with a slight frown. 'You're my business in these parts. The gamekeeper thing is just a useful cover. Personally I've no great interest in pheasants at all.'

'But... who would do such a thing?' asked Toby, again turning to the frame.

'It's mainly the work of the Towsers; those two you met today... and a friend of theirs who lives in the cottage you saw. His name's Finch – Declan Finch – a stranger in these parts, from the city.'

'I've heard of him,' said Toby. 'Does he work for the Towsers?'

'No, at least not in any way you might expect. You see, Mr. Finch has a rather dark secret and it suits him well to remain hidden as much as possible. Now, as of this moment it's time we departed from here as the beaters will be coming through before long.'

Jasper moved away once more and they quickly returned to their former position just above the farm track. The sky was clearing from the west and the weather had improved considerably. Toby also noted that a thin column of wood smoke now spiralled from the stone chimney of the cottage.

'It would seem that Declan is at home,' Jasper indicated wryly. 'He likes a little comfort.'

'Tell me more about him,' said Toby. 'Where does he come from?'

Jasper scratched his chin. 'He's from London originally, but has been here for some time – just turned up about eight or ten years back. At first he seemed to come and go, but then set up in permanent residence and has stayed around ever since. Cregan and Barnaby took to him, that's for certain, and although their parents complained, Matthew and Abigail weren't allowed to have any real say in the matter. This old cottage was just a ruin then; but the brothers had it refurbished, and he lives there rent free as far as I know.'

'Why would they allow that?' asked Toby.

'Dodgy deals, Toby. You wouldn't call Cregan or Barnaby the most honest people in the world. No, they like to make money on the side, since a little dishonesty spices up their lives. It seems they knew Declan Finch before he came to these parts – that they arranged activities he and his friends were involved in: hunting exploits, dog fights and other lucrative clandestine gatherings. It was only a natural progression therefore when things began to happen here – secret meetings, contests in the night – you name it. Finch and other unsavoury characters would come up from London to gamble on the results, and any incriminating evidence could easily be disposed of round about. It may not have been much at first, but in time a lot of money changed hands, and the Towsers were drawn in deeper. ...You see, Toby, it's best not to cross the men they're in with, because it can cost you too much. And that Declan Finch is one of the worst – a cunning and manipulative schemer. There are thugs who carry out ill deeds; and those, all too often much worse, that plan them and take the rewards. You might not imagine it to look at him, but Finch is a villain and he'll stop at nothing.'

'But why does he operate from here?' asked Toby. 'Surely he would prefer to run his enterprise from London.'

'That's what you'd expect; but living in the capital is too much of a risk for him these days. He's on the run you see... for murder. It seems that he cold-bloodedly killed a shopkeeper who was unable to pay protection money. ...Yet this little gangland execution didn't quite go to plan, for he was recognised while getting away. Ah, but our Declan is one of those clever, evil little worms who are past masters at avoiding detection by vanishing from the place of their crimes. He already knew of "Deep Spinney Farm" and decided to come here to conceal his notoriety in the depths of the countryside. So Bedfordshire has inherited one of London's maggots, a feral criminal from its dark underbelly. Life throws up any number of warped characters, Toby – and they may move among us unrecognised even in the most pleasant places. Meanwhile, by settling here, with Cregan and Barnaby, Declan Finch found fertile ground for his deeds – simply poisoning an already polluted well.

'Yet the criminal fraternity don't always have it all their own way and his plan has begun to unravel. You see, although the murder case became dormant for some time – him having melted away from his old haunts – the long arm of the law continued to grind slowly away in the pursuit of its quarry and was eventually drawn to this neck of the woods. Some of his associates were known to be visiting these parts, and Scotland Yard became interested again. Quiet surveillance was carried out and a pattern began to emerge, with the result that the net is now closing in on the lot of them. However, although his associates are certainly of interest to the police, you can be sure that Declan Finch would be the real prize... And who knows,' said Jasper turning with a crafty smile, 'this very day the beaters may unwittingly help to flush out a bigger quarry than they expect.'

'And... what would happen to him if he was caught?' asked Toby tentatively.

'What do you think?' replied Jasper. 'This is 1931 and Finch took another man's life in cold blood.'

* * *

They were now interrupted by the sound of voices calling in the woods behind, and settling back into the undergrowth, waited for the beaters to pass through. There was not long to wait, for barely two minutes had elapsed before a chorus of whoops, accompanied by the cracking sounds of flailing sticks, signalled their approach. Then the padding of clawed feet could be heard to both right and left, and as Toby watched, a number of pheasants, agitated by the clamour, scuttled by. The first of these flew up just moments later, and as if at a signal, several more followed, clattering loudly through the branches as they took to the air and broke through the canopy above. A cacophony of shots rang out, startling other birds that likewise lifted skyward; four or five almost immediately dropped back to earth, one falling just the other side of the farm track.

It was at this moment that Toby realised they were not alone in observing these events. A man had appeared in the front garden of the cottage and was looking up to watch the proceedings with an expression of delight upon his face. Jasper had seen him too, and eased Toby back into the deeper shelter behind them with his right hand. He was just in time, for at that moment Declan Finch turned to look back through the wood, briefly gazing in their direction. His enjoyment of the entertainment did not change, however, and it was clear he'd not noticed them. But in those few moments Toby had a clear view of a face, both long and pale, the mouth thin lipped. Wisps of short bodiless flaxen hair straggled across Finch's narrow forehead… yet it was the fugitive's eyes that most caught his attention – for they were cold, lifeless and empty.

After less than a minute the gunfire ceased and, evidently satisfied that the sport was over for a while, Finch disappeared back into the house. He had not been gone a minute, however, when Toby noticed a car pull up next to the beech trees at the head of the lane. Two men got out, and having briefly surveyed the scene in the field below, came on down the lane towards the cottage. They were both well-dressed, one with shining cuff links and buckled shoes, and judging from their attire, neither was evidently there for the shoot. Indeed, something in their brisk, furtive movements suggested a more pressing engagement. Soon they neared the cottage gate, took a final look around, and proceeded up the path to the front door. This was opened from the inside before they reached it, and following a short exchange of words on the doorstep, they disappeared inside.

'That will be some of our friend's London associates – down on business,' Jasper intimated meaningfully. 'But today they might not be alone…'

Toby wondered what he meant by this, and was further mystified when Jasper suggested they stay on in their current position for a while longer. Another ten minutes elapsed, and with the cold taking hold of his limbs Toby was about to suggest they might safely move on, when a second black car pulled slowly off the Northampton road and slid up behind the first. Soon after a third arrived and the unmistakable figures of a number of policemen began to emerge, before moving cautiously forward to examine the other vehicle. The owner had apparently left it unlocked and a search of the contents was made. This did not take long, and following a short discussion the officer in charge ordered some of his men to move round into the wood. Then, after a further wait of perhaps two minutes, he and three others began to approach along the lane. Toby and Jasper remained motionless as the policemen moved past their hiding place, before stopping just short of the cottage. Three of them were armed and took up positions where they could cover the front door. Then, alone, the leading officer stepped out to open the front gate. He had not gone two paces, however, when the sound of agitated voices was heard from inside and a door at the rear of the cottage burst open.

Toby did not see everything that happened next, but was aware of enough to realise that the three men inside had attempted to make their escape. One had immediately been wrestled to the ground by a constable who appeared from behind the garden hedge, while another, doubling back round the side of the house, tripped and fell heavily over a low wall to be overpowered in the front garden. These were the two they had seen enter, but Declan Finch avoided capture. Whether it was that he knew the terrain better, or was simply more nimble than the others, having evaded the groping arms of an officer waiting by the back door, he managed to vault a nearby wall before emerging once more, thirty yards further off, and disappearing from sight in the direction of "Deep Spinney Farm".

The ensuing minutes were a time of confusion. Several officers belatedly gave chase, while others emerged from the trees and proceeded to search the cottage. Additional police cars also arrived, and after a short period of consultation the two captured felons, together with the sly one and his associates found hiding nearby, were escorted to these. Finally the vehicles proceeded down the lane towards the farmyard, followed by the remaining officers on foot, and Toby and Jasper, having remained unnoticed were able to unobtrusively step in at the tail of the party as it descended toward 'Deep Spinney Farm'.

The scene there was one of bustle and uproar. Several dogs were barked loudly, while orders and instructions were being shouted from every quarter. Basil Tyler remonstrated angrily with the police inspector, and old Mr and Mrs Towser stood by the door of their farmhouse, the latter weeping. The rest of the Towser family were nowhere to be seen.

Toby soon ascertained what had happened. Finch had run into the farmyard just as the beaters and guns were about to move off to a new position. Having initially gazed wildly around, he'd rushed into the house, knocking Abigail Towser over in the process. There he came upon her daughter, Queenie, whom he dragged towards the door as a hostage. As he emerged, Cregan and Barnaby attempted to intervene, but having produced a knife, Declan Finch flourished this towards them before holding it to Queenie's throat. Forced to hold off, the two men stood aside to let him pass, and Finch made his escape with the girl along the track leading to "Maxton Tower", the two brothers following close behind.

'Why would he take Queenie?' Toby asked.

'Insurance… In her ignorance poor Queenie had been sweet on him – and this is her reward!'

'Sweet on him…?'

Jasper thrust his hands in his pockets. 'Just think about it for a moment. Having spent all her life in this dreary place, Queenie hasn't had the opportunity to gain much experience of other people. Instead she has developed into one of those unfortunate, stunted young women who seem blighted by their surroundings and the company they are forced to keep. Any ambition she may have had to get away disappeared long ago and she just came to accept what was offered here. Therefore, when Declan Finch appeared

– someone from the world outside who seemed both successful and dangerous – she was bowled over from the start, as if a film star had walked into her world. Of course this suited him just fine, because he could have what he wanted from her and she was too blind to ask questions. Now he has taken her for his own protection and she is in real danger, for above all else, Finch is evil and won't hold back from using whatever force is necessary to save his skin.'

* * *

Decisions were quickly made, and together with many others, Toby and Jasper joined the pursuit. Having passed between the outer buildings of the farm, they proceeded quickly along a deeply rutted track before tunnelling steeply uphill through an untidy avenue of overhanging trees. Emerging at the top, Toby found himself but a short distance from the deserted farm where he had slept, and to the north, across the open field, saw the familiar outline of "Maxton Tower". Several officers and sportsmen carrying guns were fanning out on either side of this; while two figures stood beside the base looking up. With Jasper, Toby made his way forward, and as they approached began to make out what was happening.

Declan Finch was crouching in one of the embrasures shaking his fist at Cregan and Barnaby Towser. It was clear they must have overtaken him, and that in fear of losing his hostage he'd sought refuge above. There had been a fierce scuffle, and as he came beside Cregan, Toby could see a deep gash on the farmer's left arm. The big man was furious and seemed oblivious of the blood dripping from his elbow as he shouted oaths at the cornered offender. For his part Finch was trapped with no means of escape – but like many desperate rogues with their backs to the wall, he now refused to give up.

'Hold off or I'll kill her!' he yelled, his eyes wide with desperation and hatred. 'I've done it before and I'll do it again!'

With these words he bent down, and heaving Queenie into view, held her round the middle with the knife to her neck.

'I swear it, take one step up here and I'll slit her throat. I'll not swing without taking another with me!'

That these were the words of blind despair was clear; but the conviction in their tone suggested that a frontal assault on the villain would be ill-advised. The police inspector wisely ordered his men to fall back a few paces while considering his options, and there was a pause in which indecision held sway on both sides.

It was then that Macken reappeared, scampering across the damp grass from the direction of "Pocket Farm". He seemed disappointed at having been absent from the proceedings so far, and anxious to make up for lost time. Looking up at Declan Finch he apparently summed up the situation in an instant, before trotting forward to the doorway and passing purposefully into the shadows within.

Finch had noticed none of this, and now hauled himself onto the parapet of the tower with Queenie beside him. She appeared to have suffered a blow to the face and hung limply on his arm as he balanced on the stonework.

'Don't nobody try anything – just listen!' he bellowed wildly. 'I want free passage out of here so you can all clear off right away – do you hear? Then send someone back with a car, a quick one mind you, and have it left parked down below with the engine running. When that's done I'll need a guaranteed passage out, or the girl dies! ... And remember, any crafty tricks and she'll be meetin' the Almighty afore I do... got the message?'

A note of cold determination had entered Finch's voice, and for a moment a short silence ensued before Cregan Towser stepped forward to meet his challenge.

'I've felt the edge of your knife, you bastard,' he said coolly. 'But I'll tell you this... if you lay so much as a finger on her, I'll tear your greasy heart out!'

Finch threw his head back and laughed. 'Such words!' he sneered. 'You're no better than I am, Towser. You have a wrongdoer's ways as much as another, so don't come that empty blather with me!'

By now he had lifted himself into a kneeling position, with Queenie's head held to his chest, and swayed out to shake his fist as the Jack Russell's sharp bark suddenly rang out from the battlements. Macken had trotted up the worn steps, scenting each one along the way, and emerging at the summit found the murderer above him, his right leg held back to maintain balance. Seeing this, the little dog leapt up in an instant, sinking his teeth into the exposed ankle so invitingly presented to him. Caught completely unaware, Finch yelped with pain, raising both arms as he did so. This proved a fatal reaction, for in a moment he lost balance, toppling forward – Queenie Towser still on his lap. She fell with him, the two turning together in midair before crashing to the ground twenty-five feet below. Finch landed a split second before his erstwhile hostage; then she, limp and unconscious, fell on top of him, breaking his neck, while suffering a fracture to her own skull.

A groan of dismay rippled among the watchers before the two figures of Meg and Alice Maddox emerged from the back of the gathering. They knelt at either side of Queenie, who had rolled away from Finch's lifeless body, the child's face mirroring her mother's concern. Others also came forward, including Coodie Trindle, who stooped beside the injured woman's head and touched her cheek with a shaking hand.

Looking on it was clear to Toby that, upon approaching a little earlier, the three had not noticed him in his heavy coat and hat, and he might have gone to speak with them had Jasper not advised against this.

'Stay,' said the little man guardedly. 'This is not an appropriate time; just watch.'

So Toby held back as preparations were made to remove Queenie from the scene. But this was not a problem easily solved. The approaches to "Maxton Tower" were bumpy and rutted for some distance, and it was evident that should one of the crude ambulances of the time be called, it would be thrown about on the uneven surface. Yet rain had begun falling again, and massed clouds swelling up from the west suggested a storm was imminent. Therefore, since the fallen woman's condition was very serious, she must be taken inside without delay, and much hasty conversation went on as to how this might be achieved. Eventually a makeshift stretcher was produced and a decision made to carry Queenie down to "Silver Link Cottage" where she could be looked after in the dry while a way of safely removing her to hospital was arranged. Thus, with the help of four volunteer stretcher-bearers, she was gently lifted and carried the short distance to Meg's home.

Meanwhile, the body of Declan Finch lay draped with a policeman's cloak waiting to be recovered, while Barnaby Towser had been escorted to the rear seat of a police car. Cregan remained standing nearby, his bleeding shoulder bound with a strip of bloodstained cloth. Both men were visibly shaken and now appeared small and deflated when compared to the braggarts Toby had encountered earlier.

Soon a police van arrived, and after photographs had been taken, Finch's body was driven off, accompanied by the rest of the law force and their prisoners. The group around the tower also melted away, anxious to be home before the onset of bad weather, until at last, as the rain came on and the light faded, Toby and Jasper were left alone with Basil Tyler, whose agitation and ill humour, which had been evident throughout, now boiled over as he faced them.

'That was your bloody dog, Shotwell!' he said, his voice low and threatening. 'And where were you today during the shoot? I didn't see you more than once! No, and it's not the first time either. I pay you good money to keep my birds safe, but you seem to go off for days on end and leave the place wide open to any poacher that strolls by. It appears to me that if it wasn't for the efforts of others, my woods would be full of vermin and there would be nothing worthwhile to shoot.'

Jasper had relit his pipe and stood before the landlord drawing upon it with slow even breaths. His face was calm, and a contemptuous smile flickered across it. 'Maybe I ain't the world's most enthusiastic gamekeeper, Mr. Tyler,' he drawled in reply. 'But it seems like the worst vermin to inhabit your woods are the ones that take such pride in killing everything that moves.'

Basil Tyler's eyes narrowed. 'Is that so?' he said. 'Well, you can collect your cards from the house. I don't pay people to do nothing... and I don't need lectures from my employees either!'

An expensive yellow limousine had appeared at the entrance to the track leading up from "Deep Spinney Farm" and now bobbed towards them over the rutted soil. It pulled up twenty feet away and Basil Tyler's chauffeur emerged to hold the door. The landowner strode towards it before turning again to deliver a parting shot as he was about to get in. 'And be warned, if I see that damned dog around here again, I'll kill it myself! …Now get off my land and take your friend with you!'

Then he lounged back in his seat and the car moved off before disappearing from sight at the lower edge of the field.

Jasper turned to Toby, grinning mischievously. 'He likes the sound of his own voice, don't he… Mind you, if he knew anything like how little I'd actually done for him, he'd be really upset!'

* * *

During this awkward interlude the sky had become increasingly overcast and the rain steadily grew worse as they made their way towards "Silver Link Cottage" where a light glowed behind the curtained windows. But instead of stopping at the door, Jasper led Toby to the stile beside the railway line. Here they paused in the shelter of overhanging trees and watched as Meg appeared in the doorway, a bucket in hand, before hurrying to collect water from the well. On her return she stood in the porch for a moment, her eyes briefly settling in their direction. She must have noticed them because she put her head on one side as if wondering why they were there. Seeing this, Toby took a step forward and Meg half raised her hand as if in recognition. He was on the very point of speaking, and would have done so had not Alice Maddox emerged at the same moment to stand beside her mother. The young woman followed Meg's gaze, then bent to whisper in her ear; and without further hesitation Meg disappeared from view, leaving Alice alone, shielding her eyes against the falling rain. She too did not wait long, however, before stepping back through the cottage door beyond the circle of light.

'Alice is a fine girl,' said Jasper, as they turned away. 'Always self-reliant and unafraid.'

'So like her mother,' replied Toby, thoughtfully.

'That is doubtless true, but it is now certain they must soon go their separate ways.'

'But Alice is still young.'

'For her it is youth itself that will provide the spur to leave… Be assured, she will not stay.'

Night drew on apace, dark hollows filling with shadow. Toby reluctantly allowed himself to be led away and they came at last to the field where the deserted mill stood. It had not fared well with the passage of time, becoming even more ruined. One of the four sails had been taken down, and the skeletons of those that remained were warped and twisted with age. Some of the wooden cladding on the upper structure had also fallen away, allowing wind and weather to penetrate the ancient workings within.

They walked down to it, rainwater cascading from their hats as a single crow, wet and bedraggled, flew overhead before landing heavily on the roof. It shook the raindrops off its dripping wings and looked beadily down as they approached.

'You'll need somewhere dry for the night, and something to eat,' said Jasper, drawing the roll of greaseproof paper containing the remaining sandwiches from his pocket. 'Take these; they'll be of greater benefit to you than me.'

'I could stay here,' said Toby, peering up disconsolately. 'But the main structure looks too dilapidated.'

'I imagine you're right, but take a gander in there,' suggested Jasper, pointing to the door of a storeroom built into the stone base of the mill. The handle of this squeaked as it turned, and with a firm tug it swung outwards to reveal a low room containing rusty milling tools and a pile of sacks. It smelt musty but was otherwise dry and would provide the shelter he needed.

'You're going again, aren't you?' said Toby, his spirits draining away at the prospect.

'I have to… but we'll meet at other times.'

'…And this will be a long night for me?'

'Perhaps… only time will tell, as they say. So you'd best wrap up warm, and I'll see you when I do.'

'Wait!' said Toby, catching Jasper's shoulder as he turned to leave. 'You cast the dice both times before…'

The little man reached into his pocket with a sideways glance. 'Then we'd best roll it again, hadn't we? …Since you're curious.'

The lid of a water butt stood next to his arm and he cast the dice upon it so that both might see. It clattered over the surface, causing vibration within, and came to rest with four spots uppermost.

'Four,' whispered Toby. 'What more did I hope for?'

'You hoped for an ending, my friend, which is reasonable enough… However, for that I am afraid you must wait until another day.'

So saying he departed – walking away into the gloom as the crow cawed loudly from above.

* * *

Now it seemed there was nothing left for Toby but to make the best of what he had. To this end he drank from the water butt with cupped hands before making a meal of the sandwiches left for him. Then, as night closed in, having kicked the old sacks into the semblance of a bed, he settled to rest. The rain still hammered down outside, while the wind blowing through cracked timbers above set up an eerie chorus of discordant voices. Unable to rest at first his thoughts wandered upon rats and mice; but hearing no sound of any other living thing beyond his own breathing, Toby rightly concluded that he alone was the sole tenant of a mill long picked clean of grain.

Thus reassured, and tired beyond further contemplation, he allowed himself to drop into unconsciousness once more and time passed.

Chapter Nine

Demolition and Change

TOBY KNEW NOTHING OF THE SUCCEEDING MONTHS and years as the old world he had briefly witnessed slipped away. Advances in electrical engineering, aviation and communication began to promise great opportunities for a brighter future: but in Central Europe and beyond evil voices grew daily in power, and once again the newspapers whispered… "War".

* * *

Long since having rolled off his bed of sacks, Toby awoke, lying upon the stone floor, to find his limbs had all but seized up and that his left arm was completely numb. He crawled upright, bumping his head on the low ceiling of the storeroom, and having managed to lever the door open with the toe of a shoe, staggered outside. Cool air caressed his face as he emerged, and in moments the scent of spring blossom began to seep deliciously into the musty corners of his brain.

There was nobody in sight and he spent the following two or three minutes hopping from side to side, slapping his useless limb with his good hand, trying to encourage life back into an aching body. Then at last, as the blood started to flow normally, a prickling sensation ran down to his elbow and he was able to bend it and wiggle his dead fingers. Toby was relieved to feel whole once more, but the accompanying pain and discomfort made him bite his lip in a pantomime of agony. Finally, having eased his thirst at the water butt, he lowered himself onto a patch of damp grass.

Judging from the angle of the sun, it was still early morning: the clear sky promising a fine day ahead. The song of skylarks could be heard rising on the breeze, while many other birds warbled and chattered in nearby hedgerows. In front, the field before him lay newly planted with spring barley, the first shoots spreading a green haze over the soil.

'March or April, I guess,' said Toby to himself, 'but which year?'

Deciding to investigate, he stood up again and began walking across to the footpath that led from "Windmill Halt" to Stavenham, but had only got halfway when a seated figure caught his eye: that of young man perched cross-legged on a tree stump, drawing on a sketchpad.

Toby approached, and as he came within a few paces the artist turned the pad for him to see. Upon it was an accurately drawn landscape with the windmill as its subject.

'I'm afraid you're not in it, since I don't draw people as a rule,' said the other pleasantly. 'I thought I had the place all to myself until I saw you moving about. Harry Clayton's the name... and yours?'

'Toby Freeman,' replied Toby, relaxing for a moment. 'You draw well; have you been sketching long?'

'Since I was a child... I write a little poetry too,' the other added as he began putting his pencils away into a wooden case.

'I admire you for it,' said Toby. 'I wish I had the time and patience.'

'Some things are worth making time for,' said Harry. 'After all, such a beautiful morning as this may not come again.'

There was a homely wisdom in these words and Toby now studied the newcomer more closely. He was dressed in well-worn dungarees, and judging by the appearance of his roughened hands was familiar with hard manual labour. His black wavy hair had been combed back from the forehead in a fashion popularised by film stars of the day, and the brown eyes in his clean-shaven face twinkled when he became animated. Yet, despite his openness, a hint of detachment in the artist's voice suggested a thoughtful and private nature lay beneath this friendly outward demeanour.

'I must be getting back for breakfast, or I'll be late for work,' said Harry, now rising to his feet. 'You look as if you could do with a bite yourself, unless I'm much mistaken... why not join me? I'm certain the wife could rustle up something for us both.'

Toby was about to refuse, but the rumblings of his empty stomach made him think better of it.

'Well, if you're sure she wouldn't mind,' he said hopefully.

'Sarah won't mind a bit. We haven't been here long, and don't get many visitors. We've only been married these last three months.'

Harry Clayton's cottage was situated close by, nestling among trees at the bottom of a yet to be cultivated potato field. It had stood empty for some years previous to the couple's arrival, but there was now considerable evidence of renovation, the roof having been completely re-thatched, although much else remained to be done.

Harry pointed up as they entered the front garden. 'I did all that,' he said proudly. 'Self taught; not bad, eh? But the rest will have to wait until I make some extra money.'

'You could try selling one of your drawings,' suggested Toby as they entered the house.

The other man stopped in his tracks and immediately became serious. 'I might try,' he said, slowly stepping back, 'but I'm not a fool. A man needs to make a proper living,

Toby. He can't draw and dream all the time. I'd love to spend my time sketching; and maybe one day I'd be good at it – but it won't pay the bills just now. I grew up in London, and couldn't wait to leave school when I was fourteen. Trouble is, since then I've had a hell of a job finding work. I trained as an electrician, but was in and out of employment for eight years. Sometimes I hadn't even got enough money for the tram fare home. I tried everything – factory work, driving – I even signed up as a steeplejack once! Yes, I've risked my neck to earn a crust, and lost my job a dozen times. If I'm honest, of course, I'd be delighted to spend my time doing something creative; but you need to make a few quid every week or little else is possible. So now I'm exercising my talents in this neck of the woods, and it would seem that there is plenty for me to do, what with so many farms and businesses going under.'

'What exactly is your craft?' asked Toby.

Here the other spread his arms theatrically. 'Harry Clayton – demolition man – what else?'

'You're a "demolition" man?' said Toby, taken aback. 'Around here... but what is there for you to knock down?'

'You'd be surprised,' said Harry cheerfully. 'I've got half a dozen projects lined up just as soon as I'm finished on my present job at the deserted farm over the hill. That old seventeenth-century tower is next on my list.'

'Would that be "Pocket Farm"?' said Toby, his jaw dropping, 'and "Maxton Tower"?'

'That's right... you know this area then?'

'A little.'

'I'll tell you what, why don't you come up there with me today and earn yourself a few bob? A group of lads are helping me complete work on the farmhouse just now, but I could use an extra pair of hands. I've got a rolling agreement with the landowner, Basil Tyler, who wants everything done as quickly as possible. The money's good, but you can't hang about or he'll give the contract to someone else.'

'Thanks,' said Toby, thinking about what he would find, '...I'd like to.'

* * *

As they went inside he was introduced to Sarah Clayton, a fresh-faced young woman of twenty; who prepared them a cooked breakfast while engaging in friendly conversation. He learned from her that the exact date was Thursday, 12th April 1936 – meaning that his most recent rest had bridged another four and a half years. Toby also gleaned that the most significant change to happen locally in that time was that Basil Tyler had begun to clear much of his land to make it more efficient for mechanised agriculture. Redundant buildings were being knocked down, tenancies terminated, and fields previously used for grazing ploughed up.

The two men left for work at seven thirty, Sarah having provided Toby with a change of clothes, with the promise that she would wash his own. However, he was careful to transfer his watch and mobile before leaving, while keeping the fleece on under his working jacket. In five minutes they had reached the railway crossing and were soon cutting down the track that skirted "Warren Hill Farm".

'That's my next but one job,' said Harry pointing up at the dilapidated barn towering above them. 'Before it collapses on someone and kills them!'

'You're going to knock "The Great Barn" down too?' said Toby, unable to conceal his surprise.

'Aye, and most of the other buildings as well.'

'But don't the Trindles still work the farm?' Toby asked, a note of dismay in his voice.

'Not any more they don't,' said Harry, turning to look at him quizzically. 'Henry Trindle gave up the tenancy at the end of March.'

Toby was stunned into silence and they walked on without speaking until reaching the outer yard where what was left of "Pocket Farm" could be seen. Even from a distance the change was stark. The trees and outbuildings around the farm had been cleared, and all that remained was the broken shell of the farmhouse. Already, some of the other men had begun work. One was on the gutted roof rhythmically swinging a mallet, knocking bricks from the chimney stack, each blow sending a puff of mortar dust skywards to be carried away on the breeze. It was evident that by the end of the day little of what had been Rose and Albert Smallwoods' home for more than fifty years would remain. Meanwhile, in an adjacent field a shiny blue tractor, followed by a cluster of wheeling seagulls, roared into sight up the rising ground drawing a heavy cultivator over newly ploughed soil.

As if drawn forward by the activity, the two increased their pace, soon reaching the ruined farm. Heaps of bricks and piles of wood lay around in various places and it was evident that systematic methods were being used. Much of the recovered material would be sold or carried off, in time-honoured tradition, to be reused or burned locally, while anything without value would be buried nearby. There had been three ponds in the farmyard and the largest of these, now drained, was serving as a tip for rubbish and shale.

'Sorry I'm late!' Harry called to the men as he approached. 'I got talking with this new lad. He'll be helping us today.'

Without further conversation they too set to work, each labouring with a will at his allotted task, and Toby was greatly impressed by the steady industry of his fellow workers. All were on piecework – being paid by Basil Tyler for the amount of work completed – and every man seemed determined to maximise his wage. The toil went on apace and by mid-morning the whole roof structure of the house, including the chimney stack and beams, was down: a start being made on the body of the building. Two tractor drawn farm carts then arrived to remove timber, piles of stone, roof slates and copper piping, while one of the men started a fire to burn rough wood and other combustible rubbish, which was soon blazing fiercely.

It was around this point that Toby began to register the absence of horses for the first time, not one of which could be seen in any direction. Following the men's progress he also mused to himself upon the capacity of human beings, who were at other times capable of such invention and creativity, to display grim satisfaction in destruction. He paused to watch Harry Clayton lever the front door off its hinges with a crowbar, then thought back just three or four hours to when he had seen him patiently working on a detailed sketch of the old windmill.

Lunchtime, a quickly taken meal of tea and sandwiches, came and went as the day progressed, and later the afternoon sky became increasingly heavy with cloud as if shrouding the last hours of the dying farmhouse. The upstairs windows were knocked out, exposing faded wallpaper and a broken mirror pushed at an angle on a bedroom wall. Then two of the men appeared in the doorway carrying Kate Smallwood's bed, the bedclothes still piled on top, while another carried out the chair Toby had slept in.

'There's a dressing-table and wardrobe with some coats and dresses in,' the latter said. 'Everything seems a bit musty though.'

Harry Clayton approached them and a short inspection ensued.

'The stuff's riddled with woodworm,' said Harry, 'and the clothes will have no value... You might as well burn it all.'

So the whole lot was carried and thrown onto the fire: a jumbled heap of unwanted furniture, clothing and bedding. The heart of the blaze now being intensely hot, within moments flames began to claw up and engulf the dry material. The searing heat did its work in no time, allowing only fragments of charred fabric and wood sparks to be carried off in swirls of grey-white smoke. Watching as he laboured, Toby thought of the loving hands that had arranged those precious things so perfectly years before – the mementos of a life long remembered, now obliterated by nature's most basic element.

By six o'clock their work was done, and all that remained of "Pocket Farm" was piles of bricks and shattered glass.

'That's enough for today,' said Harry, as the men gathered around him. 'We'll be back tomorrow to clear the rest and get on with landscaping the site.'

They dispersed in various directions, leaving Toby and Harry standing beside the dying fire, which still smouldered fitfully as if hopeful of being revived. Now, in the cool of late evening, Toby began to feel a creeping sense of desolation – as if part of his own past had been lost.

'You said earlier that "Maxton Tower" will be demolished... and "The Great Barn" as well?' he asked, turning to Harry.

'That's right: Basil Tyler wants the whole area tidied up. You see down there,' he added, pointing to "Deep Spinney Farm", 'there's a lot of work to be done at that place too. We're removing nearly all the big trees, and those black stables and barns – modernisation, he calls it.'

Toby thought of the Towsers. 'Is that what the people living there want?' he asked.

'I reckon they'll not have had any say in the matter. It seems they fell out of favour with Tyler: that he's distanced himself from them because of some embarrassment in the past. Something about a bit of trouble a few years back.

'Evidently the men were given an eighteen-month prison sentence, during which their parents were all but turned off the property. Apparently the only thing that stopped it happening was that the landlord took pity on them because they had to care for their crippled daughter, Queenie. So since Cregan and Barnaby Towser returned home they've had to toe the line; and if Basil Tyler says modernise, they're not in a position to object.'

'And what of "Warren Hill Farm"? Will any of that be improved?'

'No, as I told you, most of it's coming down; although we'll probably leave the empty farmhouse for now.'

'Empty?' said Toby, turning towards him with a sense of shock. 'But what about the Trindle family – what will they do?'

'There's only two of them there now: old Henry and his son Wesley. The daughter, Scarlet, she moved away last year; got married to a farmer up near Rushden, and old Coodie Trindle's been dead these last three years.'

'Dead...'

'Passed on in '33... worn out, according to Henry – though some say she never got over the loss of her youngest son in The Great War.'

'So Henry has to go too?'

'You might say that, but he never could make much of "Warren Hill Farm" after Mark was killed: always struggled to earn a penny, too easygoing. But he's past it now too – hasn't got the heart any more. So he's leaving to live with his cousin down at Flitton. The land he rented is being taken over by the Braylings at "High Dyke Farm". They'll do all right with it; they're good farmers, not afraid of up-to-date methods! As for big Wesley, he's got a job labouring the other side of Bedford: so by the end of the week the place will be empty and we can move in.'

Toby was stunned that so much had happened so rapidly in his absence.

'Are they there now?' he asked.

'I imagine so. Will you be visiting them?'

'Yes... I think I'll drop in on my way back,' replied Toby thoughtfully. 'To renew old acquaintances... before it's too late.'

'By the way,' said Harry, as he began to move off. 'Where are you staying?'

'At... at "The Drover's Rest".'

'That's good,' Harry called over his shoulder. 'The way you appeared this morning, I thought you must have spent the night in the old mill. Goodbye then, I'll see you back here tomorrow at eight!'

Toby followed Harry's departing figure until he had passed the brooding tower and dropped out of sight over the brow of the hill; then made off himself in the direction of "Warren Hill Farm".

* * *

As he approached he noted again that it was in an advanced state of dilapidation and decay. Apart from "The Great Barn", which had lost part of its roof, several other buildings had become derelict, while all were empty. The outer yard as he entered it had a long neglected air, the dead and twisted vegetation of previous years sticking up through discarded moss covered farm machinery. Meanwhile, the stout post where the bull had previously been tethered held nothing more than a short length of rusty chain.

Moving on he came to the archway and entered the inner yard, to be greeted by the chirruping of a few dusty sparrows. "The Great Barn" loomed before him, and apart from the absence of animals the place appeared much as he remembered it. Then, when Toby was about to walk over to the house, he heard someone whistling in the stable to his right. Coming to the door he could see, with his back to him, an old man of short stature grooming a contented and surprisingly small shire horse. The farmer wore a shabby cloth cap and a pair of ample trousers held up with braces. His shirt was rolled up at the sleeves and as he swept the brush over the horse's flank, Toby could see that he had lost three fingers on his right hand.

'Sam... Sam Milton – it's you, isn't it?' Toby called across.

The old labourer didn't seem to notice at first, but continued his work, simply changing from a previous tune to a warbling rendition of "Colonel Bogey".

'Sam!' Toby repeated in a raised voice. 'It's me, Toby... how are you?'

There was a pause in which Sam creaked upright, his left hand held to his back, before turning to locate the speaker. He squinted through watery eyes before the old, good natured smile spread across his face.

'I know you,' he said with a toothless grin. 'You're that Toby feller... Where you been all these years? It's good to see you, boy!'

Sam was now the picture of age, his face so lined and tanned by the sun and weather that it resembled a shrivelled apple. He was evidently very deaf too, and Toby had to speak up to make himself heard.

'I've come to see you!' he shouted. 'I heard the farm was finished.'

Sam, who had been leaning forward to hear Toby, took a step back and his face dropped. Then he lifted his cap to scratch his bald head as if thinking to himself.

'Aye… that's right,' he said reflectively, 'and soon there won't be anything left. Even our old Cali here has to be found a new home now they tractors have made him redundant. But I don't suppose he'll mind all that much since he's past his proper time – like the rest of us.'

Another deeper voice broke in from behind Toby's shoulder.

'That's right, and I'm thinking of selling you off too, you old devil. But I doubt anyone would pay much!'

Toby turned to see Henry Trindle smiling down at him, Wesley just behind. Both men stepped forward to shake Toby warmly by the hand; like an old friend, even though they had not met for over twenty years. Both had aged considerably, Wesley having lost the majority of his hair, but it was upon Henry that time had most left its mark. Although still outwardly jocular and good-humoured, his former easy manner and sparkle had gone, to be replaced by a quiet reserve that made him seem uncertain and hollowed out.

'Come into the house,' he said. 'I'll get us a bite to eat and make some tea.'

With no further formality, they walked across the yard together and entered the familiar farmhouse kitchen that had once been Coodie's domain. When the others were seated, Henry set to work ladling soup from a saucepan left simmering on the stove, before putting the kettle on to boil. Several packing cases and piles of clothes lined the walls – clear signs of preparation for imminent departure.

'We're off on Saturday,' said Henry in a flat voice. 'We just have to sell the horse tomorrow and then we'll be gone.'

'I heard,' said Toby. 'The men at "Pocket Farm" told me.'

Henry's eyebrows drew together, but his tone remained resigned and matter-of-fact. 'What's been done there will soon happen here, and I don't want to be around when it does… too many memories, see.'

'Would you stay if you could?'

'What… if old Basil Tyler didn't want me out? No, I've had enough of farming. Old Sam and me are fair crocked by it. Anyway, my neighbour Arthur Brayling will doubtless do a good job of looking after the land. And besides, his boys all get on a lot better with these new fangled tractors and machines than I ever could. No, since Coodie went the place has never been the same, so I don't mind leaving.'

'You lost her… three years ago.'

'Three years…' Henry mused to himself. 'Such a lovely kind woman, Toby. Therefore I mustn't be sad, must I, what with the two of us having had so many good times together? …And do you know what?' he added, brightening up. 'She never forgot you, but was always wonderin' what had happened – how you were and all. Many's the time I had to remind her that young men do sometimes just come and go like that… But you can rest assured she always hoped you'd return some day.'

'I wanted to,' said Toby, a sense of guilt seeping through him once more. '…I really wish I'd had the opportunity.'

'Well, whatever, that's all water under the bridge, as they say. But she'd rest happy to think we'd been hospitable now you have shown up. You're welcome to stay with us for a couple of nights if you've nowhere else. The bed's still prepared as before.'

Yet again, Toby was amazed at this plain and generous offer… he, the adopted prodigal son, had come home and was accepted once more without question.

They talked on together as night drew in, but before long, feeling exhausted from his day's work, Toby asked to be excused and departed gratefully to bed. His old room was much as he had left it, except that the small flower vase stood empty upon the window ledge, and having sunk wearily beneath the blankets he soon fell into the oblivion of a deep sleep beyond care.

*　*　*

Waking refreshed the following morning, a sudden and understandable dread came upon him. 'What if another leap of time had occurred… where would he be?' But the sound of someone humming below suggested that only the night hours had elapsed, and having quickly washed and dressed he descended to find Henry finishing his breakfast at the kitchen table.

'What time is it?' asked Toby.

'Twenty to eight: we thought you were never going to appear… Sleep well?'

'Blissfully – never better. I'm really grateful to you for letting me stay.'

'Don't mention it. You can come with us if you like. We're going to sell Cali at Bedford Market.'

'…I can't,' Toby replied hesitantly. 'I've been taken on by the demolition contractor.'

Henry raised his eyebrows. 'Well would you believe that?' he said with a faint smile. 'But we won't hold it against you; a man's got to make a living.'

'You have to sell the horse?' asked Toby, moving the conversation on.

'That's the way it is,' replied Henry, rising from his seat and reaching for his cap. 'Old Cali's been with us ever since we lost Caesar and Cleo nine years ago. It'll be a shame to see him go, since he's the last of the line – but that's progress for you, and there's no use chaffing against it.'

Toby mused for a moment. 'It's the second really unusual name for an animal that I've come across here… Why Cali?'

'Just a family tradition really,' replied Henry. 'You see my father was interested in Roman history and named his horses after Roman emperors and empresses, and the idea stuck. When we bought this scaled down chap we couldn't help admiring his dainty hooves, so we called him Caligula, which means "Little Boots". Of course the real

Caligula was a bit of a madman, according to some, so we shortened his name to Cali to avoid offending the old fellow, and that's what he's been called ever since.'

They now moved out into the farmyard where Wesley and Sam were waiting.

'We'd best be off then,' said Henry. 'Sam will be here if you come back early. As for us, we'll walk the horse down to the market… It'll only take an hour or so.'

They turned to depart and he waved them off before leaving himself for the demolition site, where he found Harry Clayton waiting. The other men were already at work breaking up the foundations of the farmhouse prior to removing what remained of the recovered materials from the site, and by mid-morning the final task of landscaping would begin.

Later, when this time arrived, Harry took Toby to one side.

'Look,' he said, 'we'll be starting on the Tower tomorrow and I need to do some preparation. I'd be glad if you'd come over there now to help out.'

Toby, whose hands were already rough and grazed from the previous day's work, was more than happy to accept the invitation, and they made their way up the hill to "Maxton Tower".

'This is going to take some knocking down,' said Harry as they stopped before it. 'The walls are two foot thick at the base and made largely of stone. The only sensible way to clear the site is to use dynamite, so that's what I intend to do.'

They spent the next half hour going over the building, both judging the best spots for Harry to place his explosive charges, and considering the possible value of any residual stone.

'She'll fall,' said Harry at last, 'but those Stuart engineers certainly knew how to build a powerful structure. I'm not surprised the Parliamentary guns only removed the door.'

Having almost completed their work, they were about to return when Meg approached from the direction of the railway. She was wearing a heavy shawl, pulled close about her neck to keep off the cool wind, and looked older than he remembered – wisps of grey showing in her hair.

'Toby, you're here,' she said, upon recognising him. 'I haven't had the pleasure of your company for such a time… I did think I saw you on the occasion when Queenie fell from the tower, but later put it down to my imagination.'

'I've been away,' he replied, '…on business. But tell me about yourself. Are you well?'

She smiled before looking around. 'Well enough, Toby, but this makes me angry. I don't see why "Maxton Tower" has to be removed. I think Basil Tyler is only doing it to spite me for what happened in the past, rather than for any better reason.'

'Why would he wish to hurt you?' asked Toby. 'Tyler's motives surely only stem from a desire for profit, no more.'

'Perhaps,' she said, with a veiled look. 'But I cannot see how freeing up an acre of land for wheat will do much to make him richer. He knows I love this tower, and many are the times that he has passed this way when I have stood upon the battlements. He is also aware that Mark and I came here – that it is special to me for that reason too. Yet now he decrees that it must be removed without further delay, although it has stood here for centuries.'

'Tomorrow's the chosen day,' said Harry, who had listened to their conversation. 'I never realised that anyone cared about it.'

'I have looked upon "Maxton Tower" from my bedroom window since my earliest days,' replied Meg. 'It is a part of my life.'

Harry turned pensively toward the powerful structure before meeting her gaze once more. 'I could sketch it for you, if you'd like: make a drawing to keep at your fireside. I was meaning to get around to it at some point; but events seem to have overtaken me.'

Meg smiled, some of the care melting from her eyes. 'Yes I'd like that, if you would but draw it from here; for the only other study I possess was taken from the northern side.'

'I'll fetch my pad and pencils then,' said Harry cheerfully. 'I have them down at the other site. Stay here, I can be back in a few minutes.'

With no more ado he jogged off over the field and they watched him descend towards the site of "Pocket Farm" – a spot now gradually coming to resemble nothing more than an area of ploughed earth at the corner of a rough meadow. He returned almost immediately, and seating himself next to the adjacent hedge began his task.

'Why don't you climb to the top?' he called to them. 'I could paint you there – to add some human interest and give an idea of scale!'

So up they went, to enjoy the view from the age-old vantage point for the last time.

'I shall miss it so much,' said Meg, as they stood facing each other. 'For me this is a place like no other. I need somewhere to come... that is special to me.'

'You seem tired,' Toby whispered, noting the signs of weariness around her eyes. 'Are you well?'

'Oh I survive and must not complain. It can get a little lonely out here; but I have my animals and the dog – a different one from when I saw you last: Nancy, another collie. I have visitors too, but miss Coodie a great deal.'

'Does Morwen Hughes still come?' he asked.

'Sometimes... but infrequently now. It seems that we women living alone get out less and less as time goes by.'

'But wasn't she married to George, the crossing keeper? What happened to him?'

'The railway company closed "Windmill Halt" three years ago, Toby – as an economy measure, they said. He was offered a small pension, but chose instead to take another position near Leeds. Morwen always said he was more married to his job than to her. Well, whatever the truth was: off he went. He still sends her money, which makes it possible for her to stay at the keeper's house, but I doubt he's been back more than once since leaving. He did encourage her to go with him at first; but she's happy here and couldn't bring herself to leave the trees and fields... I don't suppose she'll ever pack her bags now.'

'You mentioned other visitors.'

Meg looked up at him, her hand shielding her face. 'I see two young girls almost every day: Millie and Harriette Corrie; twins, from "Chelham Farm" down by the Molliton road,' she confided earnestly, as if seeking his approval. 'Strange little girls they are – wild children. They were roughly brought up by a father who beat them you see – always in trouble and wouldn't go to school. Their mother turned to drink from the worry of it, and there was talk a while ago of them being put in a reformatory. That was about the time when I first came across them. One day I looked out of my window, just after six o'clock on a May morning and saw them looking through the wire at my animals. Two more unkempt and raggle-taggle ten year olds you couldn't hope to meet.

'I went outside and shooed them off at first – thinking they were after eggs, or worse, but saw them creep back and realised they must be hungry. So I encouraged them to come to the porch and offered a bite to eat. They said nothing just then, but finished every scrap – and you could see the gratitude on their faces. I didn't know what to expect from that point, but they turned up again mid-morning the following day (when they should have been at their lessons) and have been coming regularly ever since.

'I've had visits from the police and other well-meaning people to warn me about their thieving, but I've never known anything go missing. Actually, since I've got to know them and taken the time to teach them things, they've both been a great help to me, what with feeding and cleaning out the animals and all. Some of their rough edges seem to have been smoothed off too; because I know for a fact they get in a lot less trouble and manage to attend school most of the time.'

'And what does your daughter, Alice, think of them?'

A shadow passed over Meg's face and she looked away wistfully.

'Alice left the day after her eighteenth birthday last January, Toby. She always said she'd want to go when she was able; and there was no persuading her otherwise when the opportunity came. She moved to Newport Pagnell to work for one of those new radio and communications firms. She writes for a newspaper too, just as you do. Life here always frustrated her, so I hope she's found what she wants. But she's too clever and intense to be really happy and I worry about what will become of her.'

'Does she ever visit?'

'Not once, so far... but she writes regularly; always saying that she's really busy, but will try to get back when things calm down a bit. She's a lot like you, I imagine – often away from her family.'

Toby felt his mind cloud inwardly. How little he had thought of Jenny, Brendan and Sophie in recent days.

* * *

146

They talked on until Harry announced that he had completed the outline of his sketch.

'I'll finish it this evening,' he announced when they descended to meet him. 'Then you shall have it to keep as a memento.'

After this they parted company, leaving Meg, who remained standing by the tower, silhouetted against a pale sky.

Further down, the work of demolition and landscaping at "Pocket Farm" was concluded, and apart from a small pile of timber stacked against a hedge, all else had been removed and dug over. With spring sowing and summer growth it would be little more than a matter of weeks before any remaining evidence of the Smallwoods' home was gone – while in two or three years, someone might pass that way without realising it had ever existed.

* * *

Toby again spent the night at "Warren Hill Farm" before getting up early next morning to help Henry and Wesley load their things onto a small motor lorry that had been hired for the purpose of removal. With it Henry would drive Wesley to his new farm before taking himself on to Flitton. Old Sam had come up to assist and was unable to conceal his low spirits.

'Looks like I'll have to find meself some new drinking partners,' he said. 'That's if anyone will have me.'

'I'll get myself over here as often as possible,' said Henry, slapping him on the back. 'We can't have you moping about all the time, can we?'

'But first things first,' he went on, turning to Toby. 'I don't suppose I'll be returning to the farm very often from now on. I'll visit Coodie down at the church from time to time, of course, but coming here would probably only make me morbid. So listen here, lad,' he said, reaching down into the pocket of his waistcoat. 'As this house is evidently going to stand empty for a while, I propose to leave you the key. The water's still on, and should someone come to turn the electric off there's oil for the old lamps under the sink. Old Basil will probably get shirty if he realises you're here, but until then why not stay on as long as you like... It's only what you know who would have wanted.'

It seemed only polite to accept, and Toby did so gratefully. Then the three men climbed into the lorry and, after exchanging farewells, drove off in a swirl of dust along the track towards Molliton.

It was the last time Toby would see them.

* * *

The farmhouse was strangely silent when he went back inside to collect his things. Although it was Saturday, the men, anxious to earn some overtime money, had agreed to work on the demolition of "Maxton Tower", and having locked the door behind him, Toby made his way through the deserted farmyard to join them. Upon approaching the site he found that a swelling group of onlookers had already begun to gather: several of them youths and small boys eager for a little weekend entertainment. The tower was a well-known landmark and all naturally wanted to be present at its demise.

The subsequent proceedings went slowly, however, as it was necessary to drill a number of holes round the base into which explosives would be placed. A mobile petrol operated pneumatic drill had been hired for the purpose, but it was midday before the work was completed and another hour until the charges were packed into position. A cordon stretching back some fifty-yards was then set up and an announcement made that blasting would commence at two o'clock. In the interval many sat on the drying grass to eat their lunches, while a number of boys began an impromptu game of football. Then, at one thirty, a reporter from the local newspaper drove up and he, with a photographer, took up position to record the event – the scene now somewhat resembling a village fete, lacking only the vendors' stalls and bunting.

Meg had also appeared on the rise above "Silver Link Cottage" and Toby went to sit with her. She seemed anxious, like a child anticipating a visit from an unloved relative; or waiting to enter a dentist's surgery.

As the appointed time drew near, Basil Tyler arrived in a stylish Rover limousine, before striding round the tower in conversation with Harry Clayton.

'This must be a big moment for him,' said Meg, a note of bitterness in her voice. 'I'm sure he won't want anything to upset his plans.'

With preparations complete, those present were at last encouraged to move to the viewing area. Toby, with Meg at his side, joined the assembly, standing only a few paces from the rich landowner. He wore black leather driving gloves and an expensive fawn mohair coat with a brown collar, and looked well pleased with the proceedings. A snaking lead had been run out to the metal detonating device and with everyone clear, a hush fell upon the gathering as Harry knelt to operate the plunger. Then time seemed to stand still as countdown began – only the anguished movement of Meg's hands measuring the final moments of a three hundred year history; a brief calm – rudely shattered moments later as simultaneous explosions split the air.

The onlookers were assailed by the blast and many clutched their ears to protect against the deafening sound; while thousands of startled and terrified birds rose into the sky for miles around. Before them, "Maxton Tower" disappeared in an eruption of dust and flying fragments, more than one of which flew beyond where the watchers were standing. There were shouts and squeals from some of the children, before a chorus of coughing and spluttering broke out as a blinding cloud swept outwards. For an entire ten seconds nothing could be seen around the place where the tower had stood; then the dust gradually began to disperse and the cowering group witnessed the extent of Harry Clayton's handiwork. All that remained was a wide swathe of scattered rubble around a curved pit, into which one defiantly intact section of the tower battlements had rolled before settling at a slanting angle, like a jagged tooth wrenched from a troll's head.

Further cries of amazement arose, then a smattering of applause, for something that would be the talk around dinner tables for many years to come – becoming in time the favourite anecdote of ageing grandparents to their grandchildren. However, few suspected that in his desire to see the tower brought down at one attempt, Basil Tyler had ordered his foreman to use twice the amount of dynamite normally required for such a job. Nor that one youth, a tall acne-faced fellow of fourteen, had avoided death by a matter of inches when a chunk of flying debris skimmed his head. Most simply began to depart shortly afterwards, their ears ringing, and soon only the workmen, Meg, Toby and Basil Tyler remained. Clearly satisfied with the outcome, despite its near fatal consequences, the landowner gave instructions to Harry Clayton regarding the clearing up operation, before walking past the two quiet bystanders to his car. He had ignored his tenant completely since arriving, and did so again, but turning suddenly, Tyler retraced his steps and looked intently at Toby.

'Don't I know you?' he said, his eyes narrowing. 'Yes, I've seen you before – and I don't like your face. You were with that Shotwell fellow, weren't you?'

His tone was arrogant and accusatory; but Toby sensed that behind the bluster lay uncertainty and displeasure at being reminded of a previous embarrassment.

'He's visiting me,' said Meg, intervening, her face set. 'An old friend,' she added.

'Humph! Is that so? Well, you can tell your *friend* to stay off my land and keep to the footpaths in future. From now on these fields are going to be worked to make money and not used as places of recreation by people that turn up when they're not needed. So I should take heed!'

With these words he left them and drove away over the scarp towards "Tyler Hall".

* * *

They watched the Rover disappear into the distance before Harry dismissed the men. Then, having promised to bring the drawing of the tower with him on Monday, he too set off for home, leaving Meg and Toby alone beside the crater.

The site was now theirs to explore and together they moved about looking for familiar objects, before Meg spoke again. 'Are you busy this afternoon, Toby, or could you perhaps spare an hour or so?' she asked a little hesitantly.

'I've nothing on,' he replied.

'Then come back with me and I'll make you something to eat. It would be good to talk again in comfort.'

So they walked back towards "Silver Link Cottage", which, as always, sat quietly in its secluded corner, the flustered geese, still outraged by the earlier explosion, each greeting them with a wary stare.

'I did see you that day, didn't I... by the stile?' Meg ventured pensively as they approached.

Toby nodded.

'I knew it, but I was so busy with other things, and then you'd gone again. Yet now you've returned once more... and don't look a day older. While me, I'm nursing grey hairs and don't know what to think...'

He took her hand in his and squeezed it. 'I barely know what I'm doing myself,' he said, looking into her eyes.

Meg smiled, and some of the strain and care upon her face melted away – like a veil drawn back to reveal something of her former youthfulness.

* * *

They reached the cottage entrance and she led the way inside, offering him a seat in the recess by the door while putting the kettle on for tea. A young border collie lying curled up before the stove looked up as they entered, then contentedly settled again, watching them, its head resting upon its paws.

'This is Nancy,' said Meg, reaching down to scratch the dog's head affectionately. 'I lost Pip not long ago; so it's she that keeps me company now.'

They went on to talk light-heartedly about a number of things; but as she sat in her armchair facing him, Toby noticed that more than once Meg's eyes moved towards the window to gaze upon the distant spot where "Maxton Tower" had been.

Thus evening drew on, and Toby had reluctantly begun to think about taking his leave, when scuffling noises were heard and the voices of children approaching from the direction of the stile. Then, suddenly two young girls pushed through the door together and began gabbling to Meg about the Tower, their backs toward him. For several seconds neither noticed Toby and he was able to watch them unobserved. They were evidently twins, but nonetheless very different individually. Both were grubby faced and unkempt; one, the taller and stockier of the two, with an untidy mop of shoulder length straw-coloured hair tied in two bunches behind her ears. She had on a shabby dress and a venerable knitted cardigan, and wore heavy ill-fitting laced boots, clearly handed down many times. The other had straight black locks that shone as if newly washed, although these had clearly not seen a comb that day. She also wore a dress, much patched and stained, that was gathered in at the waist by a piece of rough farm twine. A threadbare shawl covered her shoulders and she wore a clumsy pair of down-at-heel shoes that would have offered little protection from either sharp stones or water.

'The Tower's gone!' exclaimed the fair-haired one, who seemed naturally to take the lead. 'What have they done to it?'

There was an almost theatrical note of indignation in her voice, which the smaller girl matched with vigorous nods of her head before speaking herself.

'They shouldn't… orta done that… cos you liked it so much!' she stammered.

Then a short silence ensued in which both girls seemed to become aware of Toby's presence at the same time. They stiffened, the taller one clenching her fists, before both turned in his direction, simultaneously shrinking back. The two then crouched, looking up, one on either side of Meg's knees, their expressions showing shock and surprise. The smaller girl's bottom lip began to tremble; while the other, now overcoming her initial surprise, began to eye Toby with a sharply defiant look; such that he felt at any moment she might fly at him or make her escape through the doorway. Neither was a pretty child: but their faces were full of personality and character, with strong expressive features upon which their emotions could be easily read. They were clearly untutored in their ways and manners, the bigger one betraying an especially fierce resentment of Toby's presence.

'What's *he* doing here?' she blurted out. 'Nobody told him to come!'

'Hush, Millie,' said Meg in a calming voice. 'I invited him.'

'Well, we want him to go – don't we, Harriette?' the girl intoned as she turned to face her sister, who again nodded vigorously.

'I can't do that,' said Meg softly. 'Toby is my guest… he's a friend – like you and Harriette are to me. I mustn't just send him away as that would be impolite.'

The two girls looked doubtfully at Meg as if trying to grasp the concept of politeness for the first time.

'I will introduce you,' she went on slowly, as if tutoring them in the etiquette of social meetings. 'Then you must say "Hello". Will you do that?'

The girls exchanged glances with each other uncertainly before looking towards Toby once more. Some of the initial apprehension had gone from their faces; but this seemed to have been replaced by disbelief that Meg should ask that they have anything to do with him.

'Why?' said the fair-haired one, her top lip raised, as if dismissive of the idea.

'Because I'd like you to – for me,' replied Meg patiently.

'Alright,' said the girl shifting her weight and finally accepting the inevitability of fulfilling an act that she still clearly considered unnecessary. 'But then we want to go and feed the chickens, don't we, Harriette?'

Her sister nodded again and it was evident that the tension had subsided – that they were prepared to accept Toby for the time being.

Seizing the moment, Meg leaned forward, placing a hand on the bigger girl's shoulder.

'Toby, this is Millie Corrie,' she said brightly. 'And here,' she added, looking down at the smaller girl with a smile, 'is little Harriette, her twin sister. They would both like to welcome you!'

There was an awkward pause in which Meg, with fingers crossed, nodded further encouragement.

'Hello,' said Harriette at last, ducking her head and looking shyly toward Toby.

Watching her sister's performance, Millie puffed out her cheeks somewhat disapprovingly. 'Lo,' she piped.

* * *

After this rather awkward introduction the two disappeared outside with Meg, leaving Toby to watch through the open window as the girls moved among the animals carrying out a number of tasks. Soon Meg returned, leaving them happily at work, although once or twice the older girl did look in the direction of the cottage, as if wondering about Toby.

'I've told them to finish up and go home when they are done,' said Meg. 'They can seem a bit rude and odd, I know, but there are reasons for that...

'Now, we could go for a little walk to the village if you've got time. I don't often get out, and it's a pleasant evening.'

* * *

The sun was already sinking towards the western skyline as they prepared to leave. Meg put a shawl around her shoulders and took up a small wicker basket; but Toby noted that she made no move to secure the door.

'Aren't you going to lock up?' he asked, looking over to where the girls were still tending the goat.

She followed his glance. 'They won't take anything from me, Toby. You see they have come to understand that friendship must be rewarded with honesty and trust, and therefore won't let me down.'

Departing in the direction of Stavenham, Meg and Toby crossed the railway line and made their way down the track on the opposite side towards the deserted windmill. The view was always good from this point, and that evening Toby could see the land sweeping away northwards for several miles.

'Tell me more about the girls,' he said, as they strolled along.

Meg paused before answering. 'They have had a hard life, Toby... knowing things that children ought not to experience. Their father, Frank Corrie, is the kind of man that should never have a family, for he's a drinker and a brute. He could never make a living out of "Chelham Farm" and the family has always been poor. Then one evening, when the girls were still babies, he got into a pub brawl and stabbed a man with a broken bottle, for which he was sentenced to three years in prison. After that his wife, Mavis Corrie, did the best she could without him; but the pressure of running the farm and trying to bring up two children alone got to her, and at some point she found comfort in drink. She'd never made many friends, due to her husband's behaviour, and because of this nobody realised early enough how desperate she actually was. Then, upon his release, Frank Corrie returned to the family home with an even bigger chip on his shoulder, and, if anything, a nastier streak than before. On more than one occasion Mavis was seen with cuts and bruises – but rumours also started to go around that he'd begun abusing the girls. It's the kind of thing that most people don't like to imagine, for the twins were only six years old. They'd had no proper guidance and were now suffering God knows what at home; so it's not surprising they went off the rails and began to go wild. Some folk did try to intervene, but Frank could always talk his way out of answering the most awkward questions, and as a result nothing was done. Millie, the fair-haired one, seems to have fared the worst... but it's strange how the most abused children develop the toughest skins. She's disrespectful and no angel, (the kind of child that has pulled the legs off spiders and tormented frogs more than once), but there is another side to her; when you give her time.'

Meg fell silent, looking up. 'That's what I do: I let the girls come and tend the animals... and talk to them like a proper mother. Their father has now been back inside for more than a year, and Mavis just sits around all day... while I'm always here for them if they need me – with nobody else to care for since Alice moved away. So why shouldn't I give them my time? Perhaps they will get back to normal if I keep trying.'

Resuming their walk, they passed the dilapidated mill and shortly afterwards came to the crossing next to "Windmill Halt". The small station, once so much the pride of George Hughes, was now closed and shut up, the cream and red paint beginning to flake from neglect and decay. The railway was still very much in use, however, and as they watched a passenger train fought its way up the bank towards them. Yet this time, instead of reducing speed as it approached, the busy little engine rattled on amid a cloud of smoke and steam before disappearing round the curve towards Turnham. When it had gone, Morwen Hughes came to stand by her fence and they talked together for a while. The old lady was full of smiles; and although left by herself since her husband had moved away, nevertheless retained her pleasant demeanour, as if happier for being alone.

Their conversation lasted more than half an hour and twilight had already begun to suffuse the western sky when Toby and Meg departed toward Stavenham. A short walk to the village crossroads then brought them outside the "The Three Eels" pub, which stood, as before, with the heavy front door wide open, though now a much quieter establishment. The landlord, Davy Oldfield, still plied his trade within, but his hopes of moving on had long since withered. Now middle-aged and disillusioned, he had lost the will to be innovative and by slow degrees had allowed the heart to go out of his pub. The same few regulars continued to prop up the bar; but the younger folk of the village were no longer encouraged in and therefore chose to frequent the neighbouring "Drover's Rest" instead. Goldie, his wife, her ample bust now even more expansive, would sometimes stand and chide him for his inaction. But her waspish words – having long since eroded the last vestiges of his confidence and ambition – fell on deaf ears.

* * *

Yet Meg had not brought Toby to the spot with the intention of entering for a drink, but moved instead to the newly erected war memorial nearby. The declining rays of a setting sun illuminated the names upon it, and she stood for a moment pensively tracing a fingertip over the engraved letters. There were eight in all, two of which Toby recognised: Elijah Barnes, the blacksmith, and Mark Trindle.

'It's strange to see his name there,' Meg said at last, 'unreal really... impersonal. Coodie was always so proud – but for his life to be recorded in stone just leaves me cold... After all, what good is such a thing when the men whose sacrifices are recorded here are no more?'

Toby could see that having brought him to the place, Meg was now upset and agitated. 'It is a way for others to show respect,' he offered. 'To show their gratitude.'

'Respect? ...Gratitude?' she echoed, her words trailing to a forlorn and bitter edge. 'I for one could live without all such time-honoured sentiments if it was possible to have another hour with Mark... but the trouble is they can't come back – can they? ...But must remain shut off from us, forever... although in my heart I'll always hope to be with him again some day.'

* * *

Meg then walked swiftly on and he followed her into a narrow lane lined with thatched houses. She did not say anything more at first, and they progressed in silence until arriving at a corner where a small shop and post office stood. It was neatly painted, but in the windows the packets, tins and other items for sale – once placed to attract customers – now stood bleached and faded by the sunlight of many passing seasons. They had drawn level when the door opened and a tall man in his late sixties came out turning, as he did so, to lock the door with not one but two sturdy keys. It was the owner, Christian Mandell, and as he straightened up their eyes met. Toby remembered seeing him leaving the train on the first day; though he now looked far more gaunt and wizened than then.

His long face was devoid of warmth, as if a smile had not crept across its hollow features for a decade or more. The shopkeeper glanced dismissively at Toby, but upon noticing Meg, met her eyes with more than a hint of dislike in his own.

'Meg Maddox,' he said dryly. 'I haven't seen you for a good long time. I'm afraid you're too late; I've just closed.'

The tone of his voice amply suggested that he would have made no exception to his established routine had she begged him; but there was too something dark and troubled in the set of his face and furrowed brow.

'You used to work for my daughter when she became Mrs Tyler, didn't you?' he said, his head slightly on one side. 'Then she just went and disappeared out of my life… but why would the girl simply go off and never come back? My Charlotte was all I had in the world after Amy died; and that was that – gone! So what are we to make of it?' he added meaningfully.

Meg, her complexion now a little paler, had taken a step back; but her answer, when it came, was even and precise. 'Perhaps Charlotte didn't like her husband and position very much,' she replied coldly. 'Perhaps she wanted to get completely away – like your wife might have done if she'd had the chance. Have you ever considered that, Christian?'

The shopkeeper visibly bristled; raising a finger and peering down the line of his nose. 'I don't believe my daughter would have left Basil Tyler, no matter how unhappy he made her – she'd been taught too much about the value of money for that,' he replied stonily. 'No, Charlotte had her head screwed on better than some might think. Therefore her disappearance is a mystery that I will ponder until I go to my grave… Blood is thicker than water and the truth may yet come out.'

'Well, I'd say that you'd be wiser to consider the matter at an end,' Meg countered, her voice edged with emotion. 'Moreover, I think that on reflection you might conclude that it would have been better to have taught your daughter to love wealth rather less – and others more. But that was your mistake, Christian… and her loss.

'Therefore, *if Charlotte is dead*… let her rest – while *if she lives,* it is not for you to question her motives. Now, I must bid you "Good Evening".'

Leaving the shopkeeper standing in the lane, Meg turned and walked purposefully away without awaiting a further response, and Toby only caught up with her when she emerged onto the Molliton road. As they descended from there to a small bridge over a brook, he noted that her hands were trembling, and she did not pause until drawing next to the entrance of a quiet pathway leading back to "Silver Link Cottage".

'I must leave you,' she said hurriedly upon reaching it. 'The hour is late and it is right to be getting home.'

'I could make a detour,' he offered.

'That is kind of you, Toby; but it won't be necessary. You have work to do tomorrow… and I would prefer to be by myself for now. But do come another evening.

You mean much to me – and I'm sure the girls won't get such a shock next time,' she added, forcing a smile.

So Meg moved off, her form quickly becoming lost amidst dappled shadows among the trees.

The two would not meet again for many years.

* * *

Greatly perplexed by Meg's change of mood, Toby now trudged slowly up to "Warren Hill Farm" as the full moon came out from behind a dark bank of evening cloud. On past the crossing he went, to arrive at the deserted outer yard as night drew in. Taking the key from his pocket, he let himself into the empty house and began ascending the dim staircase to his room. The boards creaked and there was a coldness about the place that would never have been felt when the stove burned in the kitchen as of old. The family that had lived there through many changing years had gone, taking their lives, loves and hopes with them to leave nothing but quiet corners and stillness behind. Only the soft mattress of the bed offered a welcome – while outside, now flooded with moonlight, the ruin of the "The Great Barn" lay abandoned and silent beneath a canopy of scattered stars.

Chapter 10

"Odette"

ALICE MADDOX LEFT HER MOTHER AND THE place of her birth on 1st January 1936, travelling to Newport Pagnell to find work and develop a career in journalism. She showed great enthusiasm and determination, and was soon taken on by a publisher as reporter for a local newspaper. Yet Alice was not content. Having spent years longing to escape from the rural backwater of North Bedfordshire, she felt limited and frustrated by the parochial nature of local news and craved development in other fields.

She could be fiery and abrasive when challenged; once throwing a typewriter at a sub-editor who had insisted she re-write a piece about a church fete. Because of this there were times when she went weeks and months without employment as her reputation followed her through the newspaper world. But Alice was also noticed for the right reasons too. Her ability to get to the nub of an issue when interviewing politicians and businessmen, along with her linguistic skills, led her to stand out in her field, and she was both respected and feared by many with whom she crossed swords. Alice became fluent in French, German and Spanish, and this, along with her determination and courage, eventually shaped her destiny. By the beginning of the war she had already progressed to become a correspondent for the War Office, and by the end of 1940 had worked through the lower ranks of the Secret Service before being taken on by the code-breaking establishment at Bletchley Park.

There were some that considered her a liability, for she was feisty and outspoken in her views, while her left leaning opinions would win her as many enemies as friends. There were also those that doubted she could act dispassionately under pressure. But they were wrong. Alice proved herself more than once in a crisis: exercising a cool head when others came to doubt their own judgement, while leading her teams with an assured confidence that belied her years.

In the weeks leading up to the Battle of Britain in 1940 she was helping to break German Luftwaffe radio ciphers when she met a young publisher, Tom Cheetham. To some they seemed most unlike one another in character: she intense and outwardly dynamic, he more reserved and cautious. But Alice found him warm and funny, and a mutual love and understanding quickly developed between them. They married in June 1940, and within two months, at the height of the airborne conflict, Alice discovered herself pregnant. She was devastated at first, concealing her condition from all but her closest friends and family, and only once visiting her mother, whom she had not seen for four years, to give her the news.

The baby, a girl, was born on 10th April 1941, and they named her Claire. Alice was back to work almost immediately: becoming one of a team of senior analysts at Bletchley Park with responsibility for intercepting German radio signals and the development of the "Enigma" code-breaking system. Her contribution was of the highest calibre and won recognition from the top echelons of the service. Yet at the height of her success, Alice stepped back from the limelight and asked to be allowed more time with her husband and daughter. A new and more dangerous avenue was opening up before her – the support for vital resistance groups in occupied Europe, and in her naturally thrusting and intense way she hoped to be a part of it.

Many times Alice and Tom Cheetham sat into the night discussing the hazards of the field she seemed determined to move into, and how this would greatly conflict with her role as a wife and mother. But she was never dissuaded, and even her patient husband reluctantly gave his support when all lines of argument had failed. It was to be a fatal decision that would mean she saw very little of her growing daughter from that time onward, while ultimately costing Alice her life.

She became a member of the SOE ("Special Operations Executive") in August 1943 with the code name "Odette", and immediately began training for her new role. Meg received a letter from her ~~mother~~ around the same time; but partly because of the secrecy of her work the two enjoyed little contact thereafter.

* * *

What makes a good secret agent is difficult to define: an organised brain, intelligence and courage undoubtedly; but there is also room for a certain disregard for personal safety, and a definite requirement for inventiveness in critical situations. Alice proved innovative and unpredictable in training, setting a standard of her own that few others could match in terms of originality and flair. One instructor once said of her, only half jokingly, that 'She could talk her way out of any tight situation, hide in the middle of an empty room, or escape from a sealed bag without needing to open it'. He was not far wrong.

Her introduction to the service was, however, long and arduous; with hundreds of hours spent studying codes, maps and secret plans. Therefore it was not before the following spring that she was ready for service in France. The build-up to D-Day had begun, and Alice was to be landed twenty miles behind the Normandy beaches to link up with local resistance groups and undertake vital pre-invasion reconnaissance work. The intelligence gathered by her would be radioed back to England to aid preparations for the offensive. She would also carry coded plans and instructions for sabotage attacks to be carried out when the Allies made their landings, while helping local cells co-ordinate their efforts in the days that followed.

Her training complete, Alice arrived at RAF Tadsfield in Bedfordshire on 9th May 1944 before reporting to the small operations room for final briefing. The evening was warm and sunny, with no likelihood of rain, and a pale three-quarter moon had already begun to rise in the southern sky.

Alice was calm and collected. She wore a finely cut grey jacket with matching skirt, and a neat black hat decorated on one side with a cluster of five small glass beads, each fashioned in the shape of a pink Christmas rose. A white blouse and a neck scarf of soft pink set this off. She had chosen simple black shoes and grey stockings to complement her attire, and carried a black handbag over her shoulder containing her papers, a small quantity of money and other everyday items. With her precise movements and assumed faintly bored demeanour, she would pass as a secretary or office clerk if questioned. In Normandy a position had been created for her at a local corn merchant, and it was hoped that she would be able to move around, as if on business, without drawing attention to herself while gathering up-to-date information about the surrounding area. As Alice waited for departure she also had beside her a small suitcase holding the rest of her belongings.

The briefing took little time, and at nine o'clock, just after sunset, she was led out to a waiting Lysander to begin her journey. The cramped layout of the tiny aircraft, with its high stubby wings, was already familiar to her as she sat down in one of the two passenger seats behind the pilot and navigator. Little was said, apart from a brief exchange of greetings, before taxiing out onto the concrete runway. Tadsfield was a bomber base, and they passed four large Halifax bombers on dispersal pads while moving towards the open expanse of the airfield. At least eight more, camouflaged by hedgerows and earth dykes, could be seen further off in the gathering dusk.

The pilot revved his engines, and when the brakes were released the Lysander bobbed forward, taking to the air and gliding quietly away over the English countryside moments later. At first Alice was able to pick out familiar landmarks: the main LNER railway line and the spire of a church near Sandy, but soon, as height was gained, all became progressively shrouded by darkness. On they flew over towns and villages blacked out to deceive searching eyes, with only the silvery curves of meandering rivers and the mirrored sheen of lakes and reservoirs giving definition to the world below. Then a much larger expanse of pale grey began to spread across the horizon ahead, until the spy plane crossed the Essex coast and turned south over the Straits of Dover.

'This is dangerous airspace,' said the navigator turning to her. 'German night fighters sometimes lurk around here. There are some of our boys too; so we'd best hope nobody finds us and gets trigger happy.'

But they saw nothing else around them as the milky moon illuminated the wide expanse of open sky; before all too soon a darker mass appeared below and to their right. Then, after a few more minutes, the sea was left behind and, bearing eastward once more, they made their way inland over the coast of France. Alice looked down all the while, at first seeing only an unbroken panorama of fields and small woods with little suggestion of human habitation. But as they gradually flew lower, she began to notice vague shapes in the darkness: a chateau beside a lake, a moving freight train, a quiet country railway station and a farmhouse surrounded by tall poplars. Then something garish and unexpected stabbed up at them – a bright light followed by three others set in a row upon a narrow pasture between trees. Within seconds these were gone again, lost in the Stygian gloom, only to reappear as the Lysander circled closer.

Alice had flown many times in daylight, but rubbed the palm of her hands together now as she wondered at the smallness of the landing strip. Again the lights went out, as if turned off by a switch, only to reappear once more through a break in the trees as the final approach was made and the spy plane dropped down to land lightly upon the waiting earth. Almost immediately it turned and taxied to a halt, the door on Alice's side being opened from the outside. Before her stood a man holding a torch, a heavy cap pulled low over his eyes.

'Bonjour, mademoiselle,' he said with a brief smile. 'I am Henri, your guide; please come with me.'

Alice climbed out and was led off towards adjoining bushes as the Lysander moved away for take-off and turned at the other end of the clearing. Then, with engine revving at full power, it moved past them in a flurry of dust and flying grass to rise up and disappear into the enveloping darkness. Within seconds the noise too had died away, and the bright incriminating lights of the makeshift landing strip were extinguished.

'Come,' said the Frenchman, 'we must not remain here. Others will have been alerted by this; and there are many that cannot be trusted.'

They turned to go, making off through the shadows; but just then Alice's hat was snared from her head by a thorn. She turned and groped for it, feeling blindly with her fingers in the damp grass.

'Come on,' said Henri, doubling back. 'You must leave it!'

But in a moment more the thing was there: she touched the soft material, before lifting and returning the hat to her head, smiling with relief.

'We were trained never to leave evidence,' she said. 'Now I am ready – lead on.'

* * *

The next five minutes passed in a whirl as she was whisked by car down narrow tracks and lanes for about two miles, before emerging at a courtyard next to an unlit farmhouse. A small van was parked there, and changing to this they drove off once more, together with two other men, finally stopping on the outskirts of the village of Berigny. There only one other person waited to greet them; a sallow faced farmer, his chin covered with grey stubble, who immediately got behind the wheel and drove away.

'Come, this way,' said Henri. 'It is not much further.'

They moved on again down a cart track between high hedgerows, coming at last to a cluster of cottages – the end of their journey. Inside one of these sat three people: two men and a middle-aged female agent from the resistance cell operating between Cean and Carentan. Together, the two men quizzed her on her mission to judge how this would affect their plans, before leaving her with Henri and the woman.

'I must go now too,' Henri announced. 'But you will stay here with Julienne. She has offered to be your mother during your stay,' he added more warmly. 'I hope you will show her your gratitude and respect, "Odette".'

With that he departed and Alice only saw him once more. She did not sleep before morning, but spent time talking with her host and looking around her new surroundings. Then on the following day she cycled into Berigny with Julienne, and was introduced to the local corn merchant, Gaspard Frey.

'This is your cover,' said the Frenchman stiffly. 'I will take no other part in your mission than providing you with this position. But remember, should you be caught, my life is at pawn with yours. The Germans will show no mercy to those who are captured.'

* * *

So her work proceeded and details were radioed back to England at regular intervals from different locations dotted around the local area. The Nazi authorities were now on high alert as the threat of invasion grew; and with the Normandy coast only twenty miles away her papers were regularly checked in the following week. By the 20th May, Alice was well established in her role and had gained the trust of those around her through diligence and hard work. She had also begun to make regular forays on her bicycle into the surrounding countryside, going in widening sweeps in order to gain a better awareness of the landscape and local roads and railways. That morning, wearing the clothes she had landed in, she set off just after nine o'clock towards the town of Bayeux: ostensibly on an errand for her employer. The day was warm and pleasant, with bright sunshine and little wind.

After cycling through the Foret de Carisy she came to a crossroads, turned off to the right and headed for Balleroy – making a mental note as she did so of the possible importance of the junction. Thus far she had seen no sign of German patrols; but just after crossing an ancient bridge over the River Drome, Alice was passed by a troop lorry preceded by a grey staff car. A little while later she entered the village: where at a junction of two cobbled streets, she found herself approaching a newly erected checkpoint. Several soldiers stood around a wooden barrier examining the papers of passers-by, and a small queue of citizens waiting their turn had formed. The staff car had drawn up beside it and a Gestapo officer sat inside looking through a file upon his knee. He glanced up as Alice arrived, paused to scratch his smoothly shaven chin, then returned to perusing his documents.

Alice had already had her papers checked a number of times before and was used to the procedure. The soldiers involved in the activity were frequently called upon to do so several times every day, and most were normally anxious to complete the formality as quickly as possible. She was confident, therefore, of getting on with her journey without much delay.

The queue moved forward steadily, and Alice made a theatre of reaching into her handbag and applying a little more lipstick as she approached the sergeant in charge. When she was next in line, she turned to see that the Gestapo officer had left his car and was moving over towards the barrier. He was a man in his mid to late thirties, with a lean, handsome face and pale, enquiring blue eyes. His grey overcoat was immaculately brushed and he wore a dark trilby hat.

'Papers?' said the sergeant on duty.

Alice showed these as the Gestapo officer leaned forward to look more closely at her face. She smiled back at him demurely, brushing a lock of hair from her cheek.

'Destination?' the soldier asked, curtly.

'Bayeux,' she replied. 'I have a meeting with the corn chandler there.'

The soldier handed back her papers and moved on to the next in line as she remounted her bicycle... but just then a second person spoke.

'Do enjoy your journey, mademoiselle,' came a voice in a perfect French accent from behind as she began to move off. 'It is such a lovely day to go cycling.'

A little surprised, Alice turned back to see the Gestapo officer looking in her direction as she rode away – a thoughtful expression upon his smooth face.

* * *

The episode had gone off without difficulty, but the Gestapo officer's interest was troubling. Yet no attempt was made to follow her and half an hour later Alice was well away from the scene. She had entered the bocage country, a network of hedgerow lined sunken roads that would be stubbornly defended by the Germans when the Allied invasion came. She cycled lazily through Tilly-sur-Seulles, but instead of turning here towards Bayeux, rode on towards Fontenay in the direction of Cean. The countryside around seemed empty; nothing passed her on the quiet winding road, but as she came round a bend towards another forked T-junction Alice suddenly encountered a second checkpoint.

This time she found herself the sole focus of attention for the three soldiers who turned towards her. They were the group that she had encountered before, and the same Gestapo staff car was parked on a verge nearby. As Alice slid forward from the saddle, its door opened and the grey-coated officer stepped out. He came forward, waving a hand dismissively toward the soldier reaching out to take the papers she offered.

'That will not be necessary,' he said, smiling at her. 'Mademoiselle will be coming with me.'

Alice acted flustered and taken aback, drawing upon her many months of training in subterfuge. 'Why?' she asked, offering up the palms of her hands innocently. 'I am sure there has been a mistake.'

'Oh, I don't think so,' said the officer, signalling to one of the soldiers to take her bicycle. 'No... I think we need to talk. Now, if you will follow me.'

He spoke civilly, but a chill of fear ran through Alice as she faced him. He was so precise and assured in his words and actions that inwardly she could not but be un-nerved by his manner – feeling like a cornered mouse confronted by a sleek and deliberate cat.

They came to the car and he held the door for her as she sat in the back seat, before climbing in beside her. Then one of his men climbed into the driver's seat and they were driven off down the narrow lanes towards Cean.

The journey lasted little more than twenty minutes before, having entered the precincts of the city and driven through a number of narrow streets, they came to a halt outside a large municipal building on one side of a cobbled square. Two soldiers came forward, and after being led through the imposing front door Alice was escorted down a long corridor to a simple room furnished with only a bookcase, two chairs and a large polished wooden desk. The window of this room looked out onto a small inner courtyard and the gaunt, blank wall of the building next door. Alice was offered a hard upright seat on one side of the desk as a female guard, with an expressionless face, stepped in front of the closed door behind her.

The Gestapo officer first went to look out of the window; then, having lit a cigarette, slowly recrossed the room, before casually tossing his hat on the table and sitting opposite.

'My name is Karl Bruck,' he said, after pausing to scrutinize her, a genial expression on his face. 'I expect you would like to convince me that you do not know why you have been brought here.'

He spoke this time without a pronounced accent, in a voice refined and calculating. Alice stared back at him, a feigned look of surprise and exasperation upon her face.

'What... can you mean?' she stammered. 'I am a loyal citizen of the Vichy government – and now I find myself... arrested?'

'Just so, mademoiselle... just so... But I feel we should end the little charade without delay, don't you? Time is so precious; I am sure you will agree.'

'I don't understand... what reason have you for bringing me here and keeping me away from my work?'

The officer raised himself in his chair and deliberately placed his smoking cigarette on the lip of an ashtray, before leaning towards her.

'I know who you are and why you are here,' he said, narrowing his eyes. 'You must not attempt to deceive me... "Odette".'

At the enunciation of her code name, Alice felt as if placed in a spotlight, and he noticed her hesitation.

'You should have taken the direct route to Bayeux today... Then we would perhaps not have met,' he said, smiling benignly, as if admonishing an errant child. 'But not to have taken the shorter road after you left us at Balleroy... that was a bigger mistake!'

'I decided to take a detour to enjoy the fine weather.'

'A reasonable explanation,' Karl Bruck averred, placing the palms of his hands together as he leant back, 'but not one your employer would approve of, I suspect.'

'He would not mind,' she replied in a level voice. 'Today is my half-day... and I had time to see him later.'

'Your *half-day*,' the Gestapo officer repeated with exaggerated expression, 'a very *English* concept, but one rather less used in France than you might expect. And besides, "Odette", I could of course check all these things... But I don't think such steps will be necessary.'

Alice suddenly felt trapped under his questioning but fought within herself to keep up the pretence of her innocence. 'You are mistaken, Herr Bruck,' she said, sitting up primly. 'And when your mistake is appreciated you will blame yourself for the error.'

He again put the cigarette to his lips, studying her through a miasma of smoke. 'You are an actress, I see... but your prevarication begins to offend me.'

'I only say what any other would in their defence... I am frightened because you falsely accuse me... and believe me to be someone else.'

At this point he reached into his pocket and drew out a small familiar glass object, which he held up and rotated between his fingers. It twinkled upon catching the light – a delicate pink ornament in the shape of a flower.

'This was found by me eleven days ago,' he went on, 'at the site where a light aircraft from England dropped its passenger. We know from our loyal sources locally that it was a female agent. When I came upon this,' he added with satisfaction, 'I saw at once that it was from an item of clothing, and decided to keep it in case further clues might materialise. But alas, if I am to tell the truth, today when I first saw you at the crossroads in Balleroy, I had almost forgotten it was in my possession. Yet there was something about you…a little something that nudged the back of my mind… However, whether it was the warmth of the morning, or your pleasant face; I did not come to my senses straight away – for which I am ashamed,' he added, looking up from beneath his eyebrows and smiling once more.

'Then it came to me… the flower! I believe they call them Christmas Roses in England. Yes, this flower was exactly the same as those used so charmingly to decorate your hat… Why don't you check for me?'

Here he reached across, placing the ornament on the table in front of Alice, before stubbing out his cigarette and lounging back in his seat.

She looked down at her lap where she held the hat between her hands, and turned it so that the cut beads faced upwards. There were four where originally five had been; the lower one of the cluster had gone leaving only a short length of thread.

Her inquisitor sat watching her, like a hawk eyeing its prey; now with a cold dispassionate glint in his eye. 'I might have let you escape, had you not been considerate enough to fall into my hands a second time… You are a spy, "Odette", and now must tell me all you know.'

'And if I repeat that I know nothing?' she answered with a note of veiled defiance.

'Then I must warn you of your situation,' he said, nodding slowly. 'This is a place of interrogation, "Odette". Those that co-operate avoid great suffering… but those who do not come to regret their last hours.'

He paused as if considering his options before going on.

'I should remind you as well that I am the absolute arbiter of your fate and that every decision concerning what remains of your life is mine to make… If you tell me all you know it will go easier for you. If not… then,' here he glanced toward the impassive guard, 'then you will suffer.'

'You want me to talk to save my skin… to bargain for my life – to become an informant like the one you say betrayed me?'

'Your *fate* is now inevitable, "Odette". Come, *all* mortals can be tempted to deny the trust of others to avoid personal loss… or pain.'

His assumption of her weakness caused a thread to tighten. Alice looked back unwaveringly.

'Tell me who is worse, Herr Bruck – the one that reveals the identity of an accomplice and condemns them to pain… or he who inflicts suffering in the name of a cruel and callous ideology?'

Kark Bruck's face became more fixed as she spoke, as if she had struck a chord. But he replied in the same deliberate tone.

'Ah, moral issues – so convoluted… so time-consuming. But you really should try to see the position from another point of view. I am not a barbarian, "Odette". Before the war I was a university lecturer in languages, and as such I served the people... Only now, in this time of strife, must I fulfil my duty in another way. I am a hunter of spies; and by doing so serve both my country and my Fuhrer.'

Here Alice met his eyes with growing resolve. 'And is your service to the Nazis supposed to excuse the foul nature of your work? No, evil may wear many false masks and seek to justify itself a thousand times as it destroys what is just and honourable. Yet it remains what it is – a lie, and I will not aid you to save myself.'

The Gestapo officer, his head bowed, stood up and walked to the window before turning back with narrowed eyes.

'I cannot help you if you will not help yourself,' he said with cold finality. 'I hold all the most important cards in this little game of ours and can only invite you to reveal what you know to avoid personal agony. To this contest there can be but one ending. You are a spy – and in time of war spies are shot!'

These words dropped like lead upon her ears, and all that was meaningful in Alice's life filled her mind. She thought of her husband and the small child she had left behind... and more distant still, she thought of her first home among the Bedfordshire fields.

But although Alice despaired, a fierce determination had risen within her: to defy her enemy – to deny him a winning hand!

'We must begin?' said Karl Bruck, with a note of professional assurance in his voice as he returned to his seat and beckoned to the guard. 'Come, "Odette"... be sensible. What can you tell me?'

There was a brief silence in which only the mechanical ticking of the clock could be heard. '...Nothing,' she replied at last – that one word seeming to echo in the corners of the room.

The Gestapo officer froze, the triumph in his face disappearing in a moment.

He nodded. 'That is most regrettable, for now, as time is pressing, you leave me with but one option.'

* * *

Alice Cheetham did not speak voluntarily again, and although tortured constantly and savagely for more than forty-eight hours, she refused to divulge any information. Torn and broken, she was shot at six o'clock on the morning of 23rd May 1944: her secrets dying with her. To her lasting credit none of those she had been with in France suffered as a result of evidence forced from her; while it was not until the war was over that her relatives in England eventually learned of "Odette's" fate.

Chapter Eleven

Firestorm

Harry Clayton, the demolition contractor, followed his chosen career until the end of the 1930s, but was far from happy in his work. Harry was a man of artistic temperament, who would rather create than destroy, and the unceasing routine of tree felling, demolition and clearance offered him little satisfaction. He looked forward to a time when he could make a living doing something more constructive.

Ironically, the coming of war gave him his chance. A need for mechanics, electricians, engineers and construction workers quickly developed, and he was grateful to be taken on at a local aircraft factory as an electrical fitter. Harry progressed rapidly through the ranks and was soon running a section of his own (a small group of men dedicated to the repair and refurbishment of damaged aircraft). This work became essential from 1940 onwards as Britain fought for survival during the "Battle of Britain" and the "Blitz". He might have avoided active service altogether by staying on with the company, but Harry had developed other interests: in radio and electronics, for which he also began to show flair. He was particularly adept when servicing the navigation and reconnaissance equipment being increasingly adopted by the RAF; particularly that used by a new generation of night bombers; and in 1941, almost by default, he began training as a navigator with Bomber Command.

For Harry, the challenge of plotting a course by air was both absorbing and stimulating. He became recognised for his enthusiasm and skill in directing his aircraft towards practice sites and finding concealed locations both by night and day. This seemed a valuable asset, because all strategic places, be they railway stations, bridges or airfields, were now camouflaged from the air, and only an experienced and confident airman could find them. He would study the landscape as he flew over it; matching every recognisable detail with his flight charts and developing an almost encyclopaedic awareness of roads, railway lines and rivers; only matched in scope perhaps, by the street knowledge of a London cabbie. Harry was truly happy for the first time in his life; and content to ignore, for the immediate future, the implications of where his chosen career would lead. There were those that encouraged him to become involved in passing on his skills as an instructor; but Harry was reluctant to part with his new comrades and remained stationed with them. Thus, in 1942, he was posted to an active squadron based in Lincolnshire, flying Short Stirlings. It was to be a rude awakening and one that he would long regret; but the war had now reached its darkest phase and he settled to do his duty.

He and his wife Sarah (who still lived in Stavenham with their two sons, James and Edward) exchanged letters every week. But Harry would tell her little of his work, or of the fear and trauma becoming familiar to him as the bombing war intensified. He also learned that many of his specialist navigation skills were of diminishing value in the new war of the air as, increasingly, large formations of assembled aircraft followed prearranged corridors to their targets. Yet what this tactic might provide in terms of accuracy and the ability to maintain formations at night was negated by the growing ability of German radar and Luftwaffe night fighter squadrons to track and intercept the incoming raiders.

The Stirling was a big and brutish night bomber, capable of carrying a considerable payload, but vulnerable to attack from both air and ground defences. German pilots were soon able to identify its weaknesses and losses began to mount. When Harry flew his first mission, he began with the utmost confidence in the strength and security of the lumbering giant, seemingly so tough and indestructible; but the raid was not a success. The journey to the target was hampered by both poor communications and bad weather. Many of the aircraft were blown off course with few reaching the correct dropping zones, and as a result most simply jettisoned their bombs into the night sky and set course for home. It was then that the German fighters found them – creeping up unnoticed to deliver cannon fire into the unprotected bellies of the returning aircraft. Harry's aircraft was hit by a burst of fire from a fighter that peeled off unseen into a bank of cloud. A hole was punched through the fuselage from bottom to top, the shell removing the top gunner's right leg. Pilot John Timmons fought to regain control of his charge, while Harry struggled to contain a fire that broke out among the electrical equipment.

The situation was critical for about two minutes: each man dreading another pass from the fighter until the blaze was extinguished. But any thoughts for their own safety were soon dramatically eclipsed by another event. A massive ball of fire suddenly erupted among the clouds about a mile ahead and the stricken shape of a burning Stirling, with half of its port wing blown off, curved into view. The aircraft began to disintegrate as they watched it spiral down, casting sparks and flaming debris outwards in its descent. They flew through these remnants, blinded for some moments by the smoking column of ruin, each man craning his neck to maintain a sight of the other aircraft. But in seconds it had gone, lost in the cold air with all on board.

They landed safely to find that two others of their squadron had also been brought down, and that their own gunner, Douglas Hamilton, had died of his wounds. As a result, it was not surprising that having been both numbed and traumatised, Harry began to develop a savage hatred for the foe that had done this to men he had known and trained with. He had lost his naivety about the true cost of war as the brutality and horror of what he'd witnessed sank in. No longer would he see his aircraft as an inspiring manifestation of advances in technology and human ingenuity: from now on he would know it as a place of apprehension and fear – a bringer of death that in an instant could turn into a trap... a burning coffin!

Yet Harry did cope. Like thousands of other airmen in the RAF he put fear to the back of his mind to concentrate upon the present, and for a time his luck held. Nineteen forty-two turned to 1943 and his squadron underwent conversion to a new bomber, the Lancaster; a more sophisticated and better equipped 'heavy' reliably capable of carrying the war to Germany. His tally of missions rose to fifteen, making him one of the senior navigators available to "Bomber Command". But in subtle ways Harry had changed with the passing months. The sights of war were appalling to his sensitive nature, and when home on leave he would talk little about his experiences, sometimes walking with Sarah for an hour without saying a word, only to sit for another quietly sketching as she read a book. His wife longed for him to share his troubled thoughts, but when encouraged to open up he would do little more than dismiss her concerns with a weak joke. Only in drawing and poetry did he find solace; giving expression to his inner-self in rhyme and sketches – although many would remain unfinished or incomplete until the end of his life.

* * *

By the summer of 1943 the air war over Europe intensified. The United States had entered the conflict and its daylight bombers began a grinding offensive with the intention of destroying Germany's manufacturing might. The RAF matched this at night, constantly selecting new targets to sap the strength of the enemy. Huge armadas of bombers, sometimes more than a thousand strong, were assembled over East Anglia before setting off to bomb the industrial heartlands of the enemy.

These destinations varied as new targets were identified, and so it was that in July 1943 it fell to the industrial city of Hamburg to experience the full destructive force of all that could be sent against it. A succession of raids was planned, each closely following the one before, in which the city would be razed to the ground and forty per cent of Germany's submarine production capacity destroyed. A new blocking device, "Window", would be deployed; millions of tinfoil strips cut to half the wavelength of enemy radar, to blind the German tracking scopes, allowing a succession of bombers to blanket Hamburg with thousands of incendiary bombs and high explosives before returning in succeeding days with repeat attacks.

The first raid took place on the night of 24th/25th July, prior to which Hamburg had been enjoying hot, dry weather that left everywhere tinder dry. Added to this a large area of the city consisted of ancient buildings constructed of timber which would be easily ignited to burn out of control. The leading aircraft dropped huge numbers of incendiaries and within minutes hundreds of fires sprang up over a wide area. The city's fire fighting teams went into action to tackle these, but before they could make an impression a second wave of bombers swept over. These were Wellingtons, each carrying a single 2,000-lb parachute mine fused to explode 50 feet above the ground and designed for maximum blast effect that knocked down large buildings and blocked the streets with rubble. Finally another wave had dropped a mix of 8,000-lb, 4,000-lb and delayed action 1,000-lb bombs deliberately intended to collapse large buildings, destroy water and gas mains and trap the fire services in blocked streets. The devastation was incredible and more than 4,000 key personnel in the city's emergency services were killed or seriously injured. To add to the confusion, long delay fuses had been fitted to a high proportion of the bombs, which continued to detonate some hours after the last bombers had departed, frequently erupting to bring buildings crashing down on the rescue workers.

Harry, with the other crew-members of Lancaster "F for Freddy", was assigned to take part in the second wave of attacks, take-off being scheduled for 8pm on the evening of 27th July. The day was warm and sunny with a light breeze. In adjacent fields the harvest had just begun, complete with rattling binders and shirt-sleeved labourers – the perfect English backdrop to the sinister preparations being undertaken on the airfield.

'The city is burning already,' said the Station Commander coolly, as they sat in the briefing for the raid. 'Before you get within forty miles of it you'll see the glow. They're calling it "Operation Gomorrah". Our job is to go back and smother the city again: to carpet Hamburg from end to end with a cocktail of incendiaries and high explosive. We'll simply be there to stoke the fires so they stay hot enough to burn out the last rats of the place – just as the good Lord brought down his wrath upon the ancient city of sin,' he added, raising an eyebrow.

A ripple of laughter ran round the room, but Harry felt unable to add his own voice to this.

'The German radar is out so you'll have less to worry about from fighters,' the Station Commander concluded with a genial smile. 'So good luck to you – and remember, this is our chance to pay them back for London and Coventry.'

By employing the expedient of "blanket bombing", Harry thought; an indiscriminate tool that puts women, children and the old and sick in the front line.

* * *

The crews then rested while their aircraft were bombed up, and Harry wrote a final letter to Sarah before sitting for an hour sketching an old sports car that stood in front of a hayrick by the perimeter track. Then it was time, and the men, having collected their flying gear, climbed into the dark belly of the waiting Lancaster. Pre-flight checks were meticulously run through – for nothing less than maximum power would be required from the four Rolls Royce engines to lift the 8,000-lb bomb load into the sky. When ready, the Merlins were started up, one after the other, each coughing into life with a cloud of grey smoke before settling to an even rhythmic hum. A shudder of vibration coursed through the airframe, like sinews being tightened, then, with throttles advanced, "F for Freddy" moved forward and taxied towards the runway. Other bombers were also coming up: forming a queue of lumbering giants crawling to that point of no return where, with the prayers of each member of their crews and everyone else on the base, they would be hurled ponderously down the runway in an endeavour to overcome the force of gravity before clawing into the evening sky. The crew watched as three other aircraft began their odyssey ahead of them, until at last their own turn arrived. The Lancaster swung round, stopping briefly as it lined up with the central guideline running down the wide ribbon of tarmac. Then, accompanied by a mighty roar, the dark beast lurched forward, shaken to every bolt and rivet, slowly gaining the momentum it would need to break free from the earth.

There is always a point on take-off when the crew or passengers of an aircraft wonder whether the miracle of flight will be achieved – that grip of exhilaration and fear, when destiny is controlled by forces other than our own. So Harry, facing his navigator's instrument panel, calculated the aircraft's steadily rising speed and clenched his damp palms as he thought of the massive bomb held below in the bowels of the aircraft. He seemed to count an age of seconds until the blessed sensation of lift came and they were away, climbing westwards toward the setting sun.

It had been a textbook take-off and soon "F for Freddy" was circling in a wide arc over the Lincolnshire countryside before heading eastwards to the assembly area over The Wash. Other aircraft could be seen at various points – gradually coming together in organised groups stretching from horizon to horizon. But night was falling and darkness soon began to swallow up the more distant formations; leaving only those of their own squadron still visible nearby as they rose up to join the developing bombing order. When all were accounted for Harry, following the direction of the lead aircraft, set a new course and they settled down to begin the journey to Germany as night closed in.

There was high cloud and little moon as the dark expanse of England slipped away below them. The Station Commander had talked confidently about the deployment of "Window" to block the German radar, but Harry could not but help doubting its likely effectiveness, and wondered if the controllers in Denmark and the Netherlands might still have picked up the track of their approach and alerted the air defences of the occupied countries. Whatever the case, their pace was slow and lumbering as they entered hostile airspace without fighter support... At any moment a swarm of vengeful fighters might strike and tear them out of the sky.

Harry worked methodically, checking and re-checking their position against calculations of time and speed. Over Holland they flew, then across the German border – occasional puffs of flak showing that ground defences had sighted them. But the armada passed undamaged, leaving the grateful citizens of many German towns thankful for their deliverance. All was blacked out below, with only the shimmering courses of rivers and canals to indicate the changing landscape. The world of their enemies lay in darkness – a black closet sealed up by fear.

* * *

Eventually a glow began to broaden across the horizon, like the dull light of a shrouded lamp that grew as the miles decreased between the Lancaster and its destination. It gradually became more distinct, widening amid a swirling mass of cloud. Yet this was not cloud, but smoke – the smoke of a thousand fires raging in the streets of a city being devoured by flames. Hamburg was burning from end to end, a vast lake of fire, superheated smoke rising five miles into the watching sky. Burning shapes could now be made out below – of churches, factories and residential blocks – while above, the brazen silhouettes of bombers continued their unerring approach to the target. So the crew of "F for Freddy" flew on over the shifting inferno to deliver their deadly bomb into the blistering cauldron.

The scene resembled a biblical hell; for within thirty minutes of the second raid commencing, the congested dock area, comprising eight square miles of narrow streets and warehouses, had been transformed into a searing oven in which the temperature rose to 1,832 degrees Fahrenheit. This inferno demanded oxygen and in a report to Adolf Hitler, Hamburg's Air Protection Leader would write:

> *The air stormed through the streets with immense force until it became a typhoon against which all human resistance was powerless. The man-made winds of 150 miles per hour tossed human beings like so much chaff into the flames; large trees were uprooted and reduced to charcoal in seconds; citizens strove to avoid oxygen starvation in their shelters by emerging into the holocaust, only to be driven back by the rain of high explosives.*

The firestorm he described would eventually destroy over 300,000 homes, cause the deaths of more than 50,000 citizens and leave seventy per cent of its firefighting personnel dead or injured.

The Lancaster was over the burning city for more than two minutes, each crew member awed by the scene of destruction as he watched other aircraft discharge their deadly cargoes. Upon bomb-release, "F for Freddy" leapt up as if mightily relieved to be free of her burden and speed began to increase. Anti-aircraft fire over the city had been slight up to this point, but upon reaching the eastern side a more determined barrage developed as they entered a zone of concentrated bombardment – quartered by the gunners below. The crew had experienced this attempted retribution many times before and the pilot, John Hammond, hauled the aircraft up in an endeavour to escape the exploding shells. Two burst nearby, sending shards of debris peppering through the airframe, before a third struck the outer port engine, shearing off part of the wing. The Lancaster shuddered as if struck by a mighty blow, then, with control surfaces gone, tipped sideways and slid out of the bomber stream. There was another internal explosion close to Harry's seat and with the remaining propellers feathering, the stricken aircraft began its final descent. Smoke and flames filled the fuselage as electrical wire melted and caught fire. Harry tore himself from his safety harness and stood up, tipping forward as the aircraft assumed a steepening angle. He hadn't much time since, having come in low for its final bomb run, to achieve greater accuracy, the Lancaster had made little height upon climbing away. If Harry did not make it to the escape hatch quickly his chance of gaining salvation from the burning aircraft would be gone. Tom Simons, the co-pilot, stumbled against him in the smoke and confusion and together they made their way back. The co-pilot wrenched the door open and then, sitting astride the aperture, he reached across and slapped Harry on the shoulder.

'That's another fine mess you've got us into, Harry,' he shouted. 'Look me up when you get home, mate!' and with a brief thumbs up he dropped through into the spiralling sky below.

Harry remained in the aircraft for perhaps another five seconds, waiting for others to come up. But none arrived and he was finally toppled out as "F for Freddy" lurched again in its death throes before breaking in half.

The next moments passed in a tumbling blur as he twisted and somersaulted through the air. Harry had parachuted only twice before – both times over the airfield on a bright sunny day. Now he found himself falling through an eerie night of alternating light and darkness. His head swam and his eyes ran as he grappled for the parachute release, which he clasped and pulled, shoulders wrenched up as it unfurled amid a clamour of material. But as his descent stabilised, other sounds and sensations began to demand Harry's attention. The acrid stench of burning tar, fuel and wood came to his nostrils, while a hollow roar from the raging inferno below began to fill his ears.

Now he could see the world around – a world stained red on three sides by the flames. Billowing smoke was rising up in huge clouds from a hundred points and being tugged about by a strengthening wind. The Lancaster had been hit above the outer suburbs of the city, but he now realised he was descending at an angle back towards a thousand burning buildings. He became aware too of rising blasts of heat and quickly realised his predicament as the likelihood of being carried into the heart of the fires engulfing Hamburg became apparent. Suspended like a clumsy butterfly above a fiery brazier he slanted lower, passing a church already reduced to ashes and apartment blocks with flames issuing from every window, until he neared the bulk of a large factory burning from end to end.

He seemed drawn inexorably towards it as he approached the earth, a strong breeze, swiftly growing to a wind, pulling him sideways and carrying him almost horizontally over the ground. He had never enjoyed parachuting because of the certainty of an uncomfortable landing, but prayed now for the crunch of his body against terra firma. Had Harry stayed airborne for another thirty seconds he would not have survived, but just then a hot surge of smoke and ashes snatched him sideways and he was carried pell-mell towards a scorched and twisted tree standing in a small park. He crashed into it with considerable force, cracking his head, one blackened branch tearing his thigh, leaving an open gash. For a few moments he passed out and could later recall nothing about his landing. On coming to, he found he was caught – suspended with his feet dangling a yard from the ground, the parachute entangled in the branches above. The grass around was blackened and the heat from the burning factory fifty yards away began to sear his face. He could not have stayed there, since before half an hour had elapsed he would have been slowly roasted – held as on a blackened toasting fork in offering to the flames. Yet, although Harry struggled to free himself, his efforts were in vain because, pulled sideways as he was, the parachute release refused to budge under the downward stress of his own weight. His helpless position became still more critical when a corner section of the burning factory caved in and a fresh wave of heat from the newly exposed fires washed towards him. Harry reached up to wipe his smarting eyes and to protect his face – the black terror of approaching death gripping his heart.

It was then that a figure emerged from an alleyway beside the factory: a man, his head shrouded in a blanket already burning at the fringes, stumbling backwards as he retreated from the fury close at hand. He carried a spade with a long handle that he raised up as if to shield himself from the heat, or perhaps in vain gesture of defiance towards the infernal beast devouring his city. Then, throwing off the smouldering blanket, he turned and came on towards Harry, head down, stumbling over the scorched and stunted grass. He fell twice, like a man exhausted, both times rising slowly to look from side to side, as if lost and stupefied, before tottering on once more. He tripped for a third and final time less than ten paces from where Harry was hanging, and lay face down for almost a minute with his cheek pressed to the soil. Harry might have called out above the raging conflagration threatening to scorch his skin, but a sense of danger of a different kind made him hold his tongue.

The German had suffered badly. His clothes were smoking and the hair had been singed off one side of his head. Harry could also see that the top of his hands were blistered and, as he moved his knee, that his shoes were matted with tar from molten roads. Aircrew had been warned that crash survivors who made it to the ground did not always receive sympathetic attention from rescue workers; while there were authenticated reports of airmen being beaten to death by brutalised civilian mobs. Thus Toby continued to watch the newcomer, trying to judge his state of mind and how he would react.

Suddenly, as if coming to his senses, the German pulled himself up on his hands and knees and gazed forward. His eyes moved slowly up as he saw Harry and he squinted, his head on one side, as if trying to remember something. He was a young man of around Harry's age, with sharp and intelligent features, and it was clear that before the fire he'd had a beard and moustache; the tufts of tightly curled black hair still remaining upon his upper lip and cheeks. Yet his skin had suffered badly in the fire and was both red and inflamed, as if it might peel at any moment.

He sat back: his expression hardening and turning to rage as he looked at Harry and took in who he was.

'Englander,' he said under his breath. 'Swinehunder, Englander!' Then, rising to his feet, he moved forward, the spade gripped firmly in both hands.

His eyes glittered malevolently, like someone on the verge of madness...

* * *

For a few seconds Harry's life hung in the balance as the rescue worker weighed in his head all the carnage he had seen in the last days and nights against the retribution he might bring down upon this defenceless airman. He clenched his jaw, as if suppressing a fearful urge, then bared his upper teeth and strode forward with the spade raised. But the blow did not come, for he stopped less than a yard away, stiffening in a moment of spent aggression before turning and throwing the spade to the ground.

When the man looked back some seconds later he held a knife in his hand, causing Harry to fear a still swifter end, but this time the rescue worker was not bent on slaughter. Instead he clutched Harry's flying jacket and began to pull him powerfully downward while reaching above to cut the parachute cords. Harry could smell the burnt hair on his head and neck and the broken skin on the other's face brushed against his cheek.

The German worked quickly, with little regard for pain or hurt on either side, and in fifteen seconds Harry dropped to the ground. His knees buckled beneath him and they knelt together for a few moments panting with exhaustion.

'Up… we must move… Up!' said the warden in broken English before, half lifting, half pulling, he began to haul Harry inch by inch away from the flames. It was an agonising ordeal for them both. The gash on Harry's leg still dripped blood and he could not rest his full weight upon it without doubling up in pain; while in his attempts to lift Harry, the German winced each time he took his weight against burned flesh. But he would not give up, and although only light in stature, was wiry too: with strength far greater than his frame might suggest.

At last they reached a low wall a hundred yards away where Harry's saviour propped him before setting about tending his injury. The man tore a wide length of material from his own tattered shirt and bound the wound to staunch the bleeding.

'You will live,' said the other as he looked up from his work. 'You are lucky I found you… many have not been so fortunate,' he added, looking towards the sky.

Harry 'You speak English,' said ~~Toby~~, breathing through his pain and exhaustion. 'My name is Harry Clayton… and you?'

The man looked at him, his face pinched, the gaunt fatigue of three nights without sleep etched upon his brow.

'Harry Clayton,' he said reflectively, while looking up into Harry's face and drawing forth a flask of water from a smouldering pocket for him to drink from. 'I am Martin Brandt… and this,' he said with a sweep of his hand behind him, 'this burning wreck is the city of my birth.'

They said no more for a while, but moved further away still to a corner of the park where the grass remained green. Others had gathered there, many injured by falling debris or badly burned, and a makeshift treatment centre was being set up. The bombers had now departed and those that had survived in their shelters were either seeking help themselves or giving what assistance they could to others worse off. All were dazed and frightened, and few initially gave more than passing heed to Harry, who was placed under guard beside a withered cherry tree. There were however a few that looked across at him with malicious eyes, in whose faces he saw an undisguised hatred that chilled him.

Soon Martin Brandt returned and sat down heavily at his side, his head bandaged and a greatcoat pulled around his shoulders.

'You cannot stay,' he said. 'I have sent word to the city authorities that you are here. They will collect you soon: even at times like these, such things are dealt with.'

Harry ~~Toby~~ looked at him – this wasted man still so practical and collected.

'Herr Brandt,' he said, 'I owe you my life… I wish to thank you.'

The other smiled without expression. 'Hmm… you are right,' he responded wearily. 'But how strange it is that I should have had more success saving you, than rescuing my own people tonight.'

'What do you do? What is your occupation?' Harry ventured after a pause.

Martin Brandt gazed ahead. 'I am, as you see, a member of the Reich Fire Fighting Reserve of Hamburg,' he replied automatically, as if chilled from within. 'But in my daily life I am a teacher, the principal of a school... Had I not held such a position I would have been called upon long ago – to fight you. However... now perhaps it will be different.'

'Why so?' asked Harry. 'Surely schoolteachers are still needed.'

The German turned to him, inhaling deeply. 'Perhaps not... if both the school and the children have gone – reduced to ashes.'

* * *

Their conversation ended, but as long as he remained in the park Harry owed his continuing safety to Martin Brandt. Dawn eventually came, but it was to be the beginning of a day shrouded in shifting smoke and blustery winds, as fires continued to rage in the heart of the city. In the early light he felt uncomfortably exposed as dishevelled people came frequently to look at him, muttering among themselves. Then, at one point, a small girl of perhaps five or six tottered up and stood scrutinising his face. Her frock was stained with ash, and the hair on the right side of her head left curled and frizzled from close proximity to heat and flames. She seemed vulnerable and timid and Harry smiled reassuringly at her; but in an instant a look of loathing spread across her smudged face, and she spat at his feet before turning away with her head raised proudly, in a caricature of triumph. A ripple of coarse laughter ran round the watching group, accompanied by guttural oaths directed at Harry, and he looked away, spurned by their anger. It had been a salutary reminder, if one were needed, of their feelings towards him, and redoubled his feelings of the debt he would always owe to the schoolteacher.

Harry was collected during the middle of the morning and driven from the park on an army lorry, accompanied by Martin Brandt and two soldiers.

'There will be paper work to complete,' said the fire warden as they began picking their way through rubble-strewn streets where the gutted ruins of buildings still smouldered. 'When that is all done, I will leave you.'

They passed fire crews still battling blazes in shops and offices, and medical crews tending the burned and dying. In several places too they came upon neatly stacked piles of corpses; hundreds charred and burned beyond recognition, left pathetically exposed to the steadily falling rain of fine ash and particles. Harry was appalled. These were images that he would take with him all his life: to haunt his dreams and darken an unguarded waking hour.

* * *

By noon the lorry driver had successfully negotiated a path to the city limits and drove into a wide field where a number of tents and feeding stations had been set up. A constant stream of people was moving into it; some carried on doors, others slung in blankets. All wore the defeated look of those having gone long without sleep – walking shadows emerging from a night of terror. Soon they drew up beside a reception area where two officers sat at a trestle table. With Martin Brandt acting as translator, Harry was led before them and asked his rank and number before being led to one side and told to sit on the grass. The others then talked together, as the details of his capture were carefully recorded, before Martin Brandt and a soldier approached him again.

'You will go with this man,' Martin said. 'I doubt we will meet again; but at least you will now be safe if you do what is asked.'

He then turned away, only to stop after three paces and step back.

'I might have killed you last might,' he said deliberately, though with a hint of warmth passing across his features. 'It was a close thing; and I think I would perhaps have regretted it for the rest of my life... but you, Harry Clayton, must also live with the memory of your actions. When you bombed my city you did not only destroy the buildings, but also took the lives of my fellow people and shattered the hopes of those that must live on. Perhaps, while in captivity, you will have time enough to dwell upon this.'

The schoolteacher held out his hand. 'Now, goodbye... I hope the coming days will not be too arduous... and that you live to see your homeland and loved ones again.'

No further words were spoken, and with a smile of farewell he walked off across the field, a hunched and blackened figure, before disappearing into the smouldering city.

* * *

Harry Clayton spent the rest of the war moving between a series of prisoner of war camps as first the Russians and then the Allies moved into Germany. He was liberated on 29th April 1945, returning home to Stavenham two months later. No other crew member of Lancaster "F for Freddy" was ever seen or heard of again.

* * *

Two nights later, during the third of four consecutive raids on Hamburg, Martin Brandt was killed by an exploding delayed action bomb as the RAF continued in its effort to "burn out the last rats of the city".

Chapter Twelve

Home Front

THE LONG MONTHS AND YEARS OF CONFLICT passed as Toby slept; yet he was not oblivious to the sufferings of the waking world. Like shadowy thoughts the events of war invaded his dreams and touched upon the inner regions of his mind.

* * *

The growl of powerful engines suddenly rattled the windowpanes of Toby's small room and he sat up, jolted into consciousness by the crescendo of noise outside. At first, with his head struggling to crawl back to the present, he stared blankly ahead; listening as the uproar began to subside once more, a stabbing pain in his neck causing him to wince.

'That was an aircraft... American – four engines.'

Still groggy, he heaved himself to the edge of the bed, and standing on aching feet looked out of the window. The day was somewhat overcast with occasional gaps in the cloud where bright patches of sunshine broke through. A number of startled rooks, crows and pigeons were circling on a fresh breeze, and less than a mile away he could clearly see the diminishing shape of a large aircraft. The sound of its fully extended Pratt and Whitney's could still be heard as it faded into the milky distance, and as he listened the rumble of another plane began to vibrate the air. Once more the windows juddered in their frames, and he watched it come into view, flying low above the treetops; a great silver machine with tall recognition numbers on its tail: the insignia of the United States Air Force emblazoned large on wings and fuselage.

'Flying Fortresses,' said Toby aloud. 'B17s – it's wartime.'

Two others then hove into view, heavy with bombs, steadily gaining height after take-off. Squinting, he followed them until they lumbered out of sight, leaving the countryside relatively peaceful once more, although a medley of familiar noises remained perceptible on the settling air: cattle lowing, voices calling in the distance, the rumble of a tractor – and another muffled sound, as of a mass of chickens clucking and crowing nearby.

Toby threw open the window to air the musty room, pulled on his shoes and the farm coat given to him by the Trindles, and descended the stairs in search of water. His creaking footwear pinched, and the clothes on his back felt rough against the skin, but just then Toby's only thought was to ease his parched throat. Yet this was not as straightforward as hoped, for upon turning the kitchen tap, nothing came out except a dribble of rusty water.

'The mains have been turned off – now what?'

He looked around; seeing only mouse droppings and a few empty bottles on the dusty shelves. Deciding that he would need to venture further afield in his quest, he set about unlocking the front door. The hinges creaked as it swung open, as if the memory of oil was long forgotten; yet it was not this that caught his attention – for now, as he gazed out through the porch Toby could barely believe the sight that met his eyes. The farm he'd known was gone; and where "The Great Barn" and stables once stood there was nothing evident but the grey stubble of a harvested wheat field. Everything had been removed – buildings, stones and machinery – all wiped away as if by a powerful hand!

He stepped forward and looked toward where the milking shed and outhouses had been; but here too nothing remained. Everything – the preparation shed, the wall where the cat had sunned itself, and the archway between the inner and outer yards – had vanished. Only the house was left, its paint peeling – ivy and flowering creeper half covering the walls and roof.

'That wonderful barn,' Toby said to himself, feeling a sense of loss. 'How can it have disappeared while I slept?'

Forlornly, he walked to the east side of the house where the farm entrance had been and came upon the water butt Coodie once used when watering her flowers. It had an old wooden lid. Lifting this, Toby found that, apart from a light scum upon the surface, the contents within were cool and clear. The butt was full to the brim, rain having recently fallen to refresh its contents. He cupped his hands and took several swallows before liberally splashing his face. Then, shaking droplets out of his hair like a grizzled dog, he returned to the house where he drew forth a chair from the kitchen, and sat down just beyond the porch to consider his next move.

* * *

Toby quickly ascertained that the hour was still early; the air retained the crispness of morning, while the ripe berries he could see glistening in the hedgerows suggested autumn. However, beyond noting these familiar signs, his mind seemed fuzzy; and needing some form of activity to focus his thoughts, he rose again, stepping forward to poke the soil around where the barn had stood. He levered the loose earth with a stick, like an archaeologist searching for clues, and had soon turned up four rusty rings from an old chain and the crumbling handle of a sickle.

'What else is buried here?' he thought, gazing around at the bare ground and remembering the wide interior of the building... 'And who else would know or care?'

At this point, Toby was about to take himself off and explore further when his eye was caught by the approach of a large crow that circled down from the top of a nearby elm tree. It landed no more than ten paces from him, at the place where he had discovered the chain, and began poking with its long beak for the grubs and worms that had been disturbed. Yet the crow's actions seemed somewhat desultory, and it appeared more interested in Toby than obtaining breakfast: constantly turning and twisting to fix him with a beady eye. Then suddenly the creature stood up high upon its legs, head cocked inquisitively, before lifting away and disappearing over the rise in the direction of the railway.

'It's as if it knew me – like the one at the windmill and "The Three Eels",' thought Toby, and was about to follow when Macken came trotting up the pathway from the crossing.

The Yorkshire terrier was approaching at a steady pace, but when it caught sight of Toby, scampered forward, skidding to a halt just in front of him. It looked up, wagging its tail excitedly before sniffing round Toby's shoe and moving off to explore a clump of nettles beyond the farmhouse.

'If you're here, old boy, who else might turn up?' thought Toby. He had little time to await an answer, for upon turning again he noticed the head of a walker bobbing into view. It was that of a young woman of slim build, wearing a short-sleeved shirt and loose working trousers, her hair held back by a headscarf tied in a bow at the nape of her neck. She had on Wellington boots and carried a sturdy stick over her shoulder.

'A "land girl",' Toby said to himself. 'But I know her too.'

He waited as Jeannie approached.

'Toby, you look a mess; haven't you got a comb?' she chided him with a winning smile when drawing near. 'How are you?'

'I'm well enough,' he answered. 'But please tell me... How long have I been inactive this time? For if it should be years I have a right to look a little unkempt.'

'Eight further summers have passed, Toby,' she replied more soberly. 'It is Tuesday, 29th September 1944, and World War Two will soon be over.'

'I knew it... those American bombers – I watched them earlier.'

'They come from Poddington and fly almost daily... such hazardous work,' she added thoughtfully. 'But come, I have labours of my own to perform and much to show that will be of interest to you.'

'Wait,' he said, hesitating and looking questioningly into her face. 'It's been so long... but you are no older, Jeannie.'

'Neither are you, Toby,' she replied enigmatically. 'That is our little gift, you and I. We will not age here.'

They stood for some moments without speaking, Toby feeling puzzled and unsettled, before he lamely attempted to fill the void. 'Should I lock the house? …It seems wrong to leave it open.'

'If you wish, Toby – but few people ever come near it now.'

* * *

Choosing to rely upon habit, he turned the key in the rusty lock before setting off with Jeannie, who now informed him that she would be potato picking with the Braylings at "High Dyke Farm" that day. Soon they came to an open ridge and began walking down the cart track he had travelled years before when haymaking with the Trindles. Many changes had since taken place. Now every scrap of countryside seemed to be in use for growing crops or rearing animals. There were meadows containing a variety of dairy cows, cattle and sheep, while many plots of land that had previously been used to grow grain now contained neat rows of root and green vegetables waiting to be harvested. Everything was organised to maximise production for a nation made hungry by war.

But another sight also drew his attention: for as they reached a high point where much of the surrounding countryside could be seen, an unobstructed view of the Towsers' "Deep Spinney Farm" opened out before them in the valley to the south. It had been transformed; gone were the tall dark barns that had nestled eerily among brooding elm and poplar trees – everything had been felled and cleared away including much of the encroaching woodland on the opposite slope. In their place stood eight large sheds with pitched roofs in an evenly spaced and regimented group. Toby stopped to study the scene and heard again the muttering of a multitude of birds carried towards them on the morning air. Yet there was no sight of any living thing on the farm, no movement of man, beast or bird – just the huge ugly sheds standing gauntly amid the surrounding gold of autumn.

'The Towsers' chicken farm,' said Jeannie, stopping beside him. 'Egg production on a vast scale! Apparently there are more than three thousand birds in every shed; so you can imagine how many eggs they produce. Then there's the meat – hundreds of birds every month – it's a good business. Basil Tyler came up with part of the money at the start of the war, and the War Office provided the rest. So everything else was torn down to make way for what you see. The provision of adequate food supplies is now top of the agenda, and Basil Tyler is making a good profit. Cregan and Barnaby Towser have continued there as managers; but they don't have any real say in what goes on any more – while if they were to argue about anything, Basil would simply evict them and find someone else to run the farm.'

'It looks an unpleasant sort of place,' said Toby, sniffing the faintly noxious scent of chicken manure wafting towards them from the distant buildings.

'You certainly wouldn't choose to live there,' she replied. 'It's just like a factory, with too many animals cooped up in too little space. That's bad enough, but then there's the smell – and the rats. When we're finished I'll take you down. You need to see it close up to appreciate what goes on.'

* * *

They now resumed their walk and soon turned into the entrance of "High Dyke Farm". This, by contrast with the establishment Toby had just looked upon, was a picture of good order and quiet efficiency; with well maintained buildings around a spacious yard, beyond which stood pastures and enclosures for cows, beef cattle, geese and free-range chickens. There were also several sties and sheds where pigs and calves could be seen; and at the centre, a large modern milking shed with several churns standing on a platform outside. An open backed lorry had just drawn up, and the churns were being loaded onto it by two young women in frocks and pinafores who, skilfully tilting and turning these on their heavy bases, were positioning them behind the driver's cabin.

As Toby and Jeannie walked towards the spot, old Arthur Brayling stepped out of the cowshed and hailed them. He was now advanced in years, his face so lined with wrinkles that his eyes all but closed up when he smiled; but he still retained the genial good-humoured manner of earlier years.

'Good day, Jeannie,' he said, coming up and slapping his work stained hand on her shoulder – a faint aroma of pigswill and cow manure wafting around as he did so. 'Oops… I didn't mean to soil your clothes,' he apologised, noticing the mark left by his palm. 'Still, "it's all good clean dirt" as my old mother used to say. Come, let me wipe it off.'

By now the two women, Betty and Mickey Brayling, had jumped down to join them.

'You'll do nothing of the kind with those hands,' said Mickey, the older of the sisters, stepping in between. 'We'll not have our guests further covered in muck because you're too lazy to wash your mitts.'

She was a busy little woman with a lively expression and wind-blown fair hair who, although seemingly brusque and businesslike, had a twinkle in her hazel eyes that betrayed a sense of fun and good humour.'

'You tell him, Mickey,' said the other smiling broadly. 'I don't know what these menfolk are up to – you'd think they ran the place.'

Betty Brayling was in her early twenties and looked every inch a farmer's daughter. She was a round-faced girl with attentive brown eyes and wiry black hair that curled around her cheeks from beneath a headscarf. Already the years of working in the sun had bronzed and creased her skin, but her mouth, when she laughed, opened widely to show bright even teeth.

Mickey quickly cleaned Jeannie up, using water from a nearby butt, and they stood awhile in conversation as her father explained that they would be working in a large potato field down by the railway, and that his three sons had already gone there with a group of "land girls" to begin.

'It seems set fair,' he said looking up at the clearing sky, where the sun was beginning to appear regularly between clouds. 'I shouldn't wonder that we'll get plenty done before the day's out; especially if our new friend here is prepared to help out.'

The old man had turned to Toby, and now wrinkled his brow as he looked closely at him. 'Mind you,' he added, 'it seems to me I remember you helping us out some years ago – when Henry Trindle still worked "Warren Hill Farm". I don't normally forget a face. Am I right?'

For a moment Toby considered whether it was wise to confirm the old farmer's enquiry; but looking at the earnest and open expressions on the faces of Arthur Brayling and his daughters, decided that frankness and honesty were best.

'It was me,' he replied. 'I remember it well – you were very welcoming.'

'Well I'm blowed, so I'm not mistaken,' puffed the farmer. 'And I'll tell you something else…' he added, scrutinising Toby more closely. 'I don't know what you take to look after yourself, boy; but whatever it is you should bottle it. You don't look a day older than when I last saw you – and that must have been before our Betty here was born.'

His wife, Sarah Brayling, had now approached from the house conveying a large canvas bag and two heavy tea tins which she wheeled towards them hung over the handlebars of an old bicycle. She was now a stout but still active old lady, who continued to evince the charm and loving nature of someone that had never had anything but good thoughts for others.

'I remember the lad too,' she said, having caught her husband's words. 'And good luck to him if he is still lookin' young. I dare say that's what you get for livin' sensible. If you and me had our time over again, I'm sure we'd choose to keep our youth rather than growin' old… Now, it's time you were all away. Those taters won't pick themselves off the ground. Take this lot for your elevenses, and I won't expect to see owt of you again afore dinner time.'

This was not the kind of prompting that could be ignored, and together they moved off, with Betty wheeling the bicycle close behind. There was little distance to travel and Toby soon glimpsed the other labourers busily at work in a narrow potato field beside the railway. To reach them they followed the farm track over a raised shoulder of land; all that remained of the ancient dyke, before descending into a sheltered dip where a milky autumn sun had already begun to warm the air. A number of "land girls" were present, evenly spaced along a line of newly dug potatoes; each bent over a metal pail in which she collected the knobbly staple of a million English dinners. It was backbreaking but satisfying work and many of the women greeted their arrival with a cheerful wave.

Old Arthur's three sons were visible too: Bert, the eldest, now in his forties, digging out the first roots of the next row with a fork to allow the tractor drawn machine to begin its work again. He was a slim, wiry fellow, wearing a shirt rolled up at the sleeves and loose trousers supported by grey braces. On his head he wore a faded but much-loved cloth-cap, while what remained of a dead roll-up cigarette was clamped firmly between his teeth. Always someone to keep his own company, Bert was the cowman of the farm, and there were those that said of his gruff nature that he got on better with his animals than with humans. But if conversation wasn't his forte, Bert often made up for this by exhibiting a dry good-humoured wit when he did speak. He was his own man, living the life he knew best, and a more honest, hardworking person you couldn't hope to meet.

Jim Brayling, the farmer's second son, raised a hand in greeting as they approached. He was a big man in his mid-thirties, broad shouldered and strong. Clever with figures, Jim managed the finances of the farm, and it was he that had proposed plans for expanding the establishment during the previous decade after the Trindles moved on. The use of new machinery and securing a loan to purchase a tractor to replace the working horses were his ideas also. Thus, it was readily accepted by his brothers and sisters that Jim would inherit the role of farm manager when the time came; and this he had done with the skill and understanding that were hallmarks of his generous nature. Jim was firm and positive with everyone that knew him – caring not only for the members of his family, but also for the land he worked and the natural environment of which it was part. Moreover, as with the whole family, there was no cruelty in him; and while vermin and pests were properly controlled, Jim took no delight in hunting and killing for its own sake.

The youngest of the menfolk was Duke. Now in his late twenties, he had taken on the role of tractor driver and mechanic – showing skill at getting the best out of primitive machinery that frequently gave up under the rigours of daily use. Whenever a breakdown did occur, he would push his cap back on his balding forehead and, having relit the Woodbine seemingly kept permanently wedged behind his left ear, would set to without delay in a normally successful effort to solve the problem. He clearly loved his work and greeted Toby warmly.

'You been tater pickin' before, Toby?' he asked, having been introduced.

'Once or twice – but a long time ago.'

'No matter,' said the young farmer smiling. 'There's not much to it after all, though it gets to your back after a while. I'll tell you what – why don't you give me a hand for a bit? It helps to have an extra pair of eyes available when you're set upon keepin' this contraption working.'

They were standing beside the potato-picking machine that he had brought up to the beginning of the second row of the day, and Duke now handed Toby a fork, instructing him to keep the straggling heads of dead foliage from clogging the rotating claws. Then, having mounted the tractor and noisily engaged gear, he moved off at a slow walking pace. The machine sprang into action, the spinning tines arcing into the soft soil and casting out the buried potatoes amid a shower of brown earth and loose stones. The problem of the tops was almost immediately evident as a clump threatened to wrap itself round the mechanism, bringing it to a grinding halt. But by applying the fork Toby was able to free the mass in time, with Duke nodding approval from the driver's seat. In this way they continued on down the field; stopping only twice along the way – the appreciative look frequently crossing the young farmer's face providing ample evidence that Toby's efforts were valued.

'Jump up beside the seat,' Duke said, through a swirl of tobacco smoke, as he turned to drive back and begin another row. 'You can have a go at steering next time.'

And so Toby did. When the tractor had been positioned at the start of the next ridge he was invited to climb aboard, and following a brief description of the controls, drove the Fordson himself. It was a primitive beast of a thing and he initially stalled it upon releasing the clutch.

'Everyone does that first off,' said Duke, grinning. 'You just have to speak to the old girl politely, that's all!'

Toby tried again, and with a little coaxing the rugged little tractor clawed forward, transmission grinding, before beginning its steady journey down the field.

As the morning progressed the two of them repeated this process of change and change about, each taking his turn at the controls as the other walked behind, and by midday a dozen more rows had been dug. By then both they and the picking team were becoming weary from the constant labour, and all were glad to see Sarah Brayling approaching with food and drink for dinner. The day was now bright and sunny, and together they formed a group beside the railway fence; slumping restfully upon the grass to enjoy a meal of sandwiches, boiled eggs and sweet tea. There was a deal of good-natured banter between the men and the young women – most of whom could more than hold their own when telling a bawdy joke. Only Jeannie held back from the exchange of pleasantries, apparently preferring to watch and listen while the others talked.

Then, when their rest time was almost over, a chorus of distant whistles coming from the junction with the main line to London signalled the approach of a train. Such an event rarely drew their attention, as most were normally local services consisting of no more than an engine and one or two coaches. The occasional freight train also passed by; but these were usually short and infrequent and so far Toby had noted only one other that day. This time, however, the growing and determined roar of a large locomotive battling against the grade could be heard approaching; the gradually increasing volume of sound attracted them all.

'That's a big un,' said Jim, standing up. 'One of they ammunition trains I shouldn't wonder – judging by the effort it's making!'

They were at a spot on a level with the tracks and moved to a break in the hedge to observe the developing drama. It soon became apparent that not one, but perhaps two or even three engines might be involved in moving the train. Nor, it was clear, were they the small tank locomotives normally associated with the line. These were heavyweights straining against the grade in an all out effort to lift their load. By now tall columns of smoke could be seen rising above the trees and the air began to vibrate with the strident roar of powerful exhausts. One or two reached up to shield their ears as the first engine came into sight round the bend two hundred yards away, double headed with another – both proceeding at little more than walking pace. Closer they came, the long freight train in tow snaking round the distant bend in an endless column of gently swaying trucks. Not until the first engine was almost upon them did the guard's van appear; then a final locomotive, giving full voice to its assistance, emerged at the rear.

The watchers were all but deafened by the spectacle as the leading locomotives crawled past – two great 2-8-0 tender engines, their crews bent to the task of keeping the heavy load of covered trucks, oil tankers and flat wagons piled with war provisions on the move. For almost two minutes the train continued to rumble by, wheels screaming against tight curves, before the driver of the banking engine whistled triumphantly at them as it came level. Grinning down he then gave a parting wave as the whole assemblage disappeared from view in a swirl of billowing smoke and steam, the reverberating blast of the engines echoing across the valley towards Stavenham. The tumultuous sound continued to rend the air for some time afterwards as the train maintained its laborious journey up the gradient, and it took all of ten minutes to crest the hill towards Turnham before passing beyond hearing.

'That's got to be the tenth we've see like that,' said Duke turning at last. 'It's odd to see this one-horse line so heavily used. I wonder what it's all for?'

His brother, Jim, looked up. 'Supplies for the airfields I shouldn't wonder – fuel and the like,' he mused. 'One thing's for sure; I wouldn't want to be around if a stray German fighter took a pop at one of 'em.'

'Well I reckon if you were, you'd meet your maker soon enough,' Bert interposed laconically. 'And as I see it, we don't exactly live a million miles from the line, do we?'

It was a sobering thought, and one that cropped up more than once in a number of conversations when work resumed. But their efforts went on apace and before afternoon turned to evening they had cleared half the field of its valuable crop. Duke then unhitched the potato-picking machine from the drawbar and disappeared to fetch the trailer upon which they would load the filled sacks for safe storage at the farm. All were now tired but in good spirits from their labours, and when he returned set to with a will to complete this final activity. Teamwork was evident on all sides as the heavy sacks were lifted aboard, the women proving as adept as the men, each committing his or her strength to a shared endeavour. Satisfaction in a job well done was their true reward and Toby again felt at one with his working companions. When finished they rode back to the farmyard perched on the swaying load, legs swinging as the trailer lurched up the uneven track, and there Toby and Jeannie took their leave.

'Come back tomorrow,' said Duke, lighting another of his skinny cigarettes. 'There's plenty still to do and you're always welcome to lend a hand.'

'Perhaps,' said Toby. 'But I'll have to see what I've got on.'

'Now you listen,' said the farmer, catching the note of hesitation in his voice. 'Don't you let them talk you into being a soldier or some other such thing, boy. Farming's best for the likes of us: for while you may end up with a mess of aches and pains... Well at least you won't suffer worse, eh.'

Having imparted this advice, he shook Toby's hand and walked away towards the storage barn as Toby and Jeannie made off in the direction of the farm gate. On the way they passed the milking parlour – where Bert and Betty were once more engaged in their twice daily undertaking – before turning onto the track beyond.

* * *

Relishing the prospect of being able to sit down in a comfortable chair, Toby was hoping to make an immediate return to Warren Hill; but instead of going straight on towards the deserted farmhouse, Jeannie proceeded slightly ahead for a short distance, then forked left through a partly concealed gap in a hedge before leading the way downhill along an overgrown path. His guide said little, but there was a strong sense of purpose in her step. It was still early evening and the sun, though dipping towards the west, would still be up for another two hours.

'Where are you taking me?' asked Toby, who was now having serious thoughts about supper.

Jeannie looked round, her delicate features caught by a shaft of light. 'I promised I would show you more,' she replied. 'This brief detour will take but a short time.'

The path began to curve to the right and he realised that they were descending in the direction of "Deep Spinney Farm". Then, coming round a corner by a tall hedge, he found himself looking down upon the wooden sheds recently erected there. A stale and unpleasant aroma of chicken manure again wafted towards him, and the dull chatter of many thousands of incarcerated birds rose to his ears. There were no warning signs or fences to keep them out but Toby felt neither comfortable nor welcome in the place.

A minute later they arrived at the south-east corner of the block of eight, the long flat sides of the nearest stretching away before them, flanked by an encroaching tangle of bindweed, brambles and nettles that crept up from the adjacent hedge. Head high ventilation ducts covered with wire were set six feet apart along the wall, these having in most cases become partially clogged with a mixture of cobwebs, dust and feathers, restricting the flow of fresh air to the residents inside. Toby stepped forward to peer through the nearest, evidently startling a dozen or more of the occupants, for a clamour of beating wings and sharp calls erupted within which seemed to ripple away across a sea of muffled voices. He could make out little at first, but as his pupils gradually became accustomed to the low light, progessively focused upon a mass of birds milling around the wide floor. Most scratched and pecked aimlessly at the earth around them, or at each other; some as if boldly trying to establish an area of territory, but the majority merely from listless habit. They were a motley collection, many with completely bare necks and raw rumps; others hobbling or dragging a damaged leg as if injured in a recent, less than neighbourly encounter. In all there was something sordid and pathetic about the scene: as if the chickens themselves were bored and overcome by a sense of hopelessness, having realised that their only function was to provide food for others.

In this last respect the shed, as Toby noted, was clearly productive, for as the chickens moved about several newly laid eggs could be seen deposited upon the straw – while many more were to be spied in the dozens of raised nesting boxes around the walls. The birds in this stuffy and overcrowded shed alone would evidently produce many hundreds each day.

Having held his breath for several seconds, Toby stepped back, deeply inhaling the marginally fresher air away from the vent while looking across at the ends of four identical sheds forming the eastern side of the complex. Each was a wide, squat structure with a single access door set in the centre below a pitched roof. Outside them large heaps of chicken manure had accumulated, some containing the remains of dead hens. The dull reek of creosote from the slatted boards, mixing with other noxious smells, produced a fetid odour that offended his senses.

'I know this is wartime and the country badly needs food,' he said, turning to Jeannie with a furrowed brow. 'But it seems grim that this kind of thing should be necessary.'

'The Braylings would certainly not tolerate what you see,' she replied, 'for their methods are markedly different. No, what you witness is the result of neglect – the work of men who have no interest in their labour or in the welfare of animals… those that care only for themselves and what they can get out of this place.'

'The Towsers?'

'Just so: but this filth and cruelty go beyond them. They indeed carry out the daily business of running the farm, but as I said earlier, it was Basil Tyler who provided the money to set it up; and he alone will profit richly from the produce sold.'

'Tyler is still the outright owner then?'

'Most certainly, Toby: but he has never lifted a pound of chicken meal or collected an egg in his life. The Towsers are his puppets – mere tenants that must do their landlord's will. Cregan and Barnaby have no love of farming or the land; but they know well enough that as food producers they will never be called up to take arms in the service of their country. So they follow Basil Tyler's instructions; in a sullen way, mind you, for there is no love lost in that relationship. And meanwhile, what you see around you is the outcome.'

Both now walked along a little further until, when nearing the third shed, a scattering of birds inside warned of someone approaching behind the door. They stood back when it opened, coming face to face with Cregan Towser as he stepped out. The burly farmer carried an empty pail in one hand, and in the other held the feet of a dead and emaciated chicken which he tossed casually onto the nearby manure heap. He was still a relatively young and powerful man; but the same surly expression marred his features. Clad in work stained clothes, his heavy check shirt rolled up at the sleeves, he wore a cap pushed high upon his now balding forehead. A two-day growth of grey-flecked stubble covered his face and chin giving him an untidy rumpled appearance. But Cregan still had something of his former arrogance about him; like an ageing bully on the lookout for an unwitting victim. Yet something in his shifty eyes told Toby that he was also a beaten man – a lackey now reduced to keeping his place and doing another's bidding – that the old special relationship he seemed to have enjoyed with Basil Tyler was long over. Cregan re-lit a half smoked cigarette at the side of his mouth, then drew deeply upon it before puffing out a heavy stream of smoke.

'This is private property. What are you doing here?' he demanded.

'We mean no harm,' replied Jeannie. 'We were just out for a stroll and our walk brought us here.'

Cregan tossed his head back and looked lazily down the line of his cigarette, squinting as the smoke curled around his face. 'You came for a walk… to see my chicken farm,' he said, in a voice of contemptuous disbelief. 'I'd have thought your nose would have warned you to stay away.'

'The smell is rather strong,' said Jeannie coolly. 'But it doesn't seem to bother you.'

'Some of us are used to it,' he grunted, coughing and spitting towards the manure pile. 'It's one of the hazards of working with animals.'

'I'm sure you're right – and you seem to be thriving on it,' she added.

Whatever else might have been said of Cregan Towser, he was not a fool. Being addressed in this way rankled him more than a little and he now leaned forward in the abrasive manner of old.

'Happen you'd better be gone then, if you don't like the air around here. And don't imagine I've forgotten seeing this one in these parts before,' he added, pointing at Toby, 'cos I ain't... I didn't like him then and I'm no more impressed with his face on this occasion. But apart from that – strangers aren't welcome here without an invitation, and you... the both of you – will come a cropper if I find you trespassing on my property again. Now bugger off before I lose my temper!'

Although talking and acting in a threatening way, Cregan's blustering attitude lacked conviction, and Toby sensed that Jeannie had detected this also for she seemed inclined to stay in order to goad him further. However, the noise of their discussion had reached other ears and moments later his brother's bulk lurched into sight a little further along. Barnaby had evidently very much gone to seed in the intervening years, becoming overweight and flabby. Yet he was not to be meddled with, having always been a big man with an aggressive and unpredictable nature; and just then the leer on his heavy jaw suggested he'd take a savage delight in becoming involved in any trouble that ensued.

Jeannie took his approach as a signal to leave: she and Toby hastily retracing their steps before turning again when some distance away, to see Cregan evidently dissuading his pugilistic sibling from giving pursuit.

* * *

Relieved at having been able to depart without incident, Toby followed Jeannie as she made her way back up the path before emerging into the last of the evening sunshine. Upwind of the chicken farm the air became sweet again as they began to skirt the top of the rise, although below they could still clearly see the eight sheds. All evidence of life and movement among them had ceased once more, giving little hint of the ugliness and cruelty that existed there.

Having proceeded to another fork that would take them back to "Warren Hill" farmhouse, out of the corner of his eye Toby noticed a small group of men still at work in a field of turnips near where the Smallwoods' farm used to stand. There were nine in all; seven who were pulling and cutting the tops off the root vegetables, and two others standing a little apart who appeared to be bending down to stroke a small dog. Jeannie, having seen them too, moved off that way, and as they approached Toby began to glean the connection between the workmen and the two bystanders. The seven were clearly being supervised in their activity, and the sight of a rifle leaning against a tree indicated that they were under guard. Yet the atmosphere appeared relaxed, as if those in charge had long since dismissed the prospect that their charges might seek to escape. Indeed, the dog had become the centre of interest, with both the guards and the stooped figures vying for its attention. Macken was evidently in his element, constantly trotting back and forth with tail erect to receive small titbits and scratches behind the ears. However, when he looked up and saw Jeannie approaching, his manner changed in an instant and he came bounding towards her in an ecstatic rush of excitement and affection.

The men all stood erect to watch and she, noticing their interest, turned the dog bodily round before gently encouraging him to return to his new friends. Macken looked up at her with a familiar tilt of his head then, as if acknowledging her request, trotted back obediently towards the group.

'Is this your dog?' said one of the two guards as they came up. He was a middle-aged man, of perhaps fifty, and like the other wore a loose fitting khaki army uniform.

'That's what I tell people,' she replied. 'But I'm afraid he tends to suit himself, as you might have noticed.'

'We did rather think that. He just went and turned up out of the blue about ten minutes ago – simply sauntered along by the hedge; like the Lord of the Manor going for an evening stroll... Aye, but he's a great little fellow!'

'And you, miss...?' asked the other, an easygoing fellow with a squint. 'Where are you from?'

'Oh, I'm a visitor here... down to see a relative. My friend and I thought we might take an evening stroll.'

'I don't blame you a bit,' said the first guard. 'It beats standing around supervising this little bunch.'

He indicated the workmen, most of whom were again bent to their labour, although one remained upright, apparently listening to their conversation.

'Who are they?' asked Toby. 'Have they done anything wrong?'

'No, not unless you consider being captured by the British army a crime. They were all rounded up on D-Day, or soon after. They're prisoners of war – Germans.'

Toby swung round towards the men with renewed interest. He had not to that point considered the possibility that they were other than local convicts brought to work in the fields for the day; but now noted clues to their newly revealed identity. Two or three wore grey trousers of army issue; one a tunic of very different cut to those worn by the regular soldiers. He also began to distinguish words of German as the men exchanged comments with one another.

'They're a good lot generally,' said the second soldier. 'Except old Torsten over there,' he added, pointing towards a short, dark-haired figure wearing glasses, one lens of which had been all but covered over with black tape. 'He still thinks that Hitler will win the war and that we should behave ourselves to avoid punishment when the Nazis arrive.'

The little man in question had straightened up at the mention of his name, and stood looking towards them with an erect and dignified posture, the one good glass of his spectacles glinting as it caught the sun. He looked about to comment, but it was another of the group, the one that Toby had thought was listening earlier, who spoke.

'You must not mock my countryman too much,' he said softly. 'He is a proud man and has lost everything. You are to be the victors now; but it will take him a little longer to acknowledge this fact.'

'And who are you?' said Toby, stepping towards him.

'My name is Hans Klepner – once a Panzer grenadier, but now a farmer of turnips in your country. I was captured near Bayeux in France when resistance fighters blew the tracks off my lorry. They also came near to removing the legs from my body,' he said shifting his weight awkwardly to one side. 'But another less fortunate than myself took the full blast... so here I am.'

Toby now saw that he was lame in one leg and only able to move with the aid of a short stick.

'As the one that speaks both English and German well, I am chosen to be an interpreter between my men and your guards. It is a good arrangement because I fear that if I bend down too far I might not be able to get back up,' he added amiably.

Although war had deemed Hans Klepner to be his enemy, Toby was much taken by the soldier's civility and good humour. They were both about the same age, and while the other was now probably disabled for life, he did not seem embittered either by his experiences or capture. His smile when it came was frank and open: a desire for friendship clearly lying behind it. Yet his grey eyes showed fatigue too – a weariness of struggle and loss that drains all who suffer defeat during conflict.

Those around him exhibited similar signs. One, gaunt and emaciated, trembled as he pulled and cut the tops of the turnips, his shoulder twitching occasionally. Another worked without looking up or speaking, only bending to fondle Macken's ear as the dog came near his leg; while a third carried a livid scar down the side of his head that stretched from above the hairline to below his chin. He was also deathly pale and frequently raised his face to gaze blankly at the sky.

'That is Jurgen Haller,' said Hans Klepner, seeing Toby looking towards his friend. 'He was a tank driver. The Americans rocketed his convoy, killing the other members of his crew... but Hans was lucky – he was pulled out half dead. A piece of shrapnel had broken his jaw and fractured his skull... so now he has fits and cannot always control his bowels. Being sick he should not really be here; but the hospital is no good for him, for it is like the tank, he says – a prison. Like the rest of us, he longs to go home... But I think he may never see Germany again.'

'We will all see Germany again – when the Fatherland is victorious!' piped the short soldier with glasses. 'You talk like one who is already defeated, Hans, but should not voice such views, or it may go ill with you later.'

'I did not tell you that Torsten speaks your language too, did I?' said Hans Klepner. 'Oh yes, he is a brave fellow who will not accept the inevitable until all has failed... But perhaps this is because Torsten has never had the pleasure of being in action,' he added dryly. 'You see he was adjutant to a Panzer colonel and unfortunately fell into captivity when his staff car ran out of fuel... Therefore I am afraid the job of turnip picker is a little below his station.'

The two Germans exchanged glances, one angrily, the other with a dismissive gesture as a ripple of laughter rose from their fellow prisoners.

* * *

The sound of aircraft approaching from the south became audible at this point, and looking that way Toby noted the distant shapes of four or five heavy bombers flying low above the trees. They were "Flying Fortresses" returning from the daylight raid embarked upon in the early morning. Soon others began to appear, and as the throb of their engines grew even the silent German, as if aroused from a deep reverie, paused to slowly sweep the sky, a hand shielding his eyes. Only Macken seemed disinterested, and having noted that the attention of everyone was now directed elsewhere, contentedly picked up his heels and trotted off up the hill in search of rabbits and other amusements.

Meanwhile the aircraft came on in ragged formation, gradually stringing out in a line to begin their final approach to the air base seven miles away. Then, one by one, they rumbled over the silent watchers, the great silver bulk of each silhouetted against the westering sun. Most appeared to have returned undamaged from their mission, but one less fortunate aircraft had lost a chunk of its tail, while another was cruelly holed in three places along its fuselage. Still they came over, each lowering its landing gear as the distant runway came in sight, the men on board no doubt happy at the prospect of returning once again to the waiting earth. Twelve or fourteen went by, the sound of their engines gradually fading as they flew beyond sight over the brow of the hill until the skies were empty once more.

But the drama was not quite over, for one final bomber now entered the airborne stage – a straggler, seriously damaged and limping for home. It came on, trailing oily smoke from an outer engine, slanting at an angle towards them, the pilot barely able to maintain height and direction. An escorting fighter, its job of protection done, peeled away into the evening sky, dipping a wing in salute and wishing luck to the crew. Then the B17 was left alone to play out the concluding chapter in an all too familiar story of life or death.

Every man below gazed up with a mixture of fascination and awe, each harbouring his own thoughts. Some, remembering their homeland, willed the seemingly doomed aircraft to drop from the skies and plunge headlong to the earth in a ball of fire. Others prayed for it to stay on course, thinking of the men on board and inwardly begging God to bring them salvation. However, there was nothing they could do but watch as it lumbered overhead, like a wounded animal staggering towards shelter. One engine had lost power long before, its blackened cowling giving evidence of the battle fought to extinguish greedy flames – now a second feathered, white smoke left trailing behind suggesting that it had overheated and seized. The bomb aimer's window had also been blown out and a wing tip torn off. No designer would have envisaged his aircraft staying in the sky with such damage, but the rugged beast crawled on – the "Fortress" lumbering away northward over Stavenham while Toby, his fingers crossed, seemed to wait an age before the undercarriage opened. Then the heavy wheels sluggishly dropped down and locked into position.

Another minute elapsed before the aircraft finally disappeared over the distant hilltop, and like the others Toby moved up the rise to follow its progress. But none of them either saw or heard anything else (no distant roar or burst of flames to indicate its final fall) – signifying that the aircraft and its crew had safely landed to fly again another day.

* * *

With the final act now run, the prisoners were escorted back to the turnip field where an army lorry had drawn up to return them to their camp. Together, the tired men assisted their less fortunate comrades into it, with Hans Klepner helped up last. He appeared saddened and deeply fatigued as he leant over the side towards Toby.

'Our war is over,' he said, 'but it seems others must continue to their final victory. For myself I wish no harm to any man, since all must do their duty. My only hope is to return home to see my wife and son – if they are still alive.'

The lorry then moved off and bumped down the hill as Toby raised his hand in farewell; a gesture returned by Hans Klepner and one or two others. Then he and Jeannie began to make their way back to the deserted farmhouse with Macken, who had appeared through a nearby hedge, trotting in front. Jeannie, having been quiet for some time, broke her silence as they drew near to the front door.

'I must soon leave you once more, Toby,' she said, drawing close. 'But would seek your thoughts about what you have seen.'

Her eyes were bright and enquiring, and he searched in his head for the right words to give. '…I left my own age full of doubt and trouble,' he replied at last. 'So much was wrong, both with the world… and with me. So many mistakes being made that the earth itself was threatened – with both climate and nature in turmoil. …And now I have seen something of what went before – that men had as many weaknesses then as in my own time.'

Jeannie nodded. 'This is true, Toby. Men have exploited and often destroyed each other, while defiling their world, through the ages. But there is another way,' she added, as if challenging him, 'a way beyond greed and corrupt values, for those wise enough to seek it. You will come to witness this, and it is for you to see how the lasting answers are found. …Yet things must still become worse before a better way emerges.'

Toby was troubled by her closing words, but did not say more for they had now arrived at the porch where he turned the key in the lock.

'Will you come in?' he asked.

'No, Toby, you must rest, and both Macken and I have other work to do. But take these,' she said, handing him a small package containing sandwiches and dried fruit taken from the fold of her coat. 'They will keep your hunger away; and have no fear – none shall disturb you here unless time is pressing.'

She then lightly brushed her palm across his temple before moving away into the twilight with Macken trotting close by... neither looking back as they departed.

* * *

With the void of the empty house before him there seemed little else for Toby to do but refresh himself at the water butt before going indoors to eat. Later, having chewed upon his lonely repast, he fell to thinking about his lost family and home; and not until the midnight hour had passed did he again retire to seek solace in sleep.

Chapter Thirteen

The "Pom Pom Man"

For Toby another period of quiet oblivion went by as the seasons changed beyond his window. One night part of the chimney was dislodged during a gale, and having teetered for an hour eventually toppled down onto the roof, sending broken slates crashing to the ground. Thereafter, when it rained, water splashed into the loft, before seeping slowly down inside wardrobes and behind empty bookcases. Meanwhile, whitewash cracked; and faded wallpaper peeled from plaster and ceilings to settle in languid coils where mould grew. Only Toby's room stayed habitable: warmed by the passing sun and aired through a widening crack in the window frame, it became a dry haven in an encroaching sea of dampness.

For the most part he slept peacefully during this time – only dreaming when his mind occasionally drew near to the real world. Then the faces he'd known in his old life flashed before him, while others, encountered more recently, would rise up, like subconscious accusers, seeking answers to unvoiced questions.

When Toby did eventually awake, he found himself in a period of accelerating scientific, technological and agricultural change that was sweeping away the past. The Second World War was over, and Britain had emerged into a new age in which the remaining small farmers of Stavenham would experience altered circumstances, quickly leading to their demise and extinction.

* * *

Toby lifted his head like a long submerged diver coming up for air. He'd heard a sound near at hand, someone knocking at the door – not a loud banging, but a slowly repeated series of taps, as of a gloved hand striking wood. He swung his legs to the floor, wincing once more at the pain and stiffness in his body, then raised himself into a standing position before listening again.

There it was, the same series of taps: three together in sequence, followed by another after a pause, as if the one that made them was keeping time. Toby felt uneasy; but hearing nothing else, stepped out onto the landing and began to make his way downstairs. It was then that he realised the house had become a ruin: for everything smelt strongly of decay and the musty carpet squelched beneath his feet. In places spreading blotches of mould had blackened the walls and as he descended, ceiling paper, peeling from above, coiled down in musty fronds to brush against his forehead. A window in the kitchen had also come slightly open, through which stray creepers spread their clinging tentacles around the rotting ledge.

But these sights did not long claim Toby's attention, for through the misty glass of the door he now made out the bulky shape of someone standing outside. Toby froze, then sidled to peer through the narrow slit between window and frame, where he might view the visitor unseen. He half expected to see a farm workman sent down by Basil Tyler to prospect the empty building, or even the landowner himself; but the person he actually discerned was a shabbily dressed middle-aged woman holding a stick with a cloth-covered end.

The newcomer had a broad vacant face, freckled cheeks and large short-sighted blue eyes. Her lower jaw drooped slightly, in an effort of concentration, showing a row of uneven teeth between which her tongue was tightly held; while uncombed hair, streaked with grey, poked untidily from beneath a threadbare headscarf. The testament of her clothing showed that the strange woman had dressed more than amply against the cold of early morning: for she not only had on a thick skirt that fell below her calves, but also wore a lumpy woollen cardigan and a heavy tweed outdoor coat.

At first Toby thought her a vagrant – like himself in need of shelter – but then a spark of recognition came to him. He knew her face, having seen it once before in circumstances he now recalled. It was Queenie Towser, the girl held hostage at Maxton Tower.

As there appeared to be nobody else with her, Toby moved forward to unlock the door, before stepping into the porch. Queenie was indeed alone, and for a moment stared at him, as if trying to recollect his features. Then she nodded twice, the corner of her mouth drooping slightly.

'I had a feeling... there was someone here,' she stammered. 'I thought... it might be you.'

'What made you imagine it was me?' asked Toby guardedly, wondering if others might suspect the same.

She hunched her shoulders, 'I just knew... that's all. Sometimes things come to me.'

Looking at her, Toby again recalled the injuries Queenie had suffered... injuries that had changed her life and left her as she now was. She stooped before him, leaning on the stick, her body hunched and skewed to one side as if her back was twisted.

'And do your brothers know you have come here?'

She thought again, but this time her answer came after little deliberation. 'They don't worry about me... always too busy... so I'm off to see the "Pom Pom Man".'

Queenie brightened suddenly and, lifting down her shoulder bag, held it towards him with quivering hands so Toby could see the contents. It held a pear, a few washed carrots, and a handful of apples.

'You must be hungry,' she said, shifting her weight from one foot to the other. 'Go on, take some... please – they're all clean... I wouldn't give you nothing that wasn't good to eat.'

Her expression was warm and sincere, yet she spoke like a small child seeking assurance and approval.

Toby took an apple, wiped it on his trousers and bit into it as she looked on approvingly, breaking into a smile. But this only lasted a second before Queenie was overcome with seriousness once more – her forehead wrinkling with concentration.

'You can't stay here,' she said, solemnly. 'They're coming to knock it down in a few days... but I know a place where you might sleep tonight.'

Her eagerness to help and please him could not be doubted but the news that the farmhouse was to be demolished came as a shock.

'Who will come?' he asked.

'The men with hammers – they'll take it all away... But you can come with me,' she added encouragingly. 'It's threshing day today – at the Braylings – they let me help. The "Pom Pom Man" will be here soon – it's fun!'

Toby could not fully understand Queenie's chatter, but having asked her to wait by the door, rushed back upstairs to collect his things. He put on his fleece (deciding to risk possible enquiries about it) and stuffed his few belongings into the pockets. Then he opened and held up his long unused mobile, in the faint hope that it might have a signal; but as before the miracle of late twentieth-century communication remained dead – a worthless treasure of wire and plastic.

A noise in the kitchen brought him back to the present, and having taken a final look round, Toby descended again.

It seemed Queenie's curiosity had got the better of her; and having entered the house she stood gazing at a curled and faded calendar left behind by the Trindles.

'April 1. 9. 3. 6,' she read slowly. 'Blimey, that's old – lots of years have gone by since then.'

'When is it now?' asked Toby, with a cold feeling that normal time had come to mean little in his own life.

'What a funny question! ...It's 1957... March... everyone knows that, surely?'

Her tone was incredulous, almost pitying, making him feel that he must have missed out on very much.

'But come on,' she said. 'We'll be late if we don't go now – and the "Pom Pom Man" will already have started.'

* * *

So he left the farmhouse at Warren Hill for the last time – carefully locking the door in a final act of respect for its long departed owners. After this the two of them walked together towards "High Dyke Farm", Queenie shuffling at Toby's side, and as they talked he learned that the "Pom Pom Man" was the owner of a machine brought in to thresh the Braylings' store of wheat and barley. In her excited and garrulous way, Queenie informed him that the "Pom Pom" was an old single cylinder "Field Marshal" tractor used to power the threshing machine, and that its name referred to the rhythmic noise it made. Apparently most of the larger neighbouring farms had already gone over to using new combine harvesters; but it seemed the Braylings, on their limited acreage, were still using a binder at harvest time. So the yearly ritual of hiring a thresher in spring continued to be, for them, an essential part of the farming calendar. Toby also learned that old Arthur Brayling and his wife Sarah had sadly died soon after the war, leaving their five surviving children to run "High Dyke Farm".

On entering the farmyard they were met by Jim Brayling – now a mature man approaching his fiftieth birthday, though as hale and as hearty as ever.

'Good Lord, boy!' he exclaimed, looking Toby up and down. 'You *still* don't look a day older – what *is* your secret? I'm blowed if it ain't getting to be uncanny.'

His brothers and sisters then all came up, and the conversation continued in a similar vein for the next few minutes. Duke Brayling felt the material of his fleece, commenting on its softness. 'This must be one of they "Rock 'n' Roll" garments made of some new synthetic material, I shouldn't wonder,' he remarked. 'Whatever next?'

Even in such familiar company Toby once more felt uneasy, and he was relieved when, with work in mind, they all set off towards the corn stack at the far end of the yard. This had been sheeted over with a tarpaulin during the winter months, but was now stripped off ready for threshing to commence. The stack, as always, would have been a haven for rats during the barren foraging days just past; and to snare any that still remained under the straw base, a two foot high chicken wire enclosure had been erected around three sides to catch those that tried to make an escape as the work progressed.

It was approaching nine o'clock, and Jim had already twice drawn out his pocket watch to check the time when the first sounds of the approaching "Field Marshal" rippled towards them.

'That's him!' said Queenie, becoming animated. 'That's Mr Slyman and his "Pom Pom" – you can tell by the noise.'

The noise was indeed as distinctive as anything Toby had experienced before; a sound no longer heard, other than at country fairs, in more recent times. It resembled a steady pumping noise – or the striking of a padded drumstick on the skins of orchestral timpani. Sometimes the beats would rise and fall in both volume and tempo as the tractor speeded up or slowed down; but the rhythmic heartbeat always resumed its even chorus when each distant bend or obstacle in the road had been negotiated. The steady thump carried too, echoing away over the countryside like a wave of native drumming across a savannah.

Soon they could see the machine coming as it chugged up the track from Molliton hauling the old red-painted thresher, all the while circled by a crowd of curious rooks and seagulls. The driver, a little man perched on a high seat and wearing a wide floppy felt hat, hailed them from a distance. Then, cutting across the stubble of the field between, he began to steer in their direction. He was dressed in a red waistcoat, with a bright yellow choker at his throat, and appeared for all the world like a theatrical dwarf. Cigar smoke blossomed around his head, and a large shiny clasp on the leather money pouch at his hip glinted when it caught the light.

Now only fifty yards away, the noisy assemblage had begun to cause consternation among the animals of the farm. The bull started to bellow in an adjacent paddock, while a group of calves stampeded across a nearby meadow. The farm geese also set up a loud chorus, joined by the farmyard cockerel and chickens in a competition of raucous sound.

'That blessed thing's too noisy!' Jim Brayling called out as the "Field Marshal" drew up beside the corn stack. 'Fair wakes up the whole neighbourhood!'

The tractor stopped and the owner, Cade Slyman, jumped down, leaving his charge still pumping softly. He was a very small man indeed; but what he lacked in height he more than made up for by force of personality. His shoulders were broad and muscular, and rolled up sleeves revealed strong arms and hands. Yet it was his manner and bearing that most impressed – for Mr Slyman was above all a confident and clever character. Now in his late fifties, he had run his own business for over thirty years and was master of a dying trade. He answered to no other, and had contempt for any that held their status more important than their ability. Cade could not abide a fool either, and had made a small fortune from those that thought themselves better than him. A bachelor all his life, he had sworn never to encumber himself with the shackles of marriage, and would go to his grave happy in his independence. As such he was a man with few friends – while whatever enemies he made were given reason to show him respect, for he was not only wise but cunning when challenged. The words – "Cade Slyman – Corn Threshing and Milling – Old Weldon – Bedfordshire" – were painted in faded Showman's script across the top boards of the wooden threshing machine, and he glanced at them with satisfaction as he spoke.

'You'll be telling me I'm late, Jim,' he said, straight-faced. 'But I'd say that's because your ruddy farm tracks are too long.'

It was a comment that brooked no response, and the three brothers gathered round seemed disinclined to challenge him further. He eyed them all shrewdly, his clean-shaven face lean and businesslike. Toby noticed that the threshing manager wore a gold stud in his left ear and this, together with the shock of hair that spilled over his collar, and the large polished metal buckle on his belt, gave him a rakish air.

'We'd best get started,' he announced, following another scant exchange of pleasantries; then strode round to the back of the tractor to unhitch the thresher. This task having been completed, he climbed back aboard the "Field Marshal" and chugged forward to turn in the farmyard, so that the tractor now faced the machine. Within minutes of completing the manoeuvre, a wide belt had been run out between the thresher and the "Field Marshal" so that a drive cylinder on the side of the tractor's engine could provide power. Finally, when all was ready, Cade Slyman gently reversed, and accompanied by a rhythmic, "Pom... Pom... Pom... Pom... Pom. Pom. Pom. Pom." from the tractor, as it took up the strain, the whole rickety machine came to life in a whirl of revolving belts, chattering chains and rattling winnowing tables. Out of every gap and opening a cloud of dust and chaff rose from the threshing machine, filling the air with a swirling haze as if some sleepy old nursery rhyme giant had woken up and was shaking the cobwebs out of his hair before going off in search of dinner.

While Toby stood fascinated, the others began to take up their positions for the day's toil. Bert, the eldest, had climbed a ladder and was preparing to pass the sheaves down to the open platform at the top of the thresher. Here, his sister Betty stood waiting to pass them forward to her brother Duke, who would cut the strings and release the grain stalks onto a slanting feeder table above the threshing drum. Toby watched as the first was fed in; followed by a second and a third without pause – a process that would take hours to complete before the whole stack was reduced to the ground.

He now heard the bowels of the machine churning into life as the separation of grain, chaff and straw got under way; the first corn arriving at the bagging ducts as residual straw began tumbling out from the rear end, where Mickey fed it into a stationary baler. The whole scene was one of practised teamwork and organisation: with each person performing a set task to keep the process moving smoothly. Toby was allocated the job of stacking the straw bales that emerged at regular intervals from the baler – being assisted in this by Jim, who also frequently checked the quality of the grain. It was Cade Slyman who ran the show however – working with a cool authority that was to be admired. If a blockage occurred he was on the scene in a moment; and by the skilful appliance of spanner or wrench would free the affected part with the minimum of fuss and delay. Always a stickler for efficiency, he had at first looked on disapprovingly when Queenie shuffled up to offer help with tying the full hessian bags of corn. But on watching her loop and knot the first one to his satisfaction, Cade readily accepted Queenie's presence, making her his lieutenant for the day.

For her part, Queenie could not have been happier, applying herself with the utmost dedication as her untidy hair became progressively matted with fine particles of chaff creeping from the winnowing tables clattering by her ear. Volunteering to help in any way possible, she smiled at everyone who came near her – for it filled her with delight to be valued and to know that she was among friends who accepted the way she was.

So the work went on and morning progressed towards noon. Toby's arms and back began to ache, for the bales were heavy, and as the stack began to grow each one had to be lifted and carried into position. Yet, as on previous occasions, nobody complained: for theirs was a common toil, hard and strenuous, that would reap as its only reward, the satisfaction of having played a part in a task well done. Thus, by one o'clock the corn stack had already been reduced by over a half; although Bert Brayling was still faced with pitching more than a thousand or so sheaves up to the threshing platform before the end of the day. Work now ceased for lunch; the thumping tractor was shut down for an hour, and a welcome calm returned in which the song of birds and lowing of cattle could again be heard. The air cleared of flying dust and chaff, bringing relief to their lungs, and a gentle spring sun peeped through a raft of thin cloud overhead.

Mickey had reappeared from the farmhouse with a fresh brew of tea for the men, together with a "ploughman's lunch" of bread, cheese and pickles, which they sat down to enjoy. Meanwhile the women, accompanied by Queenie, went off to eat indoors. The three brothers then quickly fell into conversation about a visit to market planned for the following week, and Toby found himself sitting a little apart with Cade Slyman next to the silent threshing machine. The smell of grain and straw, mixed with the rich odour of diesel and paraffin wafting down from the "Field Marshal", filled his senses as he leaned against a sack and looked around. The threshing master did not seem interested in conversation at first, having perched himself on a wooden stool to read a newspaper. But looking up a few moments later and noticing that Toby had remained nearby, he lowered his daily and turned to speak. Known by others to prefer his own company when not at work, few folk normally ventured near when he was relaxing: yet he was somewhat intrigued by Toby and now seemed ready to share his wisdom.

'You're new around here,' he said, fixing Toby with an enquiring look. 'Not exactly used to the work… But you do your bit well enough.'

'I'm a journalist – studying country life… I'm writing an article.'

'Newspaper man, eh,' Cade returned brusquely, tapping his own daily. '…Never trust anything you read in print – isn't that right?'

Toby passed off the not unusual comment. 'I've discovered a great many things,' he replied slowly, 'and much to suggest that things are changing very fast for farmers around here.'

'They are that,' said Cade, nodding sagely. 'And will continue to do so now, until there is nothing left of the old ways.'

'You've noticed, too?'

Cade took a long drink of tea from the tin mug beside him; then reached inside his waistcoat pocket for a half smoked cigar, which he placed between his lips and lit with a match. He drew upon it deeply before turning his head towards the sky and exhaling the smoke. When he looked back his eyes were knowing and thoughtful.

'All this will soon come to an end, young feller,' he said in a low, deliberate voice. 'The old ways of the countryside are as good as over, and before long all the folk that once cared about the land will be gone. I'll pack it in too, by and by, for there's no future in this any more,' he added, gesturing toward the thresher. 'But I'm lucky I've made enough to retire on; while for others it's different. A small farm like this can't make money no more, and each year it gets worse. You need the new machines to survive these days, or you're not able to compete. I've seen new combine harvesters that can clear a whole medium sized field in a day without the need for my services later. But they cost thousands to buy, and people like the Braylings could never afford to own one of their own. They'll soldier on for a bit as best they can, of course, trying to keep up. But for them it will come to an end soon enough. Those that know the land and animals like they do will be bought out, and all the traditional methods will disappear.'

'You think so?'

'I know so,' said Cade, fixing Toby with a bright eye. 'The big landowners, banks and men from the city will soon control everything – then the land will have to look after itself. Profit will be the only word that matters in their new world, and much damage the pursuit of it may do. Why don't you tell your readers to think about that?'

The little man then nodded in affirmation of his own sentiments before going back to reading his paper, leaving his listener to consider what he'd said. Toby already knew only too well of the fall and disappearance of both "Pocket Farm" and "Warren Hill Farm" and now, looking around him, he recognised signs of decline at "High Dyke" too: a derelict outhouse, worn out and rusting machinery, and empty animal sheds. How soon would the wind of change sweep all this away as well?

* * *

The womenfolk came back a while later: the two Brayling sisters laughing and joking with Queenie, who trotted along beside them babbling her replies. Then work resumed and the short afternoon advanced toward evening. Gradually the sun drew round to the west and a breeze blew up that scattered stray coils of loose straw, sending them scurrying in eddying swirls through the farmyard. Meanwhile a chill developed in the air as one of the last days of winter drew towards its close. But all laboured on until the last sheaves were lifted onto the thresher and the final grains ran down polished corn chutes.

With the job done, Cade Slyman nimbly climbed back onto his tractor to ease it forward so that the drive belt could be taken off. Then, having packed this away, he coupled up to the threshing machine and drew it clear of what remained of the corn stack. A final coil of chicken wire was now drawn across the opening as Duke Brayling slipped inside and moved towards what remained of the straw base with a pitchfork in his hands. The others watched him step onto this before advancing steadily forward, thrusting the fork downwards at frequent intervals.

'What's your brother doing?' Toby asked Betty, who stood beside him.

'Going after the rats,' she replied. 'We heard them in there as we finished off – he'll get them.'

The farmer had stopped momentarily after an unsuccessful lunge, but having closely scanned the surface of the straw once more, then thrust the fork near his feet before lifting it up to reveal a large brown rat impaled upon the tines. The creature squealed and wriggled convulsively before Duke lowered the two-pronged weapon and despatched the rat with a blow of his foot.

'A breeding female,' said Betty with satisfaction. 'She'll have been feeding on our good grain all winter. There'll be others, you watch.'

There were. Duke skewered two more, and another ran for the wire where it was cornered and killed. A nest was also discovered, the tiny offspring destroyed by a heavy boot.

'It's the only way,' said Betty, moving off to begin her evening milking duties. 'If we didn't do them in there would be untold damage. A farm infested with rats makes no money.'

Queenie, standing slightly apart, had not enjoyed witnessing the rodents' demise, however, and as she came and stood silently beside Toby he noticed a tear rolling down her cheek.

'You'd best take her home, Toby,' said Betty, calling back. 'She never did like that sort of thing much. The men will finish off here. Come again tomorrow and we'll settle up with you.'

Toby said he would (although sensing that the possibility of his returning the following day was far from assured) then set off with Queenie in the direction of "Deep Spinney Farm". They had not gone far when the rhythmic exhaust of the "Field Marshal" started up again and looking round Toby saw the stately machine pull into view a hundred yards away at the commencement of its return journey to Old Weldon. Cade Slyman was again bobbing along on the driver's seat, a swirl of cigar smoke around his head. He waved at them, the late rays of the sun brightening his felt hat and catching the red of his waistcoat, and they stood watching as the lumbering assemblage rumbled off into the distance before disappearing beyond a copse of trees – the stentorian thump of the tractor echoing away towards Bedford.

So departed the "Pom Pom Man", only twice more to be seen that way in years to come.

* * *

Queenie now seemed anxious to get on and, pulling at Toby's sleeve, led him downhill away from the higher ground. They soon approached the chicken farm with its ugly buildings; but this time he noted that little sound rose from them, as if many were empty. The air smelt fresher too, and Toby was about to make the suggestion that they delay a few moments, when Queenie suddenly turned to the left and made off along an unkempt footpath leading uphill through bushes and trees. She seemed excited to show him something, moving as quickly as she could on her unsteady legs, her loose overcoat constantly snagging on thorns and brambles.

'I said I would,' she said over her shoulder, through short breaths. 'I've got a place specially for you to stay in – I have!'

He couldn't imagine where she was going but followed, wondering where her wild tramp would lead, and where he would stay if Queenie's idea were simply an illusion. By now they were drawing near to the Northampton road, and circling a rambling growth of rhododendron bushes, Toby suddenly saw a cottage directly in front. He recognised the place immediately, though it was now more sunken and ivy covered than previously... It was the same cottage that Declan Finch had fled from more than twenty years before.

'It's empty,' Queenie said, a smile flushing her face as she looked from the cottage towards him. 'You can stay there – nobody comes... and I won't tell.'

He felt unease at the thought of entering the criminal's former lair; but seeing her earnest expression, knew that he could not disappoint her.

'It's not locked – we can go in.'

So they moved towards the front door, and as promised, it opened when Toby turned the handle.

'The light still works as well,' she said, stepping in behind him and reaching for the switch. 'I come here sometimes – I keep it tidy.'

The room they were in suddenly lit up and Toby looked around. It was still furnished: the cushions neatly arranged on a small sofa, a wooden table by the fireplace set for two. A small Victorian doll in a flowing dress sat primly in one of the chairs. Even the curtains at the window looked reasonably clean.

Queenie grinned with satisfaction. 'I keep it nice, don't I? And the bed's made up next door for you... the toilet still flushes too!'

She shuffled off in front towards the bedroom, which as promised contained a made-up bed and a tall wardrobe with a mirror.

'You can sleep here… it's really comfy. …The mice are a bit noisy sometimes – but they won't bother you!' she added reassuringly.

Toby hardly knew what to say: only congratulating Queenie on her housekeeping and commending her generosity.

'There's no charge,' she said, earnestly wringing her shaking hands. 'And you can stay as long as you want… but I must be going… they'll be expecting me and Cregan gets annoyed if I'm late.'

He reached down and took her hand in his – realising that she had probably offered him all she owned and valued. 'Thank you, Queenie… you're very kind,' he said, smiling.

'I'll come to see you when I can… but I won't make a fuss… must go!'

*   *   *

They parted, and Toby watched her shuffle off along the garden path before disappearing down the lane beyond, leaving him alone to face the coming night. It was getting dark, the house and its surroundings silent except for a late calling blackbird. He looked around the cottage once more, opening cupboards, where he found neatly stacked crockery and polished ornaments; while on the window ledge in the toilet there stood a vase of freshly cut daffodils that had just opened. There were also apples in a polished bowl in the kitchen, and biscuits in a tin, some of which he took to eat while thinking how he might repay his hostess.

But his thoughts continually came back to the villain who had lived there and what might have happened inside those walls. In a small cupboard next to the back door he found an earth-stained flick-knife, with a thin and rusty blade, that had evidently remained untouched for many years. The handle was made of ivory with the initials "D.F." whittled on the hilt – a relic from an evil past.

Wondering why Queenie had left it there, Toby put the weapon back again before returning to the living room. Seeing the knife had given him a troubled feeling about his situation, and deciding that it was best for now to remain concealed, Toby turned off the sitting room light and sat facing the door. His only point of focus was the elegant doll propped in her chair, and he pondered for a while as dappled rays from the early moon came in at the window, faintly illuminating his mute companion. Then, leaning forward onto the table with his head on his hands, Toby fell into a deep sleep.

Chapter Fourteen

The Burning of
"Deep Spinney Farm"

T HE WINTER OF 1962–1963 WOULD BE LONG remembered. The previous summer had been cool and indifferent, giving way at the end of September to an inclement autumn. But no one could have forecast the extreme weather that arrived at the turn of the year, when an Arctic blizzard swept down from the north.

* * *

Discomfort again brought Toby back to the present: not simply the aches and pains now familiar to him at the end of his long rests – but an all-pervading cold that chilled his bones and penetrated to the core. He shivered and rubbed his face, the blue fingers of his hands feeling icy, before gradually regaining focus and suppressing a sneeze. The cottage seemed as cold as death, a cloud of condensation forming around his head when he exhaled.

The room appeared virtually unchanged, but little touches here and there told him that it must have been visited from time to time. There were dead ashes in the grate that he had not seen before, a vase with some wilted but still blooming sprigs of winter jasmine, and a home-made calendar hanging next to the fireplace. Toby moved forward and squinted at it, his hands wrapped around his middle as he drew near. Only one month remained to be torn off – the month of December 1962 – and wiggly ticks had been put against all the dates up to Christmas Day. The others remained blank, waiting for the writer to return.

'Queenie must have done this,' he said to himself.

Desperate for warmth, Toby considered the prospect of lighting a fire, and had begun a search for wood and paper when he heard a scuffling noise in the front garden – although whether human or animal he could not tell. Curiosity drew him towards the window where he looked out upon the frosty path. Nothing moved at first, but then an agile little dog trotted into sight, and having risen up on its back legs, began circling and chasing its tail. The stubby fellow quickly became completely absorbed in his game, first going one way, then the other, in a vain endeavour to seize the prize.

'Macken!' mouthed Toby, much cheered by the sight of the Jack Russell. 'But who is with you this time, I wonder?'

He had little leave to speculate upon this for the sound of footsteps in the lane told him that another visitor was approaching and, seconds later, a short figure wearing a long black overcoat and sturdy boots appeared at the garden gate. The man, who carried a leather bag over his shoulder, wore a floppy cap, and had tied a warm scarf around his neck as extra protection against the cold. He also had on a pair of thick leather gloves, and held a stick with a knobbly handle that he swung casually at the dead heads of frozen thistles. ...It could only be Jasper.

Toby went to the door and stepped over the threshold to greet him. However, as he emerged, the creases that formed on the wiry little man's forehead made it clear that the other somewhat disapproved of his own untidy appearance. For his part, Jasper hadn't changed at all: his lean, craggy features were just as knowing – his eyes as keen and piercing as ever.

'You look a mess, mate,' he said. 'You might try combing your hair and having a shave.'

From these comments anyone might have presumed they had last met only the day before. Toby felt like protesting that his appearance was due to his enforced rest rather than neglect of personal hygiene, but before he had a chance to do so Jasper eased past him into the cottage where he quickly made clear that he was equally unimpressed by the comforts it offered.

'Blimey it's cold in here,' he complained, standing by the mantelpiece. 'We'll need to get a fire started or freeze to death before the day's much older.'

As always, Jasper was both practical as well as direct, and having dropped the leather bag from his shoulder, went straight to the back door before disappearing into the yard outside. He was back within minutes carrying a bundle of logs and with the pockets of his overcoat crammed with an assortment of kindling wood.

'Step aside while I get this going, Toby,' he said, kneeling by the hearth. 'And you'd best dress yourself up a bit warmer; there's a few jumpers and things in that bag.'

Toby lifted the well used carrier onto the table as Jasper, having produced some paper from beneath his outer garments, lit a match and began to feed the small blaze that flared into life.

'You keep newspaper under your shirt for these emergencies,' Toby observed, looking over at him.

'No…' Jasper replied, with a slight note of sarcasm, 'I wear it to keep me warm – an old countryman's trick. If you'd had a few sheets around you it might have helped keep the cold away, although I admit it's not very fashionable.'

Toby did not wish to argue the merits of newspaper insulation but instead, having put on a couple of woollen jumpers and selected an old cap, settled to watch as Jasper skilfully built a fire from damp and smoky beginnings. He also lit the small stove in the kitchen in order to boil water for making tea. Then, as the cottage warmed up and the preparation of food and drink continued, he began to divulge pieces of news. Toby learned that Queenie had returned many times to watch over him, that it was now 28th December 1962, and that, due to suffering from a sudden illness, the kindly woman had not been able to visit for more than three days.

'You have talked with her, then?' Toby asked over a steaming mug.

'Talked with Queenie… not exactly, I don't always find that very profitable. No, I just let her potter around – she does no harm. But now I think her life is about to change for good, and I'm not sure how she will take it.'

'How do you mean?'

'Well… the landlord, Basil Tyler – he just up and died three months ago. The old geezer suffered a heart attack that left him in a wheelchair some time back, and now he's gone. It seems he had plans to sell everything – "Tyler Hall", all his land and the remaining farms – the lot! He'd found a buyer too – a London conglomerate by the name of "Outlandia" – one of the new agricultural management organisations with huge machines and stacks of money. They're based at Melton Wryness about three miles from here. The company wanted immediate access to all the land between Molliton and Stavenham – with a lot more besides up towards Turnham. He was negotiating to have all his remaining tenants turned off so as to secure the best deal, but died before all the paperwork could go through. As a result it seems that the Braylings at "High Dyke Farm" have retained the right to stay; as has old Meg Maddox over at "Silver Link Cottage", but this one – the disused chicken farm down the road – that's to go. Clearance of the old sheds is to be undertaken this very day – they're getting down to it right now.'

'And what about "Deep Spinney Farm" itself?' asked Toby.

'The remaining outbuilding and everything else but the farmhouse are to come down; but there is talk that "Outlandia" also want the ground on which the house stands. Whatever happens, I don't expect the Towsers to stay much longer. The men are barely fit for work, and poor old Queenie would probably be best off somewhere else.'

Toby wasn't so sure. If Queenie went she would leave behind all that she knew – and where could she go?

'Is all this inevitable?'

'Done and dusted!' Jasper replied. 'Before long Meg's cottage and the farm at "High Dyke" will be like little islands in a sea of land farmed on behalf of people nobody

around here will ever meet. And there's no real future for them folk either. Old Meg…
she'll probably be allowed to live out her days where she is, but the Braylings face harder
times. Much of the land that passed to them when the Trindles gave up at "Warren Hill
Farm" has been taken back under the agreement that Basil made with "Outlandia". They
will be left with only about seventy acres, which isn't really enough to remain viable
when there are five mouths to feed. They'll struggle on, no doubt – the last outpost in
a corporate landscape – but the trouble is they'll be undercut for price at every point
by firms such as "Outlandia" that have fewer overheads and can afford the large new
machinery. No, mark my words: if things in Bedfordshire go on as they are, small mixed
farms will inevitably die out, and only the big firms will be left growing two or three
specialist cash crops. Even the animals will disappear; for there seems little money in
pigs and cows any more, and what that will mean for nature and the countryside can only
be guessed at.'

This information gave Toby much to think about as they sat down to eat, and he
remained quiet for some time afterwards as Jasper smoked his pipe with Macken at his
heels. Toby might eventually have dozed off again had the little man not gently prodded
him with his stick.

'Don't you do that just yet,' he said. 'There's things to be seen and appointments to
keep, but you'll need to wrap up warm before leaving.'

It was not a prospect that Toby relished, but having donned a heavy three quarter
length coat found hanging behind the kitchen door, he reluctantly followed Jasper to
the porch – flinching as the cold air struck his face. But it was fresh and reviving too,
and breathing in he felt the long cobwebs of incarceration clear from his head. Thus,
together they walked down the garden path before emerging into the lane down which
Declan Finch had fled on the day of the shoot. The trees and bushes that flanked it were
now overhanging and bare of leaves, as if little traffic ever passed that way. The biting
cold seemed to encroach from all around and they strode on before arriving at the site
of "Deep Spinney Farm". It was a place wholly changed from before: the dark barns,
outhouses and towering poplars having been cleared to leave little in the immediate area
but an open wasteland of broken concrete and weed infested cobbles. The surviving
farmhouse looked dreary and brooding. One of the upstairs windows had been crudely
boarded up, while heavy curtains shrouded all the others; this last measure taken as a
precaution against the cold – although Toby could not dismiss an uneasy feeling that they
were shut up tight to conceal a guilty and secretive world within.

There was no sign of movement either, but further off a group of men could be
seen gathered around a van parked near the chicken houses. These were still large and
imposing structures, although empty for several years since the market for chickens and
fresh eggs had changed. Yet the decline of the farm was not simply down to market
forces for the Towsers' slack ways had also played a major part. The two men, whose

love of beer and gambling had always outweighed any desire to run a good business, had never carried out any proper maintenance. Roofs had been allowed to leak when felt peeled, while the birds had been left to exist in an ever-deepening layer of straw and excrement. Rats naturally prospered in this environment, with the result that outbreaks of disease had become increasingly common. Consequently, in time local shops took less and less of the farm's produce, preferring to deal with more reliable suppliers of higher quality fare, and as a result, one by one the sheds had fallen into disuse. Thus, while the farm had gone over to chicken production only twenty years before, it was now finished, its grim buildings, with their short and unsavoury history of neglect and cruelty, awaiting destruction.

The buyers, "Outlandia", had considered salvaging some of the materials from the complex, but on inspection found little that wasn't riddled with woodworm or decayed beyond further use. So a decision was taken to cordon the area and reduce the buildings to ashes. This was what the four men in the "Outlandia" van had come to do. They were all young and fit employees, each wearing orange overalls bearing the company logo as they stood listening to Cregan Towser, who argued with them.

'Why does it all have to go? Barnaby and me could have stayed on and made use of a couple of sheds.'

Cregan looked old and beaten, as did his brother who stood a few paces away, and it was evident that the confrontational stance he'd chosen to employ was making little impression on the workmen.

'This lot isn't yours anymore, Mr Towser,' said the one that seemed to be in charge. 'It belongs to the company, and if they say it's got to come down; so it will.' He, like the others, had been offered overtime rates for working in the days before the New Year and was looking forward to his bonus.

'But this is our living,' said Cregan, puffing out his flabby chest.

The other looked him up and down, as if assessing a non-existent threat, before replying dismissively.

'Look, this... *was* your farm, my friend – but... *now* it is the property of "Outlandia",' he enunciated with great emphasis. 'So, if you'll excuse us, we have work to do!'

The foreman's tone was both forceful and collected, mirroring the weather in its coldness and finality, and choking any response from Cregan just as surely as the icy wind now blowing out of the northern sky promised to freeze the words on the broken farmer's lips.

With the conversation thus concluded, the four men turned away to complete their preparations, leaving Cregan grimacing and helplessly biting his tongue as they walked off. Barnaby too slouched away towards the farmhouse and left his brother standing alone cutting a forlorn figure – the one-time friend of London's underworld, and confidant of Basil Tyler reduced to a defeated bystander as his former livelihood went up in smoke.

There seemed nothing for him to vent his anger upon but the grey sky, until he noticed Toby and Jasper watching. In an instant Cregan's eyes screwed up and he moved towards them with clenched fists.

'You two again!' he said vociferously. 'Whenever things aren't going well for me – you turn up!'

He stopped several paces away, however, craning forward and studying them with bloodshot eyes; and while there had been menace in his approach, Toby could see that his fists would not actually deliver a blow. Indeed aggression was quickly replaced by confusion and uncertainty as Cregan more closely observed their features. 'What is this?' he growled, pulling back. 'Why ain't neither of you older yet? …Why don't time seem to mark the both of yez and that other girl like it does the rest of us? …It ain't right!'

Jasper had re-lit his pipe and seemed in no hurry to reply; while Macken, having appeared from behind the nearest shed, came up and circled round Cregan's legs, giving the impression that he felt inclined to pee against them if the farmer remained stationary a little longer.

'You should look at yourself in the mirror instead of questioning others,' Jasper said at last. 'Take more exercise, Mr Towser – you'll feel better for it and become a good deal less bad-tempered, I shouldn't wonder.'

This remark was guaranteed to annoy the naturally aggressive roughneck, yet although Cregan coughed and spat, he did no more as they moved away. Their final meeting would dog his thoughts for many a day and he would live on a puzzled and defeated man until his death three years later following an ill-advised brawl in a Bedford pub.

The "Outlandia" men worked with a will and soon all was ready. The sheds stood well away from anything likely to be ignited by the heat, and the added damp and cold of mid-winter provided ideal conditions for their work. The buildings were to be torched using paraffin and old diesel oil to get them well alight; and would burn for most of the night if all went to plan. Toby tracked one of the men as he carried a heavy can into one of the sheds and began to douse the walls with its contents. It was dark and dank inside, the straw under his feet wet in places with moisture that had got in through the roof. The rank smell of a million chickens still seeped up from the two-foot layer of soiled bedding, and he thought of the countless eggs laid in that stale wilderness.

It was now late afternoon and the weak winter light began to drain from the sky. In little more than an hour all would be dark, the sun having set for the last time on another of Stavenham's lost farms. Toby would not lament the passing of this one, however, but wondered how the land would fare in coming years when the operatives in company clothes dragged their huge ploughs and cultivators across the clay soil. While in summer would the men driving their huge harvesters have any more than an inkling of what had once been there?

As he thought of these things the first flames licked up from the nearest hut, creeping and hesitant at first, before quickly becoming more vibrant as the paraffin and diesel did their work. Then another tongue of flame crept up the side of a second shed amid a growing column of choking smoke. Sparks started to fly as the four men set new fires: each offering a flaming brand to prepared sections in an orderly sequence – flitting to and fro like torch flourishing demons. One moment they would disappear in a shroud of swirling smoke, to emerge ten seconds later at another doorway, before making off in the billowing gloom to carry the cleansing flames to a further corner. It took only minutes until the whole compound was irreversibly alight, the underbelly of the encroaching night stained red and orange by the rising conflagration: an apocalyptic scene – like Dante's vision of the fires of hell as the servants of Lucifer danced among the spreading flames.

Driven back by the heat, and with the sound of burning roaring in their ears, Toby and Jasper drew off to higher ground where they could better view the scene. Each shed now blazed from end to end, and Toby occasionally heard shots ring out as the workmen fired at an escaping rat. Even from fifty or sixty yards away the heat became intense, and he would sometimes need to shield his face when the wind veered. There was much smoke from the burning straw and manure too, sometimes becoming so thick that it blotted out all that lay in front, only to be lifted up at last in a great wave and expelled into the frosty air. A grinding noise, as of a ceiling giving way, then sounded amid the crackling din and as Toby watched, the roof of the nearest shed collapsed inwards – the walls subsiding like an exhausted and defeated creature succumbing to the jaws of a hungry beast. The roof sections of other sheds similarly imploded in regular succession, sending showers of sparks and burning straw skywards to illuminate the low clouds with an eerie glow.

Night closed in, dark and brooding at first, choked by countless sooty particles rising from the scene of extinction below. But in time stars began to appear between breaks in the thinning cumulus, staring down from the purity of space upon a violent scene of cleansing and renewal. The rats ran and were dispatched; nests of mice and fleas shrivelled to nothing; woodlice filled crevices fell apart, and the noxious smells of years of neglect were blown away on the wind. For two hours they watched as the "Outlandia" men went about their task; and in that time the squalid entrails of the diseased and noisome sheds were all consumed – turned to ashes in the heat; made good again for new growth during future years. By morning only glowing embers would remain – the scant remnants of soot and charcoal picked over by curious rooks and crows – yet for many summers afterwards this low corner in North-Bedfordshire's rolling landscape would long be remarked upon as an oasis of fertility.

At last the fierce heat subsided and a chill again invaded their smut-covered clothes. Jasper took off his cap to brush away the thin layer of ash that had accumulated around his collar.

'We should be getting back,' he said. 'You need to rest; but this time it will be for only a few hours until we meet again tomorrow.'

Weary once more, Toby agreed, and they retraced their steps to the farmhouse where a single light still glowed behind a curtained upstairs window, before walking back up the lane towards the cottage. All was in darkness there: a new frost crunching beneath their feet as they approached the front door.

'Should I stay here another night? Won't the Towsers know by now?' asked Toby warily.

'Why would they?' replied Jasper. 'No… I think tonight they are probably tucked up in bed already – but perhaps you ought to move on in the morning.'

They found food to eat and stoked up the fire, talking all the while about the events of the day. But when it came time for Toby to sleep, Jasper stood up and having put on his hat and gloves, went to the door. Macken was already waiting there, and as his master pushed it ajar, passed between his legs before skipping off into the night.

'Where will you go?' asked Toby.

'I have many places to stay,' Jasper replied, gesturing toward the night sky. 'There is one in Stavenham that suits me well… though I may rest under the stars if the fancy takes me.'

'You'll freeze if you do.'

'Not I, my friend… my blood doesn't run that cold. But now you must rest in the bed Queenie has prepared for you or she will be disappointed. As for me, I'll be back soon after sunrise.'

With these words he slid round the door and was gone, with only the distant barking of a dog breaking the silence that had descended among the trees.

Left alone with his thoughts Toby sat on by the embers for a while before fatigue overtook him. Then, having walked through to the bedroom, he blinked into the darkened corners, thinking of rusty knives and dodgy money, before lying down and pulling the blankets round him.

* * *

The night passed quickly and without dreams and Toby opened his eyes the following day feeling revived. The sound of an animal softly grumbling and licking its lips then came to his ears, and looking through the open door he saw Macken contentedly gnawing on a large bone by the hearth before Jasper appeared holding a mug of tea.

215

'I don't know,' the little man said with a grin, 'some people get to sleep for years and years, but still want to stay in bed till late.'

'Have I overslept?' asked Toby sheepishly.

'Don't mind me… I'm only joking. It comes of being an early riser, that's all. Now come on, drink your tea; we've people to visit this morning!'

With this, Jasper went back to the kitchen, where he'd managed to conjure up a breakfast of toast and eggs. He had stoked the fire too and they sat in comfort to eat.

'What have you planned for me?' Toby asked.

'To see someone you already know… but there will perhaps be others along the way.'

The little man would not elaborate further, but as they carefully tidied up, Toby thought about Meg and the folk he knew.

'Never leave a mess, that's my motto,' said Jasper, looking back at their handiwork as they departed from the cottage. 'You never know when you might need to call upon the hospitality of others again.'

Toby was thinking about this as they walked down the lane, when they heard someone panting towards them and saw Queenie appear round the corner ahead. She was dressed very much the same as when he had last seen her, but was more haggard than he remembered. She was flushed too, and seemed to have a fever, her breath coming in short gasps. But upon looking up and seeing them her face broke into a smile and she waved as they approached.

'They told me not to go out,' she said in a thick voice, coughing. 'But I wanted to see you… can I come along? I'll be no trouble.'

Toby looked at her with concern. 'Are you sure you're well enough, Queenie?'

'Oh I'm alright,' she replied, coughing again. 'It's better for me out here – I've been inside with them for four days and I just feel worse all the time.'

Toby was not sure she could be right but her expression was so earnest, and her smile so winning, that he decided against sending her back.

'You aren't well, Queenie, and should probably be in bed… but you may come with us if you want. Do say if the walk is too much for you, and we can change what we have in mind.'

She seemed delighted by his words and fell in beside them, leaning on her stick and talking to Macken as if she had enjoyed his company many times before. They walked down to the deserted farmyard, and having passed through, came to the sight of last night's burnings. Smoke still rose in wisps from the ashy ruins, and here and there flames could be seen licking from a smouldering roof beam or heap of debris. But the rest was gone – all semblance of the buildings that had stood there less than twenty-four hours before removed by the blaze, leaving only faint outlines of lost structures. They hurried on, and coming to hedgerows again, began to make their way up the bridleway that once led to "Warren Hill Farm". The skyline was wide and open now, with only the outbuildings of "High Dyke Farm" standing way off to the left towards Oakwell. The Trindles' farmhouse was no more, the earth all around neatly ploughed and sown with winter barley. When they arrived at the spot where it once stood, Toby traced his steps to where the porch had been. A cold unhindered wind, with a promise of snow, caught his face and froze his cheeks.

'Nothing,' he said. 'It's all gone.'

'Knocked down just after you left the last time,' said Jasper, watching him from the track. 'But you can still see things lying around if you look carefully.'

Toby searched a little further, and sure enough found half bricks and cobbles lying around on the surface or sticking out of the ground to indicate what had been there – inconsequential relics from a bygone age. He bent down and picked up the broken end of a water butt pipe.

But Jasper did not permit him to linger very long. 'Come away,' he said after a few moments, 'it's too cold for archaeology today. We'd best move on towards a more sheltered spot.'

Toby was half inclined to stay awhile longer, but as the others move off towards the railway crossing, reluctantly fell in behind, only briefly looking back. He was soon in for another surprise, and one that would impress him even more than the first. Coming down the track to "Windmill Crossing" he saw again the familiar rooftop of "Station House" rising above the trees. The hedgerow next to the garden was still neatly trimmed, and looking through he could see evidence of freshly dug earth on the vegetable patch. There were also rows of cauliflower plants, broccoli and parsnips to be seen, and he wondered how old Morwen Hughes could keep the whole thing so well maintained. Or had she moved on, leaving someone else in residence? So preoccupied was he with these thoughts that they had arrived at the crossing before much else registered. It was here he beheld another scene that stopped him dead – the railway line had gone! Not only had the tracks been torn up, but the old halt had disappeared too, and even the boards that once straddled the crossing were no more. Only a rough screed of gravel ballast was left to allow farm vehicles to cross on firm ground. Moreover, the work appeared to have been only recently completed as deep ruts made by the tyres of contractors' lorries could still clearly be seen. Yet already the place seemed strangely deserted and empty, and looking down the gradient towards Oakwell Toby strove to recall the trains he had seen disappearing from view round the distant bend. He also visualised the mighty locomotives of the ammunition train that had fought their way up the gradient, shaking the rickety old halt to its foundations as they passed. Now both it and the permanent way had gone, leaving the spot to nature – a place only frequented by walkers, rabbits and passing owls.

'I wish it hadn't closed,' said Queenie sadly. 'I used to like the trains.'

Toby agreed with her, but knew the tracks would never return. Men and women had enthusiastically opted for the motorcar, which would come to dominate their lives instead.

The three of them took a final look around and were just about to move off along the abandoned track bed when a figure appeared round the side of "Station House". It was a man in his mid forties, but whose hair was already completely grey. He held a fork in one hand, and wore a heavy coat and boots as protection from the cold wind. At first Toby did not recognise him; but then something in his movements and the earnest look in his eyes reminded him of a person he knew. The newcomer came up to them and kissed Queenie on the cheek, causing her to blush and hop from side to side with a broad smile. He then held out his hand towards Toby, his eyes wrinkling at the corners.

'Don't you remember me, Toby?' he asked.

Toby did remember the face, but it was older and much changed, and he could not give it a name.

'Harry Clayton,' said the other. 'You worked with me some years back – down at what used to be "Pocket Farm".'

Toby placed him now – it was the demolition man, the one he had first met on leaving the old mill.

'I'm sorry… not to have recognised you,' he stammered, offering his hand in return. 'How is your wife?'

'She's well – and my three grown-up children, too.' He spoke proudly of his family, as most men do, but there was weariness in his voice and his features were worn like one upon whom distant memories weighed heavily.

'You are not in the demolition business any more then?' asked Toby.

'No, I've had enough of destruction to last me a lifetime… the war saw to that.'

Toby did not know about Harry's service with the RAF, and in the next ten minutes was given a brief outline of what he had experienced. They had now begun walking together in the direction of "Silver Link Cottage", with Jasper a pace or two behind listening – Macken having initially disappeared into a large rabbit hole, frequently emerging some way down the embankment slope to pad among the undergrowth.

As their conversation developed, Toby learned about Harry's fascination with navigation, his training, and subsequent missions over Europe. It was a story told without bravado, delivered in a flat voice devoid of emotion; but when he came to describe the Hamburg raid he spoke in a clear concise tone (like a newsreader describing the events of the previous day), every detail recalled exactly. Toby would have asked questions but kept quiet, thinking it better not to disturb the other's train of thought.

'They shot us down,' said Harry, 'and I became a prisoner, after which I was moved away from the city pretty quickly – to one grim and dreary prison camp after another. You see those films about brave airmen trying to escape, digging holes and the like…

well, it's true that there were some that actually did. But as to the people I was with: many of us had perhaps simply had enough of flying and just wanted to get home. There was sickness, too, and hunger. Germany was on its last legs trying to fight a war against half the world. The Nazis couldn't win, and it was only a matter of time before it ended. I wound up in Poland towards the close of 1944, but it wasn't safe to keep us there either. The Russians were advancing and I remember being told one morning of another projected move – a westward march back towards Germany. It was October and the summer had been hot and dry. The Polish countryside can be really attractive in the autumn – what with the trees turning to gold and the peasants working in the fields. Most of us were on foot, marching ten to fifteen miles a day, escorted by a motley collection of German guards and conscripted locals.

'On the third day out, around noon, our column was passing through open country when we noticed compounds of low buildings off to the right. You couldn't see them very well because the nearest was more than a mile away; but a series of watch towers spaced at regular intervals told us it was a camp of some kind. One or two columns of sooty smoke could also be seen rising, although little else moved except an occasional lorry. Yet there was something about that place... something you sensed wasn't right. The site was huge, and we must have taken more than two hours walking by. ...But it was the smell emanating from it that will stay with me: somehow sour and unclean it was – as if disease and death had taken hold there. I tell you we were all glad to leave it well behind.

'I saw many things on that march... some I wouldn't want to dwell on now. A prisoner of war is often made aware of the best and worst in human nature. Most of us eventually got back to England, each with his own stories to tell. For myself: I think that looking back I'd had more than enough of war, aeroplanes and fancy technology to last me a lifetime. Yet needing work to support the family, I did think of getting another job in aviation for a while... but somehow I couldn't get beyond the interview. ...It seems they knew my heart wasn't in it. So the demolition man and ex-navigator became a gardener. It doesn't pay much, I'll admit that right enough, but I'm happy now. I've brought my children up to love and respect others, spend my days growing fruit and vegetables, and gladly tend the gardens of elderly folk who couldn't otherwise cope by themselves.'

'Is that what you do at "Station House"?' asked Toby.

'That's right; I've been looking after old Morwen Hughes' garden for some time; ever since it started to get beyond her. But the way things are I'm beginning to doubt she'll be able to go back there now. You see, I found her housebound just before Christmas – couldn't hardly get out of bed, what with her bad legs and all. I helped her down to Meg Maddox at "Silver Link Cottage"; they're old friends, you know. She's still there. You might like to pop in to see them both.'

Toby agreed that he would, for he had a strong desire to spend an hour with Meg once more. Yet one question still remained in his head after listening to Harry's story, and since they had stopped briefly as Harry adjusted the weight of his tools, Toby ventured to ask it.

'You mentioned the camp you passed in Poland… did you ever find where that was?'

The former airman straightened up, a shadow passing over his features as a blast of chilly air whipped through the trees, lifting the grey hair on his forehead. He suddenly looked old, resigned and tired.

'A navigator should be able to work that one out,' he said. 'When I got home I became interested in maps of Eastern Europe, wanting to know where I had been. I found it at last, a region of Poland near Krakow – Birkenau was the name of the camp I passed that day… although it is more commonly known as Auschwitz.'

They went on together, soon arriving at the stile leading to Meg's cottage; but having closed up like a book as if to seal up his memories, Harry would say no more. There he bade them farewell before heading swiftly away down the steep slope towards Stavenham. 'Tell Morwen the garden's sorted for the winter, so she won't have to worry none,' he called back upon reaching the dell. 'Oh… and say her parsnips look wonderful!'

* * *

They watched him pass out of sight in the gathering murk then, having crossed the stile, approached and knocked on the door of "Silver Link Cottage". This now appeared old and withered with age but a promise of warmth glowed through the curtained windows. Low voices could be heard inside and a fresh-faced woman opened the door. She smiled pleasantly and recognising Queenie, who had gradually developed a hacking cough, immediately led her in out of the cold, while politely bidding the others to follow. Macken also squeezed inside before padding over to sit beside the stove where a large shaggy mongrel stood up to make way for him. The room was in fact quite full and Meg, her hair now almost white, welcomed them, offering tea. She had changed much, but her movements were still light for a woman getting on in years, and she had the same thoughtful and perceptive expression. Opposite her, covered by a large blanket and fast asleep, Morwen Hughes sat propped up in an armchair on the other side of the stove. A fourth woman, with a reserved and striking countenance, stood looking at the two men from behind the old woman's shoulder.

'Toby,' said Meg, 'and Jasper too, it's good of you to come! We don't get enough visitors – at least not any who have the habit of looking and staying so youthful. But do you recognise my two friends?' she added.

Toby looked again at the younger women: the serious one helping a still coughing Queenie take off her damp coat; the other standing smiling beside Meg.

'These are my two girls… my little project you might say. You knew them as Millie and Harriette Corrie – although Harriette, who met you at the door, is now Mrs Foxton and has two lovely boys of her own. They were the little waifs that you met many years ago… those whom no one else could control; that some predicted would turn out badly. Isn't that right, Harriette?' she added, looking up with affection at the slender and poised young woman standing beside her.

'You were our mother then,' replied the other, touching her hand. 'We wouldn't have become what we are without you.'

'Meg is a remarkable person,' added her sister Millie, speaking for the first time. The latter had begun devotedly applying herself to providing for Queenie's needs, the seriousness of which were becoming increasingly evident – for the farm girl had turned very white, her forehead was damp, and she had begun to doze while breathing noisily through her open mouth. 'Meg was really good to us: a mentor and friend,' Millie went on. 'She took us in when no one else had time for we two. The rest had given up and thought we were bound to spend a life off the rails… But Meg knew – she saw that didn't have to be.'

The note of respect in Millie's voice was unmistakable, causing the subject of their praise to blush. She shook her head deprecatingly as if such comments were entirely undeserved.

'I only did what other right minded folk would do,' she said. 'You needed help and support, and I gave it. …There is nothing special in that.'

At this, Harriette wagged a finger at her. 'No… you are special; not everyone's like you, so kind and generous. That's a God-given thing, and I won't hear you say otherwise.'

At this point Queenie stirred from her fitful rest with a painful burst of coughing, again arousing their concerns. She had clearly taken a severe chill, or worse, and would not be able to return home that night, even if proper care at "Deep Spinney Farm" could have been guaranteed. But there was a problem, for Meg had only two beds, one of which had been occupied for three days by old Mrs. Hughes.

'They can't both stay,' said Harriette Foxton, putting on her coat. 'But I could look after Morwen for a bit, and that will make room for Queenie to stay here.'

'Why don't I have her?' said her sister. 'There's more room at my place, and it's only half a mile.'

The latter option was agreed upon and a short discussion followed during which the pros and cons of moving a frail eighty-four year old woman late on a winter's evening, with snow expected before nightfall, were considered. In our time such a thing would not have been contemplated; but then people were more self-reliant and resourceful, and expected to look out for each other when times were difficult. Millie gently shook Morwen to wake her; and when she was made aware of the plan, the elderly good-natured Welsh woman readily endorsed the proposal, with the comment that she had been cooped up indoors for three days and would enjoy the walk. Amid much good-humoured talk and giggles, the sisters next set about wrapping her in an abundance of cardigans, shawls, warm hats and gloves, over which she was ultimately tugged into an overcoat that came down to her ankles. At last, muffled and togged up for her short journey, Morwen turned to Toby and Jasper, smiling kindly.

'And where are you two to stay?' she asked. 'You must go somewhere warm and dry, for it's snowing already.'

This was indeed the case: beyond the door held ajar by Harriette large snowflakes were glimpsed being carried sideways by a strengthening wind.

'It looks like a blizzard's blowing up alright,' the old woman declared, an expression of concern crossing her features. 'So may an elderly lady ask where you do plan to be during the dark hours?'

'We… have a place,' Toby muttered, remembering that Jasper had warned against staying longer in the cottage at "Deep Spinney Farm". 'It will do, I'm sure.'

Morwen noticed the note of hesitation in his voice, however, and her eyes twinkled. 'You could stay at my house for a few days until the weather improves,' she suggested helpfully. 'It's comfortable, and having someone there will help stop things freezing up. You could be my caretakers if you like,' she added, taking a door key on a length of string from her pocket. 'I'd consider it a pleasure to have you as my lodgers.'

Morwen had obviously quite made up her mind, and Toby, seeing no good reason to argue, took the key from the old lady while thanking her for her generosity.

'Don't thank me,' she said. 'I've lived too long there on my own. It will be a good thing to have a man around the house again. Make yourself comfortable; there's plenty of wood in the shed for the fire, and a bed made up. You'll be no trouble, I'm sure.'

Morwen then moved out into the night with her guides and after much laughter and a few earthy comments, the three awkwardly but successfully negotiated the stile and passed together into the enveloping gloom.

'Thank you, that was kind,' said Meg to Toby after they had closed the door again. 'When you are old there is little you feel you can do for those you come to depend upon. Morwen has had to rely on me and the girls more and more, but is still a proud and independent woman who needs to feel that she can be of use to others, if only in a small way. But now you too must go, for I will need to get Queenie to bed. She has a bad fever and must be watched closely in the coming hours. Her life has been hard, and the old injury left her far from strong.'

These words made Toby feel more than a little guilty for having let her come with them that morning; but knowing that Queenie was in good hands he prepared to leave with Jasper and Macken.

'Do come to see me again soon, won't you, Toby,' said Meg, as they were about to go. 'Your visits are too rare, and I still have much to tell you. You must not wait so long in future, for I will soon be old.'

* * *

They departed then, padding off into the night as snow began to fall more heavily. The journey to "Station House" was less than half a mile, but night was drawing in and swirling snow slowed their progress as they made their way through the rising blizzard. The little dog stayed with them, skipping in front and playfully nosing through the small drifts that had begun to form – sometimes disappearing completely under an ensuing fall, only to re-emerge moments later with a joyful bark, shaking himself vigorously. Jasper, too, seemed entirely at home, forging on with untiring steps as if he were merely on his way to buy stamps at the local post office. But this was no ordinary snowstorm, for it would last more than twenty-four hours and leave drifts ten feet deep that lingered on until spring. During "The Big Freeze" temperatures plummeted, the ice and frost going on for weeks, often paralysing roads and railways. As such it was as if a little Ice Age had returned – one that would be long recalled in years to come by those that experienced it.

Toby plodded on behind, his fingers numb and cheeks smarting; struggling to keep his feet on the uneven ground. He tripped against a discarded sleeper, and stubbed his toe more than once, while all the time constantly peering ahead in an effort to judge the distance to their destination through a driving shroud of whiteness. Then it was there, just above the snow covered cutting, and turning to face Jasper he drew the front door key from his pocket with stiff fingers. The little man was already decked in a thick blanket and looked up from under his hat, the pipe he had somehow managed to keep alight still smoking between his lips. Macken stood beside him, his head on one side, clouds of condensation coming from his panting lungs – a comical lump of snow, looking for all the world like a pantomime hat, perched upon his forehead.

'Will you be coming inside with me?' asked Toby, half expecting the answer he received.

'No, mate,' replied his companion, 'not this time. The dog and me have other errands to complete. But don't you worry about us – we can't come to any harm.'

Toby nodded, knowing there was little use arguing, before focusing his attention on the house once more and carefully negotiating the steps to the front door. Looking back, mere seconds later, he found that both had already gone – only his own fresh footprints seeming to show upon the deepening blanket. He gazed for a moment at the place where they had stood together, stunned and chilled by the unwelcome disappearance of his guides, before stepping inside and turning the key, his emptiness returning.

* * *

As Morwen Hughes had promised, the house was tidy, and although very cold at first, could quickly be made comfortable. To this end, Toby busied himself lighting a fire in the living room to bring warmth back to its walls. His fingers ached as the circulation returned to them, and he hopped around, as once before, until the sensation diminished. Then, although weary as always at the end of the day, he found tinned food to heat while considering his next steps. By easy reckoning he calculated that it was now almost fifty years since his arrival in this lost time: yet all was becoming a little more familiar to him now that the landscape was changing again and the railway had been removed. Moreover, as these years had apparently passed in a matter of but a few waking days… might the next fifty not also do the same – so bringing him back to the present? And if this was indeed possible, would he not then be able to pick up his own life as before, so leaving all this behind? …Like some waking dream – or nightmare?

Encouraged by these thoughts, and having stoked the fire, Toby sat before the blaze thinking of his family and the life he had known; dozing in and out of sleep as the night wore on. Then at around 2pm he started up, disturbed by the eerie howling of the wind outside, his body damp with sweat. 'I must rest now,' he said aloud to the four walls. 'But if I do… how much more time will then have gone by – how much closer to home will I be?'

With this thought, Toby kissed his fingertips in memory of Jenny and the children before making his way into the bedroom and there, having lain for a while staring at his reflection in the polished mirror of the dressing-table, his eyelids closed on the Arctic winter night.

Chapter Fifteen

A Close Kept Secret

URING A TIME WHEN THE WORLD OUTSIDE lay frozen by snow and ice, Queenie Towser died at "Silver Link Cottage" on 5th January, 1963. For more than a week Meg Maddox had cared for her with skill and compassion as the fever burned within the poor woman's body, but the pneumonia that had settled on her lungs proved fatal in the end and she passed away. Following this sad event, some of those that had hardly known Queenie maliciously whispered that she should have been taken to hospital where her life might perhaps have been saved by drugs and more professional care. But Queenie would not have wanted this: for in her last hours she knew she was loved and watched over by a devoted friend, and that was the best medicine of all. The Corrie sisters had come every morning and evening to help, and these once uncultured, neglected waifs – Meg's "wild twins" – proved themselves very able nurses. Yet perhaps most precious of all during those final days was the music of shared laughter that frequently brought peace to Queenie's more lucid moments – a smattering of mirth at the edge of eternity.

* * *

Twelve more years ran their course; bringing new souls into the world as others departed – Morwen Hughes and Harry Clayton among them. The young grew up and their parents became older: bowing to the endless progress of time. Toby knew nothing of it, but moved along in an existence of his own – somewhere between sleep and reality. Then, when he did become conscious again, he might have woken in a different century. Passenger jets had begun to fill the skies, motorways were spreading like tentacles across the countryside, and the much lamented steam train had disappeared forever from the railway lines of Britain.

* * *

When he opened the curtains of his room, Toby found the sun shining brightly upon a garden now overgrown with weeds and brambles. Spiders' webs hung down from the curtain rail, floating like weightless gossamer in the disturbed air; for the house had long been left as empty, shut up against unwanted visitors, and he alone had remained through all the passing days. But, being sturdy and well-built, the interior of the building stayed dry – only a few faded patches of wallpaper, caught by chinks of penetrating light, showing signs of abandonment.

Gathering his few belongings, Toby straightway moved downstairs. He was hungry and needed water, but only a dull squeak sounded when he turned the kitchen tap. There was little to eat either: only tinned food in rusty cans and the remains of dusty biscuits in packets yellow with age. He would need to look further afield, or go hungry for another day.

Outside the air was filled with sweet scents – the rampant growth of summer burdening the trees and bushes with blossom and leaves. Through a gap in the hedge he saw a field of barley, the delicate fronds of its swaying beard rippling and waving in the breeze. Birds could be heard calling from many points, or seen flying to and fro among the branches. He guessed it was the month of June; and one it seemed in which the weather had long been hot and dry, for the old track bed below appeared cracked and dusty.

'I must find out what day and year it is,' Toby thought, before walking down the path and turning west towards Meg's cottage. He hoped she was well, for in this place she had always been a point of reference. Yet if much time had passed, Meg would now be getting on in years... and how might he manage if she was no longer living?

There were signs of activity in the adjacent fields, and more than once he spotted a large crop sprayer: the long arms of the ugly machine delivering a fine mist to growing corn. But few farm animals were to be seen. Where once he might have spotted ten or more fields with herds of cattle, pigs or sheep, now only a solitary horse grazing in a paddock, or a lone pony kept to amuse a child, was evident in the countryside towards Stavenham. He passed the old mill, but this too was changed; for the great sails had been taken away, and all that remained was the mill building standing isolated on its brick base in an open field – a limbless stump abandoned under the morning sun.

Toby quickened his pace, meeting no one as he strode along; but noting signs that walkers must often frequent the line of the old railway, as the footmarks of others could be seen imprinted in the grit and ash. Looking up, he saw the vapour trails of aircraft too: while the sound of cars and other speeding vehicles now constantly punctuated the rural calm.

Thus he made his way back to the stile beside "Silver Link Cottage". But as Toby approached, he was stopped in his tracks by an unexpected sight. For tucked in under the trees where the rails had run was a little car; an Austin A35 painted two-tone green...

one he had seen before on the road between Oakwell and Stavenham. He drew near and noted that a patterned umbrella, together with a pair of lady's gloves, had been left on the front seat. But there was little else to suggest the owner's identity. It was obvious however that the car was both much valued and much used, for its paintwork shone, and the brown leather upholstery of the driver's seat was deeply polished. In addition, a faint smell of oil and petrol rising from beneath the warm bonnet suggested that it had not stood there long.

Much prompted to speculation by the find, Toby was still curiously moving round the car when a shadow passed over its roof, followed moments later by the sound of claws clasping the branch of a nearby tree. He looked up, and there, at the top of a hawthorn bush, swaying gently from side to side, sat a large crow. It was a magnificent creature, the sunlight glistening upon smooth folded wings and powerful beak; and it seemed to scrutinise him – like a sentinel set to guard its master's jewels, suspecting a thief.

'Caark,' the crow called in a husky croaking voice. 'Caark... Ktaaark!'

Was this a challenge... or a salute? Toby could not tell, but he was certain that his presence had again been logged. Becoming wary, he backed away toward the stile, the bird still beadily watching his every move, and having climbed over, walked up to the cottage door.

This appeared little changed from before, although the knocker was less bright and the varnished wood of the sign more deeply lined. The setting round about was somewhat quieter moreover: for fewer animals wandered in the enclosure, and the geese that had always been kept to warn off strangers no longer hissed and gabbled nearby. Yet scented honeysuckle still bloomed upon the trellis round the porch, and fresh petunias, lobelia and alyssum had been planted in flowerbeds below the windows.

Toby listened and hearing voices within, knocked twice. There was a short silence, then the sound of a chair being pushed back, and a few moments later Jeannie opened the door. She looked as young as ever, although her eyes betrayed both concern and sadness.

'So, you have returned once more, Toby,' she said, brightening. 'We hoped you would. Meg and I have been talking of you.'

Jeannie then stepped down into the room, and following he found Meg sitting in her favourite chair by the stove. She now looked much thinner than at their last meeting, and was wrapped up in a warm cardigan over which she wore a shawl of Bedfordshire lace. Her dress and appearance could be said to have belonged to a previous age, so inwardly composed did she look – like one whose poise and manner might comfortably transcend time. Meg smiled and her eyes twinkled like a young girl greeting a friend, soft wisps of white hair curling around her cheeks. Yet something was amiss, for the flush of good health no longer infused her cheeks – she looked tired and drawn, as if worn out by the endurance of long suffering and pain.

Such was Toby's concern for her that at first he failed to notice the other person in the room. But now, having been offered a seat by his host, Toby was introduced to a young woman, perhaps in her early thirties, who sat with a cup and saucer on her lap. Her face was refined and striking – having strong angular features that bore a close resemblance to Meg, when younger. The newcomer's eyes, too, bore the same intent expression, as of one that listens closely to every word, and has an enquiring disposition. He noted that the clothes she wore were well cut and of good quality, showing a flair for bright colours – the more sober lines of her office suit and shoes being set off by a contrasting apple green scarf and bright jewellery.

The four sat quietly for perhaps another twenty seconds before Meg addressed Toby once more.

'I see few people other than Millie and Harriette these days,' she said, wagging a shaking finger towards him playfully. 'Then up pop three visitors in one day. What am I to do?'

Her remarks made them all smile, breaking the tension and allowing a cup of tea to be poured for Toby, and freshly baked cake offered, which he gratefully accepted.

'You know Jeannie, I believe,' said Meg, turning to him again. 'But you will not have met my granddaughter, Claire Cheetham. She has come to see me today, having thought me dead these last thirty years... we have just been getting to know one another.'

Toby put down his cup and gazed at the woman. 'This is your daughter Alice's child?' he said slowly, studying her face. 'She that was killed in the war?'

'Just so,' said Meg, looking across at the other woman. 'She is my link with Alice and Mark – the truest loves of my life.'

Meg's last words were heavy with sorrow, and she sat for a moment, seemingly sifting the memories of her earlier life.

The younger woman noticed this also: involuntarily leaning towards her, clearly anguished. She shook her head.

'Grandmother... I thought you were dead... I didn't know...'

Having spoken haltingly, she looked up at Jeannie, and then towards Toby, as if seeking support.

'I was born in 1941 you see – at the height of the war. My mother and father married when they both worked for the intelligence service, and it was he that brought me up. They must have talked little about Meg; for after Alice was killed in France no mention was ever made of her. I hardly remember my mother either, for she was always away and father took charge of everything. I do know that he loved her dearly, however; and when the war was over I learned all about what she had done. It made me proud to think of her courage, but I regret having grown up without the guidance a mother can give. Father said very little about her childhood, and seemed to know few details, but I came to assume that Alice had not always been happy and didn't pry further… so as a result I had scant knowledge of my family history until recently.'

Meg had listened carefully, and now spoke with regret as she thought of her daughter. 'I think neither of us really knew your mother, Claire. It seems she was destined to be her own person always; and could not have stayed here… not with me. Sometimes it is impossible for those of the same blood to live under one roof.'

There was another silence – a pause for reflection – before her granddaughter spoke again.

'Father died suddenly two years ago, in 1973,' she went on. 'It was then that I decided to search for details of my roots. In time I learned that my mother had lived near Bedford – though at first I hadn't time to come back to make enquiries locally. You see, my fiancé is an environmental campaigner… or troublemaker, as his critics are wont to call him. His name is Jamie Tresco,' she said, breaking into a smile, 'and he is England's greatest optimist! But he worries too – about what is happening to our planet now that we are polluting the seas and destroying the forests of the earth. I am a journalist by profession, but he says I am wasted in Fleet Street while ordinary people and politicians remain largely ignorant and unconcerned about what the human race is doing to our world. So he took me off to South America – to see the logging and destruction that are taking place in the Amazon. "Give nature a voice with your pen," he tells me. "Make it more powerful than the chainsaw!" Sometimes I think he's mad… after all, how can we challenge big business and the governments that do these things? But at other times, I know he's right – for people have to stand up and do something, don't they? …Surely complacency is wrong.'

Toby thought about his own position, and about what had brought him there in the beginning. This young woman had given expression to feelings they both shared.

'I hope to marry Jamie in a few months,' Claire continued. 'I'm thirty-four and had begun to think that such a thing wasn't for me. But he's changed all that; and I now think I can be happy living with someone else.'

She had spoken frankly and openly for some time, but now fell silent, clutching her fingers as if concerned that she might have revealed too much.

'And how did you find out about me at last?' asked Meg, who had become if anything a little paler while following her granddaughter's words.

'We returned five months ago, and I began to write a series of articles about our visit. I was also doing a lot of research which eventually brought me to Bedford. During one of my lunchtimes I went down to the council offices to look at the parish registers; on the off chance… that's when I came across grandmother's name and address. I knew that she had never married, but had no idea she was still living, so I made plans to come back. I took the bus from Bedford to Stavenham this morning, and was dropped near the windmill. The last bit might have been difficult if I had not met Jeannie, who was out walking her dog and offered to accompany me here.'

Toby looked across at Jeannie, who returned his gaze with the slightest inclination of her head.

Claire was now looking around the room, as if she had lost something. 'Where is the little fellow?' she asked, somewhat puzzled. 'He was here when we arrived.'

'Don't worry about him,' replied Jeannie, looking out through the curtained window. 'He will be back in his own good time.'

They broke off for a while to prepare food for Meg – of which she could eat little. Then, when the meal was done, Jeannie propped her up so that she might be as comfortable as possible. Macken had reappeared meanwhile, and seemed happy to sit by her lap so that she could stroke him. But Meg was obviously very ill, her pulse low, and her skin cold to the touch.

'You can't stay here,' said her granddaughter, becoming increasingly anxious. 'You need to see a doctor.'

'No doctors,' said Meg, her head drooping. 'I've lived here for sixty years on my own, and can manage another few days without them. They'll only fill me up with chemicals and what not. There's no need to worry; the girls will pop in from time to time, and I've got Jeannie around too if I need her.'

Meg appeared determined to keep with this arrangement, and all could see that there was little point in arguing with her.

'I have a meeting in Edinburgh tomorrow,' said Claire, now preparing to leave. 'But I can be back in two or three days… I want you to be alright grandmother, so you must promise that you will do what is best while I'm away.'

Meg looked up with a wan smile of reassurance.

'I was here all along, Claire – and hope to be always… therefore, whenever you come back you are sure to find me.'

Her granddaughter bent to kiss her, holding Meg's frail fingers for several seconds before departing with Jeannie, who had offered to walk with her to the bus stop. Meanwhile Macken jumped down from Meg's lap and could be heard from time to time pottering around in the yard outside. So Toby and Meg were left alone in the room surrounded by the old woman's books and the small things that she had held dear during her life. In pride of place, Harry Clayton's watercolour of Maxton Tower hung on the wall beside her head where the afternoon sunlight would find it. She dozed for a while, before waking painfully with a start; and Toby had once more to arrange her cushions before bringing water. She thanked him, but he sensed there was something else she wanted to say as he sat down opposite her. A look of inner struggle had clouded Meg's features and she rocked gently, her eyes, now brighter, bringing a glimmer of lost youth, which reminded him of the day they had first met.

'I'm glad you are here, Toby,' she said at last. 'You see, I have something to confide – and know that you will try to understand. But it must stay a secret always, or I will not rest in peace.'

She spoke earnestly, like someone contemplating the end, and he leaned forward to listen, placing his hand on hers.

Meg looked down upon the fingers resting upon her own. 'You might not still wish to touch me when all is known,' she murmured. '…Some things can perhaps never be put right.'

'Try me – I've got all day.'

'Then I will; for it is nearly over,' she went on. 'I am dying, Toby – something's wrong with my insides – I won't live. It's been coming on for a year or more, and I get a little lower every day. But that's no matter; I'm eighty-one, and we don't live forever. In two days time it will be Midsummer's Day; and I always wanted to go when the flowers were in bloom. Don't imagine I've spent a lonely life either. Plenty of good folk have passed this way: old Coodie, Morwen and the girls, and I'll always be thankful for that. Then there were my animals; I wouldn't have been without them – for the many creatures of this earth make few demands and have been constant companions, my dogs especially. But I've buried them all now. Old Nancy went this spring, and she was always going to be the last. Everything passes in time… only memories live on.

'This house has been good to me too; but there is a secret here that I must tell before departing from it… something that has held me in this place. I know I can trust you Toby; for you are not like the others. Mark knew that; he said you were some kind of wanderer… or a messenger. I didn't know then if he was right; but you do keep coming back – like a traveller from another time – and it seems right that you should be here now.'

Toby shifted in his chair, wondering how much she knew.

'Whatever you are, Toby, it may be that you are here to judge me for what I have done. You knew of my affair with Mark Trindle before he went away to war: of our plans to marry and of my time at "Tyler Hall". I told you about Charlotte, too, didn't I? About her feelings of jealousy towards me… Then Mark was killed at Ypres, and my daughter Alice was born the following winter. That wasn't such a scandal really as many young women lost their men in those days, thus being left to bring up a child alone. But I had a mistress that would not forgive: someone of my own generation who taunted me for my indiscretion – who put me down because of her personal longing for fulfilment.

'I accepted this for a while: desperate as I was for money with a baby to support. Then one evening in early summer, Charlotte stopped by at the cottage on the very day of another sadness. Do you remember the dog I owned at that time, the Golden Retriever, Mr Toots?' she said, smiling at the memory of him. 'He was the most wonderful dog I have ever known, and could make me laugh a hundred times a day, even when I was sad.

He seemed to know my feelings – and was daft, loveable, giving and kind, all in one. Next to Mark, he was the best thing ever to come into my life... and rest assured, Toby, we never forget the ones we love.

'Well, having lived to the ripe old age of fourteen, he'd died only that morning and I, having just put Alice to bed, was about to go out and bury him in a grave I had prepared, when Charlotte appeared at my open door. She had taken to walking by the cottage in recent days, and looking back I feel sure she did so in the hope of having an opportunity to spite me with her words. We faced each other for a moment, before she came in uninvited and stood in the kitchen. Her attitude was haughty and superior, as it was when she stood and watched me at work at "Tyler Hall"; like one who is pleased by the control she exercises over another's life.

'"So this is where you live," she sneered. "Such is the little that fallen women can afford."

'I said nothing in reply, simply wanting her to leave me in peace as soon as possible, while I knelt down to tend the stove with the poker. But I was angry at my loss, and my pride hurt that she should so insult me in my own home. Perhaps I should have thrown her out at the start, but a mother's caution held me back. So there she stood behind me, looking down... then her eyes must have wandered to where Mr Toots lay covered up with a blanket. Charlotte could see what it was straight away and gave a short laugh of derision at my second loss.

'"So this is another judgement upon you," she smirked. "No matter... now you will have more time to attend to your duties."

'She seemed so arrogant and proud – this foolish woman that I had known at school; and could more than equal in everything but status and looks... At that moment something snapped inside me; having been drawn tight by a dual sense of loathing and despair, and clutching the poker I turned suddenly, bringing it down upon her temple – felling her with the blow. She crumpled before me with a sigh, blood from an open gash beginning to seep onto the cold stones, and for some moments I simply stood there, looking down, with the weapon clenched in my hand. Charlotte still breathed, but I had no feeling, and did not wish to touch her – as if she were suddenly some distant thing. I dropped the poker by the stove, and hearing Alice begin to cry, brought her through to the kitchen while wondering what to do. I was naturally numbed by my own actions – but a deeper concern for my child had begun to rise within me. If Charlotte should die I would be responsible for her murder... and what would become of my daughter then?

'I felt Charlotte's pulse, which was still beating, but instead of seeking help, gathered Alice up and walked away from the cottage to clear my thoughts. Perhaps a part of me planned to fetch Coodie Trindle to help... but I never arrived at "Warren Hill Farm". Instead, after wandering for a while, and sitting under a tree for an hour with Alice on my lap, I circled home as night began to fall.

'"Silver Link Cottage" was already quite dark when I got back. Stepping over Charlotte, I lit the oil lamp to see her better. She lay as before, but without sound or movement, and I knew at once that she was dead...

'It was a moment that I shall never forget – but I felt no remorse... I was simply empty, devoid of feeling – as if my last emotions had frozen up. Only the desire to protect Alice filled my head. But what possible way forward could there be? So there I sat for a while before putting my sleeping daughter safely back in her cot.'

* * *

The effort of speaking was wearying Meg. Her voice had become lower and Toby suggested that she rest before going on. But Meg revived at this, as if driven on by the need to share her secret, repeatedly clutching the folds of her shawl.

'The solution soon came to me, Toby. I needed to cover up my crime – to remove the evidence in a way that might fool anyone that came searching for her. That was when I went outside with a lamp to the place on the edge of the animal cemetery where I had dug Mr. Toots' grave. The hole was quite large and about three feet deep; but I set about making it longer, wider and deeper. It would be a short night and I wanted to be finished by morning; but the work was hard, due to the earth being dry following a long spell without rain. The place, as you know, is sheltered from prying eyes, but I listened frequently, lest any late walkers, or a courting couple, should happen to pass by. But none did: I was alone in the night to pursue my solitary task.'

Meg's voice became more even as she recounted her actions; but the motion of her hands continued as she spoke – as if her mind was agonised by remembrance of the deed.

'By three o'clock I'd finished, having made the grave more than five feet deep; but upon looking up I could already see the first light of dawn creeping into the eastern sky. I was exhausted and might have lain down to sleep, but an inner voice told me to go on until all was done... yet now came the worst part, for I had to convey Charlotte to the spot, and you cannot imagine how heavy the body of a lifeless human being is until you've tried carrying one. I struggled out of the house with her: sometimes pulling her limp and stiffening frame; sometimes rolling her over when my strength had all but gone. A kind of desperation had come over me – a sense of hopelessness worse than fear – such that I could not stop until achieving my goal of bringing her to the grave's edge. Yet this too was an awful moment, for it seemed wrong to topple her in as she was. Therefore I brought out an old blanket and tied it round her, hoping that it would not come away as she fell. Then the matter was done and she lay in the earth below. But I had to go on, to cover her before bringing the dog to the grave also. I shovelled the loose soil as best I could, then finished by scooping it in with my bare hands until she lay no more beneath the sky. After that I returned for Mr Toots. He too was a large fellow, Toby – but carrying my old and faithful companion seemed much lighter work. …Perhaps our love for the departed gives us greater strength, who knows, but burying him was easier – an ending of a proper kind.

'Thus he was covered up with the other lying there, and I placed a board with the dog's name at one end. So it was over; and I, filthy from my labours, might have kneeled then and wept – but you cannot do such things when the future of another is at stake. Already the cockerel at "Pocket Farm" had crowed five times: the rising sun beginning to colour the horizon between low clouds. Heeding this warning of the coming day I collected the tools, went inside and straightaway washed the dirt from my hands and face before changing out of my soiled clothes. Then there was just one last thing to do… Charlotte's blood had been left to congeal upon the kitchen stones and with a brush I knelt to clean it away.'

Here she looked at Toby with an expression between supplication and hopelessness.

'…But dried blood is so hard to erase. …It seems to stain a surface like no other, and although I scrubbed for ten minutes, nothing seemed to remove it all! When the place had become dry once more, a dull incriminating mark remained that only a covering would conceal.'

He looked down at the floor, where as always the ornate oval rug was placed between the stove and the door.

'Turn it back and you will see,' she said.

He did as Meg asked, and there on the centre stones a pale mark was revealed, its edges rounded as if made by the steady hand of a skilled painter. It might have been a stain left by some innocent household mishap, or by a writer's ink, but he could not mistake it for other than she had described.

Toby covered the place again and came to sit with Meg whose deathly weariness had returned. She slumped back, studying her hands.

'It is an awful thing to end another's life, Toby. I thought time would help salve my conscience… but it's never been that way. Every time I awake, that day comes to mind, and I cannot fall asleep at night without remembering it. You are the first and only person I shall ever tell of this, and I pray no others will ever have to know. I brought up Alice as best I could… but perhaps something inside stopped me giving her the love she needed.

'Sometimes I felt as if her life had been blighted by me in some way, and perhaps that was what made her want to leave as soon as she could, who can say? Whatever it was, our bond never seemed quite strong enough… perhaps because the other half of me had already gone.'

Meg seemed entirely defeated, and although Toby said much in an effort to reassure her, he could tell that the time had long passed when she might have been reconciled with the dark and tragic events of her past.

'You must be going,' she said at last, 'and I do not think we shall meet again. But perhaps a part of this story will continue as the life of my granddaughter unfolds. I wish that she and I had met before and come to know one another better, as it would have been a comfort to me to realise Alice's life was not in vain...

'Now, when you depart, please close the door. But do leave the fire made up and a drink of water near to my hand, should I need it in the night.'

* * *

It was as if Meg was giving Toby permission to depart without regrets of his own and within a few moments more she fell asleep. His natural instinct was to stay with her, but another power told him to leave her in peace and seek somewhere else close by where he could rest. So he went quietly from the cottage, closing the door with a final click before walking away into the shadows of a summer evening. Toby re-crossed the stile and would have retraced his steps to "Station House" but for coming upon the little A35 still parked by the hedge. He did not know why Jeannie had failed to return to it and looked round, wondering if she was perhaps standing waiting nearby. But there was no one else about, and all he saw, apart from a passing owl that flew up into a nearby tree, was the same black crow peering down from a lofty branch. The two of them eyed each other for a moment, the crow ducking its head once as if acknowledging the satisfactory completion of a duty.

'If you could speak – what would you say?' muttered Toby, backing towards the car, the door of which he found to be open. He chose to sit in the passenger seat where he could stretch his legs, deciding to stay on for a while where he might hear if Meg should call out. But the evening air was becoming cool, and having closed the door, he shut his eyes in contemplation before gradually, irreversibly, succumbing to sleep. So the 19th day of June 1975 came to an end and Toby Freeman dropped away from the waking world once more.

* * *

Meg Maddox was visited by Millie Corrie and Harriette Foxton over the next few days, and kept as comfortable as they could make her. When awake, she never once complained of her illness, often chuckling with them over stories of shared times. But Meg chose to die alone, as she had lived, on 1st July; exactly fifty-eight years after Mark Trindle fell at Ypres – and with her death the old world that Toby had entered finally passed away.

* * *

She had always expressed a desire to be buried beside the cottage; but in those days the giving of approval for internment in unconsecrated ground was not common. Yet the Corrie sisters – now respected members of the community – were able to argue her case successfully with the church authorities, and at last received permission to carry out her wishes in a quiet spot among trees by the disused railway. Thus, re-united once more in spirit with the only man she had ever loved, Meg was laid to rest near the canine companions of her days and the forever concealed remains of the woman whose life she had taken.

* * *

Meanwhile, her daughter, Claire Cheetham, having been delayed by business concerns during her visit to Edinburgh, eventually returned more than three weeks later, some five days after the ceremony – an unhappy circumstance she would always regret.

Chapter Sixteen

The March of King Profit

I<small>T IS SAID THAT</small> "<small>TIME WAITS FOR</small> no man" and Toby was certainly not an exception to this rule. The silent years of unconsciousness passed speedily around him just as the unwatched sand of an egg timer falls quickly from the glass. Innovation and technical development went on apace, and much that was beneficial to mankind was achieved. Diseases were conquered or controlled; new machines eased the burden of work, and the microchip revolutionised the world of science and communication. But there was a price to be paid: for as life in wealthy nations became more comfortable and convenient, so too did their citizens become both increasingly separated from the means of production and less connected to the living earth. The consumer was created – a slave to advertising and the notion of desirable social competition – a ready convert to the doctrine of "self-interest".

* * *

The A35 came to life and began to move forward, with Toby gripping the leather seat, trying to focus and decide what was happening. His head was swimming, like one recovering from a glancing blow, and at first he imagined himself to be in a dream – carried along on some inexplicable ride. But now, as his mind caught up with his senses, he remembered where he was and turning, saw Jeannie beside him. She was as calm as ever and touched him on the arm reassuringly.

'I'm sorry to have startled you,' she said. 'But you looked so peaceful that it seemed wrong to wake you too soon. I thought I would do the first part before you surfaced; but I'm afraid my little car bobs around too much.'

Her look was genuinely apologetic, but he could see that Jeannie was also pleased that he had come out of his long slumber. She handed him a plastic bottle containing water to refresh his dry throat and pointed to a bag of doughnuts on the dashboard that she had brought for him. He took one, pulled himself upright, and rubbed his tired face while beginning to eat.

Jeannie was not driving quickly, but carefully picked her way along the old track bed avoiding as many obstacles as possible. It had changed much: most evidence of the old railway (apart from the earthworks) having gone, leaving many bushes and trees to encroach upon the corridor where the rails had been. Yet it was not overgrown, having clearly been landscaped to provide a place for ramblers to enjoy. In a few years it would be very much as found in his own time.

'I've moved on again, haven't I?' he said, as they passed the place where the old mill stood surrounded by a field of ripe wheat.

'Most surely, Toby – it is now August 1986. The harvest has begun and you will soon see the way it is done these days.'

Having come to the spot where "Windmill Crossing" had been, she turned right up the track towards higher ground. "Station House" could be seen through the thick growth of hawthorn, brambles and unpruned fruit trees, its roof now stripped of tiles, the windows boarded up.

'It has been like that for some time,' she told him. 'The men from "Outlandia" came to recover materials when it was declared unfit for further use, so now it stands abandoned and open to the sky.'

Toby thought of old Morwen Hughes and her husband George, who had taken such pride in their home. He also remembered his own stay there just eleven years before and wondered if, with a little work, a house formerly so dry and secure might have been made habitable for someone else.

Moments later they emerged onto the plateau of land that Toby had noted being progressively transformed during his previous visits. But again, he was not prepared for the sights that met him.

* * *

All of us maintain a lasting impression of places that are valued because important events happened in or around them during our lives. Be they holiday beaches we loved as a child, or the home where we grew up, the images become fixed and unchanging in our minds, and it is difficult to accept they might alter, or that well-known features could disappear. We still expect the same fishing boats to be tied up in the harbour; the seemingly ever-present pink ice cream van to be selling its wares on the promenade.

Toby was not a child, but he had begun to wish for some permanence in his life as the journey he had embarked upon continued. Yet, as Jeannie pulled up beside a hedge at the junction of two cart tracks where "Warren Hill Farm" used to stand, what he saw caused him to catch his breath. This was now very like the place he had known in the early twentieth century – a landscape seemingly ironed out and cleared of all but a few widely spaced hedgerows and small trees. A column of electricity pylons had also been erected: marching out of the west and crossing the open expanse of fields before disappearing eastwards towards Bedford. Still stiff from his long spell of inactivity he stepped out of the car and moved round next to Jeannie. The day was fine and hot, the breeze lifting her hair, which she held back from her forehead with a raised hand.

'Do you recognise it all?' she asked.

He thought for a moment, looking around for points of reference from his last visit. But there were few, for although the countryside lay before him with the same folds and hollows, much else had changed. The buildings had all disappeared – not one remaining on the land between Molliton and the Northampton road, a space of two miles. And where four farms had once stood now there was nothing but fields of harvested wheat – the rows of cut straw stretching to the horizon. In the dip to the south, the last buildings at "Deep Spinney Farm" had all gone, the farmhouse with them: the whole area having been opened out. The far slope, where he had slept in Queenie's cottage, was also bare – just another wide expanse in a sea of monoculture. But as they began to walk along the track towards Molliton it was the disappearance of "High Dyke Farm" that struck Toby most. On the rising ground, not thirty years before, he had visited a still vibrant farm with a great number of buildings, many of quite recent construction. He'd been warned then that life was becoming more difficult for the Braylings, but had not imagined they too would be forced to give up completely so soon. Yet the evidence was there before him: the farm had been expunged, all trace removed, as if it had never existed.

'When did this happen?' asked Toby as they came to the place where the front gate had stood – now just a wide space between the remains of two straggly hedges.

'Five years ago,' she replied, gazing into the distance. 'The Braylings were bought out by "Outlandia". The farm was making a loss and the family were in no position to refuse. They didn't want to go, and had tried a number of things to update the business and diversify, but it was not to be. The loss of a milk contract (when the local dairy closed because all the other local producers had given up) was the last straw, and with that blow they had to move on.'

Toby looked out at the open countryside: the absence of animals anywhere in the landscape striking him once more. He also noted the scarcity of birds and other wildlife. There was a stillness all around, and where previously he had seen flocks of sparrows, starlings and other small birds flitting between farm buildings, trees and hedgerows, he now witnessed but a single woodpigeon flying away towards Molliton and a pair of dusty rooks picking about among nearby corn stubble.

'So what became of the Braylings?' he asked, thinking about the pleasant days that he'd spent working with them, and perhaps fearing they might all be gone.

'Bert, the eldest – the one who was always the cowman – he died in 1980,' replied Jeannie. 'But I believe the others are still with us. They moved to the farm of relatives in

Hertfordshire – old Jim and Mickey – to retire, but I've heard Duke and Betty still work there, although they are getting on in years now.'

Toby was glad the family had found somewhere to be together, but felt sad that he would not meet them again. They had been honest people who deserved better than to be driven from their home by what financiers coldly call "economic forces". In the way the Braylings had farmed, with their mixed crops and reliance on organic fertilisers, there was a sustainable future. But as "Outlandia" took over the management of the countryside a different ethos had begun to prevail in which the care and wellbeing of the soil and natural environment would come a distant second to the pursuit of cheap food and company profit.

What resulted was a kind of stark desolation – a landscape stripped down to its essentials, in which anything that impeded the machines or harboured a hungry rabbit was removed. Most trees and hedgerows had been unceremoniously torn down or grubbed out; while those that remained were left as neglected barriers between one prairie sized field and another. The old forms of agriculture, with all their admitted imperfections, together with the communities that made a living by them, were no more; having been replaced by something that would in time prove grossly worse – techniques of industrial farming that pay little regard to the welfare of either people or nature. So in the pursuit of profits for developers, pension funds and insurance companies in London, Tokyo and New York, the still quite recent past of rural North Bedfordshire – a way of life we have lost – had been ploughed out and erased forever.

* * *

The two moved on to where the ancient dyke that had given the Brayling farm its name reached out into the countryside beyond. Toby knew what he would find; for whereas in the time of the family's tenure there had been a patchwork of small fields and hedgerows dotted with trees round about, now the "Ninety Acre Field" was restored to the way he knew all too well – a single huge swathe of standing wheat stretching down to the line of the old railway and the Oakwell Road.

'One field,' said Toby sadly. 'One field from so many... Does it have to be this way?'

'If we are to eat inexpensive bread and cake,' Jeannie replied, with a look of irony. 'Or so we are told.'

It was just after ten o'clock in the morning and they watched as a third of a mile away a huge combine harvester heaved into the field through a gap between two small woods at the edge of Molliton. The great lumbering giant came to a halt by an old fuel tanker and very soon was joined by two similar machines. Tractors with grain trailers also appeared, and there were signs of activity as men prepared the harvesters for work.

'They will clear this wide slope by evening,' said Jeannie, turning to him. 'Less than a week ago not one of the surrounding fields had been cut but by tonight all will be finished – then the straw burning can begin.'

Toby had seen this done as a child: whole fields of straw and stubble torched to prepare the land for ploughing and to eradicate pests and weeds.

'That can be messy,' he said, remembering.

'Oh yes! But we are told that it is an efficient method, so it must be alright. Efficiency is everything in this modern age. These "Outlandia" men know their jobs: be they called upon to plough out an ancient farm, or harvest in eight hours a field of corn that would have taken our ancestors a week to collect, they work with a steady will and get the task done.'

The distant harvesters moved forward once more, the two onlookers watching as each began to crawl round the edge of the vast field. At first Toby thought they made little impression, but in a short time a wide swathe of stubble lined with rows of straw began to open up. Nor were the creeping leviathans as slow as might be imagined, but moved on at a steady pace consuming the crop before them. In time the three disappeared into a dip by the railway, and for perhaps three minutes all that could be seen was a billowing cloud of dust and particles rising up in that direction – like the dull smog from moving chimneys. Then the first reappeared, now heading towards them up the slope, the revolving feeder tines glittering as they rose and fell to scoop the grain into the harvester's insatiable bowels. The noise increased with its approach, the two other machines rising into view behind like fellow gladiators marching to war. Yet this was no contest: for the harvesters were more than masters of their task, unstinting in their steady drive to bring the harvest home: though theirs was might without beauty; majesty without art – the work of brute monsters let loose upon the land to win cheap food for men.

Toby could not help but think of the horse drawn binder used long ago by the Trindles: of the stoked sheaves and Cade Slyman's threshing machine. Such methods could never be efficient by modern standards since they required the endeavours of a whole family to do the work that one of these two hundred thousand pound "miracles" could perform in a day. Yet in those departed times all had a role in the drama of bringing the harvest safely home. Everyone, including children, took part and was valued for his or her contribution in the fields – thus coming to understand how food arrives on the dinner plate. But now only a man high up in a closed, air-conditioned cab was needed, and all others (especially the young), were instructed to keep well away lest they impede the work or be swallowed by the all conquering machines.

Toby and Jeannie stepped back behind a grassy bank as the first harvester went by, half blinded by the muck ejected from it. They could see the driver looking down at them with disapproval upon his face as if questioning their right to be there. But both stood on a public way and he made no gesture towards them. The following two rumbled past as well, the final driver, now some distance into the field from where they stood, waving before turning and moving off towards Molliton.

During the ensuing calm Jeannie, who had produced food and drink from her shoulder bag, talked more about the recent changes that had taken place.

'The countryside is suffering,' she said, 'and many folk are becoming increasingly concerned about what will happen in the future if things continue as they are. Due to changing agricultural methods many wild bird and animal species are in steep decline; while the soil is also suffering because too many pesticides and artificial fertilizers are used. Nature's natural cycle is being disrupted, and may soon be destroyed altogether; with consequences that men have yet to understand or plan for.'

She leant towards him, looking earnestly into his eyes. 'But there are good people that care about this – people that want to protect the natural world and ensure our quest for food is sustainable. You have met one of them, Meg Maddox's granddaughter, Claire Cheetham.'

'You know what became of her?' he asked with interest. 'Did she marry after all?'

'Her wedding to Jamie Tresco took place in January 1976 and they have been happy together since then. Sometimes the people we meet change our lives in ways we can hardly imagine, and this was certainly the case with Claire. She had always been a very competent journalist, but one whose work lacked the edge of any real commitment. This was, perhaps, because she had grown up in a very comfortable and protected environment, without the spur that inspires others to go out and achieve their true potential. Had she known her own mother better, I am sure that she would have been determined to make her mark much earlier. However, meeting Jamie Tresco changed that, for he encouraged her to see the problems of the outside world, and helped her focus her talents in support of a cause. She was one of the first to write knowledgeably on the subject of how present-day damage to the natural environment is likely to impact upon human populations in the future. In doing so Claire has inevitably had to accept being lampooned and challenged by powerful vested interests, learning to use their shallow mockery as a source of motivation. She knows from her own experience, and her husband's research, that her arguments are on the right track, and has developed the skill and perseverance to encourage others to listen. Moreover, having made this journey, Claire is a thousand times happier in what she does and will surely pass her enthusiasm onto her own child.'

'She has children?'

'Just one,' said Jeannie, pulling her knees up to her chin. 'Her daughter, Emma, was born on 11th December, 1979 but there were complications that meant Claire could not have more. She was ill for some while and spent two years devoting the whole of her time to Emma. Their bond has grown very strong, and the young girl shows every sign of developing the same zeal and commitment as her mother.'

'Can that be seen in a small child?' he asked doubtfully.

'I believe so. Emma Tresco will not be an uncommitted person – she has too much of her maternal grandmother in her for that.'

'And perhaps something of her great-grandmother as well,' thought Toby.

* * *

The day wore on, and by late afternoon more than half of the "Ninety-Acre Field" had been harvested. Still the harvesters clawed their way back and forth, like mighty four wheeled vacuum cleaners scouring the land and swallowing the valuable crop. There was a pleasing regularity in the resulting pattern of straw trails that grew across the open mile of countryside.

Meanwhile, much was said in their quiet conversation that Toby could link to his own life; for having been a boy himself in 1986, he knew of many of the other events she described. Thus it was not until just after four o'clock, though with the sun still bright in the western sky, that Jeannie stood up at last and invited him to follow.

'There will be more to this day for you to ponder,' she said. 'But before the shadows fall I would like to show you what has happened in another place.'

She would say no more and remained silent as they walked back to where her little car was parked. But instead of stopping she moved further on, striding across an empty field towards the place where "Maxton Tower" had once stood. Soon they came out at a point where they could see all the land on that side of the rise. Startled by their approach, a frightened hare scudded off ahead across the open waste of stubble in a reckless search for concealment. They watched it move away into the distance, its brown and white fur caught by the golden rays of the evening sun – obvious to the eye as it skipped over serried lines of straw before disappearing from sight beyond a fold in the land.

The air was now beginning to freshen as the heat of the day wore off, and a faint breeze from the north made Toby look that way.

'Is Meg's cottage still standing?' he asked, shielding his eyes. But again Jeannie did not answer, only moving off in the direction of the dip where it had stood. Soon, as they descended towards the stile over the railway, he saw that here too the site had been mostly cleared. The hedgerow, once growing before her door, still remained, as did the thicket of trees beside the old railway, but the cottage had gone as if it had sunk into the ground. The animal enclosure, too, with its untidy trees and bushes, was no more – the entire half acre of land being covered by a few wide lines of wheat straw.

'When was this done?' Toby asked, his voice trailing to a whisper.

'Three winters ago… the cottage stood empty for some years, although they did cultivate the land around. It became a haven for wildlife: foxes, rabbits, owls and the like. There were even badgers here. But that only seemed to annoy the "Outlandia" managers as time went on; for to them all such wild creatures are vermin. So at last the men came to pull it down.'

'There was a well here too. What became of that?'

'They dug down to a level where it could be sealed over with concrete, then filled it with bricks and rubble from the cottage. "Silver Link Cottage" is still here, Toby,' she added with a faint smile. 'But it lies deep in the ground where none can see it.'

'And when they ploughed the area... was anything found – did anything come to the surface?'

Jeannie looked at Toby, knowing what lay behind his query. 'No, Toby... the ploughs went deep into the soil but all they revealed were chicken bones and ancient flints; Meg's former pets were not disturbed... or any other remains.'

He breathed deeply, moving a few steps ahead towards the rusty fence by the abandoned railway. 'And what of Meg?'

'She is there, at the lowest spot,' replied Jeannie, pointing at a place caught by the late sunlight where an array of straggling dog daisies and other wild flowers grew. 'The Corrie twins used to tend her grave in the early days, but now they leave it to the care of nature. To this end they sprinkled wild flowers around; and these come back year on year to keep alive her memory.'

'She would have liked that... and it must provide a bright place in summer for any that pass this way.'

* * *

Their pilgrimage done, they turned to walk back; but Toby stopped again when crossing the place where he judged her front door to have stood. 'What of Meg's things... her books?' he asked. 'What became of them – were they thrown down the well with the rest?'

She smiled, looking back at him. 'Have no fear about that, Toby. Meg's life was not of so little value that folk would allow the things she loved to be destroyed. The Corrie sisters gained permission to empty the cottage of what was valuable before demolition work commenced. Some things were given to a local museum, while many of her volumes were presented to schools and a library. But her most valued books are still in safe-keeping; so one day you may perhaps be reacquainted with them.'

Jeannie resumed walking on ahead of him before adding, seemingly as an after thought, 'There is one other small memento of interest to show you.'

He followed her as the dying light of an evening sky filling with high cloud fell around them, sending faint shadows creeping across the fields. Regaining the higher ground they came back to where the car was parked and she beckoned him round to the rear before lifting the boot lid. Toby had expected to see some small vase or ornament; but what was revealed affected him much more, for there next to the jack, lying on a canvas sheet, was the name board of "Silver Link Cottage".

'I thought it would appeal to you,' she said, studying his reaction. 'It seemed such a personal thing to leave behind.'

He agreed, picking it up and turning the artefact reverently in his hands. 'I'm glad you took it down… It would have been a pity if it had been buried with the rest.'

Toby then placed the time-weathered item back and closed the boot, a chill now tingling his skin as the heat of the day wore off. Absently he began also to consider where to stay that night, since the prospect of another sojourn in the cramped little A35 held little appeal.

'I have a place in mind,' she said, reading his thoughts, 'a boatyard by the River Ouse at Stavenham. It is not much used and I doubt that you will be troubled there. There are one or two old pleasure cruisers drawn up that you might stay in if they are not too firmly locked.'

'So I'll need to break in… but how am I supposed to do that?' Toby asked, not relishing resorting to the housebreaker's art.

'Leave that to me,' she replied without emotion or concern. 'Such things are easy enough when the need arises.'

Toby could think of nothing to say in reply – although he did wonder how a policeman might respond if he was discovered sleeping in another's private property. But the sight of the first of the three giant combine harvesters approaching now drove this thought from his mind. Each monster had had its cutting table removed to allow negotiation of restricted entrances, and with headlights staring into the developing gloom, swung left in front of them before heading downhill in a cloud of dust.

'Contractors!' said Jeannie above the noise. 'They'll have another job to work on tonight, and another crew will be waiting to take over.'

The support tractors also came up, and following the reaping machines accelerated off in the same direction, bumping and rolling over the rutted ground. Their speed amazed Toby, and he reflected that the age old process of bringing in the harvest, once dictated by the comfortable pace of a horse, had now become a headlong charge in pursuit of the next pay cheque; with men working day and night in relays across three counties to make a living.

Very soon the convoy had disappeared from sight, though the distant roar of the harvesters continued to be heard on the still air as they made their way towards Picts Hill on the road to Turnham. No wind stirred, as was shown by the appearance of two vertical columns of smoke that began rising from a field towards "Tyler Hall".

'Fires!' said Toby, remembering the ritual of his youth. 'They're burning the stubble.'

Both he and Jeannie now focussed their attention in that direction, and within five minutes saw a dozen blazes spring up, each quickly moving forward down the lines of straw made tinder dry by days of hot weather. Then the same thing began to happen closer to them in the large field that had been created around the spot where "Pocket Farm" once stood. A station wagon had pulled up at the far end, and they watched as a labourer with a flaming torch stepped methodically across the rows spreading a curtain of fire. Now that the animals that once needed bedding and food were gone from the land it was a simple enough expedient to dispose of an unwanted commodity. Two men with sticks and a few oily rags could torch the lot in one night. But there was a downside to this simple economy, in terms of the massive pollution that would occur before morning. The rancid smoke and ash beginning to reach Toby's nostrils would be carried off on the night air, to settle by the early hours in a grey film on every window ledge and windscreen for several miles downwind. Meanwhile, any half dry clothing left out overnight would inevitably require another wash. But the profit takers in London cared little for that. If the good folk of East Anglia had to sleep through a sticky night with windows closed or to be faced with cleaning the dirt from their curtains on the morrow, it must be regarded as an acceptable inconvenience if the practice led to greater profitability for the company.

Indeed, the activity they were witnessing was evidently to be part of a major undertaking. The harvesters having completed their work and departed, the land could be prepared again for sowing, and the men pursued their task of dispensing the flames with steady zeal. Another field to their left came to life, and as the sky darkened they noted that hillsides on other estates were ablaze, adding further concentrations of soot to the carbon soup now filling the atmosphere. It soon became clear that by first light a landscape previously brushed with pale gold and yellow would be liberally scarred by wide smoking swards of brown and black.

* * *

Yet above all else, fire is an elemental thing – a force that if left to get out of control, develops a momentum of its own. Moreover, its progress can become intoxicating to those that spread it… while the demonstration of its primal energy may so overcome normal judgement that while it might take but two energetic enthusiasts to start a blaze; a hundred might be required to bring under control the myriad army of flames let loose. So it was this night; for as the two men walked to and fro about their work, firing a widening acreage, a warm wind sprang up from the west that grew steadily in strength. At first the fire-raisers seemed unaware of the danger – one passing within ten yards of Jeannie giving but a curt warning that she should move her car before stalking on through the swirling smoke towards the "Ninety Acre Field".

Jeannie wisely elected to follow his advice and together she and Toby bumped off down the track the harvesters had taken, before rising to higher ground beyond. Here, upwind of the flames, they were able to clearly observe what was happening as the fires began to burn out of control. The labourers were now nowhere to be seen, but the process of field clearance was undoubtedly taking a serious turn. The wind had begun to tug the blazing columns around, sometimes picking up burning straw and depositing it well beyond the boundaries of the cornfields into dry hay meadows and tree copses further off, while at other places a wall of creeping flames relentlessly advanced through tall stubble to engulf ancient hedgerows. In this way the casual burning of unwanted straw became something less forgivable – an act of careless vandalism.

As they watched, a section of hedge burst into flame not fifty yards from them, and within seconds more fires curled up further along. Unhindered by any barrier, the blaze, stirred by the ever increasing breeze, began to eat its way steadily forward, licking round a weather worn ash tree, the leaves of which burst into flame in a moving sheet of yellow sparks. They saw a terrified muntjac leap off into the night, kicking through the hot ashes of an adjacent field as it made its escape. Then a minute later, a fox, seemingly dazzled and bewildered by the heat and glare, slunk off before the encircling danger – its tail brushing the earth.

Similar scenes, shrouded by smoke and darkness, were doubtless being played out in a dozen other places across the valley and beyond the brow of the hill towards the old railway line as other surviving hedgerows succumbed to the scorching fires or were blackened and charred round the roots – many burned so badly that they would never grow properly again. As a result, by morning more than two miles of these valuable natural corridors, along with the trees that grew there, would be gone… time honoured and precious natural relics irreversibly scarred; their gaunt remains left exposed to the wind. Yet, when the hard-pressed fire brigade had gone, the over zealous "Outlandia" operatives would successfully protest their innocence; facing only mild chastisement from managers far from willing to part with such loyal and efficient workers while the pursuit of profit remained king.

For their own part Toby and Jeannie had endeavoured to help by stamping out the flames that threatened a hawthorn hedge near to them, but could only stand helplessly as the fires elsewhere ran their course. When firemen eventually arrived the two decided to leave quietly and drove back towards Stavenham over tracks blackened by the passing flames. The stench of smoke and ash filled the air; and would not finally be washed away until the first proper rains of autumn blew in from the Atlantic.

Not until moving beyond the railway line did they reach an area of untouched land; although before descending towards the Oakwell Road they came upon a fire engine tackling a fierce blaze among the lineside trees below "Station House". Here Toby also noted one or two anxious sightseers observing the ugly spectacle; but once Jeannie had steered the little car down to the the main road and shortly afterwards entered a narrow lane leading to a riverside boatyard, they saw no one else.

Toby now realised that the little car's lights were very weak – seemingly hardly better than glow-worms by modern standards, and the next two minutes were spent negotiating barely seen bumps and potholes before arrival at a five-barred security gate. He jumped out to open this, and Jeannie quickly passed through with Toby following into a concrete yard bathed by pale moonlight shining down from a sky of broken cloud and smoke. Moments later she pulled up in an open space where a number of craft had been drawn out of the water. One of these was a small motor cruiser, the "Isinglass", which stood on a metal stand in a corner near the river's edge, its white paint stained and mildewed from an evident period of disuse.

'Don't be put off by the exterior,' said Jeannie reassuringly. 'It's quite comfortable inside.'

'The boat is yours?'

'Let's say I know where it came from,' she replied with an enigmatic smile.

Toby hopped up onto the narrow deck; then dropped down beside the door to the cabin. Jeannie handed him a key and with it he bent to let himself in.

'There's a torch in the bedside drawer,' she called to him. 'But take care not to waste the batteries.'

'After what we've been up to I'll smoke this little place out,' he replied, summoning a half-hearted grin when his head reappeared.

'Don't worry, you smell fine, Toby. Everything will be okay – but whatever you do keep the door locked. Then you are sure not to be disturbed.'

'And you… where will you go?'

'There are no dangers for me to worry about,' she said, turning to depart. 'It is you that must take care.'

* * *

And so, having said their farewells, he stooped to make a further inspection of his new quarters as Jeannie moved back towards the A35. The accommodation did indeed appear comfortable enough: with dry sheets and a blanket stored in a box beneath a fold down bed, and a tiny galley stocked with tins and dry essentials to eat. A few seconds passed as he rummaged around, all the time expecting to hear the car engine start; but as no sound came he emerged a second time, only to find the boatyard deserted once more.

'Gone without a whisper,' he said to himself, '…as if she melted into thin air.'

* * *

Left behind in this out-of-the way location there was little else for Toby to do but lock up and await developments. He had come closer to home, in time, and his journey might soon be over. Thus, having made sure his few belongings were readily at hand, he slumped wearily onto the cabin bed. Then his vision swam, the torch falling from a loosened grip, and he remembered no more.

Chapter Seventeen

Brave New World or Dark Millennium?

THE FINAL YEARS OF THE TWENTIETH CENTURY saw mankind approach the dawn of a new millennium with increasing uncertainty. The previous thousand years of history, having begun with our ancestors unable to travel faster than a galloping horse, now ended with scientists contemplating the possibility of space exploration at the speed of light. While some, of even more expansive and romantic temperament, allowed themselves to dream of a distant future lived beyond the stars!

However, as many members of the scientific community were beginning to realise from the evidence of their own research and projections, it would be during the short period of the following century that the ultimate destiny of human beings would be decided. Would our race slide into terminal decline, amid mass plant and animal extinction? Or might it emerge at the eleventh hour, having adopted the path to a sustainable existence that would safeguard the living planet? Yet, for a few more precious and wasted years, only limited steps were taken to halt the accelerating trend towards environmental breakdown. The world's riches were still greedily torn from the soil: rainforests cleared, the seas and oceans pillaged – the very atmosphere around us choked by pollution from fossil fuels. Meanwhile oil and mining companies enjoyed a bonanza – fuel corporations making fortunes every day as complicit politicians treated oil oligarchs like emperors.

The age of convenience, mass transport and commercialism: with its seemingly inevitable corollaries – extravagance, exploitation, greed and waste – flourished beneath the darkening cloud. It became a time in which every man, woman and child in the "developed" countries was encouraged to believe they had the right to live like kings at the expense of the poor, the less fortunate and the planet – "Because they were worth it". A false premise was sown that we might save the earth without changing the way we live – that nations could endlessly expand their economies (consuming ever more each year) rather than encouraging citizens to exercise greater thrift and demand less. Meanwhile, an alternative idea – that the impoverished might have a fairer share if the rich went without their more extravagant pleasures – was dismissed as heresy and a restraint of "free enterprise". No, the economic world would surely grind to a halt and fall apart if the consumer junkie bought less! He had to be pampered and encouraged – even if it did ultimately cost the earth... To this end, highly paid government "experts" were primed to dismiss the concerns of more considered and cautious voices. 'Climate change is part of a naturally occurring cycle,' they averred, with crossed fingers. 'The planet will surely cope with all this – for another few years at least.' ...But the planet was about to bite back; and the days of reckoning were coming from which, in the light of experience, wiser and more humble leaders would eventually emerge.

* * *

By now, virtually all those living at the time of Toby's arrival in Stavenham were gone, while the few survivors would play no further part in his story. Toby had entered his own age: a time in which he and his travelling companions were destined to journey out into the wider world. He would not wake at the end of the old millennium, or witness the start of the new, and the shallow words of optimism uttered by grey suited politicians did not fall upon his ears. Nor did the bright, reassuring fireworks – extravagantly shipped eight thousand miles from China – penetrate a single corner of his dreams.

But the raucous parties, so elaborately stage-managed as he slept, would soon come to an end; and when the last embers of celebratory fires had burned out, the old problems daily affecting so many inevitably remained. The widespread unhappiness of family life in Britain continued to eat away at the social fabric of the nation. On our city streets a growing band of corrupted, dispirited and abandoned youth were left, without direction or hope, to indulge in a largely vacuous existence fuelled increasingly by drugs and alcohol. In a drive to counter this, and purportedly to make our children "better citizens", a hundred school tests were devised for them, between four and sixteen, that they might be stuffed with useful facts to take forward through life. ...Sadly, all too often the outcome of this policy was that the gaining of arbitrary attainment grades and paper qualifications would come to be seen by many as of greater worth than the development of creativity, sensitivity and understanding – the voyeuristic viewing of a minor celebrity freak show more interesting than issues relating to honesty, justice and love.

Not everything that happened at this time was bad of course. Those born at the end of the twentieth century might, as medical science advanced, expect to live for a hundred years or more; and one of these, a British Asian named Rajesh Patel, eventually became the last surviving Englishman of the old millennium. The second of three siblings, he came into this world at Hastings General Hospital on the evening of the 16th November 1999 and would live a long and eventful life. In his time Planet Earth was transformed by climate change, natural disaster and war. Yet at the end, having experienced and suffered many things – far from thinking himself unfortunate, Rajesh would feel blessed to have seen so much and to have witnessed a new beginning.

Chapter Eighteen

Trapped!

IN THE MONTH OF MAY 2013 "THE Great Storm" broke over England, and it was then that Toby again surfaced in his own time. He was roused by a thrashing sound – as of a thousand skittering claws upon the lid of an empty barrel. The cacophony around him was deafening; a drumming in his ears that came from all sides at once, disconcerting and unnerving. He found himself in pitch-blackness, unable to recollect at first where he had last laid his head – a dozen wild explanations flashing through his befuddled, sleep-weary mind. Reaching up he touched wooden boards, and to one side, the fabric of a window curtain. Had he fallen into some confined, claustrophobic place; or become trapped inside a coffin?

Gripped by panic, Toby swung sideways, half toppling out of the bunk onto a cabin floor already ankle deep in water. The sharp cold made him jump back with a yelp, cracking his head on the ceiling, and he at last realised where he was.

'Rain...' he mouthed, half relieved. 'It's rain falling on the roof of the boat!'

Listening, his supposition was confirmed. The thunderous clamour of an intense downpour, growing heavier by the second, was beating against the curved roof, as if it might break through at any moment. Toby felt closed in again; but this time thankful as well to be protected from the drenching wall of water outside, and might have settled down to ride out the storm where he was, had not the wild ferocity of the lashing rain made him consider the need to find a less exposed refuge. Stepping down, his toes became immersed in chilly liquid once more – now a little deeper than previously, as if the craft were taking on water. He considered this for a moment, recalling clearly that the "Isinglass" had been drawn out of the river onto a boatyard stand. Yet he could sense movement – as if the motor cruiser was now dipping and turning in a strengthening current.

'It's afloat,' Toby said to himself, 'drifting on the river. But how could that be?'

A sense of not being in control spurred him to action. He felt frantically for the torch, but failing to find it, decided to take his chances with the weather to discover what was happening, and having unlocked the door, reached for the handle before pushing hard and tumbling forward into the recess below the boat deck.

The unbridled fury of the elements exploded upon him as he emerged: Toby was immediately deluged by falling water and wet through in seconds, his hair becoming plastered across cheeks and forehead. Beaten and forced to stoop forward, he instinctively curled himself down as if seeking protection from a multitude of blows, before falling back into the cabin again, leaving the door ajar. His perilous position had been made abundantly clear: for in the few seconds he'd ventured beneath the open sky, not only had Toby confirmed that the "Isinglass" was indeed afloat – but through the dancing haze of raindrops lashing the water, he'd ascertained that the normally placid River Ouse had turned into a wide and swirling torrent. On its own this would have been bad enough, but from the perceptible list that the "Isinglass" was developing, he was right in thinking that the little craft, having been lifted up and swept from its previously safe haven by the rising floodwater, was now in imminent danger of sinking.

Nautical activities had never been Toby's favourite pastimes, and as he reached down to put on his floating shoes, he had no idea what to do. An old weatherproof jacket with a hood hung behind the door, and although already soaked through he put this on as protection against the downpour. Then he clawed his way outside once more, to find the wind roaring even louder as fresh blasts rushed up the valley. It was very dark, but even the blackest night allows a little illumination through the clouds, and by this he discerned the broken surface of the river being stirred into a commotion of flaring spouts by the percussion of rain. At first there seemed little else in view – no shoreline, buildings or trees – but then he began to make things out. A large shape slid by: the fronds of a willow tree brushing his face as the "Isinglass" pitched drunkenly in the turning current. A half submerged barbed wire fence came next, curving away into the darkness as he was carried across a wide flood plain; then an abandoned tractor – awash to the level of the driver's seat, like some forlorn wreck on the open sea. The boat slewed on, frequently bumping against other unseen objects, all the while gradually sinking lower until water began to lap over the prow and seep along the deck. How long could this last? The only encouragement for Toby was that the rain had now eased temporarily – the heavy droplets falling more fitfully in irregular bursts – thus allowing him an interval in which to consider his chances of escape. But there seemed no opportunity to reach the shore as the water spread away, dark and oily, on all sides. The "Isinglass" was travelling faster than a man could walk, accompanied by other flotsam carried by the flood: broken branches, the debris from gardens, and circling further off, the floating carcass of a goat drowned by the rising water. Then, as he peered forward, a building loomed ahead: a boathouse inundated to the rafters and half surrounded by reeds, with little showing of the latter but waving seed heads. The stricken boat bumped heavily against the former, before beginning to nestle among submerged stems. Had it stopped there, Toby would have perished before morning as the craft sank into the mud and debris, but the summoning hand of a strong undercurrent gradually pulled him clear, like a knife drawn from a clinging wound.

He bobbed away once more, a break in the thick cloud allowing a shaft of moonlight to glint across the hurrying surface of the river. By this Toby realised that he was being carried into the centre of the normal course towards the deepest part, where even in a dry summer the turgid water lay twelve feet deep below the keel of pleasure craft. To founder here could only lead to a watery grave, and he clung to the roof of the sinking craft, watching as the encroaching ripples began to seep down the four steps to the cabin below. When almost beyond hope, a post grew out of the shimmering darkness ahead, one that normally stood tall to indicate the level of floodwater after stormy weather. It had marker lines up to fifteen feet, but now all were covered and only the white painted crown still showed. Yet there was something else that caught his eye, for perched upon it was a large bird – a crow with folded wings that watched him as he approached. He expected the creature to take flight and lift away, but it continued to eye him steadily, swivelling its head as he passed by not three feet away. Then, as the post was left astern, the inky scavenger spread his wings, and taking flight, flew low towards the opposite shore, cawing into the turbulent night. Toby lost it in the darkness as the moon again went behind a bank of cloud, before glimpsing something further – a figure moving near the spot where the creature had disappeared from view.

He craned forward to make out who it might be, and saw a woman making her way to the water's edge. She was struggling to maintain her balance on the muddy bank, and shielded her eyes to look in his direction. Had the current continued to flow the same way he might have been carried directly towards her, but a sudden tugging of the undertow caused the sinking "Isinglass" to lurch away again around another stand of half-submerged river plant, before drunkenly turning back towards the bank once more. The pace of the boat had slowed perceptibly, partly as a result of being carried into the shelter of the lee shore, but more ominously because the rapidly filling hull was sinking lower in the stream and being held by hidden roots and snares. Toby thought of swimming to the bank as the rain began to lash down with renewed fervour, but would have been carried under in a moment in the garb he wore. Yet the vessel was undoubtedly going down beneath him – settling for the last time before disappearing below the swollen waters five metres from the riverbank.

He hardly saw Jeannie as she leaned out holding a sturdy branch, but losing balance as he took the full force of a snaring gust, found himself tipped off the deck of the floundering craft and plunged into a channel three metres deep of freezing cold water that closed over his head. For several seconds Toby felt himself turning with the current, held in a silent world then, gasping for breath, he surfaced again to see the proffered life preserver bobbing before his eyes.

'Take it, Toby! Don't give up, hold on!' he heard a voice cry above the circling spate.

Gnarled wood touched his knuckles and with the instinct of a drowning man he clutched it before being dragged under once more.

How much Toby really knew of what happened next he could not have said. The Cold numbed his mind and senses as the eager water sought to take him, but he did not let go, and inch-by-inch was drawn forward into the shallows. A hand then took hold of his wrist and another pulled at his collar as, like a discarded raft of flotsam, he was hauled onto a muddy bank.

* * *

If the decision had been left to him, Toby might have continued to lie there recovering his wits while being washed clean by the cascading torrent again falling. But Jeannie had other ideas.

'It's not safe here,' she yelled into his ear. 'We must move further off and find shelter.'

The urgency in her voice roused him to his feet, and staggering forward they began to climb together towards higher ground, frequently slipping and stumbling on the sodden earth. The two took more than five minutes to cover less than sixty metres; coming at last to a small animal lean-to in the corner of a paddock – the presence of various brightly painted jumps and obstacles indicating the place was used by novice riders practising their equestrian skills. But the roof of the lean-to leaked badly beneath the extraordinary downpour and it was clear that another more sheltered place would be needed if Toby was to dry out and fully recover.

He had slumped down dejected on a bale of wet straw and Jeannie, crouching before him, cupped his cheeks in the palm of her hands, willing him with the earnestness of her gaze to listen and take heart.

'I know of a better place,' she said. 'Somewhere dry and secure that stands above the flood. It is some way off, but I promise that the storm will not reach us there.'

'I'll try,' Toby answered wearily, feeling the swallowed water of the river rising in his throat. '…But I am tired of this wandering… you must promise to explain what it is for – or I cannot go on.'

She nodded to him, the drips of water falling from her nose making Toby smile despite the discomfort of his wet clothing.

'Come now,' said Jeannie, lifting him, 'there is no sense in waiting longer. Morning approaches and we will soon have daylight to go by.'

So they stepped out beneath the skies and went on, tugged by a fierce and blustery wind. The light grew around them, revealing a landscape strewn with fallen trees and flattened crops. It was the morning of Friday, 26th May 2013, and the storm, which had already raged without pause for more than thirty-six hours, would not begin to subside for another day. They talked little above the howling wind, but Toby recognised familiar places as their trek continued. They crossed the Stavenham to Oakwell road, before heading up towards "Windmill Crossing"; all the while stepping over, or skirting round, fallen branches and wind-blown hedgerows. Like ragged waifs they staggered forward, heads down against the gale, passing the old mill – the preserved wooden body now lying capsized in the field, its ruined sails broken and scattered across flattened barley. Through the gap leading over the disused railway track they went, then on towards "The Cross" where the corners of four fields met at the site of "Warren Hill Farm". It was a bleak and ravaged spot that morning and Toby, now chilled to the bone, stopped to look up with reddened eyes at the dark and restless sky above. The rain still poured down, and his coat collar, caught by the angry wind, whipped about his face. All around the earth had been transformed into a sea of mud and puddles – bubbling streams of water running away in all directions from the raised spot.

Yet in the midst of Toby's misery a sudden clear sense of recollection came over him… something about the endlessly battered fields. He called to Jeannie, slightly ahead, and she turned, an anxious look in her eyes, as Toby drew closer, his throat now dry and rasping.

'You haven't told me when this is…' he croaked, with shortened breath. 'What month? …What year? …Tell me, I need to know…'

A blast of storm force wind struck them, almost knocking Toby off his feet, and somewhere nearby the branch of an exposed tree snapped before crashing to the ground. Jeannie reached out to support him, struggling to make herself heard over the uproar. But when they came to his ears, her words were slow and deliberate – like a timeless chant, or an elegy. 'This is the year 2013, Toby, and the "Great Storm" still rages around us.'

For a moment he became rooted to the spot, searching for words to express his swelling feelings. 'Then this is my own time… the month of May in that year – and I might go home…'

Toby's voice trailed away as he gazed down the flooded track towards Molliton.

'…It was only ever a mile away,' he said, stepping forward. 'Yet I never journeyed there in all these intervening years – fearing what I might find. …But now I must go back!'

He began to move off, slithering over the uneven ground, but in a moment Jeannie had stepped before him – blocking his way.

'Not yet,' she said, with a strange look conveying both empathy and determination. 'The time would not be right, dear friend… Between here and your home there is much danger and devastation and you might easily be hurt or killed.'

'How can I stop now, when I have waited a hundred years for this…?' he asked in an anguished and broken voice, looking down at the whitened hand tightly holding his own. '…What more can you want of me?'

'That you live, Toby... that is all. ...But it is so important! ...Now come – without a struggle – for we must not stay longer in this place.'

He tried to pull away, but her will seemed stronger than his, and she drew him foot by foot from the path and down across a sloping field. Once Toby broke free, but beaten down again by a rush of wind, it was she that raised him from the slough and led him on – all resistance melting as an aching sense of defeat numbed his mind.

* * *

They floundered forward: crossing a swollen ditch by an ancient half submerged bridge constructed of mossy railway sleepers, before making for higher ground once more. Soon the cleaved trees of a shattered wood next to the Northampton road loomed ahead – the same one in which the gamekeeper's gibbet had been found on the day of the pheasant shoot. But now, more openly revealed, was a tall water tower constructed after the Second World War to provide supplies for a nearby hospital. It had been little used in more recent times but was still maintained in good order in case of emergency, the cylindrical structure strongly built to support a large iron tank bordered by a railed inspection platform. Access to this was achieved by ascending a metal ladder surrounded by a circular safety frame to save those that might lose their grip. It offered a relatively safe but unnerving vertical climb and to discourage unwelcome visitors, barbed wire was normally wound round the base. A large sign, now blown down by the wind, warned of the dangers and penalties for trespassers. What few passers-by noticed or knew about, however, was that there was a small equipment room set into the eastern side of the water tank, complete with a window to allow in natural light.

Together they fought their way through fallen wood and undergrowth to stand in the lee of the wind beneath the looming structure, and it was then that Toby noticed the protective wire had been cut.

'There is a place above – somewhere dry for us to stay until the storm blows over,' said Jeannie, encouraging him towards the ladder.

'I don't know if I can do it,' replied Toby. 'Can it really be safer up there?'

She stepped beside him as another fierce gust of wind rolled up from the west, tearing twigs and branches from the remaining trees of the devastated wood, one of which fell nearby sending fountains of water from a dozen puddles cascading into the air.

'You will be better protected aloft than on the ground,' she reassured him. 'The tower is strongly made and will not fall to any natural event brought on by the activities of man. Come, take courage, and I will follow!'

She seemed certain of the scheme, and the promise of somewhere dry galvanised Toby to accept the necessity of climbing. Together they rose, rung by rung, as if ascending into a lowering heaven of wind and rain. Toby's hands were cold and numb, and more than once he came close to losing his grip when caught by a fresh blast. But when he looked down, Jeannie was constantly there, just below, smiling her encouragement as they progressed aloft. Yet there was much danger in what they did, for both were like frail matchwood in the teeth of the storm, and upon reaching the high platform forty feet above the ground, each was forced to hang on tight to the guard rail for fear of being lifted and tossed into the air by the gale.

Jeannie waited for a favourable moment before reaching out with one hand toward the handle of the storehouse door, which appeared to swing open at her touch. Then, keeping it steady with her shoulder, she beckoned him to move inside. Toby did so, tumbling forward to land out of the wind against a folded chair. He jarred his shoulder, and wincing from the stabbing pain, saw Jeannie forcing the door closed behind them, shutting out the blast, although the sound of the howling wind and thrashing rain against the metal tank still filled their ears. Yet inside, at least, it was calm and dry: while the light coming in from a small window enabled Toby to see the contents of the room.

This was not large, being little bigger than a small attic, but whoever had frequented it before had not left it without comforts. There was a total of three folded chairs that might be put out, either inside or on the lofty platform, plus a table to work or eat upon. A calor gas stove was provided for cooking, along with a set of shelves containing cans of tinned food. Opening a cupboard, Jeannie also produced knives, forks and cooking utensils that they might use. But what surprised Toby most of all was the sight of a large hold-all left on the floor in the corner, for this contained more than one change of overalls and dry clothes, all of which seemed to have been recently cleaned.

'This is quite a little hideaway,' he said, looking up, 'a splendid little eagle's nest. Did you know what we would find here?'

Jeannie gave no answer but taking a box of matches from the table drawer, lit the calor gas stove to warm the room and prepare food.

'You must change out of your wet things,' she said, busying herself. 'It will not do to become unwell, and you have already been soaked through for too long.'

'And what of you?' Toby asked. 'Surely it would be prudent to do the same.'

This was a natural enough enquiry after the experience they had both shared, but as Jeannie came to stand before him, holding a frying pan, he saw that she already appeared almost dry – while he still dripped from head to toe. Nor did she shiver as he but pushing back the drying hair on her forehead, grinned with youthful encouragement.

'I don't imagine that will be necessary, Toby. The warm, dry air of the room will be enough for me.'

He looked at her with something approaching awe: this strange young woman, living on the fringes of real life – now restored, mysterious and demure, to her former self.

* * *

Time wore on and they ate as Toby thawed out, the sensations of cold and damp gradually leaving his bones. He changed into a warm sweatshirt, socks and jeans, and they left the stove alight with his discarded clothes steaming before it. The little window very soon misted up, but upon wiping it the progress of the storm could be observed. Their refuge, meanwhile, remained a very noisy place, the endless drumming of the rain making conversation difficult. But gradually, as evening approached, the weather began to moderate at last; and while venturing outside was still impossible they could at least discuss their position without needing to resort to frequent efforts at lip-reading. Jeannie found a camping gas lamp which she lit as the light dimmed, and Toby, while absently examining the moist contents of his fleece pockets, drew forth the almost forgotten mobile phone, which he placed pensively upon the table in front of the burning stove. It was damp, like everything else, and he felt sure that the earthy waters of the river must have finished it off. Yet looking towards the device his resolve to return home welled again. Whatever else might happen, he would leave next morning at the latest – no matter what Jeannie had planned.

'I must go soon,' he said, having gathered his thoughts as he sat opposite her. 'There is much to do... and Jenny will be expecting me.'

She looked at him strangely, scrutinising his face as if reading his intentions, which unnerved him.

'You already know what will happen next, Toby... The storm will end tonight, and in two days your wife and children will travel to London.'

'Yes... I do know that... but...' His voice trailed away.

'Then why should you be able to change things?' she asked, gazing into his eyes. 'Perhaps your journey will not end so easily...'

Toby was perplexed. '...Surely that is why I was brought here. To witness the past... before returning to my own time,' he stammered.

Jeannie slowly shook her head, sadness showing in her eyes. 'No, Toby – there is more to your life than that. You set out feeling troubled... searching for explanations for what has become of you and your world. That was a special endeavour. From this you have begun to see how folly and greed inescapably shape the future, making people blind to our need to protect the earth and live in harmony with nature. You have also seen that not all was well in the past – that ways which might have saved us from the desolation found all around today were progressively abandoned in the pursuit of profit and selfish gain. But this story is only half run...' she added with emphasis, leaning towards him. 'For many other storms and hardships will undoubtedly follow if men continue to rape the earth as they do. All might yet end in tragedy – but there is hope that wiser heads may some day rule; that someone already living might find the answer.'

Toby put his head in his hands and she, taking pity, touched his shoulder.

'But why me... surely another would be better?'

'There is no one better, Toby. You have an honest and questioning spirit, and that is required above all. You will play a crucial part in the coming of change – for your very existence is bound up with what is to come, and you must now move in wider circles to fulfil your destiny.'

He might have been listening to the sentence of a judge, such was the weight of her words upon his ears.

'Is there really no other way?' he asked in a voice low and detached.

Jeannie looked closely at him, judging Toby's mood, and sensing the current of rebellion that still lurked within him. When she spoke her words were measured – like a warning.

'History is many layered,' she said, 'each succeeding layer of lives and events being put down upon the one preceding it – burying the past and covering the world of those who have departed in a veil of mystery... the sleepers of time.

'You have plumbed a little of that mystery, Toby... drawing back the veil to travel the same roads as our recent ancestors... You cannot walk away now.'

* * *

Night had fallen and their conversation gradually petered away. The abating storm was subsiding over England and the distant stars of deep space glimmered again over a ravaged landscape. Toby dozed long, dreaming of an old couple tottering through the shattered streets of Molliton, before seeing in his mind's eye a small resolute woman – the one he loved, pushing a children's buggy along a road strewn with fallen trees.

Jeannie did not share his need for sleep, and coming awake after some considerable time, Toby found himself alone. But there was something else, something that had brought him to his senses... a strange sound – though one lastingly familiar. He looked round to see that the light from the gas stove had gone out and that the room was in darkness apart from a shaft of moonlight coming through the window. But was that all? Near him an object glowed, and reaching forward he took up the mobile phone... the panel was dimly illuminated – the battery very low – but a text message had been received.

Toby could hardly believe his eyes. How could it have come back to life after so much time? ...How could the device have survived being in the river? Yet there it was... with a contact from his past life. He scrolled down and read:

"We love you, Toby. Wherever you are, please come home –
we'll always be waiting.
All our love, Jenny, Brendan and Sophie xxx."

It was so short and heart-rending... and surely out of time with the present – for such a message could not have been sent when they were all still together before the end of the storm. Yet Toby took it as a sign that he was to go to them, to escape from his time of wandering and return to an existence in the real world.

Quietly he rose from his chair – realising that all sound of the storm had died away leaving only an eerie silence. The mechanism of the door clicked as he opened it, and stepping outside onto the platform Toby looked out over the surrounding countryside. The devastation was all too evident, with flattened corn and fallen trees covering the land in all directions as far as the eye could see. Nothing moved under the night sky and only the lights from one or two distant houses stood out in the darkness. But there were some signs of restorative work too: logs stacked beside the road, a cleared ditch, debris thrown into an adjacent field, and a newly erected road-sign. Yet Jeannie was nowhere to be seen and the opportunity to take his leave appeared to have come.

Toby swung himself round onto the ladder and, step-by-step, began to lower himself towards the ground – feeling like a convict escaping from an elevated cell. Down he went, watching the earth approach beneath his feet, all the while scanning for signs of life, his heart beating fast. He had already descended halfway before a movement to his left caused him to stop and glance that way. A small dog had appeared among the bushes and fallen branches and as he watched a man wearing an overcoat and a broad felt hat joined it. The latter looked up, half raising a cupped hand in greeting – a stone dice glowing faintly upon the palm. The newcomer bore a wry grin and seemed pleased to have arrived so opportunely.

'Jasper and Macken,' Toby breathed. 'How did they know to come here?'

Then Jeannie's voice floated down from above. 'You must come back, Toby. As I intimated – your stay is not yet over.'

Looking up he saw her leaning over the rail, and just above, on the edge of the water tank, sat a dark crow silhouetted against the sky. Jeannie's expression was again sympathetic but stern – like a caring schoolmistress sadly calling an errant schoolboy from the vicar's orchard.

Toby felt trapped – determined to go on, but caught in their watchful stares.

'I need to get away,' he whispered. 'This is my chance...'

'You cannot go this night, Toby... and what is more – there would no longer be any point in such a step.'

Not understanding her words, he peered down again toward Jasper who returned his gaze with a wink. Macken also looked up curiously, his head cocked on one side, as if trying to fathom what Toby might imagine he was doing.

'Don't think of passing my faithful associate,' Jeannie said, realizing what was in his mind. 'Jasper is much stronger than he looks and will not let you through.'

Jasper nodded affirmatively before casually lighting his pipe with a match struck on the side of a boot.

'It would seem that the world for me is not yet different!' said Toby, calling down after some moments. 'Yet tell me if you will… what was the number on the dice?'

Jasper looked up, as if pleased that Toby had remembered their little game.

'Six!' he said brightly, his face widening into a crafty grin. 'A good high number… yet one that can still be bettered. But that may take a while; for the interesting part is just beginning and you still have far to go.'

'Does this mean I am to stay here indefinitely?' Toby asked, sensing defeat.

'Just for a while, old chum… until the wind has properly changed and your way forward is clear. Now go back – there is nothing to be gained from dangling in the night air.'

Feeling frustrated and outmanoeuvred, Toby again ascended the ladder – his every move watched by the beady eyed crow on the water tower, which hopped from claw to claw as he came up. However, Jeannie's head disappeared from view before he had reached the last few rungs, and she was not in sight when he rose onto the platform once more. The air meanwhile seemed strangely devoid of sound, only the rasping noise from the lifting wings of the departing crow scraping at the pervading emptiness. After looking into the storeroom, Toby made a circuit of the platform before returning to the same spot and gazing eastwards to where the first light of morning had begun to glow on the horizon. It was clear that Jeannie and the others had gone once more – disappearing into the air like shadows – and left alone, Toby might have attempted to leave a second time but for a sure knowledge that the outcome would doubtless be the same.

Despondently he moved back inside where the camping light burned again, and on the table found a copy of a daily newspaper barely dry from the printer's press. He looked wonderingly over a front page filled with news of the clear-up after the storm. The headline read, "Reconstruction Costs to Reach One Thousand Seven Hundred and Fifty Billion Pounds – Four Major Insurance Companies to Default on Payouts". But it was the date that held his attention. The paper had been printed on 18th June 2013 – almost three weeks after Toby had left home on the first morning of his journey.

Clutching it, he moved back outside to look around once more. A car moved by on the reopened road, accelerating past the piled logs that he had noticed earlier, while the first rays of the rising sun cast low shadows around the debris removed from a clogged ditch.

'I should have realised,' he said to himself, '…when I saw that all this work had already been done; and that the road sign had been replaced.'

As he looked, other obvious signs that time had passed became evident: a damaged car pushed out of the way by a nearby crossing; and further off a newly erected row of pylons with the first wires strung between them.

'And if the time has elapsed, Jenny will probably have already returned to London, after coming back to search for me days ago…'

He re-read the text message, feeling desolate and lonely – unable to go back and not knowing how to go on. …Like a lost explorer gazing out from the peak of a remote mountain.

* * *

Unmoving, Toby stood sentinel for an hour as the sun rose higher, bringing light to the new world that lay before him as the window to his own time closed behind. Then he went disconsolately inside and sank into the canvas chair, feeling resigned and empty at the prospect of going on.

For a few moments the control dials on the wall gazed down like frozen faces behind glass… then these images too swam before his eyes and he remembered no more.

PART TWO

DROUGHT AND FLOOD

It's like I'm perched on the handlebars
of a blind man's bike.
No straws to grab, just the rushing wind...
on a rolling mind.

from
"Spilt Needles"
The Shins

A T NO TIME IN HUMAN HISTORY HAVE people lived unblemished lives or achieved a flawless existence. In striving to survive and move forward, the desire for power and the pitfalls of war have seldom been avoided for long. Yet, in our headlong rush towards a "developed" industrialised world, perhaps the worst error to have been made is the denial of our natural affinity to and connection with the earth.

We have too often allowed custody of the natural landscape and its gifts to fall into the hands of those whose only interests are plunder and profit: speculators, cunning industrialists, developers and business entrepreneurs. They in their turn have encouraged us to compromise our better judgement – using advertising to create an unhealthy desire for cheap food and an unsustainable standard of living – the blind pursuit of personal advantage. Yet, unless we ourselves have become sufficiently corrupt to accept greed and vanity as the sole driving forces of humanity, there is surely a better way.

However optimistic or pessimistic we are about the destiny of our planet depends upon whether we regard human beings as basically good or bad. Do we see our species as pre-ordained to a life of excess and wickedness, or as made up of right-minded, intelligent beings, willing to help shape the future of mankind through principled and rational actions? Put another way: do we assume that men and women will pursue their own selfish wellbeing at the expense of others and the natural environment? Or do we believe that given hope for the future, they will strive to protect and preserve this fragile world for themselves and their children through co-operation, sharing and kindness?

Chapter One

Emma Tresco

Emma Tresco did not have an easy life. The only child of Meg Maddox's granddaughter, Claire Cheetham, her early years were spent in a happy and loving family surrounded by committed and caring friends. For her mother, these were the best and most fulfilling times that she would have – dividing her days between bringing up her quirky, funny and intelligent little girl, and her involvement in a dozen charities and causes dedicated to protecting people and their surroundings. It was not surprising that Emma learned to care about the natural world, people and justice, for these interests were the foundations upon which her life developed. But the joy of growing up with devoted parents and coming to love them dearly is matched by the sense of loss endured when a loved one is taken away. Nine years after Emma was born, her mother was diagnosed with spinal cancer, and despite a period of painful and extended treatment, eight months later, in August 1989, she died. Left at a formative time in her young life the girl, now in her tenth year, struggled to come to terms with her loss. Worse still, although her father loved Emma and did the best he could, losing his wife had drained him more than he knew, causing an emotional space to develop between Jamie Tresco and his daughter. Thus, having each locked up a personal sorrow within themselves, it might be said that they retreated into parallel emotional worlds that the other could not reach.

Jamie immersed himself in his career in conservation and development, rising to prominence in three organisations. He also became a respected television panellist; while publishing several books on wildlife and sustainable living. It was natural that Emma would admire her father and grow up with a desire to emulate him. She prospered at school and went off to university to further her studies, gaining degrees in Geography and Earth Science, before qualifying as a teacher. These were challenging years. She was bright, lively and imaginative in everything she did – driven on to test herself at every point by a hunger to excel. During this time Emma also developed a love of music and the theatre (a natural outlet for her inner thoughts and emotions), regularly acting in a wide variety of plays and shows with increasing confidence and skill. Yet she was not truly happy. A string of failed relationships left her nervous and anxious about life – always wondering what she need do to achieve greater acceptance among others. Her fears were irrational and unfounded: more often the product of introspection and loneliness than having any basis in truth. But doubt is like a wound daily picked open, and the hurt would not go away. To those that knew her well it was as if she wore the emotional garb of two contrasting people – the creative teacher and capable actress on the outside – and that of one whose soul was tortured by indecision and doubt when alone.

If our circumstances do much to make us what we are, it is the gifts or emotional drag chains we inherit that dictate the ultimate course of our lives. Torn as she was, Emma never ceased to be a fighter. When knocked down or laid low, she would always rise up again, bruised and battered, to face a new day. Meanwhile, the men in her life came and went (some stealing off forever with a piece of her heart), all having taught her to accept a little more pain and disappointment. Yet adversity helps us appreciate what we are... to recognise our limitations and understand the need for humility and patience. Emma's wait for happiness was long and testing, but her inner strength – the strength passed down from her recent ancestors – would eventually carry her through.

* * *

Like many women that seem to have been continually rebuffed and let down by the menfolk they have known, Emma began to lose faith that she would ever find someone who would truly respect and love her. By the time she was thirty she had locked the hope of lasting romance firmly into a private cupboard of her life and, disillusioned with the mating game, settled to work and the theatre as the chief focuses of her life. She was still a willowy and attractive young woman; sometimes stern and closed up it is true – but generous and kind of heart towards children and those she cared for.

Hers now became a quieter existence, a little removed from the normal beaten track of social interaction – pottering along in a less demanding emotional backwater among friends and colleagues. She remained disappointed deep down; but disappointment was easier to accept than being rejected by someone only interested in tipping his hat at her. She would frequently sit alone in cafes or restaurants reading while sipping tea or coffee, as if oblivious of the passing world. But such solitary and quiet gems do not go unnoticed by the entire crowd – for while the brightest flowers might attract a thousand vain and lazy drones, similarly might the scent from a small unshowy bloom attract the attention of a discerning bee.

So it was that one day in April 2012, while sitting in a coffee shop off the Tottenham Court Road, she caught the eye of a young architect, Richard Anderson, who came to sit opposite her. He had seen her there alone twice before and was curious. Emma barely looked up to acknowledge his arrival and straightway went back to studying her book, leaving the other waiting, perhaps a minute, before speaking.

'Excuse me,' he said at last, in a companionable voice. 'Didn't I see you here alone yesterday… and the day before?'

Emma was surprised and a little irritated by such a forward approach. She looked up and met his gaze, her brow furrowing slightly.

'I come here most days,' she replied coolly. 'It's quiet and relaxing, and I like to get away for awhile.'

At first she thought he was a student responding to a dare; or some bored middle-aged Lothario testing his charm upon her. Such people are not rare, and she had seen others off before by responding with cold indifference or a disapproving stare. But this one was different; a young man of perhaps twenty-five with a confident yet thoughtful face, neatly trimmed flowing black hair and dark penetrating eyes. He was dressed in an expensively cut city suit, with tie loose and collar button undone as a concession to the heat. His complexion was swarthy; somewhat darker than that of white Londoners, and with the flush of good health upon his cheeks. Emma tried to sum him up – what was his motive? Was he simply amusing himself in his lunchtime? But the young man's face appeared honest and open enough, the winning smile he offered leading her to relax a little in spite of herself.

'I didn't mean to offend,' he said. 'But I felt I'd like to make your acquaintance… since we both seem to be at a loose end.'

'Why should I be at a loose end? It's good to take time out – don't you think?'

He smiled again, showing even teeth. 'You don't need to apologise; we all ought to take our leisure more seriously. City dwellers spend half their day rushing somewhere; then the other half running back!'

Emma closed her book deliberately. She was becoming a little intrigued by this stranger who had thrust his company upon her; but her practised reserve still made her wary of his motives. A direct and practical approach seemed wisest.

'Look,' she said, 'since we seem to have fallen into conversation you ought to tell me your name – that seems the best way to go on.'

He sat back, surprised and amused by her bluntness. 'My name is Richard Anderson, and I work for the architects "Barnett and Holland" in Harbury Street,' he said, as if giving details at a police station, before grinning broadly. 'Now – may I have yours?'

Emma could not help but smile back. 'My name is Emma Tresco,' she replied, looking steadily across the table. 'I am a teacher of English and drama in Holborn. I love my job, but most lunchtimes like to escape for an hour, if I can. The journey here is one stop on the tube and takes me ten minutes – I sit for half an hour, and then go back. … There you have it!'

He leaned forward; not like someone pressing his advances, but with a serious expression, as if really interested in her work.

'You teach,' he said. 'They say it is an awful profession – too much work; too little respect from the children. Yet I would say that it was the most important job of all; for what could be more valuable than informing young people about the world they have inherited?'

There was no doubting his sincerity and desire to know more about what she did, and they talked for five minutes about her career.

'But what of you?' she asked at last. 'Surely an architect's work has great worth too.'

'I'm sure that's right,' he agreed, 'and what we build may endure a hundred or even five hundred years. But the foundations of knowledge that you develop in a child's mind may still have greater and more lasting consequence.'

Did he really mean it? In her experience such profound and thoughtful comments were not the usual stuff of polite conversation or casual flirtation. Emma glanced at her watch. 'I must be going,' she said, realising that the time had flown. 'I have only a quarter of an hour left and must not be late.'

'Look… could we meet again?' he asked after a moment's hesitation. 'You love the theatre as do I – there's a play on at The Royal Festival Hall this week, Shakespeare's *A Midsummer Night's Dream*… It's Friday tomorrow and I'm sure I could get tickets. If you give me your number I could text to let you know for sure.'

Emma checked herself for a moment – she had been let down before by promises out of the blue.

'I don't know,' she replied, gathering her things and moving towards the door. 'I hardly know you – it's a nice idea, but I wouldn't want to put you out… or be disappointed myself.'

He stood in front of her as she stepped into the street.

'I won't disappoint you – If I say I can get tickets, then trust me, I will.'

The smile was again upon his lips; the earnestness in his eyes and voice reassuring.

Emma nodded, handing him a piece of paper with her number on it. 'If you let me know that you've managed it… I'll meet you there.'

'Brilliant!' he said, dashing away. 'I won't let you down… must rush – my lunch hour ended five minutes ago!'

* * *

She watched him disappear into the milling crowd before turning and completing her journey back to work. Seated on the underground train, looking up unfocused at the tube map, Emma shook her head.

'I've done it again,' she thought. 'A man's got my number; and all I've got is his promise… I don't think I should hold my breath.'

Feeling strangely deflated by the whole too familiar scenario, Emma spent the rest of the afternoon deeply immersed in work to save thinking about their meeting. After school, she went home to her rented flat in Highbury, ate and resigned herself to spending a night in front of the television preparing work for the following day. It was just after eight when his text message came – a confirmation that two tickets had become available due to a cancellation, and that he looked forward to seeing her by the steps below Hungerford Bridge at 7:15pm next day. He had signed himself, "R xx".

'It's as if he thinks he knows me well enough to be familiar already,' she thought. 'But it's often the forward ones that lose courage and don't turn up.'

This doubt kept creeping into her head and was still there when she woke next morning. At lunchtime Emma travelled again to the coffee shop; but although she frequently glanced round, there was no sign of Richard and no one disturbed her. So the end of the day came round, and while travelling home on the bus she idly read through the television schedules to remind herself what was on.

'I could stay in,' she thought. 'And if he phones, just say I forgot.'

But Emma was not the kind of person to let others down, having had enough experience of that herself. Thus she prepared to go out: selecting some of her favourite clothes and jewellery and determining to look her best whatever the outcome.

'I may be stood up,' she said, studying herself in the mirror, 'but at least I'll give the pigeons something to admire.'

With this thought, she locked the flat behind her before stepping out into the cool evening air. The day had been typically showery for the time of year, and the streets were fresh again following the end of the rush hour. Emma took the tube to Waterloo, before walking the last few hundred yards with an ever swelling mass of sightseers and theatregoers – arriving at the appointed rendezvous on the dot of seven fifteen. The area was crowded with people: tourists, joggers and couples out strolling in the last of the evening sunshine, and she looked round casually in that nonchalant way people do when determined to seem relaxed and in control of the situation in which they find themselves.

But Emma's stomach was churning – she felt like a sore thumb: inwardly imagining that everyone present had noticed her standing by herself, sensing her discomfort.

'I'll wait five minutes,' she thought, 'then go. I'd rather watch Monty Don than stay around here looking like a lemon.'

Then miraculously her date appeared through the front door of the Festival Theatre. He looked up smiling broadly, waved and zigzagged towards her through the milling throng.

'Blimey... you look great,' Richard said, breaking into an appreciative grin and brushing back the hair that had fallen across his forehead. 'I'm really glad you made it... I've just picked up the tickets from the box office to save time; so we can go straight up to the auditorium.'

They walked inside together, he talking continually about the play and other productions that he'd recently seen, and she delighted to have another opportunity to get his measure. They were guided to some of the best seats in the house and Emma, realising the cost of such tickets, offered to pay her share.

'Listen,' he said, leaning closer, 'I get paid plenty in my line of work; and anyway, I got a last minute discount on these; so there's no need, really. ...It's my treat!'

Emma felt it polite not to argue further, and they settled back to watch the play; laughing together at the absurdities in Shakespeare's masterpiece, and later discussing their mutual interest over a drink during the interval. More than once she glanced sideways at him, half expecting to see signs that he might be growing bored – that this was all a feint to cover another motive or intention. But the opposite was true – Richard seemed totally engaged in the plot, frequently whispering in her ear about some well-loved pun or the skill of the actors – until it seemed the most natural thing in the world when he laid his arm across her shoulder and drew her towards him. Emma's reserve melted as she rode a much longed for wave of companionship, and in their subsequent three hours together a foundation was established upon which a lasting, though sometimes troubled and complex relationship quickly grew.

* * *

They met again in the following days and weeks: during lunch breaks, evenings out and weekend trips away. He introduced her to the delights of sailing and rock climbing, while she tutored him in the pastimes of playing the saxophone and writing poetry. Their admiration for the achievements of the other was mutual and their time together never without conversation or challenge. But there were darker moments... some current event would set them arguing, each with their own passionate point of view upon a possible outcome or solution, and the ensuing exchange often kept them up long into the night. Yet some relationships are toughened and made firmer in the fire, and both gradually began to reveal their inner thoughts, aspirations and fears; until there was nothing that each would not share with the other.

So it was that sitting together one evening shortly after she had moved into his riverside flat, Emma learned of Richard Anderson's childhood and of a family's disturbed past.

'My mother, Margeritte, came from Florida,' he said, leaning forward on the sofa as they sat together gazing into the fire. 'She was from Mexico originally and had gone to live in the United States when still in her teens. They were not easy times because her family had stayed at home, and she had to make her own way in a new society. Margeritte worked as a waitress at first; before learning English and training as a nurse. But mother rarely had enough money, and having got into debt... more than once resorted to selling herself to get by. She was pretty then, and many were prepared to pay for time with her; but there is no dignity in such a life… she had lost her self-respect and began sliding into the despair that surrounds such work.

'Then one day while serving at the restaurant, she met a successful and respected doctor, Charles Anderson – a man twenty-five years her senior. From the moment of his first setting eyes on Margeritte he seemed to become infatuated; to want to know all about her; to set himself the goal of lifting her out of the poverty she was accustomed to. There were things that she could not say of course… the darker side of her existence she kept hidden from him – but the offer of a better life was beyond her dreams and she took it with both hands. I don't know whether my mother was really in love; but after all she had suffered, the security he provided was a comfort she readily accepted in exchange for being with him. They were married a year later at one of the biggest ceremonies of the year and I was born the following Fall.'

He stopped at that moment, looking up intently.

'Everything should have turned out well from then on in, but when I was twelve years old he found out about her past. A malicious fellow recently hired as a gardener recognised her one day when she was gathering flowers, and made it his job to tell my father how mother had once lived on the streets – so the lid came off! As I've told you, Charles Anderson could be very generous; but as well as being rich and influential he was also a bigot. He had aspirations then to become a senator, and knew full well that the shame of his wife's past would have ruined his reputation. So what might you expect? He immediately sought a separation, and would have left Margeritte with nothing if she hadn't threatened to fight him in court. Desperate to be rid of us both, he settled a sum of money on her, with the proviso that she leave America – get out of his life for good, and come to live in England where the Andersons originally had their roots.

'Margeritte did as he wanted, leaving her friends and moving to London where she bought a house in Bromley. I was already halfway through my education and she made sure I was sent to the best possible schools and university, so that I might get where I am now. Margeritte herself never lacked for anything materially… but you know what they say about a "fish out of water". That's the way she is now – just an isolated woman, living on her own in a foreign land.'

'She still lives in the capital!' said Emma, much surprised: since until then he had made no mention of any relative residing locally.

'Yes,' he said, looking up with a faint smile. 'She's only forty-eight – but in some ways mother is older… much older – like she doesn't care about tomorrow anymore. I blame him for that. He didn't have to turn her away. If he'd been more understanding… more loving – they could have stayed together.'

Listening to him, Emma felt the uncomfortable parallel between her own life and his experiences: she, separated from her father's love and confidence by the death of her mother, and he having lost the warmth of a mother due to his father's abandonment.

'It makes me nervous about relationships,' he said after a pause, 'seeing what people do to each other. I can't forgive my father for what he did to us… and sometimes wonder if I am capable of doing the same thing. I'm not sure I could be Mr Right for anybody.'

She reached forward and kissed him before resting her forehead against his – searching for words of reassurance.

'I don't think you'll make that mistake, Richard… but if you ever do, I won't give up in a hurry.'

* * *

Their relationship deepened by the day – occasionally storm-tossed and angry: between wide rafts of calm. Then one morning in mid July, feeling unwell and knowing herself to be outside the normal cycle of things, Emma visited her chemist. The results were positive, as she had expected, and although delighted in one part of her heart at the prospect before her, she nevertheless felt uncertain how her partner would receive the news. Whether it was because she was more tetchy and tired than usual due to her condition, or that he was more troubled by work and his mother's isolation, their relationship had for some days been going through a difficult patch. Tension had arisen between them on several occasions, the latest ending in an early morning row following which Richard stormed out when setting off to the office.

Emma had taken the rest of the day off, pottering around the flat, or resting on the sofa looking out at the ebbing tide: wondering how he would be when he returned. Evening was drawing on when she at last heard footsteps in the corridor. The door opened and Richard entered the room – but from the first she could tell that he was distracted and out of sorts. He put the kettle on absently; then came and slumped in the armchair without looking at her.

There was something awkward in his manner – something she had noticed before when he was out of humour. He rubbed his brow while looking down at the floor, as if trying to gather his thoughts.

'How was your day?' she asked nervously.

'Alright.'

'You seem unhappy.'

'I am… it's being here… at the moment.'

'I don't understand… what have I done?'

Richard scratched his head vigorously, as if forcing himself to say what was in his mind. 'It's just that you seem to know me too well... I tell you too much! You get me to say everything – so I can't keep anything back!'

'I never wanted to hear anything you didn't want me to know – I wouldn't pry.' Emma thought of the news she so wanted to share; but the chill between them precluded this. 'Is there anything else wrong... something at work?'

'I dunno, love... I'm just confused, that's all – I need some breathing space.'

'Breathing space?'

He shifted in his seat before leaning forward, gazing into her eyes with an anguished expression. 'It's just that right now you seem to tie me in knots... You wall me in so there's no air... I love you to bits, Emma... but... I can't stay right now... I need to get away for a while.'

The cold realisation of what had got into his head now came to her. 'Need to get away... for how long?'

'A few days... a week... maybe more.'

'Or... for good?'

'I haven't got it figured out... I can't say... I'm going to spend a while with Margeritte... I'll put some things together.'

* * *

With these words Richard stood up and busied himself in the bedroom, packing a case. Within five minutes he was ready and they stood awkwardly facing each other in the centre of the living room as he prepared to leave.

'Look, you can stay here as long as you want,' he said, 'I owe you that... but I can't make any other promises at the moment... I've got a lot of thinking to do... I'll keep in touch.'

He moved forward to kiss her.

'Is there someone else?' she asked, her arms hanging loosely.

'No one else... believe me... I did want... I do want to be happy with you. I just haven't got it right in my head at the moment.'

Then he left, disappearing quickly through the door, echoing footsteps ringing down the passageway. Emma felt frightened and hollow – abandoned to her own dark and hopeless thoughts. She did not cry at first, but sloped around the flat before standing to watch a barge sliding down the Thames with a load of refuse for the Essex marshes. Like all that suffer so, she hoped it was all a mistake; that he would come back a short time later, thus enabling them to continue their lives together. But Richard did not return that day, or the next; nor did he phone. All she received was a text to say that he had arrived at his mother's house and would contact her in due course. So Emma dusted away the pieces of her shattered hopes and went back to work. Friends and colleagues noticed that she was down: but she reassured them that things were all right, and they decided to keep an eye on her rather than invading her privacy.

Yet Emma needed to talk: her hopes and confidence had received a heavy blow and the weight of the secret she harboured began to play upon her mind and judgement. The thought of the baby gnawed at her. It is a great responsibility to bring another person into this world and she had always believed it a job too great for one. Having no family to easily fall back upon, the prospect of bringing up a child alone daunted her. Ashamed at having come to this position, a dark solution beckoned.

'I can't have a baby in these circumstances,' she thought. 'How will I care for it? What kind of a life will it have?'

Emma might have seen things differently had she had others to confide in. But left alone, a grim course of action suggested itself – one that both broke her heart and poisoned her dreams.

She might have seen her doctor; but declined this course. Destroying her unborn child was not something she could bring herself to contemplate achieving on the NHS.

'People are sure to find out if I do,' she thought. 'No, I must find another way… and soon!'

Richard had been gone for almost a month. He had made contact by text on three occasions and had spoken on the phone a week before she made her decision; but their conversation had been awkward, and when she asked if he would be coming back soon there had been a long pause before he hung up, following a promise to call again later. Now that was days ago, and Emma felt she could wait no longer. Morning sickness was becoming a problem; and her resultant lateness for school and occasional absences were causing suspicions at work.

* * *

In her growing desperation and loneliness, Emma had taken to visiting a local bar in the evenings. There she had been befriended by Kelly, the barman's wife; a worldly wise woman in her early fifties who was fond of telling the regulars about her many liaisons when she was "a young sprite of a thing". Kelly was a well-worn woman of ample proportions, with a wide friendly grin and a penchant for elaborate and vividly dyed 80s' hairdos. She had obviously "known life", and was evidently someone in tune with the underworld culture of the streets.

'There's not much that goes on around here that I don't hear about,' she announced one evening as she served Emma with an orange and soda. 'What I miss ain't worth knowing.'

Emma smiled back sheepishly, somewhat overawed as always by the other woman's confidence and ease.

Kelly now stood eyeing her appraisingly before leaning forward in an elaborate posture of confidentiality.

'Course,' she said, 'most things I can work out meself – just by using me eyes. But it's only polite to ask sometimes... as a matter of conversation.'

Emma said nothing, but looking up realised that she was being closely scrutinised.

'Got something you want to share with Kelly, then?'

'Share?'

'You're pregnant, ain't you, gel? You don't work in here for nigh on twenty years without bein' able to spot such things. Why, I imagine I must have spoken to fifty girls in the same condition as you, perched on that selfsame stool.'

Emma felt suddenly exposed and glanced around to see if anyone else was observing her. But the other drinkers were all engrossed in their own conversations – except one hard-faced woman sitting at a nearby corner table. Their eyes met and the woman half raised her glass in acknowledgement before leaning forward to resume a game of dominos with the man opposite.

'What makes you think I'm pregnant?' asked Emma, sitting up. 'Does it show?'

'Oh... it doesn't show – yet... but there are plenty of other little signs that an experienced eye can spot.'

'Like what?'

'Oh let's just say it's noticeable in your manner and complexion,' said the woman, breathing in with evident satisfaction at her professional perspicacity.

'Really?'

'Really! ... Mind you, most girls usually exhibit a bit more pleasure in their circumstances than you have – a certain glow.'

Emma said nothing. The realisation that another could draw conclusions based on her appearance and read her thoughts was daunting.

'I can see you're not happy,' Kelly continued. 'Unplanned was it?'

The bitterness on Emma's face was all too evident. 'Planned... what's that? What good are plans when someone lets you down?'

'That's some men for you, girl. It happened to me once... bad decisions – we women just don't seem able to stop makin' em, do we?'

'And what did you do?'

The older woman sighed deeply. 'Me... I got rid of it... abortion... cost me eighty quid... money well spent!'

'That's what I want,' said Emma almost inaudibly.

The older woman placed her hand on hers. 'No worries, girl... it needn't be the end of the world. I've still managed to have two kids, proper like.' She pointed to a young bar assistant working close by. 'Sid here, he's my boy and I wouldn't be without him. No, if you don't want a child it's only right to put an end to it while you can.'

'But I can't go to my doctor... I'd be too ashamed... I couldn't go through with it.'

'No need for doctors or hospitals, love... people in these parts know of other folk that can perform the same service.'

Emma looked up, suddenly alarmed at having arrived at the point where such a thing was being considered. 'A back-street abortion... I shouldn't even be thinking about such a thing.'

'Not "back street", darling!' said the other woman reassuringly. 'Just think of it as... round the corner... a local convenience.'

'But isn't it dangerous?'

'No more than crossing the road; and I know just the person – someone that's been helping out for years who has a whole list of satisfied customers.'

'Who?' asked Emma, a cold emptiness creeping through her.

Kelly leant close to Emma's ear and gestured that she look behind. The same woman Emma had noticed before was again studying them and nodded as their eyes met a second time.

'Her name's Mavis Cotley; she'll do it for you. Charges £120 for the service – never been known to fail. I can set it up this minute if you'd like.'

'But where would it happen?'

'Ah well... I can't tell you that till all's agreed. You see the law takes a dim view of such things. But when we've arranged it – then you'll know; and rest assured, you won't be disappointed.'

In her hopeless and empty state, Emma seemed powerless to avoid taking the next step and agreed that her confidante should approach the woman. She was gone no more than three minutes – which seemed the most desolate of Emma's life – before returning with the confirmation that a termination could be arranged for the following day.

'Mavis wrote this number for you to ring,' said Kelly, handing her a piece of folded paper. 'You're to call it tomorrow, at 1pm. When you contact her, that's when you'll learn where to go – but whatever happens, you must turn up alone. There's a list of the things you'll need to take on the other side. So that's it – fixed – alright dear?'

Emma thanked her for her support, before preparing to leave and slipping out like a guilty spirit, passing close to the table where the abortionist sat as she did so. The woman had continued her game of dominos, but looked up as Emma went by, as did the brawny, shaven headed man opposite her. Emma half smiled back; a creeping sense of doubt and insecurity filling her head, but the two faces that met hers were flat and seemingly devoid of any compassion or emotion – dismissing her with a glance as if she were little more than a length of wood.

* * *

Emma could not sleep that night. The decision she had made appalled her, yet it seemed the only way out. Had she called her friends they might have persuaded her otherwise; but in time of trouble she instinctively became solitary and now bore the burden of her inner guilt and isolation alone. She tried to bring order to her feelings, but had become cut-off, even from herself; as if having stumbled into a void that threatened to swallow her up, both heart and soul. During those dark hours Emma withdrew to an empty place beyond despair that only the forsaken inhabit.

The following morning she mechanically prepared herself for what was to come: driving out the enormity of the choice she'd taken just as one focuses upon the dentist's injection rather than the drill. She made her phone call at the given time, and was told to take the underground to the "Elephant and Castle" before walking on another half mile to a side street near the river known as "Keeper's Reach". There she would be met and escorted to the house used by Mavis Cotley. She was to bring her things and the £120 in cash; but if suspected of being followed the termination would be off.

The journey was not a long one, but every minute of it would remain in her memory: the wait on Highbury Station, the stuffy journey south, the walk to "Keeper's Reach" – a lonely expedition conducted without verbal contact with the general throng of London – that great mass of humanity which swarms around any traveller in the city, like cloudy water round a stone.

A part of Emma simply wanted it over. The father of her child had made no further contact, and she needed to put an end to any forlorn hope of happiness. But another side of her nature was also at work. She was not a quitter, and the stirring of her maternal instinct prompted second thoughts. The baby was, after all, hers no matter what was said or done; and in a swelling corner of her heart a part of Emma longed to see it made real. Having moved away from the main thoroughfares, and with these thoughts running through her head, she stopped at a street corner to look around as she neared her destination. It was not an attractive part of the capital. Bland two storey terrace blocks built in the 1960s and '70s ran off in three directions; and every wall as far as the eye could see was daubed with the idle tags and graffiti of a dozen street gangs. Meanwhile, at the litter strewn junction where she stood, a dilapidated pub and run down "Costcutter" shop completed the scene.

Emma had just started to take in the depressing nature of the place when a heavily built man stepped out from beneath the porch of the pub and came towards her. She recognised him immediately as the one the abortionist had been playing dominos with the evening before – the same cropped hair and blank expression.

'She's expecting you… you'd better come,' were his only words as he set off round the corner. Emma trotted to keep up – suddenly harbouring powerful misgivings about the situation before her. They had not gone far before he stopped next to the open door of a ramshackle end terrace and ushered her inside.

* * *

There are times when our minds are finally made up, not by steady and reasoned calculation; but by a combination of circumstances that tell us we must preserve our safety and integrity, at whatever cost, while there is still a chance to do so. This was the case for Emma now. She had entered an untidy downstairs' room to find Mavis Cotley seated in front of an old television set drinking a cup of tea. The woman looked up with a sour expression, as one annoyed at being disturbed, before appraising Emma with a critical eye. A lighted cigarette burned in an ashtray on the arm of the sofa and she raised this to her lips, drawing upon it deeply.

'You came by yourself?'

'I said I would.'

'Know this part of London?'

'By name... I haven't been here before.'

'And you've brought the money?'

'Yes.'

The woman's eyes narrowed. 'Do you really know what you're doing?' she said, 'walkin' around here with 120 quid in your pocket... you must be desperate.'

Mavis looked pointedly across at her dominos partner who leered back, showing a row of gold teeth.

'Well, my girl: I suppose we ought to be getting on with it. You'd best be coming upstairs with me.'

Emma froze – suddenly gripped by a combination of self-determination and fear. She had now fully decided against making this final step to an unlikely salvation, and could think of nothing but escaping from the trap she had walked into. At that moment her own safety and that of the baby she was carrying meant more than any other consequence.

'No,' she said, backing against the wall. 'I can't... I don't want to go through with it.'

The woman, who had already ascended the first three steps, backed down into the room, her eyes narrowing.

'Is that the case?' she said slowly and deliberately. 'You want to just walk out... having put us to all this trouble.'

'It would be wrong. I know that now... I should never have agreed to it.'

'But agree to it you did, my love; and in these streets such an agreement amounts to a contract. You can't just walk away... And besides – it would make us look so foolish for having arranged to help you.'

278

Emma looked from one to the other: Mavis Cotley leaning with one hand on the sofa as if considering her next move, the big man blocking the door.

'Surely you can understand…' she said with fierce despair. 'It's just not what I want any more.'

'Oh I understand, dearie…' the woman continued in a soft voice. 'I understand that you want to cheat my friend and me out of £120… That's what I'm hearing.'

Emma knew she was cornered, at their mercy; that these two corrupt individuals were part of a sordid underbelly which exists beneath the surface of all "civilised societies".

Mrs Cotley moved towards her menacingly. 'You'll pay me, or my friend here will do the job for nothing… and terminate you too if he's in the mood! Then we'll take the money anyway. …Now what do you make of that little proposal, my love?'

At the suggestion of violence the henchman laughed in his throat and drew a six-inch knife from his pocket.

Emma seldom gave way to bullies, but saw now that her options had run out. She feared for her safety and that of her baby – only getting out unhurt made proper sense.

'You can have it,' she said. 'Take the money and let me go!'

'So you can visit the police and blab on us. …What do you think we are?'

'I'll say nothing… I don't want to see you again – ever. Take all I have, but let me leave.'

It can seem an odd thing to suggest; but there is normally a spark of humanity to be found in even the most base of natures. Thus, whether it was from some kindred feeling for the defenceless young woman; or merely the sight of the roll of ten pound notes Emma placed upon the table – having counted the money, the self-appointed abortionist signalled the henchman to let her pass. She had to push by him, for his muscular frame blocked much of the door, and he leered down with cold, glittering eyes. Emma shivered as she emerged into the street once more; wondering what might have happened if the woman had not been there.

* * *

While there was no denying that she had been cruelly robbed of £120, Emma retained something more precious: a sense of purpose and worth that might have been forfeited entirely had she stayed another hour. Yet she was humiliated too – for having sunk so low and placed herself in the clutches of those that only exploit the lost and vulnerable. She journeyed home in a daze, seeing and hearing little of what went on around her; though all the while questioning her inner feelings and desperately trying to decide her next move. Arrival back at the waterfront flat brought a renewed sense of foreboding and despair. She was still by herself, with no one to guide her, and would face an uncertain future alone. Thus hope largely ebbed away once more as she turned the key in the lock.

Emma wanted more than anything to be alone with her thoughts; to have time to plan out the next difficult stage in her life, with all the anticipated hardships that it would bring. For now the flat would be a sanctuary from the outside world she would soon have to face once more – a place in which to prepare herself. Yet upon closing the door, she immediately felt another sensation as that other finer sense we all possess informed her that she was not alone – that someone else already breathed the air within. Emma froze, still traumatised by her recent experience, listening for the little sounds of another's movements – the creak of leather, a clink of china.

'Richard... Richard, is that you?' she whispered.

Someone stirred in the lounge. 'Come through...it's only me, love,' he replied.

She moved forward, turning into the main room of the flat with its wide sweeping view of the river. He was there, sitting on the sofa facing her: still wearing a city coat and clutching his briefcase between tense hands. They faced each other, not speaking – like two divers emerging into the light after many days spent a hundred fathoms down in the black depths of an ocean.

'You came back,' Emma said, turning away and moving to the window where a flight of seagulls circled above the river. 'I thought you wouldn't – that it was over.'

He stood up and moved beside her. 'I didn't know if I should for a while... and I can't fully explain why I so needed to go... There just seemed to be something in me which took over for a time. I've hurt you, Emma... I never wanted to, but I have, and that's something I'll always regret.'

He turned towards her, reaching for her hands – though Emma still gazed ahead, as if hearing his voice inside herself.

'But you must know that I still love you,' he went on. 'That's something that burns within me... It did right from the start and I'm sure it always will... I've been a coward – I hurt the one I love the best, and can't simply pretend that's ok.'

She had been following the track of a pleasure boat making its way towards Greenwich while listening, but suddenly turned, gripping the hands that held hers.

'Why did you wait so long? ...I thought I'd lost you.'

'I didn't mean to... I spent time with my mother – it's amazing how rational she can be. We talked about you, about the two of us... I tried to explain my doubts...'

'And what did she say?'

'She just kept asking... "What doubts?" and suggesting that I act upon what my heart was telling me. That was the sum of her advice; but the smile that came with it made her seem young again.'

'And what does your heart tell you, Richard? ...I need to know.'

'That I love you, Emma... that if you'll let me stay, I'll never leave you again.'

'Then we'll work on it,' she said, kissing him.

* * *

In truth Emma still had misgivings, and it took many weeks for the tangle inside to unravel. She did not tell him about the baby immediately: waiting another day before breaking the news. Having seen him off that morning, before going to work herself, the lingering fear that he might not return still chilled her mind. But he was there when she turned the key, and had begun to prepare a meal, duly served at the table by the lounge window.

Emma was not hungry, however: needing as she did to let him know of her near tragic decision. At last she reached out to take his hand.

'Richard, there's something that I must tell you.'

He smiled reassuringly. 'Go on then, love... What is it?'

'I'm pregnant – almost twelve weeks.' She felt his hand tighten around hers. 'But there's something else I must let you know... about when you weren't here – when I thought you'd gone... I got so desperate then... I stopped seeing the child as my own – when it should have been ours. I felt so inadequate... so I thought about ending it! ...And I almost did; just pulling out at the last minute,' she whispered, her knuckles whitening. 'Not at a hospital; but with someone that said – they could fix me...'

Emma felt his grip tighten, but not in anger. 'I've been a selfish fool,' Richard whispered. 'To put you through that was awful.'

'So, you can forgive me?'

'Forgive you,' he replied, his eyes moist. 'Forgive you... I'm the one that needs forgiveness... you showed courage by going to the edge and pulling back – that *was* the right thing, and I'm proud of you.'

* * *

They talked on through the summer evening and into the twilight; first sharing all that had happened during their separation, then increasingly making plans for the future. After that, with each passing day, their trust in each other gradually revived and strengthened once more; and they were married just before the New Year – the great-granddaughter of Meg Maddox becoming Mrs Emma Anderson. Her time of confinement was by then growing near, and on the night of 15th March 2013, at 2.15am, the baby, a boy, was born with Richard present at the bedside. They called him Kline, after a distant uncle; and the love between them was at last secured forever in the shared wonder at a new life.

Richard Anderson expected the tiny infant to be little more than a soft ball of clinging flesh; but to his amazement his son turned and looked up as he held him for the first time – focusing upon Richard with a look of recognition and awareness oft recalled and treasured by the father throughout his life.

* * *

This little boy – one that had come so close to death in the womb – and who was destined to be saved again in childhood by the selfless action of a passer-by – grew to be a man of courage and principle who would inspire a change in the way we live – to benefit all mankind.

* * *

Six years later Emma bore another son, Paul Anderson: who, imbued like his brother with the energy of a committed family, would also grow to become a pivotal figure in times to come, likewise helping to guide others toward the evolution of a peaceful and sustainable future.

Chapter Two

Drought

THE "GREAT STORM" OF 2013 CAUSED WIDESPREAD damage and bankrupted many small insurance companies. But recovery, slow at first, was achieved, although many were unable to return to their homes – now beyond economic repair following the devastation. Others, such as Ivy Hayden, lost their lives in the tragedy; while some of those left behind, like her husband, would never be the same again.

Yet nature and the human spirit work their healing powers and within three years the worst effects of the storm receded into the past. Services had been restored to something near pre-storm levels, accommodation rebuilt and the ravages of weather cleared away. True, the countryside looked different – a host of fallen trees, logged and carted off, leaving largely denuded spaces where woods and copses once stood. But daily new saplings were being planted, which it was hoped might in time come to rival their ancient ancestors. Everything would surely be well, the reassuring voices of government and business chorused – such natural events were only once in a lifetime occurrences. Therefore, in all probability, a similar catastrophe would never happen again.

But men had not stopped their worldwide assault on the natural environment and ever greater volumes of carbon rich gas were now being pumped into the atmosphere as the quest for recovery and restored comfort rolled forward. Thus, the ticking clock, carrying mankind towards further pain, continued its relentless march.

* * *

The water tower was already becoming hot in the rays of the morning sun when Toby Freeman awoke, his mouth dry and leathery from long hours spent without water. His eyes itched as he rubbed away sleep, while dreading the cramp and stiffness that would surely grip him when he endeavoured to move. But move he must, for the small storeroom would soon become unbearably stale and stuffy. He needed fresh air and the door was only four feet away. Toby braced himself, rising to his feet like an arthritic old man getting up from an uncomfortably low chair. It was agony! For a moment every joint of his limbs seemed to complain, a sharp spasm in his back causing him to stagger sideways.

'I must be getting old,' he thought, 'or else I've been here for a *very* long time.'

This thought made him focus again upon his situation. 'The storm... was it over? And if so... what came next?'

The door handle was stiff as he turned it, the mechanism grumbling for want of oil, but the door itself gave after a slight shove and he stumbled outside into bright daylight. Unobscured by clouds, the sun overhead was already riding high, suggesting a time towards ten o'clock, and the full intensity of its warmth radiated back from the metal platform. Although better than his little cell, it was not a comfortable place. He needed shelter and shade, but his viewpoint offered neither.

Yet Toby did not descend immediately, for the sight of the surrounding countryside held his attention. Already dramatically changed from past years by the effects of the storm, it was now blighted in another way – appearing seriously parched; as if much of the higher ground were half turned to desert and only lower areas retained sufficient moisture for the normal growth of trees and plants. He had woken in early June, but already the landscape was bleached and bare; the field and roadside grasses wilted from want of water – nettles and thistles prematurely decayed.

'So dry,' he thought, leaning over the rail to watch a passing car, its silver paint flashing in the shimmering heat... 'as if it hasn't rained for weeks.'

He looked out for other signs of life; but little else seemed to move except an occasional van or lorry, or a dipping pigeon searching for shade. Only the drone of insects made any firm impact upon his senses: the air seeming full of their muffled sounds, coming and going, rising and falling on a listless breeze. Then, when he was about to collect his things and descend without further delay, a dark shape lifted away from the broken canopy of an aged oak tree nearby. The bird, a crow, circled up and flew round the top of the tower, eyeing Toby unblinkingly. He watched it spiral closer before landing precisely on the rail six feet from him, its sharp claws curling to an iron grip.

Toby returned its gaze – face to face with the familiar creature once more.

'My feathered friend,' he said in a low voice. 'But where are your confederates?'

The bird tipped its head, as if considering this question, deftly shifting its weight from claw to claw.

'Caark!' came its only reply. But then, looking down past a shimmering wing, Toby saw a vehicle approaching on the Molliton by-pass. It was a brightly painted blue and yellow camper van, but of an old design now rarely seen.

'An ancient VW,' said Toby to himself. 'But who would own one of those around here?'

Such vehicles had already become a rare sight in his own time, being found only at alternative music festivals, or driven by dreadlocked hippies down remote West Country roads. This one came on at a respectable pace, the sound of its distinctive throaty exhaust rising to a confident hum. Watching from above, Toby expected it to pass by and journey on northward, but the camper abruptly bumped off the road onto the grass verge opposite before coming to a halt less than thirty yards from the base of the tower. The engine died almost immediately and a small figure wearing sandals, shorts and a floral shirt stepped out. He looked up from under the brim of a floppy hat fashioned from faded denim and raised a hand in greeting towards Toby.

'You can't stay up there any longer, mate,' the newcomer called. 'You'll fry before the day is done if you do. Come down and freshen up.'

'Jasper... I might have known.'

Toby was still shaking his head at seeing his old travelling companion when the crow lifted away from beside him and gracefully dropped down towards the parked vehicle, landing with effortless precision upon one of the luggage rails.

'Don't hang about, my friend,' came Jasper's voice once more. 'You make me feel hot just looking at you up there. You should have something on your 'ed too. Come now, move yourself!'

The common sense of the invitation was all too clear. Toby had become uncomfortably warm and the prospect of shade was most inviting. Therefore, without further delay, he began to lower himself from the tower. The structure seemed taller than during his previously attempted descent during darkness, and he clung tightly to each rung, regardless of the heat against his skin. On reaching the ground Toby found himself sweating freely, for the heat there was even greater than he'd experienced above. But what struck him most was how withered and shrivelled everything looked. There could not have been proper rain for weeks, since all but the hardiest growth had withered in the arid conditions. The dry remnants of parched spring vegetation were all around: grass the colour of straw, scant seed heads already blown clean of their stunted growth, plantains strangled for want of rain. It was as if a creeping desert had stolen over the land, sucking the last moisture from the soil and leaving only dry crust and ruin in its wake.

Looking up at their wrinkled leaves, Toby felt uneasy as he moved through the few remaining trees toward the road. A lorry sped past as he approached, the driver sounding his horn brazenly upon noticing the camper van.

'They can't resist doing that,' said Jasper with a twinkle in his eye as Toby crossed over. 'Something a bit unusual you see – must brighten up their day.'

'Is this yours?' asked Toby, standing back to look at the VW.

It was in very good condition, with no rust anywhere – chrome hubcaps and bumpers shinning brightly. The flowered orange curtains round the passenger windows looked fresh and new; the interior fittings well cared for. On both sides a colourful smiling sun face had been painted (with more than a hint of an artful Mr Punch about it), which seemed to wink at the passing world when the camper van moved between light and shade.

'Nice in't it,' beamed Jasper, ignoring Toby's question, while tweaking the radio aerial between finger and thumb like a proud owner at a vintage car rally. 'Just what Mr Toad might have had in mind for the open road. But we can't stay here admiring the old girl, it's too blinkin hot! I'll take you for a spin... then you can have a go. She may be an old un but she's fun to drive.

'Mind you,' he added, climbing into the driver's seat and beckoning Toby toward the passenger side, '...there's no friggin' air-conditioning, so we'd best keep all the windows wide open.'

Jasper seemed in markedly good spirits as he started the engine and turned back in the direction of Bedford.

'Lucky I came when I did,' he said, gazing over the rim of the steering wheel, the brim of his hat shading his face. 'This could be one of the hottest days so far and you can have a bit too much sun on your neck.'

'You knew I was there... in the tower?' asked Toby, studying the little man's face out of the corner of his eye. Jasper had grown a moustache since the last time they'd met, yet still looked young, as if the intervening years hadn't touched him.

He glanced back, his round head swaying slightly with the gently rolling motion of the van.

'We will always know where you are and what's become of you, mate,' he replied, with a contented click of the tongue. 'You'll suffer no serious harm if we have our way.'

'Then you protect me?'

'Well... let's say we don't let you stay in one place for too long when things need to be moving along.'

'Why would you do that?'

'To keep you safe like... in one piece... for another day.'

'But you wouldn't let me return to my own time... why not?'

'It wasn't meant to be, that's all. Some things are the same for all three of us... we don't always have a free choice.'

It was like talking to a practised inquisitor, or a programmed voice unwilling to reveal certain truths. Toby's heart sank... Where were they going; where would the next part of the journey take him?

'Which year is it now?' he asked with some trepidation after a short silence.

'It's the 6th June 2018, and we are in the middle of a mighty drought,' came Jasper's unhurried response. 'It started last year. The spring rains failed; then the summer turned out ten times drier than normal. "Unusual durations of high pressure," they called it. "Unseasonable problems linked to El Nino." But that's all become a bit of a joke now. It hasn't rained more than a drop for over a year. Rainfall has been a tenth of what might be expected and the whole of Europe is as parched as dust. They promised that the winter would get us back to normal; but it was the warmest and driest on record – twenty degrees centigrade being recorded on Christmas Day! People were barbecuing in the garden – having Christmas pudding with iced lemonade. Now the reservoirs are eighty-five per cent empty, with no end to the lack of rain in sight and unessential water use banned. You can't so much as have a bath or fill a pond. Half the county is on standpipes, with the rest likely to follow in weeks. So nobody's enamoured of the situation any more.'

They had travelled a mile or so and now turned towards the Bedford suburb of Kempsford, following the River Ouse along a new by-pass through what had once been a flood plain and water meadows. The river was almost stagnant – a sinister bloom of algae matting its surface, stifling river life below. Beside it the grass footpaths and fields were likewise devoid of healthy growth, showing only stubborn weeds and stunted crops. There were many signs of brush and hedge fires too – some probably having spontaneously ignited in the heat of the sun – others less easily explained. Upon entering Kempsford, Toby could see additional evidence of blazes that had run out of control in parks and gardens, while they frequently came upon blackened and scorched areas where vehicles had burned by the roadside.

'These fires,' Toby asked, 'are they all down to the weather?'

Jasper chuckled mirthlessly. 'No doubt some were… but others most likely began with the striking of a match. There are those who like seeing things burn!

'Before the situation got really bad we had a spate of youngsters – bored yobs – setting fire to just about anything. It seemed to become a bit of a competition last autumn. Every night there would be a dozen outbreaks – too many for the local brigade to cope with. A lot of property went up in smoke – cars, garden fences, industrial units – and folk began to get annoyed. Water was already being rationed, so the waste wasn't acceptable as you can imagine. Little was done about the situation at first – most people thinking that with the onset of the winter rains the problem would disappear, and that the young darlings would simply go back to daubing on walls. But it didn't rain, and matters got serious in Bedford when a blaze, deliberately started behind someone's garage, led to the house catching fire, putting three children in hospital with serious burns. Some said the police were doing insufficient to stop the fire raisers – that they only ever turned up when those responsible were long gone. So one night last November, a group of residents set upon a group of tearaways known to be regularly playing Lucifer's little game. They caught them torching a garden shed, surrounded them, grabbed two lads that tried to lip their way out of it, and threw both through the shed doorway into the flames amid a chorus of jeers and catcalls. One stumbled out almost immediately with his hair and coat on fire, but the other didn't emerge, having fallen and struck his head on something. Anyway, they must have waited too long to find out, because the roof fell in and he was burned to death. That caused a hell of a hullabaloo I can tell you. …It even made the national newspapers! There was considerable shock; but more than that, a call to come down harder on the arsonists whatever their age. As a result, not five weeks ago, new legislation was passed stating that anybody over twelve can now be given a term of one year in prison under the emergency drought laws; with a maximum of ten years for adults, even if it's only a hedge that's been destroyed.'

'And what happened to those responsible for killing the boy?'

'Three of them were charged with manslaughter and given five years apiece, but at this moment there's talk of them being released in two if their appeals are successful. To some folk the boys had it coming to them; so the men are simply regarded as over zealous vigilantes who happened to go a little too far when defending their property.'

'I wonder if vigilantism can ever be right?' pondered Toby, looking out at a group of passing teenagers who, having noticed the old van, stood making a variety of either approving or derogatory gestures in their direction.

'People are getting tough because they're scared, Toby. The young do not always realise the seriousness of things going on around them; but most adults know that what the country is experiencing now isn't normal any more. If we do completely run out of water, what will happen? It's not something folk want to find out through experience; and if it means dealing with troublesome kids to ensure a supply, they will.'

* * *

Jasper drove on for a while before stopping beside a local park to buy ice cream from a street vendor doing good trade in the heat. The adjacent play area was full of children, many lolling in the shade of whatever trees and bushes still managed to put forth a reasonable canopy. Toby learned that local schools had been shut down for the week, due to low mains pressure making it impossible to guarantee a reliable supply of water for toilets and cooking. Some of the youngsters came and looked around the old van; but most appeared listless and a little lost, as if the novelty of missing lessons had worn off and a return to normality would be welcome.

'Where you from?' asked one little scrap wearing loose fitting shorts and a pair of thick glasses.

'From over Molliton way.'

'Have they got enough water there cos we ain't, mister?' said the boy, squinting up at him. 'I wish it weren't so hot and dry,' he went on, scratching his side. 'I don't like this anymore – we don't get any swimming lessons now; and I hate havin' to carry water from the standpipe to flush the loo. It makes my arms ache, but Mum says I've got to do my bit.' He tipped his head questioningly, as if, as an outsider, Toby might have the answer. 'When will it end?… When will it rain properly again?'

'Soon, I expect... in a couple of weeks perhaps,' replied Toby; seeing from the longing look in the child's eyes that reassurance was needed.

'I hope so,' said the little chap, turning. 'It had better anyway, or I'm going to hemigrate.'

His final words would have been painfully comic under usual circumstances; but seeing the lad trudge forlornly away brought a pang of sadness to Toby's heart. Children can never be expected to understand all that is happening around them; but can only accept whatever inheritance previous generations have seen fit to bequeath. If the carelessness of man was indeed upsetting the very fabric of the climate, causing violent storms and desperate droughts, they, and their own offspring in future years, would have no choice but to endure the consequences.

'Time to go,' said Jasper, noting Toby's furrowed brow, 'we need to be moving. Then I'll find us a shady spot where we can decide the next step.'

They climbed back into the camper van and were soon travelling on again through the sticky streets. The air, even with all the windows open, was hot and sultry: the sun uncomfortably bright in a cloudless sky. At one point they passed a group of people waiting in line around a standpipe, each holding a variety of plastic containers, buckets or cans to collect their daily water ration. A police car stood nearby, the officer watching through an open window.

'They've had trouble with people taking more than they're entitled to,' said Jasper. 'It seems there are those that think it's acceptable for them to be able to wash the dog, rather than leaving enough for their neighbours to cook the family dinner.'

Faces looked up as they passed by: most weary and resigned, but others clearly in a bad humour and ready to argue with those around them.

'I don't blame 'em entirely,' Jasper added, noting Toby's uneasy expression. 'Nobody in authority has ever made it really clear that this kind of situation could arise if the climate went pear shaped. They were brought up to believe that whatever happened, we would always be able to cope with the effects of climate change for the foreseeable future – that there would be no serious impending hardship. Now folk realise that it won't simply be coming generations that suffer, and they don't like it.'

* * *

Toby was glad when they finally left the oppressive heat of the town behind and made off along country roads and lanes. But there was little to cheer them here either; for apart from a few small green oases in low spots, or by the side of almost dry rivers, the prospect was always of an arid landscape, burned all about by wildfires, some still smouldering and threatening to flare up again. They negotiated winding byways, coming at last to the village of Ofney, its quaint medieval church circled with leering gargoyles – the ugly carved faces of devilish beasts and grotesque birds grinned out upon the world as if in silent mockery at the folly of unbelievers. Then, having turned back eastwards, the road brought them to the village of Turnham, where devout nuns prayed: a quiet wayside place, normally pretty and tranquil in its riverside setting, but now held, like a thousand others, in a limbo of drought, its green verges parched and dry. Jasper drove through without stopping, and so they came at last to a winding hill leading down towards the hamlet of Deerden, finally pulling off the road near a dry brook. In years gone by a colony of crows had built their untidy and now abandoned nests in the bare treetops above, and from one of these a solitary dark sentinel leaned out, nodding its head up and down as if noting their arrival.

'I must be going,' said Jasper, opening the driver's door and hopping down.

Toby did likewise, following him round to the front of the camper van where his companion began giving a final polish to the VW badge with a large handkerchief.

'But what about me?' asked Toby, unsettled at the thought of being left in such a remote spot.

'You can have this,' said Jasper, looking up with a grin. 'I brought it for you – you can drive, I suppose?'

'Why, yes… but it's not mine.'

'Well look at it this way… I'm loaning it to you – for the duration. She's a good little motor, and there's the best part of a tank of fuel, so you can go wherever you fancy. You'll raise a few eyebrows, but that's the fun of these. …Consider the thing your chariot to the future,' he added with a wink.

'I don't know what to say.'

'Then don't say anything… Come on, I'll show you the controls. They're a piece of cake!'

Having climbed into the driver's seat and been given the necessary instructions, Toby started the engine.

'She's well used and can be a bit sluggish on steep hills; but the old girl's got everything you need. I'm sure you'll find her really useful,' said Jasper with satisfaction as he stood in the doorway.

'And you?' asked Toby. 'Where will you go?'

'Don't concern yourself about me, mate… I've got a hundred places; it's you that needs to look out for yourself. Just drive off and find somewhere for the night – but don't bother to come back, because I won't be here.'

'Almost anywhere I stop in this people are going to be curious, aren't they?'

'Then just park up somewhere quiet, so as you won't be disturbed… You ain't going to be as conspicuous as you might think.'

Jasper then turned and began walking across the road toward an opening where a dusty track led off across a field.

Toby called after him. 'I almost forgot… you haven't rolled the dice… and I'm curious.'

Jasper stepped back, drawing the polished stone dice from his coat and tossing it toward Toby in a single action. Surprised, Toby caught it instinctively as the little man leaned forward, a conspiratorial look in his eye. Toby opened his palm to see a single white spot upon the smooth upturned face, before in the same instant, Jasper reached out to retrieve and return the thing to the darkness of his pocket.

'Just the number "One", Toby,' he grinned dismissively. 'It seems change is still a long way off and that we're nowhere near the end yet…'

'And these conditions… the drought, will it go on much longer?'

'Oh yes, mate – and things will get critical too. But I fear that still worse must follow before the ones that are really responsible take note. Let's just hope that some of the people around today live to see it.'

With this final comment Jasper walked off a second time, as if oblivious of the afternoon heat and simply out for a stroll in the country. Toby pulled away, losing sight of him in a moment; the transmission whirring as the camper van picked up speed. Seconds later, reaching a farm gate where he might have spied his erstwhile travelling companion once more, he saw that the footpath snaking up the rising ground was entirely empty – the only thing moving in the landscape being a single black crow flying off into the eastern sky.

* * *

Toby did not travel far after this, but having driven on through Deerden, took the bypass towards Milton Keynes for a short distance before heading south on another quiet road. This led uphill along a tree-lined lane to a blackthorn copse, through which, forking off to the right, ran a dry and little used farm track. In winter it would not have been suitable for a vehicle like his, but after weeks without rain could be navigated with care. Few others would pass that way and such an out of the way spot had its appeal.

Toby had much to think about. If Jasper's assertion that he was now living in the year 2018 was correct, he had already been given a further glimpse of the future. Moreover, his children would be five years older, and Jenny might well imagine that he had abandoned her… or perhaps that he was dead! If he simply turned up without warning, how would they take it? … How would he explain so long an absence?

These thoughts revolved inside Toby's head as he bumped off the lane and began to steer down the uneven track. The many ruts were deeper than he had at first anticipated and Toby was thrown about quite violently: the stored contents in drawers and cupboards chinking noisily with each violent jolt. But it did not last, and after fifty yards he came out again at the corner of a fallow field populated with drought-strangled weeds and seeding clover. A tangled overgrown hedge stood to his left, and through its thin foliage he looked out across a wide valley dotted here and there with farm buildings, the nearest half a mile away. Clearly it was a little frequented place, providing satisfactory refuge for the time being.

Toby switched off the engine before stepping out to inspect his new home. He was hungry and found provisions stored away: fresh bread, some eggs, fruit, tinned vegetables, dried milk and cheese. There was water too in a plastic can, teabags and coffee.

'What is this?' he asked himself, 'a travelling hotel?'

Toby also discovered a clever little gas stove upon which he prepared himself a meal as evening drew on. At one point a noisy tractor came up the country lane nearby before passing through an opening a little further along. It proceeded to trundle slowly across the field in front and Toby thought about reversing back among the trees, convinced that the driver, perched high up in his cab, would notice him. The doors of the tall vehicle were thrown wide open and he could hear music on the radio – a rock band urging teenage rebellion. But the pace of the tractor did not slacken, and if he had been seen, the youthful occupant paid no heed.

'I'm certain I'd have registered this old camper sitting here if it were on my land,' Toby mused a short time later, while sipping coffee in the driver's seat. 'I surely can't go on forever without being discovered. It may be best to move on tomorrow and find somewhere quieter still... or maybe I'll take the opportunity to drive home and see what's there.'

He closed his eyes in contemplation of the scene that would greet him should a return to reality be achievable once more – such a precious meeting being something he longed for as the void of sleep again eclipsed his conscious thoughts.

Chapter Three

Silent Spring

Emma and Richard Anderson experienced difficult times bringing up their young family but they grew together, strengthened by the love that flourished between them.

Those fortunate enough to experience true happiness develop the capacity to look beyond the everyday limits of their own lives to the wider world and the needs of others; so did the Andersons come to a deeper appreciation of this troubled earth and its people. But being involved in causes that seek greater protection for the natural environment and vulnerable populations does not always make one popular, as a self-seeking, manipulative and corrupt minority will inevitably seek to blur the judgement of others in order to justify greed and complacency. However, as the years passed and climate upheavals grew more frequent and intense, the tide of public opinion turned and became more supportive. The voice of protest against habitat destruction and the over exploitation of natural resources grew as increasing numbers came to doubt the reassuring silver tongued words of untrustworthy politicians, multinational corporations and the media.

The protesters' cause was aided by the disastrous drought of 2017-2018. This halted much of Europe and North Africa's food production, driving up prices and causing widespread starvation in a dozen countries. In the following three years more than thirty million of the world's poorest people died as a direct consequence of ensuing shortages: largely ignored by complacent politicians. Yet the scar of resentment left behind would fester and deepen during coming decades.

The problem was not caused by drought alone. Another factor was at work which, while ostensibly set in motion with the laudable motive of reducing the amount of pollution being released into the atmosphere, swallowed up land – both virgin and cultivated – that might otherwise have been used to grow food. These "bio-fuels" were theoretically a good idea. The car-owning people of the developed world could go on driving their vehicles as much as they wished without feeling the guilt of knowing they were contributing to global warming. The spiralling rise in global car miles could continue to accelerate without further upsetting the climate since henceforward the driving of bigger and faster cars need have no impact on our environment. A silver bullet had been found that would allow the mad unfettered road race to go on indefinitely without consequence. All praise to those that turned their land over to producing the raw materials for these new wonder fuels – the carbon dragon had been slain!

But how much land would be needed to power a billion vehicles? …And how many prairie fields and paddies would no longer grow wheat or rice to feed the hungry?

Within a few years it became clear that the miracle solution could not work or be justified. Food production fell as population continued to rise; virgin rainforests were relentlessly cleared to provide land for the new crops, while the once green and pleasant countryside of England, as in many other countries, became increasingly covered with bland mono-crops to supply the bio-fuel industry. The rush to maximise production and profits fell heavily on the environment, with little regard for either soil health or wildlife, as previously uncultivated land went under the plough and hedgerows were rooted out. Fragile populations of birds and native animal species began to decline again following a number of years around the turn of the millennium when careful measures had been taken to conserve their numbers. Now, both poisoned and neglected by the human custodians of the land, the open fields and skies grew depressingly quiet once more: the wild fragments remaining left sadly all but devoid of life. The Andersons, seeing what was happening at home and abroad, deplored the inaction of complicit governments and threw their weight behind a push for change. Thus, when a huge rally was planned in London's Hyde Park during the summer of 2021; one of many being held to challenge the bio-fuel lobby in major cities around the globe, they planned to be there. Emma would travel down from their home in Barnet with the children before meeting Richard near Marble Arch.

* * *

As Toby shifted his weight during the last remnants of sleep, a pain shot through his leg, causing him to sit bolt upright, jamming his hand on the car horn, which sounded a loud blast. He opened his eyes in shock, simultaneously toppling sideways as the numbness in his left thigh caused him to lose balance. It was one of those awful moments when his body seemed to bear him a grudge, as if punishing him for having to endure further months of inactivity by sending a hundred pains and insults. Toby swore an oath at the windshield, while trying to extract his foot from behind the clutch pedal where it had become wedged due to his contortions.

'Bloody hell!' he winced, gingerly shifting the weight of his thigh and grimacing into the mirror. 'Why don't I ever remember to lie down any more?'

The spasms gradually died away as feeling returned, but it was a full five minutes before he felt able to open the door and risk lowering a foot to the ground. Every muscle felt stiff and he knew that a period of much more than a few hours must again have elapsed. His sole touched the soil at last, and it was only then that he noted conditions had changed. The ground was damp, and behind the van the ruts of the track were filled with deep puddles. A film of dust lay in streaks across the camper van roof while trails of mould showed where water had dripped from roof runnels. Yet in other respects the VW appeared in surprisingly presentable order, the tyres still fully inflated. The old vehicle may have come to blend with the surrounding area, but it was not yet ready to fall apart like any other farmyard wreck.

Toby tottered round to the front, rubbing his thighs and looking out over the fields. What he observed was an almost uniform sea of bright yellow. A wide swathe of flowering oil seed rape reached into the distance as far as the eye could see, sending its pungent scent and cloying pollen into the atmosphere. It spread like a gaudy blanket over the land – a four-week wonder of striking visual excess, bringing hayfever misery to millions. Where wheat, barley and potatoes had once grown, and farm animals had dotted pastures and meadows, now this victorious monster crop had marched across the landscape to dominate the scene and suck life from the soil. It was truly awesome in its awfulness – beautiful yet disturbing – a triumph of monoculture over nature; which upon running to seed (the stuff of bio-fuels), would sprawl over, ragged and unkempt, to resemble something little better than a rambling expanse of crumpled mattress dumped upon the landscape by some malicious airborne fly tipper.

'I quite like the look of it now,' thought Toby, 'but you can have too much of a good thing. It's pleasant to see a cow or a field of beans occasionally.'

* * *

He busied himself making breakfast of a kind. Every scrap of fresh produce had long gone off, the milk having turned to dust in its plastic bottle, but he was able to find tinned and wrapped food to eat. There were sardines, several packets of dried biscuits and cans of baked beans. He collected water from the cleanest puddle to boil for tea, and within an hour had fed himself reasonably well on what was available. With the prospect of returning home that day, Toby also decided to shave off the stubble on his chin with a razor he had discovered. Whatever else might happen, he now needed company and to find his true bearings.

Feeling an urge to get started without delay he then went to examine the track behind the camper van. What he saw was not encouraging, for the earth was soft and every pothole filled with water. If he turned the camper van and took a run at it he might get through; but should he meet an unseen obstacle the prospect of becoming bogged down was more than likely. In the event of this happening there would be no way that he might get further without assistance. Toby scratched his head: leaving the camper van seemed a desperate move, for although a dated and novel form of transport, it did at least offer him the opportunity to cover long distances reasonably quickly. But on the other hand, he was still near enough home to walk, and would be a good deal less conspicuous if he did.

This course having suggested itself, Toby was about to lock up and move off when a noise on the other side of the hedge drew his attention. Apart from a few cars passing on the road, it was one of the first signs of life he had heard. Only twice had he seen birds: the first time a single low flying pigeon; then later, a tiny wren bobbing around the lower branches of a blackthorn tree. Apart from this there had been nothing else – no morning chorus, no sight of a grazing rabbit or foraging mouse. What he had begun to think of as a tranquil calm was more an empty silence.

A hedgehog or a wandering farm cat might have made the new sound that he had heard, but Toby was not entirely surprised by what appeared next. Whatever the creature was it now hopped down into the shallow ditch by the hedge and next moment a small wet snout, twitching and sniffing the air, pushed through a patch of spring grass ten feet away. Then, after a momentary pause, Macken rose into view shaking off the burrs and tangled grass that had become wound round him. He sneezed before trotting over to where Toby stood, offering his head to be scratched. After receiving an acceptable amount of attention, which took more than a minute to administer, the little Jack Russell finally hopped through the still open side door of the camper van and curled up on the first available seat.

'Well fancy seeing you,' said Toby, grinning and shaking his head with amusement at the dog's audacity. 'You're welcome I'm sure – but I'm afraid breakfast finished ten minutes ago.'

Macken seemed to catch his meaning; but obviously well fed, yawned widely before resting his head on a front paw and apparently drifting into a contented snooze.

'I wish you could talk, old boy,' thought Toby looking at him. 'You certainly seem to know when to turn up… but are you alone I wonder?'

Shielding his eyes against the glare of the strengthening sun, Toby scanned the fields around, searching each corner for signs of another's approach. At first nothing seemed evident, but then he saw Jeannie; not standing, but seated by a stile a little way off, the top of her straw hat occasionally turning as she busied herself at some quiet task. She had her back to him, but her slender shoulders and the soft gold hair that flowed over them were unmistakable. He moved that way, lifting and placing his feet deliberately, not wanting to disturb or frighten her by making a sudden approach – a little nervous too that she might somehow vanish into nothingness if he came up too abruptly. But she was real enough, and he found her sitting in a grassy space; her pale yellow summer dress spread out over her knees – the white lace blouse buttoned to her throat set off with a delicate sky blue ribbon. Her chosen place had once been the entrance to an ancient meadow and was still a peaceful corner, though set amid the sea of oil seed rape that pressed in on all sides. She had been making a long daisy chain, plucking the delicate flowers with her slim fingers before expertly stringing them together in a garland of white and pink – piercing the narrow stems with polished nails as expertly as a fine seamstress creating a wedding gift for a fairy princess.

'I didn't like to wake you while you still slept,' she said, glancing back as he drew near. 'So I busied myself, and the time seems to have slipped by.'

'You have been here a while?'

'Since dawn; when the farm cockerel first crowed,' she replied, turning again to look at him with the same gentle yet mysterious eyes. 'I knew you would wake today, but another hour will have done you no harm.'

'And what day is it?'

'A special day… and year,' she answered with a wistful voice. 'Today is the 23rd April 2021 – "St George's Day" – the English Saint's day.'

'I didn't know people still worried about such things,' Toby said, looking blankly at the ground and shaking his head. '…But you say it is 2021… almost eight years since I saw them last…'

He turned, suddenly overcome, and began stumbling back towards the camper van; Jeannie rose to follow, yet made no effort at first to come to his side. 'Where are you going?' she called softly from behind.

'Home!' he replied angrily, with tears in his eyes. '…I need to get back… Don't you understand? This all seems like some kind of game to you… but for me… this is my life… it's all I have… and it's running to waste!'

'It's not a game, Toby,' she answered gently, her voice again filled with sympathy and understanding. 'I wouldn't put you through so much for my amusement. We are not as cruel as you might imagine.'

He stepped back, needing to restrain himself from taking Jeannie's shoulders and shaking her in his frustration. But her penetrating look held him, and as if confronted by a force greater than his own, he drew back.

'I have to return, Jeannie… I have to see my wife and children… or I'll be a stranger to them.'

'Not if you still love them,' she said, drawing close and taking his hand. 'That is a bond that can last forever… and wherever you go.'

'But I… I… don't have to wait!' he said, choking on the words and breaking into a contorted grimace. 'I… I can see them today… within the hour… it would only take me that long to walk.'

She took his other hand, and lifting both, kissed the tips of his fingers with a barely perceptible touch of her lips.

'You must accept that they are no longer there, Toby,' Jeannie said, with a note of finality. 'Jenny came back for a while; but when you failed to return she decided to sell the house and move to live with her mother in London. They are all well – you need not worry about them.'

'But I want to see them!' Toby all but croaked, freeing his palms and dashing the last few yards to the van to search for his fleece. 'I'll ring them on my mobile… I'll arrange to meet them!'

When his head reappeared he clutched the mobile in both hands, frantically pressing buttons and cursing under his breath. 'There's no signal again,' he moaned. 'The battery must be dead!'

Jeannie came up to him and reaching forward placed her slim hand between his clawing fingers. 'It wouldn't make any difference, Toby; the system has changed since you last phoned. You can no longer make use of it to call her.'

'Then I'll use a landline.'

'They hardly exist any more… and can you remember the number?'

Toby's shoulders slumped, and defeated he leaned back against a tree. 'Then I'm stumped… it's as if I've lost them forever… I don't know what to do.'

* * *

Jeannie put the garland of daisies round her neck before turning away to gaze over the hedge at the lurid acres of oil seed rape beyond. For a minute or more they both stood in silence: he in sullen dejection, she in contemplation.

'There is a huge gathering today in London,' Jeannie said at last. '"The Silent Spring Rally" – to protest against the rush for bio-fuel crops and the damage that they are doing to the environment. It is a big issue; for the turning over of farmland to bio crop production can cause grave problems. Growers have been tearing out hedgerows once more, thousands of miles of them, and using pesticides that destroy wildlife. There has been a crash in the bird population during the last two years – ninety per cent fewer songbirds: some, like the skylark, having been almost eliminated from the land. Even once common wild animals like rabbits, foxes and hares are becoming rare. A disaster is at hand – one caused by men in an attempt to sustain a lifestyle of waste and excess that threatens to reduce most naturally occurring species to a point beyond recovery.'

'Why are you telling me this?' he asked sullenly. 'Why should I care anymore?'

'Because your children still live, Toby… because it is their world, and whatever happens, you should want to see it protected for their sakes.'

'I do,' he said wearily. '…I just wish that I could share it with them.'

'I want you to go there,' said Jeannie, her voice assuming a practical tone, 'to be at the London rally… it is important… for another reason.'

'Go to London,' replied Toby, reviving and turning to the weather stained VW. 'What, in this old banger? I'm not even sure it will start!'

He walked round the aged vehicle again, making a cursory examination. The tyres, as he had noted earlier, did still appear to be correctly inflated, and having dipped the engine oil, he found this up to the mark as well. For her part, Jeannie had already stepped into the passenger seat and Macken, sensing that a new adventure was about to begin, positioned himself on a rear seat where he could look out on the world through the open window. So it was that when Toby looked up he found the two waiting for him. Both seemed uncannily still – she with hands folded on her lap and the Jack Russell with his head winningly tilted to one side, patiently anticipating the off. It was as if any other outcome would be impossible, and thus, having resigned himself to journeying on with his unfathomable companions, Toby climbed into the driver's seat.

'We can try, I suppose,' he said, sliding the key into the ignition. 'But going back down the track behind will be unwise. I think we are bound to get stuck if we do.'

'Then go straight ahead, for we must be getting on,' suggested Jeannie, a hint of urgency creeping into her voice. 'You will have to drive over what has been planted, but there are few around to question us. The men that own and work these fields only come rarely to spray the crops.'

'It doesn't seem proper to steer right across,' said Toby, thinking back upon the country lore he'd learned when growing up.

Jeannie turned to face him, her eyes suddenly bright and determined. 'Look, Toby, there are five million people protesting in London today because they fear that this kind of farming is damaging the earth and destroying the creatures upon it. Many millions also believe that it has brought starvation and want to half the world's population. Therefore, I don't think you should worry over much about the little damage you may do.'

She then settled back, looking ahead into the distance, her evident resolve overcoming any lingering reservations Toby still had.

Crossing his fingers, he leaned forward to engage the ignition, with Macken, his paws up on the back of the driver's seat, now craning forward and panting in his ear. Toby did not feel confident, but instead of hearing the expected click and no more, indicating a dead battery, the engine turned lazily and, following an initial wheezy cough, spluttered back into life like a reliable old Victorian barrel organ struggling to find the right notes after years of disuse. A good deal of white smoke rose up from the exhaust but Toby was both reassured and elated as the engine gradually settled to a normal balanced rhythm.

'Be of good faith, Toby,' said Jeannie smiling. 'I promise there are some things that will not let you down. Now come on; this is to be a busy day and it is time we were gone from here!'

Obeying the imperative note in her voice, Toby engaged first gear and the camper van moved off, Macken retreating to the side window, where he leaned out gulping the breeze. Toby drove directly over the growing oil seed – the tall fatty stems plashing noisily against bumper and paintwork. A rank aroma of dense pollen rose up as they moved along: hanging like a curtain in the air. Toby could not help but feel guilty as he glanced in the mirror at the damage left in his wake, but Jeannie appeared to have few such thoughts.

'There is a farm entrance at the bottom,' she advised. 'When you get there, turn left and drive on towards Kempsford. If we meet anyone just keep going; there is no time for argument.'

She seemed strangely detached for the moment, as if thinking ahead and preparing the next stage; but Toby remained conscious that if they did meet someone he, the driver, would need to account for his actions. The opening soon appeared – a gap where once a farm gate had stood – stone posts removed to allow the passage of huge modern farm machines. They reached it without mishap, bumping and churning over the soft soil like a drunken matron ploughing through the fleshy growth of an overgrown kitchen garden, but did not arrive there alone! Toby had already seen another vehicle approaching, looming above the hedgerows: a large, ugly tractor equipped for field spraying, its spidery spraying arms folded back to give clearance down the narrow lanes. The irate driver had likewise noted the VW from some distance away and seemed intent upon cutting them off before they could leave the field. Yet although he had put on speed, the camper van arrived just ahead, swinging onto the road as the tractor lurched up behind with a screech of brakes.

The cab door burst open and a gruff voice rang out. 'Here, what the friggin' 'ell do you think you are up to, you hippy twit? I'll get the law on you for this!'

'Drive on,' said Jeannie calmly. 'I think the gentleman is none too pleased, and I don't much care for his language.'

Toby pulled away as the farmer, seeing their determination to escape, re-engaged gear and began to follow. But it was an unequal contest. The cumbersome equipment carried by the tractor could not be driven helter-skelter for long, and having rounded a sharp bend, Toby looked in the mirror to see evidence that their pursuer had been forced to pull up in a shower of leaves and dust, after careering too close to a small tree.

'That's torn it,' he said. 'What if he gets onto the police to report our number?'

There was a muffled noise behind them from Macken – sounding somewhere between a bark, a yawn and a laugh.

'Don't worry about that eventuality,' replied Jeannie, settling herself comfortably. 'I don't think the registration of this particular Volkswagen will be on any vehicle licence files existing now.'

* * *

They travelled on through endless fields of gaudy yellow rape, broken only here and there by a green paddock or an occasional crop of corn. The blue skies, though welcome, were empty of birds except for one or two rooks and pigeons searching languidly over the unvarying wasteland. Then, after leaving Kempsford along a by-pass clogged with slow moving traffic, they came at last to the wide four-lane M1 motorway that would take them to London. This too was overloaded with traffic: thousands of lorries, commercial vans and business travellers grinding in a stop-start procession to the capital. It was the same modern nightmare, played out on ever wider roads, that had been seen in England for the last thirty years: as it would continue to be until politicians realised that the right to unlimited road travel had gone well beyond the realm of reason.

So they came to London, home of twelve million people – the hungry, unsustainable, sprawling capital now dependent upon the food produce of a land area equivalent to one thousand times its own size. Here too the roads were almost impossibly crowded; but as they drew closer to the centre, evidence of preparations for the march began to be encountered: police diversions and advice displayed on mobile public information signs. More than once it seemed that everything might grind to a permanent halt, but they kept moving forward, just, and taking side roads that Jeannie knew somehow avoided the worst congestion. Then at last they began to see numbers of pedestrians moving toward the heart of the city – some in ones and twos, others in larger groups. Many carried banners bearing blunt slogans like, "Monoculture is the Death of Nature", "Kill the Bio-Fuel Monster" or "Shout now if you fear the coming of a Silent Spring". The growing surge of marchers poured out of underground stations: professional people with sensible anoraks and woolly hats, families with children in wheelchairs, dreadlocked environmental campaigners in bright headscarves and colourful sarongs – Samba bands, Asian restaurant workers and Afro-Caribbean dancers – all heading in a widening column toward the great open space a few streets away.

'I must park,' said Toby, when they had been slowed to little more than walking pace.

'Soon,' Jeannie replied, leaning forward. 'You must turn right when you see a steward indicating.'

Stewards… there seemed to be hundreds of them; two or three at every corner or junction – stern young men and women in bright orange jackets, charged with managing the rising tide of humanity. How would he find one in all this? But then, as they made their way down another short side road, a tall young woman suddenly stepped off the pavement indicating firmly that he should turn right into a narrow mews.

'Park down at the end, Sir!' she called through the passenger window as the VW drove past into the quieter surroundings of "Endling Place".

Toby was a little bemused. 'Here?' he asked vaguely, as the steward slid from view. 'But surely, all the spaces will be for private residences… Won't I need a permit?'

'Not today,' replied Jeannie, pointing to a parking space just comfortable enough for them to squeeze into. 'Restrictions have been relaxed during the march; so you will be alright for a few hours.'

Having carefully manoeuvred the camper van, Toby switched off the engine and climbed out, while Jeannie released Macken from his back seat position. The Jack Russell jumped down onto the pavement, cocked a leg against a lamppost and trotted off round the corner.

'Shouldn't you call him back?' asked Toby, as he watched the dog disappear among the legs of the passing crowd.

'You know Macken,' she replied without concern, 'he'll find us again – when he's good and ready.'

Toby looked up at the tall buildings, the sun illuminating walls and polished windows of west facing residences. 'You know we were incredibly lucky to find a parking space like this,' he pondered, noting how incongruous the antiquated brightly coloured camper van looked among sleek silver BMWs and Mercedes. 'How did you know about it?'

She smiled at him fondly. 'Let's just say that in this small detail we were meant to enjoy a little luck today, Toby. ...Now, we must be going!'

* * *

Jeannie had twice looked anxiously at her watch and she informed him that, as it was already twenty minutes past one, they would need to press on in order to reach their destination in time. He followed her as she moved away into the street, where they were immediately caught up in the burgeoning crowd, sometimes becoming parted in the throng. The marchers were all good-natured however, with many people calling across to one another; while others, obviously meeting up for the first time that day, homed in using directions provided by mobile. It was then that Toby considered his own unusable device and wondered what he would do if they became separated. But Jeannie was not hard to keep in sight – the outfit she wore being easily spotted if he lost contact for a moment. She moved quickly; constantly weaving in and out through the jostling walkers, finding the least impeded route, and at last they came to a rather less crowded area near a large roundabout where the traffic still flowed. Here, too, people with banners were emerging from all quarters to join the march, but some parts of the pavement still offered less busy places where groups could stop and talk for a few minutes, or simply wait for a friend to use the public convenience nearby. A succession of buses and taxis continually drew up and pulled away, while a half dozen street vendors' stalls were enjoying good trade.

Feeling a fresh spring breeze against his face, Toby moved into a quieter space, relieved to get away from the heaving mass for a few moments. He turned, realising that

Jeannie had passed from view and searching for the straw hat she had been wearing; but none such was in view. 'She'll have stepped into the loo,' he said, only half convinced. 'That's natural enough; I'll wait until she comes back.'

In other circumstances he might have been more concerned, but what with the bright day and the colourful crowd, there was much to occupy an onlooker and he leaned back against the railings. A group of chanting students noisily crossed before him, then five others wearing comical animal outfits. There was, too, a street artist sketching passers-by, and three jugglers entertaining a group of onlookers near the subway entrance to his right. He had begun to focus on these when a young family moved into sight up the subway steps – a woman with two children. The eldest was a boy of nine or ten with a steady, serious expression, who walked slightly ahead eating an ice cream. His younger brother, seated in a child's pushchair, clutched a drinking beaker. Both were soon clearly enthralled by all the activity around them – happily distracted while their mother, Emma Anderson, took out her phone to call Richard. She had stopped close to the pavement edge, no more than ten paces away from where Toby stood as he turned to look towards them. Young Kline Anderson wore a pair of slim, square framed glasses and met Toby's glance steadily. There was a reserved confidence in his face as they momentarily appraised each other beneath the April sky and in those few seconds Toby thought of his own son, who would be about the same age. ...Perhaps he too had been brought along to attend the march? ...If Toby waited a minute more, might Jenny and the children also emerge into the sunlight...?

He was lost for a moment in a personal space and upon blinking back, found the boy had turned away to look down at a small dog trotting forward from between the legs of the crowd. As Macken came closer several other bystanders noticed him too, but ignoring their coaxing to stop and be petted, he made directly for the pushchair. The small child in it also spied him, holding out the drinking beaker while looking up at his mother to encourage her to see. But Emma had just made her connection, and for five seconds was unaware of her son's entreaty.

What happened next could not have been predicted for Macken, having made his ground, suddenly barked and jumped up excitedly at the small boy, who immediately dropped the beaker and drew back into his seat with surprise. The beaker rolled away toward the road before toppling over the pavement edge and spinning out onto the roundabout. The older boy saw it and without hesitation stepped out to retrieve the thing just as a double-decker bus came round the corner. Seeing the danger, Toby dashed up at the same instant, throwing himself between the boy and the bus and scooping him back onto the pavement with his right arm, before being roughly jolted sideways by a rush of wind. He rolled over twice, coming to rest in a corner by a waste bin, as the crowd round about began to move away towards what seemed like another incident a little further down the street. It had been a selfless spur of the moment reaction and he sat dazed for several seconds as the bus pulled up nearby, a stream of people descending from it to add their numbers to a great many more assembling near the kerb. Surrounded by anxious onlookers, Emma Anderson stood a few feet away cuddling the smaller child, whom she had taken from the pushchair, and clutching her older son close. All seemed shocked, though thankfully otherwise unhurt.

Feeling oddly calm, but realising that his mobile phone had apparently disappeared from his pocket, Toby climbed shakily to his feet and began vainly searching through his fleece pockets as Jeannie reappeared at his shoulder, and Macken, having unobtrusively skirted the throng, came to sit by his ankle. Toby turned, half smiling, and glad to tell her that no harm had come to the woman or her children.

'It was a close thing,' he said excitedly. 'It was good that I happened to be nearby!'

'I saw it all, Toby,' Jeannie replied, with a look expressing both satisfaction and regret. 'You did well... and yes it was fortunate that you were in just the right place. But now we must get you away – you've had quite a shock too.'

'But I'd like to speak to the lady,' he said, 'to ask if I can assist further in any way.'

They both looked again toward the milling throng, where several police cars and an ambulance had drawn up. Emma Anderson was being led with her children towards the latter, having now been joined by her husband.

'I think it might be best to leave them,' said Jeannie. 'They have much to worry about, and talking with us at this time might distress them further.'

It was a strange moment, for Toby was torn between a desire to make contact with those he had helped, and a sudden reserve that made him wish to melt quietly back into the crowd. The second urge would prove the stronger, and when Jeannie linked her arm with his, he allowed himself to be led away into the reassuring anonymity of the jostling mass. Not until some time later would he remember to search again for his missing mobile phone – only then confirming that it had indeed been lost... that his last link with a past life had gone.

* * *

The three went on together to attend the rally in Hyde Park, standing on the fringes of the three million strong gathering, few of whom had any knowledge of the drama that had unfolded so recently in a nearby street. A life had been saved, but as they listened to the speeches most were rightly more concerned about the immediate fate of the natural world than any individual good fortune. The afternoon continued fine for a while, but towards evening black clouds bubbled up from the west, and just before five o'clock a sudden downpour of rain and hail, of the kind now becoming ever more foul and intense, sent the assembled protesters scurrying toward the underground and home. It was a damp end to what most considered a worthwhile day, but their massive expression of concern changed nothing. The powers that be continued to make their own decisions – "based on sound economic considerations" – and the good science pointing to the need for a new approach was ignored.

So all went their separate ways and the damage went on – deepening in its consequences as the dog days of the old over-commercialised world wore out.

For his part, Toby returned with Jeannie and Macken to "Endling Place" where a uniformed doorman from an adjacent property approached them as Toby unlocked the camper van. The doorman's manner was boorish and condescending as if the wider concerns of others beyond his little patch were of no consequence.

'Excuse me,' he asked. 'Is this your vehicle?'

'It is,' Toby replied, a little sheepishly.

'Well, I don't know what you thought you were doing leaving it here,' sneered the other. 'I was about to have it clamped. We don't allow old crates like this to be parked in respectable neighbourhoods… what is it anyway, a museum piece?'

What the man didn't realise was that Macken had just then sidled up behind him and, succumbing to a temptation resisted on another occasion, surreptitiously relieved himself on the back of the doorman's sharply pressed trousers.

'No,' said Toby, grinning down towards the Jack Russell, who now sat innocently peering up between the doorman's legs. 'Just think of it as… "A chariot to the future" … and one that is definitely not for sale!'

The doorman pursed his lips, unsure what to make of Toby's sudden offbeat humour, and while loudly directing him as he turned the camper van, gave additional dire warning of the consequences that would ensue should he touch or scrape any of the parked limousines.

So at last they found themselves back in the emptying street, travelling north toward the suburbs of the capital once more. Through the outer reaches of the city they trundled; along the road to Watford, Amersham, Aylesbury and beyond; but before plunging again into the wide and deeper darkness of the countryside, Jeannie directed Toby into a quiet lay-by.

'I must leave you now,' she said, climbing down. 'You'll not need me for a while and there is other business for us to attend to in London. Search for a quiet place to rest where you won't be disturbed. …But be of good faith; our paths will cross again before too long.'

Toby might have argued but recognised, as before, that this would be to no avail. Thus, as their departing forms melted beneath the streetlights, he could do no more than offer a final wave of farewell before going on alone.

* * *

He drove for another hour: through Aylesbury and into the sweeping hills of the Chiltern escarpment, before coming at last to the beauty spot at "Christmas Common" near Watlington. With the engine whirring and rattling, he climbed a steep rise out of the valley, turning near the top into a car park among trees; and there, tucked in a remote corner looking out over the downs, parked up before preparing to rest: turning down one of the camper beds so as to recline on something more comfortable than an upright seat.

'I may sleep for a good while,' he said to himself, 'but at least this time I'll have a chance of waking without being wracked by St Vitus's Dance.' Then, having locked up, he covered himself with the blanket to await another morning.

Chapter Four

Clamour and Denial
"The Lost Children"

THE CHANGES WE SEE HAPPENING TO THE fabric of the world around us may strike fear into our hearts or become a spur to action. But recognising how these changes affect our children can also lead to an escape into denial; for they might seem to go to the very root of what we ourselves have become.

* * *

Christmas Common is a beautiful place and to wake there on a fine July morning in the year 2028, was to wake in a setting still blessed by a divine hand and touched by the supreme brush strokes of nature. The view below the rolling downs stretches off towards Oxford: a wide patchwork of interlacing fields, small and medium sized villages, farms and tree-lined roads. In the late years of the twentieth century, red kites – a species of raptor once persecuted and driven out by gamekeepers – had been reintroduced there, the number of birds growing to form a colony several hundred strong. These magnificent wedge tailed scavengers frequented the lanes and byways travelled during the day by rushing commuters, before returning to roost high in the Chiltern trees as twilight fell. There was harmony enough, despite occasional "road kills", for the colony to prosper – but then the bio-fuel revolution came. For the fragile birds looking down from their treetop nests upon the landscape of men, the diesel used by passing cars became their bane. The poisons put down to kill rabbits and wildlife that might nibble at the precious fuel crops so contaminated the food supply of the kites that their numbers dramatically decreased. Indeed, so precipitate was this fall that only a few solitary birds survived to see the dawn of the new day when Toby, raising himself on one elbow, looked out across the rolling slopes towards Didcot.

On the edge of sleep he had heard a sound, a mellow but clear call, and peering into the sun, saw a kite fly gracefully into view, soaring and spiralling upwards on a current of warm air rising from the earth below. It seemed to lift without effort, sweeping the downs in search of food, though little movement might be discerned among the scattered trees and bushes; for even here, on the protected and uncultivated area, the improved pesticides and man laid viruses had done their work. The pop-eyed and infected remnants of poisoned warrens in the valley had long before hopped blindly up the slopes to be met by their curious and unsuspecting cousins; and now the overgrown mounds and dells were empty, the underground burrows still. Toby watched as the cream and red-brown bird moved lazily away, before curving back and flying slowly overhead. It dipped its neck forward, looking down towards the small clearing where the camper van stood, then disappeared from sight beyond the trees with a last plaintive call.

Toby rubbed his eyes, and having pulled open the side door of the camper van, stepped down onto the damp grass. He stretched and breathed deeply, any tiredness seeming to fall away in a moment as the cool air flooded around him, filling his lungs. He felt refreshed, and more remarkably, found he suffered none of the aches and pains sent to torment him when waking previously. Neither did he have the parched thirst or hunger of other times, giving him time to look around before worrying about these needs. There were clear indications that the quiet location among the trees and bushes had remained undisturbed. Indeed the secluded spot must have been his alone for some time, as tall grass and thistles had grown up, giving the VW the usual discarded look of old vehicles left in out-of-the-way places. But despite this, Toby felt confident that all would still be well with the sturdy and venerable lady when the time came to move on. Yet what of the outside world… what had been going on?

* * *

At times when we lose ourselves in contemplation it is easy to become shut off from the wider reality around us – even the everyday noises made by others failing to register as we concentrate upon our own thoughts. However, now that Toby began to focus his mind upon the next step, a range of sounds – some harsh and grating – rose to his ears. It was evidently still early, but the 24/7 bustle of modern life already seemed in full flow. A procession of cars, vans and motorcycles passed along the road in the valley – many of the latter group loudly proclaiming their passage with the racket of poorly silenced exhausts. Toby followed one glittering helmet as the skinny teenage rider rasped by, producing a cacophony of noise that reverberated over the countryside and echoed into every corner of the valley. It seemed ludicrous that a single person should be permitted to assault the ears of ten thousand in a crude expression of personal freedom. There were also two or three light aircraft in the sky; one with roaring engines that tore harshly at the senses. Then a small two-seater helicopter sped up from the east, destroying the calm for miles around with the rising wash of rotor blades. Toby could clearly hear distant airliners too – their white vapour trails criss-crossing the broad canvas of the morning sky overhead. Finally, a workman's drill began hammering away at a nearby road surface, making sufficient noise to wake the inhabitants of Hades. England had come awake, and even here, away from a major town or city, the crash and clamour that expunges tranquillity had become brashly evident.

The kite had gone now; doubtless searching for quieter parts away from the gratuitous rush of this brave new world, and listening, Toby rued the audible intrusions upon his sanctuary. But the mind learns to filter sound, which is like a cake of many layers. Some noises demand instant attention, disturbing our thoughts like unruly children drumming our foreheads, while others rise and fall more subtly. This can be true of music, which plays either upon the nerves or the emotions depending upon our mood or taste. So it was that Toby began to notice the repeated muffled throb of "dance music" coming from somewhere a short distance away. It had not been evident when he first regained consciousness, but the steadily rising and falling cadence was now unmistakable – the repeated rhythm eddying louder and then softer on the moving air as it was carried along the slope of the hill.

He grew curious – who could it be? Had they been there all along… did they know of his position? Toby moved off to investigate, following the direction of the sound as he descended the scarp. But anyone that has experienced music in the open air knows that it can be deceptive and play tricks upon the ear. After five minutes walking he felt no closer to where the sound was coming from. Indeed it now seemed to be rising from somewhere a little above him and to the left, perhaps back even toward the place he had come from. Toby turned and began climbing more slowly, passing between low hawthorn trees. Then suddenly, the source of the music lay just ahead.

He could see nothing at first, but pushing through a low alder thicket, came upon a sight as worrying as it was unexpected. Three brightly polished cars, with elaborate hubcaps and widened exhausts, were drawn up in a clearing where a small festival tent had been pitched. A flagpole, supported by three guy ropes, had been erected on a swath of green nearby. From this hung a crude home-made flag with an elaborate graffiti tag upon it. The remains of a barbeque were littered around its base, or thrown into nearby bushes; as were a variety of lager cans, take-away food cartons and other detritus. The doors of all the cars seemed to be open and Toby could see figures sprawled inside them. One youth, in the driver's seat of the nearest vehicle, was slumped over the steering wheel, a trail of congealed vomit smearing his shirt and jeans. Others lay in various positions, apparently asleep where they had dropped down – crumpled like fallen dolls deprived of animation by the cutting of their strings. The legs of a young girl protruded from inside the tent, one knee raised and twisted over – awkward in the sunlight.

Toby's first impulse – made uneasy by what he had witnessed – was to turn and leave the spot. But he had not gone three paces when a movement near one of the cars caught his eye. A gaunt, tousle headed youth, wearing a loose T-shirt and sagging jeans, had staggered out from among hawthorn bushes on the further side and now began lurching in Toby's direction. He could not have been more than seventeen or eighteen, but the unconcealed ire and malice in his face were starkly evident. The teenager continued shuffling forward purposefully, pointing menacingly with a provoking outstretched hand, an empty lager can held loosely in the other.

'What are you fuckin' looking at… you pervert!' he roared, stopping to draw his hand across his mouth. 'Fuckin' piss off, you bastard! – I'll kill you if I get you!'

The flow of invective might have continued, but as he attempted to come on again his eyes seemed to glaze over. Then, painfully clutching both chest and stomach, he crumpled forward, groaning. Toby considered completing his withdrawal from the place, but realising that there had been no movement from the youth's companions, stepped back into the clearing. The young man was still moaning, his shoulders moving spasmodically; then he retched violently before becoming still, apart from a twitching of his right hand. Toby came to stand over him, the awful truth of what he'd witnessed becoming evident. The youth's eyes were still open, the vomit spilling from his mouth coloured by a bloody trace; yet the rage in his face had gone – replaced by some final recognition and fear of what was happening to him… a mute supplication to the waiting earth. Toby drew away, his eyes sweeping the clearing as he took in the postures of the others nearby: a boy curled foetus like beneath a tree, a young couple lying together, faces to the grass, the slumped driver. None moved and only the incessant endlessly repeated beat music coming from the rear of the nearest hatchback gave life to the scene.

Stunned, he circled, examining each vehicle: finding three more young men sprawled in one, a girl and her boyfriend in the back seat of another, and a young woman fallen back over the front seats of the third, her highlighted hair cascading into the passenger well – the gear stick protruding into her back arching her body in a grotesque parody of sexual provocation. All were dead; yet frozen thus far and as yet uncorrupted – the cynical evidence of what had poisoned them seen scattered around: traces of white powder, empty tablet phials… a shimmering square of tinfoil fluttering in the breeze.

'What do I do?' Toby thought. 'My God, what happened here?'

He was about to go off to seek of help when a softly murmured call made him turn to the tent. …It came again – a muffled sound, like someone halfway between wakefulness and sleep, struggling for breath. He was there in a moment, dipping down from the sun into the cool shadow within. The girl lay in the same place, but had evidently tried to lift herself up on one elbow, perhaps having heard the dying youth's angry words. She flinched as Toby drew near – hollow eyes staring out through a cloudy film, hands knuckled tightly. A spasm of fear and pain together gave her the strength to pull away – hair falling in a dampened cloud across her face.

'It's alright, I've come to help you,' Toby said, reaching forward to support her shoulder.

But she would not accept his touch – slipping down into the corner of the tent and making herself small, like a child flinching from a blow. The matted curtain upon her brow parted briefly to reveal ashen features gripped by terror.

'But I... I don't know you – go away!' she said, forcing the words out in a hoarse whisper, as if the touch and help of a stranger was an alien concept. 'Please don't hurt me... the others will get you if you do.'

Toby tried again to reassure her, but to no avail; for in her distressed and muddled state she was beyond knowing and accepting kindness from him. He fetched her a bottle of water, found near the body of one of the others, then with a promise to return soon, set off at a jog trot in the direction of the spot where he judged the camper van to be parked. Toby hadn't travelled far, however, before voices rang out. There came a shout from behind, and looking back he saw that a group of six walkers had appeared and discovered the clearing just after his departure. There were many calls for help between them, and an urgent request that someone phone the police and ambulance services as Toby doubled back to give assistance.

When he arrived he found a shocked but efficient group that had already ascertained what had befallen all but the girl in the tent. Toby moved forward until he stood just behind the shoulder of the nearest. A kind faced, greying middle-aged woman was crouched beside the girl having just lowered her head back onto the groundsheet. She stepped out and turned away.

'The poor thing's gone too,' she sighed in disbelief. '...Just dropped away in my arms...'

* * *

Toby retreated a few steps... He had never before seen sudden or violent death and his senses felt numbed and empty. One of the group turned off the relentless dirge of the sound system and all remained relatively quiet for another five minutes – several of those present still hoping that the evidence of their senses would prove false, that the victims might simply be sleeping. The lone kite briefly returned, gliding in low as if unconcerned by their presence; a curious spectator at what might have been a family picnic. The group comforted one another while Toby, left to himself, sat on the grass attended by his own thoughts until the distant sounds of sirens working their way up the valley signalled the approach of the emergency services. They were not the first to arrive, however, for soon another more brusque and demanding noise began to shake the air beyond the ridge and a black police helicopter hove into view, winging across the valley. It came on quickly, turning in a wide arc above, before landing on the edge of the clearing in a violent flurry of dead leaves, dust and scattered grass. Two officers jumped out, running beneath the thrashing blades to begin a preliminary investigation of the scene. They were not alone for long, for soon two police cars and an ambulance arrived, then more emergency vehicles; followed by an inevitable procession of press reporters and outside broadcast television presenters. Within twenty-four hours, these eager bringers of bad news would ensure that the whole of Europe and much of the world knew of the "Christmas Common Tragedy".

Toby watched from the fringes as statements were taken from the party of six... though strangely no-one seemed interested in what he himself may have seen. Later he moved here or there among the crowd, listening to the various snippets of speculation about what had happened. There was much of this. Some suggested it had been a wild party that had gone wrong; while others pronounced themselves certain that an illegal rave had taken place at which deliberately poisoned drugs were passed round. There were even a few, those with more colourful and sordid imaginations, who suggested the illicit meeting had ended in rape and suicide. All possibilities were eagerly considered, but towards evening a sadder, yet in some ways more worrying assessment, began to emerge. By now the bodies had all been removed and what remained resembled a moderately sized summer camp staked out upon the Buckinghamshire hills. Tea and light refreshments were being provided at a mobile vendor's stall drawn up next to the cordoned off site, while a small outdoor television transmission facility had been set up so that on-the-spot hourly reports could be made.

It was turning into a lovely evening; the sun sinking slowly into the western sky bathing everything in a rich and mellow light. Then, just before six o'clock a car drew up and a tall, serious man, with eyes shadowed by ample brows, got out to address the crowd. He wore loose and timeworn black trousers, a rather faded shirt, and an ill-fitting and very shabby tweed jacket. He also had on an odd shaped hat, fashioned from a square of dark material, round the crown of which was tied a grey velvet ribbon. Apart from the peculiarity of his dress, there was about him a cloistered, almost mystic aura that drew one's attention. Introduced as an expert on the problems faced by young people, the gathering was informed that the late arrival had interrupted his studies in Oxford to share his views on the discovery. A raised platform with a microphone had been provided for him to use, onto which he reluctantly rose before surveying the faces of those assembled. The newcomer said nothing at first – as if waiting for a sign – giving Toby time to move close up to the back of the listening group. When all was settled, and having looked toward Toby with the faintest of nods, he began to speak in an unassuming but engaging voice:

'Ladies and Gentlemen,

'My name is Professor Wreyford Graveling of the "Institute for Youth Studies" and I am here to give my assessment of this tragic event. Today it seems probable that eleven young people have died narcotic related deaths, due to ingesting, together with a cocktail of alcohol and other drugs, what was most likely a deliberately poisoned substance. If this is proved to have been the case we should not be in any doubt that this was indeed murder; for several other youngsters up and down the length of Britain have recently died in a similar fashion. It would seem that madmen or zealots may be at work – those determined to rid our cities, towns and villages of the scourge of youth crime and drug abuse in this most lethal way.

'But will the endeavours of such lunatics succeed? I think not... No, any moral crusader who aims to destroy the manifestation of the problem will get nowhere while the root of the illness festers on. We must also accept that the youths who came here twenty-four hours ago were not all the same kind of people; and therefore should not be tarred with the same brush. True, there were at least four with a history of substance abuse and violence; but of the others, there were perhaps a number for whom drug taking was but an occasional, even rare indulgence. These might happily have joined in the barbeque, the excessive drinking and casual sexual behaviour, but experimenting with powerful drugs was not necessarily on their agenda.'

Here the professor paused briefly, as if inviting his listeners to consider the special import of what followed:

'Yet they did, I think, all have one thing in common – a lack of respect and trust for adults. Like so many young people, most had learned to make all their own decisions very early in life – to rely upon their own judgement and that of friends, while questioning the values of their parents. So when they came here, to this place of beauty, they doubtless did so, as often before, to hide themselves from the prying eyes of too often critical and unsupportive adults – instead finding a sense of belonging within their own group. All would have hoped to enjoy themselves: to have a good time while perhaps blotting out the developing environmental and human concerns of our troubled world... problems not of their making and certainly beyond their control.

'They made a fatal error of course (young people need our guidance and will make mistakes without it) and when the poisoned cocaine was produced it is a tragedy that all, without exception, should have been drawn into that final web of shared conspiracy. But the effects of drink and hypnotic music, combined with a much deeper malaise – the loss of hope, a sense of abandonment and neglect – had done their work. Those that took the most died soonest... while others testing themselves at the fringe of addiction lingered until morning. The last to die, Heather Ferris, may have been compelled to take part; we will never know.

'So what can we learn from this? What lessons can we glean from the deaths of these and other young people who have died in a similar way? What can our "Lost Children" tell us? ...I think we perhaps need to make a greater effort to know them better – to share with and nurture in them the good and lasting values of mankind. And perhaps too,' added the professor looking up towards a kite gliding on a thermal high above, 'we should enable each to gain a true appreciation of the quiet beauty of the countryside. For then, having been made more welcome in its fields and green places – both to work and seek recreation – many would find healing beyond the often monotonous and claustrophobic streets where they live.

'It is my belief that these young people were a product of a society in which we rush too much and stand to watch too little; in which at every point we are encouraged to consider our own interests above those of others. The loud noise and din so many youths perpetually create and slavishly carry with them is there, perhaps, for little other reason than to fill up an empty void – a rude expression of the callous selfishness and over-indulgence of our time – that can only lead to a slow decline of the human spirit. Yet every child is sensitive and vulnerable when born, and cannot be held entirely responsible for their later mistakes if denied care and support during their formative years. While if those that are denied choose to live by different values in a world cut off from ours... have we a right to blame them?'

Wreyford Graveling now dropped down from the platform, passing close to Toby as he returned to his car. Their eyes met briefly – the unblinking glance of the other conveying something between a question and a challenge. Then the professor was gone, leaving Toby to reflect that in an age of noise, confusion and little peace, it was as if many, having been brought up to accept the prospect of a life spent running inside a vast hamster wheel, now found it spinning out of control.

* * *

The eleven that died would be buried amid a welter of well-intentioned hand wringing, but little changed, and the lone kite, coming in to roost at twilight, might be seen to represent the forlorn and wasted spirit of an England too frequently ravaged in the uncaring pursuit of personal wealth and gain.

* * *

Sunset came late that evening, burning livid orange at the edge of a western sky flushed with crimson. Many police officers and reporters would stay on overnight, but there was a gradual melting away of others who had been present and Toby eventually joined these in departing from the downs. Upon separating from the last walkers he grew deeply thoughtful once more, and having pushed though the thicket to where the camper van stood, busied himself making preparations to leave. Most troubling was his memory of the girl in the tent – the one who in her great need had so morbidly feared a stranger... a would-be Good Samaritan who might have comforted her in her last moments.

Unable to relax, and no longer wishing to remain in the ill-fated place, Toby bit his lip and drove off into the deepening shadows as a watchful red kite, solitary and unblinking, looked down from the high branches of an oak tree.

No one, other than the frightened girl and the dying youth, had spoken to him that day.

Chapter Five

The Renewal Protesters

T HE YEAR 2028 WAS THE LAST ANYONE could recall when the weather in Britain stayed calm for lengthy spells and avoided the violent daily fluctuations then growing increasingly prevalent across the globe. The situation for many was becoming ever more difficult as a succession of baking hot summers regularly ended in vicious storms and floods. These in turn were often followed by cold winters, either very wet or dry, in which temperatures plummeted to bring frost or snow for weeks on end. Extremes became the norm, and the task of clearing up and maintaining services ever more costly and demanding. Flood damage went unrepaired, sewers stayed blocked for days, and pumping stations remained out of action for weeks on end. There were supply problems too, as food rotted in waterlogged fields or shrivelled during drought. Closed roads frequently prevented deliveries and essential items were often in short supply. Thus the quality of everyday life, for all but a privileged few, began to decline as the effects of climate change took hold. In response, the Government did introduce some "improved packages" to provide a little help to those most seriously affected, while several struggling insurance companies were primed or bailed out to keep them afloat. But despite these measures, the vulnerable or unfortunately placed now increasingly took the full force of events.

There were some, of course, as always, that did rather well out of the gradual breakdown, by selling second homes or letting property. Yet for all the cashing in and profiteering there was never enough suitable accommodation to go round, since a significant proportion of the housing stock erected in more recent years was found to have been unwisely sited in unsuitable locations: upon flood plains, next to fast eroding coasts, or on clay lands where subsidence became common during baking hot summers. Thus, at any one time a million families might be forced to leave such areas – many never to return. For hundreds of thousands of these displaced folk, caravans or emergency mobile homes would become the usual provision, and it was normally they that suffered worst when foul or extreme weather conditions returned once more. Few of these "temporary" quarters enjoyed permanent or reliable services and many people regularly found themselves cold or short of heating fuel in winter. Overcrowding also grew common, and it became increasingly evident to observers that an underclass was being created in the very heart of England – ordinary people left with little support, preyed upon by the greedy, and regarded with more or less complacent indifference by politicians.

* * *

Having no particular plan other than a wish to put a few miles between himself and the day's events on the Chiltern Hills, Toby did not travel far during the night following his stay at "Christmas Common". Instead, he drove until signposts told him he was drawing near to the town of Reading in Berkshire. Then, having no wish to enter the place during the hours of darkness, he searched for somewhere to stop from which to move on again when morning drew near. The weather had changed dramatically, and as he approached the wooded area known as "Burnham Beeches" a clap of thunder reverberated overhead, soon to be followed by a heavy shower of raindrops quickly obscuring the windscreen. Toby switched the wipers on, but although these valiantly ploughed the water aside he found it a struggle to discern the line of the road, and was grateful to pull off soon after onto a woodland track beneath a magnificent stand of oak and beech. He then settled back to sit out the squall, but although part of him fought to retain a grip on the present, within seconds his eyes drooped and he fell asleep.

* * *

The years passed once more while he rested, and he did not wake again until ten years later, in the early morning of 15th November 2038. Toby stretched as he became fully alert – noting thankfully that, as at his previous hillside refuge, he felt barely stiff in either limb or sinew. Then, having restarted the engine and checked his instruments, he drove away across a carpet of fallen leaves to regain the highroad once more.

Although dawn had yet to break there was already much traffic about: mostly large, modern vehicles that flashed by beneath the streetlights glowing in the hour before sunrise. The majority were heading in his direction, some evidently annoyed at being delayed by his stately progress, and as part of this general flow he entered the town – a modern conurbation of 500,000 people. It was a bustling place, within easy distance of the capital – a vibrant hive of busy commuting bees, many now rushing down its crowded streets before making off towards the honeypot of London.

But as the light grew and day approached, Toby began to view Reading's other more disquieting features; for upon crossing the wide bridge over the River Thames, he noticed a street of boarded-up houses – all evidently washed out in a recent flood. Just on from this, on the open space of a nearby park, a hundred or more temporary homes had been established, around which dozens of cars and piles of household possessions had been parked or heaped upon the muddy ground. Toby also noted that of the many faces attracted by the venerable appearance of the camper van, a number were blank and staring, as if not yet hardened to a refugee lifestyle. Proceeding a little further he saw an abandoned single-decker bus that had slid into a wide concrete drainage culvert – its sides splattered with mud, the roof scrawled with freshly daubed graffiti. Then there were places where walls had been pushed over and another where litter and debris left to dry in the sun lay in a wide swathe against a line of railings: an untidy collection of plastic bottles, cardboard and worse. Meanwhile, in telling contrast to this unsightly mess, the smiling image of a belly dancer, recommending the delights of economy air travel to the warm and sunny Middle East, stared down from a brightly lit billboard above. Indeed, as the town progressively lost its cloak of darkness, it seemed that at almost every point an extravagant show, represented by the opulence of expensive limousines, brash advertising and consumerism, was countered by evidence of the grim circumstances and neglect facing increasing numbers displaced by the effects of climate change.

Toby pressed on, taking in all he saw then, having passed through the commercial hub of the town, drove out toward the eastern suburbs. Not until travelling another two miles did he consider stopping – pulling off into a quiet side road to take his bearings beneath a streetlamp. Typical of many side roads in the immediate area, it was lined with small suburban semi-detached and terraced houses built about a hundred years before. The majority of them were occupied, but he noted that others, some of which appeared to have suffered structural damage to roofs and outbuildings, were boarded up against intruders. There were also caravans parked at intervals beside the road, a light glowing behind the closed curtains of the nearest. A litter of overflowing skips, bins and containers was scattered around on the pavement, and on the playground of an adjacent school a group of six or seven mobile homes were gathered close together: each separated from the next by a two metre wide passageway cluttered with wheelie bins, bicycles, buckets, brooms, children's toys and other household items. As he watched, a tired looking woman in a dressing-gown stepped down from one of these, before tenderly placing an old ginger cat on the cold asphalt and retreating back inside. The cat hunched up for a few moments, doubtless peeved at being expelled from the warmth within, then slunk away, fluffed against the chill, through a dark forest of effluent tanks, breezeblock slabs and metal supports.

Toby followed its passage for a moment until his eye was caught by another movement – that of a crow which had dropped down from the chimney pot of a nearby house to examine the contents of a waste bin stuffed full with wrapping papers from last evening's take-away meals. It pecked deliberately at the muddle of cartons and polythene, occasionally finding an odd chip or morsel of food that it swallowed with a swift straightening of the neck. Yet, while the creature seemed to be enjoying its meal, Toby realised that it was more than a little interested in him. The bird frequently looked fixedly in his direction like a hawkish village constable recognising a well-remembered local tearaway behind a thin growth of teenage beard... The two had doubtless met before.

The certainty that he was being watched again agitated Toby, and he glanced away, looking back through the mirror at the road behind. About ten metres distant was a run-down corner shop, its tumbled collection of grocery stands reaching out onto the pavement beneath a grimy awning, and as Toby focussed on this, a small man in a heavy, full-length overcoat emerged. He wore a check muffler and a wide leather hat, with what appeared to be a long pheasant's feather held in the circling band. Having returned some loose change to a trouser pocket, the newcomer then raised a sandwich to his mouth and began moving in Toby's direction, before slipping out of sight behind the camper van. A sudden shower of rain rattled upon the camper van roof before knuckles drummed on the passenger door as Jasper's crafty, smiling face appeared beside it.

'Let us in, guv,' he called through the glass. 'I'll be drenched if you keep me out here a minute longer!'

Toby immediately reached across to unlock the door and the little man, already dripping, clambered in.

'Lor... this weather!' he said with a note of irritation. 'It damn near spoiled our breakfast. But go on,' he added, passing a brown paper carrier bag across, 'see what you fancy. It's best not to start the day on an empty stomach!'

Toby looked inside and found other smaller parcels; one contained ham and cheese sandwiches, another two hot meat pies, while a third held Eccles cakes. Jasper also produced two cartons of hot tea from somewhere in his pocket, and removing the lid from the first, held it towards him.

Toby sat with his mouth half open, a pie in one hand and hot tea in the other.

'Don't just gawp at me, mate,' said Jasper, sinking his teeth into the remains of his own sandwich and wiping away the crumbs. 'Tuck in! This stuff won't stay warm forever... and why the surprised face – you didn't expect me to let you go wandering around on your own indefinitely, did you?'

'I... I didn't have any idea you might be here at all,' replied Toby, chewing slowly. 'How did you find me?'

'Easy – how many old jalopies like this do you think there are about? ...No, when you come trundling by, I've got the eyes to see you.'

Toby looked along the street again, peering through the sheet of water still cascading down the windscreen. A distant patch of blue had now appeared at the edge of the morning sky, promising an end to the rain. The crow, meanwhile, was no longer to be seen.

'Am I that obvious...' he asked a little nervously. 'Will everyone know I'm here?'

'They'll likely take note if Jeannie or me is around,' said Jasper, yawning lazily. 'But beyond that I'll wager you'll be left in peace.'

Toby could not divine the meaning of this rather mysterious reply, but nothing he went on to ask elicited a clearer explanation. What he did learn during their conversation was more about the changed circumstances of the times he was now in, and the hardships that had become commonplace for many.

'There's going to be another big nationwide series of protest marches this very day,' said Jasper, finishing his repast and taking a long drink from his tea carton. 'A lot of people are getting tired of what they have to put up with and want something to change. Not just relief work, you understand, though there's been little enough of that to date – but a change in the way everything is managed so human folk don't keep adding to the damage they're doing to the planet.'

'But aren't governments everywhere trying to combat global warming… hasn't that been going on for a long time?'

Jasper's face assumed an ironic expression. 'A lot of *talk* has been going on for a long time, but that's not the same as getting down to solving the underlying problem. I'll tell you something – there have been discussions going on for forty years about cutting the amount of carbon we pump into the atmosphere, yet for all that, the amount of fossil fuel burned has almost doubled in recent decades. Then they went for a growth in bio-fuel production; but that only amounted to scratching the surface so rich types could continue driving their "Chelsea Tractors". No, mate – when push comes to shove we are told that the world just can't do without its oil-fix. So, while the oil companies still keep finding new supplies, everything is done to convince us it's our duty to keep buying and wasting the stuff. As a result the damage goes on – the ice sheets melt and sea levels rise. But it's what's happening nearer home that's beginning to have an effect on how people think.'

'Meaning what?'

'Meanin' the weather, that's what! There've been three serious storms already in Britain this year… wind and rain for days on end. Downtown Reading has been flooded twice, the last time only three weeks ago, and now things never seem to get fully tidied up before the next lot arrives. It's not just the water damage that gets people down either. Some of the squalls will take off half your roof and plonk it in the garden next door, and when they do it's the devil's own job to get the insurance companies to pay out. Most claim they haven't got the money anymore; which is not surprising as there are few enough people left still able to pay the premiums. I tell you… it's got serious! Folk want something done – both here and in other countries – and they ain't going to wait forever.'

* * *

The downpour had now eased significantly and Toby looked above the rooftops to where the sun peeped out between ragged clouds, although a blustery wind suggested the wet conditions might easily return. A few people had begun to emerge into the road; a small group gradually forming a little way off, all evidently interested in the camper van and curious about its occupants. As Toby watched, two of them sauntered forward before crouching to look at the number plate. The first was a tall West Indian of between twenty-five and thirty, wearing jeans and a patterned cardigan. A heavy woollen hat, knitted in the colours of the Jamaican flag, sheltered his hairstyle of short dreadlocks. He had a broad round face, puckered with dark marks, and deep-set inquisitive eyes. His partner was shorter – a white teenager with long straight hair that hung down to his shoulders beneath a faded baseball cap. The latter wore loose fitting combat jeans and a denim jacket over a T-shirt showing a glacier pierced through by an arrow artistically shaped in the form of a jet airliner. His face was thin but alert, with bright blue eyes and an expressive mouth that seemed to be fixed midway between a smile and chilled discomfort as he hunched against the cold.

Their heads all but disappeared for a few seconds, before both stood up once more, the older one walking round to the driver's side. He had a good-natured incredulous grin on his face, and following a reassuring nod from Jasper, Toby wound down the window.

'Holy Jesus, man... where did you get this motor from – a museum?' asked the newcomer in a drawling accent.

For a moment Toby couldn't summon a suitable reply, but noted that Jasper was smiling too.

'JKL451F... when the hell was this thing made?' the dreadlocked character went on. '...God, these went out with Glastonbury!'

Jasper replaced the top to the empty tea carton with a loud click. 'Nineteen sixty-seven, to be precise – the old girl's more than fully run in! Do you want to buy, Charlie?'

The West Indian, Charlie Gatlin, leaned across to shake Jasper's hand as his friend also came up.

'I've seen you going around in some weird things, Jasper,' the other said, also offering his hand. 'But you know, I think I like this best of all. ...It isn't every day that someone appears in a Stone Age camper van!'

Both clearly had a sense of humour, and Toby's initial unease quickly thawed as they offered him the hand of welcome also.

'Allow me to introduce Charlie Gatlin and Billy Appletree,' said Jasper. 'My good friends and paid-up members of the "VW Appreciation Society". Gentlemen, this is Toby Freeman, sometime traveller and king of the road... But there is one other thing. I'm afraid breakfast's over – so you'll have to get your own.'

'It's alright for you two in there,' said the fair-haired youth, 'but I'm freezing my jewels off right now. Why don't you come inside and meet the others? We've got a busy day ahead, but you're welcome to spend it with us if you can spare the time.'

'Toby and I have got all the time in the world just now,' said Jasper lightly. 'So you just lead us to your castle.'

* * *

Their castle was a small end of terrace property a little further down the street. This was bounded at the front by a crumbling wall enclosing a small cultivated area where garden crops had evidently recently been harvested, leaving but a single line of root vegetables still growing.

'Parsnips,' said Billy Appletree, stopping briefly, 'perfect for Christmas dinner when they've had the frost on them. ...And I don't suppose we'll be short of a fair bit of that again this winter,' he added shivering.

Number 6, Bagetts Road, overlooked the school next door, and having passed through a small untidy lounge stacked with packing cases, they made their way into the kitchen where through misty a window, Toby once more noted the group of mobile homes tightly clustered in the adjoining playground. There were two people standing by the nearest one – a young couple, the woman holding a baby – who waved before beginning to make their way through a gap in the garden hedge.

'Casimo and Angelina,' said Billy, lighting a primus stove. 'They'll be happy to have a cup of tea and a bit of toast. I'll make us all some if you're not too full?'

'Tea's always welcome,' offered Toby, 'but not if it's any trouble.'

'No trouble, friend,' Billy replied good-naturedly. 'We all muck in to help here; and everyone's welcome if they can stand the muddle.'

Billy was right to concede the last point; for this must have been far from the tidiest house in the street. The lounge window was broken and had been boarded up, so it was necessary to keep the light on for all but the brightest hours of the day, while the few basic furnishings were faded and well worn. The room also contained two bicycles propped together to form a clothes-horse, upon which a variety of shirts, washable nappies and underwear was drying. But the most surprising thing was a large hole knocked through a wall into the neighbouring house.

'That's our extension!' said Charlie, seating himself on a packing case to eat a plate of toast and cheese. 'The owner wouldn't give us permission to go in through the front door; so we thought we'd do a bit of conversion work of our own from this side.'

'But mightn't it collapse?' asked Toby, looking a little nervously at the gaping cavity.

'No... we're pretty sure that won't happen. We do keep a check, but I reckon there's worse things to worry about.'

Toby found it quite difficult to think there might be more important things than the possibility of having three tons of bricks and mortar fall on your head. 'But the owner... can't he prosecute you, or get you evicted?'

'He could try, if he was here, but he's not. In fact he hasn't been seen in Reading for over six months. It seems he's a property millionaire who owns hundreds of houses like this one. But his real problem is that a lot of them are in some very unfortunate areas – places threatened by the floods or affected by things like the mini-tornado that came through here last spring. This whole terrace was damaged then, and the house at the far end lost its roof! So the council has pronounced half the properties uninhabitable: while to date the insurance companies won't pay for repairs. The landlord tried to get tough at first – sent the bailiffs round when homeless squatters moved in. But many of his heavyweights had suffered the same themselves and he found it difficult to have his will carried out. Even where an eviction was successful, the same person, usually helped by local people, was normally back in by the following day. The police weren't bothered about helping either (they'd got more than enough problems to deal with), so it seems Mr Runtlett, that's his name, was left to lump it. The rumour is that he's gone to live in the south of France where the weather has been a bit calmer; though the last we heard they'd had serious storms and landslips there too. Poor chap, I do feel sorry for him!'

There was a ripple of laughter around the room, following which Toby had time to study the faces of the group as they discussed recent events. There were ten present in all, including the small baby, Jasper and himself, and he was now introduced to the couple seen earlier coming into the garden. The woman was Angelina Voltman, a bright lively twenty-six year old who had spent four years as a shop supervisor before losing her job when recession forced the chain of stores she worked for to close. She was well-informed and intelligent, with a ready wit and sense of humour; her self-deprecating jokes about an ample bust and figure endearing her to all. Fond of chunky bangles and jewellery, Angelina wore these with a relaxed poise and finesse that rich women, having spent a hundred times more upon themselves, can rarely achieve. Her partner was Arganan Bagchi – (Argie for short) – a British Asian from a large family of doctors and lawyers. He had defended many residents faced with eviction due to arrears of rent in recent times, and having met Angelina when she was forced to leave a former residence following the floods, now lived with her in their temporary home. He was thirty-two years old, with a receding hairline above a kind, reflective face and dark eyebrows. The most calm and rational of the group, Argie was always thoughtful in advance of making a decision and seldom wrong in the advice he gave.

The final three newcomers were a black African woman named Tamara Welkise, and her children Anardus, ten, and Kelia, seven, who had appeared through the gap in the wall from the rooms they lived in next door with Charlie Gatlin. They were a cheerful family, the children immediately rushing towards their father to demand that he indulge in a riotous play fight, to which Charlie readily acquiesced. Tamara was quieter, looking on with a gentle smiling expression as the children tumbled on the dusty carpet with their dad, and only stepping forward occasionally with a protective hand when one of them looked like crashing into a bike handle or the edge of a packing case. Now forty-five, she too was a well-educated woman, a teacher, who had escaped her country at the outbreak of a guerrilla war over land and shortages of water. It had been a conflict costing thousands their lives; following which the ruling junta, in search of scapegoats, blamed the resulting ills upon the educated classes. She still bore the scars of a savage beating doled out just before her departure, and would never talk about the weeks of terror she had suffered in her homeland.

'Well, time's beginning to get on,' said Billy, standing up after a while with his thumbs tucked into the top of his jeans. 'The protest starts in four hours and we need to be sure that those holdin' the strings pay attention this time – even the complacent blockheads at Westminster.'

'No worries there man,' said Charlie Gatlin. 'Half of Reading will be out on this one, and the same will be happening in another fifty towns and cities around the country supposin' our plans go right. If those in control manage to ignore us this time we'll know we're banging our heads against a brick wall!'

'...And should that happen,' Billy added, leaning forward with a determined grin, 'then we'll just have to do it all over again, won't we – until even the blindest among 'em can't help but get the message? People are hurting and the powerful need to see it!'

'But what are you protesting about exactly... How will you do it?' asked Toby, suddenly finding himself thinking aloud.

'We'll be demonstrating about the whole bloody mess, that's what!' continued Billy, growing animated. 'The way it's being dealt with – the way the rich and those still with jobs to go to like to pretend that there's nothing really wrong... Or if they can bring themselves to accept that there is – that it's probably more our fault than theirs! We want some positive steps because there'll be a disaster to follow if nothing's done soon, and we're not prepared to accept that the wealthy, the ones that rule us, should remain in denial while feathering their own nests and leaving us in the mire. Reading, like every other place anywhere near a river, is starting to fall apart and become uninhabitable, that's obvious; and we're sick of being told that we don't understand the facts when we complain... or worse, having the law sent round to sort us out!'

'Too right, man,' interrupted Charlie, now sitting in the corner with his children at his feet. 'A small group of us decided to protest outside a local supermarket about the high price of bread and milk some time back. It was a peaceful thing see – spontaneous, with women and children present. We were only calling and chanting – just explaining to other folks that they had a right to join us in voicing our complaint. I tell you... we started with about forty, but within an hour there were more like four hundred! People were coming in from all points of the compass, from every street and across the park. That's when the police arrived: a squad car initially – then a van with officers armed in riot gear. We thought it was a joke at first; just some none too senior officer overreacting… But no, the one in charge said we had to move right away – that we were causing an obstruction and restraining legitimate trade …"provoking an incident likely to cause a breach of the peace!" But that charge seemed so silly and ridiculous that everyone just started to wave their banners and shout back, sayin' how stupid the coppers looked in their helmets and visors. That's when it all turned sour. They weren't about to be ignored and moved in to break us up. Most people around me stood their ground at first; so they started beating us with batons – kicking and stamping! A little kid was knocked down and half killed, while more than a dozen people had legs and arms broken. One pregnant woman even lost her baby from the shock and battering she took. As for myself… one of those bastards caught me with his riot shield and near split my head open.'

Here Charlie pushed the woollen cap back from his forehead to reveal a newly healed four-inch scar.

'So what will you do today?' asked Toby, breaking the silence that had followed.

Angelina, who had remained quiet until then, stepped forward as if deciding to speak for them all. 'This time it will be different, Toby. There will be thousands with us today. We're going to bring the town to a halt, right during the evening rush, just when all the wealthy businessmen are hurrying home for tea with their wives, or getting off trains after a busy day in London making money for themselves. We'll block all the roads – lock up the streets for a bit to make a few more listen to what we've to say. They'll get home much later than usual and be quite grumpy, I'm sure; but maybe some will be a little wiser – and at least they'll know we're here.'

The others nodded their agreement and he could sense their resolve. They were not extemists, but thoughtful and caring people who wanted recognition and greater evidence of progress toward finding lasting solutions – a new way of doing things.

Arganan Bagchi now looked towards Toby. He had listened quietly to all that was said and summarised what everyone felt: 'What we are asking for is a period of renewal, a period of change – a move away from so many of us having to live in run-down places, while greedy landlords charge us a fortune for having a roof over our heads. Nobody wants to be at the end of the line; but the problem is that before long, if we wreck our fragile world, nine tenths of the human race will find themselves in dire circumstances… Yet we believe people can still save both the planet and themselves by sharing more and consuming less. But the rich will undoubtedly have to give up their palaces of gold and unsustainable privileges for that to work.'

* * *

It was time to make final preparations for the march and both inside the house and in the streets round about a bustle of human activity grew up. Banners were produced from hallways and corridors, musical instruments assembled and tuned, megaphones tested and sturdy boots lined up on doorsteps. There was a good deal of joking and laughing, but beneath the mirth lay a shared sense of purpose, a determination that their efforts would succeed.

By midday most things were ready and a steady stream of protesters, representing groups from roads and streets nearby, went to and fro from Number 6, Bagetts Road. The visitors too had played their part in the proceedings – Jasper having positioned himself by the primus in the kitchen to ensure a constant supply of hot tea or coffee, while Toby allowed himself to be led away through the hole in the wall to the lounge of the adjoining house where a makeshift studio had been set up. Here he was enlisted to help complete some of the home-made banners that would be carried that day: banners that demanded among other things "Justice for the Storm Victims", "End the Property Rip Off" and "Action Now to Prevent Further Climate Chaos". He found his fellow workers' enthusiasm infectious, the children taking part as eagerly as their parents – skilfully sticking and tacking or adding their own creative touches to the finished works.

The little girl, Kelia, looked towards him at one point as they stood on either side of a trellis table – her hands, forehead and the bib of her dungarees speckled and smudged with a variety of vibrant colours. She had been intricately decorating her own small banner with a border of brightly coloured flowers, tongue tightly wedged at the corner of her mouth. Now, a little shyly, Kelia held it up for Toby to admire, her eyes twinkling with inner delight as she sought his approval. He congratulated her heartily, for although Kelia seemed to have got a good deal of the thick colouring paint upon herself, the flowers were delightfully and accurately done, with little hint of smears or blotching. He looked down at his own rather ragged and amateurish efforts and was happy to concede who had proved the better artist. The slogan she'd chosen was simple and to the point – "Please Care for Everyone".

'That's brilliant, Kelia!' Toby said with feeling.

She grinned widely, showing two rows of bright, even teeth. 'It's what I really want,' she said, meeting his gaze. 'Cos if we care for each other everything will be alright, won't it?'

It was an innocent and touching sentiment that only a young child, free as yet from feelings of hopelessness and cynicism, could have uttered.

* * *

They moved off together just after three o'clock in the afternoon, most turning out into the street well-dressed against the cold air and mizzling rain. It was already late in the year, and the light, never bright even in the middle of the day, was now fading fast beneath a renewed blanket of threatening cloud. One or two neon lamps already glowed as they entered the main street leading to the centre of Reading, where the tyres of passing cars and buses sent up a thin spray from damp tarmac. The walkers gathered for some minutes at a busy junction, their numbers steadily swelling as streams of protesters spilled out of side roads and through the gates of a municipal park. Many were in good heart and voice, cheerfully greeting friends, blowing whistles, banging drums and exchanging plans. But there were others with more, serious expressions: family parties, couples, people in ones and twos, all constantly added themselves to the throng that soon began to overflow the pavement, slowing traffic.

The majority of motorists were supportive rather than critical – ordinary people experiencing hardships of their own. Many honked a lively greeting while leaning out of windows to call approval. One mini-van, full of mud spattered construction workers, pulled up close to where Toby was standing by the pavement edge, its enthusiastic occupants giving "thumbs up" signs through the glass. The one in the front passenger seat wound down his side window.

'Where are you headed?' he asked, shaking the hand of the nearest protester.

Billy Appletree stepped forward. 'To the town centre, pal! We're going to shut it off for a couple of hours – make it a little difficult for our lords and masters to get home tonight. Come and join us later if you can make it.'

A police car had just appeared, and having parked a little further along, two stern officers approached to move the van on.

'It looks like the fuzz are getting a little flustered,' said the labourer, seeing them. 'Oh well, must be off! But don't worry, we'll be down later. I know plenty of others that will turn out too when we tell them what's going on. It's time the complacent bastards that run this show were made uncomfortable. See ya!'

With that the van sped away, brushing past the policemen just as they pushed to the front of the crowd. The first officer, a wide, thick-necked constable with a cropped moustache, was clearly not happy at missing his quarry.

'Right,' he said with puffed authority to the circle of faces now turned towards him. 'Who's in charge here?'

For a moment no reply was offered as people looked from one to another. Then Charlie Gatlin turned to him, with Kelia held on his arm. 'We all are,' he said. 'All of us – even my daughter here.'

There was a ripple of laughter from the gathering; but the simple logic of his reply had summed up the general mood and an involuntary closing of ranks took place as people drew together to hear the exchange. The police officer meanwhile found himself standing on the very edge of the pavement, with buses and taxis moving past within inches; his colleague having already retreated to the patrol car, which was itself causing an obstruction further along. He clearly felt vulnerable – perhaps wondering what he might do if the crowd abruptly moved forward.

'You must all move on without any delay, or I'll have you for obstructing the traffic. Get away from here now, or else you'll be arrested. Then we'll find out at the police station who's responsible.'

It was a valiant effort at bluff, thought Toby. But how exactly might two officers go about arresting fifty, a hundred or five hundred people?

*   *   *

For their part, the protesters were happy to respond to the policeman's demands. They were nowhere near the town centre yet, which had been their target all along. So the long, winding and ever growing file set off once more – although it now overflowed the pavement to such an extent that the pace of the traffic was thereafter inevitably governed by the speed of the marchers. Further police officers soon took up positions in an effort to control proceedings, but the protest had taken on a steady momentum of its own; and as much as they might try to divert it from a chosen course, the huge numbers of walkers, if diverted from their intended route, simply blocked another road or highway, thus leading to the inevitable creeping paralysis of central Reading. The same was happening on all sides of the town: north, south, east and west, as getting on for a quarter of a million people took to the streets – many leaving loved ones at home who would have joined them but for illness or disability.

The authorities nationally had anticipated for some time that something like this might happen. But in most major towns and cities they were wrong-footed and overwhelmed that evening as a seemingly little co-ordinated demonstration brought the outflow of millions onto the streets to protest at government inaction in dealing with climate change, profiteering and corruption. Their leaders were wrong to think it spontaneous, however, for a network of contacts had long been developing among ordinary people – a bond of fellowship that brought hundreds of thousands out to stand patiently in the rain as the skies opened.

By five o'clock they stood in ranks ten deep across every thoroughfare within half a mile of the railway station and Reading's commercial heart. No vehicle could move, except those allowed through for emergency purposes, and when an ambulance did approach their ranks, the crowd would move aside as one; only to close again behind like a human door, as soon as it had passed. Yet it would be a protest without violence; the weather saw to that for while the police once or twice used strong-arm tactics early on, later, with the rain cascading in rivulets from their helmets and seeping into shoes, most constables seemed to have little will to challenge the stubborn insistence of the protesters.

Meanwhile, as disgruntled city gents earlier disgorged from packed commuter trains sat unable to move and fuming in their plush limousines, so too did peeved accountants, bankers and other members of the business community find themselves trapped in their offices as a drenched street party, accompanied by dozens of amateur bands and musicians, went on below. Hair became plastered to innumerable heads, banners ran and peeled, but few if any melted away or were disheartened.

Much of the local and national press had also been caught unprepared, although four or five London based newspapers and periodicals, acting on tip-offs, had sent reporters down earlier in the day. One of these, a young journalist from an up and coming ecology magazine, was standing with a group of fellow newspaper columnists in a large crowd outside the railway station at the height of the protest. Toby, with the others from Bagetts Road, had gravitated there too, and turning for a hundredth time to look across the heads of the dripping crowd, his eyes settled upon the man. Wet through and cold himself, he was immediately struck by the steady look and intent manner of the other. The pressman could have been little better off than he, but presented an air of composure matched by few around him, appearing self-contained and relatively dry in what were now the most trying circumstances. He wore a tailored raincoat and a matching hat that gave him the almost theatrical appearance of a 1930s' detective, but it was his face that held Toby's attention...

Toby knew it, even though he'd last seen the reporter as a child. It was the face of the boy he'd swept up from the roadside in London – the reserved yet calm and attentive expression, high forehead and elegant black rimmed glasses made him sure of it!

* * *

Kline Anderson, now twenty-five years old, stood looking over the crowd at a small but colourful quartet of protesters standing on a low platform, little more than head and shoulders above the general height of the crowd. These included Billy Appletree, Angelina Voltman and Charlie Gatlin holding Kelia. The young media man was much taken by their spirit and good humour. All were thoroughly the worse for wear: cold, wet through and tired after three hours in the rain, yet all but Billy maintained a light-hearted enthusiasm. Kelia, sitting on her father's arm, still held her draggled banner, the colours of the once delicate design now running together, although the heartfelt slogan could still be made out. An orange polythene bag had been fashioned round her shoulders and her woolly hat had sunk down below her ears. Angelina was strumming an ancient and battered guitar (half ruined by the wet) to a group of women and children behind her, while Billy and Charlie talked to a local newswoman positioned just below them. Billy, clearly perished in his thin jacket and T-shirt, hunched against the chilly breeze, but nevertheless grew increasingly passionate as he spoke – his raised voice drawing the attention of everybody close by, including Toby and Kline Anderson, both of whom moved closer to catch his words. Soon Toby managed to get within a few paces of the platform, as did the journalist, who now stood less than ten feet away intently studying the two protesters and judging the reaction of other onlookers round about.

'They tried to stop us,' said Billy, waving vaguely to somewhere in the distance, 'thought they could just turn us back... But we came anyway, and I just feel so thankful to everyone for being here.'

There was a cheer of approval, full-throated and good-hearted.

At the same moment, however, Billy, by now on the point of exhaustion from overlong exposure to the elements, suddenly seemed shaken and deflated, his shoulders slumping loosely as the rain dripped from the end of his pinched nose.

'I only hope it will do some good, that's all,' he barely managed to add with a stifled intake of breath.

A murmur, fading to near silence, fell upon the listening group, broken only by the sound of distant sirens and the muffled drumming of a samba band a little further along. The protesters craned forward expectantly, ready to hear Billy speak for them all, but he was temporarily unable to go on. It was one of those awkward moments when a gathering can begin to break up – when the impetus that brought everyone together is lost and many begin to think of drifting away to return home. That might have happened now had Kline Anderson not moved forward to speak. This had a strange effect, for as he did so, those closest stood respectfully aside leaving him in a small open space. He turned slowly to right and left before looking steadily up at Billy.

'What is it you really want?' he asked in a steady voice that drew the listener. 'What do you hope to achieve by being here today?'

Billy seemed to emerge from a trance at this point, his chilled and dejected frame lifted by the dual note of encouragement and sincerity that lay behind the speaker's words. He pulled back his slumped shoulders and gazed down; then, having gathered his thoughts, began to speak passionately once more.

'People just see everything being blown away by the storms, or washed into the gutter; but nothing ever gets done to save us from all this... The planet's had enough, man... it's paying us back. We've gotta change what we do or else the time will come when we are all left to starve and die. We're living closer to the edge now... people are angry and scared because they don't know what to do. But if things get any worse they sure are going to do something. If we can't make the powerful folks sit up and listen we're going to have to rise up like the "Big Bad Wolf" and blow their fancy houses down!'

The gathering had become quieter still, as if not only those nearby but many others further off were listening. Most heads nodded in agreement with Billy's words.

'Me, I'm not a violent person... but I'm gonna tear the head off the next weak and greasy puppet scientist or politician that tells me we can do nothing about climate change, or that we have to accept the way things are as our only future. That's just boloney, a recipe for fools and disaster – something I wouldn't wish upon my worst enemy, let alone my own flesh and blood. Therefore, someone's got to come along soon to knock some heads together and make the ones in power see sense.'

At this point he crouched down so that his and Kline Anderson's eyes were level – his next words voiced as a profound entreaty.

'I don't think places like this are ever going to work properly again – big towns and cities I mean – places run by bureaucrats and financiers who just bleed the world dry. There's no real hope here. We need to break out, to take back control of our lives – to have our own land and a place to support ourselves. Tell them that, man!'

Kline Anderson gave the slightest nod of the head, the lines around his eyes wrinkling into a reassuring smile. But just then a commotion started up at the edge of the group. A burly businessman, wearing a pinstriped suit and carrying a rolled up umbrella, had come out of an adjacent office block where he was the successful manager of an estate agent and letting firm. He'd been listening from an upstairs window and now, thoroughly annoyed that the bedraggled crowd had kept him so long from returning to a comfortable fireside deep in the Oxfordshire countryside, he had come down to sort matters out himself. If the police wouldn't take action against a crowd of idle protesters he would – the conveniently overlooked fact that the payments contributing to the success of his business came directly from the shallow pockets of many of them being of no concern to him whatsoever. A more aggressive gathering might well have seen him off immediately; but most of those present were simply taken aback by the property dealer's vociferous, headlong approach.

'What do you ignorant swine think you are doing?' he bawled, pushing people aside and giving vent to his short temper. 'Get out of here – go home, the lot of you. If I had my way you'd all be thrown in jail and not let out for a month!'

To him, it would seem, they were like children; and having started he would make sure they recognised the error of their ways – even if it meant beating some sense into a number of them! Having reached the platform on which Billy stood, the volatile gentleman jumped heavily up and gripped him firmly by the arm.'

'You!' he barked. 'You're one of the ringleaders and must come with me! I'll soon find a policeman that's got sense enough to deal with your malarkey.'

This was enough for Charlie Gatlin who was standing just behind. Still balancing Kelia he stepped forward to intervene, only for the businessman to round upon him in a renewed excess of rage.

'Try your luck, would you?' he barked. 'Don't think you can creep up on me! I've dealt with bigger and tougher thugs than you a thousand times before.'

He struck out violently with the umbrella, narrowly missing Charlie's head with the downward swipe, but clipping Kelia's shoulder and breaking in half the wet and curling banner she held. A gasp went up from the crowd and Charlie, having checked that the now crying child was not seriously hurt before putting her into Angelina's care, turned again to face his assailant – his initial look of shock turning to one of blind anger.

The estate agent manager then struck and missed again, realising from the expressions of outrage upon the faces of those around him that he had probably overstepped the bounds of caution, but still unwisely relying on bluster to carry the day.

'Come on then,' he called to Charlie, 'we'll see who's the better man. One that pays taxes, such as I – or a scoundrel like you!'

Things were about to deteriorate rapidly when a lone policeman came forward from the back of the crowd and jumped up onto the platform to restrain him. The officer had been standing to the rear unnoticed for several minutes, both monitoring the scene and sympathising more than a little with the protesters. It was his job to ensure that the businessman did not cause an affray and he now performed this duty with some vigour, forcing the gentleman's head downwards while sharply twisting his arm behind his back so that the umbrella fell to the ground.

'Unhand me, man!' yelled the property manager who, upon seeing the policeman approach, had initially imagined he'd come to give assistance but now found himself held in an ignominious position of submission.

'I'm arresting you for assault and a breach of the peace, Sir,' said the officer, stoutly tightening his grip. 'And I suggest you come quietly as there are already two or three hundred witnesses to your aggressive behaviour.'

A second cheer went up from the crowd with the arrival of another policeman and the offending individual was led away to the accompaniment of several uncomplimentary shouts and boos. Meanwhile, those on the platform were left comforting Kelia – apart from Billy Greenwood who had jumped down next to Kline Anderson.

'You saw what happened,' he said. 'Was it him or us that was in the wrong?'

'Definitely him; and you can depend upon me to tell my readers as much.'

'You will?'

'Certainly... and don't give up, my friend,' the journalist added with a penetrating look.

'The name's Billy.'

'Take heart, Billy... not all of us who wear suits or come from London are bad. A lot of us agree with you and will do all we can to give support for your cause... things undoubtedly seem set to get worse; but some of us may yet live long enough to witness better times. Now, I must be off as I need to catch my train... that's if you haven't managed to stop those too.'

He offered his hand, which Billy shook, the still heavily falling rain running over their joined palms. Then he was gone into the crowd – the dark Homburg hat passing beneath rain speckled streetlamps before disappearing from view.

* * *

By now it was getting late and the protesters, having largely achieved their aims, began to break up: first in shuffling masses, then in dozens together, and finally in small groups of six or eight – the great assembly gradually melting away toward the suburbs. But it was not until a little before ten o'clock that the marchers from Bagetts Road neared home, with Toby walking at the tail of the group beside Jasper, who had kept a low profile throughout the proceedings. Just ahead Kelia skipped along at her father's side, frequently looking over her shoulder towards them.

'Interesting people ain't they?' said the little man as they strolled along eating chips. 'But it's best that you should be getting on; for there's no sense in putting down any sort of lasting roots here, as that will only make for a harder parting later.'

'As if I could find a true place to be,' thought Toby. '…What do I know of permanence anymore?'

* * *

Thus Toby was persuaded to take his leave at the door, saying that he had other places to visit and that a night journey on uncrowded roads would make for an easier trip.

'You're always welcome to come around, man,' said Charlie, standing on the doorstep as Kelia peeped round his leg. 'I'm not the only one that would like to see you again… and there's already someone I could mention that would rather you didn't have to leave at all.'

With these words they parted, and still damp, although the rain had stopped an hour before, Toby climbed into the camper van to start the engine as Jasper sidled close to the passenger window. They now had Bagetts Road to themselves, apart from a single large bird that flew through the beam of the nearest streetlight sending a shadow across Jasper's upturned face.

'You'll not be coming with me, I suppose?' asked Toby, already knowing the answer.

'Not this time, mate. You just look out for me another time you're at a loose end, eh.'

'There is one loose end that comes to mind…' said Toby deliberately. '…That of my fortune… with the dice?'

Jasper spread the thumb and four fingers upon his right hand and held it out.

'Done earlier, mate. No repeats yet… or anything special either,' he added meaningfully. 'You must rest easy, Toby – and stay patient for a while longer.'

Then, with no word of farewell, he casually sauntered off through the glistening puddles and disappeared from view, leaving footsteps echoing down an empty road.

'So I'm alone once more,' mused Toby, still looking in the direction that Jasper had gone. 'Another episode has run its course, and what's left for me but to move on again?'

So thinking, he did – turning and setting off through the empty streets before departing into the night across the rapidly swelling River Thames.

Chapter Six

War Without Victory

(2041-2050)

B Y NOW MATTERS IN THE WIDER WORLD were moving too. Had Toby been able to orbit
the globe in a distant satellite; or if a swallow had circled the earth, each would have
seen many signs that all was not well among God's people. The rumblings of conflict
were growing at a hundred points, awakening a spark that would soon ignite a desperate
fire – a steadily rising flame born variously of fear, mistrust and simmering prejudice.
With his eye pressed to a telescope at the satellite glass, Toby would have seen, in
the eroded lands of Central Asia, desperate disputes over exhausted soil and denuded
steppe; while still further east, he might look down upon scenes of riot and murder as
hungry peasants fought for a just share of rice and grain. In South America he would
have witnessed threatened populations daily facing the bloody encroachment of corrupt
governments and businesses upon the dwindling fragments of their ancestral heritage.
While in Africa a savage powder keg was being pushed closer to the fire, as a continent
now stripped of precious food and raw materials by competing power blocks stood on
the edge of widespread starvation, anarchy and genocide. High above, Toby could only
have watched and done nothing, but those in the human boiling pot below resorted,
almost inevitably, to a step they had so often taken in former times of need and creeping
despair – they went to war.

Yet the path to conflict opening up came as a surprise to many, being more the result
of miscalculation than premeditated aggression by one nation towards another.

* * *

By the middle of the twenty-first century the governments of the USA, China, Russia, India
and Europe had refined their ability to "respond and retaliate" to any threat that another
might present. Elaborate parades of military might promised such dire consequences
for all, that a permanent stand-off between the potential antagonists seemed to have

been established. All future wars could be worked out as a simulated series of strategic advances and withdrawals upon a computerised chessboard, in which no pieces would be lost and no ground permanently gained or given. The armed might of the wealthiest and most powerful countries was primarily maintained to safeguard each nation's economic interests and need never be deployed in anger. To date, this balance of "Mutually Assured Destruction" – "MAD" – had already been in existence for almost a hundred years, and appeared set to continue. But in January 2041 a conflict erupted in the Middle East that would undermine such comfortable logic.

It began in a small way following a period of intense drought, when a group of Arab villagers, desperate to gain access to fresh water and food to feed their starving children, stormed an Israeli Kibbutz in Gaza. Rockets and high explosives were used to destroy defensive walls, and in the ensuing attack the Israeli settlers either killed or driven off. The militants' victory was short-lived however, and within hours the Israeli air force struck back, destroying the attackers; while ground troops drove deep into Arab lands seeking revenge. It had happened before, but this time the outcome was somewhat different, for the following day a subsequent air strike met with substantial losses when Russian rockets, backed by ground based technical crews, successfully broke up incoming formations.

The evidence of what had happened was unequivocal and the situation compounded when, that very evening, the Russian President announced that Russia, which had been supplying weapons to Arab fighters in Gaza, would not only do so again, but would consider itself at war with Israel if Israeli forces failed to withdraw from occupied territory within twenty-four hours. It was a foregone conclusion that this would not happen, and when the Israeli air force attacked again they were confronted in the skies by a squadron of Russian fighters. During the ensuing dogfight two aircraft from each side were shot down, a captured Russian pilot subsequntly being paraded before the western media. An escalation of hostilities was inevitable from this point and before the day's end the USA, having condemned the attack on Israel, declared itself in a state of war with Russia. Meanwhile China threatened retaliation against both should its borders or interests be threatened; while the governments of India and Europe, having initially attempted to act as mediators, were drawn in on the side of the USA following the destruction of a Royal Navy frigate by Russian missiles off the Israeli coast. Thus, within the space of seventy-two hours, the road to war had been travelled and the citizens of the earth collectively held their breath.

* * *

But the outcome was not as predictable as many feared; for although fighting flared up in another dozen places within the week, there were to be no nuclear exchanges or massed attacks by well-ordered regiments. Instead, the world slipped into the grip of another kind of conflict – one fought out increasingly over land and food, and regularly viewed on mobile telephone, computer or television screen – a twenty-four-hour news war, updated each morning and throughout the day. The images were often frightening; although for the majority, few recorded events close to home: a bombing attack on a border city in Pakistan, the overrunning of an Indonesian provincial town by rebels, the destruction of a passenger aircraft on a Warsaw airfield, the mining of office blocks in Sao Paolo. Yet the great powers rarely came directly to blows, and for months on end most of those that died were lost from among populations that had already suffered severely from the worst effects of climate change and related natural disasters. Indeed, a whole year elapsed before, in the spring of 2042, a deliberate act of invasion was attempted.

Then a Chinese army of half a million men was sent into Laos and Burma in an effort, it was claimed, "to secure the region from Indian aggression". This brought a matching response from the Indian Government, but within two days of the assault commencing, a vicious cyclone suddenly struck southern Burma, followed immediately by torrential monsoons and floods throughout South-East Asia. The Chinese advance immediately ground to a standstill as its troops, now cut off and without supplies, found themselves desperately in need of rescue. The world looked on in awe as the opposing armies melted away or were reconstituted into massive relief forces, with each soldier more concerned about battling the ravages of nature than resuming conflict with his military enemy.

There would continue to be some set piece engagements between high tech forces: as when an American strike group in the South Atlantic, defending the USA's claim to mineral rights in Antarctica, met a Russian task force sent to dislodge them. This resulted in a two-day tactical battle in which three Russian nuclear submarines and the US Navy strike carrier *Washington* were sent to the bottom – the whole episode being beamed live for television. But the affair proved indecisive when the Russians, bruised but not beaten, drew off due to bad weather and the United States, now suffering the worst series of storms and hurricanes in recorded history at home, declined to continue the encounter.

On another occasion, a Russian supply base on the now ice free coast of Northern Siberia was attacked by American marines; but having managed to destroy some of the facilities established there to service the Russian Arctic Fleet, the force, now faced with plummeting temperatures and relentless blizzards, retired to their transports before returning home to avoid isolation and further loss. Thus, while there was an element of tit for tat in these confrontations, it was nature and the weather that decided the final outcomes.

* * *

So the years of indecision, posturing and confusion passed and the bigger players, far from growing in power and might, appeared sapped by uncertainty, like closely matched bullies on a school playground – afraid to come to decisive blows for fear that the other might prove the stronger. Aggression was replaced by caution as the main protagonists progressively withdrew to their own borders, sealing these ever tighter against the outside world and only venturing out to secure, preferably by trade, the food and materials that it was impossible to provide from within.

These isolationist policies left other lesser warring nations to fight on against each other over land and resources, without the intervention of more powerful allies. Under such circumstances it would be the poorer nations of Africa that fared worst of all. In these countries, already hungry and destitute people, their lands looted by the rich powers, died in countless millions – the guns and bullets sold to warlords in exchange for oil and raw materials, often being purchased at a lesser cost than rice or bread. Indeed, there were some that surmised that if the war had gone on for another ten years, parts of the continent might have been all but entirely expunged of human beings; as surely as it was of the animal species decimated to provide food for soldiers and starving villagers. But once again nature intervened as a drought, beginning in the spring of 2048, spread throughout southern and western Africa. Arid and desert like conditions scorched vast, previously fertile areas, driving whole populations north and eastwards in search of water and food – a great migration of human kind. The world merely looked on at first: viewers witnessing once more the all too familiar scenes of misery and want so frequently beamed into their homes during recent times. Yet this was not a catastrophe limited in scale to one country or region as before, but one affecting an entire land mass, and many, now struggling to cope with the effects of climate change themselves, recognised the trauma of their own experiences multiplied tenfold on the faces of those on the television screen. Millions watched in awe as the nightmare unfolded, and it was not long before the first stirrings of humanity flickered again as people looked beyond the shadow of war for ways of providing assistance to the desperate. Within little more than three weeks the first convoy of aid, crewed entirely by volunteers, departed from the shores of Europe, viewers in a hundred lands willing it to get safely through. There were many that thought the ships would be sent to the bottom by enemy action – but they were allowed to journey on, and apart from three wrecked in a tropical storm, all reached their destinations unmolested; to be followed by others in a quickening stream. So the spell was broken and further moves to feed the starving initiated. A massive airlift was organised from China and further convoys sailed from South America, the USA, Australia and India, as people across the globe came together to ease an unprecedented humanitarian crisis.

* * *

Circling above, Toby might have wondered at such an outcome – that peace should return without a victor being declared. But as the wise were aware, another group of mighty players had taken centre stage – the swollen forces of nature, now gorged on carbon and primed to spit unpredictable fury. In future, no national interest or desire for influence could rationally be seen as of more importance than managing the powerful and increasingly challenging impacts of a changing climate. Thus, following much negotiation, an end to all hostilities was declared on 1st April 2050 – the warring nations laying aside their differences in the interests of mutual long-term survival.

Yet, for all the urgent scientific warnings and timely show of good sense, the voices urging renewed industrial expansion, increased growth and unrestrained consumption would again disastrously come to the fore.

Chapter Seven

Heatwave, Inundation and Chaos

THE FOLLOWING YEARS ENCOMPASSED A TURNING POINT for the whole world, for while the horror of universal war had been averted a more potent threat was now at the door. The searing heat and drought that had drawn attention to the plight of Africa did not abate in weeks or months, but went on, creeping across the globe, for another four disastrous years. Fertile lands in North Africa, South Asia, Central America and Southern Europe were reduced to dust – useless wastes of burned forests, dried lakes and barren savannah. In the summer months temperatures rose relentlessly to above forty degrees centigrade, leaving bemused weathermen struggling to explain "the recurring phenomenon". Industry and commerce slowed down, agricultural production diminished, transport infrastructure stagnated, while civil construction work became almost impossible as metal beams twisted or bricklayers refused to ply their trade. The hours between eleven and four became a virtual "no go" time when only the foolish and the desperate would sally forth beneath baking skies. There were some, due to the nature of their work, that did have to venture out for emergency reasons: doctors, paramedics and those bringing urgent supplies to the elderly and needy – although these began to dress more like rice farmers in far off paddy fields than health professionals, often arriving in loose shirts, straw hats, sandals and culottes. Sadly, their services were much in demand as the changing conditions took a rising toll on the old and infirm. Heatstroke and other related maladies became commonplace, leading to a sharp rise in hospital admissions. But for many, help came too late and they died, dehydrated and alone, in sweltering flats and respectable bungalows.

* * *

All this went on month after month, causing leaders in the "developed" world to wring their hands over lost production and the decline in GDP. Then, in the summer of 2051, a great industrial summit was convened at which several hundred sharp suited politicians and "business experts" endorsed without exception a massive push to restore former levels of commercial activity. Some production would now, of necessity, be carried out at night, but to speed the process of recovery the widespread provision of air-conditioning would be required in all places of work and commerce. No expense on fuel and resources should be considered too great in the drive to get the economy "back on its feet".

Within a few days of these announcements, directives were going out to increase production ten and twenty fold. By the following year every office, large and small, in London, Mumbai and a thousand other cities, had been equipped with air-conditioning units, enabling staff to continue at work whatever the heat or humidity. Steelworks, car production lines, chemical plants and refineries returned to full output, many working round the clock to supply "pent up demand",each of these temples of industry being cooled by a vast array of extractor fans and ventilation devices operating at full capacity both day and night. So the operatives returned to work and commercial profits began to flow healthily once more, fuelled by a surge in "high street demand" which quickly rose back to and then exceeded previous levels. Some did remark that the weather was, if anything, becoming even more infernally hot and unpredictable; but most accepted the received wisdom of governments and media that a little extra discomfort must be tolerated if "normal consumption patterns" were to resume.

* * *

Yet the value of any action has to be set against any negative consequences it might bring. To provide energy for this revived production, and to power the millions of cooling units making it possible, existing coal, gas and oil fired generators returned to full output; while a thousand new installations were brought into use, each pouring out a huge volume of global warming gas to add to that already circulating in the atmosphere. The result was entirely predictable, for like the straw that broke the camel's back, this ill-considered push for recovery and further economic growth tipped climate change beyond the point of no return!

The two-year long heatwave shrivelling half the earth moved into a third and then a fourth summer. Melting ice sheets cracked and began to slide into the sea, the last high mountain glaciers to melt, and sea levels – which had already risen five centimetres since the start of the century – to rise dramatically. Most preferred to give little thought to these events as they rushed about their daily lives, but those watching the developing situation in Arctic weather stations and coastal monitoring centres became more nervous about the outcome. 'What would happen in future years,' they asked, 'when the searing heat had passed, but rising sea levels and other accumulated climate effects remained?' The answer was not long in coming; for the closing months of the year 2054 became a time of climate upheaval around the globe. The drought that had spread northwards four years previously was dramatically ended by a succession of massive storms across the

Northern Hemisphere. Cyclones and tornadoes ripped through North America, Asia and parts of Europe, bringing death, disease and famine to millions. Torrential rains caused vast mudslides across the regions of the Equator and widespread flooding throughout Central Africa. While in Britain, a sudden return to colder conditions brought vicious winds and icy storms, during one of which giant hailstones the size of tennis balls battered rooftops, smashed car windscreens, brought down power cables and caused the deaths of more than one hundred people. The weather was never out of the news; each new storm bringing another extreme event; every news programme telling of another tragedy afflicting those marooned on drowning atolls, or living beneath slopes left bare by landslides. But the parlous and worsening situation at home would become most vividly clear, as a series of climate related events swept away any lasting vestiges of the false assumption that the ravages of the "The Great Storm" of 2013 had been a once in a millennium occurrence.

Britain was in trouble, for a winter of storms and blizzards had been followed by a foul spring of seemingly endless heavy rain and floods. Considerable damage to property, local services and transport infrastructure was suffered; while following four dry years, farmers now found themselves unable to get heavy equipment onto their fields to plant new crops, or tend those laid down the previous autumn. By the early morning of Thursday, 29th April 2055, the circumstances were dire, with flood alerts in force on fifty major rivers and only a brief two-day respite from the bad weather forecast. Worse still, a spring tide was at hand in the North Sea and the ageing flood defences of East Anglia and London stood braced against a massive and unprecedented surge.

* * *

On the night when Toby left Reading he made his longest journey so far. Driving into the early hours of the following morning he travelled eastwards through the sleeping outer suburban towns of the Home Counties, before heading north along the Great North Road. Then, having turned east again toward Huntingdon, he drove down onto the lowlands of the fen country and on towards King's Lynn and the Norfolk coast. Immersed in deep thought for much of the time, Toby simply wished to put a number of miles between himself and the previous day's events, and could not have realised that he was being drawn on by another more subtle impulse.

By the early hours he had travelled through the town of Wells Next the Sea and the sleeping village of Blakeney and was on a twisting road that follows the shingle coastline to Sherringham and Cromer. This is a quiet area, well-known for its reed marshes and bird reserves, the latter carefully maintained to provide a habitat for threatened species. The marsh harriers and snipe, so carefully reintroduced towards the end of the twentieth century, had now disappeared once more – dispersed or destroyed by the effects of pollution and storm damage. But small colonies of rare avocets and other waders remained, protected by man, though now frequently buffeted by turbulent Nature. Many of these birds nested low down in the reed beds and channels that abounded between the road and the tall sea defences half a mile away.

Toby was very tired, his eyes beginning to droop as he looked out upon a newly risen half moon and searched for a place to sleep, eventually pulling off the road into a small lay-by. There he stopped beneath a skeletal hawthorn tree, its fallen leaves now scattered, discarded and grey among the puddles. The saltwater beds of a nature reserve lay close by, but there was no sound or movement other than his own breathing, and succumbing within moments to a seemingly ever growing wall of fatigue, he fell gratefully into a dreamless sleep.

* * *

Time goes on with no regard for man and Toby knew nothing of the years that elapsed before he awoke again. What he did notice immediately, however, was the change of season for the sun shone brightly, and a scent of blossom filled the air. All around new growth burst forth along the roadside and across rippling meres, while a chirping of sparrows arguing in the hedgerows was evident. An onshore wind blew strongly and he could hear the North Sea swell murmuring in the distance as it rose and fell on a shelving beach. Deeply inhaling the salty air, Toby opened the driver's door before stepping down to look around. With its radio blaring, a small car rushed by on the road, but nothing else came into view as he surveyed the marsh, which was largely empty except for here or there a solitary duck or goose sailing across a man-made lagoon. A flight of seagulls hung in the air further off and he watched them turn towards the coast, stooping low into the wind before disappearing from sight behind a line of dunes.

Toby lowered his gaze, a profound sense of isolation engulfing him for a few seconds, and only upon glancing back towards the spot did he become aware of a distant figure – a young woman rising onto the shingle bank at the edge of the sea, her fair hair illuminated by a shaft of sunlight shining down from a break in the fitful canopy above. Toby shielded his brow to observe her better, and noticed a small dog come scurrying along behind as she descended onto the narrow path that snaked through the marsh towards him. He knew the approaching traveller by her graceful movement and unhurried steps – now seeming to pass over the space between as if she glided through the mist rising among the bending reed stems. Her form emerged from hollows as if treading on air... weaving carefully between deep puddles and muddy channels like the Lady of Shalott set free to journey down to Camelot.

So Jeannie traversed the dips and gulleys, to come at last before him as a roaming spirit might do. She wore a light woollen shawl embroidered with images of birds rising from a hilltop, a flowing skirt, and soft leather walking boots bright with beads of water from the damp grass. Yet it was her face that held him; her eyes and pale cheeks caught by the light of the sun, her golden hair tied in a ponytail with a white ribbon. She smiled, but looked stern – like one who, having travelled far on an important errand, has little time for the passing pleasantries of a spring morning.

'You came,' she said, looking earnestly into his eyes. 'Are you rested?'

Toby considered her question... Again he had no aches or pains – any need of water or hunger for food. He was comfortable and without fatigue.

'I am well,' he replied. 'And you?'

'Content, now that you are found. Much time has passed during the night just ended – but this may prove a longer day.'

Billowing clouds suddenly enveloped the sun, shadowing its brilliance in a misty shroud that stole all heat away leaving a biting chill in the air.

'Where is Macken?' asked Toby, looking beyond her toward the distant shingle bank.

Jeannie replied with an expression of mild reproach, etched with a faint smile. 'I told you once before, Toby... Macken is free to range as he pleases – he comes and goes. Where he is now, I have no idea; but when the time is right you will be sure to see him.'

A gust of wind shook the reeds next to them and Toby looked out again at the empty landscape. 'The little dog is such a small creature to go wandering around alone in this world,' he thought. 'Is he truly real... or just a blithe four-legged wraith that occasionally roves upon the earth?'

'We must go now!' said Jeannie after a moment, her voice suddenly more urgent. 'I have something to show you that will not wait!' And with these words she turned back toward the coast with Toby following across the boggy ground, frequently stepping over oozy patches or skirting water filled dells. Soon they came to the high shingle bank separating the salt marsh from the tidal beach and began to climb a loose path that cut through a hollow near the top. The voice of the sea had grown to a rumbling growl, though one still muffled by a million tons of stone and concrete piled high to keep it back. The sky meanwhile had turned an ominous leaden grey. Yet sheltered in the lee of the high defence work, Toby's feeling of security held until reaching the top and looking out upon a churning swell. He saw immediately that the tide was coming in: pushed towards the beach by a powerful current and driven onwards by a strong North-East wind. Breakers curled and crashed upon the shoreline; each clawing forward to drag a hundred thousand stones rattling into the swirling foam. A lone seagull, tossed and buffeted like a shred of storm blown paper, struggled resolutely against turbulent onshore gusts, repeatedly rising and veering low above the tempestuous cauldron. A wrack of broken clouds, constantly separating and closing, filled the glowering sky to a bleak horizon.

But it was the height of the incoming tide that both surprised and appalled. The wash of the largest waves already reaching close to where they stood: the water level, now spiked by heavy raindrops from a scudding squall, licking to within less than fifteen feet of the gap through which they had emerged. Toby glanced back at the low pastures and reedbeds behind, all of which would be drowned up to and beyond the distant road if the sea defence was breached. He then looked towards Jeannie, gripped by sudden realisation and fear of the situation.

'This is the morning of a spring tide!' she called above the noise of the strengthening wind. 'The flow still has two hours to run; but water levels are already exceptionally high because of the weather and rising sea levels. The bank here will hold and not be fully overtopped, but at lower reaches along the coast such luck will not be had; for the sea knows no boundaries when driven on in such a mood as this, responding only to the force of the moon.'

As if in confirmation of her words, a series of wild breakers then threw themselves upon the foreshore, frothing over the stones to within inches of where they stood, each sending a cloud of spray curling away on the wind. Soon another trio followed; the last of these, and by far the largest, lifting higher and higher as it reached towards their ankles – like a menacing tongue determined to snatch them into the boiling entrails of the sea. Toby stumbled to one side as a slithering onrush threatened to catch him, then watched as it flushed wildly through the cleft at the top of the shingle bank before washing down upon the marshland beyond.

'The sea means business!' he shouted to Jeannie, who had drawn back on the other side.

'Therefore we must go!' she answered, above the thunderous crash of another plunging wave. 'It will not do to stay longer.'

So they briskly retraced their steps, but had only just reached the bottom of the stony bank when another huge gout overflowed the gap above, sending a second cascade tumbling and splashing down around their feet. But Toby could see that the nether ground before them was already becoming wet due to another cause: for along a wide front, water seeping through the stones of the bank had begun trickling down in widening rivulets to inundate the surrounding low lying countryside, before steadily spreading out in a broadening sheen. This made the going much harder from then on; as new flows of water running off the adjacent marsh began to spring up and cut across their return path to the road. More than once Toby had to double back to find higher ground, or wade unsteadily across soggy clumps of marsh grass where the track had become submerged. Not until they had covered more than half the distance to the road were drier stretches encountered, over which it was possible to jog unhindered. Toby looked up two or three times as they fled before the advancing flood, hoping on each occasion to see the camper van; but although he knew it to be parked on higher ground, the spot always seemed hidden by tall reeds or masked by hedgerows, and only when they were very close did it emerge into view, as if from behind a shadow cast by a passing cloud.

Spattered up to his thighs with mud and slime, Toby looked back to see an expanding lake filling the pools and hollows of the nature reserve.

'Start the van,' urged Jeannie, already seating herself in the passenger seat. 'I will guide you as best I can – although we may now have to rely upon another helper.'

Toby climbed in beside her and moments later the engine of the VW spluttered into life, sending a familiar plume of white smoke swirling away toward the sea.

'Drive back towards Wells!' Jeannie commanded. 'Then turn inland at the first practical opportunity. We must get away from the coastal flatlands as soon as possible, or risk being cut off.'

So they began to retrace Toby's earlier route, but having gone only a little distance, came upon a milk lorry partly blocking the way. The amply built Norfolk driver waved them down before stepping up to Toby's side window.

'Thee can't go any further, son,' he said in a fatherly way. 'I've just had a call from my wife in King's Lynn; apparently the roads around Wells have been cut by the flood water so it seems there'll be no way through further along.'

Toby looked anxiously toward the surrounding fields, now gradually filling to right and left. The raised road snaked off along a twisting causeway; while the bubble and gurgle of water flowing into a culvert from a nearby meadow could be clearly heard. Grazing sheep were also making their escape from a field on the seaward side: nervously emerging through an open gate before trotting off down the road in front of the lorry.

'We must keep moving,' Jeannie's whispered urgently. 'If we wait the waters are sure to close around us!'

'I'm going on,' Toby blurted out to the other man in an effort of feigned confidence. 'Can I get past you?'

'Past me!' the milkman exclaimed in disbelief. 'You must be mad young fella! Look, if I tell you the road is impassable, then trust me – it is. Now don't be a daft fool – turn around and get thee back toward Cromer!'

Prompted again by Jeannie, Toby waited no longer, but easing down beside the wide lorry, found just enough room to squeeze by, leaving the lorry driver shaking his head as they disappeared from sight through the frightened flock of sheep.

By now the whole area of marsh and fields between the road and the shingle bank bordering the sea had become a continuous shimmering lake, its surface whipped into dancing ripples by a strong wind driving in from the north. The sky, meanwhile, had become even more deeply disturbed and glowering, with only fitful breaks of cloud allowing an occasional bright shaft of sunlight through to illuminate the unfolding drama. The water progressively closed in around them as they sped on, filling ditches and steadily rising up: so that on low bends they were forced to splash through widening puddles that turned the road surface to a shining glare. At one such bend Toby almost misjudged the line of the rapidly disappearing corridor: the camper van lurching sideways as it drove precariously close to the raised edge. Then, rounding another, he narrowly missed a gaggle of geese that had stepped out of a farmyard intent upon sampling the new delights of the flooded paddock opposite. It was obvious their wild flight couldn't last much longer – that the way would soon be irretrievably barred by the flood. And so it seemed to prove not a half-mile further on!

At that point they came upon a crossroads where four routes converged across low-lying land. Toby pulled up just as the road directly ahead became awash with water pouring off a field to the North-West. Reacting instantly, he quickly engaged reverse, only to see the carriageway behind disappear beneath a similar surge.

'We're cut off!' he cried. 'That's it; we're trapped!'

But then the strangest thing happened. A small brown and white shape – no more than a shadow at first – jumped up next to a footpath stile beside the junction and, having barked once, skipped across a third stream of water now curving under the camper van. The little dog froze for a moment, as if getting its bearings, before scampering off at full speed down the twisting road leading inland, his tiny legs a blur of skittering paws and spray.

'Macken?' exclaimed Toby in astonishment – momentarily forgetting their predicament as he watched the retreating apparition. 'Where did he come from?'

'It was his task to find us!' cried Jeannie. 'Now follow him; we cannot stay here, for time is very short!'

Toby pulled away again as the little fellow disappeared from view round the nearest bend, and upon reaching the same point seconds later found Macken already far in front, splashing over the ever increasing multitude of streams breaching the road. As they rushed through deepening puddles in pursuit, the camper van too sent up a constant shower: water thumping ever louder and more ominously on the underside. On one particularly sharp corner the steering went altogether as the VW aquaplaned across a lake of rippling water; and thereafter, time and again, their venerable conveyance was almost irrevocably lost to the rising tide. But whenever Toby came to the point of giving up their hair-raising ride with thoughts of seeking refuge on a barn roof, or in a high tree, Macken's headlong charge, just ahead, always drew him on to the next corner or junction. More than once, on coming to a fork in the road, the Jack Russell skidded to a halt to sniff the air with an upturned nose before dashing off to right or left. On one occasion he even doubled round towards the coast, causing Toby to beat the steering wheel with his fist in frustration.

'What is he doing?' he yelled desperately. 'The crazy animal will get us all drowned if we go that way!'

'Stay with him – Macken knows what he's doing!' Jeannie replied firmly. And so he did, for although several points were reached where floodwater threatened to sever the road, little by little they escaped the coastal flats, gradually rising into a rolling hinterland of sandy heath and cultivated fields.

For his part, Macken never tired, but seemed completely absorbed with the task of staying ahead of the watery element at their heels. Only occasionally did he turn to face Toby; always with a slight toss of the head as if challenging him to keep up, but then, as they traversed the last few yards to an open viewpoint, having darted out of sight round a final corner of the road – he disappeared!

* * *

Pulling up at the roadside, Toby scanned the field to right and left for signs of their lost guide; but saw nothing moving in the rolling landscape except a brace of startled pheasants noisily clattering away over a hedgerow. They had drawn near to the pretty village of Great Walsingham, with its shrine and nunnery, and were less than ten miles from the main east-west road linking Norwich to King's Lynn.

'What now?' asked Toby, suddenly deflated.

'We keep going.'

'But where to?'

'Away from here... home perhaps.'

He scratched his head. 'I hardly know where home is anymore... where I want to be, that is.'

'Then drive on and see where the journey takes you... Your travels will end one day; of that you have my word.'

He turned to look at her: sitting patiently; demure and seemingly so wise; yet sometimes so calculating and unworldly.

'And you, Jeannie... where will you be at the end of all this?'

'Still there to advise and comfort you, Toby... when the long road is done.'

His oblique companion would say little more, other than telling him of the year and day that he had woken into; before looking into the distance as if allowing him to decide the next step.

Yet Toby felt a million miles from picking up the threads of his old life; for while only a few waking days and hours had passed since the end of the "The Great Storm", in the world he now trod a small age seemed to elapse during each passing night.

'If this is the year 2055,' he thought, looking down at his hands, 'that makes me seventy-three... and if I am that old... then what of my family? What must have become of them?'

Troubling images rose before him, and Toby sank into a hollow reflective space within himself as he turned the ignition and drove on – feeling suddenly distanced from his silent passenger. His sense of isolation and loss had returned; and he might have been travelling to the ends of the earth rather than through his own country… the fleeting trees and farmsteads mere spectral images from another time.

* * *

Only after journeying for some little while did Toby again become properly aware of the passing scenery and take further interest in the course to be taken. Soon they came to a large roundabout outside Fakenham and there, deciding against driving westwards, where any flooding south of "The Wash" might already be severe, he chose instead to head south towards Swaffham and Brandon. Little traffic was on the roads, but already signs and diversions were in place warning drivers to avoid the low-lying fen country. However, whether it was through lack of concentration, or from some other deeper design, soon after passing into Thetford Forest Toby made a fateful decision that would take them back into danger. For some five minutes he'd been watching a police car in his mirror: one that he convinced himself seemed to be keeping its distance, as if following. Feeling uneasy at the prospect of being stopped and questioned, Toby began looking for a turning where he might pull off the main road, eventually spying a sign to the tiny village of Feltwell. Signalling at the last moment, he swung into it before accelerating once more – all the while checking his mirror for signs of pursuit. There were none, the police car evidently having more important business to attend to, and he found himself travelling in stately isolation along a deserted country lane. However, once committed to the new route, and happy to be away from the general flow, Toby dismissed the idea of turning back, choosing to drive on as the road to Feltwell slipped down from the sandy heath country of Central Norfolk. Thus he approached the flat reaches of Feltwell Fen and, looking ahead, saw what appeared to be a glittering haze upon the surface of a wide mere. Yet this was not an ordinary lake – as Toby appreciated only too well, having simultaneously realised his error…

What he saw was a spreading flood sliding far inland from the overtopped sluices and sea defences of King's Lynn. As he watched it seemed to swell and grow like a silver carpet lapping toward the horizon. The wide expanse of low-lying fields behind was not yet overcome, but an inner sense told him that the advancing waters would swiftly flow across the whole area, leaving them marooned – or worse! Moreover, this time there was no sign of Macken to guide him. …Toby would need to accomplish their second escape unaided…

'What… what lies south of here?' he stammered, a renewed determination to cheat the elements rising within.

'Littleport,' Jeannie replied. 'Littleport and Ely – but we will need to be swift!'

Toby applied his foot to the accelerator, causing the VW to lurch forward in a rush of grinding gears and smoke, and soon they came to a straight Fenland road heading in their chosen direction. This in turn quickly brought them to an area known as the "Bedford Levels": a region of sunken land beside the Great Ouse: the mighty river coursing wide and slow moving between raised dykes. What they could not see, however, was that this had become swollen with tidal water flowing in from the North Sea: a mighty reservoir ready to overflow its banks as the surge advanced. When it did, the water would engulf everything below, spreading out to form a wide inland sea.

'Don't head for the main road at Littleport,' Jeannie advised, 'but go left, making for Prickwillow and Ely. We must reach the higher ground there or be lost!'

Toby responded straightway to the imperative note in her voice and they soon passed through the aforesaid village – still quiet and apparently unaware of the approaching danger – before turning towards Ely, its cathedral seen rising above the lowland fields. Speeding on, they entered the ancient refuge just before the fast encroaching waters spilled about the feet of the city, encircling its ninety thousand inhabitants upon an island.

Consternation and panic reigned as Toby drove up into the higher streets: many attempting a last minute escape in cars hastily crammed with suitcases, household possessions and family pets. Meanwhile, others rushed to vantage points where they might gain a better view of what was happening, craning out in awe at the work of nature. Toby had to stop more than once in the confusion, or drive carefully round accidents where frightened or angry drivers had careered into one another. Progress was painfully slow, but they came at last to a small square near the ancient and beautiful building for which Ely is famous. Toby pulled up for a moment, unsure where to park. Then, when on the point of switching off the engine with a view to reconnoitring on foot, he caught sight of an old friend beneath the branches of a flowering cherry tree. Macken sat on his haunches, contentedly watching, and upon seeing that he'd attracted Toby's attention, casually got to his feet before trotting away in the direction of a nearby ivy-covered archway. It looked like the entrance to the Deanery, or to a private driveway, and Toby was unsure whether to follow.

'Go on,' said Jeannie. 'He's never wrong – there will be a place.'

So Toby kept pace with the retreating Jack Russell, passing through the archway into a courtyard where a comfortable mansion, fronted by flowerbeds and a wide lawn, lay before them. Beside this, with doors open, stood a double garage before which a silver limousine was drawn up. Parked in the shadows within rested a vintage A35 car.

'Yours?' asked Toby.

'Whenever I have need, yes... although I now prefer to be chauffeur driven,' she added with a smile. 'You may park next to it.'

'But won't the owner object?'

'Everything is arranged, Toby. Neither you nor your transport will be disturbed here.'

So he reversed the camper van into the proffered spot, away from prying eyes; then together they walked across to the far corner of the courtyard where another smaller arch led through to a quiet veranda overlooking rooftops and the countryside beyond. There, sitting together on a comfortable seat flanked by ornate vases containing shrubs and spring flowers, they looked out over the roofs of Ely toward the flooded land beyond as the hours drew on towards evening.

* * *

There were unfortunately many who did not enjoy such a favourable end to the day. Ten thousand were drowned before nightfall: trapped in flooded villages or swept away in towns along the North Sea coast and Thames estuary. The worst devastation affected London, long protected by its ageing flood barrier. Although many had warned that with rising tides and sea levels, this limited defence might one day be breached, no action had been taken to modernise or strengthen it. Adequately protecting the capital would require the expenditure of vast amounts of money, and in a city dedicated to the rough economy of profit, the case for such outlay had been repeatedly shelved. For more than forty years fingers remained firmly crossed – the gamble paying off until that fateful spring.

Then, at three o'clock on a blustery April afternoon as despairing engineers, politicians and anguished citizens looked on, a foaming surge of muddy saltwater pushed over and around the puny obstacle before flowing eagerly into the lower quarters of the city. The walls of the Embankment could not hold it back and the deluge inundated large areas of the financial and commercial centre. A substantial part of the Underground was also swamped – much of the system remaining out of use for up to a year afterwards. The Docklands Railway too was paralysed by flooding and power failure, while tens of thousands of shops and houses were ruined or rendered uninhabitable by a sea of sewage and slurry that bubbled forth from subterranean drains: spewing the noxious wastes of fourteen million citizens and a scampering army of rats into every byway and corner.

In one rotting backwater of the Thames a section of an old jetty collapsed just as the tide turned and began to ebb, part of it floating up seconds later to provide a lifesaving raft for the dozens of brown rodents bobbing round about. Many of these perennial survivors were thus given an opportunity to scratch and scramble aboard before being carried out into the mainstream of the river by the receding water. Saved by a combination of good fortune and the desperate ingenuity of their species, they were then borne off downstream, the raft slowly revolving with the eddying current as the last reaches of the city fell behind. Not until evening, as the western sky grew pink, was the hungry twitching crew cast up upon land once more; this time beached and stranded in a remote corner of the Medway marshes – there to preen their whiskers, disembark and form another community.

Back in London, however, many faced a far less fortuitous outcome as the tide retreated. For several weeks previously there had been much rain, but now, when the city needed a cleansing hand to wash away the slime and reek, the sky stayed clear, leaving a bright moon to shine down upon the soiled metropolis.

Massive damage had been done – a trillion pounds' worth in less than six short hours – more than would ever be raised to put right what was ruined: for although the emergency services might bring rescue and comfort to those worst affected, London had been all but mortally wounded, its economy left in turmoil – the people threatened by disease and shortage.

* * *

Kline Anderson looked down pensively from the window of his office in Canary Wharf upon the initial scenes of disruption. Dressed in a plain black tailored suit, the top button of his white shirt undone, he sipped from a cup of tepid coffee while observing the developing spectacle. Now in his early forties, the former journalist studied the scene with a tense, thoughtful expression. The air was filled with the sound of sirens, car horns and alarm bells, as the nightmare of what many wise heads had long predicted sent panic through the hive of human life below. It was a sad, almost surreal spectacle, and he felt angry that such misery should be visited on the city of his birth and upon the people he loved. He did not show these things on the surface, however, or join in the animated conversations of others as they grouped around computer screens showing details of the developing situation. Every street and major location seemed to be covered: with nervous reporters at pavement level describing the increasing chaos, as they themselves retreated uncertainly before the advancing waters. There were scenes of people already cut off, and of those that had desperately climbed onto walls and railings beside flooded roads. Others, wet and bedraggled, were pictured emerging with horrified expressions from the entrances of underground stations and subways. Then the chief image switched to a taxi that had become wedged at a street corner between two buses, firemen fighting to release the terrified driver and passengers as the water level swelled around them.

Encircled themselves, although high above the danger and horror, Kline Anderson and his colleagues could do nothing but watch as the disaster unfolded, leaving emergency services overwhelmed. Appalled by the sights of human tragedy, he inwardly despaired at the greed, excess and stupidity that had contributed toward unsettling the world's climate. Now leader of the recently formed "Sustainability Party" – with one hundred and thirteen elected councillors – he had been gearing up for the following week's local government elections, when warning of a likely flood disaster was announced just three days before. During the ensuing seventy-two hours he'd gone on to meet with nothing but support and sincere expressions of concern about what might befall the city. He knew that ordinary people were afraid; that they wanted someone to address the ever greater problems caused by global warming; to give them hope that solutions could be found. Hundreds had shaken his hand, promising to vote for stability at the polls.

Now, looking out, he wondered if he might have come forward too late – if the damage to the climate and environment had already gone too far. But another voice told him to have trust in the citizens of his country: that, having once come through war and great difficulties in another age, they might do so again if the prospect of an achievable way forward was offered.

*   *   *

Kline Anderson was not wrong to think this; for only six days after the flooding, and with the clear-up operation already faltering, the people of London and the rest of the country did not forget. The Sustainability Party made a great electoral breakthrough, winning hundreds of seats and gaining control of councils throughout the country. This represented a huge and popular upsurge of support for a party, and its inspirational leader, dedicated to meeting the challenge of climate change in future years.

*   *   *

Twelve months later this success would go on to act as the springboard to an even greater victory.

Chapter Eight

Kline Anderson

T HE DIFFERENT EXPECTATIONS THAT WE HAVE OF boys and girls will always provide fertile ground for discussion among parents. Should we encourage male children to grow up to be tough and resourceful – and must little girls always be dressed in pink? Whatever hopes we may have, children come into this world with their own qualities. We may endeavour to shape them in our own image, or impress upon them the need to conform to the norms of others, but we do not make them what they individually are and they must be allowed to be true to themselves when all is done.

* * *

Kline Anderson seemed different from the day of his birth: not odd, but unusual in his perception and understanding of people and the environment. From the moment he first blinked open a puffy eye, while lying in the crook of his mother's arm, he seemed to look knowingly upon the world.

Emma and Richard Anderson had no plans for moulding their child's future but were simply glad as parents to grow with him. Thus, as Kline began to develop, they were happy to share his wonder at the world and encouraged him to look, touch and listen to everything that came to his fingertips. But most of all, Emma and Richard gave him their time: time for shared play, to be read nursery rhymes and well-loved books, to walk, sing and laugh. They also talked to him and had time to listen too – which is the greatest gift that any parent can give.

It is said that some children absorb information like a sponge – which can appear a good thing until a child comes along who is so stuffed with factual knowledge that they seem too clever for their own good, having become quirky and self-absorbed. Kline Anderson did not succumb to these traits: for although quick to learn, he never troubled himself to achieve a pretentious or encyclopaedic knowledge of any subject. Yet he was interested in everything, and particularly the everyday lives of his fellow human beings. Almost as soon as he learned to speak he began to ask questions that revealed a deepening side to his nature. He desired to understand the thoughts and cares of others, what they hoped and dreamed for, and would go through life in this way, never speaking to others without listening carefully and attentively to their replies. To talk with Kline Anderson was to become the focus of his attention, a quality that earned him many friends – along with a number of enemies among those he found guilty of conceit, ignorance and lies.

* * *

His schooldays were challenging, for being near-sighted and having to wear glasses set him apart from others and like many children he was sometimes singled out for being different. He looked studious, his thin framed spectacles and drooping hair giving him a refined yet appealing look that, while irritating some of the jealous and shallow kind, made him popular among the more discerning at school.

On one occasion, soon after his tenth birthday, the classroom bully and a group of cronies cornered Kline in an alleyway. Many times he had been warned about going there alone, and on several previous occasions he'd been jostled and jeered at as he passed through with friends. But on this occasion, having stayed back after lessons for a play rehearsal, Kline was alone. It was high summer towards the end of the school year, the evening hot and sticky, when he sauntered into the alleyway still diligently practising in his head the words he must learn. The other boys, led by their shaven headed gang leader, Jimmy Bicton, had been hanging around for some time, and seeing Kline decided to relieve their boredom at his expense. It is a situation faced by thousands of similar victims every day: one that usually brings with it a churning of fear and a sense of hopelessness. But on looking up and finding himself trapped, Kline did not exhibit the usual signs of fawning panic and despair. He simply stopped as the boys closed around him, looking steadily up at Jimmy's familiar, mocking face.

For some time, as the daily taunts and threats had gradually intensified, he'd been expecting a confrontation, and now that the reckoning had come felt no great foreboding – only a desire to face out the danger and escape again to real life at the far end of the alleyway. Initially his lack of outward emotion and unease seemed to perplex Jimmy Bicton who, for a full ten seconds, was strangely lost for words. The fact that Kline was not behaving as Jimmy's victims normally did nonplussed the aspiring little Caesar, but the prospect of losing face and credibility eventually made him blurt out a sarcastic challenge.

'What are you staring at, you wimp?' he barked, bringing his spotty face close to Kline's.

'I'm not staring,' replied Kline slowly, without lowering his eyes, 'and if you'll let me through, I'll go.'

'Oh, we'll let you go… when *we've* finished with you,' Jimmy leered.

The bigger boy's voice was soft and menacing and a titter of laughter went round the other members of the group. But looking about him, Kline could see in some of their expressions a hint of distaste for what was happening – that they were merely going along with a practised charade. Three or four were children that he normally got on reasonably well with in class, or when he met them during the holidays for a kick about in the local park. Others he had never met or spoken to – small, rather insignificant boys enlisted to bolster Jimmy Bicton's ego. Kline sensed that the hearts of these too were not really in it, that they'd rather get out of the sun and go home.

'What have you got against me?' he asked, looking back towards his tormentor.

'What haven't I got against you, you poncy little prat?' said Jimmy, reaching forward and roughing his hair. 'You think you know it all, don't you?'

There was another pause, a silence filled only with breathing – like the quiet between a fork of lightning and the crash of following thunder. When Kline answered his face showed no emotion, his matter-of-fact voice resonating maturity beyond his years.

'I don't know half of what I'd like to know... and I've forgotten more than half of what I've ever learned – so why should I trouble you?'

Jimmy Bicton's forehead wrinkled as he tried to take in this ambiguous rejoinder.

'What's that supposed to mean, you little smart arse?' he snarled angrily, stepping forward and pushing Kline's shoulder.

'It means I'm not half as clever as you think I am,' replied Kline, his face still bearing the same even expression. 'So why don't you let me go?'

The gathering had become all but motionless as if the others, now finding themselves spectators to a choreographed word game, looked on as silent witnesses at a battle of wills evidently no longer favouring the aggressor.

'That's just typical of you – Mr "four-eyes" Anderson,' said Jimmy, attempting to go on the offensive again. 'All talk and no bottle – no stomach for a fight.'

'If we fight, then you win... But if we talk...' said Kline, looking round at the other boys, two or three of whom he could see from their sheepish looks were almost on his side, 'if we talk – maybe it will end there.'

The bigger boy pushed him again, though now more in frustration than from any true purpose or conviction. Then, finding that no one else joined in, he stepped aside with a contemptuous toss of the head, allowing his prey to walk on. As a relieved Kline emerged into the bright street once more, the air behind was blue for thirty seconds with Jimmy's dire threats to, "kill him" or "smash him" next time he passed that way. But these, as time would tell, were never carried out. The ensuing days became weeks and Jimmy Bicton gradually turned his attention to others more easily intimidated. Kline, meanwhile, found his reputation enhanced rather than diminished. He hadn't backed down from the school bully and that, as most people know, means a lot when you are ten!

* * *

So his early years passed and Kline suffered the usual scrapes experienced by small boys: once memorably being rescued from almost certain death in a busy London street by the timely intervention of an unknown stranger. Following this, he developed quickly and learned well – always intrigued by the behaviour and motives of others. In the family kitchen one day, when just into his teens, he glanced up from a newspaper in which he'd been reading about race riots in Holland and political corruption in Africa. His brow was deeply furrowed and his mother immediately recognised that her son was wrestling with an important question.

'What is it, Kline?' Emma asked. 'What's puzzling you?'

He did not reply straightaway, but sat staring out of the window, as if thinking of the best way to give utterance to his thoughts.

'I was just wondering why...' he answered after some deliberation' ...why, when men and women have such good brains – they so often act as fools?'

'What do you mean?'

'Well... why don't they realise that when they hurt the world and others, they must ultimately hurt themselves too?'

For a few quiet moments Emma gave careful thought before replying, knowing her firstborn would consider every word.

'Some people don't seem to care about anything or anyone but themselves, Kline. Yet it appears likely that such individuals have always been, and will always be there to trouble us... so perhaps we must learn to accommodate them.'

Kline's head came up in a flash – a look of anger flushing his face.

'But they can't expect to live selfishly all the time! ...I mean, everything and everybody matters, don't they, Mum? ...And you can't always expect to be top dog – to get your own way all the time. Even quite small children have got enough sense to understand that!'

Emma smiled back – wondering for the hundredth time at the intensity of her son's words.

'Perhaps the ones you are thinking of should consider the wisdom of children more often, Kline. Do be sure to heed the voices of the young too, when you grow up.'

'Why wouldn't I?' he said, walking to the window to look out at the grey-green vista of the rolling Thames. 'It's their world that many adults seem determined to spoil!'

* * *

So Kline's childhood ended; to be followed by six years at college and university building a foundation upon which his future years of influence would stand. He studied

"Bio Technology" and "Sustainable Energy" – graduating in the autumn of 2037 – before spending three years gaining experience as a journalist for a radical magazine. Then, encouraged by close friends and admirers, he returned to university life, being appointed within a year as senior research lecturer of "Sustainable Living" at the University of Telford. His own future looked bright, but the clouds of war had now gathered – drawing attention away from the main thrust of his work as men reverted again to older ways by which to settle their differences. There were disruptions and shortages throughout the years of struggle and little funding for methods other than those advancing the use of force and destruction. But Kline Anderson and his team went on with their research; every report of a new environmental catastrophe inspiring fresh resolve among them to discover ways to counter the global impact of man's activities upon the earth and its climate. There would, he believed, be another way forward (beyond the age of competition and recurring aggression), if only mankind had the wit to find it and the courage to live differently.

And so events seemed to promise, for as he approached his fortieth year the global conflict faltered and stuttered to a conclusion: the return to peace stimulated by profound concerns about the state of the environment. The scars of war across much of the earth would begin to heal, but the increasing devastation caused by floods and heat waves appeared likely to be without end. Some leaders listened and acted cautiously at first, but the majority, increasingly gripped by a pervading sense of anxiety very close to despair, quickly lapsed toward former solutions. Where well-informed scientists and researchers advised a reduction of carbon emissions, the strengthening of sea defences and a move towards funding more locally led solutions to environmental problems – too many politicians baulked at the massive costs and drew back from endorsing new initiatives. Everything would be all right, they argued, if the fossil fuel dependent economy was helped back onto its feet; if more oil could be supplied to the pumps, more markets created, more precious resources consumed. Then there would be money available to expand production still further; with enough set aside to solve the most pressing environmental difficulties.

Whatever the long-term consequences might be – like a hamster in a wheel, or a drunken man constantly turning in the revolving door of a saloon bar – the endlessly damaging circle of consumption must go on, despite the risk of human civilisation eventually stumbling to the cliff edge of no return – and toppling over.

* * *

In Britain the years immediately following the end of World War Three constituted a period of muddle, indecision and decline. The old vibrant and meaningful political system had broken down long before as, in their desperation to be elected, the three main parties increasingly put forward policies for long term development and environmental protection all but identical in both paucity of aims and the extent of media spin and rhetoric. Yet times were becoming increasingly hard and more difficult – climate change impacts more severe, possible solutions more distant. Some with scientific knowledge and vision were wise enough to look towards a new epoch – a time in which all use of fossil fuels would end, food would be produced sustainably, and in which population levels would be controlled by consent rather than conflict. Among these were the researchers of Telford University, quietly encouraged by their mentor, Kline Anderson.

For some time the group had considered various ways by which they might influence governments and persuade ministers to act upon the radical proposals required to bring about change. Yet politicians seemed deaf to even the most pressing or persuasive arguments. But what were the alternatives? The Telford researchers might give up the struggle to promote government action and return to their labs, hoping that more enlightened leaders would emerge in coming years. Or – and this prospect only emerged following many late night discussions – they might found a new political party in order to make their views and aims known, in the hope that ordinary people would support them at the ballot box. In the current situation their first option would probably lead nowhere; whereas a newly formed political organisation might at least have the opportunity to make itself heard over the bland and hollow calls to "weather the climate change storm" and "vigorously pursue long term recovery of the economy". But how might a frightened public be persuaded to listen and support calls for an alternative way forward? The founding group would need to give themselves a voice, and this was what they set about doing.

* * *

On a grey November evening towards the end of 2053 – an already disastrous year of blizzards, uncontrollable summer heath fires, autumn storms and mudslides – the Telford activists presented themselves to the public for the first time. They had chosen as their venue the village hall at Jackfield near Ironbridge in Shropshire – a place known by British historians as the "Cradle of the Industrial Revolution" due to its association with early large-scale iron production. There, they hoped to share their plans and explain the aims of the proposed "Sustainability Party" to anyone that might turn up to the advertised meeting.

Jackfield Village Hall was sturdy but unimposing: a simple early twenty-first-century structure, with one or two features from an earlier period. It had been built overlooking the Severn Gorge on land reclaimed after the disastrous landslip of 2015, when the previous village hall, along with several houses, collapsed and slithered down into the raging torrent below following three days of incessant rain. The building had a polished floor, high windows (in sympathy with the Victorian church above) and the usual modern conveniences provided in local authority premises of the time. However, the main considerations in its construction were that it should blend well with the heritage setting, while being able to withstand the now frequent battering of wind and weather.

Several rows of seats had been put out below the stage, upon which had been placed a heavy wooden speaker's table and four chairs, and with the clock rapidly approaching seven in the evening, preparations were in full swing. Two of the group were testing a sound system, while others set out cups and saucers for tea and coffee, plates of biscuits and other light refreshments. A tangible air of optimism was evident amid the banter of raised voices and clatter of cutlery, such as is normally found before any general meeting advertised to the public. Fliers had been sent round locally, information posted on the Internet and notices placed in local papers – good money had been spent to get the message out and a reporter from the local newspaper invited. Now all they needed were "bums on seats" before the event commenced at seven -thirty.

Kline Anderson sat on the front of the stage sipping a mug of tea and talking to his long time friend and colleague, Manjinder Singh. Always the great optimist, Manny was now going on in an upbeat way about what they must do following the evening's activities. He had volunteered to address the gathering to explain the party's aims and was working himself into a familiar state of nervous excitement. But beneath this enthusiasm, Kline sensed a level of uncertainty concerning the limited options which might be left to the group if the meeting was a failure – if nobody came.

Listening attentively as usual, Kline found his own feelings running along similar lines. Launching anything from scratch is always difficult. Publicity requires funds, of which they had precious few, and the public often took little interest in something new if it failed to catch the imagination. They had billed the *"Sustainability Party"* launch as:

The start of a new era of hope for the future.

But had such promises been made or scotched too many times before? Were people becoming tired of promises of false dawns? The lure of the fireside would surely be more attractive for most than the rain and drizzle of an autumn night. Kline himself had not prepared a speech, preferring to speak without notes if his turn should come. He had frequently lectured to several hundred students at the university; but now, looking around the empty hall, the prospect of addressing seven or eight people and a sleeping dog seemed a distinct possibility. Glancing up at the clock, which had now ticked round to 7.05pm, he caught sight of his research assistant, Sue Carter, as she approached with a worried look.

'They aren't going to turn up, are they?' she said, sitting beside him. 'Never hold anything on a soggy November evening… we should have known better.'

He looked into her anxious face, smiling reassurance. 'I wouldn't be in a hurry to rush out myself on a night like this, Sue. But I've a fancy the prospect of tea and biscuits might just do the trick… let's wait and see, shall we?'

Kline had said this with fingers crossed behind his back, but at that point the hall door swung open and an enthusiastic young man, barely out of his teens, entered drawing his girlfriend behind him with an encouraging hand. He had a lively expression, full of intelligent good-humour, and a shock of dark shaggy hair drawn into tufts and tied up at the ends with bright ribbons. The girl appeared more reserved, but upon noting the seated group, she too returned their glances with a winning smile.

'Wow, I'm glad we made it!' said the young man brightly. 'The bus from Bromsgrove was a bit slow I'm afraid. We were held up for twenty minutes because a lorry had skidded across the road – but we got here at last! There's some others coming up behind as well; we've been chatting to them on the way… but I say,' he said, suddenly checking himself as he looked round the empty room, 'there isn't any charge is there?'

'None at all,' Kline replied, smiling. 'Although you can make a donation toward the refreshments if you'd like to.'

'Thanks, I will… the name's Pete Janelka, and this is Kileen. …People say we're an item, but I say she just keeps me out of trouble – for which I am truly grateful,' he added.

Other voices could now be heard and a further six people soon entered. They were already engaged in lively conversation and observing that the previous couple had gravitated to the back row, retreated there to join them.

It was a start – but would this be all? The answer was only a moment in coming. Another couple now appeared, middle-aged folk this time, the man still wearing his day suit, the woman neat and businesslike. They sat down together at the side of the hall, just as a second group, a mother and father with their teenage son and daughter, also entered and took up position in the second row. From then on, with the clock moving round to seven fifteen and beyond, a steady stream of arrivals continued: first an elderly couple with a damp and tired looking Scotty dog, then a gaggle of students, followed by a local church party and several more families with their friends. Hot drinks and sandwiches were handed round and a gentle buzz began to grow up in the hall. In all there were seats for eighty or ninety and within twenty minutes more than half had been filled. But then Sue Carter, who had been supervising car parking arrangements, suddenly scurried in from outside. Her expression was one of concern mixed with surprise and disbelief.

'The car park's full!' she gasped. 'And guess what? Two mini buses have just drawn up – one from Birmingham and another from London. Apparently the people that hired them have been talking to each other on the Internet about our ideas and decided to make the journey to see what we are all about. They say there are at least another four groups trying to get here as well – including a sixteen-seater from Edinburgh! They all seem really keen!'

'Get them in,' said Kline, with a nod. 'We'll delay the start if we have to. It's the least we can do if people have travelled a long way.

'This is looking better than we expected,' he said, turning to Manny Singh. 'Do you think you'll still be ok speaking to a large gathering?'

'I'll do my best,' Manny replied, watching as the last available seats began to fill. '... But I'd appreciate you being around if I get lost for words.'

'I'll be there, Manny, don't worry. Let's see how it goes.'

* * *

By the time the hands of the old analogue clock reached the appointed moment, the situation inside the hall had been transformed, every seat having been taken some five minutes before, and although enough spare chairs had been found in the adjacent family room to form another row, three or four dozen people were left standing round the edge with others still arriving outside. Three visitors in wheelchairs had been accommodated near the front and an appeal to allow older people the opportunity to sit brought good-natured readjustments. The atmosphere was cheerful and expectant; the shared concerns and hopes of those present being discussed at every point.

'It's time to start, Manny,' said Kline after another five minutes. 'If we wait any longer we are going to seriously exceed our safety limit.'

Manny swallowed hard and rose to speak, but not before the rear door had been opened once more to allow in a mini bus group from Nottingham who filled the last available spaces. Others also looked in from outside – patiently standing in the November drizzle to hear what was said.

'Good evening, everyone,' Manny began, a little awkwardly. 'We are very pleased to see you all and promise not to keep you too long on such a night.'

'Don't worry, mate,' came a voice with a London accent. 'Everyone's made the effort to be here – you just tell us what you have in mind.'

Something approaching complete silence had descended, enabling the veiled swish of mizzling rain brushing the roof slates to be heard in the stillness. Manny had never before faced such an attentive audience and did his best to explain what the proposed new "Sustainability Party" would aim to do. He had carefully prepared a weighty sheaf of notes, which he fingered nervously.

'It is our belief,' he said, 'that the climate and our world are in a mess... That it is becoming beyond the capacity of our ecosystem to absorb any further man-made carbon pollution. We also feel that mankind's greedy waste of resources and excessive consumption are helping to fuel the current environmental disasters occurring around the globe. Having all but stripped our planet bare of the very stuff upon which modern civilisation is built, we think there is an urgent need to find another, more sustainable way to live. This will involve the rich nations, such as our own, learning to live more frugally – consuming much less in future; rather than ever more and more as constantly demanded now. Then the rest of humanity will be given a fairer opportunity to share what the earth can provide.

'The "Sustainability Party" will set out to challenge the everyday mantra that unfettered economic expansion, greed and global exploitation is the only possible model for human development. Our aim will be to help people to learn how to live in a state of self-sufficiency, without needing to plunder finite resources or bring the natural world to the point of mass extinctions. Those with vested interests in business and power will of course accuse us of foolishness and naivety; but we feel that the "vested interest" that we all have in our own survival and that of our children should now be given a voice.'

Manny went on to detail some of the many proposals that a growing "Sustainability Party" might present to Parliament, before inviting questions from the audience. These were many and keenly asked – some being relayed in from outside where up to a further one hundred people were listening.

The groundswell of support was unmistakable, but that support would remain tenuous unless threads were drawn together. Having got through his own part, Manny sat down exhausted and other members of the founding group came up to explain in further detail how the party would be established. The gathering was informed that all those present could become members and as such would be eligible to stand as "Sustainability Party" candidates in their own areas. On a rising wave of enthusiasm it was decided within an hour that the new Party would be represented at forthcoming local elections in London, Birmingham and sixty other towns and cities the following spring. However, there was a general consensus that their efforts would stand a better chance of success if fronted by a leader with whom the public could identify. Yet who should that be? …Who would stand as a target for the press in the stale but still hostile world of mid-twenty-first-century politics?

The man who had said least among the founding group, Kline Anderson, was the one their eyes turned to. The lecturer, who had many times quietly inspired them with his ideas and support, was presented to the audience before reluctantly taking the chair.

*   *   *

As his close friends and associates knew, Kline Anderson was an intellectual and a free thinker, but at no time in his life had he desired or coveted high position or power. Although a persuasive speaker, he remained disarmingly un-assuming and would listen to others for half an hour without interrupting, nodding his head in open approval at the wit and wisdom of his colleagues, while dismissing with a deprecating hand any suggestion of his own. The gathering patiently waited for him to speak as he returned their gaze.

'I will be a leader if you must have one...' he began at last. 'But you must never come to regard me or any that you raise up as indispensable. As a party we have much to tell people; a new way to explain, and there are many that will mistrust or mock our motives. Sustainability is but a word in itself, but will seem a daunting prospect to those who have come to depend so much upon the labours of others, while producing so little themselves. Our message may be difficult for many to accept, but will make increasing sense if people are successfully encouraged to look beyond the chaos now being caused – to visualise a future where our descendants have learned to wisely use and justly share the limited resources of our planet.'

Here he brought his hands together before him, as if to represent a small and fragile thing – a child or a feather – clasped between powerful crushing palms.

'I put this to you; that there is now no other course. Either human beings change their wasteful and damaging ways, or mankind will be progressively expelled from this earth by starvation and natural disaster; leaving behind a much emptier and degraded place to regenerate itself over many ages. We have, I believe, a stark choice... move willingly towards an intelligent and sustainable future... or like dinosaurs mired in a mess of our own making, crawl slowly to the point of extinction. Some will not wish to listen; but we must tell them anyway, for in itself that will be a worthwhile task. And if we fail, we will at least know we tried although the odds were against us.'

Total silence had fallen upon the gathering, a silence born of rapt attention – the listeners hanging on every word. It was as if he spoke to each of them personally.

'But I don't think we will fail,' Kline went on. 'The time is near when the old assurances of prosperity without responsibility will seem as empty as the people that make them. There are millions who will heed, having suffered much themselves already, and countless more who will do so within a few years. These fellow citizens of our earth must be given cause to maintain hope in the days to come – the promise of a new direction. It is our purpose to provide them with this, and I believe that in doing so we will prove ourselves neither dreamers nor fools..., but messengers. As such we must now have the courage to take our message to the people – to paint a broader canvas.'

Kline Anderson's words were not delivered in a strident voice, as so often heard at political rallies, but instead he spoke in a level, measured tone, the import of his convictions dropping into the listeners' ears with the cool weight of reason. Their impact could not have been greater, for few who were there would leave without a sense of newly implanted resolve, a will to be heard. The seeds of the "Sustainability Party" were sown in that five-minute period – it had found both a voice and a leader.

* * *

Before the meeting broke up that evening a committee of representatives was chosen to co-ordinate the future campaign, each returning home to share with others what they had heard. Further plans were made in the following weeks. Finance would be provided by two benefactors: Paulo Canacha, a Brazilian filmmaker and broadcaster, and David Kelton, the manager of Conservation World, a visitor attraction dedicated to the survival of species made extinct in the wild. Media exposure would be provided through the current affairs channels of Canacha Digital and when the local elections of May 2054 approached, each candidate began to campaign in their selected area.

There was a period at first when little interest seemed to be shown. But then, three weeks before polling day, the new "Sustainability Party" gained airtime on radio and television, from which point something seemed to click. A spark of interest grew; attendances at local meetings swelled – trust was cemented. In a steadily rising wave, new supporters came on board; voters from all walks of life. Even the national media, previously engrossed by the usual three-party dogfight, reluctantly took note. The result was remarkable: coming from nowhere, within two weeks the "Sustainability Party" began registering a five per cent rating of voter support – enough for the leader of the Conservative Party to dismiss it as 'an irrelevance in the pragmatic circumstances of modern day politics'. Progress did not fall away, however, and on polling day a total of one hundred and thirteen candidates, including Kline Anderson, Pete Janelka and Manny Singh, were elected – the "Sustainability Party" had arrived.

* * *

Gaining a voice in politics is only the first step – coming to use it well is the next challenge. Those that are committed to new and vibrant organisations often fall prey to their own naivety, showing themselves ill prepared when called upon to justify their ideals and policies. The media sharks and political strategists of the other leading parties rounded on the fledgling organisation from the start, determined to head off the threat it posed. Emerging Sustainability Party personalities were targeted: Manny Singh and Pete Janelka being invited to attend a morning breakfast show on the day their election victories were announced. Having agreed to go on without seeking advice from the rest of the leadership, and still slightly inebriated and tired after the night's celebrations, the two were torn apart. Walking into the studio they found themselves confronted by a panel of hawkish representatives from the three main parties, accompanied by the right wing political columnist for a bestselling daily newspaper. The chairman was Victor Brannagan – waspish political affairs commentator for the BBC.

Within minutes, both men, still looking dishevelled from their revels, found themselves facing a barrage of barbed questions about the party's aims and objectives:

each carefully prepared and designed to slice through the credibility of a party daring to call for a cut in economic growth at a time when, said Victor Brannagan, 'such expansion provided the only method of feeding the still increasing world population'. As the two men floundered in the spotlight, the alternative view that the sustainable and necessary expansion of food production could be achieved without an equivalent and unsustainable rise in the production of non-essential consumer goods was prevented from coming across.

Kline Anderson had returned to the London home of his ageing mother that morning and lay dozing on a settee by the window when Emma came in from the kitchen to tell him what was unfolding on the television. She switched on the set in the lounge and Kline, propped on an elbow, watched as Pete Janelka tried to offer an impromptu demonstration in mime of the various methods of alternative energy generation using solar, wind and wave power. He had again braided the tips of his long hair with a variety of brightly coloured ties, and the motion of his swaying arms and nodding head gave the appearance of a colourful and awkward scarecrow performing at an Edwardian freak show. The more Pete tried to emphasise the need for these and other methods of producing energy without releasing further climate changing carbon emissions into the atmosphere, the more ridiculous he looked. What Pete actually said made a great deal of sense, but the audience were not encouraged to listen. The visual spectacle of a young man being made to appear a fool was the entertainment of the moment, and the crocodiles seated around him were past masters at pouring scorn and ridicule upon their victim.

Ironically, beyond the blinds and glass of the studio window another torrential spring storm of thunder and lightning was in progress, the heavy, once unseasonable rains now delivering a fresh glut of water to already overflowing rivers. Growing crops were being beaten down in the fields, blossom torn from the trees by capricious winds, and slates blown from exposed roofs; while by nightfall, towns and villages up and down the country would be swept by flash floods. Yet in that warm BBC studio, the only concern was that an alternative voice of hope and change should be "exposed", routed and put to the sword!

Kline Anderson watched the cynical manipulation of his friends with a sense of calm determination.

'They're having a bad time, aren't they?' he said, pulling himself upright.

Emma had come to sit beside him, her chin cupped between her hands. 'They're like boys thrown in with vipers,' she concurred, almost wincing as Manny Singh, looking lost and unhappy, was challenged to join in the pantomime.

'They'll learn from it, as we all do from our mistakes,' said her son in an even voice. 'This is the first time the Opposition have taken us really seriously and had a real go, but it won't be the last. They fear us now and want the public to laugh us back to the fringes; but we have those votes, and the one hundred and thirteen elected councillors to give us a voice. This is a setback, but we will recover. The important thing from this point is that we continue to grow.'

He rose and stood by the window, first peering out at the pouring rain before looking down into his mother's face, his eyes reflected in the light of the lamp. 'Tomorrow I'll call a meeting for all our representatives to discuss how to go on in future. No one will fall into this trap again… that I can promise. As for the Opposition and the media, I'll be the one to face them next time. If there is still a proper job for a leader, then that would seem to be it!'

* * *

The following day's newspapers did indeed savage the new party. Headlines pronounced that the nascent political organisation had proved itself a laughing stock:

<u>The Times</u>
"Sustainability Party activists make fools of themselves"
<u>Daily Mail</u>
"New Brooms or Buffoons?"
"Don't be taken in by this farce of a Party"
<u>Newsforce</u>
"Third Rate Christmas Charade!"
"Sustainability Party proves hopelessly lightweight during first media outing"
<u>The Guardian</u>
"No Coherent Vision – Sustainability Party must do better"

* * *

The furore raged for a month – popularity ratings showing that support for the party, having blossomed so recently, had fallen once more to virtually nil. But setbacks are there to be weathered and within itself the Sustainability Party began to regain its feet. There were a few desertions, but a quiet drift back towards the embryo political voice gradually outweighed these. Known faces kept a low profile for a while; the Party concentrating instead upon spreading its message through local contacts and open meetings. By November – a particularly stormy and unpleasant one in which power cuts and supply problems dominated the news – lost ground had been recovered and the Sustainability Party began looking towards the elections of the following spring. A venture onto national television was again in prospect – political analysts pronouncing that the country wanted to see once more the colourful representatives of the organisation. To this end, and doubtless hoping for more of the light entertainment resultant the previous May, the BBC invited the Leader of the Sustainability Party to attend an early evening session of "News Forum" and he duly arrived at the studio to present himself for the seven o'clock show.

Dressed simply in a neat jacket and corduroy trousers, his shirt open at the collar, there was some surprise at first that Kline Anderson should have come alone and unaccompanied. He sat waiting calmly in the foyer, occasionally talking to members of staff who approached to brief him on procedure. Throughout, the previously little seen leading figure retained a polite and good-natured poise, smiling affably through polished glasses when brought coffee, before resuming an attitude of quiet reflection and preparedness. Many were greatly impressed by his manner; from the blonde secretary who watched him from behind her desk, to the studio briefing assistant who had dealt a hundred times before with people about to face interrogation by the legendary Victor Brannagan. Most usually quailed at the prospect; painfully clasping and unclasping damp hands, their faces pale. But here was a man who betrayed no emotion regarding the coming ordeal – simply a focused resolve. When he was called to go on stage, the operations room had filled to capacity, all wishing to view the contest and get the Sustainability Party leader's measure.

* * *

Victor Brannagan was a seasoned interviewer and a bully. An initial handshake across the table was his only concession to formal courtesy and politeness. From then on the "guest" could expect a grilling on any subject, either political, private or personal. Some were given an easier ride than others if he sympathised with their views, but those he disagreed with or personally despised were not so fortunate. An intelligent and articulate speaker, he could undermine a nervous or uncertain guest in a few words, and would then subject them to a merciless barrage that often shattered the interviewee's confidence, and with it, his reputation. He was a master of his art and like a cat with a mouse took obvious and calculated pleasure in exercising a sharp wit.

A big man with broad features, dark bushy eyebrows and a wide mouth, Victor Brannagan looked upon the relatively diminutive, slightly built, bespectacled leader of the Sustainability Party with barely concealed disdain. Then, having watched him sit, he relaxed back into his chair with the air of someone anticipating easy sport. The fact that Kline Anderson should walk into his studio casually dressed, as if merely out for the evening, giving added reason for sharpening his claws. Regular viewers would have noted the narrowed eyes, for although an unlikeable television personality because of his caustic manner, he nonetheless achieved excellent viewing figures due to the revelations and entertainment that resulted from an abrasive approach. Over seven million viewers were tuned in, few having seen the leader of the Sustainability Party live before, each curious to see how the interview would unfold. At last, Victor Brannagan, hands clasped together with thumbs raised, leant across the table, his features creasing into a sardonic smile.

'So, Mr Anderson,' he began blandly, cracking his knuckles. 'I understand that we are supposed to believe your "Sustainability Party" possesses the secret of how mankind might save the earth. Is that right?'

'Really?' replied Kline, adjusting his glasses and meeting the other's incredulous look.

'Oh, come on, Mr Anderson, surely you don't expect to be given air time on this programme and provide only single word answers to my questions?'

'I will answer all your questions in full if they are asked seriously and with respect.'

'Respect!' cried Victor Brannagan, leaning back and tossing his head dismissively. 'That is something any leader must learn to win through concise argument and clear answers, not through evasion and prevarication.'

'I will be sure to do so when you choose to make a valid enquiry, Mr Brannagan. But if you merely treat me with contempt and ask questions that no wise person could properly answer then I must wait until you have settled more appropriately to your task. I did not come here to be the butt of your ill manners, but to explain, in the few minutes that we have, what my party believes is a way out of our present difficulties. There will be many whose homes have been flooded again this night who look for some hope that we can plot a way out of endless decline – if not for themselves, then at least for their children and their descendants. That might not involve attempting to preserve the world with all the attendant luxuries that you and I have grown to enjoy. But I am sure there are entire communities now suffering recurrent disasters who will think that discovering ways to sustain a basic, but adequate and just standard of life for all human beings, is better than allowing our carbon footprint to become a gaping cavern that will lead to the starvation of millions and the end of civilisation.'

Victor Brannagan, who normally interrupted and harangued his guests as they tried to put over their views, had been uncharacteristically quiet while Kline was speaking. But now, hearing the ripple of applause that broke out among the invited audience, he felt disposed to go back on the offensive.

'What all this amounts to,' he intoned cynically, 'is just another case of the well-meaning few putting forward a "pie in the sky" solution to a major problem that only developments in science and technology can solve. You would tell us that the cure for climate change is for us all to roll up our sleeves and return to a traditional and outmoded way of life, which is nonsense, surely?'

At this point, Kline Anderson leaned forward almost confidentially, closing the space between him and the great television personality – an action that to everyone watching seemed to put both men on an equal footing. The presenter drew off a fraction, as if taken aback by the other's show of assurance and resolve.

'I'll thank you to allow a fair explanation of the views of my Party, Mr Brannagan,' said Kline pointedly. 'Firstly, may I confirm that we do indeed suggest that people, particularly in the developed world, will have to greatly reduce their demands for power and consumer goods. And yes, we will all have to travel rather less; perhaps giving up the convenience of flying completely, while using our cars more sparingly. We will also need to "roll up our sleeves" to grow more and produce more for ourselves – often without the use of fuel or power. It is not a sin to put one's shoulder to a task or rely on a strong back... But secondly, no, we are not stupid enough to think that nine billion people can be provided for without harnessing the benefits of technology. We must develop our use of solar, wave and wind technology and continue to learn new ways to recycle and reuse everything that comes to our homes. Then there will be the challenge of excavating and using again the billions of tons of materials that lie buried in waste tips outside our towns and cities. To do all these things and more, the rapid development of our scientific and technological skills will be as much a part of the way forward as creativity, innovation and honest physical endeavour.

'Therefore, don't seek to mock me, Mr Brannagan. ...Ideas are important – and we bring ideas. It is for you and others like you to give ordinary people the chance to listen and make up their own minds. Our world has changed, as the recently concluded world conflict undoubtedly showed. Wars and weaponry may have been used to build empires in the past, but it will now take carefully planned and executed measures to enable us to live with the effects of climate change and ensure the survival of our species in times to come. We in the Sustainability Party believe that there is no alternative and have confidence that it can still be achieved – since we owe as much to our children and our children's children. Now, if you will excuse me, I think I have taken up enough of your viewers' time.'

* * *

With these words Kline Anderson stood up and walked out of Victor Brannagan's studio – something that had never happened without the presenter's bidding before. There was minor uproar, but he left amid a round of applause from the audience and was followed on screen to a waiting taxi. The Leader of the Sustainability Party had made his mark – the nation would not forget.

Next day his face was in all the papers, the events of the television interview being discussed by half the nation – sometimes by people offended and gnashing their teeth – but more often among those full of approbation and excited approval. In the short space of a ten-minute interview the fortunes of the Party had been restored – its leader gaining instant recognition, together with more than a smattering of potentially dangerous enemies.

The following May, as Kline Anderson stood watching the rising flood waters from newly rented twelfth floor offices in Canary Wharf, the now steadily growing organisation planned to field candidates in over a thousand council seats up and down the country. Popular support had been running high, being recorded at around twenty-one per cent in the most recent poll of voting intentions, with every sign that this might increase during the last days of the campaign. And so it did – bringing a further six hundred council representatives and establishing the new voice in local government as the third most favoured in the country. Then, just one year later, the political world was turned on its head as in May 2056, following even more disastrous floods in London and South-Eastern England, the Sustainability Party took three hundred and sixteen seats at the General Election and in doing so rose from nowhere to become the governing party of Great Britain, with Kline Anderson as its first Prime Minister.

Chapter Nine

The New Way

LEFT BEHIND BY JEANNIE AS THE SPRING floods of 2055 receded, Toby Freeman once more retreated to the camper van – there to sink beyond reality for a further thirty-six months. As a consequence, both the renewed devastation of the following year and the momentous general election soon after, passed beyond the limits of his sleeping world.

* * *

Meanwhile, the newly elected Government faced vast problems: a capital city swamped for a second time and half functioning; millions of people temporarily or permanently displaced; food supplies disrupted and transport networks in crisis. Indeed, as some cruelly, but rightly, pointed out, the situation might have been designed to overwhelm the incoming Sustainability Party – to wash it away with the silt that had been scoured from the countryside of South-East England. Moreover, the problems did not end there; for a series of freak whirlwinds later tore through the Midlands as summer progressed, to be followed, in October, by a week long storm across Scotland and the North. Then, in early December, a vicious Atlantic gale, of tremendous force, swept onto the seaside towns of Cornwall, Devon and South Wales, wrecking many almost completely and leaving not a single coastal structure undamaged between Torquay and Ilfracombe. There was considerable loss of life, and a state of near panic in these areas, with the result that the armed services had to be sent in to give assistance and maintain order. But the magnitude of the task dictated that even with all the resources available little could be offered to alleviate the worsening situation. Power stations were out of action, water services disrupted; the transport system, where intact, left operating at half capacity, due to lack of fuel. As a result of this appalling sequence of events, it became increasingly clear that the economic life of the country was slowly being strangled and put on a survival footing; while as the crisis deepened, a mood of fear and uncertainty began to grip the heart of the country. Yet it would be a final stab in the back from another quarter that forced all but the blindest, or most deluded, to face the prospect of a new and emerging reality.

In early February 2057 the country's second largest insurance company (by now deluged with claims for flood and storm damage) announced that, due to a liquidity crisis, it was ceasing to make awards to customers until further notice. Within six days its fellow competitor companies had followed suit – two filing for bankruptcy less than twelve hours later. Thus, within the space of a week, the reassuring safety net for so long relied upon by millions to help them through difficult times, had been removed. There were widespread protests, strikes and threats of civil action. Financial and insurance premises were blockaded day and night as people demanded their savings, or recompense for valueless policies. A run on the high street banks caused an almost immediate suspension of business by three of the weakest, while others limited withdrawals. Panic buying of everything from Weetabix to shoe polish hit the shops; fighting broke out in the emptying aisles of supermarkets. It was a situation quickly getting out of control and requiring a cool nerve – a nerve supplied by a Prime Minister still less than one year into his first term of office.

At six o'clock on the evening of St Valentine's Day Kline Anderson, his personal popularity rating, and that of his party, having slid again into single figures, appeared on television to appeal for calm. In a level and evenly delivered address, offering no promises of a quick and easy solution, he reminded viewers of the enormity of the task. The combined damage of all the year's natural disasters was estimated, he said, at over seven trillion pounds – way beyond the capacity of government, the banks or insurance companies to fund from limited reserves. What was more, similar natural disasters had occurred in profusion across the globe, leaving turmoil in a hundred countries. There was a need for the people of Britain to collectively take stock of altered circumstances; while for its part the Sustainability Party would present concrete proposals for the establishment of a "New Way Forward" as soon as possible. In the meantime the country remained on what amounted to a war footing – everything possible being done to restore power supplies and maintain essential services while the planning of long-term solutions was undertaken. Until the latter could be brought to fruition, every individual must be prepared to play their part by adapting to what might prove a permanently changed situation: getting to work as before and sharing transport wherever possible. If an atmosphere of calm and co-operation was allowed to prevail, then recovery would come.

The newly elected Prime Minister's words were heard in countless living rooms, causing many to grumble vociferously at first; but gradually increasing numbers were won over by the sincerity and conviction of Kline Anderson's delivery. He finally went off air at six forty-five, leaving a national debate humming in twenty million households. In a measured and calm way he had asked each citizen to exercise restraint, patience and shared responsibility in order to prevent a descent into hopelessness and chaos. There might have been a violent reaction to such hard logic; but most of his listeners were already fatigued and frightened – with the likely risks of social breakdown becoming all too evident around them. If the new leader and his Party could indeed plot a way out of the nation's difficulties, it might be worth giving Kline Anderson's Government time to decide upon an effective programme of measures. The need to allow a period of grace having been accepted, most of Britain slept that night and went to work the following morning.

* * *

The slow process of recovery continued through the summer and into the following autumn. Several banks did partially restore their daily operations – although the insurance companies would all disappear into the oblivion of that sector's final collapse, taking the policies of countless families, pensioners and companies with them. Meanwhile, a substantial number of businesses managed to shamble along on a reduced basis – although many, like crippled and winded beasts, could only stagger to the end of each week with little guarantee of being fit to continue the following Monday. Jobs were lost, pay was cut and living standards fell. Yet, confronted with daily hardships, most did manage – just – becoming more generous and innovative when sharing, getting by with basic things and wasting nothing. Many grew leaner and fitter, while others remembered skills long abandoned in the throwaway age of convenience, as generations young and old began to learn again the rudimentary arts of self-sufficiency. Thus, chastened by another severe late summer storm, and still struggling to make damaged homes ready for winter, all now awaited the announcement of new government proposals to help the country move away from crisis. These, they had been promised, would be presented to the new sitting of Parliament at two o'clock on 5th November 2057.

* * *

It was in the early morning of this day that Toby again awoke, before venturing forth into the changing world once more.

Dozing, and only half conscious at first, he became aware of bells ringing, before rising up from the camper van bed to look out through the open doors of the garage. The sun was shining and having heaved himself from his place of rest, Toby went to stand in the open air. The rush of oxygen swiftly roused him as he looked around a deserted area decked with late autumn colours. The sky above lay cloaked by a mass of broken cloud, some heavy patches threatening rain, though at intervals looser wisps allowed shafts of sunlight to break through from a loftier region above. As Toby looked up, shielding his eyes, a fast moving mass of cumulus, warning of possibly harsher weather to come, blotted out the temperate rays, leaving an instant chill. But then, just as quickly, it was blown onwards to the east, and the sun, like a playful child peeping out from behind a high curtain, burst forth once more. It was a morning to share the joy of being alive but Toby was alone – nothing moved across the dry cobbles, or between the ivy covered walls, except a furtive wren picking among the leaf litter and an occasional passing blackbird.

He returned to the camper van considering what to do, rightly sensing that another lengthy spell of time had elapsed; but as seemed normal now, feeling no ill effects from many long days and nights of inactivity. What he did have was a sudden powerful urge to move on, to discover what had happened in the real world – to continue his journey home.

A quick assessment of the vehicle showed that again, although dusty, the battery still retained a charge, while the tyres miraculously remained inflated. Encouraged, Toby decided to leave then and there, hoping to draw as little attention to himself as possible before making firmer plans when he had driven beyond the confines of the city. Thus, having checked that the gate to the courtyard stood open, and after taking a final look around, he strode back inside to start the old VW, only noticing at the last moment a small square of paper held under the wiper blade on the passenger side. Toby reached forward to release it, the threads of a long disused cobweb wrapping themselves around his fingers as he took the discovered item in his hand. It had been folded once, the exposed side becoming light brown with age. Within a short message was elegantly written in copperplate:

"Travel to London when you are ready, Toby – I will meet you there, or on the way."

The note was unsigned, but he knew Jeannie's hand well enough to know that she alone must have penned it. Reading it again, an ironic smile spread across his face. He was to go to London – a city of more than ten million people – and she would find him there, or on his journey?

'And if I take a wrong turning?' he asked himself. 'What might happen then?'

But perhaps this should be only of passing concern… for after all, had she not already found him, more than once, on previous occasions…

Placing his trust in this recollection, Toby climbed behind the wheel, turned the ignition key and listened anxiously as the engine spun over before bursting into life in a flurry of white smoke. Like an elderly lady rousing herself from slumber, or a jaded dragon called upon to make one last laborious flight into the sky, the engine of the aged vehicle settled into a grumbling uneven rhythm, the exhaust note rising and falling as if some ancient brain composed of worn valves and pistons was trying to remember the required level of revolutions.

'That doesn't sound too healthy, old friend,' said Toby through clenched teeth, 'but let's see if you can still make one last effort.'

Depressing the clutch pedal he then gingerly engaged gear before slowly beginning an unhappy, spluttering progress into the open. The noise reverberating around the enclosed courtyard seemed more than enough to bring any listener running to investigate, but at first not a soul appeared as he crunched onto course gravel before turning towards the exit. As he passed through a young mother pushing a wheelchair looked up, clearly surprised to see such a fussy and loud apparition, but it was not until she had been left some way behind that another form caught Toby's eye in the mirror – a small figure emerging from the ivy covered wall by the gateway, to stand with hands on hips, slowly shaking his head, his eyes shaded by a broad brimmed hat. Toby could not mistake him, but in the time taken to toss a coin, Jasper dissolved once more into the backcloth of flora and stone – a wraith of light and shade dispersed by an eddying breeze...

* * *

The Ely that Toby now drove through was greatly changed from the day of his arrival. Considerable additional damage had evidently been suffered in the time between, yet he was struck by how little had been repaired in a professional way. This is not to say that buildings had been left insecure or uninhabitable; but rather that many rectifications seemed of a more makeshift nature than might be expected. Some had boarded windows, while others were retiled with slates of various sizes and colours, most clearly reclaimed from other buildings. Garden fences, even doors and windows, had been fashioned out of damaged sections taken from neighbouring premises: some crudely, others with more painstaking care, reflecting the pride of the owner. One house, standing among a number with roofs open to the skies, had been made habitable from the remains of several more; every window, panel and door a different colour – like a wacky structure from a children's playground. Yet the skill, humour and care evident in its appearance were remarkable, as if the owner had endeavoured to make a notable example of his efforts. At the garden gate stood a group of people all chatting and admiring the handiwork of their neighbour. They looked up as Toby passed, the children waving to him in surprise and excitement. That day he would see many folk similarly learning to survive by their own endeavours.

Travelling on Toby drove through streets almost devoid of motorised traffic: all the while seeing businessmen striding to work, or children journeying to school. A number turned to watch his progress, often inclining their heads and frowning at the trail of white pollution left behind in the spluttering camper van's wake. One or two angrily shook their fists and he was glad, upon passing the limits of the town, to drive into the countryside once more. Here much of the landscape had already taken on its dog day hues – the fields carpeted grey with beaten stubble, the ditches dark with standing water – although occasionally a tree or hedge, still vibrant with autumn colours, glowed red or orange when caught by the southerly sun.

With face set above the wheel, Toby drove on across lowland fen country towards Cambridge, frequently reminded that all was clearly far from well with the van. Occasionally there would be a loud misfire, then a flickering warning light came on, suggesting a discharge from the battery, to be followed shortly afterwards by the development of a crunching unevenness when changing gear that ominously threatened worse to come should Toby attempt a prolonged journey. Yet if he broke down, how would he continue?

With growing concern he skirted the famous university town, preferring to stay well away from its busy streets, and came at last to the southerly suburb of Great Shelford. Here, in a dip, the road passes over the main railway line to London – the narrow platforms of a wayside station situated just north of the crossing – and as he approached this the ailing engine coughed loudly, before abruptly expiring, leaving the camper rolling along at about twenty miles per hour. If Toby had continued straight ahead, forward momentum might have carried him down onto the railway crossing, there to roll to a halt blocking the lines. But at the last moment he saw a quiet side turning, tugged the wheel sharply and was able to swing into it. Now off the main road, the van rolled on for another forty metres, finally coming to rest under the broad canopy of a substantial horse chestnut. There seemed little prospect of his previously faithful conveyance being coaxed back to life, yet Toby was still a long way from London, with surely too far to walk. His only realistic option was to go by bus or rail – but without money how might he obtain a ticket?

'You've done your best, old friend,' he sighed, stepping away from the VW with hunched shoulders. 'Now it's down to me what happens next – although I confess I haven't much idea how to go on at the moment.'

The daunting prospect of needing to bluff his way onto a train filled Toby's mind as he retraced his steps to the crossing, before coming to a point opposite the station. At this still early morning hour the spot was busy with commuters, a steady stream coalescing at the entrance – most showing weekly passes, while others paid their fare at the ticket office. This particular building is a low structure with a traditional awning and Toby could see the attendant cheerfully greeting regular travellers, most of whom he obviously knew both by sight and name. Beyond was an automatic gate where a heavily built attendant watched as passengers swiped their tickets to gain access to the platform.

Feeling exposed and awkward, Toby sidled up, certain of failure, as a slim young woman stepped up to the ticket desk just in front of him. She was dressed like a city secretary, in a smart two-piece suit, her hair tied back under a fashionable hat with a mauve ribbon.

'Two singles to Liverpool Street, please,' she said, in a vaguely familiar voice.

'Certainly, madam,' replied the ticket officer with an amiable smile. 'I'm afraid the train is running about ten minutes late this morning, but no matter, you'll doubtless have a good trip when it arrives.' As she moved forward he touched his forehead deferentially, before calling, 'Next please!' and looking past Toby towards the customer behind.

Toby stopped, not knowing why he had been overlooked, and the attendant, realising Toby was holding up the flow, addressed him personally, 'It's alright, sir, you can go straight in... the lady has already paid for you.'

It was then that the woman turned back and Jeannie's face met his.

'We must go now, Toby,' she said, holding up two tickets between her gloved fingers. 'Come, be quick – there will be time enough to talk on the train!'

He followed her onto the platform as the 8.40am train pulled in and together they selected a quiet corner seat.

'You found me again,' he said, in a suppressed undertone as the train pulled away... in a little place like this... how do you do it?'

'It's not hard,' she said softly, her lips close to his ear. 'When you are awake, we know – for when you are up and about our attention is drawn to you.'

* * *

For the next half hour the two spoke only occasionally as the train rattled towards London and then on through the busy streets of the capital. There was much that Toby would like to have asked; but he knew that the purpose of their journey would, as before, be made clear in the course of time, and that then many of his questions would be answered. At one point Jeannie drew a newspaper from her bag, the main headline of which announced that the Prime Minister would be presenting plans for the Sustainability Government's "New Way Forward" that afternoon. She proceeded to immerse herself in the details, leaving Toby to his thoughts while looking out at the passing scenery.

As at Ely, the damage caused by recent storms and floods was to be noted in almost every street or park the train passed. Yet in the capital, too, there was much evidence of self–help and people pulling together – that the co-operative side of human nature was very much alive. He noted many rudimentary but effective repairs to roofs and chimneys, along with street shelters erected for the temporarily homeless. A smile or cheerful wave was seen at almost every corner, the faces that looked up showing fortitude and a will to overcome shared hardships. An on time arrival at Liverpool Street Station did nothing to dispel this positive impression as Toby stepped out onto a platform buzzing with activity. The main concourse was heaving, a great throng of travellers spilling from the train before steadily melting away toward the exits, each individual heading off to work without fuss or ill humour.

However, upon descending with Jeannie into the tube, Toby saw that here much was far from well. Every platform was packed with people, many carefully stepping round the belongings of displaced folk forced to sleep rough on the cold floors each night. A number, some of them young mothers with small children, still remained huddled together at the end of one platform; while a group of homeless, unemployed office workers were being served tea and sandwiches from a mobile charity kitchen. But something else, something odorous and unpleasant, increasingly impinged upon Toby's senses: a stench emanating from all around – through train tunnels, via ventilation ducts and escalator wells – a dull fetid smell of slime and stale sewage rising up from the deep subterranean bowels of London. It was all-pervasive, allowing no freshness to penetrate from any quarter, so that the station began perversely to resemble, in Toby's sight, a scene from a war zone, or the decaying capital of a corrupt dictator, rather than a location near the heart of a once proud and historic city. Now brought to the edge of collapse by forces beyond the power of man to control, such views provided stark testament to the brutal aftermath of natural calamity. Nonetheless, the people Toby saw were not broken, but getting on with their lives; still providing for their children and showing consideration for the discomfort and misfortune of others.

'From all that I have seen of the damage that has occurred while I slept, there is evidently still much to do,' said Toby as they waited by a flickering destination board.

'Much indeed,' Jeannie replied, 'though I doubt there will ever be resources or money enough to rebuild everything as it once was; for the whole world is under threat and London must now accept its share of pain. With good fortune, many parts of the city will recover in time; but I fear much will have to be abandoned for this human anthill became too large long ago.'

As if to confirm her view several hundred commuters besieged the already overcrowded incoming train – all of them pushing forward to find a place upon it. One set of doors opened next to where they stood and Jeannie, ducking under the arm of an alighting passenger, tucked herself inside. But when Toby moved to enter, he was immediately squeezed by a mighty crush of bodies, almost lifting him from his feet. Hands reached out of the carriage, some pushing, others pulling, as a loudspeaker demanded travellers stand back to allow departure, and Toby felt himself lost, unable to move, as the doors began to close once more. Then a slim but firm palm took his, and looking up he found Jeannie drawing him forward. He turned and sidestepped into a slither of space that opened to receive him, before being clamped tight again, this time between two rather surprised young women. Jeannie, meanwhile, had somehow made her way into the centre aisle, where she glanced back towards Toby with an amused, even mischievous wink.

There was little opportunity for release as the subway train trundled through stifling tunnels between succeeding stops, the same struggle to get on or off being repeated at every major station. The whole of London, thought Toby ruefully, must be on the move; with every person equally determined to scuff his ankle, step on a toe, or share the air within an inch of his face. Never before could he remember being so glad as when, upon arrival at Westminster Station, they managed to fight their way out of that moving prison, to ascend, stiff and shaken, towards the open expanse of Parliament Square.

It was a relief to be above ground once more, but here too the scene was remarkable. The successive spring floods and more recent storms had again done their worst, leaving a film of slime and silt, up to a line four feet above the pavement, on every wall and building. In some places this had dried to a flaking crust, teams of workmen being employed in an effort to remove it. But the smell of what remained, still damp and clinging to each slab or concreté block between Greenwich and Putney, filled the heart of the city with an unwholesome cloying reek that soured the air for up to a mile on either side of the Thames. Many people passed by with scarves held to their faces but only another hundred rains or more would flush away the pervading odour.

'Come, Toby,' said Jeannie, taking his arm as he looked up at Big Ben, the hands of which had long stopped at six twenty-eight, 'we must hurry; for a meeting is soon to be held nearby that I am sure will interest you.'

She led him forward across the moving traffic, then past the Palace of Westminster and onto to the lawns of Parliament Square. There, close to the statue of Winston Churchill, a series of portable offices and reception rooms had been set up as substitutes for those put out of use by flooding in the nearby Houses of Parliament. A large number of uniformed security men and police officers were present, all closely scrutinising newcomers and checking identification papers, and the two were channelled into a short queue outside a temporary conference facility, beside which stood an armed guard with an automatic pistol. Jeannie turned to Toby as they waited.

'The new Prime Minister, Kline Anderson, will address the reopening of Parliament this afternoon, to outline the Sustainability Party's policies for dealing with the present emergency. This morning, at eleven, he is due to speak to his elected MPs and most loyal supporters here before going to the main chamber. We will be allowed in if you let me speak on your behalf. Once inside there will be nothing for you to do but listen; for you have already done your part in bringing about this day...'

'What part?' Toby asked, turning to Jeannie with a puzzled expression. 'How can I, of all people, have done anything to affect what happens here?'

'Hush,' she replied. 'You have done more, and given more, than most will ever be called upon to do, and have my word that only a little extra time must pass before all is made clear.'

* * *

What Jeannie meant Toby could far from imagine, but calmed by her words he settled again to his own thoughts as they moved up to the security desk. Jeannie held forth a form when the security man spoke to her, and having allowed her bag to be searched, stepped through the entrance door into a corridor. Turning, she looked back at the attendant again and he, having closely scrutinised Toby's puzzled face, waved him through with a nod.

Once inside Toby immediately became aware of the chatter and hubbub of an already substantial gathering coming from the conference room to their right, where perhaps three or four hundred people were exchanging greetings and engaging in earnest conversations. Among them were a number of police officers and parliamentary officials, but the rest were mostly members of the new Sustainability Party, the majority MPs elected the previous May. A temporary speaker's platform had been erected at the far end, behind which a large display board announced, in the bold green and orange Party colours, "A New Way Forward for Britain – A New Start for the Earth". In front of this two or three leading members of the Government were already sitting; while to one side a raised lectern, complete with new "pinpoint" digital microphones, had been erected. Toby was immediately struck by the bearing of Pete Janelka, now more conventionally presented in a suit and tie, but still retaining his flamboyant shoulder length hair – never before can Britain have had such a remarkable Home Secretary. Beside him, Cookie Wilcox, another of the original-founding members, and now "Environment Secretary", sat in a colourful dress suit of green and orange; while gathered behind were other members of the Sustainability Party Cabinet. The Party colours were replicated at every point – on ties, scarves and rosettes – giving a carnival atmosphere to the meeting.

Yet one group were notable by their absence – the press and media being nowhere to be seen! Not a single camera or digital video recorder was evident, either in front of the platform or moving among the guests; for this was to be a private gathering, and prying, often hostile reporters were not invited.

Drawing Toby with her, Jeannie steadily worked her way towards the front until both stood by the wall at the side of the platform. The air was warm and sticky, but they had little time to endure this discomfort before two men walked onto the platform amid a burst of warm and enthusiastic applause. One, the shorter of the two, whom Toby already knew by sight, was in his late forties and had the look of a man for whom the responsibility of running his beleaguered country, although born with skill, weighed heavily. The other was younger, his tailored jacket and open shirt giving a confident and purposeful appearance. Yet upon looking out at the audience, the second seemed momentarily anxious; until upon catching sight of a group of friends, his expression relaxed in an instant, a smile spreading across youthful features. He was clearly well-known and liked, for upon seeing his reaction several voices called out and he returned their lively greetings with a friendly wave.

'That's Paul Anderson, the brother of the Prime Minister,' said Jeannie, looking up at Toby, '...the child you saw in the pushchair many years ago. He is not an elected member of the Government, but spends much time dealing with publicity matters. Paul still campaigns for the environment, as his mother and father did before him, and has won the respect of many for his firm and resolute handling of the press.'

The occupants of the room now began to settle and the older man, having declined to use the speaker's lectern, moved forward to the front of the platform. Kline Anderson adjusted his glasses and looked slowly round the gathering. He did not speak until more than a quarter of a minute had elapsed, however, seeming prepared to wait until each of the watchers had settled, allowing their attention to focus. The noise gradually died away to an expectant hush in which Toby could all but hear his own breathing. When Kline Anderson's opening words came they fell softly upon the air.

'Welcome, my good friends,' he said, slightly raising a palm. 'This is a big day and it is most heartening to see everyone here. The last six months have been difficult, since the people expect much of us, while to date we have been able to do relatively little. Every day, in the wake of tornadoes, cyclones or floods, the disturbed forces of nature leave their cruel calling cards, and governments like ours must struggle to bring what little relief we can. Hundreds were killed only this morning when a landslide, caused by melting glaciers in Tibet, buried a town and three villages, and there will doubtless be other such events tomorrow. The daily realities of climate change are with us; but how should we respond to them?'

Here he stopped and turned away to sip from a glass of water before looking back, his head slightly on one side, as if personally asking each of them to consider the question.

'Get the greedy banks to pay up,' came a voice from somewhere near the back of the room. 'Or make the failed insurance companies come up with our money,' cried another. 'They can't have lost everything!'

A spontaneous round of applause sprang up at these words amid other suggestions that the rich should foot the bill, and Kline Anderson waited patiently until the hubbub subsided once more before continuing.

'The argument that clawing back such wealth might solve the problem sounds reasonable enough,' he said slowly. 'But I think by and large securing adequate finance may only provide a part of the solution from now on. We are all familiar with the saying, "We cannot eat money", which is clearly true, but neither can we actually rebuild a house or a dam using fifty pound notes. Money is simply a vehicle for generating and rewarding human activity, but it requires the processing of natural resources and the toil of men and women skilled in using them to get things done. You say that the rich and the banks should pay; yet I would suggest that the present situation is beyond the means of any bank or insurance company to solve. Indeed many of these have long been engaged in a process of irresponsibly lending money they did not actually possess to people themselves wildly gambling upon a short cut to riches. Much of that theoretical wealth was like the notes in a Monopoly player's fist – worthless... No, we cannot simply buy or spend our way out of the present situation, for the current nationwide flood and storm damage will never be wholly put right by financial aid alone. What is more, we can be sure that other events of similar, or even greater magnitude, now lie ahead of us in the coming years. There is not enough gold or currency in the whole world to restore things to normal after every natural disaster; while if such demands were made, the whole financial system would inevitably become insolvent within a year.'

'Then how are we to survive and put right everything that keeps going wrong?' came another voice.

'I think part of the answer to your question is already becoming evident, not only in the damaged streets of our own capital, but also in every town and village of South-East England and elsewhere. Having learned that they cannot always expect the money and skills for reconstruction to come from another source, many have set about things in a different way, coming together as families and communities to collectively roll up their sleeves and set about rebuilding what they had. Increasingly, there is little chance for most to acquire new for old; so large numbers have adapted to the new reality by recycling salvaged materials. I would suggest that on inspection many will be found to have made a good job of this; most likely at a fraction of the cost which would have been required if State or private insurance money had been made available to them. With a few nails, a little power, and some sand and cement, miracles are being worked; and it is these millions of small local endeavours that the Sustainability Party must increasingly support and encourage during the months and years ahead. Meanwhile, it will be the Government's main task to rebuild hospitals, schools and the transport network, to clear sewers and strengthen sea defences.

'Today our Party will present to Parliament the policies that we feel are needed to help Britain towards a sustainable future. They will not offer a quick-fix solution to every problem, but hopefully a long-term way out of the climate change hole humankind has slipped into. We will not suggest we can put everything right for the people, but will offer proposals that increasingly enable local groups living sustainably to take control of their own destinies – building a new way for themselves and their communities. They will be backed in this by the best and most up-to-date advances that science and technology can provide – by a Government setting out to build the foundations of a positive future.'

Kline Anderson paused again, looking down with quiet dignity upon his audience.

'I invited you, as loyal friends and supporters, to meet with me here because I feel that our proposals should first be shared in simple, unpretentious surroundings – for it is surely in a million ordinary homes and villages that our "New Way" will be successfully established. We must primarily support rather than lead if the challenges of the future are to be met.'

He then announced the three new Acts to be presented to Parliament that day:

'"The Partnership Act" – requiring all local authorities to actively promote community self-help and recovery through the provision of essential resources, expertise and recycling facilities.

'"The Sustainable Energy Act" – This would promote the development of alternative solar, wind, wave and water energy production; with a target of bringing about the end of power generation using carbon dioxide producing fossil fuels by 2085. By this time, total energy use would be reduced by twenty-five per cent through greater economy and reduced consumption. (To advance the CO2target, the production of all petrol and diesel for use by road vehicles would cease by 2065.)

'Future recourse to nuclear generation had not been deemed a rational or viable option since available supplies of uranium are very limited. There remained, too, grave concerns over security of operation, and ongoing difficulties with regard to safe storage of lethal radio-active waste following decommissioning.

'"The Youth Engagement Act" – A bill aiming through education and practical training, to involve all young people in the daily processes of land management and food production; thus helping them to a better understanding of the natural world and its capacity to sustain life.'

Kline Anderson now looked around again at the attentive faces, as if reaching out to draw them with him.

'I must soon depart and make my way to the public chamber to launch these proposals, and fully expect there will be howls of protest from many quarters. But we will persevere with our programme: trusting in the resilience and good sense of ordinary people to build the foundation upon which a new sustainable economy can be established. We may already be standing, as many believe, on the very brink of climate and ecological Armageddon; but with the taking of these and subsequent steps towards the establishment of a planned and sustainable way forward, I believe Britain and the whole world will begin to pull back from the edge. For most people would surely prefer to live more frugally than be guilty of destroying the world their children will inherit.'

At this point he looked down toward an earnest teenage girl who seemed to have a question on her lips.

'I think you have something to ask,' he said, drawing nearer. 'Please take this opportunity… or else, as usual, I will talk too long.'

As if a spell had been broken, others smiled, causing the young woman to relax.

'I only wanted to say that such ideas are bound to be torn apart by some elements of the media, economic experts and our political opponents,' she said.

'Ah yes, the professional dissenting voices... You are right! But remember: devious and scheming people will always endeavour to pull the plank away from beneath a just ideology or sensible idea. Machiavellian self-interest and base cunning lie deep within the hearts of these men and women, and for this reason they must not be permitted to prevail. Moreover, if we are able to expose such malicious arguments for what they are, then I believe human beings may grow to live in a world without the starvation, cruelty and indifference that their machinations frequently bring. There is another way – but it lies far beyond a rich man's stunted dreams or a covetous life of avarice.'

Warm applause followed as Kline Anderson left the platform and prepared to depart, speaking with many as he passed; or more usually listening with head slightly bowed as those gathered round shared their feelings. Most would return home that night reassured and galvanised to face the coming challenge; encouraged by the words of an honest man without conceit or pretension.

* * *

Following the Opening of Parliament, the new Government's proposals were initially greeted, as expected, with disbelief and derision at media desks around the world; while the evening headlines were almost as explosive as the fireworks let off, in parks and gardens, to celebrate the thwarting of Guy Fawkes more than four hundred years before. But although the initial reaction among opposition commentators, politicians and parts of the business community was fierce, no such furore arose among the general public. Many tuned in to watch the Prime Minister's address following the six o'clock news and were impressed by what they heard. Tens of thousands had already begun doing much to support themselves in the face of enduring difficulties and therefore appreciated his assurance that their efforts would be recognised and supported by the Government.

Then, to the horror of many commentators, the Sustainability Party went on to steadily rebuild its support base, rising again in popularity. The need for change had been accepted, and at the General Election of May 2060 it triumphed a second time, this time with a slightly larger majority than before.

Chapter Ten

Carbon Zero

LONDON, WITH ITS WIDE THOROUGHFARES, SOARING OFFICE blocks and countless back streets, can feel a crowded, intimidating and lonely city. Those living in the capital are familiar with its rush and bustle – ducking into the tube or hopping onto buses with the assured confidence of rodents negotiating the tunnels of a vast labyrinthine warren. But to strangers, the mere transit between a few closely located public squares and byroads can be as confusing as setting foot in a North African bazaar, or taking the first step as a "fresher" student on the campus of a vast, sprawling university. A map is often essential to navigate a reasonably purposeful course. To venture without one is to be left to interpret an ever changing skyline, frequently matched at street level by a bewildering succession of eccentric place names.

* * *

When the meeting of the Sustainability Party broke up just after midday, Toby and Jeannie walked away from Parliament Square, making tracks towards the Pool of London along Victoria Embankment. A weak sun had broken through and all around intense activity continued unceasingly. A large new battery electric tug, hauling eight yellow recycling barges, glided by on the ebb tide, while one or two tired pleasure boats plied the muddy waters, their faded ensigns tugged by the river breeze. But these last craft seemed out of place amid the intense industry to right and left, as everywhere the more vital work of rebuilding and renovation progressed. The ground and first floors of every office block and building had been gutted: none escaping the high tide surge when the embankment wall was overtopped, causing riverside sewers to spew forth their filth. A cascade of noisome muck and debris had bubbled into the light searching out every opening, crack and doorsill, before seeping down again into basements, there to leech away across expensive carpets and polished floors. .Every electric circuit had been contaminated or washed out by the deluge – computer systems paralysed and photocopiers, printers and fax machines put beyond further use.

As recovery slowly got under way, much of this equipment had been dragged out into the streets for collection by recycling teams. To make way for it all, fine trees, many of them storm damaged, were felled to leave open areas where the winter sun shone down upon a jumble of discarded wreckage. In one such break they came upon an amazing sight: an old ship, the *Wellington* (long moored on the north side of the river as a restaurant and conference facility), stood beached and tilted in the roadway like the carcass of a stranded whale. A scrap recovery team was busily engaged around it and the foreman advised Toby that, at the height of the flood, the vessel had been lifted clear of the jetty by a swollen glut of floodwater driving upstream. For almost half a minute the craft had been held no less than fifteen feet above the normal height of the flow before being rammed against the embankment wall – ripping off the coping stones and having a gaping hole punched in its rotting bow. Then the venerable relic had settled back, sinking stern first to the river bottom, leaving the prow and forecastle sticking out at a near vertical angle above a churning stream. Within hours, the curious sight had become a magnet for sightseers, and soon an enterprising group of squatters clambered aboard to make a home in the *Wellington*'s skyward pointing cabin: each subsequently offering his or her services as paid models to budding artists of the unusual. But this ruse had come to a sudden and tragic end, when, during a subsequent violent squall, the ship – buffeted by both strong winds and a powerful tide – shifted sideways thirty degrees, throwing one of its newly acquired residents into the Thames to drown in the fast flowing water. The other freewheelers wisely left without delay and within days a decision was reached to break up the wreck – temporarily overriding a previous directive that all precious resources should be targeted toward the work of reconstruction elsewhere. Two powerful cranes were straightway brought in to lift the *Wellington* over the Embankment wall and now, as Toby and Jeannie watched, workers in protective headwear and grey boiler suits were engaged in reducing the carcass of the old ship to a heap of severed metal, the sparks from their acetylene torches arcing out like burning spittle.

There was a grim fascination in the spectacle and Toby might have stayed longer but Jeannie drew him away to witness other scenes – leading on past partially reopened offices and legal premises outside which lawyers and secretaries in prim suits picked their way through rumbling generators, churning cement mixers and piles of builders' waste. The City of London Authority was evidently determined that its commercial heartland should remain a going concern but here, at the very centre, it was subject to a massive recovery effort that would ultimately never be fully costed or completed.

* * *

The short winter day gradually drew to its end: lengthening shadows stealthily filling quiet corners before spreading out across busy thoroughfares. Streetlamps began to glimmer as twilight fell, and in another half an hour night descended upon the capital. Having taken a winding route, the two travellers wandered many streets during the short afternoon – Toby noting a thousand times the resilient way the populace went about their labours; some darting to catch a bus or train – others laughing or whistling as they loaded a van, or called down from the scaffolding bridging every pavement. But the working day was coming to a close – the queues at bus stops and a general flow towards the underground increasing as five o'clock approached. For perhaps an hour their direction had been away from the river, heading north. Looking ahead, Toby realised they were drawing near to the busy dual concourse of St Pancras and King's Cross stations when Jeannie turned to him.

Although roughly nudged by a passer-by, she managed to smile, though seeming a little distracted and sad.

'It is necessary that we part again, Toby… But I promise you will not be alone for too long this time,' she added, drawing back a wisp of stray hair. 'Now go where your feet take you – trusting that the path is set… though ever looking out for me during the coming years – for we are destined to travel another road together…'

A question sprang to Toby's lips, but before he had the opportunity to speak, Jeannie turned and immediately merged with the crowd. She disappeared in a moment, and not until several seconds had elapsed did the throng briefly part at a distant pavement edge, allowing a further glimpse of her head and shoulders. Then she seemed to drop from view as if swallowed by the rushing tide of commuters. Toby endeavoured to follow; but having stumbled at the kerbside, he caught only the briefest final sighting of her before she glided from view through the portal of King's Cross station entrance, her hat eclipsed among a sea of bobbing heads.

Toby hurriedly made his way to the spot – finding a newspaper seller stooping to gather something at his feet. The vendor slowly drew himself upright – oblivious for a moment of the milling crowd and a slightly irritated customer holding two coins towards him. In the seller's hand was a mauve ribbon that fluttered in the draught from the street like the downy feather of a bird.

'Funny thing that,' he mouthed absently, looking past Toby as if talking to himself. 'Just seemed to vanish as she walked past me… there one moment, gone the next!'

He took the glasses from his nose and wiped his eyes, staring again at the length of ribbon.

'Must be me old blinkers… the wife says I should change me specs. …Odd though… 'cos there was someone, really… weird, eh?'

He might have been a million miles away, his hand relaxing as he spoke, allowing the mauve ribbon to slide between finger and thumb before twisting and curling away on a lilting breeze to land beside a polished seat next to a ticket machine. Nobody else seemed to notice it and the vendor, having apparently emerged from a trance, resumed his normal banter.

'*Evening News*, sir – that will be ninety pence...'

Toby moved across to the seat, carefully picked up the silky ribbon, and put it safely into his side pocket before moving on.

* * *

After retreating to a quieter spot, the necessary consideration of what to do next occupied Toby once more. He had little practical knowledge of London and – cast adrift during the evening rush – the immense city seemed to surround him like a vast maze. The added problem of being without money also remained a major drawback and fully half an hour elapsed before, having vainly looked about for mislaid coins, he decided to try his luck beyond the station confines. The sky was now regularly illuminated by the bright flashes and colourful bursts of celebratory fireworks and the night had grown chilly, with a hint of coming rain, making the prospect of a prolonged journey less than pleasant. However, Toby resolved to travel on in a northerly direction, hoping to reach the outer suburbs where a dry and sheltered spot might be found to rest during the night. Through Kentish Town, Cricklewood and Mill Hill he trudged, gradually rising away from the heart of the city until, just before ten o'clock, he came to the Borough of Hendon. Increasingly fatigued by his wanderings, it was here that Toby began looking for a suitable place to stop and rest. He passed several bus shelters; but these, with their Perspex sides and narrow seats, provided neither comfort nor privacy. Then, having travelled another half mile, approached a wide park surrounded on all sides by low blocks of flats and private houses. There were still a surprising number of people around, and he quickly realised that this was because a late night Guy Fawkes bonfire had just been lit on the far side, which even at a relatively advanced hour attracted a fair crowd. Coming to a gate, Toby walked inside and following behind a group of boisterous teenagers, made his way towards the smoky blaze. He had no great wish to mix with other people, but the chill seeping through his thin coat, combined with the bright glow of the fire, drew him toward the festivities. There was much merriment: children held burning sparklers, the fire crackled and sizzled, while a well frequented burger bar stood beside railings at the roadside. A rocket suddenly shot into the sky – bursting in a brilliant shower of pink, green and yellow sparks that brought a chorus of delighted 'Oohs' and 'Ahs' from a wide crescent of upturned faces.

Only when he was within fifty yards of the gathering did Toby steer off to the left, toward an area of shrubberies and flowerbeds where, protected by a decorated Victorian canopy, he found a four-sided park bench offering a place of ease and shelter from which to watch the proceedings. A light rain began to fall as he sat down, but not until leaning back to rest his head against the weathered boards, after following the antics of a 'Jumping Jack', did Toby realise he was not alone in recognising the value of the vantage point. A slumped figure, drinking regularly from a beer can, already occupied the opposite end of the bench. Clearly in an advanced state of alcoholic submersion, the old chap paid no attention to Toby, but sat observing the display with a mixture of pleasure and grumpy disdain.

'Bloody smoke,' he growled, sitting up with a loud cough and staring blearily forward as the fire roared up. 'That'll do wonders for me bleedin' asthma. I wish people would take their stuffing fireworks and shove them somewhere, so that others like me might be left to enjoy a bit of peace and quiet.'

But then, as another rocket burst overhead, sending out a cascade of beautiful silver and gold streamers, his mood changed in an instant. 'Ah... now ain't that lovely?' he remarked, a bleary smile widening puffy cheeks. 'I reckon we should 'ave more of them as makes such a pretty show.'

So the curious and sometimes amusing monologue went on throughout the display; with Toby apparently ignored for the duration, and pleased, in such unpromising company, to retain his anonymity. There was a satisfying variety of fireworks and Toby, now warm and content, hunched down in his corner seat to enjoy them with his inebriated fellow spectator. They were both still looking on an hour later when the fire began to dwindle and the watchers, now left standing in a steadily falling curtain of rain, started to drift home. Eventually only a small number of youths remained: one or two of them larking around beside the dying fire kicking up the embers. The air became still and quiet once more except for an occasional distant laugh or shout and the soft swish of rain upon the shelter roof. Now entirely fatigued, Toby's chin sank into his coat collar, the soft even breathing of the drinker telling him that his companion had already passed beyond caring to sleep off an excess of Special Brew. Glancing sideways he saw the old man's crumpled form curled over the arm of the seat, an empty beer can still lovingly clutched in the hand limply draped across one knee. Thus assured of remaining undisturbed for a while, and gratefully taking the other's cue, Toby allowed himself to sink into a comfortable repose.

* * *

Another slippage of time followed. The hours came and went; some well used in the waking world, others dismally wasted – but all adding to a deeper history. Babies were born, while many departed the stage as the ever moving bus of life rolled on.

* * *

On the bright, sunny morning of 1st July 2060 Toby was at last aroused from his rest by a thumping sound on the roof. He found himself alone again, the adjacent bench empty – the stale aroma of his former companion long dispersed. The shelter had been freshly painted, and a play area, neatly bordered by green and yellow railings, newly erected twenty metres away. A pleasant breeze blew across the park, the air warm and richly scented with the smell of cut grass, but as yet no living soul seemed abroad. It was still quite early, perhaps before six o'clock, and the few human sounds to be heard seemed strangely muffled and far away. At this tranquil time birds and animals have such places to themselves and one of the former was responsible for having woken him.

A scratching of clawed feet sounded again on the tiles above, followed by the swish and "thump" "thump" of a winged arrival making its way from one side to the other. Such was the effect in the quietness, that for a moment Toby imagined a large and exotic creature had got up there – an escaped macaw or peacock perhaps – but before his imagination had chance to run further, a hefty crow hopped into view and dropped down onto the grass a short distance away. It was a sleek, well-fed and beautiful animal; coal black from beak to tail, with an amusing waddling gait that made it resemble a rather pompous dowager duchess with overtight stays. As Toby watched, the scavenger quartered and inspected the patch of land where it had alighted, occasionally stabbing its beak into the ground to pull out a worm or grub. Yet, on close observation, it appeared little concerned with eating; often tossing away a find to go off in search of other quarry, then turning and circling in his direction once more, as if intent upon keeping Toby in sight. It was the recurrence of a somewhat familiar ritual, and Toby felt little surprise when the crow eventually flew gracefully up onto the top rail of the line of swings, where it settled and eyed him steadily.

Unmoving, Toby returned its gaze for perhaps three minutes, made steadily more edgy and irritated by the bird's patient, intent stare. He felt exposed, uneasy that others might be drawn to the spot and find him there – that the crow might point him out. At last, unable to tolerate the tension any longer, he rose from the shelter seat and stepped out into the bright sunshine before moving towards the place where the creature perched. Immediately registering his movement, the crow lifted its head and paced three steps along the bar before becoming still again, allowing Toby to close the space between, which he did, coming to within little more than a metre from where the crow had positioned itself. He knew from experience that such birds are normally prudent and wary animals; but this one did not budge, confidently standing its ground and peering down with bent knees, his head cocked on one side in an attitude of rapt curiosity. There could now be no doubt that they had met before.

'Well, old fellow,' Toby said, looking up, 'it seems you know me.'

'Caaark… Ktark!' came the bird's reply, the last sound short and clipped.

'My thoughts entirely, but this conversation may be of little value if you cannot make yourself better understood.'

The crow looked down at its claws as if considering this problem; then glanced skyward for a moment before abruptly swivelling round to face the other way.

'Oh,' said Toby, a little surprised. 'So now the cat's got your tongue.'

The smooth head swung back briefly, as if its owner was mildly offended by this reference to a less than respected foe; then the crow turned away once more, this time looking toward the northern perimeter of the park where the chattering sound of an approaching vehicle had become audible.

* * *

A long circular road bordered the green space, along which Toby saw a vehicle moving. The familiar blue and yellow shape of the camper van had come into view, the sunshine face, with its Mr Punch grin, becoming live and animated as it moved between the trees. The VW slowed before pulling up by the park gate, Toby having recognised another familiar figure behind the wheel.

'Jasper,' he said to himself, as the crow took to the sky and flew off. 'But how did he get the old thing going again?'

Toby set off in pursuit; jogging up as Jasper, rag in hand, emerged from the driver's side and began polishing the front windscreen.

He looked up with his usual cheerful grin. 'I thought I'd give the old girl a wipe over since we've got a moment. She's been standing around for a while doing nothing and could do with a proper clean.'

This was certainly true: the camper was layered with dust and smears of mildew but nonetheless appeared in uncannily good order beneath the grime.

'How did you get it going?' asked Toby, thinking back to the morning he'd left the ailing machine near Cambridge.

'Oh I have my ways,' replied Jasper, winking and artfully touching his nose. 'I'm not just a pretty face, you know.'

Just then a newspaper delivery boy cycled up, stopped in front of the VW and gazed at it with a mixture of disbelief and disdain. One of those pert, street-wise London kids that confidently speak their minds with adults, the lad wasn't going to let a golden opportunity pass him by.

'Whew… what an old wreck!' he guffawed. 'Where the 'ell did you get that from – a dump or something? Even my grandad wouldn't be seen dead in that contraption… and he's over an 'undred.'

'You want to keep your lip to yourself,' said Jasper, turning and brandishing his rag. 'This is a much loved old friend, and the likes of urchins like you can't be expected to appreciate such things.'

'Old friend! What are you talking about?' continued the boy, completely unimpressed by the challenge. 'Are you some kind of ancient hippy or something? Haven't you 'eard that motors like these ain't welcome on the roads no more? I thought I sniffed something bad as I was coming along, and I was right – you can smell that old jalopy miles away! Surely you've read about the new pollution laws?'

'What new pollution laws?' asked Toby.

'Lor, don't you start as well, mate! Where 'ave you two been for the last few years? The new "Carbon Zero" laws bein' brought in are supposed to cut transport pollution to nothing before long,' the little juvenile explained, looking hard at the camper van as if willing it to disappear. 'The plan is to turn old crates like this into spoons, pronto – or even sooner if possible!'

Jasper was now clearly becoming vexed with the boy's attitude but the approach of a dog walker and two middle-aged female joggers provided a useful chance to end the exchange. Seizing the opportunity, he retreated to the driver's seat and restarted the engine, beckoning Toby to climb inside. By now the first jogger had stopped next to the newspaper boy, shaking her head, and all seemed amazed and fascinated by the old vehicle's noisy utterances.

'You'll never get fuel for it!' the woman called. 'They won't serve these old high-emission vehicles anymore. I do hope you've got enough petrol to get home.'

The well-meaning lady seemed genuinely concerned for them but the boy had no such charitable thoughts.

'They might have thought of that before they brought it here,' he said. 'Better still, they should ride a bike or rely on "Shanks's Pony" like the rest of us!'

The sound of his voice was then lost below the roar of the VW's engine as it pulled away, and Jasper, with foot hard down, seemed to delight in sending a denser cloud of white smoke than usual towards the diminishing figures, some of whom could be seen pinching their noses in disgust.

'Bloody kids!' he said, turning, the old sly but genial grin back upon his face. 'Don't they know a limousine when they see one?'

* * *

The following ten minutes were a revelation, for on this morning the streets seemed to carry less than half the traffic Toby remembered – much of it made up of buses and delivery vans. People were just beginning to get about; many riding bicycles rather than going on four wheels; while the pavements filled with people heading towards shops and bus stops on their way to work. At one point they pulled up at a huge junction equipped with batteries of traffic lights, where five major roads went off in different directions. There, forced to pause at a red light next to a centre island, they stood for a full half-minute in splendid isolation drawing the attention of cyclists and passers-by, who stared curiously as if at an apparition from a bygone age.

The construction of a tramway was under way on the road they were crossing, while at the next junction the installation of overhead wires showed that power was being provided for another form of transport. The work was evidently almost complete and a team of engineers could be seen making final checks to a power box and bus stop nearby. Noting this, Jasper swung the camper van into a lay-by next to a cemetery so that they might watch what was happening. The street was reasonably quiet at this point, although a little further on, beyond the bus stop, they could see people steadily disappearing into a tube station. The engineers had recently placed barriers across adjacent side roads and seemed to be waiting for something.

Toby looked up at the shimmering power lines, their supports often cleverly fitted onto adjacent buildings or combined with lampposts to reduce environmental impact.

'What is all this new equipment for?' he asked, turning to Jasper.

'Government works, mate! They're putting in trolley buses here and on lesser routes all over outer London. Closer in, and where the services are more densely used, it'll be tram lines such as you saw going down back there. It's being done quickly too – seeing as how things have got so bad with the climate. The plan is to get most people out of their cars and onto public transport within a year or two, so that the city can become carbon free as soon as possible. The power will initially be provided by wind and solar energy, but later much will come from tidal energy provided by the new Thames Barrage.

A rising flurry of activity among the engineers drew their attention, and looking down the road Toby saw a brand new silver and blue double-decker bus approaching. It glided silently up to the bus stop, but only when a small spark flashed above the aluminium roof did he realise this came from contact between its curving pantograph and the slender overhead supply cable. The trolley bus waited at the stop for about ten seconds, then moved forward, accelerating quickly and smoothly away before disappearing from sight – the very image of modern efficiency. However, the two had only a few minutes to wait before it returned again, this time filled with volunteer passengers, several of whom waved and pointed in their direction upon spotting the camper van.

Noting this unwelcome interest, and the renewed attention of some of the men working near the spot, Jasper turned pointedly to Toby.

'I think it's time we were heading on, old chum, as it appears likely one or two of the natives may be contemplating saying hello.'

Here he nodded casually to his left, where the local church vicar, watched by a growing gathering of pedestrians, had begun to approach.

'Best not hang around to be interrogated by a man of the cloth, eh?' quipped Jasper.

He started the engine, the abrupt roar of which drew further interest, and swung the camper van into the roadway just as the trolley bus stole into motion once more. It came up close behind and they were followed for the next two minutes by the sleek machine, looking for all the world like an ancient museum piece being effortlessly pursued by an earth bound science fiction spacecraft. Front passengers at the upstairs windows peered down: some amused and fascinated by the old vehicle, others clearly making uncomplimentary remarks about its less than environmentally friendly progress. The driver, a thin moustachioed man with a menacing expression, seemed intent upon staying a little too close, as if hinting that with a slight increase in power he might easily shunt the trundling camper van into final and ignominious retirement. Toby was somewhat relieved, therefore, when the brightly polished vehicle pulled up at the next stop before dropping out of view as Jasper drove on round a sweeping bend in the road.

By now the city had fully come to life: children with lap top satchels and lunch boxes were on their way to school; mothers with prams made for the shops; a uniformed nurse in a tiny electric car stopped at the curb to make a home visit; while early morning delivery tradesmen completed their rounds. An air of reassuring calm and good order thus pervaded the scene, yet there was much to remind a passing traveller that here, too, in the suburbs of the city, the effects of violent and unpredictable variations in the weather had made their mark. A recent freak tornado had traversed the area, carving an arbitrary path through side streets and gardens, several of which had lost trees, walls and fences in the blast. From a line of terraced houses, chimney pots, roof tiles and satellite dishes had been torn off; and these now lay piled among heaps of debris and twisted scrap, waiting for collection by the recycling department. Another fallen tree had damaged a water main, the force of its lifting roots tearing through strong plastic pipes to send a river rippling down the road. Further on a crushed car lay abandoned upon a shattered driveway, and close by the awning of a shop front had been unceremoniously dumped inside the play area of an adjacent nursery.

Much of this damage was already being worked upon as they passed, while the evidence of restoration work following previous storms could easily be recognised; functional repairs, skilfully executed for the most part, using wherever possible reclaimed materials fashioned to suit the needs of reconstruction.

These efforts would be worth a detailed study in years to come, but Jasper was determined to get on and quite soon began heading out of London along the A1 motorway to York and Edinburgh. The weather was still fine but blustery when they passed through the tunnel at Hatfield, the road becoming increasingly clear and free of traffic. Powerful diesel lorries occasionally passed in the opposite direction, their speed now strictly regulated to a stately fifty miles per hour; while a variety of other smaller hydrogen fuel cell and battery powered vehicles came and went along slip roads. But long distance road travellers like themselves were few, and for whole sections at a time the camper van was often the only moving thing in a half mile stretch of road.

'Why is there so little traffic?' asked Toby.

'Fuel's too expensive to waste,' Jasper replied, 'and the old diesel and petrol-powered vehicles are being phased out due to the tougher carbon laws. There are new types of road transport, using other forms of power, but these have their limitations; so most long distance passenger journeys and freight movements are made by rail.'

At this point they came to an inclined curve, and looking to his right Toby could see the old established railway line to Scotland. As he watched, a long crimson and gold passenger train of eighteen coaches sped by, while from the other direction, a lengthy double decker freight train rattled towards London – dozens of brightly branded containers catching the sun and giving the impression of a moving circus or shopping mall.

'Travel is not as easy now as it was a while back,' Jasper went on. 'People can't use cars like they did a few years ago, and not much goes by air any more. But there will be other ways of getting around soon, as you saw in London; and when the new high speed railway lines come on stream things should improve a lot.'

'New high speed railway lines?'

'That's right: two to the north – one to Glasgow, the other to Edinburgh. Then there's the "Wales and West" lines to Swansea and Plymouth, and the "Anglian" line to Norwich. They are being constructed at the moment, with completion due in five years' time: two hundred and fifty mile per hour railways that will run at fifteen-minute intervals, day and night – with off peak travel offered at a quarter of the normal fare. Every train will have twenty-four or thirty coaches offering seating for up to fifteen hundred people. When the new works are completed existing routes will then be turned over to local traffic and freight only. Some reckon that freight trains in the future will be up to a mile long – each one taking as many as eight hundred lorries off the road.'

* * *

They were now making their way to the top of a long rise near the village of Welwyn and the VW again began to produce some of the ominous noises that Toby had experienced during his journey from Ely to Cambridge. The oil pressure warning light had come on and a rather thicker stream of white smoke clouded the road behind.

Jasper turned to Toby. 'The old girl's getting tired like you and me, Toby. I'd best pull off for a bit and give her a chance to cool down.'

The sign to a lay-by and picnic area appeared just ahead, and coming to a short slip road Jasper swung off the motorway before driving in among a stand of sycamore and oak where picnic tables had been placed for the use of travellers. The site was now little used however, although the peace and seclusion it offered were pleasant enough, while a break in the trees on the western side gave a view over a valley and well established parkland beyond. A few of the surrounding trees were splintered and storm damaged, but most had escaped the worst effects of the weather and stood with age-old resilience, spreading their branches towards the sky. Birds and squirrels moved among them, but apart from these the travellers found themselves alone at the spot.

Jasper switched off the engine, lit his pipe, stepped out of the VW and went to sit at the nearest table, puffing contentedly.

'Much seems to have been going on since I went away,' Toby ventured, having joined him.

'You're right there.'

'What can you tell me?'

'That Kline Anderson's Sustainability Party has got itself elected again and has some serious policies lined up.'

'Such as?'

'Well,' replied Jasper, sitting back comfortably against the edge of the picnic table. 'You take the new "Carbon Zero Act" they are about to introduce – the first to be made law anywhere in the world. This will bring to an end the use of all diesel and petrol powered vehicles by 2065: replacing them where appropriate with cars and vans using other forms of energy. Power generation from fossil fuels is also to cease no later than 2085. It's a big step, but necessary if we are to stop adding to the climate damage that's already been done.'

'But what about aircraft… and ships… won't they still need aviation fuel and diesel?'

'If they do, it won't be coming from traditional sources; and it's highly unlikely any bio-fuel will be in production by then.'

'Why not?' asked Toby, already trying to envisage a world no longer dependent upon coal, gas and oil.

'Because the production of bio-fuel has been a bit of a disaster in the past, that's why. All that land turned over to growing the crops needed for it led to mass want and starvation in many parts of the world – not to mention the destruction of virgin forests cleared to produce the stuff. No, it wasn't the answer, and nobody except a few blind fools now questions that. All this has led to folk having to find ways of using less energy, but most are learning.'

Jasper went on to tell Toby about other government acts in the pipeline.

"The Sustainable Communities Act": This, he said, would promote a move towards local self-sufficiency in food and water resources, energy, health care and education services. With government backing, production and recycling facilities would also be sited locally – while where communities were found to be unsustainable at their present location, these would be progressively relocated. (The ultimate long-term goal of the act would be for nothing to be produced outside the area of consumption.)

<u>"The Protection of Wildlife and Natural Habitats Act"</u>: Under provisions of the bill, legal protection would be given to all natural habitats in both town and country, while henceforward the deliberate destruction of wildlife would be classified a criminal offence. The lawful holding of firearms for hunting or sport would end; with all pest control or culling of wildlife undertaken as necessary by licensed local wardens.

'There is one more,' said Jasper, 'and this has raised a few eyebrows, I can tell you. It's called <u>"The Death and Natural Burial Act"</u>. When passed in 2072, it will require that all future burials be of the "woodland" type, carried out within the local area of the deceased's place of birth. Cremations using fossil fuel would end, and only those held in accordance with religious traditions, requiring non-fossil materials, would still be permissible. The Prime Minister has said that it's a logical step and consequently something he wants for himself when the time comes.'

'I can see that might cause a stir,' said Toby thoughtfully. 'People don't like to imagine that what happens to them after they die might be controlled by the state.'

'That's one way of looking at it, 'said Jasper, getting to his feet and stretching. 'But I'd say being buried near to where you have lived your life, with a tree above to provide a bit of shade, is a very pleasant idea. More than that, it will also help to fix some of the carbon in the atmosphere, which can't be bad.'

As if to emphasise this link to the weather, the sky then clouded over with unseasonal speed and a fitful wind began to whip around them.

'Another bloody squall coming,' said Jasper. 'Let's hope everyone has got their runner beans tied up nice and tight or they'll find them blown over when they get home tonight.'

They returned to the camper van as the first drops of rain began to fall from a sky that had been clear and azure blue only fifteen minutes before.

'I'm going to take you on a little way further,' said Jasper, looking up from beneath his eyebrows. 'Not too far mind, because I'm almost done myself for a bit. When we get there I'll be leaving, but don't worry, you'll find your own way home – no sweat.'

Not waiting for a reply, he drove off to rejoin the motorway, the camper van groaning and complaining at every bump and gear change. Meanwhile, the downpour soon built in intensity – driven against the windscreen in slanting gusts that blocked out both sky and road between feeble wiper sweeps. Yet it was not to be a long cloudburst, just enough to cause an unpleasant drenching, and some unwelcome damage to crops and gardens.

Less than a mile further on they left the deserted highway a second time, soon drawing near to the small village of Kimpstead in Hertfordshire. Like many old and well-established places in rural England, this had an interesting history – as well as two very different public houses. The first of these, oddly named "The Duck and Dagger", stood in a main street lined by pleasant cottages and carefully restored former labourers' dwellings. It was spacious and relatively modern, with a burgeoning reputation for good food and entertainment. The other, standing in a secluded back road known as Coward's Lane, was smaller and far quieter, being frequented only by locals and the eccentric characters that naturally congregate in out-of-the-way corners, Named the "Tinker's Rest"; parts of the ageing fabric reputedly dated from Georgian times when mail coaches had passed through. Then, it was said, travellers wishing to avoid the unwelcome attention of dangerous thieves and revellers in the main thoroughfare had made their way quietly past its doors by the gentler and less frequented route.

Now, in the twenty-first-century, the hotellery had been brought up-to-date with some of the usual attributes of a modern pub: an Internet games room, facilities for karaoke and live music, and an outside television screen provided for the benefit of smokers sitting alfresco in a sheltered lounge area by the front door. It was beside the "Tinker's Rest" that Jasper pulled up as the rain ceased and the sun peeped out again between ragged clouds. Having told Toby to wait for him in the smokers' lounge, he went inside to order drinks, returning shortly afterwards with two pints of beer.

'This one's on me, Toby,' he said, sitting back and closing his eyes. 'I reckon we've had a few interesting times together and it's nice to be sociable at the last.'

'You're going away... and must leave me here?'

'That I am... and I'll be taking the van too,' Jasper affirmed, enjoying a long sip from his glass. 'The old girl's more than ninety years old, with a hundred and ninety thousand on the clock, which is plenty respectable enough to be drawing a pension... She'll be able to put her feet up from now on as it were.'

'And you, Jasper... what will you do?'

'Oh... I'll be around... never far away – just in case there's a need.'

'And me... what further steps should I take?'

'Just keep on for a bit longer, mate,' Jasper replied, some of the colour and life seeming to fade from his features in the shifting light. 'But don't trouble yourself none – the end to all this will soon come round. Whatever... I must be off!' he concluded, rising hastily after a moment's thought. 'Evening draws on and my good steed awaits her final oats. You yourself would do best to stay here for a while, so I've asked the landlord to bring out a bit of grub at six o'clock, which you can eat when the news is on. Just remember not to miss what is said during the broadcast, as I vouch there'll be something more for you to ponder. After that I can't say exactly what will happen – but your travels do not end here, so you must be ready to leave when the time comes.'

Jasper then returned to the camper van, and having coaxed the engine into life, leant out of the window. 'Whatever happens, simply keep moving with the flow, Toby. Oh...

and if a friend of mine should come this way – don't hesitate to follow where he leads. …Take care now!'

With these parting words he drove away, leaving no trace upon the muddy road, and as the sound of the camper van receded to nothing in the distance, only a faint smell of petrol fumes remained suspended upon the drying air.

Toby continued gazing forlornly towards the spot for some while, and not until upwards of ten minutes later did he realise he'd forgotten to ask about the dice…

* * *

Undisturbed by passers-by or patrons of the pub, Toby sat alone for another three hours. The sky cleared, leaving a golden light that enriched the dappled colours of tree and hedgerow while bathing the front of the pub in a mellow glow. The still air, meanwhile, became warm and humid, the evening perfect for doing little or nothing at all. Coming wide awake again, after a period mulling over his recent travels, Toby found himself struggling to cope with an uncomfortable and growing suspicion that he might be dropping below the compass of those in the ordinary world. There was the incident with the newspaper seller at King's Cross, and then the tramp in the park. This nagging doubt was to be bluntly reinforced only five minutes later when the landlord of the pub backed through the door carrying a tray containing a ploughman's lunch and a pint of beer. He turned and stopped abruptly, just six feet away, sweeping the smokers' lounge with puzzled and apparently unseeing eyes – his gaze passing directly across where Toby reclined comfortably in a shaded corner seat. Then, having apparently satisfied himself that his customer had gone off without staying to eat the requested meal, he shrugged his shoulders and stepped back inside.

Soon afterwards a similarly inexplicable thing occurred. This time Toby was facing the blank television screen when an old lady approached, muttering as if in conversation with herself. Clearly in a hurry to reach the pub for a given time, she shuffled straight by him, and having pushed through the entrance door, hollered peremptorily across the lounge bar, 'Oi, Randolf, switch the telly on will you! And pour us an arf of stout while you're at it!'

Her voice was raw and throaty, full of the crotchety imperative of the aged and self-reliant. Almost immediately the screen on the wall flickered into life, and having reappeared a few moments later, clasping a half of Mackeson, the old woman settled herself on the end of the bench nearest to it. She was white haired, with a lined and freckled face in which her sharp but watery eyes peered out below surprisingly large and heavy silver eyebrows. A pair of quaint steel rimmed spectacles, the right hand lens cracked, sat on the bridge of her nose – the defect causing her to squint. For this evening's regular sojourn at the "Tinker's Rest" she wore a pale, rose coloured dress beneath a white pinafore embroidered with dancing elephants, while her head was adorned with a curious, knobbly Tam o'Shanter hat. A loose cotton shawl, a pair of ancient woollen boots and a brown cotton bag fringed with yellow lace complemented this quirky attire. Ignoring Toby a second time, and for the moment preoccupied with the process of making herself comfortable, she settled to watch the news.

As the introductory credits rolled his new companion then produced an ornate chromium plated cigarette case from her bag, and lighting a filter-tip to the accompaniment of a chesty cough, peered short-sightedly forward through an enveloping haze of smoke.

A cheerful, casually dressed newsreader greeted viewers, but the news of the day would be almost universally disturbing.

'That Maxeena Kaur,' grouched the old lady, piping up, 'what does she look like? Fancy coming on wearing that – she might have a bit more style!'

A deep sip from the glass of stout sufficed to assuage her ire however, and having merely affirmed her unflattering appraisal of the newsreader's apparel with a loud, 'Tch tch!' the old girl intently listened to each ensuing report.

The first of these informed viewers that recent mudslides in China and Indonesia were estimated to have killed almost two million people: another ten million being left homeless. Also, the death toll from North Africa's three year long drought was believed to have reached five million; while fires in Siberia and Kazakhstan had destroyed fifty million square miles of forest during the previous month. That very day, the cyclonic flooding of low-lying islands in the Indian Ocean – long threatened by global warming – had swept away an estimated fifty thousand islanders. A final article then made it poignantly and depressingly clear that the polar bear stood on the point of extinction in the wild, due to the accelerating disappearance of ice fields in the Northern Hemisphere.

'Gawd, what's wrong with this world?' complained the old lady through another rising plume of smoke. 'These disasters keep happening; it's just one thing after another.'

The newswoman finished her accounts with an almost apologetic air before announcing that the next article would be a recording made that day of the Prime Minister speaking at the "World Economic Recovery Summit" in Quito, Equador.

'Not him again,' remarked Toby's companion with hunched shoulders. 'What's Mr. K.A. been up to this time? ...These bloomin' politicians ought to try actually sortin' out the mess everything's in rather than just spending the whole day gassing.'

It was clear that she considered herself to have known much better times and took the opportunity each evening to berate the nation's leaders for their ineptitude whenever they appeared on screen.

The broadcast now changed to show a reporter dressed in a high necked overcoat, standing before a conference building surrounded by a phalanx of multi-national flags – the high sunbathed mountains of the Andes beyond.

'Welcome to you all,' he began seriously, 'on what may prove to be an important day for Britain and other major industrialised nations. The Prime Minister, Mr. Kline Anderson, has been speaking to world leaders here this afternoon, and has astonished many with his frank and demanding position on the climate issue. We would now like to show you just part of his speech to the Summit.'

'Summit?' said the old lady, coughing again and chuckling to herself at the same time. 'I should think it is – if you ask me the whole thing seems to be taking place on top of a mountain.'

The interior of the conference room now appeared; the ranks of world delegates arranged around a central dais where Kline Anderson stood addressing his audience. He was dressed as usual in a simple plain black suit, one hand resting upon the reading lectern, his left raised in emphasis of a point. An open smile occasionally passed across his lips, but the presence of the Sustainability Party leader and the force of his delivery firmly held the assembled national representatives.

'He's only a little fellow,' the old woman remarked to herself, 'but he scrubs up well, don't he? I like to see a man make an effort when he appears in public.'

* * *

The British Prime Minister had been outlining his Government's policies for its coming term of office (with the "Carbon Zero" and "Sustainable Community" Acts central to his theme), and his voice now sounded clearly in ten million living rooms – the message stark and uncompromising.

'In my country, as in so many advanced nations,' he said, looking directly into the camera, 'we have chosen to live unsustainably for decades and centuries past; trusting to others to provide our food, and the foundation of our wealth, without considering the consequences for the poor, or the environment. Countless numbers have been left to starve in poverty while we have felt ourselves justified in stealing food from the mouths of the less fortunate.'

He paused for a moment, sweeping the assembled audience of presidents, prime ministers and dictators with a steady challenging gaze.

'A not insubstantial number of those residing in the developed lands have come to live like kings, when compared to their ancestors; selfishly using fuel and power to meet their every desire and whim, while children suffering at the other end of the human scale are left to die as a result of this damaging profligacy and greed. Like bloated sultans or maharajas, the materially wealthy have demanded that every machine and gadget be made available to them; that every convenience is placed at their disposal – thus enabling all too many to become both gross and lazy in their selfish enjoyment of wealth and luxury.'

'He's right about that,' said the old woman shifting on her seat. 'I could do with losing a few pounds; I reckon just about all of us could.'

Kline Anderson now cupped his hands in a familiar gesture.

'Fellow leaders, we have a duty to all mankind to move away from the previous policies and economic models that have brought us to this hopelessly unsustainable situation. We must turn from the relentless pursuit of economic, commercial and military power that will inevitably lead to irreversible damage to our planet and the slow decline of humanity into a universal state of need. This will involve a sea change in our thinking and behaviour, but it is not yet too late. As nations we must develop the skills that will enable us to live again in sustainable communities, where we predominantly depend upon resources grown and sourced locally. We must control our numbers and ensure that, wherever they live in the world, our children are educated in the new ways, so that each is able to contribute to, and share in, the creation of those things they and succeeding generations will need in the future.

'Do not dismiss this as fantasy – for I am no backwoodsman coming to you with some idyllic vision of a return to a virgin frontier. Indeed, that frontier no longer exists in our modern age. The wild places are now all but gone, and those pockets that remain can only be saved in the form of wildlife reserves where generations yet to be born may marvel at the remnants of an extraordinary natural legacy already recklessly consigned to the past.

'No, we must urgently plan for a new era in human history, in which the future of our nations will be based upon the best and most up-to-date application of science and technology. Reaching this goal will require diligent research into new and sustainable methods of production. It will demand the continued development of our minds and intellect to stay ahead of the great and terrible disaster of ecological collapse. The contribution of our innovators, scientists, colleges and universities will never have been more vital in plotting the difficult course towards our own long-term survival. The future I envisage will be one of shared technology and co-operation, a world of mutual ownership in which all are given just access to the land and resources upon which we depend. In that time a fusion of high technology and the best in traditional methods will have been reached: a viable mix of scientific excellence and home-made sustainability.'

At this point, as if coming to the essential nub of his argument, Kline Anderson leaned forward, pushing his glasses slowly back onto the bridge of his nose.

'But this is the vital twist, ladies and gentlemen – the great ingredient and driver of this change,' he emphasised deliberately. 'We, the great and powerful leaders of this world, must be prepared to stand down and relinquish our authority; for what is most needed now is that our citizens learn for themselves how to create and live this new sustainable existence... while allowing us to join with them in achieving that essential aim. In doing so we must all curtail our current ever increasing demands for power and finite resources; instead relying again more than a little on a degree of honest sweat and physical labour to get things done.

'Some will gnash their teeth at such a prospect and doubt my sanity for expounding it. But my capacity for rational thought should not be held in any greater doubt than that of the ambitious and prattling fools who imagine our current mismanagement of the planet can continue. The upheavals we witness every day on our television screens must warn us that only worse will follow, unless we as a species are prepared to change and adapt to a new reality. The game is already up for international finance and self-interest; instead the future will depend much more upon astute local management and co-operative endeavour.'

He stopped at this point, head bowed, and upon looking up, did so with a rueful, almost boyish face.

'I hope you will agree with me upon some of the points that I have made. I love my people, as most of you love yours. For me, power can have no value if by hanging on to it we come to live in a world of despair and poverty. Personally I wish to leave nothing behind me when I am gone... except perhaps the memory of my name and the worthy things I strove for.'

Kline Anderson then dropped down from the dais as a ripple of applause rose from the assembled leaders. A number clapped sincerely, some even rising to stand in expression of enthusiastic approval, and a general hubbub of animated discussion pervaded the conference hall. There were a significant few, however, who maintained a still and silent posture, their eyes fixed straight ahead – while others gravely consulted advisors on mobile phones. The ovation lasted less than a minute, but the implications of his address would go on to echo round the corridors of power for many years to come.

* * *

'Lord, he makes a good speech, don't he?' said the old woman, still staring at the screen as the weather forecast came on. 'Most politicians talk a lot of rubbish, but that Kline Anderson knows how to make an impact. Not that his ideas will work, mind you.'

She now stood up, and having gathered her things disappeared into the pub. 'Did you hear him, Randolf? ...Just imagine – a world in which people run their own affairs! ...Seems like a pipe dream to me...'

* * *

Toby did not catch the landlord's reply but left alone, fell to considering what he had heard. The prospect of a future in which power at the centre had been relinquished in favour of local organisation and initiative was beyond what most people would consider possible. Yet Kline Anderson's conviction made such a thing seem plausible – a model for the future that at least offered food for thought. Toby continued to mull over various points and only when the light began to fade as night drew on did he again consider how to spend the night. An owl hooted nearby and a fox barked in a thicket further off soon after. Two lovers strolled by along the road and the muffled sound of drinkers inside the hostelry could occasionally be heard, but Toby was not disturbed as few regulars ever came or went by the quiet entrance next to which he sat.

He had already mused on for some while, not sure whether to leave or stay, when an inky shape hove into view from the direction of a disused farm building beyond the hedge. Toby watched the crow circle, wings dark against the starless gloom, before dropping down onto the disk of a half obscured 30MPH sign a few yards away. The bird settled before tucking its heavy beak across a shoulder, as if preparing for rest, but a glow of gold reflecting from the lamp shining above the pub door showed that one eye remained observant and wary.

'Is it you again, my feathered friend?' said Toby, suppressing a yawn; part of his brain feeling inclined to seek a closer encounter with the watching sentinel. But the hour was late – the remainder of his being now suddenly beyond caring – and in seconds he drifted out of consciousness once more as a pale three quarter moon looked down upon the shadowy portals of the "Tinker's Rest".

Chapter Eleven

Assassination

For the first time since the beginning of his wanderings, Toby dreamed long about Jenny and the children – the two of them now surely grown-up, perhaps with youngsters of their own. His heart ached with the deep realisation that this must be true: that he was witnessing a future long hence and had forgone the cherished experiences of family life...

Was he to blame for their parting? And if they were ever to meet again, what would he do or say to make up for the lost days and years – to show that he had always loved them, and no others, with enduring affection?

* * *

Waking from such reflections on a grey spring morning might easily have prompted Toby to close his eyes once more in a state of melancholy. But as he focused, he felt himself urged by another force – one deep within – a latent but powerful need to move on. Responding to this, he stood up to look around the smokers' porch; gradually recollecting events at the conclusion of that earlier day. The warmth and comfort enjoyed then were now entirely gone and breathing in the moist air he shivered as a damp breeze played against his cool and puckered skin. Yet there had been no real welcome for him at the pub and now, with a hundred regrets milling in his brain, Toby wanted only to be away from the spot, to continue his travels. ...But where should he go? ...Which direction should he take?

A great sense of loneliness welled deep inside, and with head in hands he looked up toward the cloud filled heavens... a movement which roused another sleeper. At that moment the crow, still comfortably perched on the traffic sign, blinked open an eye and finding Toby about to venture forth, croaked a throat-clearing greeting, 'Cawk... Caaaw... Ktaark!'

The sound fell stridently upon the morning air and Toby, having failed to note the continued presence of the creature until then, turned sharply towards it. His sometime companion bobbed from claw to claw as their eyes met; but instead of flying up, simply flexed a feather and settled once more, as if content to stay a while longer.

Toby studied the devourer of scraps with a mixture of curiosity and mistrust. If this *was* the same bird that had followed his progress, where would it lead him now? What he most wanted that morning was to discover the truth about his own life and the ones he loved – yet here again was his enigmatic winged shadow, perhaps about to lead him on another wild goose chase across half of England. He sidled towards the creature, every second expecting it to take off and soar away to a branch or treetop where, out of reach, it could continue to monitor his movements. Yet as he gradually closed the gap between, it did no such thing; but seemed instead to become ever more intent and curious as Toby drew near – dipping a shoulder and craning almost questioningly towards him.

In those few creeping seconds an affinity briefly grew up between the two: the crow in undertaker's black – sleek, yet drawn of necessity to carrion and death – and he, the man, wracked by thoughts of guilt and betrayal – half inclined to take out his frustration by wringing the neck of an all too patient and vigilant spy. Soon there was but a yard between – a space of three feet that Toby might have crossed in a second before taking hold of the crow and throttling out its life. But the creature stood his ground, its beady eyes seeing beyond Toby's anger to the uncertainty that lay beneath.

'Well – Lucifer, Darkness, Bad Penny – or whatever you call yourself... What is it this time?' enquired Toby, enunciating each word with an unaccustomed feeling of disfavour. 'Have you come to lead me another merry dance? ...Or will you show me a way out of this unworldly theatre of loss and longing? ...As of now my greatest greatest need is to reach the end of all this – and if you can help me towards it, then I will happily follow.'

The crow skewed its head to one side, as if deliberating, then dropped down to peck at a worm recently washed from a nearby bank by the rain. It proceeded to swallow the leathery scrap, with a backward toss of its beak, before flying up once more; this time landing a little further along on an old wooden gatepost. A scant few seconds had elapsed, however, when with a summoning snap of the beak, it lifted away again, gliding on this time to a point just out of sight beyond a bend in the road – brittle claws rattling upon bare metal moments later. His curiosity aroused (despite an inclination to let the bird go and be rid of it), Toby came on behind with halting steps, and arriving at the spot where it had passed from view, found his mysterious winged guide perched this time on the chrome edged screen of a long abandoned sports car, left propped at the side of the lane on a support of bricks and timbers. Twice more Toby was similarly encouraged to follow, until the crow had led him beyond the shady reaches of Coward's Lane to a point on the village green where a duck pond lay in a pleasant tree lined hollow beside the main street.

At this early hour there were few people around – those to be seen mostly coming and going in the vicinity of a tiny village shop nearby. Parked next to this stood a rather elderly open backed furniture van with the name "Hinton's of Bridgenorth" hand painted in tall letters on the side. As Toby watched, the two occupants, men wearing workmen's overalls, dropped down from the cab and walked into the shop. This motion seemed to be interpreted as a signal by the crow; for having watched them disappear, it flew across from its perch in a cherry tree, landing on the tailboard with a hop and skip. Then peering inside like a curious estate agent inspecting a vacant property, it seemed to spend a few moments deciding on the suitability of the conveyance, before bobbing out of sight with a loud, 'Caaark!'

Toby had never witnessed such behaviour before, and after looking around to assure himself that nobody else had noticed, he too jogged across to examine the removal van. The interior was dark, but he could see enough to realise that a quantity of furniture, garden tools and household items had been neatly stacked and secured inside. There were chests of drawers, beds and wardrobes lashed to the sides, and near the back, held securely by a leather harness, a comfortable armchair sat facing the rear as if to provide a stately seat from which to view the retreating countryside. The crow had hopped onto the mirror of a ladies' dressing-table in the far corner and appeared settled, as if ready to spend some time on its chosen perch. It glanced towards Toby, apparently wondering why he hesitated to sample the delights within.

'It's just the job – warm and comfortable,' he seemed to intimate with an inclination of his head. 'So why are you standing around out there?'

This was a moment when Toby might have taken his leave by pulling the canvas tarpaulins together and making off, leaving the crow trapped inside. But another stronger compulsion suddenly told him to climb aboard, and obeying he heaved himself into the furniture van seconds before the two men emerged from the shop door. His pulse began to race when he realised how close they had come to witnessing the move; but he was considerably more alarmed when the face of one peered inside to check that the load was still safely secured. Yet, having apparently looked straight at Toby; the removal man simply pulled away without any sign of hesitation, barely pausing in his conversation with the other. Both their voices now sounded clearly as the two moved forward to re-enter the cab.

'The Sustainability Party have done it again,' said one. 'What's more, they've got in with a majority of two hundred this time.'

'Crikey!' exclaimed his companion. 'Well, if Mr Anderson means what he says, we should really see some changes now.'

'Let's hope so! Give the bloke a fair chance, I say. And it would seem people have – so we can only hope it works out.'

Toby heard the doors slam, and lowering himself into the welcoming upholstery of the armchair, felt the heavily laden lorry steal into motion and pick up speed.

* * *

The journey now underway would prove both comfortable and relaxing. The old lorry, on its huge leaf springs, rode as smoothly as a royal coach, and as Toby reclined in his armchair, the care laden thoughts that had beset him at the "Tinker's Rest" gradually drifted to the back of his mind. The crow too seemed equally at ease: swaying gently with the motion of the lorry and occasionally preening itself in a half-awake doze. Their progress was dignified and unhurried, the removal van frequently slowing to a very sedate pace when passing through towns and villages where new twenty-mile per hour speed limits were in force. Standing by the rear tailboard and holding the tarpaulin for support Toby could then observe all that went on. The lorry first passed through Hitchin, before making towards Milton Keynes: the "new city" now alive and bustling with morning travellers. Yet this was no longer the place of hurtling cars and high-speed roundabouts that he remembered from previous visits. Begun as a sprawling green field development one hundred years before, it had become home to half a million people, with mature tree lined avenues, parks and thriving local centres. Here, as in London, a tram system was being developed, and almost every junction saw teams of men at work establishing the rail system and energy supplies required to power the new vehicles. During the interim period, fleets of buses were operating – ferrying citizens to school, work, or on shopping expeditions. Meanwhile, all around, on pavements, cycle paths and in underpasses, hundreds more were seen walking or riding to their offices. There were still a number of cars and lorries, but unlike the one he travelled in (soon to be compulsorily retired when the new "carbon zero" laws came into force), most were battery, electric or hydrogen cell powered creations, the soft bleep of warning sirens signalling their proximity as they approached. Toby also saw banks of retractable solar panels being installed at the corners of south facing parks, on office roofs and on public buildings, while at a thousand other locations – by riversides, in open spaces and around business parks – the turning blades of wind generators, large and small, rotated in quiet harmony.

However, for all these positive signs, there was also evidence that the city had not survived unscathed by recent extreme weather. More than twenty fallen poplar trees lay partially logged beside the canal, and later the van had to slow to pass an abandoned warehouse wrecked by a squall; while above the main retail centre a tall builders' crane stood twisted and broken – its wrecked arm curving towards the earth like the crooked finger of a witch. But these sights would no longer be left to blight the landscape for months and years as previously, for now a dedicated local army of skilled workers had been formed to speed the process of clearance and redevelopment.

So the removal van moved on, heading north-west through the rolling landscape of middle England: first passing through Buckingham and Banbury, then on to Stratford on Avon, the home of Shakespeare. Here it slowed again to negotiate the busy streets, where a considerable throng of visitors, as always, moved among the elegant buildings. All was well-maintained, in homage to the bard, but the old town had not escaped a great many enforced changes. Modern windbreaks, many designed to be raised when severe weather threatened, were now provided to protect historic and vulnerable structures. Other buildings had been elevated on decorative stilts to keep them from falling victim to flash floods; while every house or cottage with a traditional roof saw the thatch protected by a transparent Perspex covering as safeguard against storm force winds or torrential downpours.

Travelling into the heart of the town they came at last to a large crossroads by a newly developed play park. There the lorry was held for more than a minute by a temporary traffic light, erected to protect workmen clearing and enlarging roadside drains blocked by recent floods, and it was at this juncture that Toby learned of the exact day and date. Looking surreptitiously out from behind the tarpaulin, he saw that a large new public telescreen had been installed on one side of the play park, around which decorative benches were installed to allow folk to sit and catch up on current events. A group of viewers was there now; many of them parents keeping an eye on children playing on toddler swings and equipment.

The date, 7th May 2064, was displayed at the top of the screen in elaborate Elizabethan lettering, below which beamed the headline:

Sustainability Party wins Third Term in office with 200 Majority

A newscaster read a report about the day's result, and below her a second headline read:

The Prime Minister, Kline Anderson, will present a statement about his Party's future proposals at Jackfield Village Hall near Ironbridge this afternoon

Toby returned to the armchair, sinking down into it as he took in the fact that another four years had passed. He sat silently for some time, no longer taking an interest in the changing scenery as the furniture lorry drove on. Only once did he turn to where the crow was perched, but it simply looked steadily back at him, quiet and unruffled, as if waiting for journey's end before rousing itself to further activity. ...That end came quite soon.

* * *

Droitwich and Kidderminster were next on their route – then the valley of the Severn to Bridgenorth and beyond. Due to recent heavy rain and subsidence the old "A" road northward was much broken and rutted and Toby, finding himself increasingly thrown about as the lorry weaved round fallen trees, stood up to investigate at the very moment it slowed to a halt upon entering the tiny roadside village of Matton Suddock. The sound of whirring chainsaws filled the air, and looking out he saw several men hard at work logging the remains of splintered oaks and horse chestnuts that had until recently blocked the road. The removal van rolled to a halt beside a row of houses, one with a "Sold" sign outside, and as Toby watched from his concealed position, the driver and his companion stepped across to where a middle-aged couple waited by the front gate. A falling tree had damaged the house next door and the new owners both wore apprehensive expressions. A conversation developed in which the couple, ever more earnestly, endeavoured to negotiate for their furniture to be taken away again. However, the removal men seemed equally adamant that it should be left where it was so they might drive back to their families in Bridgenorth in time for tea. The outcome of this disagreement still remained in doubt when Toby, deciding to take advantage of the noise and the fact that the men's attention lay elsewhere, dropped unobtrusively from the far end of the tailgate, before sidling round to the blind side of the lorry. His escape would have been perfect had not the nearest workman clearly heard the sound of feet crunching on gravel. The tree operative switched off his chainsaw and stood up, scratching his head and staring blankly at the spot from which Toby had just departed – while he, having apparently remained unobserved in broad daylight, casually sauntered off past the front of the lorry. The man was then made even more puzzled and suspicious when a large crow flapped down onto the tailgate from inside, looked around with a slow sweep of its head and lifted up to follow Toby's progress.

Aware that his presence had undoubtedly registered, in sound if not sight, Toby moved on, all the time expecting a challenge from behind. But he made it to the first bend in the road without being called back, and having increased pace was soon beyond earshot of all but the fading rasp of metal on wood.

He slowed a mile further on, able to relax once more, before stopping and turning briefly… where to now? …The way back was not sensible, but would he fare better by going blindly on…?

If Toby's geography had been better he might have realised he was already less than four miles from the old industrial heritage centres of Ironbridge and Coalbrookdale, where at that moment members of the Sustainability Party, media journalists and other invited guests were gathering to meet the Prime Minister at Jackfield Village Hall. How easy it would have been for him to take a wrong turning, or double back via a quiet lane in an attempt to retrace his steps another way; but Toby had an ally, a guide, who having circled for a while above the trees to check his bearings, now stooped back towards the lone figure standing astride an empty road below. The crow, having brushed – as at their first meeting – within a whisker of Toby's left ear, bobbed to a halt on the tarmacadam twenty paces ahead, before examining a smear of recent road kill.

Toby was vexed at this sudden intrusion upon his thoughts, and irritation briefly flared in his head as he watched the loathsome actions of the bird tugging at its find. But then his mood changed, for as he watched, the grisly forager hopped off down the road, its head cocked artfully on one side as it looked back inviting him to follow once more.

'That game again,' said Toby to himself. 'It would seem that I must allow myself to be at your beck and call a second time.'

Before long his feathered friend began to disappear over the brow of a rise in the road, and not wishing to be left behind, Toby trotted forward, the same pantomime of bob and follow being repeated as he drew closer, then again a little further down the road; until the two had fallen into a regular pattern with the bird apparently content to exercise its stubby legs for as long as Toby continued in pursuit. In this way steady progress was made, only occasionally disturbed by a passing car or van.

After travelling for over a mile the edge of a deep cleft in the landscape became evident and the two began to descend steeply downhill to the picturesque village of Coalport in the Severn Gorge, where the River Severn cuts through the ironstone hills. From there, having traversed the turbulent waters below via a narrow foot crossing, it was but a short trek through winding lanes to Jackfield.

* * *

Tucked away on the edge of the gorge, the location, with its tile museum and church, was far from quiet that day. Hundreds of officials and security personnel had moved in to police the coming event, and although every effort was being made to present an air of normality, the sheer presence of so many visitors made this impossible. On every corner were media vans and police cars – while press tents had sprung up in gardens and on any available open space. Everywhere watchful security guards with machine guns, and event co-ordinators with plastic coated identification labels, moved to and fro busily endeavouring to ensure that the hastily scheduled meeting would go off without incident. But as efficient as preparations may seem on the surface, it is always difficult to cover every eventuality. Even after the best laid plans have been made things can go wrong. The highest level of security still sometimes leaves a corner unwatched that a determined villain might exploit. ...One such circled now, undetected: sliding in with skilful subterfuge among hospitality tents and scurrying waitresses.

Having come to a junction close to where Jackfield Village Hall stood, Toby watched as the crow flew up to perch upon a nearby rooftop. Then, as he considered what next to do, he began to pick up the gist of a conversation between two armed security guards standing a few feet away. One was a strongly built officer in his late thirties, with a long career in the police force behind him – his partner, a younger man, brightly efficient but still learning his trade. Both kept a wary eye out as they talked, the older, Special Firearms Officer Dave Maitland, frequently frowning as he observed the increasing flow of activity. The first guests had arrived; some in security cars with blacked out windows, others drawing up in coaches and government mini vans. From these a steady stream of people began to make their way into the hall, beside which stood a catering tent on the small adjacent playing field.

'This is bloody risky if you ask me,' said Dave Maitland biting his lip. 'Bringing the Prime Minister and a whole lot of top bods to an out-of-the-way place like this – there's just too much that can go wrong. If I was a terrorist or the like I'd think my birthday had come right now!'

The other turned to him, a doubtful expression wrinkling his fresh face. 'You worry too much, Dave. This place is crawling with security; a gnat would only have to cough in a bomber's underpants and we'd be onto it. There were four checks carried out on the press and catering personnel before any of them could get themselves a pass to come within a mile of here, and you can't get near the village hall without going through two more.'

'Hmm… is that right?' said Officer Maitland, caressing the barrel of his machine pistol. 'But what use is that if people aren't equally vigilant at every point? I've seen folk walk straight up this road unchallenged; while others scurry from one place to the other, flashing their ID and getting in without a by your leave. I tell you, I've got a funny feeling about this here setting; it's too comfortable – too bloody pretty… Nothing is ever supposed to happen here. But it's in places just like this that something can turn up. I've been twenty years on the force; eleven doing this job, and I'm telling you – I've never felt more iffy about the arrangements made to prevent a security incident.'

The younger officer was about to counter again with an assertion that his colleague was being over pessimistic, but seeing the vigilant aspect on his senior's lined features, thought better of it. 'Where do you think we should tighten up?'

'Try everywhere,' replied Dave Maitland, moving forward. 'Double check every ID card every ten minutes; patrol every corner – that's exactly what I intend to start doing right now. You'd best stay on here, while I take a little wander… somewhere off the beaten track a bit. I'll see you later!' Having thus resolved, he walked across the road, before beginning a wide circuit of the area where the village hall stood.

Toby mulled over what had been said as he looked up to see the crow still patiently surveying all from its chosen viewpoint. Then, curious to learn more about what was going on, he fell in with the flow of people heading toward the village hall.

This had been extensively rebuilt and extended in recent years, the original stucture being re-roofed and enclosed by a family meeting room complete with refreshment lounge overlooking the gorge. Revamped toilets, together with a theatre annexe, had also been provided. These improvements raised the overall capacity to more than three hundred; with an elevated gallery provided at the back for use by sound and lighting technicians during drama productions. Today this was given over to press and television crews, a large contingent of whom had been moving in and out all morning. There were door personnel and security guards at every entrance, carefully checking the identities of those attending, while a special forces group had been assigned to monitor both the gallery and hall below. Admittance without the required documents would, it seemed, be impossible and as Toby drew near to the door he realised that his chances of being permitted inside were apparently negligible. But here a sequence of events conspired in his favour, giving some credence to Dave Maitland's concerns.

He had reached the point of being next but one in line when the man and woman in front, two delegates from the French Government, realised that the lady had failed to put her rather large and unflattering security pass round her neck. Immaculately dressed, she had evidently elected to keep it handy in her shoulder bag rather than wearing the item and now, having been politely asked to show it, was forced to delve to the bottom in a fluster of scent and tissue.

'Oh my goodnez,' she said, a little peeved. 'Zis is zutch a fuss over nozing! Vy must we troop around like ze cows at a market?'

'I'm sorry, madam, but those are the rules,' said the security guard, patiently waiting. 'You will need to keep it on when you are inside, I'm afraid, in case one of my colleagues should want to inspect it.'

'Oh you Eenglish, you are so pedantic. How long have we been your European partners? …Yet still you mistrust us – it eez not fair!'

'I assure you, madam, that we treat all our visitors the same – regardless of their nationality. Now, I must ask you to move to one side as there are many more people waiting to come in.'

'Oh, enough!' said the woman, irritably producing the item. 'So now I must look like a clumsy parcel when I am photographed …Believe me, I shall 'ave words with my ambassador ven I get 'ome!'

She then endeavoured to slip the pass over her expensively styled hair, but at the point when her gloved hands were raised the crow suddenly flew low overhead, spraying a trail of droppings upon the hapless tightly packed group. The muck missed Toby by inches, but a shriek arose from the lady standing behind who had been struck squarely on the shoulder of her smart suit. Meanwhile the Frenchwoman slowly drew three soiled fingers from her crown, realising that her previously immaculate hair had been liberally coated with the noxious mess.

'My God!' she screamed. 'Zis is ze final insult… vat iz 'appening to me!'

There was a flurry of movement as the woman, now almost hysterical, swung round to make her retreat. In doing so she bumped into the other female delegate, who was only a little less put out, and together they managed to send the French lady's male companion tumbling to the floor. This in turn caused them both to stumble and Toby had to move quickly forward to avoid the two crashing into him. Three armed security officers immediately pushed their way though the queue of people to ascertain what was happening, and in his efforts to avoid the jostle and muddle Toby stepped inside the door of Jackfield Village Hall. He had neither planned this move, nor expected anything like it to happen, but now found himself facing the stage together with a considerable crowd of waiting guests. At first he froze, not believing that his entrance could have been missed, but as the seconds passed no one stepped through the door to investigate. Quietly relieved, and following a short wait during which he closely surveyed the faces around him, he was thus able to move forward inconspicuously before taking up position at the foot of the stage.

* * *

It was fortunate that the afternoon was not too warm as the room soon became tightly crowded. A considerable number of those present were obviously Sustainability Party Members of Parliament, or supporters, but there were many others in addition to the press corps and numerous security staff. A large group of government representatives from European countries also made their way in; and present were several dozen more from much more distant parts of the world, including delegations from India, Japan and Egypt. A festive spirit enlivened the occasion, enhanced by a party from Brazil dressed in bright samba costumes and native Indian bonnets. But the buzz in the air also bubbled with a tense undercurrent as if an announcement of great import was about to be given. Outside, meanwhile, heavy clouds had gathered and the rumblings of a storm drew near.

Then, at the stroke of three o'clock, an expectant hush descended as a single bright spotlight illuminated the stage. A formal introduction, or the playing of stirring mood music might have been expected, but instead Kline Anderson simply stepped out from behind the tall theatre curtains. The audience applauded warmly before falling silent again, waiting for him to speak. Meanwhile, his brother Paul also appeared, before standing a few feet from Toby.

Kline Anderson, now 51, waited for the final latecomers to settle, the last movement being that of a darting member of the catering staff making her exit through the fire door at the rear of the auditorium. The Prime Minister was dressed more casually than many had seen before, in a plain brown corduroy jacket and tan trousers – his bright green and orange Sustainability Party tie adding a splash of colour against the familiar white shirt – and Toby thought he might easily have come to address a family gathering rather than an international audience. However, the cares and responsibilities of leadership and government were, if anything, more deeply engraved upon his features, while as always there was a soberness about him – the quiet reserve of a reflective man.

'We meet here again,' he opened confidentially – as if addressing only his nearest and closest supporters, although half the world's media was present. 'Back where it all began …It seems only a short time ago, just ten and a half years – yet we have all come a very long way since then. But have we changed anything? Perhaps: if only to have opened the eyes of people to the possibility of living another way. And was it worth it? …Again, only time will tell – for human beings are fickle and often take backward steps when they lose hope and are afraid. …Yet they need to be challenged to make the best decisions, and that is what we have endeavoured to do.

'So what is the next step? Do we proceed in the same way, constantly providing support and direction in order to lead our citizens toward a vision of a new and Promised Land? …No.'

Here he paused, smiling humbly – like someone preparing to withdraw from centre stage.

'The next step is the greatest of all – the one that is both the most difficult for us, and the most demanding for everyone beyond these four walls… We must now stand back and allow the electorate to build their own futures without relying upon others to guide their every effort.'

At these words many heads tilted quizzically.

'I can see you are a little puzzled by my comments – then I must make the feelings of the party leadership known more clearly. In essence, my friends, they come to this… that we must relinquish much of our power over the people that voted for us. While I, as Party leader, must give up my office and resign as Prime Minister.'

There was stunned silence for a moment, during which a pin might have been heard to drop, before in excess of three hundred voices rose together in protest.

'You can't mean that!' came a shout from the back. 'If you stand down, won't that simply mean that someone is elected in your place?'

Kline Anderson waited until calm had returned before continuing, his tone clear and concise.

'I have travelled much in these last few years; visiting many countries and witnessing the struggles of so many to rebuild their lives following the natural disasters that have become commonplace across our planet. Climate change has brought death and great hardship to almost every part of the globe, but there is hope for the future wherever people are given reason to believe in tomorrow. In those countries where governments have promoted and supported local initiatives to rebuild there has been great progress. The people have come together more readily as communities to support each other's efforts and pool both skills and resources. They have shown initiative in using and re-using the materials available to them, and have become skilled in growing food, thus providing for their families. These folk accept and utilise fresh ideas and new technologies where they are made available, but are wise enough to reject or abandon modern innovations or machinery for which sustainable supplies of fuel or energy cannot be provided. In old parlance, they have "Gone Green" of necessity, and are not foolish enough to imagine there is another viable alternative for the future. But do they live worse lives? Almost certainly not, for few would choose a return to the old ways. Of course many are indeed less rich materially – less surrounded by the expensive and energy consuming products of a "consumer society". But their children are now usually well fed and educated, their elderly cared for, and they have hope for better days ahead – a growing belief in an ability to stay in control of their own lives and destinies.

'Now contrast this with the existence of those living in countries where the state is still firmly in control, where dictators maintain command, or in any place where the wealth and resources that people daily require remain in the hands of a selfish few. There we all too often find poverty, disease and starvation – a paralysis in government when disasters strike that fosters hopelessness and despair among the people at their inability to rebuild. In such countries, ordinary citizens are prevented from exercising their own will and judgement, but must wait for lamentably corrupt, ignorant and incompetent leaders to provide assistance, that so often never comes. They are simply there to be worked for profit by political and economic masters, to be sold food and energy they can barely afford, while being taxed at every point. And when the people complain, or other nations question such policies, their masters threaten only violence and war – swift retribution for those that question the right of a few to indulge their greed and lust for power. These callous people will always have their supporters and cronies… Indeed there may even be one or two here today that have time for hereditary kings, billionaire oligarchs and oppressors – those unworthy few that use might and influence to maintain authoritarian rule, while turning a blind eye to the suffering of their fellow men.'

Here Kline Anderson leaned forward, looking into each face as if seeking to reach all personally, even down to the most hard-nosed press reporter.

'We *must* now move toward a more rational, a more sustainable and a fairer world: one in which greed and the lust for power and self-interest are no longer cynically held to be the only true and basic driving forces of human behaviour. As for me, I have nothing but contempt for such failings. Therefore, with a desire to provide a necessary example to others, I will stand down this year on 6th August – the still remembered anniversary of a murderous act once perpetrated to end another tyranny.'

A gasp went around the audience.

'This may seem too soon, or too rash; but there are others that I think will follow where we lead – for the plotting of our survival in a world afflicted by the ravages of climate change must now become the new priority. Selfish nationalism and war can only delay that process and lead mankind to catastrophe. Should we succeed our example will become a beacon, and I know of only a few dark and oppressive regimes that may hope to undermine or oppose our aims. The governments of France, Germany, Brazil and Japan have indicated that their leaders will stand down within five years of my doing so, should all go well; while our friends in India and twenty other countries have pledged themselves to follow. As such, I trust my action will set a ball rolling that may not be stilled.'

At this point a clap of thunder sounded nearby and in the silent room the first rattle of raindrops could be heard above.

'So there you have it. My cabinet and I will relinquish our present positions in three months' time; and on the 1st January 2065, the Sustainability Party will formally sit for the inaugural time as a "Government without Leaders". The necessary Act will come into force at the beginning of the New Year and it is my hope that its passing will herald the dawn of a new and enlightened age.'

A flash of lightning lit up the windows and another burst of thunder echoed overhead – the sound reverberating round the steep sided valley before rumbling away down the gorge. Then the thrash of a cascading downpour began lashing furiously upon every surface, rooftop and stone.

'It seems the elements will wait for us no longer,' said Kline Anderson, looking up. 'Or perhaps God is listening after all.'

Speaking above the restless sounds he went on to explain that the "Sustainability Party" proposed bringing in additional legislation in the form of the "Motorway Closure Act". This, he said, would involve the gradual removal of all but a few of the country's neglected and now underused motorways; to be replaced by lesser highways, dedicated freight railways, restored farmland and new housing. Some former routes would become "living corridors" – winding natural pathways, liberally planted with trees and wild flowers, containing cycle tracks, community fields and gardens. He smiled by way of conclusion. 'At last we seem to have overcome our long addiction to the motor car and lorry – therefore it is time to reclaim some of the useful land previously sacrificed to build the concrete and asphalt carriageways for them.'

The rain stopped and calm once again settled upon the gathering, a shaft of sunlight breaking through a side window as heavy clouds parted in the sky outside, its warming rays causing the first shimmers of evaporation to rise from surrounding roads. Now, glancing in Toby's direction, Kline Anderson checked for a moment as their eyes met – although Toby sensed that the other looked through him to a place beyond sight. When the Prime Minister turned away again, he seemed suddenly drained and tired – like a man thinking about his life at the closing of a book. His final words to the gathering were profound and personal, as if drawn from deep within.

'I sometimes think of myself as a rock at the edge of the rising water: trusting that when the people are set free to govern their own lives I will be overflowed and washed into the deep ocean of history. Such is my wish – that all assumed power will end and that these words will be accurately recorded – allowing those that support our principles to go forward in good heart. But all here must remember this… To speak and share such just convictions can be a dangerous thing – for the devil hates an honest man.'

Straightway he moved forward, amid a rising volume of applause and walked down the steps into the audience. Flashlights burst as a hundred people came to shake his hand or ask questions. Many begged the Prime Minister to reconsider, while others praised him for his boldness and offered support in the weeks to come. Newsmen emailed reports around the world, and before twenty minutes had passed the story of Kline Anderson's intentions spread across the globe. Few left Jackfield Village Hall at first: most milling around discussing his words in a buzz of earnest conversation. Toby remained quietly on one side, listening to a score of excited voices and studying the animated faces of those nearest. Most seemed full of admiration; although some among the more cautious and sceptical, questioned the wisdom of his decision. One man, a diplomat, vociferously proclaimed that while he was the British Premier's most loyal supporter, he couldn't believe any other country would take the UK's lead in moving forward without central leadership. This drew a number of assenting nods, but before being allowed to bask in the satisfaction of having made a sound point, a tall gentleman next to him stepped forward.

'I can assure you that Mr Anderson is not alone,' the newcomer said. 'I am Jaled Asmi, the Bangladeshi Ambassador to England, and must say that my country is committed to following his lead if all goes well. We admire your Prime Minister for taking this step because his policy of settling power with people locally can, we believe, do much to help our citizens cope with the disastrous changes in climate that have devastated much of Bangladesh.'

The ambassador was straightway welcomed into the group to further share his views and Toby, having watched the doubters gradually won over, decided to make for the nearest exit with a view to departing. He emerged into sunshine to see widely broken clouds, already scattered by a freshening north-east wind, clearing towards the west. A number of people were milling around, some of them guests that had made their way outside to enjoy the fresh air; others a mixture of media technicians, security men and event officials. Another exit was open at the far end of the hall, where more people were emerging in a steady stream before heading toward the hospitality tent. The thought of slipping away to somewhere less conspicuous beyond the security cordon occurred to Toby, and he was about to sidle off behind a television van when three shots rang out. A woman screamed and a chorus of shouts went up, amid which one strident voice ordered others to 'Get down!' Then came a chatter of machine gun fire and further confusion.

Toby stepped back instinctively, but was then immediately carried forward as virtually everyone present began to gravitate in the direction of the sounds. Security officers appeared at several points, their arms held wide to keep people back, but he soon found himself close enough to see what had happened. Near the exit to the hall, and now circled by a ring of police officers, lay the slumped body of Kline Anderson; while ten yards away, just inside the hospitality tent, the legs of a woman wearing an apron could be discerned. The Prime Minister, his head cradled in his brother's arms, had been shot in both chest and neck, his blood staining the damp earth around. A doctor kneeled beside him, searching for signs of a pulse. There was none – Kline Anderson was dead!

* * *

The evening news report later pieced together the events of the afternoon.

Kline Anderson had made his way through the crowds of well-wishers towards the back of the hall, patiently answering all their questions. He had looked greatly fatigued and it was suggested that, with his brother and Manny Singh, he might seek refreshment in the hospitality tent. Apparently having heard this, a young waitress offered to prepare him a cup of tea, moved swiftly away and reappeared shortly afterwards carrying a tray.

The stern face of Special Firearms Officer Dave Maitland now filled the screen, his complexion grey – like that of a man who had done something he would prefer had stayed outside the line of duty. A reporter queried his part in the affair.

'I'd taken up position at the north exit to the village hall while the Prime Minister was speaking inside,' he replied grimly. 'The weather had become foul by then, but I decided to keep up a presence outside, knowing my fellow officers would be equally vigilant within. The skies opened, rain falling so heavily that most people took cover. Fewer than a dozen brave souls were still moving about: one of these a waitress – a small slim woman of Eastern European appearance. I noticed her come out of the hospitality tent and make her way over to the door of the hall before opening it to look inside. I did think it a tad odd – her being interested in what was going on at that moment... while getting so wet. But she seemed purposeful, rather than agitated – even managing to smile at me as she trotted back... pretty girl really – reminded me of my daughter – so I just decided to keep her in mind.

'Well, the rain stopped and gradually the audience began to come outside. There were a number of hospitality people about – all very busy now that the main meeting had broken up. The waitress reappeared twice more as I remember, and my attention was again drawn to her when she found time to step aside behind a catering van to use her mobile phone. Then she moved briefly into the hall before coming back outside again seconds later. The young lady brushed past me in a great hurry, and seemed to be on an important errand, but with so much else going on I thought little of it. Then there was Mr Anderson, stepping into the sunlight and talking over his shoulder. I focused on the Prime Minister for a moment, before realising that the girl had reappeared at my shoulder. Glancing down I saw she held a tray evidently containing nothing but a folded tea towel and an empty cup. At this point the Prime Minister looked across at us, apparently remembering something, and smiled towards the girl. But she remained straight-faced, as if programmed to act, simply drawing her right hand from underneath the folded cloth to produce a small revolver. I had no time to react before she pulled the trigger and shot him three times – deliberately and at point-blank range. The first bullet went clean through Mr Anderson's neck; the others were aimed at his heart. …The Prime Minister must have been dead before he hit the ground. A poorer shot might have injured or killed someone else; but this girl knew her business – she made no mistake…

'It was one of those moments you dread in this profession. It's as if you're frozen for a second… but then the girl turned towards me and seemed to come out of a trance. I watched her step back into the entrance of the hospitality tent and take aim at the P.M's brother. That's when my training took over. I turned and fired – just a short burst. …Now I wish I'd followed my instinct to question her earlier… But I didn't.'

The reporter thanked him and further summaries about the shooting followed. Later it would emerge that the assassin was Lydia Maranek, a twenty-two year old Montenegrin national with links to right wing nationalist groups in the Balkans. She had been working in England for two years, but little was known about her movements, and there were no clues that she might have been involved in any plan to kill Kline Anderson. Nevertheless she had done her job well, the great-great-grandson of Meg Maddox was dead – the first leader in history to be murdered at the very point of handing power back to the people.

* * *

As he had wished, Kline Anderson was buried without ceremony near his place of birth in South London, at one of the new woodland burial sites then being created throughout Britain. His mother, Emma, died one month later, aged 84.

* * *

The proposed date of his resignation, 6th August 2064, "Hiroshima Day", was later honoured as the official day when the office of Prime Minister was discontinued – the first "Government Without Leaders" being inaugurated five months afterwards on New Year's Day 2065.

Chapter Twelve

A World Without Leaders

FROM VERY EARLY IN MAN'S HISTORY ON earth there have been those that have claimed the right of leadership, power and dominance over others. A determination to beat down, subjugate and if necessary destroy dissenting voices has been the central tenet of a thousand realms, dynasties and dictatorships. How many past and present rulers have stolen the land of once free and independent people by theft, rape and murder, then fashioned their own crowns for others to bow before? And why, more surprisingly, do the sycophants of the present day still fawn and bend a knee to the descendants of such unscrupulous masters?

Power and privilege undoubtedly go together, and this has held back human development throughout history. How many good, intelligent and forward thinking individuals have been imprisoned, beaten, tortured or murdered by rough, overbearing kings and dictators? How often has physical power, intimidation and the wielding of arms been used to oppress the rights of the common man, or to silence those that challenge such abuses?

In prehistoric times, during the raw infancy of civilisation, some might well suggest that such oppression was inevitable, but to maintain, in the modern age, any vestige of such crude behaviour surely goes against both justice and reason, as to do so inevitably suggests that it is beyond the capacity of ordinary citizens to live their lives without others enjoying pre-eminence, advantage and authority over them. Might it not also be contended as a corollary that those who continue to follow so obsequiously at the shirt tails of wealth and privilege, are themselves people who view the upholding of such traditional feudal rights by an elite as justifying the enjoyment of lesser, yet equally convenient and satisfying powers and prerogatives of their own?

If universal education gives young people anything of value, it should be a determination to challenge the self-proclaimed rights, excesses and dictates of their so-called "social superiors". Rather, our children should be encouraged to become skilled, imaginative and discerning adults, each able to take control of his or her own destiny, and all willing to display personal conviction, resolve, initiative and courage. Such is the worthy course toward true freedom – and in a world constantly ravaged by the effects of a changing climate these qualities, as Kline Anderson recognised, would be essential.

* * *

With the swearing-in of elected representatives to the first "Government Without Leaders" on 1st January 2065, and the annulment of the last reigning monarch's constitutional powers, the UK came under the spotlight of the world. How could a nation move forward without a head of state? How would seventy-five million people – many highly skilled and intelligent – possibly manage to live without the daily direction of one person and a small cabinet elite? The nation's economy would implode – our shores would face immediate invasion from an aggressive neighbour. Yet neither thing happened. True, there were many hardships, but these were caused by extreme climatic factors, together with a further tidal surge in the North Sea, rather than any financial or military threat. Damage and crop losses again ran into countless billions; shortages of food, water, energy and resources became critical both in Britain and across Europe; while major infrastructure assets – roads, railways and airports – were put out of action for days and sometimes weeks on end. Yet when recovery plans were put in place the following winter – while the blanket aid and state directed intervention preferred by other countries often faltered – the model adopted in the U.K. began to achieve success. Here, self-help and local initiatives, rather than wholesale aid, were generously supported by freely available technical back-up and access to expert advice. Emergency supplies and resources were, when essential, directed to areas of critical need; but elsewhere, communities now briefed to expect no such aid (and long having learned to live without the safety nets of personal insurance policies) showed the ability to rebuild, recover and move on. Local power supplies, increasingly provided by solar and wind energy, could be quickly restored, allowing the normal rhythm of life to continue. Citizens' assemblies took responsibility for assessing the need for small-scale technology projects – with national finances generated and used to provide larger capital-intensive infrastructure. Funding for any requirement this year that might lead to greater self-sufficiency in the next, was found wherever possible. Meanwhile, science and technology departments in schools received liberal enhancement; as did university faculties dedicated to research into the support of sustainable living initiatives, plant development trials or recycling projects. A concurrent start toward introducing more localised policing, hospital management and healthcare programmes was also undertaken; while future provision for the care of the elderly, preferably at home or in the immediate neighbourhood, became a priority.

In less than two years, towards the end of 2066, the English model had begun to bed in and fellow European nations, Holland and Germany, followed suit with their own governments without leaders during the coming January. Then, in the spring, the first major world nation, India, announced that for an initial period of six months it would do likewise following elections in July. A year later, six further countries, including Japan, Egypt and Brazil, had also changed their government structures to the new model. The rest of the World looked on – wondering if the process would break down due to an opportunist attack, or some other endeavour at outside interference. But it appeared there was little prospect of such acts as the final months of 2068 again proved ones of great upheaval in the natural world, with millions dying in freak cyclones, mudslides and blizzards across Asia, Africa and Central America. Moreover, as another new year dawned amid widespread climate chaos, those countries that had adopted a "Government Without Leaders" were seen to be faring at least as well as any other.

* * *

By the summer of 2069 Fanny Grimshaw and Maxine Fairweather were living one mile north of Silverdale in North Lancashire, in one of the newly created "Land Communities". The site overlooked Morecambe Bay, with Arnside Knott, 159 metres high, to the north, while the now little used M6 motorway passed by about three miles away in the shadow of the Pennines. On the morning of 2nd July they were hoeing turnips and parsnips on a newly created small field, their bicycles propped against a nearby gate, when a small electric van came along the lane from Silverdale, before pulling up by a gap in the recently planted hawthorn hedgerow nearby. Several more stooped figures laboured in fields round about, and a small, wheeled, hand operated electric cultivator could be heard at work in a soft fruit plantation just beyond an adjacent hazel copse. Three seagulls flew overhead, mewing and calling as they glided down towards the shoreline.

Observing that the man behind the wheel had begun writing on a pad, the two girls resumed their work, occasionally looking in his direction as they chatted and exchanged jokes. It was not until ten minutes later that he emerged. The newcomer, perhaps in his early fifties, had dark hair, slightly greying at the temples, and wore a green polo shirt embroidered with the Sustainability Party's oak tree logo. Having donned a cap he struck out towards them with easy, purposeful strides, and while the peak of his headwear partly shaded his features, Fanny Grimshaw vaguely recollected having seen him somewhere before.

She herself was a plump, buxom, kindly Lancashire girl of nineteen, and having ascertained that the new arrival was old enough to be her father she prepared to meet him in a relaxed but respectful way. Visits by Sustainability Government officials sent to discover how new communities were doing were not uncommon, and she was mindful of making a good impression in case the time should come when they would need to enlist his assistance in seeking a government grant. Her friend, likewise wearing the loose shorts and sleeveless top of a field worker, also observed the stranger. Both girls had their hair tied back with a scarf and both were deeply tanned; their bronzed arms and shoulders glistening beneath a noonday sun only occasionally obscured by light banks of white cloud moving in off the Irish Sea.

Maxine Fairweather, twenty-two years old, was thinner and slightly taller than her companion; and while Fanny's hair was both dark and tightly curled, Maxine's grew naturally fairer and finer. Now, moreover, having spent many days in the previous weeks working out of doors, it was bleached lighter still – loose wisps, caught by the breeze, floating about her face as she looked up. Although older than Fanny, Maxine was naturally more reticent and initially content to let her long time friend do the talking; but when drawn into conversation later would express strong and thoughtful opinions of her own. It was Maxine in fact who had developed the greater understanding of agricultural matters, while also volunteering to work alongside the menfolk on a project to develop the community's solar panel strategy. Following the new arrival's movements she gave a slight nod towards the other girl as he came up, and for a moment all three faced each other without speaking.

The man removed his cap and wiped his forehead in an unguarded way, revealing gentle, intelligent features, his grey-green eyes straightway breaking into a disarming smile. It was one that invited and received the same response from the two; yet behind the pleasant openness lay another level – one of care, duty and resignation, perhaps hinting at loss.

'Good morning, ladies,' he said warmly. 'I hope I'm not disturbing you too much.'

'Ooh no,' said Fanny in a broad Lancashire accent that contrasted sharply with the other's more modulated southern tones. 'We needed a break – it can get warm, us being out here in the fields most of the day, as you can imagine.'

'I certainly can, but the sea air is healthy, and I would vouch that it beats being in an office, as I often am!'

'You're reet, we wouldn't change it now – it's tons better than livin' in Manchester, anyhow.'

'You were one of the first groups in the North West to be dispersed, they tell me. How are you finding things?'

'Moostn't complain… it's 'ard work like, but it 'as its compensations too; and at least we can sort out things that go awry for ourselves. Back 'ome in Manchester there were always far too many people chasin' after the same thing whenever owt went wrong – an' that's no fun I can tell you. No, we'd rather be 'ere, wouldn't we, Max? And you know that they say "'ard work never urt anyone".'

Maxine nodded and the stranger turned to her. 'I'm here to collect some information about new communities such as this,' he said. 'To learn how the government can help you further. As you know this is not a short-term programme, so there is a good chance of you being here permanently from now on. We really do want to help everyone make a go of it.'

Addressing the second girl, he sensed that she had a different, perhaps more studied response, to offer; her face becoming serious and contemplative as she turned to look out over Morecambe Bay toward the twenty-six huge wind turbines turning in the distance.

'It's a good place to be most of the time,' said Maxine, 'and I do love it... but I often miss the hustle and bustle of Manchester; even though there always seemed to be something amiss. You may not believe it, but I was a bit of a tearaway in my early teens... went off the rails like – always writing graffiti everywhere and things. I were into drink and drugs then as well, like a lot of people I knew. One of my friends, Trina Melcott, overdosed when I was only fifteen... She didn't make it, and that could have happened to me too. You see, a lot of us didn't really care about ourselves and living for the future back then – what with so much climate trouble happening, and being told about animals becoming extinct all the time, it didn't seem as if anything was going to last much longer! Nobody ever really seemed to listen to us either... you know – young lads and lasses. So I just sort of said "stuff 'em!" That's where Fanny here helped me; she were me best mate – the only person that could make me laugh, and help me see a bit o' sense. Without her I don't think I'd be here now.'

As he observed the young woman's still youthful profile, the telltale lines of earlier cares around eye and temple gave evidence that she had known the emptiness of a life short on hope.

'But these days it's all go, in't it?' said Fanny, chipping in cheerfully. 'Always plenty to do and a laugh to be had! Eee, you should see some of the scrapes us and some of the others have got owerselves into out here. Talk about a "learning curve"! But we're gettin' there. You soon come to understand things when you have to do them for yourselves – and a lesson properly learned is one not easily forgotten!'

'I agree,' said the man, smiling at her good spirits. 'It would be nice if everybody in the world could learn as fast as you; then we would really make some progress. But I'm hopeful that will come in good time. Now, I'd like to be shown around and told what will be needed in the future. I can't promise you everything, as you know, but we don't want you simply to exist here either. Ideally your life should be made as pleasant as possible – for this is not intended to be a quiet withdrawal back to a hand-to-mouth existence, but a new beginning.'

* * *

So the girls led him off on a tour of the few acres of land that had been made over for them. It was by no means a large settlement and the three soon came to an encampment of temporary caravans and mobile homes – enough for forty people – that had been established next to a small farm. There were twelve vehicles in all, more than half showing signs of weather damage and subsequent improvised repairs. One caravan appeared to have had its side pushed in quite recently, for the windows were still covered with a layer of hastily applied transparent plastic. Fanny Grimshaw saw the newcomer looking that way and burst out laughing.

'Lor', I shouldn't really find what 'appened so funny!' she said, swallowing a giggle. 'The whole thing almost ended in tragedy, really. You see we had a sudden squall come in off the sea two weeks ago – just blew up in the space of twenty minutes. Ali, Tim and Janita, who live here, had gone to bed about half an hour before. Then along comes the wind – Bash! On average we have serious blows about once a fortnight, but this one was a real shaker, I can tell you! Would you believe, it toppled them over in one go... sent the whole ruddy caravan tumbling upon a pile of old concrete sleepers we'd got hold of for one of our projects. Fair stove in the side you're looking at, and two others next to it went the same way. The noise brought us all running, and when we eventually got inside we found Tim and Janita trapped against the wall, all neatly bundled up in their bed sheets. But Lor'... our Ali were in a worse state!' she chuckled. 'He were just hanging out of his bunk bed in the room next door, halfway between the ceiling and the floor, like – unable to free himself or move an inch. None of them was hurt, but if we hadn't been around I think they'd still have been stuck there come Christmas time!

'Seriously though,' she added, becoming earnest again, 'extreme weather is our greatest challenge. ...And I expect that will remain the case as long as we stay. Freak storms can build up and sweep in from the Irish Sea within an hour. We've had caravans pushed over three times – as well as losing greenhouses and having crops washed out or blown away. It can break your heart when you've worked hard for two months to grow a row of sweetcorn or courgettes, only to see them wrecked overnight.'

There was a pause while Fanny went to speak to three young men who had just walked in from the nearest field. They had a small wheelbarrow piled with garden produce, and it was evident from their conversation that this would be divided among the residents to provide the day's supply of fresh vegetables. Left with Maxine, the Sustainability Party man had another chance to seek her opinions.

She, meanwhile, had been studying his features as he watched the others, and when their visitor looked back he noted that she checked herself.

'Is there anything wrong?' he asked.

'Oh no... not at all. ...It's just that Fanny nudged me at the start about having seen your face somewhere... and now she comes to mention it...'

'That's possible,' he replied. 'I represent the "Sustainable Communities and Technological Support Department". You might have seen me on our website or printed circulars.'

'Maybe...' Maxine considered thoughtfully. 'But it's strange, as your appearance seems even more familiar than that... Oh well, never mind – it'll come to me later.'

The young woman was clearly very curious and her guest purposely moved the conversation on.

'Tell me a little more about this project,' he said encouragingly. 'I know the land was acquired for you by the government when the previous owner moved away. Is the forty acres you have been given sufficient?'

'Now there's a question,' Maxine responded, turning to face him squarely. 'No... at the moment there is no way that we can produce all our food, let alone everything else we require. And there will always be things – some items of clothing, essential materials and supplies etc that we will have to acquire from other sources. But we are making progress as we learn the ropes. For example, how do you sweeten your food without sugar? Well, you can plant sugar beet and try growing it – but you still have the problem of refining the crop, which requires power. As a desperate alternative you might choose to go without altogether, which of course is very dull! Personally I prefer rhubarb sweetened, don't you? ...So what's the solution? The solution is to try your hand at bee-keeping. We have, and our take from the hives last year almost got us through the winter months. We were lucky with the weather, mind – but are hoping to do at least as well this summer. We have fifteen hives now, which is also good for the pollination of our crops. The bee is a farmer's and gardener's friend, as we have discovered, and the end product of his labours also gladdens my sweet tooth.'

Relaxing once more, Maxine smiled openly and their conversation continued as she led him on a circuit of the farming enclosures, gardens and fields while her friend was engaged on an errand.

'Do you believe that the land you have been given here can ever be made productive enough to meet your needs?' he prompted as they moved on.

'As I said,' she replied, 'we are not expected yet to produce all the food we eat – although in the future we hope to be able to do that and have enough surplus to sell, or barter, for other things.'

'Just exactly how much food can you grow on an acre of land, Maxine? Have you been able to work that out?'

They had come to a small, low roofed pigsty and Maxine leant over the rail to scratch the back of the nearest sow with a forked stick.

'That question is a bit like asking "How long is a piece of string?"' she replied. 'You see, it's all a question of what you want out of the land – what you rear and grow. Then there's the question of fertiliser. We've decided not to buy that in for the present, so we really need animals like Priscilla and Jemima here. They mostly live on scraps – vegetable tops, leftovers and suchlike – giving us the benefit of recycling those in the form of good quality organic muck. We also plan to have a go at processing our own bodily wastes, just as happens in many other countries, although there are a few that want us to hold on until we know that we can safely manage any health risks. But looking back to the question of having animals here: there is always going to be a downside to that. We keep two cows and their calves for milk and meat at the moment; and have a flock of twenty sheep grazing on the poorest land down by the sea, which provide us with meat and wool. ...But that may have to change. Animals need food and space, and when you only have forty acres to play with, the chunk that is needed to provide grass and other fodder for them amounts to a considerable percentage of what is available. Our initial target is to achieve sixty per cent of our food needs by 2075 – then to push on toward providing one hundred per cent, or better, by 2085. There are many that don't think it will be possible, but much of the land we have is very productive, or could be made so if it was improved. We might have to cut down on the amount of meat we eat to reach our most ambitious targets; but is that the worst thing that can happen? It's about learning to live and support ourselves in a different way. An acre of land will grow a lot if managed properly – staples like potatoes, root and green vegetables, fruit and some grain. We have the sea on our doorstep, too, and that, sensibly harvested, will give us something. I see no reason why we should starve. It's a challenge and challenge is good!'

Left alone to share her ideas with the stranger, Maxine Fairweather became ever more confident and expansive. She was clearly a very intelligent young woman: full of ideas and constantly thinking of potential solutions to problems faced by the fledgling community. Taken out of the city environment of her birth the young sustainable living pioneer showed few signs of actually wanting to return to her former home. The challenges associated with endeavouring to live self-sufficiently upon the land had already surfaced a thousand times but together, she and her fellow community members were clearly committed to overcoming them.

* * *

Maxine moved on; pointing out farm buildings, greenhouses, and wooden windbreaks being erected on the windward side of homes. 'We'll need mobile shields to protect vulnerable plants in the growing season,' she advised, 'otherwise too many losses from the weather will wreck our plans.'

As if coming to the main purpose of his visit, her listener drew a writing pad from his pocket and prepared to make notes.

'If I asked you to provide a wish list of the things you think you most need, the things that will help to make this community sustainable in fifteen years' time – what would you ask for? You know the score; the government will provide no luxuries, but we will do our level best to come up with the essential resources and technology to make life viable. I think you are on to something here and I want to see it work! New and resourceful communities like this one are at the forefront of the move towards sustainable living and will receive all the help we can provide.'

As he was speaking they began walking back towards the farm compound where Fanny Grimshaw, fresh from helping some of the men clear a ditch, rejoined them.

'Lor', I'm a mug,' she said, smiling and wiping her hands on her dungarees. 'Whenever the lads see me coming they manage to get me into situations where I'm the one that gets most dirty!'

'They do it on purpose!' said Maxine. 'You're just too ready to muck in.'

'Aye… and that young Jack Carsley keeps offerin' to soap me down afterwards, an' all!' added Fanny, with feigned umbrage.

Maxine then explained what their visitor had offered and Fanny became as serious as she when offering her own ideas.

'We need to make sure life isn't over hard, or else some folk will think it's just too difficult and lose heart,' she said. 'We're all young at present, but in thirty years' time the way we live now will seem very hard and may easily get beyond us. We need permanent homes. Homes made of brick or wood, with wind defences on the side facing the sea; or else protected by earth ramparts. Then there's also a requirement for a proper storage bunker, where we can keep our produce and valuable resources – somewhere that provides a place of safety, too, if something really catastrophic rolls in from the Atlantic. We believe this should be set into the lee side of the rising ground just beyond the farm compound, to prevent it from flooding. It was with the thought of building such a place that we acquired the old railway sleepers to give us a start on the base and flanking walls. But what will undoubtedly be most valuable to us are sustainable energy sources which we can maintain and control! Solar panels to provide heat for our greenhouses would be great – so we can grow food all year round, as well as providing hot water and heating for our homes. We also need our own wind generators to provide extra power in winter – and as a back-up in foul weather – plus a storm generator capable of operating in extreme conditions when the normal wind turbines and solar panels have to be shut down, or are out of action.'

Fanny suddenly fell silent – as if it had occurred to her that what they were asking was merely the stuff of dreams, and that the man she faced might only be able to offer a fraction of what was required.

'I expect you think we have been going on too long,' she said with a wan smile. 'Like a bunch of kids making a Christmas list.'

Their visitor replied slowly and deliberately, 'Not at all, Fanny… you must believe me when I say that I admire what you are doing here. And if you should be allowed to fail… what will you become? …Little better than refugees perhaps – just more mouths for others to feed, with no way of supporting yourselves. This way you have a chance to move on in these changed times. You are all still young, and I hope will settle happily enough to bring up a new generation here who will learn the ways of sustainable living from their earliest years.

'Meanwhile we will still have our town and city workers to provide essential services and manufactured goods; for the world we envisage will not be one without fridges or computers. Indeed, as Kline Anderson often said, it will be an age of high technology and innovation – though one fed and supplied, as far as possible, by resources produced locally. This is where I believe you have a crucial part to play. If we in government provide support toward developing the productivity of these few acres of land, then others staying on in urban surroundings will benefit also by having the opportunity to buy and share the wholesome surpluses you achieve by your labours. Because of this we must and will help you, both now and in the future, when sensible proposals are presented. Together you are learning the truths about a new way of living from your own daily experience and my department will ensure that no problem is allowed to become insurmountable. Now, I must leave you with my good wishes. I have much to do to persuade others that what you ask is worthwhile and affordable – a task in which I do not intend to fail.'

With these words, the official shook hands with all those present before returning to his little electric van and disappearing down the road. So Paul Anderson, now chief researcher for the "Sustainable Communities and Technological Support Department" took their wishes and recommendations away with him – most of which were met during the following five years.

Chapter Thirteen

Time Capsule

TOBY FREEMAN FELT NUMBED AND HOLLOW WHEN he realised Kline Anderson had been shot. It seemed unreal that a person he had been watching and listening to not more than half an hour before, should now be beyond life and lying in a pool of blood upon the cold earth. There was clamour and movement all round: a pushing forward of press photographers, a close gathering of the mawkish and curious, together with genuine dismay among the Prime Minister's friends and admirers. But for Toby, the place had become above all a scene of tragedy – from which his only wish was to depart without delay.

He eased back through the crowd, made his way to where the crush was less intense and drew apart from the rest. A chorus of sirens could be heard approaching from three directions, and as he paused to look towards the roadway a speeding ambulance came into view, before pulling up close by. Two paramedics jumped out, one passing within inches of Toby as he hurried to open the rear doors; then three police cars and a further ambulance rushed onto the scene. Within moments all the available space in front of the village hall had been filled, effectively barring his retreat. Unable to move without impeding those around him, Toby felt uncomfortably exposed as the business of recovering the two bodies went ahead. A dozen people must have moved within inches of where he stood, and more than once it seemed he would be bowled over. But the fateful push or shove never came – nor did an apprehending hand or questioning voice. Indeed, Toby might have had a perfect reporter's pitch to review the proceedings, for it was as if he stood in a separate place of his own, beyond the sight or hearing of those around him...

'They don't seem to notice me,' he said to himself, '...just like on the other occasions... but why?'

It was a thought that added to an already deepening sense of unease about his condition – a feeling that he had become little more than part of the backcloth of those close by... like someone shielded by a veil.

On an impulse Toby stepped forward as one of the paramedics returned to collect a clipboard from the cab of the ambulance, partially blocking her way. Without breaking stride the woman turned sideways involuntarily, like someone easing past a solid object; but having almost brushed against him, continued on without comment or apology – as if he were no more than a fold of curtain or a refuse container. Had he existed for her at all Toby wondered... and how might others react?

To find out, he sidled up to a group of journalists loudly endeavouring to berate a government representative into making a statement about the shooting. Yet although Toby actually stepped between the pressmen and their quarry, neither the reporters nor the minister paid him the slightest heed as they continued their exchange. A sudden chill at having confirmed something only previously half suspected, ran down Toby's spine as he moved off through the gradually thinning mêlée of people and vehicles towards an unimposing brick-built Victorian church standing a little distance above.

Upon reaching and drawing back the heavy door, the calm sanctuary offered within seemed to beckon: that cool silence which exists inside most religious buildings, their great walls and high windows blocking out the harshest and most intrusive sounds of the wider world. But Toby could not be at peace, and sitting at a corner pew stared back toward the entrance stones framing a sweet pea entwined fence beyond.

'Jenny...' he whispered into the cloistered air... 'Where are you... and what am I? ...How can all these years have passed? ...I need to get back – but there doesn't seem to be a way...'

No sound or voice came in reply and Toby sat on in dismay and misery as evening turned to twilight – awakened at last to the certainty that his own life, and the lives of the ones he most loved, might have changed and slipped away forever. More than once he distractedly placed a fingertip upon wrist and cheek – feeling for warmth: a normal radiance and reassuring pulse meeting his touch... except perhaps for a smooth, unblemished evenness of the skin only belonging to the young.

'...I am real!' he cried aloud into the stillness as the deepening veil of night descended. But the returning echo did nothing to calm the frightened voices in his head. He might have called into the depths of a well, or cast his words into the deeps of the ocean for all the comfort his repeated words could bring.

Meanwhile the winding street outside became quiet; police and guests having departed to their constabulary offices and hotel beds, leaving only late birdsong and the gentle stirring of the river below. The woods and fields beyond the high windows and shadowed door might have been another world – a land beyond the stars now beginning to glimmer in that distant heavenly realm far above. Thus, nursing a renewed sense of despair and loss, Toby hunched into the corner of the pew as darkness silently crept into the church, allowing sleep to draw a veil about his restless thoughts.

* * *

The years sped by again and another eight had run their course before he awoke once more on the bright early morning of 3rd October 2072. Then, upon opening an eye, he heard the first tumbling leaves of autumn rustling past the church door and saw, looking towards him with twitchy curiosity, a squirrel silhouetted against the light. Toby watched as it warily hopped forward. But the tiny animal was no more than an inquisitive opportunist; attracted perhaps by the stale smell of a dropped peanut, or the scuttling of a mouse, and having looked up at the vaulted roof, it bobbed back outside, doubtless content to exchange the exploration of dusty church corners for more fruitful adventures among the high treetops of its own realm.

Toby stood up and stretched (a cobweb separating between knee and elbow), before following through the porch, where a flower rota pinned on a notice board told him which year would soon draw to a close. Few others were about, except an elderly woman dead heading roses in a nearby garden and a young man walking a small dog. As Toby expected, neither showed any sign of having marked his emergence; and feeling that for the time being this was probably for the best, he set off at a brisk walk with the intention of clearing his head.

The curving lane quickly brought him down to a sheltered pathway –"The Severn Trail" – created around one hundred years before on the straight track bed of an old railway that once ran along the upper edge of the gorge. Feeling that this must eventually lead to a place where he would be able to get his bearings, Toby set off along it, heading north. Two joggers approached in the next mile, another passing from behind; but he was left to himself until emerging at last into a public car park next to the "Station Inn" at Ironbridge. The town, as its title suggests, is named after the venerable iron structure that crosses the River Severn at this point. Many thousands of tourists once flocked there during the summer months to visit the site, together with other industrial heritage museums round about, and even now, when travel was much more difficult and expensive, a fair spattering of school parties, visitors arriving by coach and touring cyclists still enjoyed excursions to the place. To cater for them, a number of gift shops, pubs and small restaurants remained in business on either side of the bridge, giving the location a lively atmosphere.

Having reached a more populous part, Toby slackened his pace to observe what was going on. The pedestrian only bridge bustled with movement and he was glad, upon reaching the arched centre, to begin descending the other side. Then, while weaving through a meandering huddle of garrulous pensioners, he saw a tiny two-seater "Chipmunk" battery-electric car pull up across the protected exit to a public thoroughfare a short distance further on. It was like a little model, or futuristic plaything – a small wonder of scaled down engineering that could run for five hundred miles at a maximum speed of forty mph without recharging. Moreover, as the makers proudly proclaimed, it might then be parked in a space little bigger than required to store two wheelie bins. When first introduced the revolutionary design had been derided as too small, slow and insufficiently sophisticated by those that might afford to buy one. But now, with ever-stricter energy efficiency laws being introduced, the Chipmunk was among the most common and reliable vehicles on the road, with over ten million sold in less than eight years.

For Toby, this was the first one that he had seen, and he crouched to look inside upon approaching it. The electric window wound down as he did so and Jeannie greeted him with a smile as she leant across. She was dressed in attire that matched the more fashionable of the women walking by, her fair hair, as always, loosely tied back in a ponytail; this time using a ribbon of a colour between pale blue and silver.

'You'd best get in quickly, Toby,' she said with a hint of amusement in her voice. 'As I fear we may have attracted the attention of an unwelcome passer-by.'

Puzzled by this comment, Toby looked up to see a somewhat portly parking attendant stalking diagonally towards them from the other side of the road. He had clearly noted both the car and Toby, and the mixed look of annoyance and triumph on his face promised only one outcome should they tarry longer. Toby hopped in beside Jeannie and the little car began to glide forward at the very moment the attendant, breathing heavily, drew level with the open window. He had already placed one hand on the sill, as a prelude to presenting Jeannie with a parking ticket, when he felt the car move beneath it.

'Think you can get away, do you?' he called after them, as the Chipmunk pulled into the traffic. 'Well you're wrong, you're on CCTV and the fines treble for people driving off without paying!'

The stout fellow was quickly left behind, hands on hips, a look of assured satisfaction that the penalty fine would soon drop on Jeannie's doormat creasing his features as he dropped from view.

'It looks like you might have torn it this time, Jeannie,' said Toby ruefully, looking back over his shoulder.

'I think not,' she replied calmly, continuing to steer straight ahead. 'You see this little car has a habit of disappearing when necessary – and I very much doubt that *my* address could possibly be traced by the Shropshire Traffic Department.'

'But even so, that warden *did* see us, didn't he? I've got used to being ignored recently; but that one certainly knew we were there!'

'Quite so, Toby,' she affirmed, turning towards him, 'both you and I are evident, while together. That is the way of things.'

'And... when we aren't?'

Here she looked back with a slight inclination of the head. '...Let us just say that when you are alone, things become much more indistinct...'

* * *

The suggestion behind Jeannie's reply again struck a hollow chord and Toby fell silent once more, concentrating instead upon the changing scenery as the Chipmunk climbed out of the gorge on the road to Telford. Soon they began negotiating the complex ring road to the town, busy with cars like their own, together with a variety of hydrogen cell buses and battery-powered delivery vehicles. There were also many tree lined cycle tracks, and a new orbital tramway to serve the perimeter estates of the large conurbation. For more than five miles Jeannie stayed with the general flow before steering down onto the almost empty and weed-strewn motorway that would take them to Wolverhampton and Birmingham. Due to the presence of works traffic a strict thirty-mile per hour speed restriction was in force – the outer lane being cordoned off to protect workmen in yellow suits engaged upon the task of removing central crash barriers. Some of the overhead destination gantries had also been taken down, while at several locations preparations were in hand to demolish over bridges.

'This seems like a full-scale clear-up. What are they doing?' asked Toby, as Jeannie pulled up at a temporary traffic light provided to allow safe passage of scrap recovery vehicles crossing from the centre reservation.

'This motorway is to cease operation at the end of the year,' she replied, following the progress of a large slab sided vehicle bearing the Sustainability Party logo and the words "Transport Regeneration and Construction Dept" on its side. 'The only reason that we have been directed to use it today is to allow the final refurbishment of traditional routes in the area that will carry all remaining traffic in the future. If you travelled the length of Britain, from Scotland to the West Country, you would see the same thing happening at a hundred locations. From next year most of the old long distance motorway system will be at an end, with only local sections in some towns and cities remaining in use for a little longer.'

'But won't that cause chaos?' asked Toby, wrinkling his brow. 'I mean… where will all the traffic go? Surely it will simply gum up the old main roads and stifle population centres as it did in the past?'

'That is what many claimed would happen. But things seem to be turning out rather differently. You see, there simply aren't the same number of journeys being made any more – and less journeys mean less congestion. Most business is now carried out electronically, allowing more people to work at home or in their local communities, while there is less freight because many more things are produced and distributed locally. The remaining long distance goods traffic is normally conveyed on the upgraded rail network, which also carries a majority of inter-city passenger traffic. By train you can now travel between any major town or centre at approaching four times the strictly enforced fifty-mile per hour speed limit permitted to road traffic. Since rail also costs less than half as much, that is what most travellers are happy to do. There is more traffic around urban conurbations of course; but here too good public transport alternatives have been introduced and most are gradually moving away from using their cars for all but a few journeys. So all in all, as you can see, there is less demand for roads, particularly motorways. The passing of the "Motorway Closure Act" was Kline Anderson's last wish, and it was brought into law just over two years ago, on 14ᵗʰ July 2070 – with final shutting down scheduled for New Year's Day this coming January. The motorway that we are on has already had a stay of execution, but the M54, like every other route, has proved hugely costly to maintain. Having been in use around a hundred years, most now require complete renewal of bridges, flyovers, drainage and lighting. Therefore, as the Government has fewer avenues to generate revenue for public expenditure; and as it serves no purpose to renew an asset which is no longer required when the money can be better spent upon more useful long-term communication projects, complete removal is the most sensible option. So the motorways will soon become history, necessitating that we fall back to using the restored roads our ancestors once relied upon. In place of these abandoned thoroughfares, some of the land previously covered over with concrete and tar will be returned to agricultural use – now more vital than ever as we attempt to move towards a self-sufficient future – while in other locations eco villages, local parkland amenities and cycle tracks will be developed. In a number of regions there are projects to develop rail corridors, tram systems and guided bus ways too. Thus, while our motorways may have temporarily become construction sites again, before long they will have made way for much that is urgently needed and of far greater value.'

Listening in silence, Toby was amazed by Jeannie's words; all the while thinking back to his own life in the late nineteenth and early twentieth centuries, when relentlessly increasing road traffic volumes had led to an ever-expanding network of motorways and bypasses. The concept, then, of a world in which traffic figures would decline once more, would have seemed impossible. The nose to tail progress of thousands of diesel hungry lorries was the norm – endless traffic tailbacks a constant experience; as too was the unending toll of death on the highway. Yet at that time there had seemed no other alternative but to simply grin and bear the daily misery of wasted hours.

'So it would seem we are to be among the last that will make this kind of journey,' Toby reflected aloud, looking ahead at the virtually empty carriageway.

'That is so.'

'And is that why you have brought me here… to experience an ending?'

A smile lit Jeannie's face as she replied. 'No, Toby, my aim was not as ordinary as that. My true desire is that you should come with me to witness something much more intriguing. We are going to Central Birmingham – to the location known as "Spaghetti Junction". There, as here, much redevelopment work is in hand, and having already removed most of the road decking, the contractors are now at work demolishing the concrete columns that supported the elevated motorway and slip roads. There were five hundred and fifty-nine of them in all, and it was known that one had in its base a "time capsule" – a box containing items of memorabilia – put there to be opened at a future time when the structures were replaced. This was done at several new construction locations when building proceeded, as it was thought amusing to speculate upon what those opening such a box... a hundred, perhaps two hundred years later, would make of the relics found inside. Some, such as a copy of the documents authorising the commencement of construction, were predictable enough as you can imagine: while there were the usual pictures of civic dignitaries at signing events and first sod cutting ceremonies. In addition, memorabilia to do with the modern age might be included: items of clothing, pop records, photographs of film and television personalities, etc. A few other artefacts were also sometimes slipped in, perhaps to raise the eyebrow of an archaeologist.

'Well, I must tell you that the time capsule at "Spaghetti Junction" was indeed found in one of the tallest columns: being subsequently opened just over a week ago amid much media interest. Its contents are to go on show in Birmingham City Museum as soon as possible. However, the matter is not to end there; for last evening, during the demolition of an adjacent supporting pillar, a further, smaller "time capsule" was unearthed near its base. The latter is known to have been erected just over one hundred years ago, in September 1970, but there is no record of the placement of this container in the construction documents. Yet, when the box came to light there could be little doubt what it must be, and although slightly crumpled by the demolition claw, it remained both safely locked and sealed. An attempt at opening might have been undertaken then and there, but the demolition foreman decided against this in favour of informing the "National Office of Works and Historic Research" who promised to send their archaeological survey representative, Clyde Brasher, this morning. He is due to be there at ten o'clock, and until then the immediate area of the structure has been cordoned off. The two of us will be permitted to observe the proceedings if we can successfully make our way to the site, so that is where I am heading.'

It was now possible to proceed again and with a clear road ahead they made good progress, soon drawing near to the curving slip road to the M6 that in previous years would have taken them south towards their destination. The motorway in that direction had already been closed, however, and Jeannie was directed instead onto the old main road to Walsall and the "Black Country": their progress frequently being slowed by the myriad new works being undertaken. Sometimes the traffic was channelled into single file through streets where tram extensions were being established; while at others new pedestrian precincts and open spaces had replaced intimidating dual carriageways and desolate retail car parks. Often, the remaining embankments and elevated sections of the fast disappearing motorway passed in and out of view, frequently lined with rows of spoil lorries ready to take the recovered materials away to nearby railway yards for onward transportation and recycling.

Meanwhile the quartz dashboard clock ticked remorselessly on until by ten o'clock they had made their way to the heart of Birmingham and were nearing the vast thirty-acre demolition site that was once "Spaghetti Junction". Eighteen roads had previously converged there, crossing three canals, two rivers and a main line railway, but now all was being re-developed less grandly and intrusively, with efficient bus and tramways, a light railway system and landscaped pedestrian zones. When completed in 2080, "Spaghetti Junction" would become the "Kline Anderson Centre", complete with sporting arena, community park, wildlife centre and theatres – a starkly different place from the barren area once given over exclusively to thundering cars and lorries.

The Chipmunk briefly drew up at the site office, where Jeannie spoke in low tones to the attendant before bumping on into the heart of a wilderness of piled rubble, grinding caterpillar tractors and noise. At a dozen points the mechanical jaws of demolition machines dipped and rose like nodding dinosaurs – each filling the air with dust and swirling particles as they ripped and tore away at the surviving roadways. Great derelict spaces had already been opened up, where an assortment of different heaps of rusty steel, reinforcing mesh, aluminium railings and general debris climbed up to tower over the declining ruins round about. While high above it all, a small forest of cranes swung and turned overhead – a gathering of carrion feeders continually reaching down to savour the entrails of torn and broken structures below. As such these angular monsters gazed out upon a field of plenty, for although the work had already gone on for eight months, it would be another six until the site was fully levelled and the City of Birmingham Planning Department's brave dream began to rise from a sea of rubble.

Toby and Jeannie drove for some distance before approaching a section near the centre that had been cordoned off with bollards and warning tape. A little less than one hundred metres away a final section of decking, spanning four remaining motorway columns, was coming under the attention of the demolition grabs, great puffs of concrete dust and fractured asphalt bursting out as the structure succumbed. But where they finally stopped was calmer; and although fine particles continually circled and settled all around, within the cordon an unraised voice might still be heard – as if the insidious din of destruction could not entirely invade every corner.

A number of people were already present: four or five local reporters, a small party of history students and the site foreman. They were greeted by the latter, a heavily built Brummie in his fifties standing near the remains of an approach road column, of which only a three-foot high section had been left intact, the severed ends of rusted steel reinforcing cables stabbing skyward. The column was about two meters wide at its base and there, in a recess left by a fallen slab of masonry, sat a metal box about two feet square, temporarily returned to the position from which it had initially been dislodged by the attentions of a powerful demolition grab. The top and sides were badly dented and scored, but the container had retained its shape and there seemed a good prospect that most of the contents remained undamaged. As Toby and Jeannie came up the foreman made a point of apologising on behalf of his late coming history guest.

'We'll just have to wait a bit,' he rumbled dismissively, as if referring to an unreliable relative. 'Some *expert* from Loondon is coomin' up. I'm expecting him any minute, but you never know when these academic types will actually appear.'

His comments could have been a signal, however, for within thirty seconds another vehicle approached, a small electric van with the words "National Historical Archive" hand-painted in fine royal blue script across the side panels. It bobbed rather comically towards them through deep ruts and puddles and then turned, before reversing up to the stub of the motorway column. A man of mixed white and Afro-Caribbean race casually climbed out, and without a word to anyone went round to unlock the rear doors. As he did so a pronounced click sounded from inside – a digital camera switching itself on. Then, having satisfied himself that everything was ready and in good order, the newcomer returned, whistling contentedly.

Based in London, Clyde Brasher was an archaeologist and social historian who had built a reputation on television and radio for his skill in interpreting archaeological finds from the industrial and post-industrial period of British history. He was very tall, almost six feet six, and genial in his approach; but meticulously thorough when examining new finds, relying in his work upon the most up-to-date techniques of recording and data storage. Of his dress sense, it might be said that this could sometimes be flamboyant to the point of being ill-judged; and today he wore a pair of green corduroy jeans below a vivid yellow shirt and check waistcoat that made him appear somewhat like the jolly giant from a commercial. Yet his looks, as is so often the case, were deceptive. At less than forty years of age, Clyde Brasher had become the foremost expert in his field; and the value of his work and methods would long survive him. Turning to face the site foreman, he grinned broadly: smile lines around his eyes and mouth emphasising the features of a handsome face.

'You made it then,' said the foreman, clearly giving a heavy hint that he also had important work to do and didn't approve of being kept waiting.

'I have indeed, my good man; and am ready to begin as soon as you permit.'

The colourful archaeologist spoke in a casual yet refined way that his friends knew and loved, but which the uninitiated might easily construe as pretentious and dismissive. Such was the effect on the foreman, who cocked his head on one side as much to say, 'We've got a right one here!'

'I at least have got serious work to do,' he replied shortly. 'So I'll be pleased if you'd get on with your examination. This particular area is due to be flattened and graded by the end of the month, and I have little time to waste on formalities.'

'Then let us go to it,' said Clyde, 'for the contents of this "Pandora's Box" surely deserve to see the light of day at the spot where they have lain undisturbed for so long.'

The two men then walked to the rear of the van, while Toby and Jeannie tagged along at the fringe of the following group before taking up a position just to one side of the column base only six feet from the rediscovered container. Meanwhile, Clyde Brasher had begun to busy himself in a final act of preparation by unfolding an aluminium trestle table on which to arrange the contents of the time capsule.

'I see you're recording everything,' said the foreman, studying the van's interior. 'Will that be for broadcasting on television?'

'Possibly,' replied Clyde, jumping up beside the box. 'That depends what we find. You see there is no guarantee on that score. Sometimes it amounts to nothing of importance – an empty container, a load of junk, or the kind of items we've all seen a thousand times before. ...But then again,' he added with a mischievous glint in his eye, 'it could be something grand – even fabulous – like the lost crown jewels of Stuart England... or perhaps a flying medieval demon that seizes my throat and throttles me before your eyes!!

'Should that occur,' he chuckled, 'there would certainly be something worth recording! So, as I'm sure you'll agree, it is best to let the camera run at all times.

'Now... if you will step back, I'll begin.'

The watchers complied, and he reached down to lift the box, which was clearly quite heavy, even for a big man – and they all heard a large object move a fraction inside as he tilted the container slightly upon regaining his balance.

'Not all newspaper cuttings and cuddly dolls, at any rate,' said Clyde Brasher. 'Nor the rotten contents of a sandwich box either, unless I'm very much mistaken! And I have to tell you, ladies and gentlemen,' he smiled, raising an eyebrow and playfully wagging his finger, 'that I have indeed unearthed more than one rather ancient cheese sandwich. There is simply no accounting for some people's sense of humour!'

The history man now crouched before them in his slightly elevated position, the damaged metal box held between outspread knees. A small inexpensive brass padlock secured it, but there was no sign of a key.

'It would seem that we will need to resort to the housebreaker's technique if we are to see what is inside,' he said, looking towards the foreman. 'Pray hand me the small hacksaw in my toolbox, if you please, my good fellow.'

The foreman visibly bristled for a second, before reaching inside the van, presently producing the required tool. Then all watched intently as Clyde Brasher began methodically working the blade back and forth across the projecting loop to which the securing padlock had been attached. The metal was of poor quality mild steel and before long he had sawn to a point more than halfway through. The whole box vibrated softly as he did so, producing a low humming sound akin to a muffled snore. Pausing briefly, the big man looked up from his work and catching the eye of a female reporter, showed his teeth in an artful grin.

'Perhaps I have woken something up… like the genie of the lamp,' he winked. 'Will he allow me to be his master this day – or perhaps choose to punish me harshly for my audacity?'

It was a ridiculous conjecture, meant purely in fun; but the oddity of the event, together with the growing suspense of the moment, engendered the spice of possibility in the mind of each watcher. Then the rasping note of the saw changed, as the teeth cut through a last shard of metal – the loop, complete with padlock, falling to the ground.

'Now for it,' said Clyde Brasher, at last becoming entirely serious as he gripped the top of the box with both hands. 'Now to reveal what has lain here so long – and in doing so, take a glimpse of history.'

He gripped the container tightly, pulling gently but firmly round the rim… At first nothing happened, but then, as if some film of rust or snag of metal had been overcome, the lid slid up with a squeak and was lifted away.

* * *

Just as the princess of Ancient Greek myth expected to find jewels or perhaps the secrets of life and love in her forbidden box, so did some of the curious onlookers hope to see revealed a startling treasure – or maybe some lost half forgotten icon of the 1960s. If Geoff Hurst's hat trick ball from the 1966 World Cup had rolled out, or Ringo Starr's drumsticks, it would have well fitted their mood of expectation. But what was actually found at first appeared unremarkable – a miscellaneous collection of seemingly unrelated items.

Clyde Brasher took a camera from his pocket to photograph the contents and then, one by one, began carefully removing them. The first to be brought forth was a rabbit's foot, the fur perfectly preserved, the stubbed nails still smooth and shining in the daylight.

'What's that?' asked one of the students, clearly less than impressed by such a mundane thing. 'Putting that on top seems a little primitive to me.'

'I doubt it was meant that way,' replied Clyde, meeting her gaze. 'It was more likely placed in last as a good luck charm – a simple token left by an ordinary man to bless the new motorway above and protect those that travelled upon it. It may even have been put there with a smile, but perhaps has served its purpose.'

Clyde stepped down and reverently placed the tiny relic at the top left hand corner of the table, before returning to reach into the box again. This time he lifted out a coloured photograph of four men dressed in construction workers' overalls. The dyes had faded with age and there was a tinge of brown at the edges, but the freshness of the men's smiles as they posed by a dumper truck was undimmed by the passage of time. They might have been looking forward to knocking off and going for a drink that very evening – though all had surely been dead for many years. Their names were written beside each face, giving them life and character. On the right, making a "thumbs up" sign, stood Carl Wilson, a twenty-five year old Scotsman with long shoulder length fair hair falling down below his hard hat. A Glaswegian, with two small children, he'd been the joker of the pack; always playing pranks upon his mates. But Carl had been honest and reliable too, always sending the majority of his pay packet home at the end of the week to support his wife and family. Next to him were "Chipper" Cunningham and Tim Bradford, each with his arm around the other's shoulder; two long time friends from Birmingham – both married and in their early thirties. They too had the shaggy long hair so fashionable at the time – "Chipper" with the addition of a theatrical droopy moustache that gave him, perhaps intentionally, the appearance of a Mexican bandit in a "Spaghetti Western". Yet there was nothing forbidding about the craggy smiles and open expressions of men clearly full of good humour. Crouching below them in front was the fourth, Gervais Malcolm, a Jamaican born West Indian, also from Birmingham, his round, bearded face looking up from beneath greying eyebrows. The eldest and most serious of the group, he had come to England ten years before, making his way up by hard work to become section foreman. A writer of poetry about his past life in the Caribbean, Gervais was kind-hearted, level-headed and reliable – "a regular good bloke" – whom the other three had come to regard as a father figure.

Clyde Brasher held up the photograph to his audience. 'These, it seems, were the players in our little mystery…' he pondered reflectively. 'I wonder what other clues about themselves they have left us?'

The next item to be lifted into the light was a vinyl record, *Hey Jude* by the Beatles – a worldwide hit at the time the motorway junction was under construction. This was then followed by the folded sports section from the *Sunday Mirror* newspaper containing a Wembley ticket for the 1968 FA Cup Final between West Bromwich Albion and Everton. The game had been the first at Wembley to be televised in colour and Jeff Astle, the scorer of the only goal in the third minute of injury time, had become both a local and national hero, having netted in every round of the competition.

'No doubt some or all of these men were there that day,' said Clyde Brasher, having read out brief details of the game. 'And what a valued token to have left for posterity!' he added, holding up the ticket. 'For you can be sure it was much treasured by the owner. West Bromwich is but a short distance from here, and men need good reason before parting with such a memento.'

Next came another folded newspaper, dated more than a year later; its front page dominated by headlines about the war raging in Vietnam. A large picture showed a flight of B52 bombers over Hanoi: while another was of a burning village, with terrified children running towards the camera.

'They have included this too,' he said, turning the familiar image so that all could see. 'Once more, I feel, because they wanted to record what influenced and affected their lives… for those were becoming solemn and changing times after the post-war optimism of the 1950s and early 60s. The clouds of conflict around the world had gathered again – an escalating confrontation in South-east Asia, the "Troubles" in Northern Ireland. Then there were new environmental concerns too: the loss of life due to a landslip at Aberfan in South Wales – followed by the disastrous *Torrey Canyon* oil spill off the Cornish coast. In any event, I would conclude from the presence of this additional record of the time that our construction workers had a serious side.'

Subsequently to emerge came something more homely: a bottle of home-brewed beer, the colour still dark and clear; although the tarnished lid was etched with a film of rust… then a metal model of a digger, a "Dinky Toy", still in its box, as if ready even now, to go on proud display in a collector's cabinet. After this appeared a small *Penguin* paperback, such as might still sometimes be found in local museums and secondhand bookshops, which the historian turned in his hand.

'Ah, *Chocky* by John Wyndham!' Clyde Brasher piped. 'A popular science fiction author of the time I believe… now let's see, if my memory serves me right it is the story of a boy who holds conversations with people inside his head – an activity some would doubtless consider a sure sign of insanity. But Wyndham was always one to explore themes beyond our normal understanding, or the usual parameters of life. It would seem that one of our men enjoyed indulging in such interludes and saw fit to select such a book from among the normal fare. I wonder what he would have made of the new world we are endeavouring to build in these times?'

Next out was a cinema ticket to a showing of *Butch Cassidy and the Sundance Kid*, followed by a shiny copy of *Mayfair*, a men's magazine – the pretty girl on the front cover smiling coyly, her bodily curves faintly concealed by a veil of fine chiffon.

'Hmm… the portrayal of a beautiful woman,' said Clyde, with the hint of a smile, as a few wry comments passed between those before him. 'Such will forever be the temptation and delight of men – sometimes artistic, often provocative; with no doubt many more alluring images displayed inside the glossy covers.'

With equal care he laid it together with the other finds, before going on to the next. This was a booklet containing a full set of collectors' cards depicting African wild animals, the colours still as fresh as when it had last been opened. But then something more touching was drawn forth – a child's maternity band, carefully cut from where it had encircled the newborn's wrist – a precious thing, with lasting relevance to the parent.

The name "Kathy Wilson" had been neatly written upon it in blue biro and Clyde held the tiny item towards them upon his massive palm.

'Now we get a little closer still to one of their number,' he said with quiet gravity. 'It is my guess that each of the friends placed something in their time capsule that they valued greatly. For Carl Wilson, regularly separated from his family for weeks on end, it would appear to have been this. Not only, perhaps, did he want to put in the box an item of lasting personal significance, but also to record for posterity the existence on this earth of a much loved daughter.'

There remained only three things inside, but two were by far the largest and most bulky. The first to emerge was what appeared to be a large folded flag, but which on closer inspection was found to be an engineering union banner; the fine embroidery and trailing cords still pleasingly bright and in good order. Signs of wear did exist, however, down either side where the poles would have been attached, these worn folds and creases indicating that it had been proudly carried in procession many times. ...But with the demise of the union, due to falling membership or amalgamation, the time must have come when, no longer required for its original use; it had been saved as a private memento before being passed down to one of the men. Now revealed again in the light of day, the banner represented a poignant reminder of Britain's industrial decline, while commemorating a former age of worker solidarity.

'Another strange thing, you may think,' said Clyde Brasher, 'but one of the most important, nonetheless. Many thousands must have walked behind this with pride in their industry and craftsmanship during days gone by; and while they themselves are lost to the earth, it has endured to remind us of their former sense of purpose and community.'

Now the final items came forth: the first a railway enthusiast's notebook, much battered and worn, with many numbers and names carefully underlined. Inside, neatly folded, was a photograph of a streamlined locomotive, polished and shining brightly beneath a sunny sky. It bore the name "Kingfisher" and possessed a sleek grace that would still have turned heads. Then, reaching down to the very bottom, Clyde flexed his muscles to lift the very last – a curved metal plate with the name "FIJI" presented in raised letters.

'FIJI?' said the nearest reporter, hunching his shoulders. 'What has something bearing the name of a South Pacific island got to do with Birmingham?'

'Nothing directly, in terms of the place and location, perhaps,' replied the historian. 'But this artefact has, I believe, got another association with the area... you see it is a steam locomotive nameplate, and one among only a few of its kind that would have been small enough to fit in our box. I have gathered from my research that during the nineteen fifties and sixties, countless boys grew up to become railway enthusiasts; and having found both this and the previous book, I think we can be reasonably certain that one of our men had developed the spotting bug. Yet the period was also one of change and modernisation – a time when old and past technologies were being superseded and erased. The steam locomotive, alive and exciting as it was to many small boys and young men, was swept away and consigned to the scrap heap in a few short years. By the summer of 1968 they had all gone; cleared out amid the march of progress. To the enthusiasts this was a minor tragedy. Many gave up their hobby when the steam engines were no more, turning their attention to other pressing things such as girlfriends and family, but most retained a few nostalgic items. Collections of magazines, spotters' manuals and station objects were carefully hoarded away, while some were a little more adventurous in securing mementos of their hobby – removing whistles, number or nameplates from abandoned locomotives awaiting a tow to the breakers' yard. This was often done with the shed foreman's consent upon the exchange of a few pounds; but it was sometimes achieved in a more clandestine way – after working hours, or in the dead of night when few prying eyes were about. I suspect the locomotive that carried this name ended its days at one of the Birmingham engine sheds and that one of our men, having discovered it there, returned later with a suitable spanner to remove this nameplate. It was now his to keep; but perhaps in time his enthusiasm for seeing the lifeless treasure mounted upon a bedroom wall declined. Then, we may well surmise that along with his trusty spotters' book and a picture of his favourite engine, one of our four decided to leave it sealed away with the other things discovered here – a once prized artefact of a now all but forgotten age, left for us to ponder at our leisure.'

Having completed his task, Clyde Brasher stood back from the collection laid out on the folding table. 'So there we have it, an eclectic selection, pooled by four ordinary men. No doubt having witnessed the placing of the official box shortly before, the construction employees secretly sealed away their own time capsule for us to find; and among its contents we have a simple record of their loves, interests and passing passions. In doing so, they have provided us with tokens of their world – a connection with a time now beyond living memory. As such we should treasure these things for what they are, since they remind us of how our recent ancestors lived, and of the past from which we spring.

'In the short term I intend to remove them for further examination and cataloguing; but they will soon be returned to your city museum for display so that the people of Birmingham may enjoy and learn from them. Now I must be off, but I would like to assure you that you have witnessed something every bit as important as the opening of the official time capsule seven days ago. The lives of ordinary people are all too easily overlooked; but they are revealed and laid before us when such finds are made.'

After carefully labelling and putting the items into a series of wooden containers, Clyde Brasher drove away across the scarred moonscape, leaving the small gathering to break up as the dust of his departure settled. Before long Jeannie and Toby were clear of the haze and turmoil too, travelling south-east through Birmingham and beyond. Toby spoke little… thinking about the four men whose lives had been lived so close in time to his own.

'Those workers…' he said at last. 'Surely I could have passed any one of them in the street – yet now they are doubtless long departed?'

'Most certainly,' replied Jeannie, realising the direction in which his thoughts were moving. 'Men do not live forever – that will always remain an iron law.'

* * *

Passing on through fields and hedgerows bright with autumn colours, Toby settled again to contemplation. By mid afternoon they had circled Coventry and came at last to a secluded canal basin on the Grand Union Canal a few miles south of Rugby. Several traditional barges, long restored to their former glory for use as pleasure craft, were tied up, while many other modern cargo transports lay moored close by. These latter vessels were all fabricated from tough, recycled plastic sections and had been equipped with electric propulsion engines for the task of carrying freight on recently upgraded waterways between London, Birmingham and the North.

One ancient barge – the *Amethyst* – beautifully decorated with the scrolls and lettering beloved of Victorian boatmen, lay moored on a shady reach below a willow tree and it was next to this that Jeannie drew up. The soft whirr of the Chipmunk motor died away, and when it fell silent all that could be heard were the occasional calls of moorhen and coot. Having surveyed these new surroundings, Toby looked towards Jeannie, who slowly turned the ornate bracelet on her wrist.

'This is it again, isn't it? You're off once more, and I'm to stay here.'

'That's right, Toby… I must leave you this last time. You will find the cabin of *Amethyst* open and may rest there undisturbed as long as you will.'

'So I won't see you again… this is the end?'

'Not quite – for us there will be a final meeting… but no journey beyond.'

'It's impossible! How am I to complete the last part? …You said that I was on my way home… but when will I get there?'

Jeannie turned to him – a look expressing something more than sympathy alone in her eyes. 'I have not misled you, Toby. The next and concluding part of your travels will indeed take you back where you belong. This is but a penultimate station, where you must wait again for a while.'

Toby wrung his hands. '…But can't you see I'm afraid, Jeannie… afraid of what I have become… and what I can never be again.'

She nodded meditatively while turning to follow the graceful progress of a swan. 'Yet you are brave too, my good friend. Brave enough to pass another interlude of dreams until your truth is revealed... now I will tarry no longer, while you must stay to enjoy the delights of a fine autumn evening.'

'Wait!' he called, seeking to delay her departure another moment. '...I have one more question to ask... one that has puzzled me for many days.'

'Then say it.'

'It concerns a bird – a crow... the one that so often seems to observe and shadow me when I am awake. ...What do you know of it? ...Does it have a name?'

Jeannie faced him again, noting how he searched the treetops as if expecting to see the creature peering down.

'His name is "Tark"...' she replied softly. 'But to understand why he is so called, you must think back to those occasions when the two of you have met before. As to the first part of your question – let us say that he has been a most diligent observer, and has therefore played an important part in your history... beyond that I can tell no more.'

Toby could see there was no hope of delaying Jeannie further and waved farewell as she glided away along the towpath before passing from view. Then, after ambling a few paces further off and gazing more than once into the murky water, he returned to the *Amethyst*. One or two figures had appeared among the low buildings where the modern barges lay tied up a short distance away, but none took any heed of his presence, and accustomed now to anonymity, Toby saw little point in approaching them. Instead he hopped up onto the painted deck, and finding the door to the cabin open as promised, stepped down inside. What he found within was a place of charm and history: a bargeman's comfortable kitchen and living quarters equipped with a wood-burning stove, copper kettle, cooking utensils and colourful flower vases, all brightly polished as if they had been cleaned that very day. He read the labels on drawers and food containers – each finely scrolled by a master signwriter – and found ornate knives and two-pronged forks that might be set for a cosy meal. ...But Toby could summon no appetite for food, and experienced but a remembered thought for water. Rather, his mind had become increasingly focused on a single end – to complete his journey home – and with this in mind he sat on the barge roof as a mellow October sun suffused the western sky with a tinge of gold.

* * *

Much later, as he lay to rest for the last time, curled in the bargeman's cot, returning to Jenny remained the one thing that gave an enduring purpose to his life.

Chapter Fourteen

The End of the Beginning

NEW ORDER YEAR ONE, THE YEAR WHICH more than one hundred national governments had agreed would mark the virtual end of their dependency upon fossil fuels, dawned on 1st January 2085. However, at no stage leading up to or following this new beginning was the event celebrated with loud fanfares, mutual congratulation or mass celebrations. Rather, the whole process was seen as part of an ongoing development – a stage in the long walk away from the extravagant misuse of resources that had unbalanced the climate of planet Earth, threatening the civilised existence of those living upon it. The need for change had been embraced by all but a blinkered few, and a world had begun to emerge in which progression towards self-sufficiency and sustainability was accepted as a central requirement for long-term survival. Yet it would not be a future, as some cynically portrayed, for "hippies living in wigwams", but one in which people and their families – supported by the development and application of advanced technology – came to live in a new way, with less demanding and wasteful aspirations. The ultimate beneficiary would be the natural world upon which all depended: the seas, oceans, forests and grasslands no longer carelessly pillaged and abused, but managed wisely for the good of everyone and for generations yet to come.

Sadly the wild tigers, apes and migrating beasts of the earth had vanished; the lands they once roamed now taken by human populations gradually learning to pursue more contained and viable lifestyles to safeguard their own existence. A symbol had been chosen to commemorate the coming of this "New Order" – a crouching snow leopard looking up towards the beating sun – a creature long driven from its once frozen mountain habitat by the profligate and careless actions of man.

* * *

Every month of the calendar year has its special scents, sights and character. From the cold of a freezing February morning, when the hoar frost clings to the trees, to the golden glow of a September evening, each one, even damp and blustery November, can delight our senses. The minute Toby came awake, on 10th April 2085, he would know from the sweet fragrance in the air around that spring had arrived; while the angle of the sun peeping through the lace-edged curtains of his sleeping cabin told him it was morning. However, what he could not fathom at first was the warm sensation cosily penetrating his middle.

He opened one eye, focusing again after countless hours beyond sleep, and surveyed the objects around him. The decorated pots and copper kettle were there as before, so too was the Toby Jug and the small clock in its wooden case – the spidery hands still showing half past four. These articles glowed and glinted where the light caught them, as if some patient hand had recently returned to wipe away the settling dust, or revive a dimming surface. But something else of much greater import also caught his attention. …The cabin door was open!

It was then, his caution suddenly aroused, that Toby looked down and saw Macken comfortably curled in the curve of his stomach. He watched as the little dog's chest expanded and fell with the gentle action of his breathing, a look of relaxed bliss upon the sleeping face. Then an eyebrow lifted slightly, no doubt in satisfactory contemplation of a well-earned meal, and his nose twitched, as if the scent of squirrel or rabbit, promising a chase, had brushed across a paw-licking canine dream. Never before had Toby seen the little Jack Russell so calm and restful – as if the coiled spring that was so much a part of his temperament had unwound for a while, allowing a welcome interlude of peace.

Although surprised to find him there, Toby felt reluctant to wake the sleeping animal; but was forced to acknowledge the likelihood of being unable to rise without disturbing his infrequent visitor. As it happened, Macken himself brought an abrupt end to this speculation; for he suddenly lifted his head, before tottering up a little shakily to lick Toby's face. It was a damp, rather unwelcome greeting, but one taken in good heart by a recipient glad of renewed companionship.

'I'd ask you where you've come from and how you found me here?' mused Toby, playfully holding the panting animal from him. 'But as always, my little friend, I'm sure that you will not be able to tell. Are we to go on together, I wonder? If so you must lead me… for I am far from sure about the next part.'

Macken put his head on one side, then dropped to the floor, before skipping up the five steps to the tiller deck. Toby followed into the light, shielding his eyes against a sun reflected in shimmering ripples from the broad surface of the canal basin. No one else moved nearby, and the only creature to be seen was a mother Mallard duck with an early brood of chicks. Startled by their sudden emergence the matron hastily gathered her family, then waddled off along a grassy track towards the safety of the canal, her eight tiny charges scurrying behind. Toby smiled at the effect of their sudden intrusion, while Macken, sitting alertly upon his haunches, clearly eyed the retreating party with thoughts of giving playful pursuit.

For a few moments Toby deeply inhaled the fresh air, his senses quickly reviving as the last effects of long inaction dropped away. A renewed urge to move on came too, an inner feeling that the day should not be wasted and that in all likelihood he still had a number of miles to travel.

'What next, old fellow?' he asked, looking down at Macken who had settled to gnaw at a stick. 'If you do know the way, lead on… unless, that is, we have to wait here for another.'

This last conjecture could be immediately dismissed, for the Jack Russell straightway tossed the frayed morsel aside and jumping to his feet, trotted over towards the canal. Then, upon reaching it, he raised his nose to sniff the air, before popping out of sight behind a rustling patch of last year's reed stems and making off along the towpath.

*　*　*

Following in pursuit, Toby could see that the day's weather promised to be mixed and unsettled. There was more of a breeze as he left the canal basin behind, and this stirred the dead grasses and old reed heads into a rustling murmur. Yet new growth was evident also: the fatty stems of cow parsley, nettle and other lush plants breaking through moist soil after six winter months lying dormant. Patches of primrose and flowering dandelion showed round about, while one field, stretching back to a crumbling waterside residence half covered in ivy, lay carpeted with bobbing daffodils. The sky overhead meanwhile, grew alive with the puffs and plumes of passing clouds – one moment coming together in threatening heaps, only to break up again seconds later, as if involved in an ungainly frolic. Such was their rapid, uneven progress, that while one minute the sun would break out to spread its rays in a wide patch of blue sky, by the next it frequently became eclipsed by billowing patches of grey gloom that threatened anything from a sharp shower to a burst of hail or sleet. In all, it was a morning for staying wrapped up, for the chill of recent winter had not entirely lost its grip.

Macken was but a short distance ahead, and having waited patiently until Toby drew level, walked close at his heels, often looking up, like a busy court advisor in conversation with his royal master. There was very little activity on the water; which seemed odd when Toby recollected the number of working barges moored at the canal basin, and taking the opportunity to rise onto a quiet over bridge, he was able to look further afield. It was then he noticed one of the modern, silver painted craft – large and bulky in the rural setting – moving through a meadow about half a mile to the west. A short while later another hove into view, coming up from the south, gliding silently onwards at six to eight miles an hour with a cargo of wood, potatoes and garden vegetables for Coventry. Both travelled along the new and wider canal that had been completed eight years before as a part of a revived and extended national waterways network. Powered by almost silent electric propulsion units, they were designed to operate day and night, even through densely populated urban areas, without disturbance to sleeping residents or hindering other traffic; thus providing a viable alternative to rail and road transport.

After watching for a short while, Toby descended once more to the towpath before walking on; drawing close soon afterwards to a railway line standing on a newly constructed embankment – a section of the recently completed high-speed railway line from London to the West Midlands, Manchester and Scotland. The services on it were operated by a specially built generation of double deck "Ultra Trains", one of which swished into sight. Twenty-four carriages long, travelling at two hundred and twenty-five miles per hour, it flashed by in little more than the blink of an eye, safely carrying two thousand five hundred people on their journey. The contrast with the old canal that he walked beside could not have been greater; a contrast that became sharper still when Toby glanced back in the direction from which they had come to see a horse drawn barge coasting round the nearest bend. Except when disturbed by trains, the location at which he stood offered splendid isolation, where only the lap of water around reed stems or the call of a plover broke the stillness. The wind, meanwhile, had begun to moderate, and the sky, although still not without a lingering threat of rain, would stay fine for a while, the clouds having closed together into a more general mass. Turning on his heels, Macken made back towards the approaching craft, leaving Toby to stand and watch alone as it drew near.

The barge was another of the traditional narrow boat variety meticulously converted for use by holidaymakers following the termination of lengthy working careers after the Second World War. Most that still survived in use, while formerly converted to diesel power, had been more recently fitted with battery electric motors, but this one was restored to its original horse-drawn form, and now, newly repainted in contrasting colours of maroon and Brunswick green, made stately progress towards him. It was pulled by an old, superannuated shire horse named Goliath; a regal fellow with a taste for wayside grass and an easygoing pace that far from overtaxed his still massive strength. Standing more than seventeen hands high, Goliath was very grey around the muzzle, with a jet-black coat, white fetlocks and a snow white blaze down the bridge of his nose. This elegant marking, it must be said, had made him highly prized in earlier years, but now long retired from his days of fame, he spent a quiet retirement occasionally hauling travellers enjoying a pleasant day out on the canal. Those aboard today were of this carefree ilk, although as Toby discovered, they comprised a very mixed and varied group.

The barge, previously named *Barnacle* and before that the *Royal George,* had now been rechristened *Wren* and she had been adapted to provide accommodation for parties of visitors with varying degrees of disability. Some of these could only enjoy the trip as passengers; but others – those sufficiently well and mobile – were encouraged to take on the role of crewmen, tying up at landing stages and helping to negotiate the many locks along the way. The group currently aboard had done so many times; becoming so confident and familiar with life on the barge that they could virtually run it themselves without assistance. Providing support when needed were three-able bodied helpers, one of whom was Paul Anderson.

Now well into his sixties, greying but with a full head of hair, Paul sat on the rear tiller rail talking to a girl with Downs Syndrome steering the barge. He was dressed for the day out-of-doors in casual jeans, cotton shirt and a green fleece bearing the "Sustainability Party" logo, and wore a floppy grey waterproof hat to keep off the sun or showers. In a crowded room Paul Anderson could still cut a notable figure, but dressed as here, on the waterway, he might easily go a whole day without drawing a second glance. Yet having seen him before, Toby was not deceived; and from his reaction as the barge drew alongside it was evident the former politician had some perception of having previously met him also. He looked directly towards Toby, and then leant forward to call the young woman leading the horse: asking her to pull up so they might take the opportunity to talk. At the same instant Macken, who had recently reappeared from beneath the towpath hedge, trotted up and sat beside Toby's feet, tongue lolling from the side of his panting mouth as he concentrated upon the faces turned towards them.

'This time he saw me from the start,' thought Toby glancing from Paul Anderson to Macken. 'But I'm sure he didn't on the last occasion – How can that be? Unless… the dog…?'

Soon the barge had lost headway, and aided by the efforts of a stolidly back stepping Goliath, the girl at the tiller smoothly guided her venerable craft to the canal side.

'Hello,' the latter said, 'my name's Carol. You can come aboard if you like.' The young lady was dressed in loose fitting jeans, a pair of old trainers and a massive pink T-shirt that reached almost to her knees. But to preserve an air of nautical dignity and authority, she also wore a navy blue captain's cap complete with silver badge. Carol Croucher had thoroughly learned how to steer and handle the *Wren* two years before, and now considered it her duty to skipper the vessel whenever the party was abroad on the canal. She did so with a studied vigilance that all had learned to trust, and although never at any time more than three metres from the towpath, diligently maintained her concentration as well as any fabled "Ancient Mariner" strapped to the helm of a galleon in the Southern Ocean. Yet, unlike that ill-starred traveller, she was a humorist; a "card" – always full of fun and ready for mischief. Toby could see no good reason to turn down such an open, well-meaning invitation and made ready to embark. Meanwhile, in her impression of a rakish buccaneer, Carol tipped her cap at him as he clambered up.

'Welcome aboard, lubber! You're lucky we had time to stop, since we're in so much of a hurry.'

'Don't worry about our Carol,' said Paul Anderson, who had now moved to sit on the cabin roof. 'Our bucko pirate captain will make time enough if her first mate asks it. Now, I hope you don't mind joining us. Seeing your solitary figure on the towpath, I considered it quite likely that you would enjoy the ride, and besides...' he added, winking at Carol, 'the present company was getting a bit boring, so I thought it would make a nice change.'

'Charmin', I'm sure!' flounced Carol, feigning indignation as her face flushed into a wide smile. 'I'll get back to me job then.'

With that they cast off once more; but catching sight of Paul Anderson looking towards him, Toby couldn't quite dismiss the idea that his host had another reason for picking him up.

* * *

As the day drew on Toby soon got to know the rest of the group. The girl leading the horse was Jill Carraway, a regular carer with the "Paul Anderson Trust" to which the barge belonged. She was one of those remarkable young people that are entirely committed to helping improve the circumstaces of those whose lives have been blighted by injury or disability. Jill was tall and thin, preferred to go without make-up and only ever wore clothes for practical comfort rather than style. With a degree in psychiatric care, she could have worked for a much bigger organisation; but having been interviewed in person by Paul Anderson when the trust was initially founded five years before, and greatly inspired during their meeting by his commitment to providing the best possible care and opportunities for the disabled, she had worked for the organisation ever since. Sometimes considered too serious by those who merely knew her in passing, Jill nevertheless had a vivacious and beautiful smile when relaxed and among friends, together with an abiding love for the people she worked with. They in turn had grown to love and trust her, knowing that however serious their misfortunes, she would always treat them with equal affection and understanding.

Walking beside her now was a teenage dwarf named Davy Striker. Davy was very slight, with remarkably short legs, and beside Goliath and the slender Jill, resembled a small child dressed in clothes beyond his years. He had long light brown hair tied in a pigtail beneath a much travelled Coventry City baseball cap, and had cultivated a droopy moustache to make his cherubic features appear more masculine. The pride of Davy's wardrobe was a hand tailored, chocolate brown bomber jacket, worn now above a pair of wide corduroy trousers, the lower apparel having an unfortunate tendency to make his bottom appear oddly large and out of proportion with the rest of his diminutive frame. But he, like all the voyagers that day, had a sense of fun that could look beyond the difficult hand fate had dealt. If Toby caught anyone off guard, staring towards him, his favoured response was to strike a pose, with hand on hip, before looking over a shoulder to enquire, 'Does my bum look big in this?' in such a casual and dismissive way that good-natured laughter and discourse invariably followed.

When invited below, Toby met Jolene Temple, a girl paralysed from the waist down at birth. Unable to move independently, and with the additional disadvantage of having a withered arm, she was seated in a wheelchair on the lounge deck of the barge, where she fished one-handed with a rod and line through a wide rectangular opening in the panelling. Institutionalised all her life, Jolene had never once caught anything larger than a stickleback or minnow; but would sit for hours watching the water slide by as she dreamed of pike, or more often the handsome Frog Prince who would one day sweep her away to walk among the fields. Toby was also introduced to Mohammed Tamal, crippled by multiple sclerosis and wheelchair bound too – yet nevertheless strong enough at heart to force a crooked smile while performing a handshake of magisterial gravity. Then he met young Wallace Minder, condemned by a spinal injury sustained in a road accident to similarly sit out his days. Yet Wallace still had valid aspirations to appear at the Olympics, and when set down on the towpath, would show all the determination in the world to successfully perform the duties of a shore crewman.

However, Jitan the kite flyer, and little Maisie Archer, were the ones that Toby would most remember when looking back. He met Jitan Mistry in the converted open bow well of the barge where she shared the changing delights of the spring day with Naomi Peters, the third helper. A petite, pretty and infectiously enthusiastic teenager, Naomi was always a pleasure to be with. She constantly chattered like a sparrow; interested in everything and everyone as if the next minute would always be more amazing than the last. But Naomi had learned to listen too: to smile encouragement when others less lucid then she attempted to shape their thoughts into coherent gestures and words – cheering them when they became frustrated or distracted.

What a contrast then with twenty-three year old Jitan, the mute quadriplegic: fixed and secured immobile in her chair – her head held and clamped in a supporting brace. Jitan, who could neither walk nor move, but who, through the special sensory control tube placed in her mouth, was able to look towards the sky and fly her kite. She too knew how to smile at a friend, to thank her helpers with a blink, or just to grin at chance. Yet, most marvellously, through the creative skill and patience of an inventor she would never meet, Jitan was, with an action of her tongue, able to draw the delicate threads that linked a cruelly earthbound existence with the dancing freedom of the kite above.

…But it was Maisie Archer, her face constantly drawn with the strain of living with cerebral palsy, that inspired Toby above all. Maisie – only seventeen – who would break into an involuntary grimace when frustrated or in pain, or burst into a fit of giggles when amused. A girl who could light up any room with her smile and cause others to fall about with shared laughter by making wry, self-deprecating comments about her own tragi-comic antics. Toby only realised what a marvel of bravery and determination Maisie was when they approached a canal lock and the shore crew disembarked to raise sluices and open gates. These duties were carried out under the supervision of Jill Carraway, but it was Davy the dwarf, Wallace Minder in his wheelchair and Maisie Archer that did most of the work. Maisie suffered the indignity of walking with the clumsy, poorly co-ordinated gait of those suffering from her disease, her back awkwardly stooped and twisted; but when ashore she set off with the others at a determined shambling trot – like a little "Mother Courage" bravely going off to seek her fortune in a cruel and troubled world. There was no hesitation in her step, no reaching for another's hand, only a stout and unwavering assertion of her right to take part fully – to be considered an equal on life's unequal playing field.

Thus, although taking a little longer perhaps than would have been the case had a less challenged team set forth, between the four of them the jobs were always done, and soon skipper Carol was able to steer through to the other side; while the feelings of satisfaction felt by Davy and the returning shore party might have puffed out a dozen much broader chests.

* * *

The day was now well past noon and they had entered the county of Buckingham, where the old Grand Union Canal passes through the tunnels at Blisworth before gently meandering on towards Stoke Bruerne. Davy Striker had been hoisted onto Goliath's back by Jill, where he sat, with legs dangling on either side, like a ploughboy riding off in search of cheese and ale to some long forgotten market. The sky meanwhile drew threatening, with heavy clouds blowing up from the west; a freshening wind promised showers to come. Looking toward the declining sun, Toby sat on the barge roof with Paul Anderson as a patchwork of small fields and community farms slid by. With the spring planting season under way, there were a number of people, both adults and children, working round about, one or two of whom hailed them as they glided by. Ranks of new solar panels were being installed in one place, while in many others, wind generators, both large and small, had been erected to supply energy to the national grid and local farms. In sheltered spots there were animals too: not large herds, but half a dozen cows in a small pasture, or a sty with a sow and piglets. Toby also noted occasional flocks of farmyard geese or chickens, and sheep grazing areas of low-grade scrub. Gone however were the huge fields that he remembered – the hundred acre prairies given over to a single crop to be turned into bio-fuel or cattle feed – these having been replaced by highly productive fields, orchard gardens and soft fruit plantations providing local communities with a wide range of fresh produce.

'It has all changed very much, don't you think?' said Paul Anderson, looking towards Toby with a searching expression.

'Very much indeed,' he replied, watching a woman in a nearby field raising one of the new electrically operated windbreaks already noted at a number of other locations.

'And you have seen these changes, Toby… perhaps have even known a time long before all this was thought of?'

…These words, simple yet probing, dropped like stones into a pool – like a much-denied truth cast upon a bright table… Temporarily silenced by uncertainty, Toby looked blankly towards the older man; no ready answer coming to his lips.

'I feel I know you,' Paul Anderson went on, 'that we have perhaps met before… I had that impression earlier; the moment I could distinguish your face as you stood on the towpath. Such imaginings are ridiculous of course, since in all probability we have never seen each other in another place… But there is something in your look and I am glad to have the opportunity to talk with you.'

He seemed to hesitate before going on.

'I wonder if you could have known my brother… that you might perhaps have been connected with his life in some way? …I am not a romantic, but I sense that he would have wanted to meet you.'

Toby struggled to decide what he might say. The insight of his host had penetrated the veil of secrecy he chose to maintain – but a wish to impart something of what he'd discovered encouraged him to lower his guard just a little.

'To confirm that we have met before… or that I knew your brother, might be going too far… but I do know something of your family history – of the corner of Bedfordshire, only a few miles from here, where one half of his and your own story has its roots.'

'I thought so!' said Paul Anderson, earnestly leaning closer. 'But how could you have learned of such things? …Are you a journalist? …Have you studied my family?'

'I am not a journalist… nor is anything written about what I know,' replied Toby, looking down at the passing water. 'But there are things I have come to understand in my travels.'

'And did your travels take you to that part of Bedfordshire of which you speak?'

Sensing that it would be unwise to allow the conversation to trap him further, Toby met Paul Anderson's eyes more guardedly when he turned back.

'Let us say that I lived there for a while, thus enabling me to learn something about your ancestor, Meg Maddox. …She was evidently a good woman – but tell me, what do you know of her yourself?'

Paul Anderson's brow wrinkled and his face became both serious and puzzled. '…I know part of me springs from her,' he replied after a lengthy pause. 'And I have searched for more information about the life that she led. …But it seems she was something of a recluse – a strange old woman who kept herself to herself having brought up her only child alone. My family are not ones for producing large families, as you may have gleaned, and I am, as far as I know, her sole surviving blood relative. As to what else I have learned of her, there is very little; other than that it has been suggested she may have had a secret… a secret that she took with her to the grave.'

'Country folklore, perhaps?' said Toby, thinking back to his visits to "Silver Link Cottage". 'The stories meddling folk want to believe about people they do not fully understand.

'Trust me, Paul. …She was not odd… neither was she always old. …And all of us have our secrets…'

* * *

They talked on for a little longer, Toby revealing some of the things he knew also about Alice Maddox, Claire Cheetham and his companion's mother, Emma Tresco. But he was careful all the while to steer away from conveying any detailed knowledge; their conversation eventually turning by degrees to the general affairs of the modern world and the part Paul Anderson had played in this since the assassination of his brother.

'I have done a little to help many people resettle and bring about the changes that must happen,' he said. 'Changes that are, wherever possible, being carried through with a supportive and sympathetic hand. Moreover, we poison nothing now with toxic chemicals – for the industrial assault on nature is done! The land is for all, both young and old; and all must learn, as their right, the skills that will enable them to live in harmony with the natural world.'

* * *

They now passed close to a half-acre field where newly planted kitchen vegetables grew. It was alive with young workers and as the *Wren* drifted sedately by four or five broke into an impromptu jig to the accompaniment of a wind-up radio.

'As you can see,' Paul Anderson continued, 'there is little demarcation now between the roles of the young and those that are older. Each is taught how to work the soil and all are given equal responsibility for its management. We have encouraged our children to connect with nature – to be challenged and strengthened by an affinity with the land and wild things.'

He smiled towards Carol who, still stolidly holding her course at the tiller, winked back in her favoured imitation of a carefree sailor.

'Something that we have also kept in this time of change and upheaval,' he went on, 'is our willingness to invest in such as the crew and passengers of this barge, for a nation that properly cares for the disadvantaged is a nation with a heart and soul. There is no perfection here (as is equally true of the wider world), only harmony between the barge and the canal – between the able-bodied and those somewhat less fortunate.

'...Remember, Toby, everyone is worthy of respect and a share in what we have.'

* * *

The sky had darkened now, promising a sharp spring shower or worse – one of the now regular sudden storms that could do great damage to crops and property if drainage was improperly maintained or precautions not quickly taken. Toby had witnessed the raising of protective shields earlier, and now in a number of places field workers and the owners of houses hurried to batten down equipment or secure window shutters. The wooden covers to greenhouses and cold frames were also being closed to minimise damage should the winds or any downpour become extreme. Jill Carraway brought the barge to a stop beneath an overhanging willow tree where Goliath could shelter; then, having tied up, she jumped aboard with Davy as the first strong gusts brought a spattering of heavy raindrops. It was but a brief overture in advance of what followed: for after another short lull, the heavens opened and a barrage of freezing rain and hail began to beat upon the roof of the accommodation cabin. The noise was loud and threatening and through the opening where Jolene Temple still stolidly sat with her rod and line, the surface of the canal turned to a boiling froth of churning and bobbing hailstones. Jitan, her kite reeled in, began to whimper nervously, and it was then that Naomi Peters suggested they all join in singing a song while the shower lasted. The proposal meeting enthusiastic approval, five hearty choruses of "Ten Green Bottles" were subsequently rendered before the rain and wind began to abate, the sound of cheerful voices often distorted by the noise above; and what with forgotten words, out of tune harmonies and bursts of giggles, it was far from being the best rendition of the old ditty. But never can the perennial favourite have been sung with such good humour and gusto. For ten minutes *Wren* was a haven of mirth and merriment, of throaty groans and trilling whistles, where the Devil himself might have rattled on the roof without bringing a lessening of the good spirits within.

When those who were able eventually emerged again to sweep the decks, the sun, now dipping low into the west, had broken through fleeting clouds once more, and all who laboured shared a collective resolve to get under way as soon as possible, with the aim of reaching their destination in Milton Keynes before nightfall.

* * *

Within less than eight minutes the onward journey had been resumed; the old horse seemingly not the least put out for having remained uninvited to the uproarious gathering. Soon Stony Stratford was left behind and as evening drew on the barge began to glide among the housing estates, allotments and recreation areas of the now long established "New City". The poor weather had largely cleared away, leaving a heavy atmosphere of spring scent and rising vapour as a warm April sun dried streets and rooftops. Before long they were approaching the landscaped canal basin where *Wren* would be moored and Toby noted two electric mini buses waiting to take the day-trippers back to their community residence. He moved forward and stood beside Paul Anderson to watch the shore crew land and tie up, a smiling Maisie Archer proudly leading the operation.

'As you can see, my brother's legacy is more than simply a world without leaders,' said Paul Anderson reflectively. 'It is a world in which everybody can have the confidence to fully play their part; young and not so young, men and women. For myself, I believe we are at last truly engaged in the process of building a sustainable future – a world in which all are respected and listened to, and in which everyone is encouraged to play a fair and equal part.

'That was his dream... and the manifestation of his spirit is here.'

* * *

There was then much labour and toing and froing as the day's expedition came to a close, the travellers and their belongings being safely loaded into the two conveyances. Soon only Paul Anderson, Toby and Macken remained standing together on the towpath; Goliath having been led away to nearby stables for a well deserved brush down and feed. Carol called to Toby through an open window of the nearest mini bus as it prepared to leave.

'You can come next time too, if you want,' she said. 'It was fun, wasn't it?'

'Yes indeed, Carol... and thank you all,' he replied, with a smile for each of her companions. Then, with these pleasant exchanges completed, the two vehicles pulled away accompanied by a tooting of horns liberally arranged by Maisie Archer.

'These have been a good few hours,' said Paul Anderson, reflectively looking down at Macken, who had again dutifully taken up position beside Toby's leg. 'And may I thank you also for joining my happy crowd on their day out... although I have a nagging feeling none of us will experience the pleasure of your company again.'

This note of finality struck a painful chord with Toby. 'You cannot be sure,' he replied, 'there may be another time.'

'No... I don't imagine so, my friend. ...You must go now, with the dog – wherever it leads you – and I doubt others may traverse the same country: which is unfortunate because I have enjoyed meeting you and will not forget our conversation. As for me, I must leave in another direction. I have a meeting at seven thirty to help decide how the "Friends of the Grand Union Canal" can increase the catch from its waters. You see, we have stocked parts of it with carp; and I must confess that I have begun to develop a taste for the fish. So goodbye, and farewell; I trust that you will journey safely from this time... wherever you may travel.'

With that they shook hands and Paul Anderson briskly walked off to a nearby bicycle rack where, having put a token in a slot and removed the local authority "Borrow and Return" bike, he mounted and cycled away into the lengthening shadows.

'So it's just you and me again, Macken,' said Toby, looking down at the little dog, which eyed him enthusiastically at the prospect of moving on. 'But where to, boy?'

Toby had barely uttered these words before the answer seemed to emerge of itself from the clouded recesses of his own thoughts. '…Where have I wanted to go all along?' he said out loud, looking eastwards into the darkening sky. 'Home of course… where else? And now I am again within reach – so that is where my steps must take me!'

* * *

Macken had already moved off at a skittering run and stood some twenty metres ahead, cocking his leg against a tree while giving Toby a 'Hurry up' look. Toby followed into a lighted avenue where electric cars and vans occasionally passed and the two made their way beside this for a while until, upon reaching the outskirts of the city, the route eastwards curved off into the countryside. Night was rapidly drawing in and soon Toby walked the near deserted road towards Bedford with little more than the glow from a distant and watery moon to light his way. It had grown cold, too, though he didn't feel it; a rising mist gathering in shrouding banks that swirled and eddied, obscuring the highway ahead. Once or twice Macken passed out of sight in the enveloping murk, only to reappear again a little further off. …But he no longer made a sound of any kind, and only the calls of the night – a hooting owl, or barking fox – broke the silence.

Then, seconds later, Macken melted away completely… there one moment, he simply vanished into the moving cloud to be seen no more. Toby walked on as straight as possible, hoping his so oft dependable companion would show; but a minute passed… then two.

'Alone again!' Toby cried aloud to no one. 'Is that how the final episode is to come in…?'

Then, like Macken, he too merged with the gathering vapour and was gone.

Chapter Fifteen

A Wanderer Returns

S O THE WHEEL OF TIME ADVANCED AS another three decades all but ran their course, while for Toby, it might be said that he walked, at last, out of a waking dream: his feet touching the cool surface of a metalled road in the first hours of 29th May 2113. Within seconds his senses revived, allowing recognition of a familiar remote spot on the winding country lane leading uphill from the Northampton Road toward Stavenham. He paused briefly beneath the canopy of an overhanging oak, taking courage from the reassuring touch of weathered bark against fingertip and palm, then set off into the approaching day of his final homecoming.

* * *

It was that grey hour around dawn when slow moving banks of high cloud shroud the last dimming stars, and taking in the well-remembered shapes and folds of the countryside, Toby walked on through a sleeping landscape, past open fields and silent hedgerows. The light gradually strengthened, and as it did both life and colour gradually returned to the changing canvas before him. First, the dappled leaves and growing crops took on a dozen shades of green; then an awakening dawn chorus of birds grew up, led by the ever-sweet song of a single skylark rising upon the mellow air. Toby heard the ascending chorister with a gladdened heart: yet at alternate moments felt strangely hollow too – as if his frame was no longer entirely whole, but something paper thin and wasted. Stopping, he held forth an upturned hand to study the lines – the etched tale of life and destiny sketched upon hardened skin; then walked on into the widening expanse of morning.

* * *

The road to Stavenham soon dips sharply down between earthen banks left following the removal of an old bridge once carrying the Bedford to Northampton railway line, and by turning right at this point, an easy climb brings ramblers to the country walk traversing the disused track bed toward Molliton. Well knowing that he had come within a half hour trek of his own front door, and urged to complete the last leg of his journey by the shorter route, Toby might well have taken these steps had he not heard the soft electronic bleep of an appliance automatically switching on in a newly constructed bus shelter nearby. He stopped to look and was amazed at the welcoming glow that sprang up. Evidently erected to serve the needs of walkers returning home after spending an enjoyable day in the country, the structure nevertheless bore scant resemblance to the blandly functional, often vandal damaged examples he had known in his own time. This particular shelter was a work of art: the pleasant, decorative canopy being modelled in the sweeping shape of a bird's wing; the interior equipped with five comfortable plastic seats, all recently cleaned and polished. The frame was made from clear recycled plastic panels, blue tinted to prevent glare from the sun; each corner being enhanced by freshly watered hanging baskets filled with an array of petunias, geraniums and trailing lobelia. As Toby watched, a small wind generator, set within a stainless steel cowling upon a post, activated and turned with a mellow hum, the whole device being amusingly topped by a weathercock modelled in the form of a drunken owl hailing passers-by with a tankard of ale. It seemed as if Toby really was being welcomed to enter, and the agreeable tones of a telescreen, now shining at one end of the interior, further enticed him to step inside.

A twenty-four hour news programme was showing: with further channels offered for the benefit of would-be travellers facing a lengthy wait before the arrival of the next bus. Beside the telescreen a printed timetable showed that services commenced every morning at six o'clock, before running half hourly until midnight; while underneath a glowing digital time display indicated that it was 04-30 on 29-5-2113. There was, in addition, a polished rack containing three recently published magazines (all neatly folded and left for the next reader), a stainless steel drinking water fountain, and a small heater, powered by a solar storage panel in the roof, that gave out a gentle warmth. In all the shelter offered a good degree of comfort and order, like the small neatly maintained conservatory of a suburban residence. Yet it was unmanned and unattended – left open for the use and convenience of all, at any hour.

Toby sat down facing the screen, his eyes drifting towards the information display and date upon it. 'Twenty-one thousand and thirteen,' he thought, '…exactly one hundred years since I left…'

This news could only add to his strange sensation of emptiness, and suddenly desirous of hearing another's voice, he reached towards the screen where a menu panel advised, "Touch for sound" – the volume swiftly growing until the speaker's words were comfortably heard. The presenter had previously been covering a range of everyday news: some to do with adverse weather events around the world, and another about the opening of the new and heightened Thames Barrier in London. Now she had reached her closing items: beginning with one announcing the death of Rajesh Patel, the last surviving Briton of the previous millennium. Born in November 1999, Rajesh had lived an impressive one hundred and thirteen years; witnessing all the major changes leading to a sustainable new order of everyday living.

Mr Patel was like 'a Time Lord', the newsreader said. 'A man who had spanned the ages, as he had spanned two millennia!' A witness of world war, environmental collapse and human revival; he was the great survivor of a recklessly extravagant age that would be finally consigned to history with him. Plans were in hand for his natural burial at Rye in Kent the following Wednesday.

'The last survivor of the twentieth-century,' murmured Toby. 'Then what of Jenny and me... and the children?'

He was left to mull this over as the weather forecast came on. A young woman wearing an orange blouse, with an embroidered lightning flash logo, stood before a digital screen, where the most startling 3D graphics gave an impression of the weather to be expected that day. 'This,' she announced, 'would be very changeable in all areas; for while most seemed likely to enjoy some warm sunshine, the majority could expect sudden and possibly dramatic changes as the day wore on, with violent, thundery spells developing before evening. Extreme weather might be expected locally and the need to maintain crop protection measures in a state of readiness was emphasised. Otherwise, it would be another normal day,' she concluded, wishing her viewers good fortune.

The loop, evidently updated every hour, began to run again, and Toby stepped forward to turn down the sound. He was now occupied with his own thoughts once more: unsure what he would find on his return to Molliton, but now prepared to wait a little longer until the world had woken up. To fill the time he took a magazine from the rack and just three pages in came upon an article that made him stop in his tracks. It was in *"Turning Page Monthly"* and presented a brief review of the life of Paul Anderson, who had died only a week earlier. There was a large full colour picture of the man he had met (it seemed only hours before) but who had in fact died more than twenty-eight years later at the age of ninety-four. Tributes were paid to his career in helping bring about the resettlement of the ten million people returning to live and work in rural areas, together with others celebrating his activities promoting the "Paul Anderson Trust". The article concluded that the man who had so ably stepped forward into the vacuum left by his brother's death would be greatly missed by all who knew and loved him. A footnote also added that the Anderson line was now at an end, since neither of the brothers had married.

'This is worse than odd,' Toby whispered to himself, returning the magazine to its place. 'Now he too has gone – like all the rest... another contact left behind... another ghost?'

He sat waiting, eyes closed in meditation, until the sun rose higher and the first signs of human activity became evident. Two cyclists wearing straw sunhats made their way uphill; then a sleek little electric mini bus drew up beside the shelter, though the driver, as Toby expected, merely looked briefly inside before driving away down the slope. Having watched the bus depart, Toby moved outside into brightening surroundings, becoming fully aware for the first time of subtle changes that had happened since his most recent visit. Firstly, where previously barely a soul would have been seen at work on the land at such an early hour, now he noted four or five people at various points: cutting vegetables, tending animals or walking among fruit trees. Meanwhile, nothing was on the large scale of previous years; for all the land had now been divided up into many smaller units, most lined with newly planted hedgerows, where an abundance of different crops grew. There was still grain and some evidence of domestic animals to provide meat and fertiliser; but it was the overall variety of produce and enhanced productivity of the land that impressed. Even small corners were sown with a few things: a half dozen maize plants, a row of soft fruit, or an apple tree to provide food for urban mouths, and all were worked in with plants and vegetation offering a habitat for bees, insects and birds to aid fertilisation. Toby nodded approvingly and then climbed to the old track bed before setting off purposely towards Molliton.

But within one hundred yards, a second reminder of the change in himself was made cruelly obvious when he came upon a young girl wearing a beekeeper's hat examining a hive at one side of the tree-lined walk. Insects buzzed in abundance all around and Toby stopped for a moment to watch. The girl worked away with skilful hands, before stepping back beside him, removing the cumbersome head protection to brush her face as she did so. Toby remained motionless – though positioned very much in her line of vision should she look up. But upon raising her head the young woman paid not the slightest attention; merely staring through and beyond the spot where he stood, before collecting her things and making off toward another hive nearby.

A similar thing happened five minutes later when two men carrying hedging tools and heavy canvas bags approached. They were deep in conversation, blithely laughing and joking about the events at a party the previous evening, but as Toby quite deliberately stepped in their path, barring the way, both merely sidestepped by on either side before continuing on without breaking step, as if he were no more than a rooted post.

'…Am I really as nought to any of them?' he thought, rubbing his temple. '…A mere nothing?'

* * *

Disquieted afresh, Toby shambled on uncertainly, coming at last to the isolated corner where Meg had lived. Here at least much less had changed, for although "Silver Link Cottage" and her smallholding had been grubbed out more than one hundred and thirty years before, something of the former calm and tranquillity of the spot remained. …

Indeed, Meg might have been there waiting by the stile, or tending the flowerbeds beside her front door.

He went to the hedge to peer through, finding the stump of the original stile, now rotted and covered with moss, next to a new structure that had replaced it. In front meanwhile, the place where she had lived lay empty; except for an overgrown corner beside the railway embankment, covered by a straggle of nettles, seeding thistles and common mallow. The two or three acres round about had been left to provide grazing for half a dozen sheep, while further off were small plantations of fruit trees and patches of ground given over to chickens, rows of new potatoes and celery. Two field workers in straw hats, a man and a woman making adjustments to a solar panel, stood straight ahead of him about two hundred metres away across the shimmering land. They might, he thought wistfully, have been two others that he'd known long before, except for their modern overalls and the nature of their work.

But just then, as Toby was about to drop back onto the country path, an additional couple appeared at the edge of his vision – apparently solid enough, but seeming to have materialised in a moment. One was a young man wearing a cloth cap, his sleeves rolled up to the elbow; the other, a youthful woman wearing an ankle length dress similarly reminiscent of a bygone age. They walked with a Golden Retriever on the higher ground where Maxton Tower had once stood, the grey muzzled animal bouncing heavily around the woman's ankles like a playful puppy. As Toby observed their progress she appeared to hesitate and turn towards him, caught for a moment in a shaft of bright sunlight, her hand raised in silent greeting… a vision on the edge of the sky. The old dog too seemed to follow its mistress's gaze, and, as if recognising Toby also, barked joyfully before bounding forward with loping strides – only to disappear, having covered less than half the distance between, in a flurry of swirling grass and dust.

'…Mr Toots!' said Toby, staring at the point where the dog had vanished, before looking back to where the couple had been. …But they too had disappeared and no one stood within half a mile of the tower mound, except the pair of diligent workers patiently adjusting a solar panel…

'Am I going mad,' Toby mouthed to the trees, 'to imagine I have seen those that have been dead so long…'

Shaken, he turned and stepped back into the shade of an overhanging oak as another trio of field workers walked by, before continuing on his way past Stavenham Windmill: the sails he had once seen turning, now propped and supported by stout metal poles to protect against powerful gusts and flailing rain. Then the site of Windmill Halt was reached; all trace of which was long removed together with the substantial house, formerly home to its stationmaster and gatekeeper. A hundred years on, the shallow cutting had been landscaped with young trees, wayside ponds and wild roses; while the spot where Morwen Hughes once tilled her well ordered garden was edged with buddleia and flowering shrubs providing a tranquil wildlife garden – a quiet place for families to picnic on a summer's evening. Time and nature had clearly worked their subtle arts upon the location, but the screeching of a bird still occasionally provided a haunting reminder of a train whistle echoing upon the drowsy air.

Toby sauntered on more slowly now: as if reading the last page of a long book that he had no desire to finish. The country walk, once almost straight in parts as it followed the course of the removed railway lines, had now been altered to present a gently curving and undulating avenue. Much was neatly maintained, with wayside seats and picnic tables provided at regular intervals wherever a view was offered through the trees; or where some natural feature, such as a pond or nesting area for birds, might give reason to pause and stay awhile. He also passed a wild untended corner where a profusion of poppies and nettles grew, from which colourful butterflies fluttered up on silent wings: a gathering of mottled orange and brown tortoiseshells, five peacocks, a brightly beautiful red admiral and a delicate painted lady.

Rounding another bend, the place came into view where he'd first noticed a length of rusty track protruding at the foot of a mound of earth. But no such reminder peeped from the soil now. Instead, the area had been built up to provide a place for wild things, the evidence of several fresh holes and scrapes showing that badgers had accepted the invitation.

Morning progressed toward noon, with frequent changes in a sometimes-fretful sky, when quite suddenly, as Toby approached a grove of white may blossom and delicately coloured wild flowers, there came a warm interlude in which the restive breeze fell away completely. A woman and her daughter were there – a little girl toddling at her mother's side in a summer dress of pink and blue. The light shifted and glittered as if through dappled glass, but he knew them as a good man knows his own heart… Sophie holding out a daisy chain towards him… Jenny's face breaking into a welcoming smile. Yet this image lasted no more than a moment, and as Toby watched they seemed to pass into a veiled space, fading like wraiths into the scented air – such that when he came to the spot, there was no more to be seen than a quiet corner carpeted with buttercups, foxgloves, violets and pink campion…

Toby vainly searched for them, pushing between thorny bush and briar; then stumbled on again, clutching at the vision within his head… More bereaved than those able to view and touch the recent dead.

Not until his steps had blindly taken him a further half-mile distant did he look up once more, to see a familiar dark bird gliding between sun and earth – the late watchman of his nightly sojourns, wending its solitary way above the trees. Toby cursed under his breath, bending the while to clutch a stone that he might hurl towards the creature in his despair…

…Then he saw it!

Upon stooping down, Toby's eye was drawn to a bright patch of sunlight at the edge of the path. Something glinted there, smooth and mottled – a polished shape of worked stone… the dice Jasper had owned!

He stepped forward, crouching to touch it with the tip of a finger. White spots stood raised on an upturned face: a simple pattern of marks to represent the fortune of a throw – seven in all…

Seven! …Toby lifted the thing in his hand, counting again – his brain seeking to reason the impossible from his sight by registering a number between one and six. But no… there were seven – two above and two below, with a line of three across the middle.

What had Jasper said? '…If this dice should show a seven, then you'll know the world has changed.' …Was this confirmation that it had…?

Toby turned the dice in his hand, establishing that the others were there – 1 – 2 – 3 – 4 – 5 and 6. …Then again to make sure… and a third time. Always six faces now – six numbers, no more… the seven having dissolved back into granite! …And although he might revolve the dice a thousand – even ten thousand times – he would see it no more…

'What am I to do?' thought Toby, as he stood on the deserted path. '…Is this what it all leads to… the finding of a dice?

'…But no, there is a reason to go on… perhaps to discover yet what part I have played. …If that is truly to be made known to me.'

* * *

Having arrived at the concluding stage of his long journey; Toby wandered on to the end of the twisting country path, before stepping out onto the Molliton Road and making his way towards the "Ninety Acre Field". Then, after rising up towards higher ground, he looked out once more across the familiar landscape that had previously been a treeless prairie.

It had been transformed beyond all recognition: now more resembling a rambling allotment garden or park than a place of intensive agriculture. Gone were the sweeping reaches of bland mono-crop rape, wheat or barley, to be replaced by a rich and varied vista of growing plants, tended by diligent farm workers both young and adult. There were many others present too: mothers walking babies, students reading, a play group in session beneath a grove of trees and a teacher pond dipping with a science classs. Elderly people were also much in evidence, many sitting and talking together on shaded benches, or simply dozing and taking the air. He might have been viewing a model landscape or garden village; for this was an outlook entirely without intrusive buildings or large structures. There were low storage buildings at various corners, all made either of wood or recycled plastic, and quaint shelters with covered verandas where refuge could be taken during times of searing heat; or where workers might meet for lunch or conversation. Wind generators of various sizes and pumps for powering irrigation hoses stood in many places; while neat, compact solar panels, automatically responding to the strength and direction of the sun with a soft 'click click', were grouped beside track ways or placed in open spaces to provide power and hot water for cold frames and greenhouses. These vulnerable structures, plus the many beehives and fragile growing plants such as sweetcorn and runner beans, were protected by electrically operated screens programmed to rise and give shelter when inclement weather threatened; while other manually erected wicker screens, stored in neat piles, could be lifted or moved to wherever they might be needed in an emergency. There were, too, many ponds and carp pools containing reeds and wild flowers bordering the landscape – the former to offer a haven for frogs and toads in an endeavour to promote the natural predation of slugs and soil pests – the latter to provide food for local families. Toby also saw composting areas where plant wastes from homes and fields could be stored and broken down in large enclosures neatly capped with recycled carpets and cotton sheeting. Yet it was a building close to him that most drew the eye, causing Toby to forget other pressing thoughts for a while. A block of flushing earth toilets, now becoming delightfully fringed by a covering of honeysuckle and ivy, had been provided for the field workers. These were primed by rainwater collected in a raised header tank and subsequently drained into discreet scentless purification beds a little way behind. Neatly painted signs had been put up over the doors to the male and female entrances: the one over the "Mens" pronouncing that "It's clean and not mean to the environment" and the other inviting users to "Come and take a comfy break". Three workers passed by on their way to these, each, as expected, ignoring Toby's presence; but strangely, another elderly man, wearing time-worn clothes and smoking an ancient clay pipe, meaningfully touched his cap and smiled knowingly upon emerging from between two drooping rows of raspberry canes close by.

'Luvly day,' he muttered confidentially, crossing within three paces of where Toby stood. 'But I expect we'll be in for a shower later.'

More than a little perturbed at being spoken to, Toby was left open mouthed – any reply dying upon his lips. But the old fellow appeared unconcerned and simply strolled away down an avenue of plum saplings… seeming to fade and blend with the foliage as he passed from view.

Puzzled and rather unnerved yet again, Toby began to make his way forward on the last lap to Molliton. The wide sky above was now a rolling ocean of broken cloud moving eastwards on a current of warm air. No aircraft filled it with a distant roar or vapour trail; neither did any speeding lorry leave a callous mark upon the peaceful sun filled morning. But activity went on all around as men, women and young people alike moved among the planted rows with cane baskets and wheelbarrows, thinning new growth or collecting produce for the table. In one place he saw a group of children picking early strawberries, all laughing and joking as they sampled the juiciest fruit; while in another, a party of volunteer pensioners, in home-made straw hats, were hard at work erecting netting around long rows of blackberry bushes to keep off hungry birds. The whole menu of food for the table seemed to be evident: areas given over to potatoes and a dozen root vegetables, kitchen gardens for salad vegetables, together with spaces providing every variety of brassicas, onions and beans. There were sweet herb gardens as well – of mint, parsley, thyme and many more varieties – all maintained with skilful, knowing hands to provide scent and flavour for the dinner table.

Toby marvelled at it all: from the small but efficient electric tractors that ploughed harvested areas for replanting, to the smallholding with its chickens and pigs and the carefully maintained orchards of fruit trees, their branches already set with the coming autumn's fruit. But it was the small copses of trees dotted across the landscape (separated a little from the growing areas) that began to fascinate him. Many of the saplings in any one grove had grown quite large, giving a peaceful shade; but there were frequently others that had evidently been planted more recently, each clearly being tended and watered daily to ensure good growth. Toby moved across to a group that stood near the track, two maples and an oak, to see that each had a brass plaque set at its base – a nameplate commemorating the person buried there.

'The Natural Burial Act,' Toby said to himself. 'Are they really all interred like this?'

Preoccupied with this thought, he turned absently and realised that his movements had been noticed by another; for perhaps fifty yards away, near a second grove, sat a young man in a straw hat before an easel – a painter, looking for all the world like a latter-day Van Gogh – or a sitter for a French impressionist. Having apparently taken up position to sketch the iris lined carp pond that lay between them, he even had the artist's brown beard and sandy eyebrows… yet something in the other's look implied recognition – perhaps a desire to communicate. Toby looked away for a moment (knowing that he had been seen a second time), his head seeming to spin before he glanced back to confirm what had happened…

…But the place was empty now; just a quiet spot among four trees… Had there been time for the painter to move away? …Or had the light played tricks upon Toby's sight? …He touched his forehead before moving on – a sense of loss weighing heavy upon him once more.

* * *

And so, as he reached the low ridge where the land slopes down toward the alleyway leading to Hawthorn Drive, Toby came to the end of his journey and found his travelling companions waiting by the open gate. It was the old camper van parked beside the hedge that he noticed first; its yellow and blue paint still bright, the cheerful sunshine logo boldly presenting a mischievous smile as always. The little two-tone green A35 was there too, parked on the other side by a fence quaintly festooned with flowering sweet peas. Nearby, the patient, steely-eyed crow sat on a post, occasionally reaching under its wing to preen a glistening feather; before craning forward with outstretched neck and beady eye, upon noting Toby's approach, as if welcoming a late-coming guest to a long arranged gathering of old associates. Jasper, with a knowing glance, also watched him draw near: all the while leaning casually back in a folding easy chair whittling a stem of weathered oak wood across his thigh. His wide brimmed leather hat was, as ever, tilted at a familiar roguish angle, and the court jester's half-smile and penetrating look upon his sallow features remained unfathomable to the last. At Jasper's feet lay Macken, one eye open as he witnessed the coming of an old friend – though seeming for a second time more content and restful than before, as if knowing that a long pursued task was finally done.

It was Jeannie who spoke first as he came up – stepping before him with soft tread as if to bar his passage to the gate.

'You have returned at last, Toby,' she said. 'And I am pleased for you, since it has been a long and challenging journey.'

'And now I must travel the final few yards… to see what is left,' he replied, looking beyond her shoulder toward the alleyway – the fences on each side of which were neatly painted with countryside murals.

Jeannie slowly shook her head, the breeze lifting fine wisps of flaxen hair from her forehead. 'No, Toby, I think we both appreciate there will be no point in that… you need go no further to learn all that is still to be made clear.'

Toby's first impulse was to protest, to force a way through, but her steady look held him and as once before his initial resolve ebbed away – the last corner of a grieving mind finally coming to accept that his former existence had ended long ago.

'But what was it all for?' Toby asked, his eyes filling with bitter tears as he turned to look back towards the field. '…And why did I have to lose so much!'

'Why do the bright flowers of spring wilt and die, Toby? …Why does cruelty still stalk the earth? …Because you were chosen for a purpose, and to see things no other has witnessed. You, who became a living agent of other forces: selected for a task which only an ordinary man – a simple traveller like yourself, could perform.'

He turned to face her again. 'I still don't understand! …What task can you possibly mean? …Why couldn't I be allowed to live my own life?'

'If you had, then the world would not have changed the way it has – for Kline Anderson would not have lived and his ideas would never have been made known to the people of an ailing planet sinking under the effects of climate change.'

'But… did I do that?' asked Toby, scratching his head. '…When?'

'You will remember the day if I remind you – the time we attended the march in London together… that afternoon when we saw Emma Tresco and her two children in a busy street. You will recall that a drinking beaker was dropped and that the older boy reached into the road to retrieve it as a bus appeared. …But for your selfless intervention he would have been killed – for it was you who scooped him to safety while placing yourself in the way. Your injuries were massive and you died within moments – to be hurried away by me into a changed and very different chapter. Since then you have not been part of the living world for a great many years… but more an onlooker, a passer-by. The hour you were struck by the bus was your last as a living mortal and all since then a reprise enjoyed only by the spirits of the air. You are among equals with us, dear friend,' she said, sweeping her arm towards Jasper, Macken and the crow. 'The quick and the dead have always walked this world… but it is only for the latter to see all.'

'You say my life is over… but in my heart I always thought I'd be able to get back.'

'And so you have; but alas not in your own time.'

'But my family – Jenny, Sophie, Brendan… what of them?'

'Like you they have lived their lives, Toby. …And you must take solace when I tell you that theirs were long and often happy. Jenny returned to Molliton two weeks after the Great Storm of 2013, only to find the house empty and that you had gone. She was distraught and stayed for several days, having informed the police of your disappearance and put lost person notices in shops and newspapers. Jenny also walked many miles in search of you: but there was no sign, no trail for her to follow – for you had disappeared from normal space and time. So she returned to her mother's home to be with Sophie and Brendan. Jenny raised them well, Toby, always hoping that you would come back – that you would appear on her doorstep to continue life together once more. …And so the years passed…

'She sold the house much later when it had been repaired, but never remarried – preferring to fill her days instead with the hard work of providing for and bringing up her children rather than giving up your memory and perhaps risking a second loss. Jenny passed away in 2080, in her ninety-second year, having spent her whole life thinking of you, even in her declining days.'

'And my son and daughter?' Toby asked, in a trailing whisper.

'Ah yes,' said Jeannie, breaking into a comforting smile. 'You can be very proud of them. Sophie grew to be determined and strong-minded. She became a nurse and then a ward sister in a London hospital – someone well respected and loved by her patients. She always said that they were her second family and many still have good cause to remember her excellent work. Sophie bore a daughter of her own, Ferra, who still lives in London. She qualified as a doctor and practises to this day in Highgate.

'Then there was Brendan… Brendan, who could never really let you go – the one who never stopped wanting to learn about your life and what you were like. He did well enough at school, but could never really settle to anything after leaving college. Having first tried teaching, he went on to manage a shop, but landscape painting eventually became his life. At first he set up in an attic studio in London, but still wishing to trace the lost threads of your own life he eventually sold up and moved back here upon learning that No. 84 was for sale. Brendan was married then, but his wife Karen died shortly afterwards, so he settled to making a living on his own during the coming years. It was he that had the idea that Jenny should come and live with him some time after she had retired and was getting frail. Then, fifty-one years after your death, when the new natural burial laws were established in 1972, they were at last reunited with you.'

Somewhat lost, Toby looked intently at Jeannie, not sure if her account had taken her on a tack beyond his comprehension. 'You said they and I were reunited... but that's wrong, surely?'

'I apologise, Toby. I didn't mean to confuse... but the story does come full circle... You see there was one link that no one had been able to use until then...

'When you died and were cremated after the accident, your ashes were kept in a vault at a local records office, along with your wedding ring and mobile phone. They stayed there for many years, forgotten and unheeded, as the world went through its upheaval. Then Kline Anderson promoted the concept of natural burial, by which all, when they died, would be laid in the earth near the place of their birth, with a tree planted above them. Gradually the process gathered momentum, and it was subsequently decided that all other stored human remains should likewise be returned to their place of origin for internment. This brought attention to those that had been locked away, like yours; which, simply bearing a number, because you yourself were unknown, might then have been buried in a special plot being prepared south of London but for the mobile phone. You see, although this had been very badly damaged in the accident, it was taken away a second time to be re-examined by an expert, who was able, using new techniques, to restore its memory and discover the dialling number. From this they were then able to go back to old phone company records and find your address. Thus, in due course a letter dropped on Jenny and Brendan's doormat telling them that your ashes had been found.'

'You say the memory was also restored...was there anything on it? ...Only, I was unable to use it more than once due to the battery being low.'

'There was a message,' Jeannie replied. 'One that it is sad you were unable to receive.'

'You know it, Jeannie? ...What did it say?'

'...What is the simplest message of all?'

> *"We love you, Toby... please come home...*
> *Make contact soon... Jenny, Sophie and Brendan xxx"*

'I think you meant the world to them.'

'And they to me,' he replied with sorrow.

'So Brendan went to work. He collected your ashes himself and brought them back to Molliton, where a family plot had been set aside at the far corner of the "Ninety Acre Field".'

Toby now looked back over his shoulder toward the place where the spot must be.

'Sophie came down too,' Jeannie continued, 'and they scattered the ashes there under an oak sapling. A slow growing tree was chosen, so that it wouldn't get too large before they came to join you. Jenny died eight years later, followed by Sophie when she was eighty-four, and they are buried beneath a maple and a mountain ash. But Brendan, as I said, never really let you go... and perhaps always hoped that you would return somehow. Meanwhile, he painted almost every scene from the changing landscape; patiently recording each step towards the new while skilfully recording on canvas so much of what was passing.'

Here Jeannie looked up at Toby with a faint smile once more. 'Perhaps he is doing so still, if you will but choose to go and look... he only left this earth five years ago... his tree is fittingly an oak like yours.'

Their conversation was interrupted by passers-by emerging into the field from the alleyway. A mixed group of eight young people rambled through the gate, "Field Volunteers" laughing and chatting among themselves, their green polo shirts embroidered with the "FV" symbol on a smiling sun. One stepped by within a foot of Toby, turning and dropping his shoulders a fraction as if brushing past a bush, before striding on and gesticulating to the others in an expansive parody of an ape.

'They walked past us as if we are not here... as if we are the unseen,' said Toby, watching their progress.

'We five are invisible to them, Toby... and now that you have returned our role in the conscious world is at an end. We have played our part and their continuing awareness of our existence serves no purpose. In more recent days, Jasper, Macken, the crow or I could sometimes make you visible to others for a while... but now that too is finished. We are the long departed, lost in the ether of time – although my history and Jasper's are infinitely older than yours will ever be.'

'And Macken?'

'Did I not once advise you, Toby – that Macken is his own master and weaves another story?'

* * *

Toby turned back toward the group of figures now fanning out across a vegetable patch they had come to hoe and weed.

'It is good to see the young folk here,' he said wistfully, as they looked out together across the undulating plain of trees and growing crops.

'These are the children of today, Toby. It is their time and has become as natural for them to spend daily hours in the fields helping to grow food for the evening meal, as it was formerly to be all day in the classroom They now learn many diverse skills in science, technology and agriculture, and most can as easily repair a solar panel, or install a wind pump, as lift a row of potatoes. The children and adults of this new age form a community of equals, but the young must still be guided well, for as always they will be the citizens and guardians of tomorrow when their parents are gone.'

'So different then from one hundred years ago,' thought Toby, 'when only an ugly tractor, grinding day and night, occasionally tilled or sprayed the "Ninety Acre Field" – a place where both young and old, often treated as unwelcome intruders on the land, were at risk of censure if they should deviate three feet from the line of a narrow footpath.'

'We must part soon,' said Jeannie at last. 'But before we go our separate ways, tell me what you have learned on this journey.'

Toby thought back to his time with Meg and the dissimilar farming folk of Stavenham – to the protesters in Reading, to Paul Anderson and all the other committed people he had met.

'I have learned that it is not the descendants of lords and ladies, or the rich and the powerful, that pull us through; but most often those from more ordinary stock... like the small woman I came to know who lived in an isolated cottage a mile from here. Yet I have also learned that the past was in many ways a far from golden time – that many, as now, were flawed. Perhaps we humans will always struggle to live with our shared imperfections; but here...' he said, looking out again upon the fertile acres where a hundred willing workers were engaged in their labours, '...here I see evidence that a better future can still emerge from the damage that we have done to our planet... that a start has been made.'

'You do well to note these things, Toby, and have perhaps already witnessed enough to appreciate that neither powerful men nor millionaires are likely to be needed from this time forward. Instead, people will have to work together and pool their talents to ensure their descendants can still enjoy this place a thousand years from now. This is not the model for a new Utopia, but the only practical response to problems so carelessly created in the past. Neither will it always be easy and without hardship, for the unsettled elements are now often against men, but it does offer the way to survival – to a more lasting and sustainable future. The end of civilisation that some predicted has not come to pass. People have become less demanding and more cooperative at the very time in history when circumstances require them to be genuinely skilled and empowered, and there is a sense that this change has its roots here among the ordinary people of Stavenham and Molliton. Therefore it is right that this is where we should end. In what was once the "Ninety Acre Field" you have an example of what all who seek a sustainable future might aspire to, and although they will never learn of you, Toby, there are millions as yet unborn who owe a debt of gratitude for the part you played in bringing Kline Anderson's vision to the world.'

* * *

Jeannie now took Toby's hands, her beautiful eyes looking deep into his – her soft hair, for once untied, flowing loosely around her cheek.

'And what of the others I have met on my travels?' he asked. '…Are they here too?'

'Yes, those that were born or lived in these parts – Meg Maddox, her daughter Alice and the departed folk of Stavenham. But for Emma Tresco, and her mother, Claire Cheetham, with roots elsewhere, it will be different. …Spirits only walk where they truly belong, Toby – so for them, together with Kline and Paul Anderson, there will have been another way home.'

Gently removing his right palm from hers, Toby reached into his pocket. 'I have something to give you… or rather, something to return,' he said, producing the mauve ribbon found at the railway station when she left him last; a little faded now with age, but neatly folded – a precious thing kept safe since then.

'It would always have reminded me of our time together, but now I think it better that you have it back… perhaps to remember me by.'

She took it from him gladly, and with a skilful touch tied back her flowing hair in the fashion he had always known.

'Thank you so much, Toby,' she smiled. 'I will wear it often. …It was ever a favourite of mine and I am glad you saved it as a keepsake.'

'…And may I kiss you?' he asked in a failing voice.

Jeannie turned to the sun, the bright rays accentuating her pale complexion, then looked back, placing one finger upon Toby's lips in token of the space that must always endure between them.

'No, Toby… there is another who has always loved you more than I ever could. … Now you must go to her.'

She then stepped back towards the others, where Jasper remained sitting comfortably in his chair.

'I'll see you around, young fella,' he drawled enigmatically. 'Go easy while you're out there.'

'I have something for you too,' ventured Toby, drawing forth the dice from his pocket and holding it up. 'A treasure found upon a path nearby.'

Jasper eyed the thing from beneath the curve of his hat. 'No… You keep it, Toby,' he replied after a pause '…as a memento, eh – to bring you luck, perhaps. …After all – it is but a trinket and I can always conjure another.'

So it was done and Toby turned to go, Tark the crow having flown to the topmost branch of a nearby tree, where he sat silently observing them with an ever veiled and watchful eye.

Jeannie raised her hand, the slender fingers slightly spaced in a gesture of parting.

'Now it is ended, Toby... You have seen both the past and future days and your time is done. In these fields both the living and the dead are united and you must not feel cheated when able to be a part of this forever. All those that you have known, respected and loved travel beyond the grave. They are among a thousand ghosts of mortals met in the days gone by – the walking spirits of time. Above all, no longer mourn those that you have most dearly loved, for you will be with them again before evening comes.'

With these closing words she waved farewell, and Toby Freeman, with Macken trotting by his side, walked out of sight beyond the ridge as a ragged cloud shrouded the baking sun and the air was filled once more with the sweet song of a skylark rising.